Madoc's Legacy

Madoc's Legacy

Published by RiverRun Select
An imprint of Piscataqua Press and
Riverrun Bookstore

142 Fleet Street | Portsmouth, NH 03801 | USA
603.431.1952 | www.riverrunbookstore.com

Printed in the United States of America

ISBN: 978-1-393739-24-7

www.piscataquapress.com

Madoc's Legacy

Edward Swanson

Ubi sunt qui ante nos fuerunt?

Latin: Where are those who were before us?

Acknowledgements

The author would like to acknowledge the indispensable help he received from a number of people in the writing of this book.

First and foremost I would like to thank my father, Ed Sr., for his meticulous editorial assistance. For wading through the very rawest (and error-ridden) form of the manuscript, and all of the locked horns and subsequent wrangling over fight scenes and other content that ended up making the book a finer finished product, many thanks.

Thanks to Shane Sirles for both editing advice and accompanying my father and I on one memorable research/road trip to Upper Michigan. On the topic of Upper Michigan, I'd like to give a shout out to the crew of Munising's Shooters Firehouse Brewpub for the extraordinary degree of knowledge regarding local history that they helpfully imparted.

Thanks also to Chris Devine for combing the manuscript for flaws.

And to Craig Cushing, a former professor of mine who continued expertly editing the manuscript even after falling gravely ill, I am not only thankful for your crucial assistance but am also still bowled over by your perseverance.

Dedication

For my wife, Jacquelyn. Without your sacrifices and unceasing encouragement, this novel would yet be sitting on the backburner. Thanks, toots.

Prologue

Upper Michigan. Mid-October 1823

Lake Superior's southeastern coastline, the very picture of serenity just an hour ago, now writhed in elemental fury. Amidst slashing rain and a fiercely keening wind, a frothy cavalcade of nine-foot whitecaps battered the sandstone cliffs that comprised the Pictured Rocks. Only occasionally did these soaring, multi-colored walls of rock, natural arches, and sea caves give way to isolated beaches, yet the shipwrecked captain and crew of the doomed schooner *Otter* were fortunate enough to find themselves on such a beach. Had their ship gone down a bit closer to the cliffs they would surely have been drowned to a man.

Captain Elijah Thurgood acknowledged this, although he was also acutely aware that good short-term fortune would soon give way to long-term suffering. Hands clasped behind his back he stood apart from the others, straight-backed and unflinching even as the elements tore at his coarse, rawboned face.

Drenched in icy lake water and thoroughly disgusted with his fate, Thurgood resigned to the fact that he should have stayed out among those hissing waves and gone down with his floundering ship. Many would accept a ship's captain doing so as a matter of course, and that nagged him.

In defiance of gravity, water collected at the tip of his hooked nose in a rapidly swelling drop. This he blew off with a quick, contemptuous puff of air, gritting his teeth as he continued to stare hypnotically at his forsaken vessel. From atop his vantage, a rocky promontory just above the beach, he solemnly watched his ship convulsing in her death throes.

The Hudson's Bay Company schooner *Otter*, his beloved craft, listed heavily to her right side eighty yards out into the heaving lake. The forty-foot vessel of fifty tons burden would not last much longer. Hammered by waves and taking on water, she continued her inexorable descent into the yawning depths of Lake Superior.

Even as he watched the waves consuming his craft, he could not help but marvel at their color. That luminous, crystalline aquamarine water was oddly tropical in appearance, totally belying the frigid water temperatures and harsh climate of

Superior's southern shore. That color never failed to amaze him, even now, when almost certain death loomed on the horizon upon which his ship was currently sinking.

Yes, he should have stayed aboard. But to his credit events had transpired with astonishing speed. One moment he was struggling to pilot his crippled ship; in the next, it seemed, he was in a violently pitching birchbark canoe with the remnants of his panicked crew. That canoe now lay hopelessly shattered on the beach, of no use to anyone. Formed from bedrock, the beach stretched out into the lake like a natural wharf, half its length submerged in shallow water. The waves had driven them headlong into the shore, a match even for the vaunted skill of the voyageurs guiding the canoe.

This late season run to Fond du Lac at Superior's southwestern corner had been routine, the return trip smooth until now. When the storm descended, their homeport of Sault Ste. Marie was but a short day away. But hopes of making that safe haven were dashed when a jagged rock from an unseen reef staved in the hull near the stern, snapping off the rudder and splintering the keel.

Silently he cursed Bechard and Alrinach, the demons of tempests and shipwrecks respectively. If he listened closely enough, he fancied that he could hear their mocking cackles amidst the wind-churned waves.

As he continued watching, the *Otter* gave a sudden lurch that submerged all but the prow, figurehead, and bowsprit. Those too began to sink; the rough-hewn, wooden otter that served as a figurehead seemed to stare with lifeless eyes at Thurgood, silently imploring him to take action and save it from so wretched a fate. Shortly thereafter the tip of the bowsprit disappeared altogether, and with that the wrathful lake was once again unsullied by the mark of man.

Sweeping off his black, tri-corner oilcloth cap, the captain placed it over his heart with due reverence. Recalling the times, both fair and foul, that he'd had aboard the *Otter,* a void slowly expanded in his heart until it consumed his entire chest. Heralding Nature's victory, the knife-edged wind gusted with a hollow roar, setting Thurgood's voluminous overcoat to billowing.

"Ave atque Vale," he muttered softly. Hail and Farwell. Nodding gently to himself, one corner of his mouth slowly lifted and curled into what might have passed for a self-deprecating smirk.

He had made a serious miscalculation in his effort to survive; life was only to be treasured when sustainable. And here, on a cold, rugged wilderness shoreline that rarely saw the presence of man, with exceedingly limited supplies and winter fast approaching, how sustainable could life possibly be? Hope had taken wing, leaving them for the vultures.

Yes, he'd miscalculated for sure.

The smile faded by slow degrees, leaving Thurgood's wind and rain-lashed face stony.

Huddled together in a ragged assemblage, the twelve surviving crewmen all stared intently at their captain as he turned to address them.

"Well lads, another one lost to old *Gitchi Gummi.*"

The Hudson's Bay Company had first conceived of the idea for a fleet of fur-trading ships on Superior around the turn of the century, so as to combat increased competition from their hated Northwest Company rivals. And sure, the HBC might have outlived the Northwest Company by dint of absorption in part because of Superior's streamlined trade, but was it worth the price? The better part of the fleet lost along with the lives of their crewmen?

For of the five ships, the *Speedwell* alone now plied the untamed waters. And with a mistress as tempestuous and capricious as *Gitchi Gummi*, how long could the *Speedwell* possibly hope to last? The legacy of the Superior fur schooners would come to rest on the mighty lake's bottom along with the ships themselves.

As one of the few Company employees with any serious sailing experience, Thurgood had been swiftly (and perhaps impetuously) installed as a captain at the tender age of twenty-one. The life had been lonely and dangerous, with no reliable charts to guide him (his own attempts were now lost to the lake), none but a few irregularly shaped natural harbors to seek refuge in.

"What now?" inquired a swarthy half-breed named Henry in a hollow voice.

Thurgood's dark eyes took in his crew at a glance. Most of these men were not proper sailors. That had not helped matters. Six of his eight able seamen had been lost along with some trappers and their entire cargo. He, a Liverpool lad whose scouse accent attested to his maritime heritage, was a proper son of Neptune who would be able to hold his own aboard most any vessel. But the majority of these men were trappers by trade. Trappers merely heading east from Fond du Lac who were expected to lend a hand on the ship while they hitched a ride.

Yet looking more carefully at them, he reminded himself that yes, most of these remaining men were indeed trappers, hardened voyageurs. Resilient men accustomed to hardship and wilderness survival; some among them had probably survived worse situations. Perhaps they needed only a bit of leadership to overcome the shock of shipwreck. As if stirred by wind, a spark of optimism swiftly rekindled in his breast. It was time to take charge.

"What have we for provisions?"

A towheaded man rooted through a sopping hemp bag. "Mmm, not much Ol' Hoss. Some sowbelly, hardtack... bit o' pemmican."

Thurgood snorted sardonically. "Well, that caps the bloody climax. Is that fowling piece serviceable?"

"Somehow stayed pretty dry. She's loaded with swan shot, should be able to take down something with it. I can tend to that, if'n you like."

"A sound idea." He observed that most of them still had knives in their belts, which would be a big help. A bunch of knife-toting voyageurs at his side- he had been far too quick to dismiss this situation as lost.

"Do any of you have knowledge of nearby trails, however old or unused, that we might take to Sault Ste. Marie? I realize that this place is little traveled, but mayhap one of you knows something?"

The men looked at each other as if he'd just made a rather weak attempt at a joke.

"Sorry boss," replied Fisher, "none of us have ever trapped this ground. Hell, only one crazy young bastard named Marcel Durand would dare that. Bad things happened to the early voyageurs who strayed into this area. Rumor has it some Jesuits went missin' back in the day too. Injuns fight shy of it, have for some time. Cursed land, they say. Hell, there are probably some well-defined game trails, but we're all going in blind if we take a land route. Best bet might be to try and lash a raft together, but storms is awful common this time o' year..."

Henry pursed his lips. "Well, let's get a raft thrown together, then we study the clouds and winds, see if decent weather is likely. Although hell, this storm sure came outta nowhere. But if it looks good, then the Soo will be our best bet."

"Very well. Sault Ste. Marie it is. Let's get moving, men."

Stepping off of his rocky perch, he led the way towards a sandy beach that lay on the other side of a narrow river. Crossing the shallow river mouth with authoritative stride, Thurgood suddenly caught sight of Migizi, a Chippewa brave, kneeling on the sand. It appeared that he was fiddling with something in front of him.

"Migizi! What's the matter, man?"

Migizi rose, his sodden black hair obscuring his face as he solemnly turned towards his captain.

"Make offer," he explained in highly accented English.

"To what end?" demanded Thurgood. He could see it now, a low altar of driftwood, atop which were carefully arranged bits of copper, vermillion, carnelian, and tobacco.

The Indian tried to explain in English, but ended up lapsing into Chippewa, a tongue in which Thurgood could claim little comprehension.

"Christ's wounds! English, man! Or French, if you must."

Slocum, a veteran trapper of considerable renown, translated. Thurgood did not like the growing look of concern on his grizzled face.

"He's making an offering to appease the *manitous* that haunt these shores. Bad *manitous*, Cap'n. Malevolent gods of the copper, he says. An offering must be made- damn, he even wants to leave his knife."

Upon hearing this, the rest of the crew began staring into the dark, fog-festooned aisles of the blazing maples and massive, gloomy hemlocks that marked the beach's edge. As they watched, a deep, howling sound tore through the shaking trees, quite unlike the shrieking of the wind.

The men exchanged grim looks, obviously rattled. Thurgood himself felt a chill- that had been a most abnormal sound...

"You know," muttered Slocum uneasily, "I coulda sworn I saw a figure up on the rocks wachin' us 'fore we went down, thought I was just seein' things..."

Thurgood spat bitterly. He had seen how Indian legends could rattle half-breeds and even seasoned white trappers. This was the last thing he needed now, a spooked crew... especially when the rugged, virtually unexplored territory around the Pictured Rocks offered little in the way of comfort. This was *terra incognita* for men both red and white. Of all the places to go down, it had to be here, the place avoided by Indians and trappers alike due to rumors of an ancient evil lurking amidst the cliffs...

"These people and their bleeding superstitions... tell him to pick up the shit he has arranged there, we may need it to trade. And you lot, grab a hold of your codpieces and stop quaking, that was the bloody wind and you know it."

His voice increased in volume as he began rapping out orders. "We need to get a fire going and get out of these clothes posthaste. Perkins and Fisher, you're in charge of that. The fire, that is." The men chuckled, an encouraging sign. "Henry, as they collect wood, you look for a decent spot to erect a shelter."

The men began straightening up, putting on brave faces as they strove to impress their admittedly young, but undeniably game captain whose leadership now extended beyond the decks of his ship.

But still they kept one eye on the dim forest.

"And we'll need- blimey! What in God's name are you doing, Migizi? Eh? What did I just tell you?"

He tipped over the altar with a fierce kick, yanking the intractable Indian up at the same time. "You will follow my orders, damn you-"

Migizi groaned suddenly, and Thurgood wondered if he had hurt the man. Then a spear hissed past his face, leaving a thin trail of blood on his cheek before slicing into the waves beyond. He swore bitterly and, throwing himself into a sideways roll, sprang up by his men.

Now he could see the arrow jutting from Migizi's chest; had he not lifted the man, that arrow would have taken him instead. Indians! He did not understand why Chippewa Indians, the dominant tribe of this region, would attack them. They were on good terms with whites, but obviously this rogue band sought blood. Although maybe this was a Sioux war party come far east, but that was unlikely. And wait- did not Indians avoid this area altogether? It simply did not add up, but reaction, not deliberation, was the order of the day.

That demoniac howling sound again tore through the air, above even the shrieking wind, and in its wake a hair-raising, barbaric shout went up. Figures could be seen flitting between the trees; figures that seemed to move awfully fast for men, even Indians.

A fusillade of arrows and spears poured out of the wood line, some finding their mark among the momentarily stunned men. Recovering, they began racing down the shoreline, but dark figures poured out of the forest and onto the sands about a hundred yards away. Mindlessly, in primal panic, two of the men sprinted straight into the raging hell that was the lake, as if they hoped to find deliverance in the embrace of glacial waves. Perhaps, in a way, they did; as he spared them a half-glance Thurgood saw their dwarfed, pathetic forms swallowed up, *consumed*, by the unrelenting surf.

There was nowhere to go, nowhere where safety might be found. Hopelessly exposed, outnumbered, and outgunned, they were caught between the Devil and the deep, blue sea.

He could not speak for the others, but Captain Elijah

Thurgood was not going out on a passive note. Blood rushed into his head and with a wild roar of his own he drew his short sword and rushed out to meet his concealed foes. He was heartened to hear some of the men follow.

Bursting into the ill-lit forest they were immediately engaged by their assailants. To his left Thurgood saw Henry, a man of considerable strength, hurled like a ragdoll into a tree. It was damnably hard to see, as the giant hemlocks blotted out most light. But he could discern well enough the hulking, man-like form as it rounded on him. The ship's captain thrust hard with his weapon, sticking his enemy squarely in the throat until he felt the blade scratch against bone.

He then spun around, jerking the blade out to viciously slash another comer across the face, but after that the sword was batted aside by a copper-tipped club, which slammed into his gut on its next swing. Then powerful, tattooed hands seized him, swung him aloft, and tossed him a considerable distance. He fair flew for a second or two before coming down hard upon a rotting log.

Screams of pain, roars of anger, the clash of weapons; the sounds melded into a dreadful cacophony as the fight raged on. Few of his men remained standing and all faced multiple opponents. Through vision blurred and spotty, Thurgood could make out Perkins as he fired the shotgun. A clanging sound accompanied the resultant shriek of agony, as if the shot had struck metal.

Two dark forms came up from behind the voyageur, pinning Perkin's arms behind his back as a third figure slashed viciously with a long sword, spilling his organs onto the leaf litter.

A sword? What manner of Indians were these?

Thurgood staggered to his feet and began stumbling through the woods, where to he did not know. But the fight was knocked out of him and he had simply to get away from this scene of butchery.

Turning to look behind him, he saw an Indian in pursuit- but how could it be? Torso clad in copper, his pale skin stood out starkly against the saturated bark of the trees. Beard hanging long and shaggy off his black-painted face, he leered evilly as Thurgood gazed upon him in abject horror.

He had never known Great Lakes Indians to sport metal breastplates. And they sure as hell didn't grow beards. A disturbing sense of unreality set in as he sped through the dank woods. Thurgood's mind tried in vain to formulate a plausible explanation for this madness while his legs pumped furiously.

He chanced another backward glance and beheld a veritable horde in hot pursuit. Then the ground abruptly gave way beneath him and he was falling, falling… finally coming to a bone-crunching halt next to a stream at the base of a small cliff. Shadow-dappled figures gathered at the cliff's edge, silently staring down at his supine form.

The Indian legends were true, then. Imagine that. As the darkness embraced him, Elijah Thurgood grudgingly arrived at this conclusion.

The legends were true and may Heaven help those who invoked the wrath of the copper gods.

Part One
Stirrings of Madness

"A true adventurer goes forth aimless and uncalculating to meet and greet unknown fate."

O. Henry, *The Green Door*

Chapter 1

Chicago, Illinois. July 5th 1847

Much change had been wrought in the land around Chicago since a mulatto trader first put plow to earth in the 1780's. Jean Baptiste Point du Sable's lonely lakefront cabin and small farm had given way to a city now churning with agriculture, industry, and most importantly potential.

The seed of American civilization, late in germinating at this particular location, had at last taken firm root during the past decade.

Having swiftly evolved from a frontier-trading town into a burgeoning mercantile power on the cusp of industrialization, "The Mud Hole of the Prairies" now boasted various indicators of modernity. These indicators were, however, yet tempered by the dogged persistence of frontier traits. For while factories, hotels, homes, and church steeples formed a decidedly city-like silhouette on the horizon, they lay scattered along a chaotic confusion of squalid, unpaved, animal-filled roads.

Along one such road a man ran for his life, though he hardly knew or cared about Chicago's rapid development as he raced down the near-empty, moonlit street.

His name was Richard Tansworth, and his was the gift of speed. Slyness, sleight of hand, charm, wit; these too were strengths but speed was his true gift, a divine bestowal in his opinion, and one that he prayed to God above served him well at this particular moment in time.

For a lifelong proclivity towards crime and brutality had culminated in his fleeing from a lawman of almost mythical standing. The usual Chicago city constables could never put him to such protracted, undignified flight, though time and again they had tried. That gaggle of sluggish buffoons posed no real threat to him, what with his quickness and ability to meld into crowds, to sniff out a trap. But this- this was a new threat altogether. The threat whispered of by fearful criminals in the shadows of ill-frequented places, he who moved like a wraith among the denizens of the Chicago underworld.

The one with a titan's strength and a beard that shone hellfire-red. The one who struck like a hawk with no notions of mercy in mind. He from whom there was no outrunning, no hope of eluding.

Such was the avenger he now sought to evade.

And the bastard was gaining on him.

Putting on an impressive burst of speed as he turned right onto Randolph Street, he risked a fleeting look back. *Shit.* The lawman was still on him, as Tansworth knew he'd be, almost casually trailing him by a distance of about fifteen yards.

It was July fifth and tonight a legion of bands played, men gave speeches, and general merriment filled the air as Chicago celebrated the nation's independence a day late. And here he was- *he*, Richard Tansworth, running for his life with tail firmly tucked. How had it come to this?

A bloody scourge of London he had been, a feared criminal of multifarious talents with a lengthy catalogue of infamies laid to his charge. As a highwayman, burglar, sneak thief, and garrotter, the phrase "Your purse or your life" was not one that he employed flippantly. Hell, three times had he audaciously stuck up aristocrats' carriages under the very shadow of St. Paul's steeple, holding the occupants hostage until a tidy ransom was paid. One of them had even been a member of Parliament. Not many folks could walk the dismal lanes of St. Giles without fear of bodily harm, but Richard Tansworth once trod those streets with impunity, safeguarded by unshakable confidence and a fearsome reputation. Here in Chicago easy pickings should be had, yet his own arrival in Slab Town coincided with the appearance of this accursed righter of wrongs. As a first-rate criminal who rose quickly to prominence anywhere he went, deep down Tansworth had simply known that they were destined to meet. It had only been a matter of time, really.

Striving to control his breathing, he ruminated over the incident of ten minutes ago, the one that led to this parlous game of cat and mouse. She had most assuredly deserved it, she had, the cackling painted lady at that Wells Street house of ill fame. Sure, there had been that slight problem on his part in terms of arousal, but whiskey will do that to a man, as well she knew. A titter would almost have been understandable, but that insipid *cackling*- well, that he simply couldn't abide.

So he'd gutted the bitch from navel to sternum.

His initial intentions were only to mar, yet the sight of spilt blood, the enchanting melody of her shrieks and pleas... their appeal to his senses had simply been too great. Even the blade in his hand seemed to sing to him in a voice both firm and seductive, urging him on to further exploration...

Even in a city choked with them, killing a harlot was a glaring breach of underworld protocol. Naturally, certain parties would take grave offense, the proprietor and the law in particular. But generally, enough coin placed in the right hands soothed even the sorest tempers in a bawdy house, buying one at least enough time to slip away before the law got involved. There might be honor among thieves, but he had yet to see it among whores. Savage wretches, the whole stinkin' lot of 'em. Yet that demon of a lawman fell upon him before spondulicks could grease the palms of the attendant Madame. For from a corner table where it appeared that a hunched old drunkard sat, a massive form had burst into action. Imagine that, a disguised watchman daring to venture into the heart of the Chicago's darkest and most corrupt district in the dead of night. The man had some serious dash-fire. Even the crushers of London weren't quite so bold.

His mind returned to the present and to the chase as he ran down a crowded Randolph Street. The city's population had temporarily boomed due to some river and harbor convention that Tansworth gave no shit about. But an extra ten thousand people to lose oneself among- that he had current use for. People on their way to and fro the Public Square shuffled through the cloying mud that slowed Tansworth's progress. Mud aside, this did bode well for him; he could slip into the throngs like a wisp of fog, then lay low until he could head back down to St. Louis or New Orleans, where the riverboat gamblers faced no such menace from the law.

Unexpectedly, a veritable gauntlet of decent width was being cleared for Tansworth and his pursuer as people noticed the desperate chase that was underway. For the first time Tansworth felt torpid in his movements. This was most uncharacteristic. Perhaps the booze was to blame, for of late habitual intemperance was something of which he was certainly guilty. Primal fear could also have played a role at this point, he sheepishly admitted to himself. Whatever the case, breath came to him in sharp gasps as a knifing stitch stung his left side. The mud seemed a thing alive, intent on dragging him ever deeper into itself. He could hear the squelching of the lawman behind him- *was it just him, or was the blighter even closer?*

He veered towards a wooden sidewalk, knocking an elegantly dressed woman out of his way to several vehement imprecations of outrage. Many of the roads in this area lacked a uniform grade, resulting in stepped sidewalks with frequent ups and downs. He fell down one such set of stairs, but upon rising Tansworth felt his boots find good purchase and with renewed vigor continued his getaway.

Some yellow fireworks illuminated a nearby street-sign;

Dearborn it read, and turning left onto it he weaved his way in and out of milling groups of people. Another backward glance told him that his pursuer had lost ground, and it was about bloody time.

Time to lose this bastard for good and all.

Slipping off the main road with a quick sideways lunge, he found himself at the rear entrance of a large riverfront warehouse- Newberry & Dole: Storage, Forwarding, & Commission. The back door was open; Tansworth consistently paid a worker, one of those dim-witted Famine Irishmen, to leave this door unlocked each night in case he needed a lurk in a hurry. After sundown this location was quiet, out of the way, and possessed river frontage in the event that he needed to leave Chicago for a bit. From here he could easily hitch a ride on a southbound schooner at first light if he wanted. At present that course of action held much appeal. He would cut a fine figure of a Southern gambler by his own estimation, what with his quick hands, sleek, dark hair and sly eyes.

Darkness and silence presided in the merchant house, although he became acutely aware of his own noisy breathing as time passed. Hurriedly he barred the door behind him. Looking through a window, Tansworth watched for an excruciating minute to make sure the man had truly lost his trail. Satisfied that such was the case, he leaned against a table upon which sat a small mountain of dried beef. Snatching a piece and tossing it into his mouth, he considered his escape.

A close call that'd been. A close call and no mistake. The man had appeared out of nowhere in that whorehouse, swinging a copper-tipped truncheon that just barely missed his skull. Were it not for his superb reflexes, it would almost certainly have found its mark.

Bending over, Tansworth rubbed his sore legs, legs hastily pressed into service. And they served him well, as they always had. Many a footrace was won on these legs of his, many a crusher had been made to eat his dust through their exertion.

Reaching into a cabinet where he stashed a flask of whiskey, he took an energetic pull and allowed himself a small sigh.

"Rest easy, Dicky. Come dawn's first rays it'll be back to St. Louis with you, where coppers are laggards and whores know their place."

"I fear that St. Louis is a precluded possibility," said a deep voice through the nearest window.

That awful tone of voice galvanized him into frenetic action. He needed barely a moment's time to recover from the shock- his mind and body acted in unison, launching him away from that sinister voice.

The door he had entered by exploded off its hinges in a shower of splinters. Tansworth sprinted for the opposite end of the building, but through the windows saw torch-wielding men waiting outside.

Dash it all! How could they have known about this lurk of his? He had told no one of it save the Irish dullard, and that man feared him too greatly to snitch.

Fortunately, there was a backup plan in place. Hurtling up the staircase in the center of the room, he soon burst onto the third floor, panting raggedly. Still running full tilt, he threw his shoulder into the grain elevator that lay on rollers. It rattled across the floor, smashing open the loft door on the other end of the room. With a groan the grain elevator began a sharp downward descent, but that was abruptly checked as its far end made contact with the South Water Street dock some thirty feet below.

This elevator was used to deliver grain and other goods directly into ships from the second story, saving both time and effort. At the moment, Tansworth hoped that it would save his life.

Leaping onto the elevator's top, feet pointed at the dock below, he began a fast but controlled slide down it. Once upon the docks he would dive into the waters of the Chicago River, then swim the short distance out into Lake Michigan.

If you're born to be hanged, then you'll never be drowned...

If he made the swim, he could then enter the deserted Fort Dearborn via the old sally port that connected it to the lake by means of subterranean passage.

He heard the shouts of amazement from below as he slid; let them marvel, the bastards. How gallant, how heroic he must look at this moment! With his astounding good looks and nonchalant grace, his casual sliding maneuver down this elevator must have been a sight to behold.

Yes indeed, he truly was a-

The elevator listed violently to the left, pitching him off. He landed heavily in a manner most undignified, feeling a pang of disappointment at not having completed his maneuver. That and a considerable amount of pain in his left side. Looking up, he saw a large, dark figure staring ominously down at him from the busted loft door.

How in the hell had the man shifted that elevator off its rollers? The piece of machinery was massively heavy; it should have taken at least two men to move it so.

A pair of rough hands hauled him up, but the seasoned

criminal instinctively drew his push-dagger and thrust hard. The blade bit through thick wool, entering flesh beyond but only by a small margin. This did, however, have the desired effect of causing the man to release him. Another watchman, this time swinging a torch, bore down on him, but Tansworth sidestepped and neatly kicked his legs out from under him.

Summoning every ounce of remaining strength, he went for broke as he desperately strove to reach the Dearborn Street drawbridge, which spanned the width of the Chicago River. One final trick lay up his sleeve. He'd beat these confounded lawmen yet.

A plank road led to it, upon which his feet beat out a hard tattoo. Just ahead lay the bridge- this could very well work!

Racing across the trembling bridge, he pushed a perplexed passerby off the side of it, who entered the river below with a splash and dismayed yelp. Tansworth needed the drawbridge cleared for this to work. He crossed the three hundred foot bridge with speed born of desperation. Grabbing a hold of the crank that raised and lowered the bridge, he furiously spun it.

"Leave or die!" he snarled at a young girl who stood watching him in disbelief.

Bit by bit the two halves of the bridge rose and separated. Even now, the gap would be too great for a man to possibly leap. With a feeling of deepest satisfaction he observed the two watchmen he'd gotten past standing on the far side of the slowly rising bridge, looking useless and thoroughly defeated.

"Bugger off, you bastard whoresons!" exclaimed an elated Tansworth. Then, to the rhythm of pounding feet, another figure tore past them and wildly flung itself across the widening gap.

He made it.

The relentless bastard actually made the leap, and even as he turned to continue his flight, Richard Tansworth conceded that his end was nigh.

Sure enough, he felt a great explosion of pain that was preceded by a whirring noise. The lawman had cast his club and cast it well. Spine badly damaged by the blow, Tansworth wheezed horribly as he twitched and fell, poleaxed.

Tansworth reflected on his days on this earth. A life of infamy come to this. So much for his leisurely sojourn in America. Who'd have thought that butchering one insignificant whore would prove to be the instance of his grossest folly? After all the evil committed by his hand, the death of one blasted strumpet did him in?

It had been a whore that brought him into this world, an irony that was not lost on him.

Through shimmering red mists of pain, he spotted an upraised club then watched it sink. He shrieked like a wounded banshee as his right kneecap shattered with an awful crunch.

The face of his pursuer, his tormentor the phantom lawman, came into sharp focus a moment later. In the glare of some blossoming fireworks, he took in the well-defined cheekbones, the dark hair and red beard of his vanquisher. He tried to say something witty but couldn't quite find the breath.

"A spirited effort," acknowledged Alvord Rawn with a curt nod, and his club fell once more.

Chapter 2

The Public Square through which Alvord passed teemed with activity. Chicago's Fourth of July celebration had been postponed one day for the sake of the River and Harbor Convention that had drawn these massive crowds. Thus, this muggy July fifth night roiled with people celebrating their nation's independence. A sizable number of recent immigrants to Chicago were present; Irish, Germans, and Norwegians who made merry with every bit as much alacrity as the rest.

Underneath the sprawling tent pavilion constructed especially for the Convention, brass bands sent their notes blaring across Lake Michigan's still waters, which were at intervals illuminated by the eruption of fireworks. Alongside troops of soldiers, floats evincing patriotic themes were borne along by groups of drunken men. At three separate podiums men in silk top hats and tailcoats harangued the multitudes, striving desperately to be heard over the bands, the dull thud of pyrotechnics, and the unhappy bellowing of the cattle horde that had been herded back into The Common for the night. These noises, along with those generated by many thousands of people drinking, singing, and dancing, amassed into a grating chorus that rendered sleep all but impossible for Chicago's more retiring inhabitants. Midnight might be fast approaching, but the festivities continued with zeal unabated.

Alvord moved as quickly as he could through the din and commotion. He heard one of the big-lunged speakers delivering a verbose speech on canal tariffs and decided to increase his pace. Already today the most esteemed politicians and orators present for the River and Harbor Convention had electrified audiences with their poetical speechifying. Among them were the likes of his close friend Horace Greeley, Ohio Senator Thomas Corwin, The Reverend William Allen, and a tall, soft-spoken Illinois Congressman named Abraham Lincoln. *Those* had been some speeches to lend an ear to, as Alvord had himself done. But these late-night speeches were merely dry rot spilling from the mouths of imbeciles, agonizing to intelligent ears.

While he might strive to ignore the chaos before him, Alvord himself did not pass by unnoticed. In fact, he was the recipient of many a startled look. The milling crowds actually parted to allow him passage, watching in stunned disbelief as he dragged the limp, wasted body of Richard Tansworth behind him by one leg. This occasioned many a gasp from women and many questions from men. These he silently shrugged off, indicating the copper badge on his chest while steadily wending his way towards his destination at the corner of Clark and Randolph Street. A growing pack of dogs loped in his wake, curiously sniffing at the criminal's bloody carcass.

Boots thudding on the plank sidewalk that stretched above an abysmally muddy road, Alvord passed by a structure that was uncharacteristically ornate for what he considered to be a raw, frontier city. Though dwarfed by the five-story Sherman House that loomed behind it, Chicago's First Courthouse, erected in 1835, was an impressive building in its own right. Sporting fluted, Doric columns and a large pediment of marble, it served as architectural confirmation that America's obsession with Greek Revival had followed the nation's westward course. These Classical accents seemed outlandish when compared to the rest of the building, a mottled combination of brick and limestone, but the attempt at Classical grace had been made. Alvord did not favor the style himself (he preferred more sober Federalist and Gothic structures), though he did pause for a moment in front of the building to cast his eyes upon it. Manhattan, his former place of residence, boasted many marvels of architectural engineering, but here in Chicago most buildings were simplistic and practical in structure. So this frontier interpretation of Greek Revival pleased his eye despite the flaws he considered to be inherent to the style.

"Jefferson and Latrobe would be most pleased," he muttered to himself dryly.

Behind the Courthouse stood the city watchhouse. Beyond that lay the jail buildings, but given Tansworth's condition the city morgue would be a more logical depository. Before attending to that, however, Alvord needed to check in with the City Marshall.

Before an unauthorized attack on an Irish gang cost him his job in Manhattan some months back, Alvord had enjoyed a position as a Captain in New York's Municipal Police Department. Back then his clean, spacious watchhouse had been located inside Manhattan's imposing City Hall. It could not have differed more from Chicago's watchhouse, a fifteen by twenty foot shack comprised of upright oak boards cut in the very roughest of manners. This was no proper timber frame but rather one of those balloon frame buildings, structures that Alvord had grown to hate. This building technique had originated in Chicago over twenty years ago, one that employed long, vertical 2 X 4's to build the exterior wall. Extending from the floor to the roof, these studs were held in place by mere nails, rather than the chiseled joints and wooden pegs that secured traditional buildings. The term "balloon framing" actually arose when someone joked that a stiff breeze would likely carry off such flimsy buildings. Alvord felt that, if afforded a good running start, he might well be able to knock one over. And that was bearing in mind the sheathboards and weatherboards nailed to the sides for protection from the elements. Those extra layers had actually given rise to another moniker for Chicago, that of "Slab Town."

They did not require skilled labor to erect; like so many things these days they could be constructed by unskilled laborers rather than craftsmen. That was increasingly the way of things, it seemed. Meticulous work and pride in that work would yield to the expediency of cheap, rapid production and shoddy workmanship.

And that, in Alvord's opinion, was a damn shame.

He knocked with firm hand upon the door, which shook loudly on its leather hinges. Constructed with green wood, like so many other structures here, the walls of this watchhouse stood warped and twisted from the torrid daytime heat.

"Enter," came the curt order.

He stepped under the doorway through which his shoulders barely fit and into a room dark and spare, dimly lit by the flames of several brass chamber lamps. Standing a shade over 6'1 in an age when the average American male stood just under 5'7, Alvord's brawny form seemed to take up half the dingy room, in which an oversized desk and a few chairs served as the only furniture.

Behind the desk sat a man of thin, slouchy form and steely hardness of manner.

His name was Phillip Dean. Alvord had developed a hearty disliking towards the dour, cantankerous old devil during his time in Chicago. He served as both City Marshall and Street Commissioner and was a strict, by-the-books breed of lawman. Undermanned and ill-financed, Chicago's Marshall nevertheless waged unremitting war against the rising tide of crime that assailed his city, so long as that war could be waged within the strictest confines of the law.

Lamplight gleamed off the thin film of perspiration coating Alvord's face as he dragged Tansworth's carcass into the room.

Powerful though he might be, towing one hundred and fifty pounds worth of dead weight for several blocks took its toll. The slain man's boot clunked hollowly onto the floor as Alvord let go of his pant leg.

Running a spindly finger down one of his wiry, graying muttonchops, Dean eyed Alvord's charge.

"Another one?" Dean inquired in his sharp, cracking voice, his hand holding a quill pen motionlessly over some papers.

"Another one," Alvord solemnly affirmed.

Dean leaned forward in his chair to take a closer look at the body. He slowly withdrew as his nostrils crinkled delicately.

"Given the stench, I assume that he shat himself postmortem?"

"Right in one."

"His death *was* justified, I trust?"

Alvord's light gray eyes levelly held the Marshall's incisive stare. Dean's tone implied that he very much doubted that the criminal's death was warranted.

"Indeed it was. This oozing sack of shit eviscerated a whore in a Wells Street brothel not an hour ago. I attempted to detain him at which point he forcefully resisted. He fled, I pursued."

Dean cocked a thick eyebrow in a rare display of emotion. "Death without trial for killing a whore under unspecified circumstances? I think it a bit extreme, Mr. Rawn."

"I think you did not hear her screams, Mr. Dean."

The two stared unblinkingly at each other, deaf to the raucous sounds of merriment muffled only slightly by the thin walls of the watchhouse. Only the thunderous clap of some fireworks succeeding in breaking the ponderous tension. Their eyes broke off in an uneasy stalemate.

Dean nodded slightly, to himself more than to Alvord. "Well, let us not belabor the point. The terms of your contract do grant you more leeway than the rest of us."

Alvord had spent the past three weeks in Chicago, and for the sake of keeping busy and making some money, he decided to work with the local police department. When he found the department to be both nascent and unorganized, he sought a role not as a poorly paid deputy but rather as an independent contractor whose role as patrolmen/detective had proved to be most lucrative. Alvord knew that Dean, though undeniably wary of him, recognized the value in having a veteran lawman from the nation's largest city work with his department. Grudgingly, the man had approved his position as an independent contractor after a close study his credentials. Luckily for Alvord, there was no mention in those documents of his abrupt dismissal this past April.

What's more, the man granted him the ability to function independently of the strictures that bound the other patrolmen, so long as he operated within the broader boundaries of the law.

Not that he was *always* able to manage that.

"Be it known," Alvord added firmly, "that he also attacked Pahlman and that red-haired kid who volunteered to help during the convention. Both were lucky. At present they are at that brothel, collecting witness testimonies for me. This they offered to do."

Dean looked closely at Tansworth's frozen, pallid face before he leaned back in his chair, tilting his stern visage up to stare at the ceiling. Lifting his well-preserved, beaver skin top hat, he pensively ran a hand through his hair.

"I recognize the man as Dick Tansworth. A newcomer to Chicago and of the Devil's own brood, that one. Slippery as an eel, too. Several times in the past weeks he has eluded my men, by dint of both speed and his ability to vanish seemingly into thin air. How did you come to track him down and dispatch him?"

The man's tone did not betray the curiosity contained in his words.

"A combination of my own careful observations and a useful network of informants, both in the Chicago underworld and among the general citizenry. That is how I came to know of his patterns, his predilections, and most importantly his hideouts. A footrace brought us to his favorite lurk near the river, so with the help of your two men we flushed him, allowing me to bring him down at the Dearborn Street drawbridge."

Dean nodded to himself again, eyes losing focus. With a sigh he spoke with measured words.

"Phil Mitchell, Patrick Finley, now Richard Tansworth, hmm? You are racking up quite the body count among the criminal elite of this city, not even taking into consideration the criminals you bring in alive. I am a man much constrained by the strictures of the law, Mr. Rawn. Had I or one of my men apprehended him alive, I would have been forced to give the man a fair trial, and who knows how that might've played out? At times I truly long for your autonomy. I see its benefits, even though the attendant downsides are not to be taken lightly. At this junction in time, with the rising tide of crime flooding our shores and thousands of outsiders occupying and judging this city, you were a fit. That is the reason I allowed you to hire on as an independent contractor, despite the fact that I care not a whit for either you or your style. Disguises, degenerate informants, lurking in the very bowels of the underworld... such tactics are as gauche as they are reprehensible. Yet it stands that they are effective."

Smirking, Alvord performed a sardonic half-bow.

"As it happens, Mr. Dean, my stay here in the Gem of the Prairie is coming to an end. You will have to abide my glaring lack of tact no more. You may recall that my contract is due to expire this week? In three days time I depart for Michigan's Upper Peninsula."

The Marshall's eyes squinted slightly in surprise. "Whatever for? Aside from the copper mines there, the place is a desolate wasteland fit only for Indians and half-breeds. And Frenchmen, perhaps."

"It is a trapping expedition I embark on, so the more desolate and unscarred by mankind the better, I'd imagine. For such a purpose it is a most inviting tract of wilderness."

"A former Manhattan lawman seeking adventure on the frontier? I sense that there is more to your character than meets the eye, Mr. Rawn." Folding his hands, Dean pursed his lips as if pained by what he was about to say. "Well then, now is the time, I suppose. If you are willing, I seek your counsel."

Alvord's eyebrows rose in surprise. "What did you have in mind, pray tell?"

Dean opened a desk drawer and from it withdrew a pile of papers. Placing these on the table, he tapped them pointedly with his index finger.

"I am beset on all sides. Horse stealing is rampant, Erie and Huron sailors tear up the town at least once a month, Sunday liquor laws are ignored by tippling houses and groggeries, prostitution and gambling are out of control. Chicago boasts more gambling houses than either Cincinnati or St. Louis, in fact. Robberies, burglaries, and murders are all on the rise, and on a lesser, more absurd note, droves of pigs, dogs, grouse, and prairie chickens are overrunning parts of the city. I have too few men at my disposal and lack adequate funding from City Hall. You hail from our nation's largest and most corrupt city. Having spent a few weeks here, what steps do you think we can take to improve on our model? For improvement is an absolute necessity, lest vice rides roughshod over this place. Already Chicago has the unenviable reputation as a place of wickedness and iniquity."

Alvord weighed these words carefully. Here sat a man who hated him, thinking him overly violent, unpredictable, and unwilling to play by the rules. Yet the fact that Dean approved his contract in the first place spoke volumes about his mentality. He might feel threatened and overshadowed by the presence of a lawman decidedly above his station, but he still saw the value in allowing Alvord to serve the city. And presently, he knew the benefits of picking his brain for ideas. Alvord could respect that.

Though he had not been entreated to do so, he took the seat across from Dean.

"I will be brief and direct, as I have somewhere to be. Crime is on the rise and will continue to rise in Chicago due to the rapid modernization it is undergoing, of which magnified crime is an unfortunate but invariable excrescence. Firstly, your men, while gallant, fit, and willing, lack direction and organization. That accounts for the majority of their failures. The fault lies partly with you and partly with City Hall and its refusal to work closely with you. The establishment of well-defined wards was a good first step, but their mere presence is meaningless in and of itself. Men are currently assigned to these wards, but they cannot walk about willy-nilly, as now they do. They need regular, predetermined foot posts. These beats can be altered as is seen fit, but your men *must* be a constant, visible presence in the community. And likewise must their duties be clearly defined, for men of the badge should not be running around killing stray dogs and flocks of grouse when there is actual crime to be fought."

Dean scribbled a bit on a piece of paper at intervals, but mostly sat and listened. Without warning Alvord swiftly rose and began pacing around the room, his hands clasped pensively behind his back.

"Secondly, you need to develop a proper rapport with the community. This is a tightly-knit town-"

"City," Dean interrupted piercingly.

"City," acknowledged Alvord with a deferent nod, raising his voice to be heard over the baying of some nearby dogs. "But that is no excuse for the state of things. Your men either mix too freely with the populace or remain too aloof from it. While a patrolman *is* a man apart, you need to temper professionalism with sound and, most importantly, *consistent* community relations.

"My last bit of advice is that you revise your ranking system. It is not good when one man sits at the helm and the rest of the men all possess the same rank. Several of your men have demonstrated definite leadership qualities. You should retain your rank as City Marshall, but William Wesencraft should be made Head Constable or Captain, depending on what terminology you choose to employ. That man has got some serious potential, you mark my words. Next, there should be at least two patrolmen to each ward. At least. This one ward, one patrolman nonsense is laughable and criminals and citizens alike realize it. You know these men better than I, and would be the best man to match them up. Aside from that, mounted units would be beneficial during the less muddy months, especially given the number of superlative riders within your ranks. And if City Hall remains unobliging then send petition after petition demanding reconsideration, and raise public awareness about your plans."

Dean concluded his note taking with a few last raspy scratches of the quill.

"Well then," said Alvord summarily as he headed for the door, "that said, I must be going. I will drop by tomorrow to receive my standard rate of pay for this week, with the apprehension of two murderers, three horse-thieves, six sneak-thieves, one rapist, five sots, and fifteen drunken brawlers added to the sum."

"Oh," he added as an afterthought cropped up, "and I'd be beholden to you if you kept Francis Macintosh off the chain gangs once he recovers. Perhaps just have him leave town. He is rumored to be dead, slain by my hand, and though I shall soon be gone I prefer that my reputation remains."

"No and no."

Alvord froze in the act of opening the door. Turning back, face flinty, he witnessed an unsettling change come over Dean's demeanor. Was the man trying to frown or smile? Alvord had rarely witnessed the man offer any indicators of emotion, so this sudden transformation struck him as unusual.

"No?" asked Alvord, somewhat amusedly.

"You are a rogue who is unfit to uphold the law. I am withholding your payment, Mr. Rawn."

"The devil you are. I suggest you mind your tongue ere it leads you astray, Phillip."

He watched the fellow clench his stubbly jaw, but his scowl soon gave way to a delighted, albeit sinister smile. Alvord cocked his head to the side, a bit confused. He had never before seen the man even come close to smiling.

Eyes blazing, Dean continued. "I confess that I now know just who you are, and just what stains darken your past. Some fellows from Manhattan came for the River and Harbor Convention and apparently recognized you. And then, whilst dining with those New Yorkers, some associates of mine were informed of your shadowy past by those same men. A disgraced ex-Captain of Manhattan's Municipal Police Department, eh?

When you stated that you had experience as a lawman in New York, you should have specified, Mr. Rawn. Had I been privy to that information, I'd have turned you away at once. I knew there was something about you that I distrusted, and my suspicions have at last been confirmed. So, you led an unauthorized raid, did you? That in itself reveals your arrant contempt for protocol. But even that could not sate your bloodlust, could it? So you slaughtered the wounded in the aftermath. Killing defeated men, be they gangsters or not, is barbarous and lowly in my book. A vituperative action if ever I've heard."

Alvord took a long, meaningful step towards Dean, whose rigid form tensed but remained seated. This ignorant bumpkin knew nothing of the details of that attack, knew nothing of the vengeance that had fueled it. The features on Alvord's sharp, rectangular visage contorted into a fearsome glower.

"You're digging yourself into a hole, Marshall." His voice slowed and deepened, as always it did when his ire was roused.

"Am I, now?" Dean spat maliciously. "You forget yourself, man. *You* are the stranger in this city, not I. *You* have broken countless laws in pursuit of what passes for justice in your mind. *You* are a scoundrel and an arrogant knave who considers himself utterly above the law you so boldly claim to uphold. You withhold information from me, ignore the terms of your contract, and this is what happens. Consider it a life lesson. Now turn around and see yourself out, Rawn, before I choose to pursue drastic recourse."

Dean reached into a drawer and pulled out a Colt revolver, which he cocked and placed in front of him on the desk with theatric deliberation. Sneering triumphantly, he waited for Alvord to leave.

He was kept waiting. Alvord did not turn to flee, but rather took another step forward into the light. Dean hurriedly picked up his revolver, but seemed hesitant to point it. The flickering lamp threw into sharp relief Alvord's severe, chiseled features, particularly the old scar on his left temple and the newer, raw-looking one on his right cheek, a disfigurement that left a gap in his trim red beard.

This situation was all-too reminiscent of another that took place a few months back, after his retaliatory slaughter of the Irish gang called the Roach Guards, the incident Dean had brought up. Then too, he had been ordered to leave a city due to perceived excessive force by some smug, clueless prick perched behind a desk.

Alvord's tone mirrored perfectly the contemptuous look on his face. "You dare to ask my advice before turning on me like a filthy viper? Skulls have shattered for far less, *worm.* My soul bears its scars, as does any. Your own sags under the weight of a sin so heinous that you'd be run out of town for it."

He paused, watching as that moment of dawning comprehension made itself known on his enemy's face. When he resumed speaking it was with grave deliberateness.

"I am not so easily duped, Phillip. That dapper young lad, Art Bramson, could tell me all about it, now couldn't he? Especially if plied with those candied walnuts he favors and some of that quality Madeira you routinely gift him with, no? A *very* young lad, isn't he Phillip?"

The mock regret he employed in that last sentence had the desired effect. Phillip Dean's face grew blank, taking on an insalubrious looking shade of gray.

"Dead useful, those 'degenerate informants' of mine, wouldn't you agree?" Steely-eyed, Alvord put his hands on Dean's desk and leaned closer. "*My payment,* Phillip."

Dean licked his dry lips and blinked rapidly.

Alvord adopted a weary tone, standing tall once more. "Unless, of course, you want me to reveal this delicate piece of information to City Hall? Ah! I see your eyes straying to that Colt. Go ahead, I entreat you, but be warned that my informant has been instructed to spill your secret should anything happen to me during the remainder of my stay. I myself have signed the papers she will deliver, and my reputable character will be vouched for by Horace Greeley, a good friend of mine from back in my Manhattan days. His speech given earlier today was well received by Mayor Curtiss and the rest of Chicago, I daresay. So, are you really prepared to kill a man and your career in one fell swoop, over so trivial a matter as violence towards criminals and the omission of certain truths?"

Dean slowly lowered the hammer of the revolver and put it down. He reached into a desk drawer and withdrew a leather pouch. This he threw roughly at Alvord, who deftly caught it and rattled its contents close to his ear.

"A fine sound, the jingling of hard-earned coin. Goodnight, Phillip, and don't worry- your secret is safe with me. A wonder, is it not, how one morsel of information can transform a man of influence to one of very little consequence? Oh, and since I have been officially decommissioned, you can have the pleasure of dealing with this suppurating carcass." Casually, with only the barest indication of gloating, he tossed his badge onto the desk.

Dean's eyes and voice exuded pure venom. "You'll swing for this."

"That I tend to doubt," Alvord stated briskly over his

shoulder, leaving that drab shack to reenter the babel of chatter and revelry beyond.

Chapter 3

A young harlot named Lizzie winced against the lurid guffaws filling the second story of Freneau's Billiard Hall. The source of all this ruckus stood boldly under the soft luminosity of the gaslight chandeliers hanging over a billiards table. Quite comfortably did the man preside over the motley assortment of humanity before him, among them both high and lowborn men, politicians and common criminals.

Lizzie sighed petulantly, finding the sordid tale the trim, sly-looking Irishman related to be distasteful in the extreme and a dreadful bore to boot.

Leaning idly against a billiards cue, the storyteller pressed relentlessly on above the roar of drunken mirth.

"So another dram of the stuff sends me for a right old loop, drugged it must have been, and when I regain me senses what do I come to perceive? That beefy, pockmarked gal has me slung over her shoulder like a sack of spuds and is toting me up the bleedin' stairs! And gents, only dark deeds transpire in the rooms beyond and such words ain't fit for delicate ears. In my enfeebled condition, I figured me doom to be pronounced. As I eloquently voiced my disapproval of the situation, she looked at me and grinned with green teeth- I tell you now, a nastier sow did never muck up a Waterford pigsty."

Turning away from the speaker, who artfully paused as the hilarity of his listeners crested, Lizzie prepared to quit the place. He was the focus of all eyes, this besotted Irish dog. It was hard to work one's prurient charms when such a figure was busy stealing the show. Yet this hardly ruined the night, for she possessed an unusual degree of flexibility for a whore. Aside from working Madame Worth's brothel, she was also paid to fossick about the city for the sake of luring men back to the whorehouse. So long as she did not stray onto rival turf, that was. Such a move could provoke dire results.

So she would leave this raucous pool hall, but would not have far to go. This *was* Wells Street, after all, where many places existed for a whore to ply her trade, where many a foolish soul would part with his dignity for a few schillings worth of carnal delight.

Deep in thought, she bumped into a large, powerfully made

male form. She looked up at the man, a hasty apology poised upon her lips, but the breath caught in her throat as she suddenly recognized him.

For this hulking, stern-visaged fellow was none other than the lawman that the darker elements of Chicago had come to fear of late. His name remained a mystery, but his appearance was unmistakable. Several times he had been pointed out to her from afar. Even at a distance, his height and regal bearing, dark hair and incongruous red beard were readily detectable. Even at a distance, one could perceive the stark austerity of his features.

Up close, it turned out, those features were all the more forbidding.

Lizzie's mouth dried up, her throat tightening most uncomfortably. Her apprehension was well placed. America's vagrancy laws, as ill-defined and poorly enforced as they might be, did officially render her profession unlawful. A profession made all too obvious by her suggestive attire and rouge-smeared cheeks. The stories whispered of about this man and his private war against vice suggested a temperament towards illegal behavior that could engender grave consequences for her. Could it be that he now planned to run the whores out of town? It seemed far-fetched, but then again so were many of the rumors surrounding him... how would she travel, having saved precious little of her earnings? Ah, the money had she pissed away on opium and frivolous trinkets!

A thrill of trepidation passed through her when her dark brown eyes met the glacial gaze of his gray ones. Harsh judgment and loathing lurked therein. To communicate this more deliberately, his lips and nose slowly curled into an acrid sneer.

Though rightly startled, Lizzie had the presence of mind to slip deeper into the welcoming embrace of the shadows.

After watching the young harlot leave, Alvord took in the scene at a glance. It was your usual ragtag assortment of class and race that these frontier billiard halls seemed to attract. The upscale Manhattan billiard halls that he was accustomed to, more formal in both design and atmosphere, did not permit folks to mix so freely. But here on the frontier the attitudes regarding social class and ethnicity were far more relaxed, he found. Where else would statesmen and wealthy businessmen rub elbows with woodsmen, half-breeds, hoodlums and the like?

Through the swirling haze of cigar and pipe smoke he beheld

his Irish friend, Finnbar Fagan, loudly recounting one of his more objectionable exploits to the crowd.

"So I'm floundering about like a landed pike, stripped down to me bloody unmentionables, and she-"

"My, I'm so glad I get to interrupt this," Alvord said to no one in particular as he stepped out from the crowd.

Finnbar's clean-shaven face lit up. "Alvord! I do hope this evening finds you well, lad! If not, lend me your ear as I finish this tale of mine, which is sure to put a smile on even that dour mug of yours!"

Alvord almost smiled in spite of himself; the Irishman's good-natured personality could be terribly infectious.

"Riveting though your story undoubtedly is, I am afraid it must come to a premature close. We are to dine with Horace in an hour, as I'm sure you remember."

Finnbar pursed his lips thoughtfully. "Hmmm, does ring a bell, however faintly..."

Alvord's sudden appearance, meanwhile, stimulated an overt change in the crowd. Much of the laughter stopped dead in its tracks, supplanted by speculative whispers. Tales of his deeds were well circulated in this, the shadiest part of town, where underworld denizens had grown intimately acquainted with his forceful brand of law enforcement.

Not everyone was so interested or impressed, however.

"Hey you," grunted a callous voice redolent with indignation and inebriety, "why don't you let the Irishman finish weavin' 'is tale? 'Twill only take half a mo'. You've no right to make 'im stop."

The assembly grew stiller yet and watched absorbedly, man's age-old love of drama holding them hopelessly in thrall.

Alvord clenched his jaw, bowing his head in an effort to restrain himself. He was a man accustomed to being accorded a certain degree of respect, and it showed. In Manhattan, reputation alone would have been enough to deter such insolence.

"Let us retrieve Marcel and be off, Finnbar, lest my patience wear any thinner. It has been a rather trying night."

"Hey you," the man persisted, courting disaster, "in case you're hard of hearing, I'll tell you one more time to let 'im finish."

Alvord spun round to assess the impudent speaker. Blonde, of average height and stout build, the man's pugnacious face leered nastily at Alvord. He bore the unmistakable stamp of a sailor, his attire consisting of filthy, tight-fitting white pants and a blue vest, with a small, rakishly angled hat of black leather surmounting his head. Further evidence presented itself in a dangling gold earring and the heavily tattooed arms that rolled up sleeves revealed. Four men of the same mold hung around him, all of whom appeared to have reached an aggressive stage of drunkenness. They stared with narrowed eyes, like wolves assessing a potential prey item. Rough men, hard men, but men whose whiskey-befogged minds could not distinguish between a good idea and a rather bad one.

"Are you having a good night?" Alvord asked of the man with disarming sincerity.

Quite taken aback, the sailor sputtered, "I well, ah, I mean, I suppose so. What of it?"

"Because unless you start minding your own damn business, you syphilitic, deck-swabbing imbecile, it is about to end on an awfully sour note."

The sailor and his chums visibly bristled and advanced a step or two, fists tightly clenched. The crowd broke its expectant silence to loudly roar its approval. Men began yielding ground so as to clear the center of the room, as if in preparation for a cockfight. Money changed hands as bets were swiftly placed on the outcome of the impending altercation.

The ringleader sneered amusedly. "Oh, so you think you're going to just roll over the five of us, big fella? Just like that? Listen, why don't you let the mick finish his yarn and we'll let you walk your arrogant ass outta here. Otherwise it's gettin' carried out, *savvy*?"

A darkness swept across Alvord's face, one that mingled with perfect balance the emotions of anger and cynical amusement. Anxiously the assembly leaned in, a single organism with a single-minded wish.

"You're out beyond your depth, mariner," Alvord assured him with baleful deliberation.

The man looked from Alvord, who stood alone but tall and supremely confident in the center of the room, to his own glowering shipmates. "Think we'll take our chances."

A most wicked grin slid onto Finnbar's clean-shaven face as he stepped forward to take up position beside his friend, who glanced his way and nodded crisply. The Irishman's smile broadened to reveal a gold upper canine that gleamed in the fulgent light of the chandeliers. Wildly spiked, dark red hair further lent a wild aspect to his appearance.

Alvord allowed himself a mordant smirk of his own; now here was man to draw blood beside.

"Easy there, boyos. A few deep breaths would do ye some good. Come Alvord, we shouldn't fritter away our time like this, bandying words with the scum and froth the tide hath cast ashore..."

With a rowdy yell, the sailors charged as one. Three of them made a beeline for Alvord as the other two raced each other to get at Finnbar, who sloshed the remainder of his beer into their snarling faces.

The man closest to Alvord swung a savage, overhand shot at him but met only the air Alvord had breathed a second before. Stumbling along, his momentum carried him onto a nearby pool table. Having neatly side-stepped his first assailant, Alvord went about dealing with the rest. The blonde man he dealt a cracking backhand to the chin that all but robbed him of his senses. He staggered sideways before going down, nearly colliding with Finnbar, who was busy belaboring his two sailors with a pool cue.

The third man rushed boldly in, heedless of consequence. Alvord took a swift step forward to meet him, using his superior reach to land the first blow, which took the form of a cracking jab to teeth. His next punch was a vicious right hand to the heart. A move that he had often employed in the past, Alvord watched with grim satisfaction as it did its job, leaving the man clutching his chest and hoarsely gasping for breath. Just as he repositioned himself for an uppercut, the first man made a wild leap off the pool table. Landing on Alvord's broad back, he drove a hard knee into his kidney before seeking to choke out his larger opponent. Before he could sink the hold, Finnbar spun and promptly broke his billiard cue across the sailor's back.

Alvord heard the cracking of the stick in concert with man's grunt of pain. Reaching back, he grabbed him by the hair and bodily heaved him to the floor. Alvord stomped with finality on his stomach before slamming a fist into the mariner's beaky nose, which released a sharp crack along with a fine, red mist.

Men shouted mostly foolish advice and roared with drunken pleasure as injuries were doled out. They groaned in nearly universal disappointment as they watched Finnbar get tackled to the ground by his remaining opponent.

The man proceeded to rain uninterrupted, hammering blows upon him. Seeing a sudden opening, Finnbar managed to stab his thumb into the flesh just below the sailor's jaw line, hitting a pressure point. The man reared back, away from the digging thumb, allowing the Irishman to capitalize on the shift of weight and flip him over. They grappled awkwardly for a bit before Finnbar gained the upper hand. He dropped three quick knees into his ribs, opening him up for repeated punches to the face.

Meanwhile the blonde sailor, once again steady on his feet,

reentered the fray. He blindsided Alvord with a wild but largely ineffectual right hook, swung as it was with anger but ill form. Alvord laid the ruffian low with a blurring right hand-left hook combination. Though he never fought for spectacle or money, Alvord's boxing background gave him a decided advantage in most scraps. During his time in Manhattan Alvord had trained with such illustrious figures as heavyweight boxing champ Tom Hyer and Bowery B'hoy bigwig William Poole, another feared bare-knuckle fighter. Two years back, while leading a police raid on the Sawdust House, he overcame the famed prizefighter Yankee Sullivan after a savage barroom brawl that left him nursing a host of injuries but also a keen understanding of precisely what he was capable of.

Panting, Finnbar surveyed the bodies littering the floor. "I guess the saying holds true, then."

"And what saying might that be?" inquired Alvord as he began steadying his own breathing.

"'He that would go to sea for pleasure, would go to hell for a pastime.'"

In a mule-like manner the crowd brayed its appreciation.

Finnbar stroked his chin in mock thoughtfulness. "I wonder if they still qualify as "able-bodied" seamen. Eh? Eh?"

The crowd's rousing laughter at that one firmly attested to its dissipation.

"This is a lake, you know," Alvord archly pointed out.

Shaking his head hopelessly, the Irishman countered, "If comedy was a thoroughfare, my friend, you'd be a pothole of legendary proportion."

Alvord threw back his great head and let out a rare rumble of laughter.

"Well done, Finnbar, coaxing those oafs into quarrel. They had need of a proper thrashing."

"And who better to administer it than us?"

Bowing his head, and spreading his arms in mock solemnity, Alvord replied, "Verily, they have met with their reward."

Some of the sailors were beginning to stir. The blonde-haired leader of the bunch tried to rise but reeled about the room before resuming his place on the filthy, trash-ridden floor.

An onlooker, staggering with drink, began savagely kicking one of the fallen. Before he landed his third, however, Alvord sent the heels of his hands crashing into the drunkard's shoulders. The man soared across the room before the wall checked his progress.

"He didn't earn that right," he stated clearly and firmly.

Those nearest them hastily drew back. Hank Freneau, the

establishment's rotund owner, pushed his way past his patrons and began ordering them to help him throw the sailors out.

"Sir," he turned to Alvord with a deferent little nod of his bald, perspiring head, "Please accept my profuse apologies. These men are sailors, just some rowdy b'hoys passing through and trying to find a decent watering hole. They knew not of your position within the city, nor of your character. What transpired was-"

"Nothing more than men blowing off steam, some more efficiently then others..."

The man breathed a noticeable sigh of relief.

"Ah. Alright then, so-"

"Business appears to be booming tonight and should remain as such. By all means, Hank, carry on."

Gingerly feeling his right cheek, which sported a rising bruise, Finnbar jerked his head towards a door at the other end of the room.

"Marcel is over yonder, Alvord, hope he's making out better'n I... 'twas feeling lucky this eve, but alas ended up loosing a fair bit o' coin at the billiards table, I did."

"*Gamble*, of course, being the root of the word gambling..."

The Irishman shrugged carelessly. "Always more from whence it came. One of the many perks of having a noble lineage."

Finnbar hailed from County Cork in Ireland. If his stories were to be believed, his ancestors were noblemen whose wealth had been passed down through the ages. Free as he was with his money, of which he always seemed to have a goodly store, Alvord tended to believe him. Curiously enough, one of Alvord's ancestors, Sir Walter Raleigh, had actually fought against Finnbar's rebellious forbearers under England's banner.

An aspiring writer, Finnbar had come to America after fighting as a mercenary in the Uruguayan Civil War. Seeking literary inspiration, he wished to travel for a tidy spell before hunkering down to write. He spoke often of his "associates" back home in Ireland, and in each new city he passed through mentioned having business to attend to, but Alvord could only speculate on what that business might be. The Irishman generally spoke and offered up information without restraint; that he kept mum on his "business" was highly uncharacteristic, but then again it was *his* business, not anyone else's.

They passed through the door, entering upon a scene that mightily contrasted with the rowdiness of the billiards room they'd left behind.

Here a quieter atmosphere prevailed, in keeping with the dim lighting and somber countenances of the four men who sat around the room's only table. All four held cards in their hands, cards they stared fixedly at when they weren't shrewdly assessing the faces of their competition.

Alvord and Finnbar watched as their friend Marcel Durand, veteran trapper and wanderer of lonely lands, assessed his hand with expressionless, deep-set eyes. His weatherworn, fringed buckskin clothing, while not entirely out of place in a frontier city like Chicago, did stand out against the sumptuous velvet vests and muslin evening coats of his fellow players. His strong French features, however, were every bit as deadpan and unreadable as his opposition's. Clothing did not necessarily make the man in this game.

"I'm out," one of the men suddenly said with a sigh as he laid his cards down. Easing back in his chair, he lit a cigar and took a conciliatory puff.

One man let the ghost of smirk slide onto his face. He peered slowly around the table, closely studying the demeanors of the other men.

"Anyone else suffering from lack of luck or dash?"

Alvord knew the speaker: one John Sears, a professional gambler *par excellence* and rumored to be among the best poker players in the country. A soft-voiced Southerner of French descent, his exceptional looks and charming nature had earned him a solid reputation in the city, despite his dubious profession. Female gazes were wont to linger on this man, who was touted as one of Chicago's best-dressed.

His inquiry was greeted by three grunts of "In" and the movement of money upon the table. Marcel did not even bothered to look up from his cards, but instead took a moment to inhale a nonchalant lungful off his cheroot cigar.

"Alright then. Bets have been made- let us see who Lady Fortune favors this time 'round."

Sears clutched a pair of jacks. The two men on either side of him, Walt Winchester and King Cole Conant, held three sevens and nothing of consequence, respectively. They were part of his crew, which consisted of the most courteous, easygoing gamblers Alvord had ever encountered.

Without any flourish or detectable conceit, Marcel put down his cards to reveal a nine-high diamond flush.

"Read 'em and weep, gents."

Winchester and Conant swore good-naturedly, but Sears's only reaction took the form of a few small nods of resignation.

"Well played, trapper. By the by, that barely perceptible

twitch in the corner of your left eye- were you using that all along to indicate unease in the hopes of using it falsely in the future?"

"That'd be tellin', *mon ami.*"

The gambler chuckled appreciatively. "*C'est la vérité.*"

Marcel's bushy eyebrows rose in amused curiosity. "You play any whist, Sears?"

The professional gambler smiled slyly. "Against you, friend- no. Not tonight. I'd be willing to wager that you are quite the tactician when it comes to that particular game, and I have lost more than enough money on this most inauspicious of evenings."

"I hear you, mate," Finnbar remorsefully commiserated.

"Marcel," Alvord said, taking advantage of a pause in the conversation, "I hate to be a killjoy, but we should get a move on if we are to make dinner on schedule."

An unrestrained snort of laughter erupted from Finnbar. "Who d'ya think you're kidding, Alvord? You relish the role of the killjoy! Never, and I do mean never, have I seen you happier than when quelling enjoyment!"

"True enough. I was merely being diplomatic."

Sears turned to assess the two new arrivals.

"The wry Irishman himself! Back for another fleecing, then?"

"Oooh, not quite. Once bitten, twice shy, Sears. Anyways, this poor son of Erin hasn't two coins to rub together after the billiards tables had their say. Lady Fortune proved specious and fickle tonight."

"Unenviable qualities in any mistress," nodded Sears understandingly.

His gaze turned to Alvord, where it lingered until recognition flooded his dark eyes.

"Aha! The dark avenger whispered of in sordid places." He spread his arms out to the sides, grinning. "Am I next- art thou come hither to torment me before the appointed time?"

Alvord nodded appreciatively. "Mark 8:29. A Bible quoting career gambler, eh? Peculiar."

"I've got Shakespeare and Burns at my disposal as well."

"I don't doubt you. To answer your question- no, I am not here for you. For a gambler, you are oddly well mannered and, what's more, well regarded throughout the city. Aside from an unwholesome addiction to gambling, your record is unblemished from what I have gathered."

"Ah, you'll have me blushing now! But enough about me. So- much skullduggery afoot this night?"

"About the usual. Significantly, though, the Gem of the

Prairie is now unsullied by the presence of Richard Tansworth. He'll be collecting flies before the morn."

"Finally got him, did you? Well done. A rogue through and through, that one. I did not much care for his company, although several times I did win plenty of spondulick off that Brit imbecile."

Marcel rose and collected his winnings. He stood a squat and burly five foot six, with heavy musculature straining at the chest and shoulders of his buckskin shirt. Scratching at the old powder burn on his right cheek, he addressed the gamblers genially.

"Good playin' with you fellers. Happy Fourth. Fifth, actually, but you get me. G'night."

"A parting question, if you will," Sears quickly requested of Marcel. "Where in Heaven's name did you learn the craft?"

Shrugging nonchalantly, Marcel answered in his gravely voice. "Played a bit as a young 'un on the Mississippi flatboats and steamboats, then honed my skills at Trapper's Rendezvous in the Rockies. Won a small fortune off o' Joe Meeks back in '33 at Horse Creek. To his credit, he was rightly stewed at the time. And then hell, I really cleaned house eight years back at Green River. And now I play when I feels the urge and have the means."

Sears held out his smooth palm. "A fine showing, trapper. See you around."

After genially clasping the proffered hand, Marcel joined Alvord and Finnbar as they walked out of the room and made their way through the animated crowds of the billiards hall. With rueful eyes Finnbar stared as the mountain man transferred his ample winnings into a plump leather pouch.

"You made out alright then, did you?"

"Better'n your sorry Irish ass, I can tell."

"Truer words have rarely been spoken," Finnbar admitted sheepishly.

Alvord led the way downstairs and swung wide the main door. "Let us be shot of this indecorous place."

They left behind those smoky rooms and cackling men, stepping onto muddy, malodorous Wells Street

Chapter 4

Getting muddy: an unavoidable by-product of pedestrian travel in Chicago this time of year. "The Mudhole of the Prairies," as America had mockingly christened Chicago, was a nickname most aptly applied.

To traverse the sixty-six foot wide, miry roads was pure nightmare. The majority lacked adequate sidewalks, although in certain areas planks had been thrown down willy-nilly in an effort to provide some crude form of a walkway. Along the waterfront and in the more respectable areas of town, some tentative efforts at paving were underway, but by and large Chicago's road systems were a noisome chaos of muck, debris, animal shit, and filthy water.

No one had planned Chicago. Most American cities were formed by venturesome groups of pioneers whose carefully chosen sites were conducive to settlement. Here, private landowners had put in roads on whim, resulting in glaring discontinuities and heterogeneous districts that lacked centrality. True, Slab Town did lie near the southernmost point of Lake Michigan, astride a major river and thus nicely situated to link Great Lakes trade and commerce with that of the Mississippi Valley waterways. But the city, as it developed piecemeal alongside the Indian and fur trades, arose amidst a squalid collection of bogs and sloughs, alongside a sluggish river choked with wild rice and rank growths of wild onion and skunk cabbage. The city actually derived its name from the Illinois Indian's name for the Chicago River, which they had dubbed *Checagou*, meaning onion or foul smell.

The arrival of civilization did little to improve the conditions, although the river's flow was made better due to dredging and the widening of its mouth, formerly clogged with sand, driftwood, and vegetation. The smells and the mud, however, that thick and clinging mud so often associated with Chicago, remained and was rather worsened by the traffic of sixteen thousand inhabitants and the various beasts that accompanied human habitation.

Epic sludge puddles sat stagnantly in the road, in which pigs wallowed by day, and from which legions of frogs gave vent to their passions come nightfall. Signs had been planted next to some of the more expansive pools, bearing sardonic captions like, "No bottom here!" "Quickest route to China!" and "Abandon all hope, ye who enter here!"

Finnbar, ambling along with his customary spryness despite the slippery conditions, scrutinized some such inscriptions and burst into appreciative laughter.

"Gotta love humor in the face of adversity! My, how I shall miss this place! This city has character and no mistake! What say you fellas?"

"I too shall miss certain things about it," admitted Alvord, kicking an unwary prairie chicken out of his way in an eruption of feathers. "It is a most interesting study. This city lies at the cusp of frontier obscurity and entry into the modern sphere of America's commercial and industrial enterprise. Soon after our departure the Illinois-Michigan Canal will be completed, linking Chicago to our vast transportation nexus and thus ensuring its economic future, at least in the short term. I also found it fascinating to observe how an essentially rural population waits with bated breath as modernity draws apace. With the steady increase in population these past few years have witnessed, Chicagoans will soon make the leap to being residents of a thriving urban center, and they know it."

"I see. And what about you, trapper old friend?"

Marcel cast an unimpressed eye around the street, with its rowdy occupants and unwholesome looking log and balloon-frame buildings. He sniffed the air only to grimace in apparent disgust.

"I ain't much fer cities. And truth to tell, I don't much grow attached to places fer the most part. 'Cept fer two spots, that is. One such location is called Shoshone Basin, deep in Indian Territory in the Wind River Mountains. T'other is the very place we're headed fer up Michigan way. Both are remote and untainted by man- you get to see God's original handiwork pure and unblemished."

Alvord and Finnbar looked at one another, eyebrows cocked. Rare were the moments when Marcel evinced any signs of sentimentality; rarer yet were the times when he waxed poetic.

"You aren't getting soft on us now, are ye Marcel?"

The stocky mountain man promptly gave the lean Irishman a shove that sent him staggering.

"Just tryin' to describe somethin', is all. I guess I got better uses fer my tongue than spewin' out flowery words all the livelong day."

"Aye, you need only ask the last whore he was with," added Alvord in an atypical display of crass humor.

Chuckling heartily, the three men turned left onto Lake Street, where their grateful feet found the crudest semblance of plank road. When the sun held sway this part of town would once again please the ear with the rustling of silks and tempt the nose with aroma of spices and imported fruit. But for now the crescent moon and stars reigned supreme, and darkness and drunken revelry predominated. A fresh crop of fireworks threw into sharp relief the carriages that squelched their way past the row of brick retail stores lining the street. Above them jutted a forest of masts from the steamboats, clippers, canal boats, and brigs that clogged the river after having delivered to Chicago its swarm of recent visitors. To the north, the clamor of that crowd, still many thousand strong despite the late hour, issued from the Public Square, over which towered the massive Sherman House.

Alvord had met Finnbar and Marcel back in April. After being dismissed from his position with the Municipal Police Department, he accepted a job offer from the mother of a renowned frontier painter, Charles Deas, who was caught up in dangerous occult activity in St. Louis. For a considerable fee, Alvord was to journey to St. Louis and retrieve Mrs. Deas troubled son. Finnbar's path crossed his own on the journey out, and they had met Marcel shortly after their arrival in the city. Through adversity and a shared sense of justice, they had become fast friends. All three of them had been swept into the madness that dogged Charles Deas, a madness that had taken the form of the mysterious occult science of mesmerism. And all three had risked their lives in a desperate, all-or-nothing battle against an evil mesmerizer whose powers had ultimately rendered the painter's mind all but shattered. Vengeance was wreaked but alas, the damage was already done.

Alvord had escorted the ailing Deas home to Manhattan, where he was once again with family, but that festering sense of failure was something he had yet to overcome...

Finnbar cast a backward glance towards the oppressive gloom of Wells Street.

"Quite the rookery back there, isn't it? The poor blighters who dwell amidst all that squalor... although plenty of Famine Irish have it just as bad not far from here at Hardscrabble. I do hope this canal brings widespread prosperity around here... some good folks are to be found even down that dismal lane..."

Consumed by thought, Finnbar nearly knocked a woman of ill repute off the plank road. To his credit, he did recover in time to smoothly catch her falling form as it sped towards the waiting mud below.

"Do pardon the momentary lapse in this Irishman's concentration, m'dear," he apologized, adroitly setting her back on her feet. "Lots swirling about inside this noggin o' mine, sometimes I get a bit distracted, even when the scenery is as eminently lovely as it has just become..."

"Ever the gentleman," remarked Alvord to Marcel.

"Scoff if you will," Finbarr retorted as the woman went on her way after flashing him a dazzling smile, "but does it really speak ill of me that I stooped to show her a kindness? What, would you have just let the strumpet fall?"

"Yes," replied Alvord, promptly and bluntly. "So long as I did not think she'd come to any real harm. Though I find it repellant in the extreme, prostitution is a most practical indecency. Consider this- if men did not have that outlet in which to pour base desire, what would become of the girls and women whom we so carefully shelter and protect? All guns would be brought to bear on them, so to speak, and the social walls that safeguard them would crumble. Even our most concerted efforts to shield them from it would be met with failure. Men with no other option would risk death for the sake of sex, and many females would find that reality romantic in the extreme. The end result would be an unruly and tasteless free-for-all. I think that eventually women would grow every bit as ill mannered and libidinous as we men. A shame it would be, for at the moment they are so much nobler than us in those regards. So yes- with whores to reliably rut on, men are kept in check, and are actually tamer as regards lust."

"Oddly pragmatic of you, Alvord. You generally come off as something of an idealist."

"No doubt," he admitted to the Irishman. Contrary to character, he felt impelled to chew the fat after much time spent alone in Chicago's fetid underbelly.

"But that idealism is tempered by a streak of rigid realism. Anyway, it is gamblers who are to blame for the proliferation of that seedy industry in this city. They form the true advance guard of the criminal world. In their wake inevitably trail the pimps and their whores. Then follow the hoodlums, rowdies, and bookmakers, the sneak thieves, pickpockets, and burglars. Assassins come next- gunmen and garrotters, with the highest order of criminals, the con man and the counterfeiter, setting up shop once all else has been established. That is the usual progression of crime as near as I can see it. But it is gamblers and whores who act as the fundamental props of the underworld. "Most Slab Town gamblers are men kicked out of Natchez and Vicksburg during the uprising against sharpers that swept through the Mississippi Valley in '35. Having honed their craft on the riverboats, they simply followed the rivers north until, by twists and turns, they found themselves here. This is the most important gambling center north of New Orleans and west of the Alleghenies. More gambling houses are to be found here than in Cincinnati or St. Louis, I'm told."

Nodding understandingly, Marcel inquired, "So d'ya hold it against professional gamblers fer movin' into new territory and spreadin' the pestilence, so to speak?"

"Somebody's got to be held responsible for the sullying of decency."

"Oh, I don't know," mused Finnbar mildly. "Gamblers are not necessarily bad folk. The logic of Simonides comes readily to mind- *For me, a man's good enough as long as he's not lawless, and if he has the common sense of right and wrong that does a city good — a decent guy. I certainly won't find fault with a man like that. After all, there's an endless supply of stupid fools. The way I see it, if there's no great shame in it, it's all right.*"

He raised a finger and nodded sagaciously.

"All right, you two, enough o' the lofty philosophizin'..."

Alvord looked at his trapper friend. Having seen much violence and privation during his years as a mountain man, Marcel walked with a bowlegged swagger well earned. That swagger was misleading though, for his finely attuned senses, Alvord knew, were constantly at work. His keen, dark eyes sought out each flicker of shadow along the street, his ears seemed to catch noises that Alvord's own failed to. As oblivious as Finnbar outwardly seemed to such things, Marcel addressed them with all the wariness of a wild animal.

Having developed into something of a loner after the passing of his family, Alvord realized that despite what he saw in them as shortcomings, he was glad to count these men as friends. Lust, inebriety, gambling- he uncharacteristically found himself able to look past such things. Getting to know others was so often a tainting kind of knowledge, but both Marcel and Finnbar were so barefaced in the way they confronted life that he already knew most of their vices along with most of their commendable qualities. The fact that these were men on whom he could unequivocally rely further lent a sense of validity to their friendship. He even found that he had grown surprisingly accustomed to their group dynamic. He, the orderly, stern moralist with a barely submerged dark side who acted as the unofficial leader of the group in many situations; Marcel as the coarse, canny, and dauntless survivalist who met life head-on as it came his way; and Finnbar- the puckishly witty, understated intellect and keen observer of humanity whose taste for irony Alvord had yet to see surpassed. There was a depth to this Irishman's thoughts that he tried hard to conceal, lest his jovial nature seem overshadowed by profound reflection.

Scattering a pack of half-wild dogs, a group of men in high-quality top hats and tailcoats passed by them on the plank road. One of them gave Alvord a quick nod of recognition, but offered no verbal salutation.

"Do none of these townsfolk know your name? Finnbar asked of Alvord curiously. "I have heard you mentioned during my time here, but only as "that damned lawman" or "the red-bearded shit."

Alvord gave something of an amused grunt. "Only a select few are privy to my name, and they have been instructed to keep quiet on the matter. A name begets familiarity, you see. Lack of one breeds wonder, uncertainty, and dread in the minds of criminals, aloofness in mine. Cultivating such a mystique was in my best interests. As I knew that we would not tarry here long, I presented myself as an enigma, a nameless something to be feared rather than understood."

Marcel chuckled lightly, taking a drag off his cheroot. Finnbar merely shook his head in wonderment.

"Machiavelli would be ever so proud. They should write a book about you one day- too bad Sir Walter Scott wasn't born a generation later."

"Scott wrote only historical novels."

Finnbar peered with twinkling eyes at the sliver of crescent moon. "*Precisely*. Alvord, me inscrutable mate, I get the feeling that one day our deeds will be transmuted into the very fabric of history. What say you, Marcel?"

"Damned if I know," the trapper grunted disinterestedly as he paused in the chalky darkness of an alleyway to make empty his bladder.

Chapter 5

In his lodgings at Chicago's popular Sauganash Hotel, Alvord considered his appearance in a looking glass. His favorite frock coat of charcoal hung just above his knees, which were covered by trousers of the same color. A pleated, black satin vest covered a newly starched white shirt. No fancy embroidery, no puffed-up shoulder pads or bejeweled buttons; unlike many of his day, Alvord preferred simplicity in dress to the foppish fripperies that people sported if they could afford to.

Running a comb through his dark, oiled chestnut hair one last time, he grabbed his good black top hat of silk and carefully placed it atop his head. His outfit complete, Alvord's gray eyes strayed from his reflection.

The quarters that he, Finnbar, and Marcel had secured here at the Sauganash consisted of three modestly sized but well-furnished rooms. Three cots served as beds in one, with a generous sitting room and a washroom/earth closet comprising the other two. Flush toilets, while available in the more refined of American cities, were as yet an unheard-of luxury this far west. Their predecessor, the earth closet, while not nearly so convenient, was nevertheless preferable to the outhouses or cesspools used by most. Perhaps having been spoiled by middle-class life in Manhattan, Alvord would not venture to call this place tasteful, but the rooms served their purpose and easily accommodated he and his two companions.

Marcel, blatantly refusing to make use of the brass spittoon that sat nearby, sent a globular dollop of tobacco juice plummeting towards the uncarpeted floor. Although this struck Alvord as patently uncouth, in truth it hardly mattered. The floor had been hopelessly tobacco stained when first they laid eyes on it, so what real point was there in striving for cleanliness in that regard? He did not approve of chewing tobacco, a rampant practice across America. Sure, in the folly of youth he had taken snuff a few times in an effort to cultivate a manly bearing, but plug tobacco had always struck him as unpleasant and unwholesome as smoking.

Dubiously looking over his own form in another mirror across the room, Marcel sniffed with manifest suspicion the sleeve of the bright red calico shirt he had just donned.

"Somethin's wrong with this here shirt. Don't smell right."

"Although no doubt foreign and confounding to your olfactory, that is the smell of cleanliness, Marcel me boyo," Finnbar informed him crisply as he pulled on a form-fitting black coat. "We are dining tonight with a man of great station, after all. I had that pert little washerwoman downstairs go to town on it. Quite the pong the poor lass waged war against, I'll have ye know."

Marcel gave the shirt another critical, distrustful sniff and crinkled his nose in revulsion.

"S'the way a man should smell," he grumbled. "Musky. I feel like a dandy in this damn thing now..."

"A dandy! I very much doubt ye'd meet the qualifications! Have you *ever* bathed, for instance?"

"When it's hot, sometimes I take to swimmin', but proper washin' only needs to be done a time or two a year. And that's a fact, ask any mountain man."

Finnbar chuckled and shook his head in amazement. "A regular Beau Brummel, you are."

"Beau *who*?"

"Beau Brummel. He was this chap, a proper coxcomb, over in England and France, quite into fashion and this whole hygiene trend. He is credited with establishing the white tie dress code that we in the civilized world currently adhere to. Bathed too much, if you ask me- once a day, if ye'll believe it!"

Finnbar snatched up an ornately carved cane he sometimes carried and distractedly twirled it until it moved in blurred circles before him.

"Where did you learn to brandish a stick so well?" Alvord asked of him curiously. "You demonstrated ample skill whilst belaboring those sailors with a billiards cue earlier."

"An old gypsy taught me back home in Cork," Finnbar replied absentmindedly. Leaning close to the mirror, he secured his green ascot with a stickpin that sported a golden falcon head at its tip. Grabbing a detachable collar, he tucked it into place and turned it upwards. His claret-colored hair, newly spiked, would not be mussed by the application of a top hat, Alvord knew by now. The Irishman refused to don one, despite it being considered a quintessential piece of Victorian garb.

Content with his ensemble, the Irishman tipped himself a crafty wink in the mirror. Whistling an unidentifiable tune, he strode over to the liquor cabinet next to the room's large horsehair sofa and removed from it a half-drained bottle of whiskey and three shot glasses.

Splashing some of the amber liquid into each glass, he

proposed, "Let us toast the night and our impending frontier escapades, shall we?"

"A sound proposition, Finnbar. But let us be quick about it, for we do need to be getting to dinner over at the Lake House."

Marcel grabbed the bottle and looked it over, scratching the old powder burn that marred the flesh under his right eye. "Ah. This is the corn whiskey I bought the other day, comes from Kentucky. I guess some Dutchmen-"

"German," Alvord corrected him, as if automatically. Most Americans had an absurd habit of calling German immigrants Dutch, confusing that word with the name of the Germanic homeland as spoken in the native tongue.

"Some *German*, then, started a distillery a ways back and apparently it's takin' off. S'good stuff. Had myself some last night."

Alvord stared pointedly at the half-empty bottle. Some indeed. His eyes sought out the label. *Old Jake Beam.*

"Let us give it a go, then."

Together they took an investigative snort.

"Whew!" Finnbar shook his head clear before pouring another round. "Vivifying, that was."

"*Vivifying*? You drunk or sober?" Alvord demanded of him, eyebrows arched in suspicion.

"Somewhere in betwixt. Got into some of that grand auld Monongahela Rye earlier today. Worry not- faking sobriety is a role that Finnbar Francis Fagan can play to the hilt. Glasses up then, boys- here is to some rippin' good times up Michigan way!"

"Here's to the bold men who seventy years back carved out this republic, and to those who shed their blood fer it. And to showin' two greenhorns the ropes of trappin' in God's own country, of course."

"And," added Alvord in the moment before they chinked their glasses, "to the untold glories that await us there."

"Aye!" endorsed Finnbar and Marcel in unison, and in the next moment the former Manhattan Police Captain, hardened mountain man, and roving Irish writer sucked down the piquant liquid as their thoughts strayed to what the wilds of Upper Michigan might have in store for them.

"Hope we don't have to wait too long fer vittles once we get there- I'm damn near wolfish."

"Do ye not mean peckish, Marcel?"

"Peckish? Birds peck, Finn. Peckin' is dainty. Wolves slash and tear and eat up to twenty pounds o' meat in one go. So at present I'm wolfish, not *peckish.*"

They passed through the downstairs dining hall of the Sauganash, in which merriment and its attendant ruckus were nowhere lacking. This was widely hailed as the most convivial tavern of the northwestern frontier, and also served as the social center of Chicago. Shouldering through the jostling crowd, Alvord led the way towards the front door. Though his eyes swept around the room, he was only dimly conscious of the frivolity around him. He did not delight in loud music and rowdy dance the way many people did, and wished only to get to away from this undue display so as to meet his friend Horace Greely and get a good meal in him.

Jolly Mark Beaubien, the ruddy-faced proprietor of the place, capered atop a table while vigorously sawing on a fiddle.

A girl, her speech and youthful face marred by dissipation, stumbled heavily into Finnbar, who swept her up with polished ease and nimbly danced her around in a brief, exuberant distortion of a waltz before bowing summarily and rejoining his friends.

Alvord hailed from a station in society wherein dancing was a formal and upright affair, one that he still disliked but not nearly so much as he abhorred the relaxed morals of this frontier city. Dancing wildly with a girl whom you had not been formally introduced to? It was right up the Irishman's alley, he knew, but Alvord himself heartily disapproved. In the world he knew, any man who danced so rowdily with a women in a public place would have come under some serious fire, especially so obvious a Hibernian as Finnbar. But who was he to spoil sport on such a night as this?

Finnbar sauntered back over their way, grinning like a mule eating briars. "My, that Frenchmen can really set one's feet to moving!"

"Yep, Ol' Jolly Mark there sure knows how to make them strings up and dance!"

Bringing his latest song to a rousing close, Jolly Mark suddenly noticed Marcel from his vantage and raised his fiddle in salute. This Marcel acknowledged with a casual wave.

"You two know each other?" Finnbar wondered aloud, staying in Alvord's wake as his large friend pushed his way towards the door.

"I've spent some time here over the years," Marcel answered, shouting gruffly to be heard over the noise. "Good man, that 'un. Comes from one of the earliest Chicago families. Done much fer this place, they have. That bunch has got a loose rein over their libido, though. Bastard and his brother spawned over forty children between the two of 'em, mostly half-breeds. His brother Jean Baptiste bears the nickname of "Squawman."

"Forty wee ones! Those are some busy fellows indeed..."

They found the disorder of the hotel's interior to be soundly matched by the rumpus they encountered outside the place. People, horses, and carriages clogged the streets, with men singing drunkenly and coach drivers squabbling over right of way.

Alvord flagged down a stagecoach that bore the words "Lake House" on its side. Many hotels and eateries in Chicago utilized private fleets of carriages and baggage wagons to both advertise and offer people direct transportation to their establishments. Indeed, the road before them was fair congested with carriages bearing inscriptions like "Sherman House," "Baltic," and "Planter's House."

Getting into the empty coach, they settled into the uncomfortable seats and braced themselves for the ride. Coach travel was rarely a relaxed affair, for even on a good road, aboard a good coach piloted by a good driver, one could still expect a considerable amount of bone-rattling bumps and constant jostling.

Moving at a lively clip, the coach rattled over the bridge at Dearborn Street. Looking out towards Lake Michigan, Alvord could see the dark, cheerless bulk of the deserted Fort Dearborn. Originally built in 1803, the first fort had been reduced to a pile of ash by the Potawatomie Indians after the Battle of Fort Dearborn during the War of 1812. It had been rebuilt in 1816, only to be decommissioned and left to rot come 1837.

Finnbar and Marcel, thoughts unspoken, also gazed out the windows. The Irishman cradled his chin in his right hand, brow deeply furrowed. Contemplatively stroking the stag handle of the Bowie knife he always carried, Marcel likewise stared out towards the lake. Alvord could tell that their impending trapping expedition featured centrally in his mind. Though he would never give voice to the sentiment, Alvord genuinely appreciated moments like this; the ability to tolerate companionable silence was a quality he favored in others.

Muddy wheels squelched to a halt where Kinzie Street intersected Rush. The latter, named after the famed physician and educator in medicine Benjamin Rush, was also home to the impressive Benjamin Rush Medical College. Alvord paid the hard-bitten coach driver the fare before hopping down to join Finnbar and Marcel. Together they mounted the steps that led up to the Lake House, which appeared crowded but a good deal less unruly than the Sauganash.

As they approached the imposing, three-story brick building, a lightweight phaeton carriage rocketed past and overturned not far from them, flinging both driver and passenger across the road. Women's shrieks and men's exclamatory oaths followed the noise of the crash until the carriage flipped onto the horse, whose panicked screams beggared description. That sound rendered all others inconsequential, and hustling over to the wreckage Alvord drew his Colt Walker. Noting the snapped, flailing front legs of the wild-eyed dray, he promptly drew the hammer back. The horse lay still in the instant before he shot, its wild right eye locked on his own. It was a familiar look, one that he had beheld in the eyes of man and beast alike.

Mercy, it silently implored.

His bullet tore its path through the horse's skull, into the space between the eye and ear. Blood issued from its foaming mouth as it breathed its last. And then it lay perfectly still, wrapped in Death's icy embrace.

Nearby, the passenger of the carriage rose up on shaky limbs, cursing the driver as a fool and a madman.

"Vot of him?" asked a Norwegian woman in the accent-laden English of the recent immigrant, gesturing to the still form of the driver.

"To hell with him," Alvord responded firmly, tucking the smoking pistol back into his belt as the acrid but not altogether unpleasant odor of gunpowder filled his nostrils. "He endangered the lives of others and is lucky that no one was injured or killed in the crash. Someone might fetch a physician, but that someone will not be me."

"Poor beastie," remarked Finnbar tenderly, staring down at the horse's carcass. Shaking his head sadly, he joined his friends as they left behind the wreckage, the carcass, and the growing crowd.

"So- what should we expect from this Greeley fellow?"

"Well Finnbar, he is a newspaperman by trade. Horace is the founder and editor of *The New York Tribune*, touted by many as the most influential paper of our age. His vaunted editorial skills have allowed his fledgling paper to rival the *New York Herald* in sales in just a few short years. We're talking about a businessman *par excellence*. But to only judge him as such would be a grave mistake. He is far, far more than a mere newspaperman. His temperament is characterized by an inborn need to be productive and, more importantly, self-improving, whether in an intellectual or physical context. Never before have I met someone so possessing of restless energy, nor someone so adept at focusing that energy in a productive fashion.

"A voracious reader and writer, he has political aspirations and the backing to someday pull it off. Opinionated might be too soft a word to describe the fellow, yet his frequent lyceum lectures, which encompass a wide array of topics, are often found favorable by Whig and moderate Democrat alike. He is man who broods over the injustices he beholds while applying his multifarious talents and connections towards ending them. Both he and his paper are bitterly despised in the South, as he is an outspoken critic of slavery. His many eccentricities have raised more than a few speculative eyebrows over the years, even among those closely allied with him. But I would wager that his fans outnumber his critics- for instance, tourists literally gather *en masse* outside of his newspaper building in the hope of catching a glimpse of him. His is rapidly becoming a household name. Overall he is a good man, a superior man in many ways, the breed of astute nation-builder that every young country needs."

"So what yer tellin' us is we're dinin' in rarified air, eh?"

"You could say that, Marcel." Alvord paused a moment, weighing his words. "But boys, if you believe me to be a dour moralist, then I do suggest you brace yourselves."

Chapter 6

They found Horace Greeley sitting apart from the Convention's other luminaries, of which there were a goodly amount inside the well lit and elegantly furnished Lake House. Reading a crumpled paper that bore the title *The Gem of the Prairie,* he sported a set of small round spectacles that he benignly peered over upon detecting their approach.

"Horace Greeley!" Alvord boomed, smiling hugely.

"In the living flesh," his friend replied crisply, rising from his seat to shake hands.

The man's appearance could not have contrasted more than with that of Alvord's. Greeley stood of average height but decidedly sub average build, while Alvord was considerably taller than the average man and far thicker in limb. A wispy, graying, goat-like neck beard hung around the newspaperman's collar, a far cry from his friend's trim but thick full beard of red. While Alvord was handsome in a rugged, severe sort of way, calling Greeley an attractive man would have been stretching the bounds of credulity to bursting.

Poor sartorial taste seemed also to plague the man. Despite it being summer, a full-length wool coat clung limply to his thin shoulders. He might have done well to sport a top hat, which would have helped to conceal a hairline in the early stages of recession.

But the eyes- his eyes had an arresting quality about them. As unimpressive a specimen as he might outwardly be, the eyes of Horace Greeley danced with a light that bespoke both genius and the capacity to apply it. There was intellect there, an insatiable hunger for knowledge too. And, if one chanced to peer deeply into those olive colored eyes, they might realize that here was one of those rare, inexplicable beings to whom genuine fear was something of a stranger.

"Horace, two recent acquaintances of mine. I present Marcel Durand."

Greeley turned to Marcel, whose hand he pumped vigorously as his eyes roved over the mountain man's countenance, attire, and knife.

His voice squeaked with unreserved excitement. "Ah, yes, the mountain man! I have never had the opportunity to converse with one of your mold before. At least not at length. I have a host of questions regarding life on the frontier. Upon his return to New York, Alvord informed me of your exploits in St. Louis- it is good to meet you gentlemen in person. And if memory serves, your name is Finnbar Fagan. Am I right?"

"That y'are."

"A pleasure, Mr. Fagan. Irish, I presume?"

"By the grace of God. With a name like Greeley, have you Irish blood yourself?"

"Ah, Scots-Irish," replied Greeley delicately.

"Ah, my mistake," smirked the Irishman in amused acknowledgement.

"Forgive me," Greeley swiftly requested, tilting his head in an obeisant nod, "but I grew up in a region, and in a family, where that distinction was ever stressed."

"No umbrage taken, lad."

"Shall we, then?" asked Greeley, indicating the table. "Sorry to meet at this late hour but my schedule has been socially paralyzing. I've been forced this day to endure nearly constant meetings and events, stifling in their formality; the result being a decided lack of food intake. I've heard tell that the victuals offered here are generally first-rate."

"First place to employ French chefs and printed menus, at least," Alvord added, picking up his own. "A sensible first step. Though from what I heard this place has not been a great financial success."

"Pearls before swine, I'm sure," stated Greeley, waving a careless hand.

They settled into their chairs, and after consulting their menus for a few moments Greeley energetically motioned at a waiter to come their way.

Alvord ordered roast wild duck, while Finnbar and Marcel both opted for mutton. Greeley chose fresh-caught Lake Michigan whitefish without any butter or sauces, much to Finnbar's astonishment. This perplexity was only magnified when Greeley ordered water rather than beer to wash it down with.

"Fish and water? Did ye not say you were ravenous? You know they serve pigeon potpie, fricassee of prairie chicken, venison, buffalo... from what I have observed Americans are great consumers of meat. Much more so than Europeans. It would seem that you break the mold, Mr. Greely."

"There is no accounting for tastes, now is there? You are quite right- I'm afraid that I am something of a Grahamite," answered Greeley, politely turning down a cigar offered to him by the waiter.

Alvord too waved a cigar away, but Finnbar and Marcel gladly accepted the complimentary smokes.

Finnbar frowned as he slipped his cigar between his lips. "Grahamite? Sylvester Graham, that name strikes a familiar note..."

"He is a dietary reformer of considerable renown," Alvord supplemented as the Irishman's voice trailed off. "I myself incorporate some of his doctrines into my dietary habits, as do many Americans of the middle and upper classes. Horace here takes it to the next level by entirely abstaining from tea, coffee, tobacco and alcohol, and eating sparingly of meat."

"That is abnegation the likes of which is above the likes of me. I have rather grown fond of the heavy meals you Americans serve, and in fact favor them over dainty European ones. I would venture to ascribe diet as to the reason your people are taller on average than ours."

"And, in cities at least, a bit thicker about the waist. You may be right, Finnbar, but regardless I strive for moderation in all things." Suddenly looking over Finnbar with a scrutinizing gaze, Greeley's brow knit in apparent bewilderment.

"Just a minute! I thought I recognized you! Did you not feature in the five o'clock showing of *King Lear* over at the Rice Theatre? You acted out the part of the Fool, correct?"

"A singular talent of mine," Finnbar responded airily, striking a match to light his cigar. "'Twas a charitable deed, really. They had just wrapped up their showing of *The Artful Dodger* and the proprietors were at their wits' end. The thespian who was to play the role of the Fool had taken ill. His understudy, as it were, was detained by some delicate business in a house of ill fame (gent's eyes were bigger than his cash wad, turns out), so having had some acting experience in my youth I offered me services. Hardly a professional job done on my part, but better that than to have them substitute *Stage-Struck Yankee* for the likes of Shakespeare."

He abruptly stopped talking to utilize the match's flame before it sputtering out of existence.

Greeley nodded in assent. "Charitable indeed. Though I rarely frequent theatres, by my estimation it was a fine showing and performed in a decent building to boot. It is no Park Theatre, of course, but still..."

Alvord, meanwhile, shook his head in wonderment. Never had he met such an Irishman before, one who so effortlessly mingled that essentially Celtic wit, blitheness, and fire with legitimate refinement. Imagine that, Finnbar Francis Fagan of

County Cork just waltzing onto stage and spouting out randomly memorized Shakespeare!

The mind simply boggled.

"And speaking of talents, I must doff the proverbial to you, Mr. Greeley. That was some speech you furnished today."

"I'd second that opinion," added Marcel after a hearty swig of ale and a belch. "If ever you venture west, you'll be favored by the red man. They respect boldness of manner as regards speechifying, they do, and you go that in spades, Greeley. Voice could use some deepenin' but still, you had me rooted in place. Didn't quite grasp all of it; talk of tariffs and legislationing and whatnot gets me flummoxed."

Smiling sheepishly, Greeley shrugged off the compliment. "Thank you, but others deserve to be lavished with praise much more so than myself. Senator Thomas Corwin of Ohio fair electrified that vast assemblage today, as did Abraham Lincoln, whose able speech made short shrift of David Dudley's defense of President Polk's biased policies. Imagine suggesting that publicly financed, public works should be limited by the Constitution in this of all cities!"

"Dudley? Stringy sorta feller who was heckled from the floor?"

"The very same, Marcel. He showed some dash, the fellow did, defending Polk in a city like Chicago, but even his rather adept oration fell upon decidedly deaf ears. And rightly so."

Swallowing a gulp of lager, Alvord spoke. "And Lincoln was that tall, dour specimen from Illinois?"

"Yes. Elected to Congress from the only Whig district of that state. This was in fact his first appearance and speech before a national audience. There he is now actually, speaking with Mayor Curtiss and Edward Bates."

Following Horace's gesture, Alvord saw the Congressman conversing with two men whom he towered over. He stood even taller than Alvord, his large stovepipe hat nearly tickling the ceiling like an iron-stained stalagmite. Clad uniformly in all black and wearing a long overcoat, his resemblance to a mortician was further compounded by a rather grave, chiseled visage. And, as Alvord watched, he observed Lincoln's attention suddenly drift from the conversation to a dimly lit corner of the restaurant. Nothing but shadow lay claim to that corner, yet the man's gaze lingered. A profound detachment flooded his face but neither of his interlocutors took notice, so intent were they on their dialogue. The pronounced lines around his eyes and mouth sagged under the burden of some unknown angst. This lasted but a fleeting moment before he recovered himself and returned to the discussion, the darkness gone from his face as if by magic.

Frowning slightly, Alvord felt as if he had been granted a fleeting glimpse of an inborn gloom, a lurking demon with whom the man wrangled. He recognized that every man and woman, no matter how outwardly jovial, upbeat, or virtuous, harbored in the gloomiest recesses of their souls an inner darkness. No one escaped from this world unscathed. Those who possessed the wherewithal to suppress their darkness were fortunate- his own often threatened to take the helm aboard the *S.S. Alvord Rawn.*

"That gent's a proper misery, ain't he?" asked Finnbar of Greeley.

Alvord shifted his gaze to the Irishman, whose raised eyebrows communicated both curiosity and concern. Little missed the writer's discerning, dark green eyes, and what little did Marcel's impenetrable eyes of darkest brown were apt to catch. His heavily hooded stare yet lingered on Lincoln, but in keeping with his character he offered no comment. Nor did his face betray any thoughts he might harbor. But Alvord knew him well enough to guess-

Reckon it ain't none of our business.

"Yes," Greeley answered, shaking his head sadly, "it is said by some that he is given to dark spells, times of intense inner turmoil. There are rumors afloat that madness has stalked his line for generations, a madness that has found fertile grounds in yon Abraham. But I defy you to find a more forthright and able politician. He still has stairs to climb in the political arena, and may one day lead the Whig party to greatness."

Alvord heaved a sigh of contentment, wishing to tip back in his chair but unwilling to do so in front of the etiquette-abiding Greeley. "Refreshing, Horace, is it not, to set foot in a city where we Whigs are not a besieged minority?"

"I could not agree more. Manhattan is fast becoming an undesirable place for any ardent Whig and opponent of President Polk to call home."

Finnbar, steel pen poised above the pages of a small, leather-bound book that had suddenly appeared on the table, posed a question to Greeley. "So what exactly is it about his Nibs Polk that makes the blood of these Chicagoans boil so?"

Chuckling while dodging around a rank, drifting cloud of cigar smoke, Greeley answered. "Polk and the Democratic Party as a whole are detested here on firm grounds. He blithely vetoed the 1846 River and Harbors Appropriation Bill, thereby provoking the wrath of Northern Democrats and presenting

Whigs, like Alvord and myself, a rather auspicious political opening. For too long have Southern statesmen and business leaders challenged the North for the trade of the Northwest and Far West. We in the North therefore rallied together, casting aside political boundaries so as to unite against Southern supremacy. The vetoing of that bill denied northwestern cities like Chicago much-needed opportunities to make strides in the field of commerce.

"Planned on since Illinois's statehood, this canal will divert much trade away from the Ohio Valley and Mississippi route, thus granting Chicago opportunities that were previously the province of St. Louis and New Orleans."

"Like many American cities," Alvord added, "Chicago is a merchant's town, one born of preindustrial impulses that nevertheless lies at the cusp of agricultural and commercial prominence and radical industrialization."

He had been reading extensively on the topic of the canal, had discussed it at length with locals, and had listened closely to the speeches given earlier that day.

"The much spoken of canal, upon its completion, will secure Chicago's place among our nation's important economic centers." Greeley paused to take a sip of water before launching back into it. "The costs of transferring lumber, grain, and merchandise between the mid-west prairies and the East will be drastically reduced, as the Great Lakes system is now a viable route. A great blow will be struck to Southern control of this region's trade. This city, despite its dismal location and the cloying mud that seems to cling even to its reputation, shall rise fast on the brawn of Irish, German, and Scandinavian immigrants. Especially now that it is free from the dross of strict Democratic interference and reliance. Do you know that a meager six million dollars was raised through the sale of federal land grants to Illinois for the purpose of funding the canal? Additional private capital was required to properly fund the project, achieved through public bond issues. This canal will do for Chicago what the Erie Canal did for New York. The moniker of 'Mud Hole of the Prairies' will soon yield to the less commonly applied, 'Gem of the Prairies.' We need only to wait for the completion of this canal. Although I am also of the opinion that this will be the last of the great canals. Already there is talk of establishing a railroad here, which will ultimately overtake canals as a means of transportation both personal and commercial."

Scribbling energetically, Finnbar mumbled, "Good to know, good to know."

"I'll say this much," grunted Marcel as he looked around at the restaurant's tasteful décor and elegantly clad patrons, "This city sure has seen some change since last I clapped eyes on 'er. Seems that she's taken to modernizin' lock, stock, and barrel. I can recollect the days when red skin outnumbered white in this region, when Chicago was naught but a cluster o' cabins and shanties. You could still see elk and bear on the outskirts of town, could still find the pugmarks of the catamount and lend ear to the howling of wolves... think I preferred it that way..."

His expression grew distant, his dark eyes unfocused.

Their food arrived, effectively stemming the flow of conversation as all present energetically tucked in. Alvord's duck, liberally smeared with red currant glaze, proved downright ambrosial. Finnbar and Marcel, meanwhile, launched a headlong, full-scale assault on their gravy-smothered mutton. Alvord had noticed a steady change in the Irishman's eating habits over the last few weeks. Whereas initially he had dined with the cautious palate and delicacy of a European, at this point his enthusiasm for heavy American meals was at an all time high. He had not put on a pound, though; his was the body type that seemed to process food with amazing speed. Having escorted many an esteemed European tourist around Manhattan as a patrolman, Alvord knew all too well of their revulsion at the presentation of "insoluble" American cuisine. They had a valid point, he must concede, for American meals were awfully heavy on meats, gravy, butter, cheeses, puddings, sweets, and attendant booze of all varieties. And the copious amounts of tea taken afterwards to help digest it were often nearly undrinkable in their potency.

"Damn fine grub," Marcel commented through an inordinate mouthful of mutton. Dripping strands of gravy clung to his thick beard but he hardly seemed to mind or even notice for that matter.

Finnbar too moaned his approval, his mouth being too crammed to achieve actual speech. Peering over the steel rim of his spectacles, Greeley frowned disapprovingly but offered no comment. Though he consumed his own fare at a decent pace, he compulsively wiped his mouth between each bite, no matter how brief the space of time that elapsed between.

As they finished their meal amidst sporadic talk of the day's impressive festivities, a young man with a gleaming copper badge pinned proudly to his coat came cautiously towards their table.

"Mr. Rawn," the fellow greeted Alvord with a courteous nod before addressing the others. "Gentlemen, I hope this evening finds you well."

These words he delivered with the clipped exactitude of the clearly rehearsed.

"Ah, young Pahlman!" replied Alvord. "How's that knife wound of yours?"

Pahlman was one of the few Chicago patrolmen that Alvord had come to respect in his time here. The kid had also been born in Manhattan, to German immigrants who had later emigrated to Illinois, so the New York connection also existed between them.

The patrolman let out a somewhat sheepish chuckle. "Owing to the thickness of my coat and Tamworth's lack of strength, I can happily report that it's merely a flesh wound. Now, I realize that you are in the middle of dinner, but I know that you are to depart soon. Me and some of the boys are over at the bar," he indicated a group of badge-sporting men who raised their drinks in hopeful salute, "and were wondering if, well, perhaps if you weren't too busy here would you join us for just one quick drink?"

"On us, of course," he added hastily before Alvord could respond. He then fell silent, face brimming with hope.

Alvord took quick stock of the situation. True, he was in the middle of dinner, but then again he would be leaving this city soon enough and would probably never see these men again. What's more, he knew that he had attained celebrity status in their eyes, a former Manhattan Police Captain with an indisputable knack for bringing undesirables to justice. They looked up to him, plain and simple. Having once been a rookie, he could appreciate the sentiment.

"You don't mind?" he asked of his dinner companions.

"Not at all," smiled Greeley amusedly, who knew well of Alvord's aversion to most social interactions, "'twould be churlish of you to refuse."

"Splendid!" Pahlman exclaimed. "Allan Pinkerton will be most pleased, he was hoping to speak with you about that detective agency he is thinking of starting."

"*Briefly*, of course," he appended, hard on the heels of his previous sentence.

Alvord slowly rose to follow the triumphant rookie back towards the bar, looking back and shrugging in hopeless fashion at his three grinning friends.

Chapter 7

With incisive eyes Greeley watched Alvord go. "That man is a force of nature, you know."

"Huh, you don't have to tell us," replied Marcel, tipping back in his chair. "That feller'd charge Hell with a leakin' bucket o' water."

"Like I said, upon his return to New York he informed me of your adventures down St. Louis way. A rogue mesmerizer, eh? The horrors he described to me... you are braw lads, it would seem. He spoke quite highly of you two- not something he is in the habit of doing."

"Braw we may be," Finnbar acknowledged, "but you should have seen him in action, Horace. No hesitation, no uncertainty. It came to pass that we got separated before we could all mobilize against our enemy, so he launched an assault by his onesies against the mesmerizer's manor, leaving a broad trail of destruction for us to follow. And as if facing the mesmerizer Abendroth wasn't enough, Alvord also went toe to toe with his giant Prussian bodyguard. What was that hulking bastard's name again?"

"Otto Volkmar," answered Marcel with distant look in his eyes. "A name to remember."

"And so the mesmerizer fell," stated Greeley after a petite bite of whitefish and a quick wipe of the napkin. "What mistake did he make?"

"Like all madmen, he overestimated his own power whilst underestimating that of his foes," Finnbar responded, puffing reflectively on his cigar.

"Yes, Alvord is not a good man to underestimate. Nor is he one to shilly-shally when it comes to distributing justice. The fellow takes crime by the throat and throttles it. He is, understandably, a feared figure in Manhattan. Men still shake their heads in incredulity in remembrance of his deeds."

"Yeah, figgered he had quite the rep back home."

Greeley regarded him seriously. "Aye Marcel, a reputation forged in blood. I agree with neither capital punishment nor the wanton killing of criminals, but I cannot deny the smothering effect that his presence has on criminal elements. I heard tell earlier today that he has been working as a watchman in this crime-ravaged town."

"Yeah, the dregs of Slab Town have learned fear at his hands. Feller's on the warpath. And the agreement is that the city's gotta pay him a standard weekly rate *and* an added sum fer each piece of slime he brings in. And that number is climbin' high. This week alone he brought to justice a proper mess o' murderers and thieves, not t'mention a host of more petty criminals."

Greeley sat back and whistled softly. "Whew. Glad it's not coming out of my coffers. The man does know how to make his presence felt. I tell you, back home even the Irish gangs showed him deference. Until the day poor Andrew O'Farrell was laid low by the Roach Guards. The lad was an Irish patrolman in the platoon that Alvord led. But the gang suffered accordingly. Unfortunately, likewise did Alvord."

Finnbar and Marcel exchanged puzzled looks.

"What d'ya mean by suffer, Greeley?"

"Well, the Roach Guards were slain to a man in a retaliatory raid that Alvord personally led. Not an hour after O'Farrell's death, a woman showed up at the stationhouse to report it. Alvord, suspecting that his chief would want him to hold off on any retaliation until the situation had been properly analyzed, decided to mobilize his men and conduct an unauthorized raid on the Roach Guards. How he managed to track them down so swiftly is still a matter of some conjecture, but in the aftermath of the fight nary a Roach Guard drew breath."

"An Irish gang offing a fellow Irishman? Strikes me as patently odd."

"Well Finnbar, Manhattan's Irish gangs view any fellow Hibernian who dons the copper badge to be a turncoat through and through. Such men are invariably ostracized and, in extreme cases, beaten or killed."

A verbal quarrel erupted across the room. One man had brushed up against a woman as he passed by, and another man was vociferously demanding his apology. Words flew back and forth for a bit, with tart insults and even a challenge to a duel being buffeted about. The two florid-faced, bellowing men then charged one another, but the sudden intercession of Alvord and the other patrolmen put a swift end to it.

Watching Alvord and the others bodily heave the struggling men out of the restaurant, Greeley chuckled.

"He seems happy. Content. I have not seen him like this in recent times. Since the passing of his family, he has grown increasingly reclusive. Though never one to count many folks as actual friends, he stopped seeing even the few he had, aside from myself. He ceased to attend balls and plays and even functions put on by the Municipal Police Department. Deepest gloom seized firm hold of him; that trip out to St. Louis seems to have snapped him out of his melancholia. And the promise of adventure in yon blue, distant hills has lent further buoyancy to his newfound happiness."

Finnbar and Marcel glanced at each other, visibly troubled. Alvord had not offered up this information; this was quite the revelation.

"How did his family die?" Finnbar inquired, voice hollow.

Greeley frowned confusedly. "Has he not told you? Disease claimed his wife and daughters. Katherine, a woman of the rarest order, was taken by consumption four years past. She was preceded by her two daughters, who died early in their voyage of life. One of them died an infant, of no perceivable medical reason. Little Isabel, the youngest, was struck down by cholera at the age of five. Dreadful thing, that. Truly dreadful."

"He mentioned bein' a widower once, but didn't have much to say on the matter... we just let it be."

"His losses have been beyond what most have to endure in this life. It would have been easier if it had happened in one fell swoop, I think... that succession of tragedy could only be maddening. And as if losing his wife and daughters to pestilence wasn't enough, just last year his son Elihu, a bright and impressive young man of sixteen, was killed at the battle of Resaca de la Palma. Or at least presumed to be dead. His body could not be positively identified- he took part in the celebrated cavalry charge that silenced the Mexican guns. But before they fell silent, those guns exacted on awful toll. I myself delivered one of my papers to Alvord that bore the news- I did not know how else to go about it. His face was immobile, his expression as if etched in stone, but his eyes..." here a shudder rippled through Greeley, "...it looked to me like he wanted the world to burn as payment for his losses."

"When sorrows come," intoned Finnbar somberly, "they come not in single spies. But in battalions."

"Shakespeare's word ring true in the tragic case of Alvord Rawn. People lose family each day to disease and war, but family was perhaps the only thing tethering him to this world, or at least to society... but perhaps I should not have spoken to you of these things. Sometimes I speak too freely... if these were memories he himself has refused to furnish, then it was not my place to shed light on them... fiddlesticks, I think all this cigar smoke is going to my head."

Finnbar and Marcel sat in silence, considering Greeley's

words. It suddenly struck them as odd that neither of them had ever really pressed Alvord for details regarding his past. Both began to wonder what other harsh secrets their friend might be harboring.

Finnbar absentmindedly asked the waiter for another beer. At this Greeley leveled a critical stare his way.

Taking notice of it, Finnbar frowned and turned to look behind him in search of what the newspaperman stared at.

"Is something amiss?" He asked confusedly when he realized that the fellow was looking at him.

"I mean not to pass judgement, but is that not your third drink?"

"A bird never flew on one wing."

Greeley arched an eyebrow as he retorted in the same vein. "Nor three. Ill profits the man who drowns himself in booze, particularly an Irishman."

"As ill fares the man who attempts to admonish this particular Irishman." A glint, at once playful and dangerous, sparked in the olive eyes of the Irishman.

Smiling broadly, Greeley sliced the air with his hand. "Diamond cuts diamond- our wits are evenly matched, Finnbar. Carry on, I will admonish no further."

Immediately upon finishing this sentence, his head turned as if on a swivel to regard Marcel.

"Are you an unlettered man, Marcel?"

"Nah, I can make my mark just fine."

Greeley cocked his head in birdlike curiosity.

"I'm kiddin', newspaperman, I can read a bit. Jed Smith taught me."

"I have heard that some mountain men are rather well learned, some are even devout men of faith. You would think that the wilderness would cause man to regress in such regards, but such are the complexities of the human character... I think it a shame that the skin trade has declined so. What an interesting strain of American it bred. Imagine so simple a thing as a change in fashion resulting in the deterioration of so great an industry as furs! It also did not help matters that the coypu, or nutria, of South America has fur quite comparable to our beaver and is far cheaper to obtain. The westward tide of American civilization played its role as well- farming and homesteading go hand and hand with reductions in game populations."

"The West grows tame," Marcel admitted with a wistful squinting of his eyes, recalling times past. "But it'll be awhile before she's settled good and proper. And some areas never'll be, as they are too rugged or simply poor sites for settlement. And as the West tames, my kind'll slowly be forgotten, we'll go the way of the Injun. Not that most of us give a hang."

"I respectfully disagree. Your sort will never be forgotten. You are of the breed that comprises America's marrow. The intrepid, the hardy. Mountain men acted as the torchbearers for American civilization. Artists depict you in their works; writers fill pages with your exploits. Were it not for such incursions into *terra incognita*, settlement would not be possible."

"You support wholesale settlement out there?"

"But of course. Settlement in those lonely lands is not only inevitable- it is destiny. The notion of the 'Great American Desert,' as perpetuated by Stephen Long, is a pathetic farce. As you know there is singularly rich soil out there, I have heard it said by leading experts on the matter. We would do well to settle it and put plow to soil."

"And of the red men livin' in much of that territory?" Marcel's voice contained interest laced with the slightest tincture of irritation.

Greeley shrugged his narrow shoulders. "They must learn to tolerate and intermingle with us, perhaps even become real Americans. The alternative is far less pleasant."

"Were I them, I'd take up the tomahawk and fight to the bitter end, Greeley. And many a white skull would feel the sting of my scalping knife." Marcel locked eyes with the delegate, face immobile.

"Hmm, most interesting..." Greeley pursed his lips as he returned the stare, deep in thought.

Alvord rejoined them, a thing of which both his fellow wayfarers were grateful for.

"Sorry lads, got caught up talking to this Pinkerton fellow, he is thinking about starting up a detective agency shortly down the road."

"Pick your brain, did he?"

"'Til little gray matter remained, Horace. I notice no blood has been shed- am I to gather that you are all still getting along?"

"Famously," replied Finnbar briskly.

Alvord took something out of his pocket. It was the ivory-handled push-dagger that Richard Tansworth had wielded in desperation earlier that day.

"The boys recovered this from the waterfront. It belonged to a criminal whom I ah, remonstrated rather harshly with a bit earlier. Finnbar, as this gamblers weapon does not suit me, would you like it? Marcel has his famous pig sticker and a small arsenal of other blades, so I figured you could use it more."

Finnbar took the knife, testing its point appreciatively. "A fine gift. Many thanks, messmate."

Alvord took his seat, hastily shoveling the last bite of succulent duck meat into his mouth. "They were discussing the town's early history over at the bar. The topic of the Fort Dearborn Massacre came up just as I took leave. While I have heard of it, the finer details elude me. Odd how it was done at the hands of the Pottawatomies, who later ended up paying half of the expenses of the first bridge that connect the south and west sides of Chicago. Never heard of Indians willingly paying for such a thing as that."

"Hey, the Choctaws sent seven hundred and ten dollars to relieve the sons of Erin once the Famine set in," Finnbar piped up. "And that was not all that long after that dreadful Trail of Tears affair, too. That memory could only have been fresh in their minds, yet they nobly sought to relieve beleaguered whites an ocean away. D'you know that the Ottoman Sultan actually offered ten thousand pounds for Irish relief, and Her Corpulence Victoria asked him to reduce it to one thousand, as she had only offered two herself?"

Alvord shook his head sneeringly. "Pathetic."

Greeley, finishing his meal at long last, wiped his mouth with finality and asked Marcel, "You've spent time here over the years, right? Surely you know the tale of the massacre? I myself have read accounts of it, but-"

"You go ahead... I ain't much of a story teller. Do like listenin' though."

"Yes, Horace. You have always been a fine teller of tales."

Stroking his scraggly neck beard, Greeley sighed. "Very well. I suppose, in all candor, that I do have a certain knack for it. About a month after we declared war on England in 1812, General William Hull ordered the evacuation of Fort Dearborn, fearing that it would fall as Mackinac had not long before. The woods were alive with a host of skulking Indians waiting with sinister patience to unleash all the wrath in Hell. The garrison, meanwhile, consisted of a paltry fifty-four regulars and twelve militiamen. On August 15th Captain Heald ordered the destruction of all surplus food, munitions, and whiskey lest it fall into enemy hands. Captain William Wells and John Kinzie, widely hailed as the father of Chicago, had returned to the fort posthaste upon hearing of its perilous situation with fifteen Miami Indians at their side. Shortly before the march out of the fort, the chief of the St. Joseph band offered him escape via canoe for himself and his family. Kinzie himself gallantly declined, but accepted it for his wife and children."

"Good man," Alvord stated.

"There can be no doubt of that. Theirs' was a situation without much hope. To the caprice of the red man they were unpromisingly subject. As the fort's occupants departed, the band defiantly played the Dead March. Captain Wells, who had been raised among the heathens, dressed in Indian garb and painted his face black in blunt acceptance of his fate. As the group wove its way through the sand hills to the east, the Miami warriors precipitously abandoned them, and as they departed the Potawatomie descended, numbering in the hundreds. In the ensuing battle the Indians' initial charges were savagely repulsed, and one soldier managed to bayonet Chief Naunongee before Heald surrendered. During the first stage of the battle, half the soldiers were killed during their desperate defense of the wagons containing the women and children. Wells and Kinzie reportedly fought like demons to protect the wagon. It is believed that Wells personally laid low eight of the fifteen Indians who were slain that day. When the savages began killing children, Wells became so possessed by rage that he leapt onto a horse and rode off towards the Indian encampment, intent on killing their innocents in reprisal. He was riding and shooting all the while, but was eventually brought down."

"He met well his fate," Alvord commented, nodding his approval.

"The savages quite agreed. Indeed, they showed him the highest honor they knew."

"And what did that entail?" Alvord eagerly pressed.

Illuminated by the subdued light of the restaurant's perforated tin lanterns, scattered hit or miss about the room, they witnessed a fleeting look of what could only be labeled madness pass over the newspaperman's face. He ran his hand over the smooth walnut handle of the umbrella he had propped up against the wall, while in a corner of the restaurant a drunken fiddler gave voice to a morose, fitful melody.

Through the creeping, diaphanous tendrils of cigar smoke that filled the Lake House, Greeley broke his momentary but ponderous silence.

"They ate his heart."

Chapter 8

Alvord stood alone at the end of a dock, one jutting out a considerable distance into the starlit gloom that was Chicago Harbor. Head inclined, he stared up at those stars as they glimmered coldly against the velvety black of perpetuity. Basking in the silence and solitude he lowered his gaze to observe the water mirroring the celestial brilliance above, eerie in its stillness. As he watched, a light, vagrant breeze kissed his impassive face, whispering secrets unfathomable before leaving him to his reflection once more.

His boots might be firmly resting on the uneven planks of that dock, but his soul was very, very far away.

Horace, Finnbar, and Marcel had retired after post-dinner conversation wound to a close, but compelled by an urgent call to thought Alvord sought out a place of seclusion. He knew from experience that this urge would not allow for sleep unless indulged good and proper. He had been keeping irregular hours lately anyway and was not unduly tired despite it being after midnight.

The first few lines of a Keats poem, "To one who has been long in city pent," idly drifted across his mind.

To one who has been long in city pent,
'Tis very sweet to look into the fair
And open face of Heaven- to breathe a prayer
Full in the smile of the blue firmament.

The open face of Heaven might lay an inky black above him rather than blue, but it smiled on him all the same. He tasked in vain his mind to recall the rest of the poem, there had been a time when he knew it in its entirety... ah, no matter- those few lines rang true, and its very title spoke directly to him in his overcast state.

Drawing in breath, he held it for a contemplative moment before exhaling. A sound, caught somewhere between a sigh and a snarl, escaped his curling lips. His distrust of mankind was at an all-time high. First Manhattan this past April, where he had lost his job of fourteen years with the Municipal Police Department. Never would he forget the expression of outrage and horror that overcame the face of his superior officer and onetime-friend, Chief George Matsell, when the details of his unauthorized raid were revealed. And for what? For wreaking vengeance upon the swine who brutally murdered one of his patrolmen? His brain still futilely struggled with the concept. And now that rank, bungling amateur Dean had the gall to confront him in the same vein, had attempted to withhold his rightly earned payment over the selfsame issue? Who were such men to pass judgment on him? As if he did not have to live with the knowledge of what he had done each and every day?

Ah. Such was the price of justice.

It was high time for a change. He'd had his fill of men and their cities. Urban centers, which he had lived in all his life, were for the first time beginning to elicit in him feelings of disquietude. The noisome stench of horse shit and unwashed bodies, the ever-growing crowds, the frenzied pace- these days he seemed more finely attuned to the more unsavory aspects of city living. The transparencies of society were more accurately delineated to him, as if a veil were drawn away; disenchanted with what he saw, he determined to leave the world to its designs.

An outburst of gunshots and rowdy laughter crassly intruded upon his reverie; if one ventured to look closely at him they might have glimpsed a chilling sneer flicker across his chiseled visage.

These days, interaction with most people served only to deepen his gloom and darken his vision of his fellow man. There were exceptions of course, two notable ones being Finnbar and Marcel. Yet it still stood that he could find precious little common ground with the majority of folks. There were moments wherein he asked himself- *If these people meet the standards of normality, how am I to be judged and found?*

The question stood, then- just what had he become? He was no longer a good family man whose sinister side was restrained by those he held dear. Nor was he a thing of outright darkness; no, anger and true malevolence should not be freely compared. Instead he hovered in uncertainty, in limbo somewhere betwixt the two, the light and dark each vying for ascendancy.

At the moment he felt that a balance had been struck, that the angel and demon that perched on his shoulders had worked out an uneasy truce. Yet there were times, mostly when he maimed or killed, when that inner demon danced in delight as it urged him on to further acts of violence in a voice so seductive, so convincing...

With a deep breath, he regained his composure and looked

out into the lake as far as his eyes could perceive, beyond the moored sloops and schooners, beyond even the questing flash of the lighthouse, where the glimmer of starlight was eventually swallowed up by wholesale darkness. Since his boyhood, the woods and wilds had fired his imagination. However, his job and his family, the latter of which he had valued above all else, had prevented him from pursuing that interest. The job he was no longer tethered to, his wife and daughters were lost to disease, and his son more recently in the war with Mexico.

Moments like this, when he could get away from it all and breathe deeply of fresh air, were the only moments in which he did not feel that cloying sense of being caged. For it almost felt like the civilized world was closing in around him, threatening suffocation unless he sought an avenue of escape.

The time, therefore, was well nigh. He could vanish, wraithlike, into the frontier and barely be missed by a soul.

One corner of his mouth curved slightly upwards as once again a breeze sought out his face. From across the vast, somber wastes of Lake Michigan, the frontier beckoned to him as it never had before.

And now, at long last, he would finally answer its call.

Chapter 9

Just South of Marquette, Upper Michigan.

As Alvord Rawn regarded the black throat of space over 400 miles to the south, a lone Welshman also cast his gaze upward.

The heavens themselves wore a melancholy cast, as if to reflect the darkness of his thoughts. The yellow sliver of beleaguered moon made an appearance brief and sudden, only to be strangled yet again by the prowling tendrils of cloud that preceded a menacing eastbound thunderstorm.

Owain Derog Crowder, failed physician and, more recently, luckless miner, heaved a ponderous sigh. Fate, in which he firmly believed and habitually ascribed a female persona to, had not been kind to him in recent times. One paltry mishap and the medical world had cast him aside, and now one fleeting, uncharacteristic moment of naïveté and this as the end result...

Wales, and actually Great Britain as a whole, would have been a rather injudicious place to stay. Allegations of malpractice had a way of dogging your steps over there. America, by his reckoning, would be a fine place to start anew, a massive land with a swelling population and, most importantly, an ocean between he and the prowling ghosts of his past.

He had landed in Boston two years back, entertaining thoughts of revamping his failed medical practice, but was shocked by the roiling mess that was the modern American medical scene. He had come from the Old World with the hope that the New might prove more... *simplistic*, yet in truth this fledgling nation was host to a raveled medical mess of its own. Homeopathy, herbalism, Water Cure, phrenology, Thompsonians, Grahamites- how could a practitioner of conventional medicine possibly find his footing amidst such a whirlwind of conflicting articulations? Even his thorough Edinburgh training had not properly prepared him for success here.

So it turned out that in terms of a medical practice American was no more conducive to triumph. But luckily, he was a man with an avaricious eye for business opportunities. Of course, that same avaricious eye of his was precisely what had gotten him into trouble back home in Swansea, where he had not been above ripping off those he felt deserved it. Couple that with an unfortunate proclivity towards inquisitive tinkering with different elixirs and herbal preparations, (which ultimately led to the death of a patient of significant status) and you had yourself a recipe for bloody disaster. Legal action had been swift, but not quite swift enough to prevent his covert crossing of the Atlantic aboard a coal shipment.

After seeing far too much in the way of competition in American cities, his nimble mind quickly drifted to other schemes. As distasteful as the notion struck him, he prepared to depart the comfortable familiarity of city life for the various unknowns of the frontier, where it was said that folks were desperate for competent physicians of any brand.

It was then that he first heard talk of the mines.

On the remote Keweenaw Peninsula, in the howling wilderness of Lake Superior's south shore, mine shafts sunk into the purest copper deposits known to mankind were beginning to yield impressive quantities of the prized metal.

So he had swooped in, talons outstretched. Crowder had assumed the identity of what had come to be known in Copper Country as a White Pawnee. There were honest opportunities here, but also ones that involved preying on the weak, the foolish. So many men flocked to this new Mecca of copper miners without the necessary permit, or temporary land lease. It was a simple task, really, to file one ahead of time with the War Department and arrive in mining country with one in hand. Issued in blank, the permit was transferrable from one man to another, so if the spot held promise it could then be sold at a massive profit to impatient prospectors who had a bit of extra coin and a nagging urge to get underway. White Pawnees were the men making those massive profits through permit transfers.

And if you were a White Pawnee who was wily enough to get your mitts on a large number of permits- well, his own coffers spoke to the lucrative nature of that venture. Before he threw in his lot with Cadwallader Jones, that was. He had invested most of his worth into this proposed iron-mining scheme...

A shrewd man, Crowder possessed an ability to peer into the future with a stark clarity that eluded most. After conducting careful research into the matter, poring over deposit maps, land sales and permit speculations, and the fluctuating price of copper, he came to the realization that copper mining would be a boom and bust scenario here in Michigan. Despite that particular mineral being the latest craze in mining, despite the camps of hell-roaring miners lining the Keweenaw, copper mining, as far as his discerning hazelnut eyes could see it, was simply unsustainable.

It was a luxury metal, after all. Miners from the world over, landing at Copper Harbor, Eagle Harbor, and Ontonagon, would pockmark this wilderness by dint of pick, jack, and powder, but for all their toil copper had few practical uses. Copper pots and pans might be flaunted as symbols of status, and the Navy and Merchant Marines did need it to sheath the bottoms of their ships with, but the limited demand simply did not balance with the presumptuous supply. And the supply itself was hardly meeting expectations, with only the Pittsburgh & Boston Copper Harbor Mining Company and Copper Falls Company producing anything of note. This was rather basic economics as far as Crowder saw it.

But iron... now there was a metal to pursue. Since its discovery somewhere in the murky chapters of the past, iron had played a central role in the life of the more advanced societies. Time's onward march engendered only an increasing importance for iron, as industrialization seemed to be the catchword of any country worth its salt. And without iron, industrialization would hit an impasse. For instance, just last year iron wire, with its greater tensile strength and more durable nature, had replaced copper wire for use in telegraphs. Yet another reason to favor iron over copper right there. Additionally, the War Department had recently been supplanted by the Treasury as the dispensers of land permits, with Congress also allowing for their outright sale. His role as a White Pawnee had come to an end and the lure of iron mining pulled hard on him.

Douglass Houghton, the renowned geologist whose pioneering study of the Keweenaw had made the mining of the district possible, spoke only in passing of iron deposits in the region, unaware of the vast quantities that were actually to be had. East of the Keweenaw, the Marquette Range showed great potential, and Crowder eagerly sought land in the area for he and his crew to work. They were good, worthy men, and given the chance would make great things happen.

Just last year Upper Michigan's first iron ore shipment of two hundred pounds demonstrated that iron should not be blithely overlooked. The little harbor camp of Marquette, named so for some famous Frenchie priest, was home to a small but growing number of men who sought the green and red rocks that betokened iron deposits.

Soon enough the region around Marquette would resound with the exhalations of blast furnace that would rival any of Vulcan's.

It was the Grecian fables that told of the fire god Vulcan

being cast out of Olympus by Jupiter. Landing on the Island of Lemnos, he recovered from his inglorious descent to establish iron forges with which he created objects of untold splendor.

Crowder professed no allegiance to the Christian God and upon his arrival in Michigan felt a curious kinship to Vulcan, in fact. Flung from paradise by the powers that be, only to land in a place where he could set his own forges to blazing, metaphorical or otherwise. This was not a wholesale kinship, however. Vulcan had been deformed, born ugly and club-footed in fact, and his love-goddess wife Aphrodite had had a well-publicized affair with Ares, the dashing god of war.

Dropping his gaze to the hard rock beneath his feet, Crowder scowled deeply. Perhaps there were more similarities there than he cared to reflect on. For while Vulcan-ugly he might not be, the reprehensible actions of that blasted trollop, that fork-tongued wench Gwendolyn Williams made him question at times his looks, his innate worth...

Ah, bugger it. There were more important things to mull over. Like his impending financial crisis, for instance... why had he put even a modicum of trust in another human being, even if that trust seemed to hold so much promise?

Best laid plans o' mice and men.

"Gang aft agley," he muttered bitterly, spitting onto the lichen-smothered chert that formed the little promontory he stood atop. Wind, mild and sultry, ruffled the shoulder capes of his travelling coat, one of the popular Garrick pattern. For all his careful planning, he had, alas, been well and truly duped. This stung with an acuteness beyond what the average man would have felt upon such a realization, for Crowder was a man of rare intelligence, one accustomed to using people with the practiced ease of a master deceiver. The growing anxiety that accompanied the realization that he had assumed the role of the Fool in this farce was proving ever so difficult to swallow.

Jones. It was he to whom this disastrous duplicity could be traced. That swarthy bastard of a Welsh-American whose influence around Superior's southern shore was unsurpassed. Cadwallader Jones had betrayed his trust, had led him a merry dance with talk of iron ore and its attendant riches.

Partners, Jones had promised with honesty kindling in his amber eyes, partners they would be who each owned half the iron mining company that they would soon jointly begin.

Ancient diggings, the devious blackguard assured him with such a pretense of confidentiality, ancient diggings just like the ones found all over the copper country, had revealed iron ore instead of the usual copper. Enough exposed iron ore, in fact, to suggest an initial strike that would warrant acceleration into immediate production. With the Jackson Mining Company already operating an iron mine and Catalan forge nearby at Negaunee, the time was ripe to swoop in and stake a large claim. The Jackson Mine, producing slowly but steadily as it was, would only attract others.

Crowder resigned to the fact that he had been well on his way towards a proper buzz at the time this was being explained, but Jones was an aloof man who never approached anyone, one who kept to himself and his ship's crew and was always accorded much deference and respect. Yet there he had been, eagerly engaging Crowder in mine-related conversation in a congested dram house. It struck him as a singular opportunity to wring the most out of this mining game. Jones walked as a god among the mine owners of the region; Crowder, having acquired a reputation for himself since arriving in the area, figured that having a partner would be a sound idea. He recognized in Jones the ablest candidate and entertained high hopes.

Hopes raised to Heaven only to be dashed to Hell. What thoroughgoing folly on his part. There was to be no company; this he was now keenly aware of, and the land that he had fronted cash for, that he had outfitted his crew to work, was nothing more than some barren sandstone bluffs, a goddamn lake, and some chert outcroppings that his frenzied searching revealed to be bereft of any iron trace. Jones had even furnished him with a false map- who went to such lengths to ruin a man he barely knew?

It simply did not add up.

He conceded that he might have had this coming. His instinct to take advantage of others had not diminished upon his move to America. Sure, he wished to mine, but when men allowed themselves to be fools, as he had now done himself, it stood to bloody reason that they would be taken advantage of. Such was life.

Without conscious volition, a sneer twisted Crowder's thin, sly-looking face. Vengeance would be swift and absolute. He had nothing left to lose, after all, and a string of past failures to stoke the fires of his rage. He stood now as a man with remarkably little to lose- Jones would soon find that out, consequences be damned.

A stick snapped back by some towering white pines. Their branches swayed gently with the balmy breeze, and as Crowder watched and listened he detected movement accompanied by another crack of wood.

"Hello?" His voiced echoed hollowly off the useless sandstone cliff he had purchased. "Bingham, that you?"

His inquiry was not answered by the gruff voice of his crew's foreman, but rather by maddening silence. Who ever it was, for human form he could now discern, was not concerned with being quiet. Was it a savage, perhaps? They were allegedly peaceable around here, but one could never trust them wholly...

"Announce or reveal yourself!" he barked, angry and unwilling to play games at this late hour.

A hulking figure obliged him, breaking free from the wood line and standing there, staring at him in silence.

"Who are you?" Crowder's voice quivered lamentably.

The moon broke through once again, but was quickly enveloped once more by stringy clouds, which resembled the tendril pseudopodium of the animalcules that science was just beginning to understand and that Crowder had once observed under a microscope in medical school. Before it was swallowed up, however, it did serve to illuminate a large piece of metal, something that covered his stalker's broad torso.

Armor, was the word that came to mind, but Crowder knew this could not be. Likewise was the weapon in his hand oddly Old World in appearance, leaf-bladed and somewhat Celtic, he wanted to say. Yet how was it that a metal-clad, sword-wielding warrior fit for the early medieval battlefields of Europe, came to be transplanted in this North American wilderness?

He felt like he was being toyed with and suddenly the night seemed darker, more menacing. He took several involuntary steps backwards, intent on getting away from that big, menacing antagonist of his, who remained motionless and silent.

As he made this move, several more figures emerged from the night, taking their places next to the first man. Though the night was dark, Crowder's eyes had adjusted to the point where he could make out each individual.

No words were spoken, no gestures made. Breath began coming to him rapidly and shallowly; his gut wrapped itself into a tight knot. As a strong sense of dread washed over him, sweat speckled his now-pallid face.

Crowder's camp lay just a half-mile to the north, a location that he promptly turned and began running towards, thoughts of vengeance momentarily put on hold.

Chapter 10

On the breath-warm morning of July 8th, dawn's glaucous, pre-sunrise light washed over the waterfront of a Chicago already very much awake. The rattle of wheels belonging to every form of carriage mingled with the brisk tattoo of hoof and foot upon the plank roads, creating a lively concert of human locomotion.

From Slab Town's muddy plexus of ill-paved streets people descended on the waterfront, like ants from a trod-on nest. The wharves teemed with bodies, some scurrying about in a rush while others impatiently waited in lines to board their homeward bound ships, checking their timepieces and anxiously shifting their weight from foot to foot.

The smell of fish hung heavy in the air, drawing in flocks of screeching gulls. Pelicans yawned hugely from their perches on the docks, as if bored with the proceedings but unwilling to budge. Many visitors were departing Slab Town this morning, although the Convention's delegates would be staying on another few days to discuss the secondary issue of railroads. Soon enough this frontier city would resume its accustomed pace of life, population no longer swelled by the presence of ten thousand exuberant outsiders.

A truly gargantuan steamship, the Cleveland-built *Empire*, was being noisily boarded at this time. At twelve hundred tons burden, it stood far and away the largest boat present. A shade over three hundred passengers would ride upon this behemoth, whose accommodations were widely hailed as elegant and first rate.

From the chaos of the wharves Alvord eyed the vessel that would take them close to Sault Ste. Marie, Michigan. The gateway to Lake Superior, the Soo, as it was colloquially called, would be their final stopping point before they embarked for the Pictured Rocks region of Michigan's Upper Peninsula. According to Marcel, whose knowledge of the wilds Alvord saw no reason to doubt, this remained one of the few areas around Lake Superior that had not been hit hard by various fur companies in years past.

Their mode of conveyance to the Soo was a most novel boat, a twin screw propeller ship. Outwardly resembling a three-masted schooner, the extended cabin housed a steam engine that powered the screw propellers. This recent innovation was the brainchild of the renowned Swedish-American engineer John Ericsson, whose engineering genius had won wide acclaim.

Two hundred feet from stem to stern and one hundred and eighty tons burden, the *Hellion* sat sleek and imperial at the docks. Painted white towards the top, the lower half of the freeboard gleamed deepest, glossy black.

The crew, busy loading cargo and making ready the ship, seemed competent enough; little in the way of yelling or confusion occurred, a scene unlike many of the other ships at dock. They wasted no motion in their preparatory work, demonstrating economy the likes of which Alvord heartily approved.

"Fine lookin' craft, ain't she?" Marcel observed, eyes roving over the vessel.

Horace Greeley, who had tagged along to see them off, looked up at the fore and aft rigging that flapped gently in the easy breeze.

"An impressive one for sure. These screw propeller boats will one day revolutionize travel. While quite functional now, I foresee rapid improvements that shall usher in a new age of steam-powered travel upon water."

"I have seen a few in the past," divulged Alvord, "but this will constitute my first ride upon one."

"And a fine ride it shall prove to be!" interjected a loud male voice laced with a Liverpool accent. A thirtyish man of stately bearing approached them from the dock, long blonde hair and beard gleaming in the early morning sunlight. His suntanned face, rough looking at first glance, was revealed upon closer inspection to be one that easily held a smile.

"Captain Elijah Colson," he offered, extending his hand towards each man. "Of the good ship *Hellion*. My crew is making ready as we speak, and our departure will made be in roughly ten minutes. You should have porters transfer your belongings to my ship's crew at this time."

"Sure thing," said Marcel.

"So none of you have traveled upon a propeller ship, I take it?"

"Finnbar," Greeley said quietly as Marcel and Alvord engaged Colson in conversation, "a word, if you will. I would speak in private for a moment's time."

Looking a bit taken aback and a touch amused, Finnbar nevertheless followed the newspaperman a few paces away.

Turning abruptly, and rapping the umbrella he always

carried onto the ground in a business like manner, Greeley launched right into it without preamble. "You are a most rare individual, Finnbar. These last few days have amply demonstrated that to me. You are possessing of an impressive intellect, and despite your wish to mask it, your heart glows more warmly than most. We are very different men in our comportment; many of your words and actions I find distasteful in the extreme."

"I thank you for that decidedly lukewarm endorsement, but-"

"Just hear me out," Greeley requested, holding up a placatory hand. A gleeful boy on a velocipede tore past them on the rickety two-wheeled contraption, a menace to all those around him. Having neatly dodged around him Greeley continued.

"What I am getting at is that one endowed with manifold gifts by the Almighty, as you are, might consider serving his fellows. It would require sacrifice on your part, much drudgery too, but I do not doubt that you could make a difference in this fallen world of ours. Have ever you felt such a calling?"

Finnbar met Greeley's level gaze and nodded perceptively. "I thank ye for the compliment, Horace. You're a good sort- the world could stand to spawn a few more of your mold. And as for the call, I am currently in the process of answering it. I do mean to help my fellows, and when I have concluded my North American peregrinations I shall return home to ensure the bright future of Erin. I am here now spreading the word and recruiting followers. And I am not alone in the undertaking."

A half-smile, as close to a smirk as Finnbar reckoned Greeley ever got, followed these words.

"Part of the brotherhood, are we?"

Finnbar flashed a grin of his own at this inquiry, sun-lit gold accentuating its cavalier aspect. "Whatever might ye be speaking of, Greeley me boyo?"

"Very well, I shall press no further." Greeley closed his bespectacled eyes, tilting his head up towards the sun. "Yes. Liberty and independence- the driving principles behind our celebration here a few nights past. I wish you luck in your endeavor, Finnbar."

Greeley gave him a quick nod and returned to the others, who were busy handing over their bags and valises to some Negro porters.

"Careful with that one there," Marcel sternly cautioned two of them, rather skinny sorts who struggled as they worked in unison to lift a large crate. "Good deal o' coin dropped on it, wouldn't want to see it damaged."

"And what might its contents be?" Alvord wanted to know.

"Well that'd be tellin', now wouldn't it?"

Finnbar let out a chuckle. "Marcel Durand, consummate man of mystery! Bet I could guess what it is in three tries, but I won't. I likes me some suspense."

"Balderdash," Alvord accused with a snort. "You will puzzle over the contents of that box to an excruciating extent. I have seen you try and handle suspense before and it is none too pretty a sight."

"Yeah," replied Finnbar with a sheepish shrug as he considered the crate once more, "I'd wager it's not."

"Well," said Greely summarily, "I should be off. But perhaps I shall see you soon. Like I said earlier, I will be handling the affairs of the Eagle Harbor Mining Company on the Keweenaw quite soon. Nothing permanent, just a change of scenery and a desire to help out during this important phase in our history. Our first real boom! And involving my favorite metal, no less. So I know you will be in the hinterlands, but feel free to visit Eagle Harbor, or perhaps we could rendezvous in the Soo sometime. It seems that I will be out that way about a year from present."

"By the way, he continued before anyone could reply, "there has been talk. It would seem that there have been stirrings of madness up that way, boys. Strange rumors abound of ambushed miners and men snatched out of their beds in the night. Some claim an unknown tribe of devils has declared war on those working the mining country. The Indians themselves are unsettled; they speak of desecration and vengeful, pale-skinned copper gods. Just so you know."

"Well, many thanks," Finnbar answered, "bloody encouraging news."

"Nothing we can't handle," Alvord reassured his longtime friend.

Greeley nodded understandingly. "Perhaps you're right. I mean, after the recent occult madness in St. Louis and that shady business you dealt with in New Jersey after the Mary Rogers murder..."

"Ah, we needn't get into that, Horace. In truth I failed in that instance, anyway." Alvord's face had grown steely, unreadable.

"From the stories I heard, somehow I doubt that, Alvord. But very well. Just be careful out there."

Greeley gave them each the firmest handshake he could muster along with a stiff nod. "Nice meeting you boys. Alvord, old friend, a pleasure as always. God keep you, gentlemen."

He turned to leave.

"One question," Finnbar requested, his curiosity evident.

"Why is it that you always carry that umbrella? It hardly looks like rain today."

"One never knows." Grinning broadly, the eccentric fellow disappeared into the milling crowd.

"Damn," said Marcel wistfully, "I could use a mentality like that."

A young, plumpish sort of fellow sporting a pair of purple-lensed spectacles stumbled past them, arms over-laden with wooden boxes. The stumble progressed into a fall, wildly distributing the boxes around the dock. From some of them spilled rocks and gemstones, from others skeletons and preserved animal specimens. A bundle of books tumbled towards the edge of the dock, but with the keening lisp of steel against air Marcel's elk-horn handled Bowie knife impaled the foremost, knocking the books flat and ending their advance.

"Oh, dash it all!" The man spat, round sweaty face reddening most brilliantly. He wore a shabby vest that hugged his stomach along with a large necktie that was starting to unravel. Rubbing his torn trouser knee, which had borne the brunt of his fall, he began snatching up his fallen possessions.

Some of the crew and a nearby female passenger could not help but laugh at the floundering figure before them.

Finnbar, stifling a grin of his own, moved in to help the struggling man. Feeling obligated to help himself, Alvord did the same. Their trapper friend, however, merely collected his knife. He spared the man a pitying look and a shake of his head before boarding the *Hellion*.

In a few moments' time they had collected and put back into place the fallen items.

"Many thanks, many thanks, gentlemen," the man panted distractedly, "I would make introductions but must get these dratted specimen boxes aboard ship."

They boarded the ship along with a few others. As they put foot to deck some incensed voices began casting oaths their way.

"Look yonder, Alvord! 'Tis none other then those gents we thrashed t'other night! Hey boys, nice and colorful faces ye got there! You with a traveling minstrel group or something?"

He and Finnbar received some dire threats from the men, who were working on a nearby clipper ship.

"Ha ha!" Finnbar raised two fingers at them to let them know what he thought of their fulminations, before grabbing his manhood. "Bite the back of 'em, ye whore-begotten arslings!"

Alvord, quite unconcerned with the raging verbal conflict, ran his hands over the rail, which he surmised to be rot-resistant white oak. Adventure awaited them in Upper Michigan; he needed only to endure this boat ride. The vessel rocked gently underfoot, reminding him as it swayed of how much he disliked riding aboard ships. River or canal travel was one thing, but the ocean or a large lake... ah, for his own sake he should just stop thinking about it.

As the ship was moved away from the dock, the unmistakable hiss of pumping pistons issued from under the cabin. A whirring sound by the stern ensued, and soon the propellers aided the sails in bringing the ship further from Chicago and closer to their destination.

Breathing deeply of the myriad smells of the lake, Alvord took one last backward glance at Chicago, where the din of iron could now be heard in between blasts of steamship whistles. Sounds from Slab Town's nascent industrial districts added to the clamor that betokened the progress of this once-backwater city as Irish, German, and Norwegian immigrants poured into mills, tanneries, shipyards, lumberyards, and factories. Black smoke issuing from the recently established McCormick Reaper Factory rose in a lazy coil above the forest of masts into a cloudless sky of aquamarine.

Marcel too took a quick glance back, though like Alvord did not give voice to his thoughts. Finnbar, predictably enough, did not suffer from this bout of pensive silence.

"Ah, good 'ol Slab Town. How I shall miss thy dens of iniquity, hives of degenerates, and houses of ill fame. And how they shall miss me in turn. Fare thee well, Gem of the Prairies! We hardly knew thee!"

"Are you quite finished?" Alvord asked of him.

"Am I ever?"

"No," replied Alvord and Marcel as one.

The ship had few other passengers making the northward journey; most of the room was taken up with cargo. The crew toiled busily aboard the deck, and Alvord and the others sought to stay out of their way. They stood by the stern, watching the propeller blades hack at the water.

"Well lads," said the thickly accented Irish First Mate, "we've got calm seas and a serviceable wind at our backs. Should be a fine day of travel before us."

"Calm seas. That's good."

The man regarded Alvord curiously. "Ye ain't prone to seasickness, are yeh now?

Alvord let out a deep breath, staring down at the churning, brilliantly blue water. "Ah, well..."

Chapter 11

The eighth time Alvord spewed his stomach contents into the turbulent waters of the lake was no more undignified than the previous seven, although the increasingly painful spasms in his gut did make it an altogether more painful affair.

Grimly he clung to the rails amid ship, wiping clean his mouth with the back of his sleeve. With eyes bloodshot and bleary he stared down at the lacy foam of the water below. Due to the storm the lake's color, a magnificent crystalline blue in sunlight, took on a hostile, steely gray that perfectly mirrored the gray of his eyes. Just when he thought that this latest bout of retching was concluded, it returned with renewed vigor.

The first day of travel, blessed with both clement weather and a favorable breeze, had presented no problem to him. Indeed, yesterday scarcely a ripple disturbed the peaceful waters of Lake Michigan, which shimmered merrily with dancing sunrays that few clouds impeded the designs of. Early this morning, however, a very different scene presented itself. Wind and clouds swept in from the northwest with a vengeance, soon descending upon the *Hellion* and the various other ships that charted their course along the western coast of Michigan. Waves reared out of the lake as wind-driven rain beat against man and ship alike. While hardly gale-force, the mounting storm raged powerfully enough to set Alvord's innards to dancing.

Seasickness, if that was the term properly applied to illness experienced on a lake, had all but laid him low. This was a perennial problem of his, not to mention one of an ignominious nature. As a man who prided himself in his dignified bearing and stoic comportment, few situations could provide more embarrassment.

Confident in the conclusion of this latest bout of retching, Alvord decided to move, for watching the violent waters did little to aid his condition. Gasping for breath, he staggered past some toiling crewmen and over to the aftcastle, where he collapsed in a wretched heap. Leaning up against the structure, he focused on controlling his ragged breathing. He took a sip from the bota of water he carried, swishing it around to wash the acidic taste from his mouth.

He felt the eyes upon him, knew the crew to be judging and mocking him among themselves. Not that he blamed them on a personal level, for he knew that most men reveled in seeing a large, rough-looking b'hoy like himself reduced to a quivering heap. It served to ease their own self-doubt and rendered him more relatable in their eyes, less insurmountable.

For a while he had confined himself below decks where he assumed the fetal position atop his meager cot, hoping to ride the storm out that way. Yet the darkness, in combination with the scurrying of rodent feet and the disagreeable staleness of the air down there, served only to accentuate the ship's lurches. So gamely he dragged his ailing body topside to face indignity. But here at least fresh air was to be had, and the lake provided a more substantial basin in which to spew forth. No easy feat was retching into a moving bucket aboard a heaving ship.

His eyes suddenly closed, his face took on a waxen immobility as he struggled to orientate his body to the rising and falling of the ship, to its sudden and violent sideward pitches, to the repetitious surge of hull upon waters that hissed like Hell's own serpents...

Damn, but this simply was not working for him.

He drew a borrowed oilskin cloak more tightly around his body, seeking protection from the rain. The rain, a few hours in age, was slowly giving way to a drizzle, but Alvord harbored no desire to get any wetter than he already was.

Captain Colson, noticing his plight, handed over the wheel to his First Mate, the Irishman who went only by the affectionate moniker of Mick. Although a mite stormy out, Colson had seen far, far worse in his day, having served in the Royal Navy for five hellish years. These lakes held their perils, only a fool would take them lightly, but they were still unworthy of comparison to the raw fury of Poseidon's realm. He could use a brief break from his vigil behind the wheel, anyway, and Mick was as competent as they came.

He disappeared below deck, reemerging a few minutes later with something carefully held between his hands.

"Here," offered Colson to Alvord, squatting in front of him and holding out a steaming tin mug. "'Tis peppermint tea, pipin' hot, should aid the gut in overcoming its miseries. And you might try fixing your eyes on a certain point on the horizon. Old mariner's trick."

"Much obliged," Alvord thanked him in a gravelly voice, sitting up as straight as his cramping stomach allowed. He reached for the cup- how he wished he were not quivering like some palsied wretch! Colson's doing this served as a gesture of both consideration and respect; he could have easily ordered a man of lesser rank to deliver this tea.

"I would rise, Captain... you'll have to excuse my pathetic state, but-"

"Seen worse cases than yours, Mr. Rawn. You needn't apologize, nor worry. After the storm passes you'll be right as rain. And she'll be passin' soon enough."

Rising, he strode off, movements easy and unaffected by the swaying of his vessel.

Alvord respected that man. He possessed a hard sureness about him; Alvord knew from experience that such a quality was crucial in the leading of men. Demonstrate but a little hesitation, allow the merest suggestion of doubt to creep into your orders, and it was only a matter of time before men began second guessing you, began wondering if they were better equipped to call the shots themselves.

As soon as his mouth could tolerate the heat, Alvord gulped down the tea. If nothing else, it would give him something to throw up when the time came.

From the *Hellion's* bow Finnbar and Marcel took in the dying storm as the stiff easterly wind drove it ever closer to the mainland.

Beneath them the prow bore the brunt of the waves' force, bursting them asunder with great splashes and heaves. They were forced to hold onto the rigging, else they would have slid down the deck with every rise. This did not prevent Finnbar from taking a few venturesome steps up the bowsprit, however.

"Careful now," the lissome, longhaired boatswain cautioned as he checked the knot connecting the jib topsail to the bowsprit, "Can't be losing any landlubbers on this trip. Captain'd be none too pleased about that. And you don't want to see the gent when his ire is up."

Finnbar obliged the man, stepping back to resume his position next to Marcel, who grinned fiercely into the rain.

"Never been on a ship this size before!" he revealed in a joyous bark. "Nice, it is. Far preferable to a bateaux in such weather! Let's a body enjoy the elements as they rage rather'n have to worry 'bout being consumed by 'em!"

Looking at his exultant friend, Finnbar decided that he hardly looked the part of the mariner. His fringed buckskin pants and bright red flannel shirt, both thoroughly soaked, were strikingly out of place. And while some sailors sported facial hair, it often was sculpted. Marcel's untamed black beard was anything but.

But then again, one did not have to don the apparel of a sailor to enjoy a ride upon a ship.

"A bateau, you say? What other sorts of crafts did you take the last time you were up this way?"

"Keelboats, birchbark canoes, fur barges, small sloops a couple o' times. Nothin' like this beauty."

Eyes sweeping the stormy horizon, Finnbar commented, "Might as well be an ocean unto itself, no?"

Marcel clapped him on the back, a move that rattled the Irishman's spine and ribcage. The mountain man's short, burly body contained great strength, and at times he seemed not to know its extent.

"You just wait'll yeh clap on *Lac-Supérieur, mon ami*! Not only is she a mighty 'un, she's also desolate and unforgivin'. This lake is bein' fast tamed, but Superior can boast of only a handful of fledgling settlements. Nature still holds dominion over those lonely shores. You'll find plenty to fill them pages of yours with once we set paddle to that lake."

Finnbar, taking a quick step away lest his friend get over zealous again, inclined his head so that the rain pelted his face. "That is a fervent hope of mine."

Looking up at the rigging, Marcel made out two crewmen clambering about. The boatswain moved around them, placing a hand on Marcel to move him aside as he made for the foremast.

"S'cuse me, boys."

He mounted the ropes and began hauling himself up rather gracefully. In a flash however, Marcel jumped up onto the ropes himself, and if the boatswain was graceful, then the burly mountain men was downright fluid. Like an ape he hauled himself past the astounded man, climbing ever higher. He soon passed the two riggers as well, to some shouted oaths of surprise.

Whistling softly, Finnbar stroked his smooth chin. That was a feat of daring that the Irishman was simply not willingly to replicate.

Know thy limitations, he thought to himself. *Your magnificent brain would do the world little good if it were oozing out of your skull in the aftermath of a fall from that height, after all. Greeley would be ever so disappointed.*

Converting his impressed whistle into the tune of an old Irish dockside shanty, he strode onward, eyes never at rest as he took in the world around him.

Another figure approached Alvord through the mists of rain, though with none of Colson's smooth assurance. On the contrary, the man staggered about as if legless with drink, slipping and sliding and threatening to go down at any moment. Ungainliness notwithstanding, he made towards Alvord with almost comical determination, and grabbed hold of the aftcastle to steady himself.

It was the clumsy young fellow whose specimen boxes had made such a mess upon the docks yesterday. Humphrey Demetrius Duddersfield, whose parents could only have loathed him from birth. How else could you bestow upon your child a name like that? Alvord remembered him from the brief introductions they'd made after boarding the ship.

He stood an odd personage, one of timid bearing whose young, porcine face seemed always aquiver, whether from a nervous tic or a merely an excess of fat Alvord could not quite say. His brown hair, the color of raw umber, sat plastered to his head in a most untidy fashion, some spilling onto his round glasses with those outlandish purple lenses.

"Mr. Rawn!" he hailed in a piping tenor. "It is I, Humphrey Demetrius Duddersfield! Recall you our meeting?"

With a name like that, how could I forget? "But of course. I hope this afternoon finds you in better straits than myself."

"Quite so. Actually, I observed from across the deck your acts of disgorgement. Normally I am the type to let Nature takes its course, but since you did me a kindness by helping me collect my things yesterday, I have decided to intervene."

Alvord sighed. He was definitely heading back below with the rats. Better that than become anyone else's charity case.

He stared at Duddersfield with hollow eyes. "Ah, okay."

"I offer this."

With trembling hand Alvord plucked the item out of the proffered palm. It was a stone of some sort, quite smooth and oddly pleasant to the touch. Placing it closer to his eyes, he saw that it contained concentric bands of varying shades of green.

"Please consider it a gift. It is a piece of polished malachite, a copper-based mineral long believed to be an antidote to seasickness. Although for a rather sizable specimen like yourself, perhaps I should have given you a larger stone. Or maybe two average sized ones? Ah, never mind it. That particular piece has its origins in France; that is to say, it was harvested in France. When you consider the myriad geological processes by which such carbonates are formed, who knows where its actual origins lie?"

His voice, high to begin with, precipitously rose by a solid octave. "It matters little if one adheres to the theory of uniformitarianism or that of plutonism. While they are competing theories, either way they illustrate that the inner workings of the earth are so wonderfully complex. In fact, I was just reading an article in the American Journal of Science and Arts by this fellow James Dana, who theorizes that-"

"I thank you for the stone," Alvord thanked him firmly. He had dealt with these science types before; lend them an ear, and they'd give you an earful, a lecture free of charge. And if you failed to cut them off after a few sentences... this stone would do naught for his seasickness, of that he was positive, but it would be impolite to turn down so thoughtful a gift. This Duddersfield was an odd one, sure enough. Twice Alvord had observed him sitting by himself on his cot, looking at different stones under a magnifying glass and scribbling notes into a small notebook. He would speak to himself too, employing an inaudible whisper, sometimes drawing the stones close to his ear as if in the vain hope that they would talk back.

Who knew? Perhaps they did.

As Humphrey drew in another enormous lungful of breath, an all-too-familiar voice cut through the air, and not a moment too soon.

"Avast, me lovelies! Stand fast and stow the gab, you filthy bilge rats, or I'll have your guts fer garters! Batten down the hatches! Splice the main brace!" Finnbar, swaggering past a knot of sailors, spoke with boyish glee and excitement.

"You wouldn't want to be doing that, brudder," said Mick, giving him an affectionate shove. "T'main brace is the largest and most important of all the rigging. Ship's all but unmaneuverable without it. 'Cept if you got a screw propeller handy, o' course."

"Lucky that we do, then. Do pardon me exuberant ignorance, messmate. Just trying to get a handle on these new nautical terms."

"That's great, warms the cockles of one's heart, that does. Now how's about ye practice somewhere where you ain't distracting the crew?"

Finnbar made friends with an ease that Alvord could not hope to imitate. He would not venture to ascribe jealousy to it, for he liked keeping aloof of most people, but he must admit that the Irishman had a way of getting into people's good graces, be they sailors, socialites, gamblers or whores.

Finnbar moved along, noticing his ill friend. "Alvord! Still taken with seasickness?"

"Oh, and what was your first inkling?" Alvord's vomit-bespattered clothing and wan, pallid countenance spoke more than a little on the manner. He took in another mouthful of water and, swallowing half, used the rest to rinse his mouth again. That damn taste simply would not fade.

Ignoring him, Finnbar gave Humphrey a hearty clap on the back that sent him staggering.

"Humphrey ol' boy! What brings you out on the deck in the midst of a storm?"

Pushing his glasses back up his pudgy nose and steadying himself, he replied, "Never before have I seen a storm from this vantage. From a beach, yes, from atop a mountain too once, but this is an altogether more sublime view of Nature's wrath. As a man who understands the machinations behind such atmospheric events, at times I simply like to clear my mind and revel in the power of the natural world. At the moment I feel as vigorous as an Argonaut, or bold as good Odysseus, pitting myself against the fury of the sea god and laughing all the while!"

He threw back his unsightly head and laughed in what might have been a hearty manner had not his voice jumped up the scale once again.

Mad as a hatter! Finnbar mouthed to Alvord, who snorted appreciatively despite his ill condition.

"Is that not how you feel, Mr. Rawn? Like *Odysseus*?"

"I feel more like Argos, his dog, sick and waiting atop a mound of shit for this story to be over."

Looking at him strangely, Humphrey took his leave, but not before casting back a second look of pure perplexity.

"Do believe you sent that lad for a loop, Alvord."

"So be it. He's an odd one through and through, and I can only abide his presence for so long. He did see fit to give me this, however, so it is in poor attitude that I speak ill of him."

He showed Finnbar the piece of malachite.

"I have one of me own," he said, showing Alvord a malachite ring on his right hand. "Mother Fagan fancied that it brought out my eyes, bless her heart and soul. And I must agree with her."

Alvord rose unsteadily, putting weight on Finnbar's shoulder that nearly collapsed the man. "Where is Marcel?"

"Ah, *aloft*. We were by the bowsprit earlier, but now he's up among the riggings," Finnbar told him, jerking his head upward. "Near the foremast, last I saw. Climbs as well as any of the riggers aboard, even better than that wiry boatswain."

Alvord looked upward, but could not make out Marcel's stout form amidst the ropes, rain, sails, and spars. The sails had been partially reefed to reduce surface area during the strong winds, but enough fabric remained to effectively block visibility.

"Better he than I."

In truth his condition was improving, but whether it stemmed from the malachite, the tea, or the slackening storm he could not say.

"Are you really descended from Sir Walter Raleigh?" Finnbar asked of him. "He was quite the seafarer you know."

"A fact you know that I know. As I told you before, I am his descendant. On my mother's side I have some Cornish blood, and from that blood stems my connection to Raleigh. I think my brother Anscom has the documentation verifying it. He always felt a close kinship with Raleigh."

"Another seafarer in the family, right? He owns and pilots his own merchant ship?"

Alvord led the way towards the starboard rail, feeling far better and eager for the breeze upon his face. "Indeed he does. We worked for a merchant in Boston in our early years, and then again when we both decided to relocate to New York. Eventually I drifted towards the night watch, he towards the high seas in a mercantile venture of his own. He is now in California, having settled in San Francisco with his wife and my two nephews. He is a solid sort, my brother, and I may track him down one day."

"So he roamed the frothy brine while his younger brother went on to become a shining exemplar of justice, eh?"

Blue sky became exposed at intervals, allowing an oblique sliver of sunlight to break through the melancholy expanse of clouds. It glimmered brightly, disrupting the darkness surrounding it in an almost cheerful manner.

"I don't know about shining," muttered Alvord as he watched the shaft of light get swallowed up by the clouds.

Like that ray, their talk soon fell dead, replaced by the flutter of slackening winds against the sails, and the gentle patter of rain upon the deck.

Finnbar, a smile playing about his lips, grabbed a nearby rigging and stared westward, where the steely sky met waters of similar hue.

Alvord placed his hands firmly upon the rails and likewise fixed his gaze on the horizon, beyond the ship's undulating bow, where God knew what adventures awaited them in Michigan's untamed northland.

Chapter 12

Owain Derog Crowder, gently coming out of the tenebrous void of unconsciousness, became aware of the languid warmth of a merrily crackling fire perfumed by hillside heather, heard the gentle lilt of his mother's voice as it sang in his native Welsh.

He was home again, and blissfully so! A child once more, he felt safe and content in his home, laying with his eyes closed before the hearth with the family dogs, and basking in the feeling of security and closeness.

Mam Crowder crooned to him in tones gentle and mild, but his smile faded by slow degrees when he realized that he could not properly comprehend the words being sung. A dull pain began throbbing towards the back of his skull, making it difficult to focus. Every other word he got, but the rest was simply bastardized Welsh, as if an imbecile of inferior mental capacity were speaking. The cadence was proper; he could also recognize the familiar, voiceless sonorants that made Welsh so very unique among European languages. As he listened further, he found that he could pick out the soft, nasal, and aspirate mutations that also typified the Welsh language.

But something was definitely off.

Brow furrowed in confusion and against the deepening pain in his head, he ventured to open his eyes. The world appeared to him in images blurry and disjointed, lending further uncertainty to his situation.

As the room slowly solidified before him, he started. This place bore no resemblance to his family's cozy home, none at all. He was lying facedown on a dirt floor, cheekbone sore from the angle of his head. The walls, constructed in stone but not in the same manner as his boyhood home, were alight with the flicker of flames.

A vague feeling of dread intruded upon his delusion as reality slowly but surely wrested control of his mind.

The events of the past few days returned to him full force, edging out any fanciful notions of safety, comfort, or familiarity.

With a rush, the truth returned to him in all its terrible enormity- the chase, the slaughter, his capture. The copper-wearing men whom he encountered in the clearing had given chase, tailing him with almost mocking ease back to his camp, where his frantic yells failed to muster his sleeping crew into a proper state of readiness.

The copper wearers had descended upon them like wolves upon day old lambs, slashing, clubbing, and howling in delight. A few of his men rose to fight, lashing out at their assailants with pick-axe and hammer. Crowder distinctly recalled the hollow clunk of a double jack against a copper breastplate, accompanied by the rewarding scream of the fiend who wore it. But alas, the odds were stacked firmly against them, and swiftly enough their desperate, defiant stand was silenced.

Crowder too had fought, like a madman he thought it fair to say, but the copper men kept knocking him to the ground, as if to keep him from the fray. His repeated but undisciplined charges, full of wrath yet lacking much experience, were repulsed with an ease that disgusted him. The darkness made it impossible to perceive their foes with any clarity... it was faceless devils with whom they had clashed, devils who used no firearms, who moved with such swiftness and lethality as they struck with sword, axe, and spear.

After his men were slain or lay dying on the leaf litter, Crowder had been dealt a sharp blow to the head, which rendered him unconscious for some time. But he remembered in snatches scenes of being dragged through the woods in some sort of travois, watching the sunlight gently filter through the canopy above. Then darkness. Then it was night again, and some vile concoction was being forced down his gullet, knocking him out good and proper. How much time had passed he could not say with much certainty, but the length of the rough stubble on his cheeks suggested no more than a couple of days.

The fire, which smelt of soothing heather only in his mind, hissed somewhere behind him. He heard sudden movement and lay quite still, afraid of what might lurk behind him. Part of him did not want to know what manner of men these were... something told him that savage times lay ahead of him...

The figures, coming closer, cast jerky, skeletal shadows upon the flickering wall, causing Crowder's overloaded mind to recall Plato's Allegory of the Cave. What he observed on the wall contained only a modicum of the truth. But unlike the chained prisoners in the story, he possessed the power to turn around and face reality at any time. Sure, he could remain still and ascribe appearance and substance to these hollow projections. Yet his mind, ever at work, urged him to turn round and quantify whatever it was behind him. With a deep breath, he reluctantly forced himself to role over.

Upon doing so, he perceived a serried structure before him. A cage! He had awoken in a bloody cell... not exactly his heart's nearest wish. A mounting anxiety welled up in his throat, but he set his jaw and strove to relax his breathing.

They must have kept him drugged for the majority of that time, for this was the first instance in which he had come to in a cell. All he remembered aside from this was endless trees, the thud of feet upon earth, and an occasional glimpse of Lake Superior.

It was a small, torch-lit room the cell sat in, low ceilinged and possessing of a dismal ambiance. The fire blazed in the middle of the room, encircled by stones.

Drums began playing loudly from the other side of the wall behind him, not aiding his efforts to calm himself. For he was alive, but that fact alone was hardly cause for celebration, as he was wounded and a prisoner to boot.

The beat of the drums, deliberate and resonating, made him wonder just what sort of place he was being held captive in. Never had he known Chippewa drums to sound like that... the throb of the instruments was surely primitive but in a very different way...

Ah, perhaps this was just some tribe he knew nothing about. But the Indians in these parts were hyped as being placid and peaceable, two words he would most assuredly not employ in describing his captors.

Movement distracted his befuddled mind from the drums and sounds of outside. Two figures drew near.

They were men, he could tell from their robust limbs and the breadth of their shoulders. No copper graced their forms; they were bare-chested, clad only in deerskin pants. Tattoos that looked oddly familiar to Crowder wove their way around their torsos, spreading even to parts of the face.

Silently they stared at him, features half concealed by shadow so rendered all the more unreadable. Crowder saw what appeared to be a beard on one of them, but that was impossible, as red men did not grow beards. He said nothing, although his mind was filled to bursting with questions- his dry mouth and tightening throat made sure of that.

The drums continued beating, rhythmic and wild in the same instant, while the two men persisted in their wordless staring. He struggled to his feet, moving closer so as to grab the wooden bars of his cell for support. Hunger swiftly assailed him in massive pangs, but even that primal need could not rival his insatiable need to know what the unholy hell was going on.

The men in turn moved closer to the fire, revealing more of themselves and eliciting a startled gasp from Crowder.

Watching the frenetic dance of the flames upon the pale, tattooed faces, an old story scudded across the wind-swept plains of his mind. Owain Derog Crowder, in a moment of epiphany, recalled from the mists of boyhood a legend told to him by his grandfather. A Welsh legend swathed in mystery, passed down through the ancient bardic odes, a legend that his scientific mind had long scoffed at, yet one that at present seemed to offer perhaps the only tenable explanation to the mounting madness around him...

Chapter 13

The sun dawned on a glorious morning, damn near cloudless and attended by a pleasant warmth. Already up (he rarely slept well aboard ships), Alvord surveyed the shoreline as he chewed on a savory piece of smoked whitefish. Finnbar and Marcel were both still slumbering, so he stood alone. Although that Duddersfield character lurked nearby, intently scribbling upon his notebook.

It was a picturesque extent of country they passed by, replete with softly rolling dunes and sandy beaches interrupted at intervals by dim forests of stunted pine. Densely wooded hills formed a backdrop beyond them, where larger timber reared skyward.

Gulls floated in the air, making occasional plunges into the water after herring or shiners. Scattered about the shimmering water sat flocks of cormorants and the odd loon. Twice he spotted immense schools of fish alongside the boat, silvery bursts of glittering scales. At one point a large, primeval looking specimen that he surmised to be sturgeon broke the surface with its spiked back.

The sun shone cheerily upon his face, causing his beard to smolder with its light. Although a pallid cast still hung around his eyes, he felt immensely better than yesterday. With a heave of his chest, a contented sigh passed through his nostrils.

He moved off, eager to stretch his cramped legs.

Having been stricken with seasickness during much of the storm, he had failed to appreciate the crew's competence during that rough spell, or Captain Colson's skillful tacking into the northwesterly wind. His foremost thoughts while taken with illness were the sharp canting of the masts and the incessant throbbing of the hull as it was relentlessly battered by waves. But now, having risen from the darkness of his sleeping berth in fair health and good spirits, he marveled at the efficiency of the fifteen crewmen on board. Each attended their task with apparent competence; few orders were given and he could detect no aggravated yelling from the Captain or First Mate.

He walked up the aftcastle stairs over to the helm, where Colson kept his vigil. Though he still sported his captain's hat, he had taken off his embroidered blue coat due to the early onset of heat. In a casual pose he leaned against the large wooden steering wheel, sleeves rolled up and golden hair gently tossed by the breeze.

Upon noticing Alvord, he quickly straightened. "Back in action, eh?"

"Yes. I have a recurrent problem with rough seas, one that reared its ugly head yesterday. Calm waters present no problem, but that incessant swaying and undulating gets me every time. Peculiar, as I am descended from sailors... oh well- 'tis a landlubber's life for me, that fact notwithstanding."

"Who in your family sailed?"

"My father fought in the United States Navy during the late war with Britain, dying in the savage battle between the USS *Chesapeake* and the British frigate *Shannon.*"

Colson nodded, looking up at the azure sky. "A noble way to die, serving one's country. Especially aboard a ship, where privation and isolation are often more acutely felt, and where there is little room to run once battle is joined."

"It seems that my father's death was indeed noble. One member of the marine detachment on board wrote my family afterwards, stating that he was one of the only crewmembers who obeyed Commanding Officer Lawrence's dying order. It consisted of fighting to the last gasp and not giving up the ship no matter what the cost. Upon being boarded, he and only a handful of other crewmen stood alongside the marines to make a desperate stand against the British boarding party. Apparently my father's cutlass found the skull of *Shannon's* Captain Broke, whose brain was laid bare by the blow. The man survived, I have since read, but never fully recovered. After that my father received a mortal bayonet wound to the chest, dying almost instantly."

Alvord paused, watching a nearby gull off the stern side as it hovered effortlessly above the lake. "Of course, that message bore slight meaning to me initially. I was but a mere slip of a lad at the time, and the information it contained held little consolation."

"Is your family long in this nation?"

Alvord shook his head. "Both my parents immigrated from England just after the turn of the century. How long have you been here in the colonies?"

Colson tossed back his leonine head and chortled at the self-deprecatingly applied term "colonies", one that well-heeled Londoners often used to refer to the United States.

"Having been here for four years, I can assure you that I don't consider this grand place a mere colony."

He gave the wheel a few rightward turns and jerked his head towards shore. "Muskegon lies ahead, where most of your fellow passengers will be disembarking. Booming lumber industry in this region now; it'll be cleared and properly settled before long."

A ragged cluster of fishing shanties lined the shore of a marshy lake that fed into Lake Michigan. Beyond them sat more buildings, these of sounder construction and neater arrangement.

They lapsed into a companionable silence, which Alvord decided to break with a compliment he felt Colson quite deserving of.

"I am most impressed with your crew. Efficiency seems to be the watchword aboard the *Hellion.* In the past I have been aboard my share of poorly crewed and commanded ships; if I may, what is your secret?"

"I am blessed with a fine bunch of boyos," Colson answered modestly, a fact that Alvord could appreciate. "Of the crewmen, five are former Jack Tars, or Royal Navy, two are U.S. Navy, four previously worked aboard merchant ships, three as whalers, and one was a lubber who took to this life with surprising ease. Two others you may not have seen; they serve as engineers, working the steam engine below. Their conduct is as upright as any realistic man can expect of sailors, and they are fiercely loyal. I am fortunate- most ships captains have it far worse, and are forced to dole out much-needed punishments. My men tend to stay in order."

As if on cue a commotion broke out on deck below them.

Alvord turned towards Colson, a poorly concealed look of apologetic amusement on his face as he went to investigate the source of the ruckus.

It turned out that the outburst was not one betokening dispute but rather excitement. Unsurprisingly, Finnbar was involved.

He and Marcel held smallish bows in their hands, from which they were loosing arrows at fish in the water below. Alvord guessed them to be Marcel's weapons; the man carried a small arsenal north with him in preparation for the trip. Quality weapons could be bought in Chicago, and he had expressed concern in not being able to find such quality anywhere north of Slab Town.

As he watched, Finnbar fired a shot and in the next instant dropped the bow excitedly, grabbing for a thin coil of twine that was on the deck beside him. Hauling it in vigorously, he pulled in a briskly struggling, impaled fish over the rails. A bit too energetic in his efforts, he tugged the four-pound fish right into his face, where it promptly slapped him with its tail.

He stumbled backwards into his large friend. "What ho, Alvord Rawn! You're looking to be in fine fettle at long last! Clap your eyes on this- second bloody shot!"

He held up the writhing fish, face aglow with pride. The rope was secured to a long-tipped, barbed arrow.

"Nicely done, my friend. Should make for fine eating."

"Damn straight! Marcel says this is a shoal of walleye, which are first-rate eating in his book."

Duddersfield, tripping over a wooden scrub bucket as he hastened over, scrutinized the dying fish with pursed lips. Flipping through the pages of his notebook, he adjusted his glasses and peered at a page, lips silently forming words.

"Hmmm," he said after a moment, "more likely a sauger, judging by the milky glow around the eye and the stark white of its belly. A close relative of the walleye and a fish often confused with it."

Marcel squatted on his heels, looking closely at the fish as it gasped through its large, unsightly mouth. "Damned if 'e ain't right! Sauger it is! Used to call 'em pikeperch back in the day. See, also got them dark blotches on its scales and a spotted top fin."

"Ah, *dorsal fin*," Duddersfield corrected him tartly, shaking his head hopelessly.

Marcel rose slowly, his sloped, powerful shoulders set in a way that made Alvord fear for the blundering youth, who suddenly noticed to his abject horror the trapper's abrupt and menacing change in demeanor.

"Son, I was guttin' these things 'fore you was off Mother Dudderfield's saggin' tit. When I wanna be corrected about something that nobody rightly cares about in the first place, I'll be sure to let ya know. 'Til then, why don't you mosey yer cockchafin' ass outta here?"

In the face of this upbraiding Duddersfield immediately indulged his request, scampering away in a manner most undignified to the hearty laughter of the crew.

"Man alive! Is this what sorta folk this country's breedin'? May the Almighty have mercy on us."

Alvord clapped his trapper friend on the shoulder. "That quaint fellow just sets your teeth on edge, doesn't he Marcel? Just a fool of a youth, is all."

"Yeah, true enough. Shouldn't get puckered like that. Bad fer the heart, you know." He stopped talking to take a sizeable rip off his morning pipe.

Alvord indicated the bow. "Now, you mind if I give this a go?

Looks to be capital sport."

A broad smile crept across Marcel's wildly bearded face. "Sure thing! Let 'er rip amigo!"

It turned out Alvord was no great shakes with a bow. It was only after four tries that he finally managed to put one of the wickedly barbed arrows through a fish. Hardly a significant accomplishment, for thousands swum around the boat in a teeming, tightly packed shoal as they fed on baitfish. But it was oddly satisfying nonetheless.

Some of the crew began expressing interest in trying their hand at it.

"Back to work, you idle loafers!" roared Mick, scattering the sailors who observed the proceedings.

They anchored a hundred yards from shore, waiting for some canoes from the shoreline to reach them. These would ferry the other passengers aboard the *Hellion* to the coastal town of Muskegon, were the hollow thud of axe upon tree floated across the still waters to the ship.

Most of those who left were women and rugged looking men still early in their voyage of life. Frontier towns needed their like; tough, young sorts whose strength, skill, work ethic and fortitude was crucial to taming the raw wilderness around them.

Another school of fish, this time actually walleye, hung around during this stop, so Alvord and company passed the time shooting more fish, whose meat would constitute a welcome change from the hard-bitten cook's bland meals.

After an hour and a half of lowering passengers and their baggage into the ferry canoes, they were ready to depart. All went smoothly until they were past the dunes north of Perre Marquette early that evening.

"That's where the Jesuit Jacques Marquette is buried," Marcel informed Alvord, pointing towards the sandy shoreline. "Only thirty-eight years of age, too. Imagine what that feller'd have accomplished given more time on this earth? It always impressed me that a priest, a damn *priest*, could be so intrepid. He traveled all over these lakes, hell, was even on the Mississippi all the way back in 1673. I ain't properly religious, I guess, but I ain't afraid to admit that such a journey attests to the power of faith. What else could fuel it?"

"Priests and religious men actually have a long history of roving. Look at the Apostles and St. Paul, who traveled far afield in their quest to spread the Word. Or the many priests and monks who traveled to the war torn, inhospitable Holy Land in the company of crusaders."

It was at this point, about three hours north of Muskegon that a ripple of unease passed through the crew. A faint ripple it was, but not quite faint enough to escape Alvord's notice, nor that of his friends. They made no immediate inquiries, but instead silently watched as the men pointed to a disturbed area of beach. Pine boughs and large quantities of bark lay scattered across the disturbed sand, where it was obvious that a fair amount of work had taken place. The men began quietly conferring as they worked, motioning towards the beach and the thin black column of smoke that rose above the tree line from the undulating woodlands beyond, into which a rough road had been hacked.

Mick and Colson held a hushed discussion by the helm, shaking their heads and looking out onto the horizon at times. Alvord directed his gaze at them until they concluded, whereupon Colson noticed his attention and hastily looked away with a troubled expression on his face.

"Everything alright, Mick?" Alvord queried in a causal voice as the Irishman passed by.

"Aye, for now."

They did not have long to wait until the source of the vexation was revealed. Mick, looking absorbedly through a telescope at the bow, suddenly hailed his captain in a tone that caused Alvord's head to snap to attention. Even the stoic First Mate could not keep his voice from betraying a definite strain of worry.

"Cap'n, ye'd best come take a gander at this!"

Chapter 14

The *Hellion's* anchor splashed noisily into the lake as all hands and passengers gathered for an emergency council.

Contrary to character, Colson appeared out of sorts, overcome by the mounting sense of concern his furrowed brow connoted. Silently he stood before the expectant men, eyes directed at the deck until his thoughts were properly gathered.

"We have a decision to make, one of no small importance. Though I want all present to hear me out, I address only my crew, as what I am about to propose I could never ask a passenger to have a hand in."

He fell silent, features stormy. The crew began exchanging glances, as did Alvord and his companions. They three and Duddersfield were the only remaining passengers on board, the rest having disembarked at Muskegon.

Colson looked up suddenly, expression marked by fierce determination. His next words were delivered quickly and with the coolest of deliberation.

"We have sighted the schooner *Hywell* less than half a league north of our current position. I have been informed by members of The Great Lakes Patrol that this ship and its crew are responsible not only for rampant timber piracy along the federally owned woodlands of coastal Michigan and Wisconsin, but also for the claiming of innocent lives along the way. I know that you men have heard the stories as well. These pirates are wanted dead or alive. I therefore propose that we pursue and engage the *Hywell*, as lake authorities have failed to do."

A decent number of the crewmen grimly nodded their concurrence. Not everyone so readily agreed, however.

"*Pursue and engage?*" one man spat in immediate disbelief. "You would suggest that we *attack* another ship and what, arrest or slaughter its fucking crew? This is not wartime, Captain, and this is hardly our affair."

"As I damn well know, Billings," Colson shot back, fixedly holding the man's indignant stare. "The Great Lakes Patrol has gathered information firmly connecting those aboard that ship with the murder of a man whose land they took timber from, a man whose wife and daughters they raped before slaughtering. That was a month ago; judging by the smoke coming out of the forest by that beach we passed, another land owner may have fallen by their hands, or at the very least had his home destroyed."

Without conscious volition Alvord's jaw clenched. Suddenly the squalling of the gulls and lapping of minuscule waves upon the hull faded away. Of all the criminal elements he had grown to detest over fourteen years of law enforcement, rapists comprised the muck at the bottom of that suppurating barrel. Rape was among the blackest of crimes in his mind, one that screamed out for brutal retribution. In that instant he knew that he would soon pander to his dark side, for Colson could count him in. A perfunctory glance at Finnbar and Marcel told him that their thoughts mirrored his own, for fire smoldered in their eyes.

A rare breed were the two men who stood alongside him, and for that he was thankful. Knowing how your friends will react in most given situations saves a body a lot of agonizing guesswork.

"We are under your employ as sailors aboard a cargo ship," another crewman said to his Captain, "you cannot simply abandon us here for the sake of chasing glory! Your days in the Royal Navy have passed!"

"Don't be daft. 'Tis justice I seek, Maynes. Glory is what self-important fools seek at the expense of their men's lives. *Vengeance* is what I would have, and would honor any among you who wish to join me in its pursuit."

Vengeance- there was a word that Alvord recognized the power of, one that he had lost his very job for the sake of. His emotional range had long ago been seared above the intricacies that ordinary folk experienced, but retribution- ah, for him it was an emotion unto itself.

"You are not the only one who has stock in this ship," Maynes was firmly pointing out to Colson.

"I will remind you that my shares in this boat and venture exceed all others. You all knew that when you signed on with me back in Cleveland. And yes, to be clear, as captain and rightful owner of this vessel I am proposing that we engage that ship of hellspawn."

"You've done lost your mind!" Billings's voice was strident with incredulity.

"*Ayehh...*" the Captain growled, the noise of a Liverpool man whose temper threatened to flare presently.

"Just report this sighting to the Lake Patrol! Let them deal with it- its their damn job, after all, not ours."

"The *USS Michigan* is currently on Huron, making its pass along the Canadian border before it enters these waters. And, as you know, that is the sole ship comprising the 'Great Lakes Patrol.' The lakes are expansive. This timber schooner has slipped right by them before; it could easily do so again. We can act *now*."

Maynes crossed his arms and bit his lower lip, shaking his head unconvincedly. "What happened to those folks, if true, is unfortunate but I still don't see how this is our problem."

Alvord, standing off to the side, came forward at this point, his hobnail boots rapping authoritatively on the well-scrubbed deck. Taking up position next to Colson, he called to mind the speech he had delivered to his own men this past April, when vengeance had driven him to do what most did not have the gall for.

He stood taller than any man present, more rugged of feature as well. His gray cotton shirt strained at his chest and broad span of shoulder, and rolled-up sleeves revealed the densely corded muscles of his forearms. The two scars on his face lent further severity to his chiseled countenance as he sternly regarded the crew.

They waited in silence for him to speak. This was no longer the seasick man pitifully retching over the rails.

He let his deep voice resonate from his chest. "It is up to men like us to right the wrongs of this world, and sometimes that requires unpleasant duties. Take our kind out of the equation and evil reigns unopposed. If you cannot bring yourselves to help us, then by the Eternal we shall do it ourselves."

He turned and held out his hand to Colson, who after a moment of puzzlement firmly grasped it, vigor and confidence renewed by the presence of a kindred spirit. Finnbar and Marcel were beside them in the next moment, adding further momentum to the growing faction.

"You sure of this?" Colson asked Alvord in a whispered aside.

"You hazard far more than I in this undertaking- perhaps you should direct the question inwards."

"Who else joins us, then?" Colson asked of the crew after a swift moment's reflection. "I condemn no man who does not. If you are among that group, you are welcome to the rowboats and provisions. Upon our victory we shall come back and retrieve you. On that I give my word."

A surprising number of men stepped forward, Mick and the longhaired boatswain among them. Some did so immediately, others stood in place for a bit, weighing their options and, perhaps, wondering exactly what values they were willing to stand and bleed for.

Maynes hung back with Billings and four others, restively

toying with his gold earring. "Not my funeral, Cap'n. I'll be taking my leave of this vessel now, along with any others who still retain their sanity."

He strode briskly off towards the rowboats, followed by the other five. The two engineers promptly followed that faction, but the squat, grungy cook, who had been standing near them, stood fast.

With a green, snaggletooth grin he drew the meat cleaver from his belt. Holding it close to his face, he began walking towards the stairs leading below deck.

"Best be gettin' a fine edge on ye, Molly," he whispered to it gleefully, "for we'll have some real meat for ye to sink yer teeth into 'fore long!"

He disappeared down the stairs, cackling madly to himself.

"Well, glad that chappie is on our side," Finnbar remarked flippantly as he watched the cook go.

Humphrey Demetrius Duddersfield, meanwhile, flew down after the cook, presumably to collect his various specimen boxes and books. A crashing sound soon followed, indicating his falling down the steps.

"Least we got ridda him," commented Marcel, looking on the bright side.

Colson solemnly turned towards Alvord.

"Who are you?"

"Until last year, I was Captain Alvord Rawn of the Municipal Police Department of Manhattan. As of now, I am merely Alvord Rawn, an unattached man with a roving disposition. And one to whom the dispensing of justice is yet a specialty. I stand a ready enemy of yonder swine."

The captain looked him over more closely, as if in a new light. "Gotham, eh? Well then, I suppose you have seen your share of shit. Quite glad to have you at my side, Captain Rawn. And you two, I extend my thanks to you as well."

"S'been awhile since I had me a good fight," Marcel said unconcernedly, scratching his scraggly beard. "And filth like yon pirates deserve whatever they get. Last real scrap was down St. Louis way, tackling that rogue mesmerizer, eh Al?"

Colson arched a white-blonde eyebrow. "Rogue mesmerizer?"

"Story for another day," replied Alvord crisply.

"And you, Finnbar? Likewise full of vim, are we?"

"To the fucking brim." (Here Colson beamed at the Irishman's use of a common sailor's curse word). "Can't be filling me memoirs with dry rot, now can I?"

"I do believe there is more to you fellows than meets the eye."

And Colson indeed let his pale eyes sweep over them; a

hulking former police captain, an unflappable trapper, and a red-haired Irishman with a devil-may-care smile plastered across his clever face.

"How soon until we are upon the *Hywell*?" Alvord inquired absorbedly.

"We shall have her in a jiffy. She rides low in the water, no doubt heavy laden with timber stolen from both privately and federally owned lands. Rumor has it that she sails to Milwaukee to deliver timber, so I'd imagine that before long she'll swing westward to make the crossing to Wisconsin Territory. Not before we intercept her, however. But first, down to my quarters to set forth a plan of attack."

"Aye-aye, Cap'n," said Finnbar, saluting him with a wry twist of fatalistic humor on his lips.

Colson's quarters, dimly illuminated by several oil lamps, could barely accommodate the men assembled in it. Colson, Mick, the boatswain, and Alvord and company all squeezed in to hold a quick meeting regarding the impending conflict.

"So, the *Hywell* being as weighed down as she is, and slow to begin with, presents no challenge in terms of our overtaking her. We need one man to do the work of two and stay down below in the engine room until the battle is joined, so as to feed wood into the fire. We will need full steam. Now onto the question of how to engage the enemy."

"Could ram her," the boatswain offered.

"Peter, I am unwilling to so blithely sacrifice the integrity of this ship. We would incur damage if we approached it in that manner, any way you slice it. The last thing we need is to deal with a sinking ship while facing a crew of timber pirates."

Mick impatiently toyed with the handle of his hatchet. "What d'ya propose, then?"

"I have a more deceptive plan in mind."

Colson laid it out in plain terms, and when he was done all present agreed that it was the best course of action.

"Have this," Alvord said to Colson afterwards, offering his Colt Walker to the gaping Captain. Although revolvers were gaining in popularity, flintlock pistols were far more commonly employed as weapons, being cheaper. This style of Colt, not yet a year on the market and exceedingly rare, trumped any flintlock known to man, overall lethality being the main factor. Having six .44 caliber balls at one's disposal could afford one a nice edge in battle.

"I can't accept that, it is your weapon and a fine one at that, you should be the one to-"

"I have other guns. Take it and return it after the fight is won. I do my best work in close, anyway."

Colson grinned appreciatively. "Of that I have no doubt, friend. In that case, I propose a trade. Take this."

He reached into the room's closet and pulled out a cutlass, still in good shape but bearing unmistakable signs of use.

"Served me well in the Royal Navy against Chinese pirates, and I hope it does the same for you against the men we soon face."

"Much obliged. Ah, good ol' Sheffield steel!" Alvord admiringly ran his hand over the blade's cold length.

Back in their quarters, Marcel and Finnbar were distributing weapons from the mountain man's stock. Knives, tomahawks, hatchets, flintlocks pistols, and rifles were dispersed. Marcel grabbed a bow, this one larger than the bows used for fishing, and strung it in one deft, fluid motion. Testing the draw, he nodded his approval. Finnbar, meanwhile, loaded a Harper's Ferry Model 1803 rifle with patent proficiency. Alvord sometimes forgot that he had fought as a mercenary, one of the Irish "wild geese," in the Uruguayan Civil War not too long ago.

Alvord opened one of his valises and took from it his Elgin Cutlass pistol. A .54 caliber smoothbore flintlock, this pistol was custom designed for the purpose of boarding an enemy ship, and Alvord would see it used to its fullest extent. A twelve-inch Bowie knife blade, six inches of which extended out past the barrel, made this pistol a versatile one in such a circumstance. He loaded it with bird shot rather than a single ball, as he figured a sweeping pattern, though less lethal, would find its mark more easily in crazed battle conditions.

Colson ordered that a box of muskets that they transported be opened and put to use. He also took down two old boarding pikes from his Navy days that he used for decoration in his cabin. Before long each man was armed to the teeth and eager to put the Captain's plan into action.

Alvord reached into his pocket and retrieved a locket containing a daguerreotype of his deceased wife, Katherine. Opening it he beheld her flawless face, ringed as it was with a nimbus of strawberry-blonde hair that shades of black and white did not do full justice to. Her beauty and poise, even within the still confines of a portrait, never failed to lend him strength. The phantom of a smile drifted across his face as he walked across the gloomy gangway and mounted the stairs down which the sun idly cast its golden rays.

"Full sails and full steam ahead!" roared Colson after each man reached the deck.

The crew, though diminished, was still sufficient enough to man the ship, and in a short span of time the *Hellion* was speeding towards its target. Colson took the helm while Peter went below to feed wood into the steam engine.

Upon hearing the wind fill the sails with the sound of a distant thunderclap, Alvord felt his heart accelerate. At this stage in his life, as a thirty-six year old childless widower, fear was not something he had to grapple with anymore. Death was death, shorn of all possible complications; no one relied on his continued existence any longer.

How very liberating.

Rage. In moments of philosophical musing he sometimes sought a softer term for the emotion, this tingling warmth that flooded the body, the lightness in the head that accompanied the grinding of teeth. Yet even in his most reflective moments, he eventually resigned himself to the fact that rage was simply a shadowy facet of his being. As well he knew that it was rage indeed that he would soon lose himself to.

The *Hellion* steadily sliced through the water, its smokestack coughing black puffs of sweet-smelling smoke into the flawless sky above.

Alvord, breathing deeply of the freshest air his lungs had ever enjoyed, allowed himself a grim smile. He embraced the giddy lightheadedness and let that tingling warmth course slowly through him.

"Finally found your sea legs, Mr. Rawn?" asked Colson, standing nearby.

"And not a moment to soon."

The Captain turned to face the suddenly mounting wind. His head tilted upwards, eyes closed reverentially.

"Aye. It seems that Heaven has smiled upon our undertaking."

"And as Heaven may smile, so does Hell hunger for the wicked," replied Alvord, his gray eyes a darkening tempest as he stared hypnotically at the ship they drew ever nearer to.

And the devil on his shoulder danced in delight.

Chapter 15

"Ahoy *Hywell!*" Colson's voice, rendered stentorian by the speaking trumpet he spoke into, carried across the still waters and reverberated off the dunes and wooded hillsides. No other ships were in sight; most tended to chart a course deeper into the lake at this point so as to head directly towards the Manitou Islands.

"Ahoy there!" came the gruff reply, though the captain of the other vessel employed no voice amplifier. "What be your business, and why stray you so close?"

The foghorn voice, laced with suspicion and a trace of annoyance, could not have been less welcoming.

"I am Captain Edmund Colson of the steam propeller *Hellion*, and chary though I am of making my dilemma that of another man's, I come seeking aid."

Colson, standing at the starboard side rail, cast a measured glance at the enemy ship. The *Hellion's* deck was roughly six feet higher than the *Hywell*, which afforded him a good view of the two-master timber schooner. He guessed her to be one hundred and fifty feet from bow to stern, with a beam of fifty or so feet. While decidedly wide for your average craft of that length, this was a necessary component for a timber schooner so that a sizable amount of lumber could be stacked on deck without compromising stability. And sure enough, three large piles of timber, roughly hewn into manageable pieces, sat on deck. A primitive crane hung from her aftmast, with which lumber could be loaded and unloaded.

Without being obtrusive in his assessment, Colson's keen eyes swiftly took a head count. Twenty-three men on board including the captain- an absurdly high number of men to crew a ship that size, but when one considered that they also acted as a logging crew it made sense. Swords hung from the belts of the nameless captain and one of his men. Some of the others carried knives, two had hatchets in their belts, but no guns were in evidence. A stack of axes by the forecastle glinted in the streaming sunlight.

"And, pray tell, precisely what might that aid entail?" The false, lordly tone of his voice left no man wondering as to what he thought of charity-seekers. "Cause if you're looking for wood to fuel that smoke belcher you can piss off right quick."

"We ask only for a bit of food. We can pay." Colson's manner was a subdued one, as if he were something of a defeated man. Certainly not someone to worry about, anyway.

"Fancy ship like that, one would think that provisions would be plentiful and first rate." The timber pirate crew sniggered at their Captain's words.

"Fancy is what got us into trouble. 'Twas canned food we had aboard, but it spoiled on us. And we lost some other provisions during the storm."

Hywell's Captain snorted and shook his head hopelessly. "Canned food! Poor choice, matey- that stuff never keeps. What have you to pay or barter with?"

"I have cash, and also a Pottawatomi squaw for sale. She was slavish enough to start, but yesterday that damn she-wolf came at one of my men with a knife. Too wild for us. For additional food, she's yours if you want, but keep her away from items sharp and shiny."

The man cast an enthusiastic look at his crew, who lit up with brutish glee at the mention of the imaginary squaw. Many of them came to the rail hoping to catch a glimpse of the maiden, and Colson fancied that he could see them salivating.

"Bitch ain't syphilitic, is she?"

"Nah, plenty of my men can attest to that."

"Then swing 'round and send us some lines so we can make fast for our trade."

Ordering his five visible men to toss ropes over to the *Hywell's* crew, Colson gently maneuvered her abreast of the other ship.

The boats clacked softly together, the *Hywell's* crew using staves to slow the *Hellion's* approach. This accomplished, they tied the ropes off and waited impatiently for the trade to take place.

"Give me half a mo' and I'll go down and fetch the wench. You sure you want that hissing hellcat?"

"You just toss her our way and we'll make a proper lady out of her in no time!"

At this his men hooted and cheered, and the crew of the *Hellion* joined in. None aboard the *Hywell* noticed that those smiles and laughs did not quite reach the eyes of the other crew.

Colson threw back his golden head and chortled merrily. "Well then, in that case, boys-" (here his voice underwent a swift, sinister transformation) "*send them to fucking Hell!*"

Alvord shot up from his position behind the gunwale, rifle

settling into his shoulder as he reached his full height. Shrugging off the canvas tarpaulin he had used for cover, his brain and body worked in flawless unison to get the gun into position. He and the rest of the men on board had been hiding under the tarpaulins next to the gunwales, looking for all the world like miscellaneous cargo.

A feral smile slid onto his face as he centered his sights on the chest of a shocked sailor across from him, for it was wailing time for the debauched crew of the *Hywell.*

In the instant before he squeezed the trigger, he saw the other captain's mouth begin to roar something that was obliterated by an eruption of gunfire. Alvord heard the sharp crack of the percussion cap a split second before his gun kicked. Through the white clouds of gun smoke he witnessed the damage wrought by the .69 caliber musket ball at this close range. The man's chest spurted the brightest of blood upon the deck beneath his feet, which he collapsed onto a moment later. He was not alone in doing so.

"That oughta take the starch out of 'em!" Marcel roared exultantly above the bedlam, loosing the arrow he had strung in the instant after his first was launched.

A goodly number of the pirates by the rails were down after that withering opening salvo, enough to hearten the *Hellion's* war party. A rousing cheer went up as men scrambled to either reload or make ready their hand-to-hand weapons. Alvord himself drew his truncheon with his right hand and snatched up the cutlass Colson had lent him. It was a bit small for his meaty fist, slightly top heavy as well, but it would make for a fearsome weapon in his capable hands.

His father had nobly fought and died in such a manner, aboard a ship fighting in savage, close-quarter combat. If Fate marked Alvord out this evening, then at least he and Benjamin Rawn would have something to discuss in the afterlife.

Those of the *Hywell's* crew who still retained the ability fled to various parts of the ship, some roaring out shocked oaths as they sought cover and others scrambling to arm themselves.

Finnbar dropped his rifle and pulled out a flintlock pistol, which he took careful aim with and fired at the only pirate still up in the rigging. He missed by a small margin, but startled the man sufficiently to provoke a fifteen-foot fall to the deck below. Weapon empty, Finnbar drew his wickedly sharp, double-edged dagger.

"You ready, *mo chara*?" He yelled exuberantly to Alvord in the moment before they boarded.

Alvord flashed him a steely smile by way of reply, and

launched himself over the rails.

He was not the first to do so. Immediately upon discharging his blunderbuss, the cook went at the enemy head on, wielding his sharpened meat cleaver and a hatchet with unbridled enthusiasm. His first victim was a wounded man who was dazedly trying to stuff his intestines back in.

Intent on finding more mobile quarry, Alvord swept past as the cook gleefully fell upon his target. He *was* ready for this-keyed up for it, even. And it went beyond his intense hatred of human malice. It was the losses that really fueled his shadow half, the vivid memories of his family withering before his very eyes, which drove him to altitudes of rage that most men could never hope to achieve. Every sense seemed keenly heightened. The world was more sharply delineated before him, and he became keenly aware of each sound that supplemented the riotous cacophony of battle.

From around a pile of logs a shirtless, bellowing man came at him, swinging a stave with both hands. It was a powerful but frantically aimed blow, one that Alvord avoided with a quick backward jerk of his head. The man backed off a pace, eyeing his unfazed enemy warily, then launched himself towards Alvord, stave held high for an over handed blow. The sword checked its downward progress, while the truncheon's copper tip shattered his left elbow. Howling madly, the pirate used his unbroken arm to bring the stave whipping around towards Alvord's skull.

He waited coolly until the furious momentum carried the pole harmlessly past his face, at which point his over-rotated enemy was powerless to defend himself. His thrust skewered the man's right bicep; with a twist of Sheffield steel in flesh and a quick sawing motion that muscle flapped wetly about, no longer attached to the lower arm. The man did not even have time to scream before the cutlass pommel cracked him in the temple, flooring him in a flash. The reinforced tip of the blade then sank into the hollow of his throat, causing his limbs to convulse spasmodically.

Blood bubbled out of the man's mouth and flowed onto his beard as he stared helplessly up into Alvord's pitiless eyes.

He wrenched the cutlass out summarily and moved on.

The noise of battle assaulted his ears; he heard screams of distress, roars of anger, a deep booming of gunfire, and the rapid thud of foot upon deck as the *Hellion's* crew sought to put a swift end to the engagement. He could see that the battle was to be two-pronged: the timber stacked in the middle of the *Hywell* separated the two groups of attackers. The element of surprise aided their cause, as many of the timber pirates were initially unarmed, facing oncoming men who wielded a variety of weapons with reckless abandon. Disorganization led to sheer chaos.

A man holding a knife aloft charged him next, but before he could engage Alvord felt a rush of air pass by his face and heard the meaty thud of Marcel's tomahawk as it buried itself in the pirate's chest. The man's eyes went wide with surprise, as if he could hardly believe his end. At a run, Marcel then grabbed the rope hanging down from the ship's crane and swung around to bring his feet crashing into an enemy chest.

Alvord continued his advance. To his left, between two stacks of lumber, he could see Finnbar engaged in a savage fight with an adversary, the knives of both men flashing as they desperately sought flesh. In the short space of time his eyes lingered, he saw the Irishman take a shallow cut on his arm, only to return the favor by smashing the man's head with the butt of his reversed pistol. He could only move on and hope Finnbar came out on top, as the space between the piles afforded a man of his stature little room to lend aid.

A hatchet-wielding foe rushed Alvord, whose sword severed the hand holding the weapon as it was brought down in an overhand swing. Twin truncheon strokes found his skull next, the copper tip producing a hollow clunk with each blow. Legs giving way, he crumpled like a rag doll.

A group of timber pirates managed to get to the stack of axes, and now attempted to make a stand near the bow of the ship.

"They're nervous," Marcel remarked as they advanced on the men.

"They ought to be."

As Alvord swept towards them, a shot rang out from somewhere behind him and one of the men sank to the deck with an outpouring of blood. A crewman wildly rushed the cluster of pirates with a boarding pike, ramming it through one of their stomachs before having his spine severed by the swift stroke of an axe.

Overzealous, the poor young bastard...

Then Alvord and Marcel were upon them, with more at their back. These were rough and ready men, these fiends in human form, loggers and sailors whose lives were not cushy affairs. Long days of grueling timberwork turned muscles and tendons to iron. Alvord could see the tensed power in the set of their shoulders- these were hardly your average men in strength and staying power. And with fury borne of desperation they made their stand. Their faces, though evincing signs of panic, mingled with it bitter sneers of defiance. But the axes, though wielded by experienced hands, had not the polished exactitude of the deadly weapons they faced.

Marcel fluidly ducked a massive swing and was then inside their guard, his recovered tomahawk and great Bowie knife deftly slicing crimson patterns into the hide of the algerine filth. Nearby, Alvord systematically hacked and clubbed them into nothingness, turning aside their frantic strikes and counterattacking with ferocity that none of them could equal. He fought with a cold, calculated fury that stirred his emotions but still allowed him to retain complete control over his movements.

Weapons crossed, Alvord stopped the progress of a sweeping, sideways axe swing. Freeing the cutlass, he whipped it around and imbedded the blade in the man's skull. He retrieved the gray-smeared sword with much noise and difficulty, but it mattered little as no enemies stood before him any longer.

For as his shipmates fell before his eyes, the last timber pirate of the group took to his heels and hurled himself over the rails.

Alvord sheathed his truncheon and walked over to the side of the ship with baleful deliberation. He drew his Elgin Cutlass pistol and began raising it. A sailor suddenly rushed him from across the ship, but his progress was stopped by a crushing kick to the sternum. The blade of the cutlass pistol then took him in the throat. Eyes wide, he tightly clutched Alvord's arm as he mumbled something hoarse and unintelligible.

Alvord forcefully tossed the dying man overboard. His eyes then sought out the swimming figure of the pirate who had ditched over the rails. Taking purposeful aim at his violently swimming form, Alvord squeezed the trigger. The gun barked and spat smoke and flames; when they cleared, the man floated lifelessly in the steadily reddening waters. Pleased with the results, Alvord cast no more concern his way.

The battle slackened off in a gradual diminuendo. But near the stern of the ship the noise of combat yet persisted, so Alvord hastened over to see if he could lend aid, leaping over corpses and dying, screaming men.

From behind a pile of logs came two forms, one of whom was Finnbar. He tackled his freely-bleeding adversary to the ground, mounting him and driving his knife hilt-deep into the meat just below the man's sternum. Unable to retrieve it with ease, Finnbar drew his push dagger and, amid garbled screams of pain and disbelief, frenetically stabbed the man's throat until he keeled over onto his side, wheezing horribly.

"*Holy shit!*"

"Finnbar!" Alvord, checking to make sure no enemies were about, knelt beside him. "Are you badly injured?"

The Irishman, right eye closing due to a hemorrhaging bruise, could barely muster his voice. "Arms are nicely diced, got this scalp wound that's bleedin' like a stuck hog, but you keep going, I'll be alright."

Clapping him on the shoulder, Alvord obliged him, intent on finding the source of the din nearby.

Chapter 16

Racing towards the stern, Alvord rounded a stack of lumber just in time to see one of Colson's crewmen tumble flaccidly down the aftcastle stairs, blood spurting from a mortal neck wound.

His shirtless vanquisher leapt over his body and down the staircase in a move both lithe and decisive. Upon landing, he threw a hard shoulder into another advancing crewmen, bowling him over and smoothly thrusting a long, wickedly sharp knife down into his chest. Wielding dual hatchets Mick set upon the sinewy man, whose lank black hair fell wildly about his snarling face.

Mick fought ferociously and with evident skill, but his heavily tattooed opponent was simply his better. The man methodically batted aside his increasingly wild swings, whilst opening up injuries on the Irishman's shoulder and thigh with his knife and multi-edged weapon that was most closely akin to a battle-axe.

Seeing an opening, the pirate feinted and went for an overhand strike that perfectly exploited Mick's bite on the maneuver. The swarthy face shone with malicious triumph. The strange axe swept down towards the First Mate's unprotected skull, but was promptly checked by Alvord's cutlass blade.

Exerting his strength to its fullest, Alvord stopped the downward progress of the weapon before it struck Mick, then thrust powerfully up and backwards, sending the man stumbling. Shoving the Irishman out of the way, he went out to meet the pirate, who whirled like a dervish and brought his weapons around in a high-low arrangement. With a resonant clang of copper on steel, Alvord's truncheon sent the knife spinning harmlessly to the deck, and the cutlass stopped the oncoming axe dead in its track. Before the man could react, the club was thrust upward into his chin. As blood shot out of his mouth, Alvord booted him squarely in the chest, sending him to the deck.

The man recovered most impressively, rolling nimbly to his feet though winded from the kick. For a moment he kept his distance, eyes cold and appraising. Those eyes clearly conveyed his thoughts- *this was not a foe that would be so easily dispatched.* Spitting a fine spray of blood at Alvord, he sprang back into action.

With both hands upon the axe he attacked in a series of short, controlled chops, seeking an exploitable gap in Alvord's guard. His footwork, nimble and precise, sought to reposition Alvord so as to get closer to his fallen blade. But his larger, stronger foe would simply not be muscled or maneuvered out of position, and seemed able to predict his every move. The cutlass then missed his chest by a hairsbreadth, putting an end to his series of questing strikes. He had been attacking too guardedly- the man gave his next series of swings all he had.

The effort far exceeded the reward.

Hard on the heels of a dexterous riposte Alvord renewed his attack. With relentless energy he drove the pirate back, back, and quite suddenly the man was all defense, not able to find intervals to launch counterattacks between frantic parries. His face mirrored his ever-increasing desperation and fatigue, those burning eyes widening in awe with every backward step.

Alvord knew well that look- the look of a man who had lived this scene before, only to realize that this time he would not walk away from the fracas. Such looks accompanied the moment when the distressed brain comprehended that the body could no longer respond to its desperate urgings with proper dexterity, while the taxed body implored the brain to simply quit and be done with it. He found flashing in his enemy's deep-set eyes fear of a primal brand- the dread anticipation of blade finding flesh, the pain that would accompany it, and the looming immensity of death and all its attendant mysteries.

It was panic, but it was still dangerous, a point made all the more clear when his enemy's blade nicked Alvord in the side during a panicked thrust. His answer to that was a neat bit of swordplay; positioning the truncheon on the outside of the axe, the sword on the inside, he performed a swift inward turn and jerk, dragging the weapon out of the pirate's grasp with his own. Alvord then elbowed the shocked man in the face, crushed his right kneecap with a deadening swipe of the truncheon and, digging deep with an upward cutlass stroke, opened him up slantwise from hip to shoulder.

Now on his knees, the tattooed pirate stared up at Alvord, hazel eyes glazed and unfocused as they beheld his impassive face slowly contort into a glacial sneer. Feebly, the man's hands attempted to restrain his oozing gut sack, the cloying stench of which assaulted Alvord's nostrils.

"Tell the Devil Rawn sent you."

Holding the dying man's inscrutable gaze for a fleeting moment, he chose the ever-dependable truncheon as his agent of ruin and with finality brought it crashing down on the timber pirate's skull.

He slumped heavily onto the deck, robbed of life.

Alvord, striving to get his breathing under control, took a moment to spit on the wretched carcass at his feet. Returning to reality he noticed that the *Hellion's* crew clustered together off to the side, many of them blood-spattered and some nursing injuries. They stared at him as if seeing him for the first time. Judging by their lack of activity, he surmised that this savage reprisal had come to a close.

A hand clapped him on the back. "Ye've sprung a leak, me hearty."

Alvord checked the cut on his side, which stung a bit but was by no means a serious wound. "Is that supposed to be some sort of nautical pun, Finn?

The Irishman cocked his head to the side. "No, but now that you mention it...

"Well, if I have sprung a leak, then it would appear that you've taken a full broadside. Perilous man you were up against?"

His friend grimaced, using pieces of fabric torn from his frayed sleeves to bind up the cuts on his arms. "Best I've faced. Nearly had me there, but Fortune smiled upon me as always she does."

"Luck of the Irish, I daresay."

A man was dragged across the deck screaming for mercy, but Colson and Peter the boatswain had no ears for his pleas as they roughly threw him into a pile of lumber. He slumped dejectedly against it, hand pressed against his stomach to stem the blood flowing from an incapacitating gunshot wound.

"What is this shit, eh? You lot ain't Lake Patrol, what'n the hell are you doin' this for? You've slaughtered my whole ship! This ain't lawful, what you've done!"

Colson purposefully cocked the Colt Walker and placed it against the pirate's forehead.

"The questions are mine to ask. And if you do not oblige me then my cook will be only too happy to reduce you to mincemeat. Slowly."

The man stared wide-eyed at the leering cook, who tipped him a wink of pure madness as he wiped his cleaver on his ragged apron, leaving behind a glutinous trail of blood and gristle.

"I'll answer what I can," he assured Colson hurriedly, eyes flicking from crewman to crewman and finding none of the mercy they'd hoped to. Though a large, rugged looking man, he was thoroughly cowed as a result of the whirlwind defeat and hopeless situation that he now faced and faced alone.

"I was informed that this schooner is not only used for the illicit transportation of pirated timber, but that its crew is responsible for the murder of several private land owners who resisted your attempt on their lands. The women were raped. We know you are responsible for this. We spotted a burning cabin just south of here. Did you and your crew again engage in rapine and slaughter?

He pursed his lips in mild protest. "And who informed you of all that?"

"An unimpeachable source."

"I know nothing, I'm naught but a timber man."

Alvord went over and with a face as cold as the north wind cruelly dug the truncheon's copper tip into the man's gunshot wound. Marcel smiled tightly as the pirate shrieked in agony, trying and failing to push the probing club away.

"Okay! Okay! Please, *no more...*" his words trailed off pathetically. Alvord removed the truncheon, lest the man lose consciousness. Interrogation was a longtime forte of his; he knew that balance must be struck between the application of fear and pain and the human threshold for both.

"Tell me." Colson said, voice a little unsteady as he watched the copious amount of blood seep from the wound.

"It is true... I am sorry, Lord Christ am I sorry for what happened... things just got outta hand, at first we never meant 'em much harm, but once we had to kill the menfolk it just..."

"Save your excuses for Saint Peter. Was this venture financed by Jones?"

A gull squalled somewhere above them, and the pirate's gaze rose. Alvord knew precisely what thought passed through his mind- *to be that gull right now, to switch places with that wretched seabird and be shot of this nightmare...*

"In God's name I ask that you believe me- I don't know. Only the Cap'n and a few others did, and wouldn't let the rest of us in on it. I know of the name Jones, hell everyone on the lakes does, but I don't know if this was him or not. Some say he has shady ventures going on every lake, but as for this'n I don't rightly know." He eyed Alvord's poised truncheon warily. "Please, you've got to believe me. I'd tell you if I knew, maybe one o' the others-"

"Your shipmates are all wrapped in the tomb's embrace. You are their mouthpiece now, and if that's all you are willing to tell me..." Colson's eyes strayed lazily to the cook.

"NO! Okay, please, I do have more to say, don't know if it'll help but I'll tell you somethin' strange."

He took in some air and then moistened his bloody lips. "There was two men aboard who weren't like the rest of us. They didn't speak much English, actually spoke some eldritch tongue that none of us was familiar with. Knew all the Injun languages too. They was covered in strange tattoos, some of us thought they might be from some eccentric tribe up Canada way."

"Is that one of them there?" Alvord inquired cuttingly, indicating the man he had just slain.

"Yep," answered the pirate promptly, "can't even give you a name though. That tattooed feller right there was savage as a meat axe. Merciless bastard, too. He and another cast in the same mold were aboard, word was that the moneyman wished them to be. One of 'em up and killed a crewman after the man got drunk and took a swing at him. They did their own thing, mostly. Helped with the tree work, were damn good at it actually, but only working as a pair. Knew their way around a ship but only helped out sometimes. Cap'n didn't seem to mind."

Marcel and Finnbar stood over the body, examining it.

"Ain't like any Injun tattoos I've ever seen," Marcel remarked, bushy eyebrows knit in contemplation. He picked up the strange war axe and turned it over in his hands, slowly running a finger over the broad, bloodstained blade.

"Odd," said Finnbar, rolling the carcass over to look at the back, "these symbols are unusual, never seen quite their like, and yet..."

His voice was supplanted by a thoughtful silence. Pulling down the collar of his shirt, he revealed a Celtic tattoo over his heart, the whorls and interweaving lines of which bore a subtle similarity to the pirate's own.

Marcel looked over the man's face closely. "Think there's some redman's blood in this feller. Just a hint, though. The cheekbones, nose, skin tone... odd lookin' specimen all told, ain't he? Look at those yeller eyes..."

"Got another over here," cried a voice from around the timber piles. "Older by the looks of him. Must've been jerked to Jesus in that first volley. Tattoos, strange weapons..."

"That'll be the other one, then." The pirate confirmed conversationally, like he was trying to make friends at this point, clinging to some desperate thought of emerging alive from this ordeal alive. "Here is the real strange part now. Twice in recent months the *Michigan* caught sight of us and gave chase. Those two would disappear below deck when it happened. The Lake Patrol would nearly be upon us, and outta nowhere a dense fog would cover us up, shielding us from view and allowing for our escape. My mate Bill said he saw 'em down there one of the times, huddled around something and making motions with their hands, chanting all the while..."

Alvord and Colson looked at each other confusedly.

"So that's that. That's all I know. Sorry I can't offer more, Cap'n, but I can't."

"I am not your Captain," Colson deadpanned.

A note of panic crept into the pirate's voice. "Come on, now. I'm just a hard-lucked feller who needed money, and the money was good in this. Times is tough, I ain't that bad a sort. Yeah, I freely admit to bein' a part of this, and I done a sight of things that I ain't proud of, but please, give me a second chance. Do the godly thing here... I beg you."

Colson stepped back and took careful aim.

"Fine then," the man spat savagely, unapologetic face contorting in fear and rage, "and to the devils of Hell with you lot! I hope-"

With a biting thud the bullet took him in the skull, effectively silencing him.

"I'll bet Jones was behind this," Colson said as the gun smoke swept past his face. "That blackguard has got his tentacles spread across this region, and whispers of his illegal ventures have been heard by the Lake Patrol. A pity more of the men did not survive the battle... especially the Captain, who definitely knew the truth."

"What of the Captain?" Alvord wished to know.

"Your pistol is an accurate one," Colson praised, handing it back to its rightful owner. "My bullet found his groin, as was my intent. He bled out quickly enough."

"Right in the cod, eh?" Marcel said. "Fittin' end to a goddamn rapist. How many of your boys fell?"

Mick shook his head sadly. "Obadiah and Len fell to the swarthy shit that Alvord dispatched. As I nearly did meself. I am indebted to ye, brudder."

He nodded graciously to Alvord, extending his hand.

Alvord returned the gesture, firmly grasping the Irishman's mitt. "We all do what we can in the madness of combat."

Peter approached them, unscathed but visibly shaken. "They got young Silas, too. At least it was quick- he took an axe to the spine."

"Not before he ran a pirate through with a pike," Marcel assured him. "Fought bravely, the lad did."

Colson gathered what remained of his crew, including several badly wounded men who were promptly tended to. Alvord, Finnbar and Marcel joined them. Men embraced and slapped each other on the back, some shedding tears of mingled relief and sadness. Alvord could see that for some of them this was their first taste of real combat. Emotions ran high after that, he knew, recalling his initial taste of battle many years ago.

"'Twas a true honor fighting alongside each of you men; this day is not one I shall forget. We should gather our dead, and then finish this good and proper. But first, let us thank the Almighty for seeing us through the events of the day, and pray for the souls of our departed brothers." Colson bowed his head and led the blood-dappled men in earnest prayer.

By the time night fell they had scuttled the *Hywell* and set her ablaze, the bodies of her crew still aboard. The flames licked greedily at the inky sky above, casting a ruddy aura around the ship as the wholesale blackness of the lake and the heavens slowly swallowed her up.

Chapter 17

Two Days later.
Arch Rock, Straits of Mackinac, Michigan

As he had done for the past four days, David MacTavish made his way to the center of Arch Rock on Mackinac Island. This he accomplished with little difficulty, as the land on either side of the natural limestone arch rose to meet it, so all one had to do was walk out onto the rock with measured steps and steer clear of the edge. MacTavish, however, moved with bold, lengthy strides that implied either utmost confidence in his own surefootedness or a scornful disregard towards a one hundred and fifty foot fall.

Or perhaps a dash of both.

Thus situated, he was afforded a commanding view of the Straits of Mackinac, where the mingled waters of Lake Michigan and Huron merged with the southbound flow of St. Mary's River, the sole outlet of Lake Superior.

He basked in the crisp heat of the midday sun, letting his eyes rove across the crowded scene before him. With a sharp pang of nostalgia he recalled the halcyon days of old, when the occasional schooner was still hopelessly outnumbered by flotillas of canoes swiftly paddled by intrepid white men and Indians alike. He had only known such days for a short span of time, but still recalled with fondness the desolate aspect the larger lakes had retained back then.

Ah, little use in pining over it. There was simply no resisting the tide of civilization, particularly American civilization. Whereas Canada was being settled piecemeal, the United States seemed rabid in its determination to fill up empty territorial holdings as quickly as possible. Of course, Canada's terrain did pose more challenges to swift settlement and development; dense boreal forests heavily interlaced with meandering waterways and mosquito-infested prairies offered many obstacles to those who would travel across them.

No- the immense pageant of American westward expansion, the surging of the human tide, was not to be found north of the border. Oftentimes it was small family groups who slowly and independently wended their way through that primeval northern wilderness by mode of foot, canoe, and Red River cart. The massive Conestoga wagon caravans that wore deep ruts into the

Great Plains proved laughably impractical in much of Canada. The trails too narrow, the waterways too frequent and impassable for a large wagon, the capacious Conestoga was cast aside in favor of smaller and more maneuverable modes of conveyance.

MacTavish might be able to recall the days when canoes held dominion, but here at the Straits of Mackinac, on this day of July 14th, *Anno Domine* 1847, canoes were piloted with utmost deference to larger craft, and wisely so. For a veritable armada of schooners, sloops, brigs, barques, and steamships crisscrossed the strait before him. He shifted his moccasined feet, setting his hands firmly upon his hips as he stared fixedly out at the strait. Never before had MacTavish seen so wide an array of ships swarm over the waters of the inland seas that had been his home for- well, he had actually lost count of the years, along with his age. When he was seventeen he'd left his native Scotland behind, and somewhere within a lifetime of trapping the American and Canadian wilderness his ability to recall with exactitude his own age had ceased.

He scowled with craggy features at a two-masted paddle steamer as it noisily chugged its way towards Huron, befouling the air of an otherwise flawless midday sky with vile clouds of black smoke belched from its dual smokestacks. It did his soul little good to observe the sullying of the natural world. Good thing he still had Lake Superior, where nature yet held dominion. Already he yearned to be back upon her shimmering waters and gaze at shorelines undefiled by the presence of man. But such was the course of civilization- frontiers required the skills of the advance men, the trappers and explorers, whose abilities were valued only until they could pass the torch of nation to settlers who would ensure more permanent fixtures in the land. Commerce and politics then followed in their wake, something he now saw before him and hated with a burning passion. Soon enough there would be no place for he and his breed... what role could they possibly play in a land grown tame? Extinction loomed on the horizon, and in the meantime he was forced to gaze upon steamships as they defiled his lakes? He should avert his eyes lest he become nauseas...

Patience. It was a thing alive inside him, born of years spent sitting and standing motionless in the woods waiting for game or enemy to make an appearance. It seemed like his other half, the side that took the helm when being a mere man did not cut it anymore and required the dogged persistence of something inhuman. Or at least something not white; Indians seemed to be born with a degree of patience that far exceeded that of most men and animals alike. Whatever it was, he had to exercise it now, for watching the vast array of ships sully this otherwise grand vista made his tendinous jaw muscles clench after a while.

A mosquito alighted on his forehead, which he batted away unthinkingly. They were thick on this island, but by noontime the sun tended to banish them from open areas. The forest might still be chock full of those dreaded bloodsuckers, but atop this rock they were mercifully few this time of day. MacTavish could easily recall from memory days when such insects had blanketed his skin, when they had driven him to the very brink of insanity. But then again, what voyageur couldn't? The man due to meet him at this island once spent two fitful days with him in horrific conditions, wherein they had resorted to rubbing mud on their skin to repel the flying pests, as they had not even the tools to make a fire...

The man he was to meet here had two more days to make it to this island, in accordance with the pact they had made four years ago. And yet, so much could have happened in four years; he had survived many a brush with Death himself in that span of time, but would freely admit that the life of the voyageur was far more conducive to keeping one's scalp than that of the mountain man. He had been living in a dangerous land, though not nearly so barbaric as the Indian Territory that his old trapping partner had dwelt in since last they had clapped eyes on one another...

He twisted his rangy torso from side to side in an effort to work out some yet-lingering kinks, irksome tokens of a poor night's sleep. Lean but clearly outlined muscles were visible under the thin linen of his dark blue shirt, the top buttons of which were undone.

Some Indians who were camped on the white pebble beach below stared up at him, but did not offer the censorious fulminations he knew they longed to. They merely smoked their dreadful kinnikick and ate fish, silently watching him. Their suspicion was understandable, he supposed, as he was defiling hallowed ground in their eyes. Trespassing upon this rock formation was expressly forbidden among red men, as well he knew. The tribes of the lakes treated any prominent natural formation or oddity with reverence. *Manitous*, or spirits, dwelt in such places, which were appeased with small offerings when happened upon. MacTavish could not quite bring himself to call it a religious offering, though. Indians never went out of their way to make pilgrimages to worship in spots like this, and when they did present offerings it was by way of cheapest trinket or old, unusable tool or weapon. And at times they simply did not make an offering at all- and if MacTavish despised one thing it was blasted inconsistency. Perhaps it was that ingrained Presbyterian sense of devotion and belief in grace through unshakable faith, but he simply had a hard time wrapping his graying head around native religion. Now converted Indians- there were some devout folk. Among the most pious and upright he had encountered, truth telling. But the progress made by the Jesuits of old and other missionaries was being undone in many places around the lakes. Many tribes were trending towards a reversion to old, familiar ways.

As for himself, he had never put much stock in Indian superstitions and largely ignored their spiritual belief system. Plenty of white trappers he knew would have kept their respectful distance from Arch Rock in deference to those beliefs, but David MacTavish could give a five-farthing damn.

So there he remained, form outlined by the azure expanse of sky as he stood, a lone and brooding figure, atop the geological marvel. Darkly attired in his shirt and black canvas pants, he appeared as if a presiding doomsday prophet bereft of a flock.

Eyes straining against the sharp glare of the midday sun, David caught sight of a sizable dugout canoe being borne along by three capable paddlers. It approached from the southwest and seemed to be taking a direct route towards Mackinac Island, skillfully cutting through the wakes of larger vessels.

Thirty minutes later they dragged the heavily loaded canoe onto the beach not far from where the Indians cooked some mussels and herring. After accepting some food offered by them, the three continued their unhurried trek towards the spectacular rock formation upon which MacTavish kept his vigil.

When they got close enough, he took in their forms; size, stride, bearing. One was tall and heavily muscled, moving with a slow, assured confidence across the pebbly beach. This fellow noticed him almost immediately, and held his stare as on he marched. Another had a spiky crop of dark red hair that gleamed in the sun and was both shorter and leaner than his hulking companion. This one's head swiveled left and right, up and down in a pattern of voracious curiosity. Once he even paused to scribble something in a notebook.

And the third, whose bowlegged stride and dark, unkempt beard and hair looked all-too familiar, stopped the group once they were parallel with the rock and folded his arms across his broad chest. He stared up at the arch, head cocked smugly to the side as if to say- *Here we are.*

Gradually, the left side of MacTavish's mouth curled into a pleased smirk and he shook his grizzled head, amazed.

"Well I'll be damned..."

Chapter 18

The man who peered down at them from the height of the stone arch had vanished from sight, and Marcel came to a halt underneath it. He stood quite still, arms crossed and feet firmly set, offering no words of explanation.

The land before the natural limestone curiosity fell away in a rocky, sparsely vegetated slope that terminated in the white pebble beach under their feet. The leaves of the young birches that sprang up between the rocks shivered tremulously, stirred by a wind that Alvord's other senses could not confirm the existence of.

"In mid July of 1812, the first land battle in the late war with Britain was fought on this island," Alvord announced to no one in particular as he stood staring up at the now-unoccupied, peculiar rock formation. He finished the piece of smoked whitefish the Indians had generously given them upon their landing, pleased to be eating but not altogether overjoyed at the overpowering saltiness of the meat.

"Alas," he continued, "it resulted in the sound defeat of our forces and the subsequent capture of Fort Mackinac by the enemy, but it still stands that a strand of history was woven on this ground."

Marcel grunted his assent. "A strand indeed. More strands were woven here than most know, and I'd wager more'n we'll ever know. Injuns seemed to have been here for quite some time. Alexander Henry, fur trader active last century, hid in Skull Cave, barely a mile west o' here, after Fort Michilimackinac fell in 1763 during Pontiac's uprisin'. Found it to be aptly named- the cave was either an old Injun burial ground or massacre sight, for crumbling skulls littered the cave floor."

"The Henry who organized the first mining venture up on Lake Superior?"

"The very same. Been readin' up on local history, have we?" Marcel raised an unruly eyebrow in amusement.

"Come now, Marcel," Finnbar chimed in, "history is a valuable and oft-neglected weapon."

Alvord tossed back his head and let out a deep-chested laugh, for Finnbar was quoting a line that he himself had employed back in April, when they had first walked down the historic streets of St. Louis.

"So you really made a pact with this gent four years ago to meet at this very spot?" Finnbar held his right shoulder and moved his arm in a circle, trying to loosen it up after an exhausting morning spent paddling their over-laden dugout.

"Yep."

"And that was it, then? You both parted ways and hoped that the other would show up within the allotted time frame? Not even a full week in July of 1847? That was the plan?"

"Yep."

"You rave, man." Finnbar ribbed.

"Well, kept in touch via fur posts a time or two, but fer the most part we minded our own affairs."

In keeping with his taciturn nature, Marcel had divulged virtually no information regarding the man they were to meet upon this island, and the past few days, taxing as they were, did not find Alvord or even Finnbar making many inquiries.

You'll meet 'im when we get there, his gruff response had been.

"To those of us who are as familiar with these lands as the gentry are with their manicured gardens and lawns," Marcel responded, "reckoning time of arrival even over long distances is easy. Hit a slight snag with that whole timber pirate business, we did, but luckily had some time to spare."

Colson had gone back for those of his crew that had not taken part in the battle against the pirates. He had also voiced intentions of finding those murdered in the *Hywell's* most recent act of pillaging. But Marcel had insisted that himself, Alvord, and Finnbar be dropped off on shore before they did so. Along with their gear they were dropped off on shore at first light, at which point the mountain man asked them to watch over their possessions for a few hours before heading south at a brisk trot. They did so, tending to their wounds in that time. Finnbar's lacerated arms and cut scalp were healing slowly but surely, and the small, stitched-up slice in Alvord's side was also on the mend.

Marcel had indeed returned in a few hours, paddling the dugout they now used with the assistance of two Indians, residents of the Winnebago village he had run to. They returned home on foot, leaving the three white men to pack their belongings into the canoe. From there they had paddled almost nonstop, night and day, towards the Straits of Mackinac, pausing only for bland, rapid meals and calls of nature. Alvord, used to an alert, primed, but ultimately laidback Marcel Durand, watched in amazement as with single-minded intensity the indefatigable trapper paddled tirelessly towards their destination, outlasting Finnbar and even Alvord himself, who exercised on a daily basis when he could.

But he had to admit that exercise was no substitute for work like paddling. His hands had blistered within the first day, and now he wore rags wrapped around them to give them some cushion.

Finnbar had expressed great interest in exploring the shores of the magnificent Manitou Islands, only to be bluntly informed that time was not their ally at the moment.

But after two and a half grueling days in which they passed over one hundred and sixty miles of lake water under their canoe bottom, here they were.

None of them could feel their arms or backs, but here they were.

Marcel's head suddenly swung to the right as he perceived movement. A solitary figure emerged from the dim aisle of trees where beach met forest, heading their way with long, loping strides.

He was a lean man, but one whose leanness did not exclude the possibility of coiled power beneath his dark clothing. Wiry hair, with an even distribution of salt and pepper coloration on the crown, glinted a regal steel-gray along the sides. Clean-shaven, his sun-kissed, weathered skin bore a jagged collection of scars- two on the forehead, closely placed, and another that ran slantwise from his left cheekbone to his jaw line.

Two flintlock pistols were thrust into his broad brown belt, which also contained a fiercely gleaming tomahawk and a knife to rival even that of Marcel. It looked to Alvord to be a Highland dirk, a large, straight-bladed thrusting dagger. In a leg sheath he also carried a Bowie knife with a smaller blade length. The man came to a halt a few paces from them, angular visage immobile. Light chestnut eyes, shielded by an overhanging brow, flickered over Alvord and Finnbar before fixing on Marcel.

"Och! Marcel Durand!" he hailed in a resounding baritone, a massive smile materializing on his face that contorted the scars. "Does me heart good t'clap eyes on ye once again! Tell me- how've ye been, lad?"

Alvord could do without most English and Irish accents, and could not abide French-tinged attempts at his language, but Scottish accents he found pleasing to the ear. Mellifluous almost, although he did his best to avoid using flowery words like that.

He left that to Finnbar.

"Been through times both hearty'n lean, agreeable and downright hellish. Business as usual fer those of our trade, no?"

"True enough, true enough."

He clasped Marcel in a bone-cracking bear hug. Alvord noticed that half of his right ring finger was missing. When they broke it off the man stepped back and hooked his thumbs into his weapon-filled belt.

"Ye boyos look rightly tuckered. Tough few days?"

"Paddled from Pere Marquette in two and a half days. Didn't have the luxury of much rest either."

"Two days- not bloody bad. I did harbor a wee bit o' concern that ye'd not make it in time. You're generally nothin' if not punctual."

"We was northbound from Slab Town aboard a steam propeller, but had a run in with some timber pirates few days back."

"Heard tell o' them filthy rapscallion types. Dealt wi' accordingly, were they?"

"You could say that," replied Finnbar slyly, sun glinting off his gold tooth.

The Scotsman grinned savagely, eyeing the Irishman's bruised face. "Braw one's ye brought along, eh?"

"Braw's the word fer it. They ain't pink-eyed weaklings, that's fer damn sure."

"Men you trust, then?"

"Men to ride the river with, Dave."

Dave nodded deeply. What was good enough for Marcel Durand was good enough for him.

"David MacTavish, pleased to make yer acquaintance."

Alvord returned hearty handshake. "Alvord Rawn, a pleasure."

"This feller here was Police Captain in Manhattan, in the hairiest ward of the city. Formidable man if ever there was. Dealt with them blood-crazed Irish gangs, devilish as any group of red men on the warpath."

Alvord lowered his eyes and tried to appear modest. He was ever embarrassed in these situations- never would he grow comfortable with people boasting of his exploits.

MacTavish carefully looked him over again. "So I've heard."

"And this here is Finnbar Fagan."

He turned to Finnbar, who smiled pleasantly and offered, "*Latha math*, brother."

"I had ye pegged for a fellow Caledonian, and am glad to have ye along! Where do ye hail from in the Auld Country?"

"Though flattered, I must come clean. I am actually a Hibernian by birth, a Cork lad through and through, but we Celts all share a common bond, do we not?"

"Aye, that we do. Some would say otherwise- religion does divide many in our nations- but I d'not count meself among 'em. So, what be your claim to fame?"

"Oh, just rapier wit, a dizzying intellect, and looks so good they're damn near supernatural."

Mactavish cackled wildly. "I likes me his manner, I do! It'll be good to have two more white men with us, be they greenhorns or otherwise."

"Greenhorns?" said Alvord, a flash of annoyance making itself known. Did not his paddle-weary shoulders earn him a more flattering title than that?

The Scotsman spread his scarred hands in placatory fashion. "Forgive me, big fella, I seek no quarrel with the likes of ye! But alas, ye don't bear the stamp of the trapper. 'Tis not to say ye ain't game- ye merely have some learnin' to do."

"So," asked Marcel, "how's the old crew fairin' these days?"

The Scot shook his head darkly. "Most of 'em aren't. Passed to grass, the bulk of them. DuBreil mired himself in some serious shite- got himself an Indian haircut three years back."

"Cree got his scalp, then?"

"Piegan. Strayed a bit too far west, he did."

"And what of Fergus?"

MacTavish laughed hopelessly "Ended up playing cat's cradle with his neck, the bovine lummox."

"Hanged, eh? What fer?"

"Up in the Red River Country he tried to rape some Métis woman and nearly killed her husband when caught in the act. He paid the price and rightly so. A certain darkness washed over him after he spent a winter starving up in the Athabasca country. Barely made it out alive, and his sanity didn't make it out at all. Some said he even went *wendigo*."

"Shame."

"Ah, I'm well rid of 'em, along wid a few others," MacTavish assured Marcel dismissively. "They were becomin' liabilities in their latter days. Lightfoot and Gordon are still kickin' though, an' will join us up in the Soo."

Marcel, peering eastward towards the mouth of the St. Mary's River, narrowed his eyes in satisfaction.

"And from there s'off to a place that has seldom been tainted by man."

"Why's that?" Finnbar promptly asked.

"Cursed land," Marcel answered matter-of-factly, and continued staring hypnotically at the river that would bring them one step closer it.

Chapter 19

Sault Ste. Marie, Michigan

Genevieve Connolly was bored. Dreadfully so. Inwardly she knew she this to be a patently foolish and egocentric emotion, as a state of boredom was far preferable to some of life's more miserable conditions. For while here she sat in a large house, perched atop a gently sloping hill overlooking the pristine St. Mary's River replete with all the trappings of wealth, there were others in this drowsy little frontier town whose lives' were nightmares of deprivation and uncertainty.

She reclined her head back onto the soft velvet of the couch she was perched upon, staring impassively at the dust-strewn shafts of sunlight as they idly streamed through the oriel window. Toying with the white lace of her modish muslin dress, she reflected that since becoming Cadwallader Jones's ward at the age of three, she had ever been presented with what amounted to an embarrassment of riches. It was her mysterious guardian's only detectable character flaw- lavishing her with more earthly possessions than she knew what to do with. Aside from that Jones was disciplined, ascetic even, possessing moral fiber and rectitude that she had yet to see matched in another man.

Now, at eighteen, those qualities came into sharper focus and she appreciated them all the more. Having dealt with a bevy of "gentlemen" callers in the last two years, Genevieve watched with guarded eyes as men did their best to impress her. Well did she know how the glossy veneer of virtue wore thin once guardians and chaperones drifted out of the equation. On private walks and horseback rides men invariably sought what she was unwilling to so quickly give them. The majority of these fellows might be gentlemen on the surface, but the base animal lurked just below. It was naught but the specious appearance of propriety and it sickened her. Their increasingly brazen attempts at physical affection were fast souring her on the prospect of finding a suitable husband.

Jones himself was a tart critic of other men, the bulk of whom he regarded with scorn. Likewise did many men of the Soo, envious of his wealth and success, spread defamatory rumors concerning, among other things, his relationship with his young ward. After all, they pointedly noted, he was a lifelong bachelor.

Never were insults delivered to his face, though. Danger lurked behind the incisive amber eyes of Cadwallader Jones, danger buttressed by his well-set form and skilled hands. Once Genevieve had witnessed him beat to death a drunken half-breed after the man attempted to accost her in a stable.

The mistake had yet to be repeated.

Rumors might be spitefully flung around, but never once had Jones demonstrated lecherous intent towards her. And it was not because her face and form were found unfavorable by the opposite sex. Quite the contrary, in fact. Half Irish, with an even amalgam of French and Chippewa blood from her mother's side, Genevieve was a rare specimen of beauty.

Lustrous hair of a medium brown hue contained saffron highlights that lightened in the summer sun, which also bronzed her naturally tan skin. Her face was characterized by marked elegance of feature, with high, regal cheekbones complimented by a straight-edged nose and smoky olive eyes.

The problem with her finding a fitting spouse then lay not in her appearance, but rather in the region in which she lived and the manner in which she had been raised. Her first three years were naught but distant, hazy recollections; indeed, she could scarcely recall her birth parent's faces or what influence they may have had on her early development. But her earliest memories of life here in Jones's mansion were ones of structure, refinement, and education. He hired a retired schoolmarm from New York to move to the Soo and educate her, as the local, tiny schoolhouse did not meet his stringent requirements. Lessons prepared by Jones himself were carried out by the elderly but fierce Ms. Ellsworth. And so Genevieve had received a topnotch education, like the sort people would in the east, on the frontier's edge in Michigan's oldest city.

So perhaps it was her formal education, or her proclivity towards idealized romance novels, but these frontier men simply weren't her cup of tea. Each one seemed to demonstrate at least one fatal defect, and undesirous of the title of coquet she invariably ended things quickly. They were all of them unable to carry on piquant discussions and generally bored her with their talk of trifles. Not that she disliked them all. Some of them evinced signs of dignity, but often those that did she found lacking in looks, superficial though it was. There were tough, hardy men among them, but even they could tell after awhile that despite having lived in the same town, they were essentially a world apart.

It was a dismal commentary on the town that it lacked even a proper newspaper, though there was talk that one was in the works. How could she blame these fellows for their lack of sophistication?

She was beginning to feel like the character of Elizabeth Bennet in Jane Austen's *Pride and Prejudice*. Elizabeth too saw fault in every man who sought her hand, her prejudice too strong to overlook the manifold failings of the opposite sex. Though Genevieve could not boast of Elizabeth's enduring optimism in the face of disappointment. Rather, she was of late harried by an overpowering sense of narrowing walls... perhaps there would be no dashing, urbane Mr. Darcy to her Elizabeth...

What lengths would she eventually be willing to go to in order to avoid the dreaded title of spinster?

And yet Jones had always looked out for her, given her everything... surely he had a plan in mind for her imminent future?

Tossing onto the couch her most recent copy of *Lady's Book*, the nation's premier fashion and etiquette magazine, she rose with a sigh and walked downstairs. While debutantes in New York and Philadelphia prepared for debuts and attended lavish cotillions, here she sat on the frontier's fringe with not one suitable suitor to be found.

Striding out onto the immaculate, sun-drenched back lawn, her eyes flicked southward, towards St. Mary's Falls. Those dancing rapids, the endless surge of which was just barely audible to her, looked awfully inviting. Never before had she chanced to take a canoe down them...

Such adventure could prove tonic to her tedium. Under Jones's tutelage she had learned to ride, shoot, paddle, and even sail a bit. There were those who viewed this as scandalous, for ladies of refined upbringing were not routinely instructed in manful arts like that.

She saw the vague forms of people down by the water. There would be Indians down there, Saulteur Chippewa whom she was accepted by through ties of consanguinity. Some of her cousins might even be among them- Jones had always encouraged her to embrace her bloodlines, be they Indian or otherwise.

She called to mind his words to her when she was younger.

"Always be proud of your heritage, Gen. Without pride, no race can stand the test of time."

"Pride goeth before destruction," she had primly quoted, recalling a Bible passage he had recently read to her.

"Pride in how the Almighty perceives us as we perceive ourselves is not pride of the same species."

There were white men in Sault Ste. Marie who would never consider pursuing her romantically due to her partial Indian heritage. This stung a bit, but she tried to pay it no mind. By her reckoning, men who took that stance were not men worth wasting thoughts on.

Still she stared at the rapids, the spray of which glinted a celestial white in the sun. She would require a change of attire if she was to shoot the rapids. An older dress would suit her better. She turned back towards the brooding Gothic Revival that was her abode. An odd choice of architectural style for one's home, but then again Cadwallader Jones was an odd man. She hesitated to label him as such, for the word odd she often associated with eccentricity, a brand her legal guardian was wholly undeserving of.

Jones was entirely self-taught. Yet as Genevieve knew, he could converse with scholars and scientists alike with an ease that put many of them on the defensive. With a dazzling mind for business and a sponge-like memory for history and natural science, it was no surprise that the man had amassed a small fortune in his day. Cadwallader Jones had shipping and fishing fleets operating on Superior, Huron, and Michigan, as well as a highly profitable venture in the recent copper boom, both selling tracts of land and mining for the metal. In fact, he had produced decent quantities of copper before anyone really cared about its abundance in the area, quietly selling it to men out of Quebec. Now, as the copper craze reached an incredible height, his land holdings in the Keweenaw Peninsula netted him astounding profits. By the thousands miners flocked to the Soo before shipping out to Copper Country, but none would receive the blessing of laboring under Jones. He kept a crew of his own that no one ever saw and mined in undisclosed locations.

His secretive accumulation of wealth only invited men to further speculate on his code of ethics.

They were wrong to do so, Genevieve knew. Jones was merely different, and in a way that she was beginning to find ever so alluring. The chiseled ruggedness of his face, the set of his shoulders, the perfect backward sweep of his long, steel-gray hair… ah, she would do well to stifle thoughts of that nature. He was her Guardian, after all, and had never evinced the slightest romantic interest in her.

With an anxious intake and release of breath she steadied herself and asked one of their servants to fetch an old dress for her.

Chapter 20

The interminable hissing of St. Mary's Falls was a welcome sound to their ears, as it signaled the end of a long and onerous day's paddling upriver.

For two days Alvord, Finnbar, and Marcel had indulged in some much needed rest on Mackinac Island, where Marcel and David had introduced the others to their old trapping friend, William Johnston. William's regionally famous father, John Johnston, had been the first white, English speaking settler of Sault Ste. Marie, and together with William's Chippewa mother Susan took a lead role in the development of the town. Once the importance of the fur trade dwindled and the family sold their own fur business to the American Fur Company, William had traveled extensively around the upper Great Lakes country, and proved to be an excellent tour guide as he showed them the island that was his home.

He had escorted them around Mackinac Island, filling Alvord and Finnbar in on its history. This came as a welcome thing to Alvord, who was grateful to be on *terra firma* once again. They walked among the gradually decaying ruins of the abandoned Fort Holmes and then hiked to Skull Rock, the Sugarloaf, and Arch Rock, geological curiosities that Finnbar had pored over with child-like avidity.

"A shame, 'tis, that we don't have a *camera obscura* handy," he had lamented. "These rocks would make for some fine daguerreotypes."

Alvord had silently concurred. For if that island was but a muted foretaste of natural marvels to come, as Marcel had assured him, then some means of documenting the journey would be nice. If only he could draw or paint...

He returned to the present and eyed the broad rapids, which reached their terminus some fifty yards away. Dropping over twenty feet from the level of Lake Superior to the level of the lower lakes over a distance of three quarters of a mile, the falls were an insurmountable obstacle to large vessels seeking passage to and from the Superior, Father of Lakes. Indians and half-breeds speared and netted fish in the deep, eddying pool that the rapids emptied into, pulling in astonishing numbers of whitefish. This ancient fishery and meeting place provided for the Saultuer Chippewa as it had countless other Indians through the ages.

"I still can't believe that ye opted fer a Winnebago dugout," MacTavish wondered aloud for the umpteenth time. Along with the others he dug his paddle deep, as the cumbersome, heavily laden canoe required forceful propulsion as it fought against the sluggish but inexorable current.

"I told ya," Marcel explained yet again, "a birchbark woulda been too small and light to pack all our things into, and these fellers here have nail-studded boots on that woulda chewed up a Chippewa birchbark real quick-like. Belay the whinin'. You've gotten spoiled, Scotsman, accustomed to luxury."

"Oh yes," Finnbar chimed in, "I'm sure he's a regular Sybarite."

"I am the only one in this canoe who knows the meaning of that term," called Alvord from the rear of their craft.

"That's fine," the Irishman countered, "being around me *should* be a learning experience."

"Oh, its an experience, alright," Alvord mumbled to himself, grinning. He seemed to be doing a lot of smiling lately- the promise of adventure in a new and wild land had him almost giddy at times.

Almost.

The land they had passed through in the past two days of paddling had grown progressively more desolate. Thinly peopled islands in the St. Mary's River like Drummond and St. Joseph showed the effects of settlement, but by and large the shoreline was an unbroken mass of primeval pines and hemlock interrupted at times by bright green patches of maples and birches. Even here, at the most significant population center for many miles, Nature still held considerable sway. For although the town of Sault. Ste. Marie was visible up on the left, the land around it seemed untamed. There were no visible symptoms of agriculture or manufacturing on the American or Canadian side (where stood a far smaller "town" of the same name).

It was hard for Alvord to believe that a town could exist in isolation amidst the howling wilderness of Lake Superior, but given the amount of people present the settlement couldn't be doing too badly.

He was lost in such thoughts, paddling automatically and unthinkingly, when Finnbar shot to his feet in the canoe and promptly performed a neat dive overboard, setting the boat to rocking. Spotting an overturned canoe at the base of the rapids, Alvord himself rose to see what was going on.

* * *

The birch bark canoe Genevieve occupied pitched violently as it cut through the final leg of the rapids. She kneeled in the middle of the craft, which appeared in her eyes increasingly flimsy as the waves grew ever larger and the rocks more salient and jagged.

Piloted by a Chippewa buck and a half-breed, the canoe battled the rapids that were made turgid by some recent rainfall. Though the men had evinced signs of hesitation when asked to guide her down this turbulent stretch of river, both knew better than to hazard the displeasure of Cadwallader Jones by refusing a request made by his ward.

Chilly river water reared up and over the bow of the canoe, splashing her face and already-soaked dress. Jones had always encouraged her to be adventurous, but perhaps she was out beyond her depth here. As they raced towards the massive waves that marked the final drop and the rapid's end, an electrifying thrill of fear passed through her. She had watched from the shore many a time as men demonstrated their courage and paddling prowess on this river, but never did she consider how terrifying the cascading waves might seem to one actually among them...

Suddenly too full of water to respond to its paddlers, the canoe yawed as it was struck abeam by a crashing wall of water. Genevieve could hear the two men yelling in a panicked fashion- hardly a comforting sound.

Where the rapids met the large pool that marked their end the canoe shot into the water at too great an angle. The craft flipped stern over prow, and Genevieve saw the world in brief snatches as she was flung out into the water that came up to meet her with considerable force.

She saw a bright burst of unimaginable color as her face made contact with the surface, and everything faded to gray... then black.

Dazedly she felt hands upon her chest, was conscious of being pulled powerfully through the water... but it all seemed so very far away. Voices yelling, cold water splashing around her mouth- she perceived such things confusedly, as if from the far side of a veil.

"Be you alright, lass?" inquired a soft voice, laden with concern and the melodic lilt of Ireland.

She recovered herself in a flood of senses. Sitting upright, she realized that her position was rather a pathetic one and attempted to counteract this with a sharp remark.

"Now that you have unhanded my chest, I am just spiffing, thank you."

Finnbar Fagan gave her a gold-lit grin. "Come now, 'twas but an accidental grope. Your canoe flipped and you were flung quite a ways, and forcefully so. So I dragged ye out, perhaps not entirely conscious of where my hands might have found purchase."

His playfully twinkling eyes abruptly swept all thoughts of appearing aloof from her mind. "I meant not to be cross about it. My head is fair ringing from the impact… I feel like Charybdis just spat me out of her whirlpool."

"Now, that's the second *Odyssey* reference I have heard in recent days. Not bad given the brain-rattling spill you just took."

Olive eyes met those of darkest emerald. Genevieve felt herself flush a bit; there was genuine concern mingled with dancing amusement in this young man's eyes that she found ever so enticing…

The Irishman, every bit as soaked as she was, offered his clammy hand to her and swiftly brought her to her feet. The sun infused his claret-colored hair with a golden nimbus of light, lending a celestial cast to his appearance. His handsome, crafty-looking face bore the faint signs of a recent fight, but his smiling eyes and upturned lips held her attention more than that.

Each held the other's gaze a mite longer than convention allowed for. They broke it off half-sheepishly when nearby a tall, strapping Indian upbraided the men who had piloted the ruined canoe in a thunderous voice.

Finnbar watched him, mirth playing around his lips.

"What were you thinking, lass, taking such rapids in a flimsy canoe? In the future, I'd suggest you at least choose more competent guides- you might've sustained serious injury there, a genuine crime for a form so flawless as yours."

She held out her hand. "Although you speak too freely, even for an Irishman, I would have introduction. I am Genevieve Connolly."

Finnbar urbanely clasped her hand and stooped to brush his lips against its smooth skin. Just barely. Her flesh sizzled as he did so.

"Forgive me. 'Tis been some time since I have been graced with the presence of a proper lady. The name is Finnbar Fagan."

"I extend my heartfelt gratitude, Mr. Fagan. I wish not to break off our conversation so hastily, but I must be going- these sopping clothes are none too comfortable."

Her wet dress clung to her form and revealed her gently tapering waist and shapely chest. She saw his eyes give her body a quick sweep for the first time. It was not a lingering gaze of lust, which she was by now quite accustomed too, but rather one of succinct appreciation.

She found she did not mind that so much.

Finnbar gave her a knowing smile and a courtly bow. "Be on your way then, Genevieve Connolly. My compatriots and I shall be tarrying here for a few days. Perhaps I'll be seeing you around."

"'Tis but a wee town," Genevieve pointed out in a passable Irish accent.

She flashed him a toothy, saccharine smile of her own and was on her way. Though soaked to the bone, she held herself regally, though her hair was beginning to unravel.

Still, Finnbar had to admit, the lass had some serious swagger.

"Soon to be star-crossed lovers, I take it?" Alvord posed drily as he drew up alongside Finnbar.

"Outside forces, be they astrological or otherwise, shan't thwart the likes of us. I am going to marry that girl," Finnbar announced matter-of-factly, staring after her pleasing figure as she went. "Now let's secure us some vittles, I'm positively famished."

Chapter 21

"Bear witness to *this*, gents."

Finnbar, lips pressed tight and eyes squinting with focus, took three measured steps forward and released the polished wooden ball from his palm with a flourish. It rolled smoothly down the lane until it made contact with the pins arranged at the other end, knocking down eight with a resounding clatter but leaving one to resume its stance after rocking back and forth tauntingly.

His subsequent attempt to fell the lone pin failed by a narrow, tormenting margin.

"Bloody Hell!" he exclaimed vehemently, running a hand through his hair.

"A lively attempt," Alvord attempted to console him.

"Aye, one met with damnably little success."

He walked over the to rough benches where Alvord, Marcel, and David sat. He sidled in next to Alvord and deftly snatched up his drink. It was a shade past two o'clock and they had all worked up a powerful thirst paddling against the river's current for half the day. Alvord generally did not drink before four, but after that accursed upriver paddling, battling legions of mosquitoes all the while...

"At least the booze is first-rate," the Irishman stated after a fortifying gulp of brandy.

David took a slug from an un-neglected whiskey bottle. "Damn good thing too, 'cause those vaunted bowling skills of yers are anythin' but, laddie buck."

They all had a chuckle at his words, for Finnbar had done little else but boast of his skill earlier that day. Sault Ste. Marie, they had been assured by many an authority, was a begrimed, rough-and-tumble frontier town comprised of little more than substandard brothels, groggeries, billiards halls, and bowling alleys.

And yet the ninepin bowling alley they sat in surprised Alvord in both its size and class. The first shock was wrought from the fact that they actually had indoor bowling lanes here on the edge of civilization. Alvord could recollect with clarity when the first indoor bowling alley had been constructed back in 1840. Christened Knickerbockers, the establishment provided citizens of Manhattan with an indoor alternative to a traditionally outdoor game. He was among the first to use those lanes; though he had rarely capitalized on the many favors that were offered to a patrolman, in that instance he could not help himself and played for free. He thoroughly enjoyed bowling and was reasonably proficient at it. Horace Greeley and Edgar Allen Poe had both lost to him that day.

His face suddenly fell when he realized that Katherine had still been alive then, and vitally so. She had always taken pleasure in bowling, and possessed an uncanny knack for beating him more often than not.

His gloom deepened. He should be able to reminisce about such things with fondness, yet all he felt was a sharp stab as tentacles of misery coiled in his gut. If only he could view his time with Katherine through rose-colored lenses, rather than with the stark clarity of realized loss... far too soon had the grave yanked her from his arms...

"You're up, Alvord," Finnbar informed him.

He gladly returned to reality, letting his senses override his thoughts. Taking in the welter of sounds filling the room, he let his eyes rove around the alley with the practiced vigilance of a veteran patrolman. This frontier alley was neatly kept and elegantly lit by chandeliers. There were six lanes, all of which were occupied. Rough-talking copper miners comprised the bulk of the patrons, although some trapper sorts were also present. A bar, not wanting for attention, stood near the entrance with an impressive array of liquor arranged behind it.

Tobacco smoke hung densely in the air, a ubiquitous feature of life but not one that Alvord viewed with approval. He rose each morning without having to pause to cough up a lung, and that was enough for him.

When his turn came about Alvord rolled twice and, succeeding where Finnbar had failed, managed to secure a spare. That was the last roll of the game, a game that Marcel unsurprisingly won, edging Alvord out of the top spot by a few points. In the realm of hand-to-eye coordination and dexterity, the gruff mountain man was without equal.

"Alright boys," said Marcel summarily, "cough it up."

He, David, and Finnbar had laid coin towards the outcome of the match. Alvord, never having been a gambling man, had abstained.

Finnbar checked his pockets. Frowning, he turned and asked Alvord innocently. "Spot me a V note?"

Sometimes Alvord felt like he was dealing with a wayward younger brother when he dealt with Finnbar.

"What a spendthrift you are," he chided him mockingly. "You ask five whole dollars of a man who had no stake in this to begin with, and one to whom gambling is a term of opprobrium?"

"Yeah, yeah. Do you approve of mining, my sainted Anglo-Saxon friend?"

"As he skillfully tacked in another direction," Alvord mumbled. "Yes, of course I do. It behooves a nation to utilize the natural riches God hath provided."

"And do all mining ventures succeed?"

"No..."

"And can men lose money in the endeavor? Does the enterprise sometimes become the very instrument of their ruin?"

"Of course, but-"

"So is that not a gamble, the same as whist or faro? The fact of the matter is that life itself, my austere friend, is the greatest gamble a man can undertake, and oftentimes the price to be paid is far greater than a wee bit o' coin."

Alvord began to reply but then stopped, cocking his head to the side thoughtfully. Eyebrows raised and lips turned downwards in consideration, he gave a sideways nod.

"You may be on to something, Irishman. But it still remains that I am not the one asking for money."

He dropped the bill into Finnbar's hand, giving him a lighthearted shove towards the bar.

Game concluded, prize money collected, and philosophical musings at an end, they bellied up to the bar. Gnawing on some stale pretzels, they waited few moments before the heavyset barkeep ambled over to them. One of the man's ears bore the scars of a past fight- the upper rim had been bitten off.

"What'll it be, fellas? Just rattle 'em off, my memory's sound."

"Spruce beer," grunted Marcel.

"I'll have me a phlegm-cutter," David announced enthusiastically.

"Let me get a whiskey."

"Do you serve moral suasions here?" Finnbar asked of the man.

The fellow chuckled humorously, if a bit wryly, and rested his thick forearms on the bar. "Depends on whether you intend on walking or staggering outta here."

"Then a moral suasion it'll be," replied Finnbar, much to the man's amusement.

Slowly they supped their drinks, glad to be at ease after a good many days of nonstop activity.

"Oh," said Marcel suddenly, "forgot to ask how yer better half's been fairin' these days."

David snorted cynically. "Up and left me, the auld crone. Took me youngest born wid her, but me other boy Thomas elected to stay behind. He's a Company man up in Athabasca country now. Saw him aboot a year back, seemed to be doin' arrat."

"Hudson's Bay Company?" Alvord asked of him.

"Aye. Only skin comp'ny still worth much these days. And that much ain't all that much. The American Fur Company is hurtin', turned to commercial fishin' to pick up the slack."

"So is it the HBC that we shall answer to?"

Marcel looked at him oddly. "We'll answer to no company. Guess I forgot to tell ya. We'll be free trappers, livin' as freely as a man can in this life. Beholden to no one but the fur market."

"Independent living. Now that's the life for me," Finnbar said. His head then swiveled to the right in a blur.

"Half a mo..." he stared across the room as if transfixed.

From an end lane strode the majestic creature he had plucked from the river earlier that day.

Hair neatly bundled atop her head in Continental fashion, her elegant figure was covered by a quality but not flashy muslin dress of dark green, which brought out the rich olive hue of her eyes.

She was strong of limb, Finnbar noticed, but not so much so as to render her masculine in any way. Her dark skin spoke to her exotic heritage, perhaps she had a touch of Indian blood in her...

She was flanked by a large, severe-looking man clad in a low-hanging, black oilskin coat, the collar of which was turned up. His longish hair, the very darkest shade of gray, was combed back to sweep onto his thick neck. He had a large, blocky skull that matched well his square, powerful body. Well-defined cheekbones and heavy brows encircled startling eyes of amber. His skin, while not quite so tan as Genevieve's, was weathered and dark enough to make a body wonder as to his ancestry.

Leveling a measured gaze at the four who stood before him, his face mirrored nothing his mind might be harboring.

"Gentlemen," he rumbled, offering naught else.

David and Marcel grunted and nodded; Alvord tipped his black top hat and Finnbar merely gaped at the beautiful girl who likewise held his eyes with her own.

"Hello again!" trilled Genevieve to Finnbar. "I was hoping that we'd see one another after that chance meeting this morning."

"As was I, m'dear. 'Tis but a small town indeed, isn't it?"

The man extended his hefty hand to the Irishman. "Gen informed me of your daring rescue earlier. I thank you; she is dear to me, and her safety is of paramount importance. My name is Cadwallader Jones."

The man's surname name stirred something in Alvord's memory, but he could not quite put his finger on it...

Finnbar nodded. "Ah, and she is your...?"

The man moved his mouth and eyes in what approached a smirk. "My ward, as she has been since she was three. For all intents and purposes she is my daughter."

The Irishman visibly brightened. "I see."

"And, it so happens, she has voiced her wishes for you to be present at a dinner party I am hosting tonight at five o'clock following a business meeting. It is most propitious that we should encounter you here, for I would she her wish granted, and would very much like for you to attend."

He turned courteously towards Alvord and the others. "You gentlemen, I assume, travel with Mr. Fagan here? So I likewise extend the offer to you. My servants are hard at work and there will a bounty of victuals. Roast pig, fresh fish and venison, and plenty to wash it down with, should you accept."

They all glanced at each other, silently communicating their desire to do so with alacrity.

"We would be honored," Alvord assured him.

Jones gave them a curt bow. "My house lies at the end of Welsh Drive, which is off of this main thoroughfare roughly a mile north of our present location. Until later, gentlemen. I shall secure a lane for us, Gen."

Genevieve beamed, a ray of sunlight amidst the diffused lighting of the bowling alley. "Splendid! I could do with some wit and mirth tonight. These soirees can be very stuffy affairs sometimes..."

"If its laughter you're after, then I suggest you steel yourself. Finnbar here can provide you with innumerable things to chuckle at..."

Alvord clapped him heartily on the back, chuckling. Finnbar feigned laughter whilst glaring death at his large friend.

Arsehole, he mouthed, but the shadow of a grin threatened to take solid form on his face.

"'Til then, lass," he said to Genenvieive, and after final smile and a brief bow of his own he led the others towards the door.

They left the bowling alley behind and stepped onto the town's principle road, Water Street. The town paralleled the river for three miles; true to rumor, this section of the main thoroughfare was by dominated dram shops, bowling alleys, and billiards halls, all of which were receiving ample patronage from trappers, miners, and half-breeds.

A clutch of miner's, dead-drunk, stumbled past them as they roared out some lewd shanty. The Soo was the principal place of embarkation for copper miners looking to get to Copper Harbor or Eagle Harbor up on the Keweenaw Peninsula to the west.

A portage road, akin to a small railway, coming up from the riverbank, ran along part of the road before angling off towards a large warehouse used by John Jacob Astor's once-mighty American Fur Company. Two lumbering oxen, saliva dripping from their gleaming snouts, bore a cart along the tracks that was piled high with fish.

"Yep," Marcel remarked, "like David said, commercial fishin' and freight haulin' is becoming more important to the American Fur Company than furs is. Makes sense to... to ah-"

"Diversify," Alvord and Finnbar offered in unison.

"Yeah. Still, a right shame it is. Dreadful whiff, that of too much fish in one spot... hold up a sec. Speakin' of odors- Finn, if plan to put hand to my clothes fer the sake of washin' before tonight's party, then you'd best be ready to part with said hand."

He rested a palm on the elk-horn handle of his Bowie knife to stress the gravity of his threat.

Finnbar, looking off into the skyline where towering cumulous clouds hung in their billowing majesty, merely sighed with manifest contentment.

"Do what you please, trapper old friend, for tonight Lady Fortune has showered favor upon the likes of Finnbar Fagan."

He strode along with a spring in his step, whistling the tune of "My Bonny Lass She Smileth."

Chapter 22

Jones's sullen Gothic Revival home stood shielded from the persisting harshness of the afternoon sun by the boughs of several impressive white pines. Within that interlocking network of branches a congregation of grackles nested, their grating calls growing frenzied as Alvord thrice rapped the knocker against the door.

"An unabashedly opulent dwelling for a quiet frontier town like this," he commented to David, eyes flicking from the decorative tracery of the pointed arch windows to the steeply pitched gable roof. The brass knocker, which was cast in the form of a monstrous dragon's head, glared back at him defiantly. No voices or footsteps could be heard inside, but behind them creaked the wheels of the departing carriage that had borne them to this place.

"Aye, and an odd fella who calls the place home."

"I want to say that I have heard his name spoken once before."

"None too surprisin', Alvord. Cadwallader Jones's has got a hand in everything but the skin trade here on the Upper Lakes."

"An iron in nearly every fire, interesting..."

"Gent's worth a pretty penny. I've eyed this place many a time, covetously I suppose, wonderin' what it'd look like inside."

"My dear Scotsman," said Finnbar, taking a short pull from a gleaming silver flask before handing it off to Marcel, "I do believe you're about to get your wish. Although it seems that they are in no hurry to admit us."

"Or perhaps," suggested Alvord reprovingly, "they are concerned that we are naught but a flock of tipsy revelers. You might hide that flask lest you be labeled a Lushington."

"Come now, no party is any fun unless seasoned with folly," he retorted imperturbably.

"Erasmus, *In Praise of Folly*?" Alvord posited, head cocked to the side uncertainly. It was an ongoing game between them that they sought to stump one another with quotations.

"Right in one."

"Plus," Alvord tutted, checking his timepiece, "we *are* late. Twenty minutes so. Had one of us not been fussing over his appearance for quite so long..."

"Yeah Finn," Marcel added, roughly nudging an elbow into the beleaguered Irishman's ribs, "nervous, are ye?"

"*Brimming* with confidence, thank you very much..."

With a drawn-out groan the door opened to reveal a short, stocky form silhouetted by the golden glow emanating from within the house.

The man offered no words, welcoming or otherwise, opting instead to stare at what was, admittedly, a mixed bag of fellows. Alvord and Finnbar, both fashionably appareled in dark, single-breasted frock coats, stood in stark contrast to their two trapper friends. David's voyageur garb, while clean, was a far cry from formal, and the long, violently red toque hat surmounting his head seemed patently outlandish to Alvord. Marcel, reliably deaf to Finnbar's freely dispensed fashion advice, sported ashen-white buckskins that were quite regal looking, but again were hardly appropriate for a formal dinner being hosted by a man of status.

"Alvord Rawn, sir, here at the invitation of Mr. Jones along with Finnbar Fagan, David MacTavish, and Marcel Durand."

"Ah yes, do come in." The man, clad in black servants' livery, promptly turned and led the way into the house.

They passed through a cool, dimly lit antechamber before entering a capacious entrance hall. The servant relieved Alvord of his top hat (Finnbar never wore one) and took Finnbar's intricately carved cane. He dryly announced each of their names before withdrawing once again into the darkness of the antechamber. They stood in an indecisive knot, not sure if they should proceed or wait to be acknowledged. Neither host nor other guests could be seen.

Alvord let his eyes sweep over the entrance hall. A host of landscape paintings graced the walls along with a smattering of tapestries depicting medieval themes. At the far end a red-carpeted, imperial staircase led in an easy pitch to the second floor on either side of the room. Elegantly furnished with gilt chandeliers, the room was tasteful without being overly ostentatious.

By Manhattan standards, that was. For Sault Ste. Marie, a rough-hewn frontier town lying on a colossal wilderness lake, this house was the very height of flamboyant. Alvord, a man of mostly sober tastes, had watched in dismay as Manhattan grew increasingly extravagant in its architectural makeup. Gothic and Neoclassical mansions, Italianate behemoths- such structures were swallowing up his cherished Federal buildings and quaint Dutch colonials at an alarming rate.

Oh well. Little he could do about it. Perhaps one day he

would erect a nice, stately Federal-style house of his own, built with redbrick and boasting a flat section of roof that he could walk out on to gaze up at the night sky...

The sound of lighthearted conversation abruptly snapped him out of his daydream. A flock of gaily chatting people then drifted into view, among them the tall, dark-clad form of Cadwallader Jones. Taking notice of them standing uncertainly in the hall, he approached them, looking every inch the gracious host. Oiled and neatly swept back on his head, his dark gray hair was nicely complimented by charcoal trousers and a claw-hammered tailcoat.

"Good evening," he boomed in his sonorous voice, polite without being cordial. "I bid you welcome to my home."

"Thank you," replied Alvord affably, "and do pardon our lack of punctuality."

His was not a temperament that enjoyed issuing apologies, but by the same token he hated when people arrived behind schedule.

"Not a problem. Trouble finding the place?"

"No. Merely a crisis of fashion." He indicated Finnbar a jerk of his head and the faintest of smiles.

A twinkle issued from the amber eyes of their host, who was presently joined by his stunning young ward.

Finnbar's breath caught in his throat as he beheld the object of his desire. Genevieve Connolly strode majestically towards him, attractively clad in the French style of transparent muslin, which floated diaphanously over a green silk shirt and tights. Silk satin half boots of ivory white covered her feet. Her hair fell about her neck in thick, glossy ringlets through which were woven harebell flowers of violet-blue.

"Gentlemen!" she greeted them brightly, her gaze stalling upon Finnbar for a moment. "How splendid that you all came! Perhaps now the arid talk of business will be appreciatively supplanted by topics of a more agreeable nature."

"Come now, Gen," her Guardian remonstrated gently, "those fellows *are* business associates of mine, after all."

"Not that this is a business dinner," he quickly assured his tardy guests.

"Well, you have yet to broach a topic of conversation that is not business related..."

"Fear not, Gen. I would not have all this talk of mining and lake commerce reduce your delicate female brain to so much mush."

He smiled broadly at her; Alvord got the distinct impression that Genevieve was one of the few people on earth who could elicit that particular facial expression from the man.

"Regrettably, you gentlemen did arrive a bit late to partake in our round of pre-dinner cocktails. Though for some," he glanced back at his other guests, "it was rather more than a single round. Let us repair to the dining room, for the food is ready."

He guided them into the high-ceilinged banqueting room, where the rest of the dozen or so guests stood impatiently behind their chairs, waiting for their host to take his seat. Alvord attempted to size up those present but realized he would have to wait until his eyes adjusted to the contrast of light and dark that created a striking chiaroscuro before them. For candles were present only in strategic locations, creating an aura of golden light around the long table whose white tablecloth fair glowed with a celestial softness.

"Hmm, nice ambience," commented Marcel admiringly, looking around the fashionably oak-paneled room. Finnbar and Alvord stared at him.

Jones addressed his dinner party, the candlelight educing deep shadows under his cheekbones and around his eyes. "I would make introductions, but I am confident that you can find the time to meet those around you during the course of the meal."

"That'll likely depend on how good the tucker is," quipped David to a hearty round of chuckling.

Jones took his seat at the head of the table, and pointed to indicate that Alvord and the others should join him towards the front of the table. They did so as the servants began bringing out steaming bowls and platters of food that sent forth a savory, blanketing aroma.

Finnbar, apparently oblivious to the decadent smells filling the room, watched fondly as Genevieve sat in her seat with maidenly precision. They would be sitting across from one another, and Alvord could see the satisfaction that his smitten Irish friend could not quite conceal.

The other guests, meanwhile, began chatting busily and helping themselves to bread.

No Grace? Alvord wondered to himself. For some reason he would have expected better from Jones. He then caught a mouth-watering whiff of what had to be eels and without much trouble his mind swept aside his disapproval.

"Yer *shittin'* me!" Marcel suddenly expostulated, gruff voice loaded with shock. His disbelieving eyes were locked on the man who had just occupied the seat to his immediate right.

"Aha, Mr. Durand! What an unexpected pleasure! Salutations my good man! This is shaping up to be one corking party, isn't it?" It was none other than Humphrey Demetrius Duddersfield, his voice as thin and reedy as ever.

Marcel stared at his reflection as it appeared in the purple lenses of Duddersfield's eccentric spectacles.

"What in the name of Old Clovenfoot r'ya doing here, kid?"

"In Sault Ste. Marie, or here at this soiree?"

"Why don't we cover both, eh?"

"Well, I am embarking on a private geological expedition to the Pictured Rocks region, and this is the only logical shoving-off point. I am currently at this table at the behest of Mr. Jones, whom I met whilst bowling earlier today. He told me that I would be an interesting addition to his dinner party. By the by, that is a fetching buckskin outfit- frontier *soigné*, if I might coin a term."

Marcel turned to look, flabbergasted, at Alvord and Finnbar, who wholeheartedly shared his incredulity.

"You'd best hurry, young Duddersfield," Jones commented in a teasing manner that everyone but Duddersfield could identify, "If rumor can be credited, the great Louis Agassiz will be touring Gitchee Gummi next year on the first significant scientific expedition of this, the greatest of lakes."

"Greatest in terms of surface area," the undaunted lad was quick to point out, "at an estimated 31,700 square miles. Lake Baikal is greatest in terms of volume. Do you know there are seals there, the world's only freshwater seals? And some consider the Caspian Sea to be a lake, as it *is* land-locked, so that would actually be largest. Then again, there are those who would argue that Lake Huron and Michigan are truly one, as they are connected by a strait, which has no consistent flow direction, rather than a river. *And-*"

"Thank you Mr. Duddersfield," Jones interrupted with finality. "Your limnological knowledge is most impressive, and I am eager to read your findings when they are published. Or, were you willing, perhaps I could even be afforded a coveted glimpse of said findings beforehand?"

A clever tactic, Alvord had to admit. Firmly cutting the windbag off only to temper the move with a balsamaceous compliment. Indeed, Duddersfield was beaming with unalloyed delight. Jones excelled at reading individuals, it would seem, and Alvord could not help but wonder what the man was able to perceive in him. There was something about the man's stony visage and piercing, yellowish eyes that bespoke singular powers of observation.

He eyed people as an owl might, with coolest detachment and deliberation, and, it might be said, wisdom.

"But of course! This lake is your home, and I could only stand to benefit from utilizing such a resource as you."

"Grand, grand. Now, let's have at these victuals, shall we?"

"Hear hear!" a good many of the guests roared out lustily, Finnbar and David among them.

Alvord stared fixedly at the smoked eels that gaped sightlessly back at him from their platter, which sat conveniently next to a towering heap of sliced roast beef. He waited for an attractive young brunette across the table to take her food before helping himself. For his sense of propriety he received a dazzling smile- flattering, but not quite enough to take his mind off of the steaming cornucopia before him. Giving her a polite nod, he filled his plate and enthusiastically tucked in.

The dinner proved to be patently enjoyable. As Marcel had pointed out, the room possessed an agreeable ambience, and additionally provided much for the eye to feast on, not to mention the manifold delights that were offered to the belly. The taxidermied heads of deer, moose, elk, and caribou peered somberly down at them, bearing silent witness to the unfettered spectacle of gluttony before them. The pelts of everything from mink and lynx to cougars and bears were tacked to the wall; Alvord was strongly reminded of a scene out of Washington Irving's *Astoria*, in which the Scottish men of the Northwest Company held a sumptuous feast that bore the stamp of Old World warmth and tradition. If his memory served, that part of the book actually took place at Fort William, which was situated on Thunder Bay on Lake Superior's desolate northern shore.

"There was no stint of generous wine, for it was a hard-drinking period," Irving had penned of that, the heyday of the trapping industry. The industry might be but a pale shadow of its former glory, but the hard drinking nature of the time had most assuredly persisted to present day.

Wines of the choicest vintages, brandy, whiskey, gin, chilled lager beer- all were present in riotous profusion and received no shortage of attention.

And the food, ah, the food! Rarely had Alvord overindulged as now he did. Perhaps it was simply a lack of proper vittles since leaving Chicago, but at the sight of the bounty before him his stomach seemed to expand in fond anticipation. The eel and roast beef, paired with potatoes and green beans, did not last long and were soon replaced with lake trout and grouse. And there was even more to be sampled- duck, goose, and a roast suckling pig. From this latter dish Marcel promptly ate the cherries that took the place of its eyes, as well as the apple out of its mouth, while Alvord indulged in one of its oysters- the slip of meat located beneath the cheekbone, which was fatty, moist, and packed with flavor.

This surfeit of quality food and drink engendered an understandably quiet atmosphere during the early stages of the dinner, but for the rasp of fork against plate and the odd belch.

Perhaps the only attendant downside was that it was insufferably hot, a problem hardly assuaged by the presence of a crackling fireplace. As Finnbar was fond of pointing out, Americans were prone to have a fire going even in the sweltering summer months.

As he paused to mop his glistening brow with a napkin, Alvord became more cognizant of the piquant bits of conversation around him.

Finnbar was engaged in lively discourse with the young Miss Connolly, who, Alvord had to say, was a rare beauty. Obviously not purely of white heritage, but a rare beauty regardless. He had read that some Métis women possessed stunning good looks, an assertion this girl definitely backed up. She and the Irishman were good-naturedly comparing and contrasting European and American literature, a favored topic of conversation for Finnbar.

Marcel was doing was doing his best to ignore the blathering Duddersfield, who somehow managed to speak without pause around immense mouthfuls of food.

"So I bowl me a strike on my second frame, and Mr. Jones, in the lane next to me, suggests that I join he and Genevieve, as it was a shame for such talent to be bereft of competition."

"You were playin' by yer lonesome, kid?" Marcel asked with just a hint of pity creeping into his words.

"Well who else was I, a lone traveler, to play with? Like I told you- I had been paddling nonstop for the better part of three days in a birchbark that I bought off those red men down in the Lower Penninsula. After my arrival and a generous amount of sleep, I was in dire need of *some* form of entertainment. So I proceeded to play with them, and won handedly. Genevieve said she had never seen the like! She also picked my brain about natural history, which as you well know is a topic on which I can speak exhaustively.

"And," his squeaky voice dropped to a conspiratorial whisper as his eyes darted towards her, "I do believe she took a liking to me."

He nudged Marcel's arm and lifted his queer purple glasses to tip him a decidedly awkward wink.

At this Alvord snorted into his Yorkshire pudding. The nonplussed mountain man simply gaped at the delusional young scientist. The pretty brunette across from him was conversing with both Jones and a corpulent man with a monocle and a consumptive cough about the fishing industry.

"But Mr. Jones," she inquired in a velvety voice, "are not sturgeon an unfortunate byproduct of trawling? They hold no real commercial value, do they? I have seen fishermen simply stack them like so much cordwood on beaches to die when they are brought to the surface alongside trout and whitefish."

Jones took a leisurely sip of Bordeaux wine. "For most, Miranda, that does hold true. Yet someone, and I can't imagine whom, recently started a rumor that Lake Superior and Michigan sturgeon roe is the rarest of delicacies, far better than any other variety of caviar. The result has been a growing demand for it in Montreal. There also exists a small but lucrative market for sturgeon steaks in that city, one that I am fortunate enough to have a stranglehold on. The flesh of smaller fish I actually find to be delectable, but that of older specimens grows bland and chewy, much as the quality of lobster meat lessens with age. But such meat is still quite serviceable, offering capital nutrition as dog food. Speaking of fish- did you find the lake trout to your liking, Mr. Rawn? My cook employed a new glaze and garnish."

"Nothing short of delectable," Alvord avowed. "It has been some time since my *bon vivant* days, but I still declare without hesitation that this feast is second to none."

"Splendid."

"So what brings you to the Soo, Mr. Rawn?" the monocled man wished to know. "As I have not seen you around before, I surmise that you are either a traveler or newcomer?"

"You deduce correctly. I suppose the label of traveler could be applied to me. I, along with Finnbar, Marcel, and David here, will be embarking on a trapping expedition in a few days' time."

"Where to?" The man, whose name was Richards, pressed him.

Alvord's eyes briefly met those of Marcel, who had been listening and at this last question stiffened a bit.

"Along Superior's southern coast," Alvord answered vaguely before taking a small bite of redcurrant-glazed grouse. It stood to reason that like a secret fishing hole, a prized trapping location should be kept undisclosed. Alvord did know that they would be initially camping on Chapel Beach in the Pictured Rocks, but what business did Richards have knowing that?

"I see," said Richards, visibly put off by his evasive answer.

The man paused to hawk some phlegm onto the floor; like smoking, this was common practice in America, but once again not one that Alvord partook in. "Though the fur trade as an enterprise is all but moribund, one can still make good money off of lynx, bobcat, fisher, and otter."

"I take it that you and Mr. Rawn are new to trapping, Mr. Fagan?"

"Aye, Mr. Jones," Finnbar responded cheerfully. "Neophytes we are. Or greenhorns, as we have repeatedly been called."

"Are you concerned with finding a market for your peltries? I am not directly involved in the skin trade, but do have certain connections..." Jones directed his words at David and Marcel.

Marcel nodded in deference. "'Preciate it, but we'll be goin' through Ramsay Crooks's commission house in Manhattan. He was rising fast in the American Fur Company 'til it started backslidin' in '44, and a year after he opened that commission house and slapped the old Company name on it. As he's got erstwhile American Fur Company men operatin' here in the Soo, all's we gotta do is drop our peltries off at the fur warehouse in the downtown fer transport to New York."

"Aye," added David, "Crooks has made himself a nice mint with this commission house, far better'n what was being done with the Company before it dissolved."

"Ramsay Crooks?" Alvord was surprised. "I know the man, at least in passing. That commission house you mention is indeed a very successful venture... I actually helped save the building from a fire that erupted in a neighboring structure just two years back, when first it was constructed."

"You were a fireman in Manhattan?" the brunette, whose name Alvord had not heard spoken, asked excitedly.

"I was a patrolman, actually. Captain of the Sixth Ward in the Municipal Police Department, as well as a private detective."

The answer was an honest one, so it came naturally, but it was one that he immediately regretted offering. All other conversation suddenly stopped, and people were either staring at him raptly or whispering to one another. Jones peered with hooded eyes his way, as if seeing him for the first time.

Judas Priest. They would press for stories next, unless someone came to his rescue...

Several huge, long-legged dogs with wiry gray coats loped into the room and began prowling around the table. Their precise, deliberate steps and dignified bearing suggested an inherent regality that most other breeds could never hope to attain. Dense hair created something of a mane that shrouded the animals' regal necks and deep chests, lending the dogs an even more impressive demeanor.

One of the beasts, an older pup verging on adulthood, sniffed the polished, patent leather of Alvord's boots under the table before whining loudly for scraps.

"*Cerberus*!" The authority crack in Jones's voice made many a guest snap to attention.

Alvord gave the dog a quick pat under the table in gratitude for the distraction.

"I've had a devil of a time with that one."

"Obstreperous?" Alvord inquired.

"In the extreme."

"What breed? Never have I seen such a dog. Fine looking beasts, they are."

"Half Scottish deerhound, half Irish wolfhound. Loyal pets and capital hunters of deer and wolves, but Cerberus here has been growing refractory. It is my own fault; I have been busy of late and have not had the proper time to train him as I did the others.

David looked over one of the dogs. "Deerhounds were the hunting dogs kept by the Scottish *lairds* of auld. Beasts of the nobility and the royal dog of Scotland, in fact. The fall of the clan system saw the decline of the breed, but I've heard they're on the rise once more. And often crossed with wolfhounds to help reinvigorate that breed, which likewise saw a drop in numbers. The wolfhound blood has made 'em a sight bigger'n sturdier, but might slow 'em down a touch. Still, these are truly impressive beasts, and not one's I'd want hunting me."

Jones noticed Alvord fondly petting Cerberus, who gazed back up at him dotingly with hazelnut eyes. The dog had come out from under the table and now stood beside Alvord's chair. At nearly three feet at the shoulder, the dog was eye-level with most of the seated guests. The young hound's musculature and proportions were downright inspiring.

"You know what? If you wish, you may have him. He is still young enough so that the transfer from one owner to another will not be dramatic, and he could prove useful to you during your trapping expedition."

Alvord could tell the offer was a legitimate one by Jones's tone and facial arrangement. He silently mulled things over for a bit. A dog meant responsibility and attention, but he had never had a dog before and suddenly found himself amenable to the notion. Plus, as Jones had pointed out, Cerberus could come in handy in the wilderness.

Nodding, he ran his hand over the dog's coarse back. "I accept. Many thanks, Mr. Jones. Know that he shall receive ample care."

"Of that I have no doubt. You are welcome, Mr. Rawn."

Genevieve rose summarily. "Well, this dinner has certainly been one of fine food and sparkling conversation, but I do believe that I will now take Mr. Fagan on a tour of the house and the grounds, if there is no objection. Mr. Fagan, shall we?"

Finnbar looked confusedly around the table, obviously a bit ruffled. "Um, well, I mean if there is no objection?"

Alvord knew there would not be. He did not approve of it, but in America young couples were often permitted to spend time alone, without the presence of a chaperone. Oftentimes such occasions were spent in secluded places that were conducive to engaging in certain acts that one might not be inclined to engage in out in more public settings. Finnbar, a European of a reasonably good breeding, was undoubtedly use to stricter practices and was, as a result, understandably flustered. Alvord almost pitied the poor Hibernian, whom he had never before seen ill at ease.

"But of course, Gen," rumbled Jones with a smile that was almost genuine but stopped just short.

Behave yourselves, it warned.

Finnbar, rising to join Genevieve, looked back at his friend, silently imploring them for help.

"You kids have fun now," Marcel told them with a toothy smile as he took a drag off his pipe.

Chapter 23

The sumptuous dinner wound to a close shortly after the precipitous departure of Finnbar and Genevieve. Dessert was a more spartan affair, which came as a blessing since most present could scarcely cram another bite down their gullets. Indeed, the lingering blend of cooking smells no longer came as a welcome thing to Alvord, whose bulging stomach was busy cursing his lack of restraint. As he had eaten past the point of satiety he availed himself of a gin-sling, a gin-based drink made with lemon, sugar, and bitters, so as to help the meal settle.

Marcel, on the other hand, had sampled nearly every dish and was still powering through treacle pudding when Jones finally signaled that his servants should begin clearing the table. Head down, jaws working furiously, one would have thought that the mountain man had not eaten for days. Alvord had read that Indians were capable of eating inhuman quantities of food in one sitting; it seemed Marcel had taken careful lessons from them on how to shift grub. He sometimes wondered how the fellow stayed in shape, for although he was burly in form he had only a small suggestion of a gut and carried it well. Perhaps he merely ate like a starved wolf in preparation for their impending departure into the wild, where the assurance of food would be no more. The recent and appalling story of the Donner Party, whose travails had been made public news only in the last few weeks, showed what desperate lengths human beings would go to for the sake of sustenance. Bound for California, a wagon party of eighty-six souls had become snowbound in the Sierra Nevada during the winter of 1846-47. Many of the survivors had resorted to cannibalism, to the profound shock of the nation. Upon reading the articles Alvord told himself that starvation was preferable to dining on the flesh of one's fellow man, but then again he had never been pushed to the outermost limits of hunger, when it no doubt became a thing alive, writhing inside of you...

After dessert Jones suggested that they retire into some adjacent rooms, in which he had hung a clutch of newly acquired paintings. The guests followed their host *en masse* out of the dining room.

Alvord, still munching on a piece of pineapple, watched

Marcel staggering painfully along.

"Never had you pegged for a gourmand, my friend," he joked.

"S'worth it. Ain't taken down chow like that since... damn, probl'y never. Really brought out the fatted calf, didn't he? We'll be eatin' fare that's a sight more plain in the none-too-distant future, so's I figgered it wise to overindulge. Stomach ain't well pleased with the decision, though..."

He put his right hand, the one that bore a corresponding scar to the powder burn on his cheek, to the protuberance that was straining at the seams of his white buckskins. David, caught in a similar predicament, lurched stoically alongside him.

Alvord swallowed the last of the pineapple, savoring its tangy, tropical flavor upon his lips. In Manhattan he had eaten pineapple whenever it was available; he opined now that this might be his last taste of the exotic fruit for quite some time.

A final taste of civilized living...

He suddenly felt a small hand curl firmly around his bicep. Turning his head in surprise he beheld Miranda, the attractive brunette who had been eyeing him during dinner. With a come-hither smile she tightened her hold and began inquiring as to his thoughts on the meal. To each of her questions he responded in the courteous fashion of a well-mannered man, smiling from time to time and chuckling appreciatively when an attempt at wit was made. Only a person possessing of keen perceptive faculties would have noticed his aversion to the whole situation.

The girl's attention turned elsewhere for a moment, affording Alvord the opportunity to slip out of his pocket the small locket containing Katherine's daguerreotype. The seemingly chronic hardness around his eyes softened by a few degrees.

When, as was now the case, he chanced to engage in close conversation with an attractive female, he invariably began judging her against the ever-present memory of Katherine. And, as always, he arrived at the conclusion that his wife had been a woman without peer. This young lady before him was pretty and charming enough, but compared unfavorably to his deceased wife. It was nothing against the girl, but he would just as soon avoid this situation.

There was more to it than that, as well. It had to do with an ingrained sense of loyalty that even death could not undo. Some of the Irish, he recalled being told, considered a second marriage to be an unspeakable insult to the dead spouse. He forgot the name of the old mick who had told him this, but the man went on to say that in certain neighborhoods, residents would go so far as to apologize for having to reveal that one of their neighbors had remarried. There was much about the Irish that Alvord did not care for, but their sense of spousal loyalty, even past the point of the tomb- well, that he could firmly identify with. For while he would concede that it was pleasant to have a pretty face smiling at your comments, to watch as she carelessly tucked an errant strand of hair back in place... that gratification contained within it a mounting feeling of betrayal.

And so he would be polite and somewhat receptive lest he seem outright rude, tempering the farce all the while with a scarcely detectable degree of aloofness. Suppressing a grimace as Miranda steered him along, Alvord wondered how Finnbar might be faring.

Genevieve had shown him all around the house before the others had stirred from the dinner table. The tour concluded in her well-furnished room, much to Finnbar's shock. This seemed awfully suggestive... back home this would be considered conduct unbecoming of a lady...

Still struggling with the degree of freedom they were being permitted, he perched uncertainly upon a plush couch of Persian blue. Not much dialogue had passed between them during their stroll through the house; Genevieve had simply given him a tour of her home, doing most of the talking and answering his questions when he posed them. He supposed now was the time to display the dazzling skills of conversation he had given her a taste of during dinner.

"So ah, no chaperone to ensure the observation of proprieties?"

Genevieve's delicately curved lips twisted into a wry smirk. "Not unless I feel the need for one. Why, should I be concerned about an attempt on my honor?"

"Should I?" His gold tooth brilliantly caught the light of the room's chandeliers. At this playful exchange he felt considerably less tense, casually propping his arm up on the couch's lyre arm as he recovered his customary swagger and savoir-faire. With inquisitive eyes he followed her form as she distractedly neatened up a desk across the room, arranging the books that lay upon it in a neat pile.

She was, as Sir Walter Raleigh had once phrased it, formed in the best proportions of her sex. Shockingly beautiful, really. The bronzed skin accentuated by the white, transparent muslin that hovered ethereally about her, the gold-streaked hair interlaced with flowers: she seemed more of an artist's imagining of a goddess than base flesh and blood.

Her teeth were white and straight, which came as a profound relief. Among Europeans, American females had an awful reputation when it came to the state of their pearly whites. Finnbar had heard stories of otherwise beautiful young women with unsightly green teeth. Someone also told him that they would have rows of perfectly good teeth ripped out, so as to have fake ones inserted! He was lucky then, he supposed, that Genevieve's dentition seemed near perfect, aside from a tiny gap in between the two front teeth that he found ever so endearing.

And, he noticed to his satisfaction, just above her mouth she bore the pinprick of a mole, an ancient Irish sign of a soft tongue and winning ways.

Her manner was genial and she seemed confident and self-possessed, attributes he also favored in females. There was nothing quite so unappetizing as a girl whose emotions held dominion over the rest of her faculties.

She seemed fond of reading, which was another check mark on his list of encouraging qualities. On the table in front of the couch several books sat side by side. He swiftly read the titles: *Historical & Secret Memoires of the Empress Josephine* translated by some fellow he'd never heard of, *Sense and Sensibility* by Jane Austen, and *Twice Told Tales* by Nathaniel Hawthorne, an up and comer in the arena of American fiction.

She finished neatening up her desk and primly lowered herself onto the couch. Her mere proximity to him was enough to excite some of his more impure passions, but these he quickly corralled. Although he could wench with the best of them, Finnbar actually possessed a deep respect for proper ladies. Never did his eyes linger on them lustfully and he despised it when other men spoke of what they longed to do to the women they gawked at. Whores; well, who really had respect for those who trod the primrose path, and who could begrudge a man the use of their services from time to time? Dirty water quenches fire, after all. Like most men of his time, Finnbar expected that proper ladies be pure of mind and body, while men should be free to consort with women of ill station. It was simply the established order of things.

Genevieve looked at him, trying to unveil what those dark green eyes might be concealing. "You and your compatriots are like characters out of a novel, you know."

"Aye, fiction made flesh, at your beck and call."

"I do not say that in jest. Many men with big ideas, big mouths, and bigger opinions strut through our door. You are a standout group of men- surely you've noticed that most eyes turn your way when you enter a room?"

"Ah, you'll have me blushing now! Of our merry band, though, I am least like a character from a fictional realm. Marcel and David are the trappers that have stalked across the pages of books by Washington Irving and James Fennimore Cooper, and Alvord at times seems like a hero out of a Sir Walter Scott novel."

"What of you, though? If I may, your character seems more complex." She did not bother to mask her genuine interest as she pressed him.

"Oh, me? I'm just your average Hibernian swashbuckler, writer, dizzying intellect, erstwhile mercenary, and soon-to-be trapper."

"I believe you forgot to mentioned your unsurpassed modesty."

He cackled loudly at that, clapping his hands together in appreciation. "Ah, of all the things to forget, it *had* to be my most salient quality!"

She tittered quite adorably. "On the topic of modesty, what is your friend Alvord like? He said precious little tonight. And to categorize him as being a hero out of a Scott adventure is too vague, as Scott wrote many books containing protagonists who do not fit into a common mold. What, would you say, is his character?"

Finnbar folded his hands together and thought for a minute before speaking. She asked about Alvord not out of romantic interest, he could tell, but rather out of sheer curiosity.

"Between you and I, lass, Alvord likes to think that his character defies convenient categorization, but is mistaken. His is, admittedly, one of the rarest sorts, one that demonstrates moral uprightness and the impulse to uphold justice, coupled with impressive physical prowess and intellect enough to set him apart from the great unwashed. Set apart, perhaps, for some greater purpose. Men like him used to look fondly upon times past, believing that there was once an age wherein good men were not so damnably scarce, only to realize that the present is naught but the past repeated, and most men have been worms throughout history, worms pathetically squirming their way through its muck. Out of a novel, you say? Of us all, Alvord Rawn belongs to the realm of fiction more than he does to this one. He seeks detachment from a reality in which he simply does not perceive a place for himself."

He paused and looked down at the floorboards a bit sheepishly. "I'd be beholden to you if you did not mention any of this to him. I should not have spoken as I did... it is his business, not mine or yours."

"Of course, Mr. Fagan. I thought I saw something of a dark streak in him. You trust them, then? Your friends?"

"Without reservation," he stated firmly. "We are boon companions and have each other's back to the last, bloody gasp. To be blessed with such friends as I have been... it is beyond the potency of words. And do call me Finnbar."

Genevieve nodded understandingly, pleased with how Finnbar complimented himself only in jest and was willing to speak well of other men. Too many times had she listened to men talk poorly of others in a not-so-subtle effort to build themselves up.

Finnbar pulled out a small silver flask and began unscrewing the cap.

"Are you a bit of a Lushington, Finnbar?"

"Far worse. I'm an Irishman. Which," he paused to take a fortifying swig, "does lend itself to certain abuses."

He offered her the flask, which she politely declined to take. "I should like to journey to Ireland some day. My father was an Irish immigrant."

"Really? Where from in the Old Country?" he asked interestedly.

"Where exactly I do not know. He died when I was quite young, as did my mother."

"And what was *her* heritage?" He kept his voice casual, not wishing to sound like he was prying.

"I wondered when we would get to that," she replied lightly. "She was half Normandy French and half Chippewa Indian."

She paused, anxiously awaiting his reaction.

"And here I was thinking that you merely had a nice tan."

She felt a flood of relief as he continued talking.

"So Mr. Jones became your guardian after your parents passed?"

"Correct. He had known them reasonably well before they died, and was the first to offer his guardianship."

"Do you enjoy being his ward?"

With an expansive gesture she indicated the opulent room they sat in. "He is extremely rich, extremely kind, and an extremely respectable man to boot. I am blessed to have him as a Guardian. There are some downsides, but they are far outweighed by the good. Yet if I am being honest, he *is* gone on business quite a bit; sometimes I accompany him but more often I am left here, where-"

"Lonely inner monologues soon grow stale." He looked at her closely, almost tragically, seeing more now than he had before. As a youth, he himself had been left to his own devices in his family's commodious ancestral manor on more occasions than he cared to remember.

Riches cover a multitude of woes...

She fell pointedly silent, staring for a moment's time out the window. While she did a cat with a stark, luxuriant white coat dropped onto Finnbar's lap from atop a nearby grandfather clock.

"Ah," he said, throat tightening in instinctive fear. "A cat. How, how *nice*."

He despised the creatures and always had. The beast stared at him with cold, dissimilar eyes, one green and one blue.

"His name is Orestes and he is a Turkish Angora. And my confidante to boot." She stroked his fur, causing him to arch his back pleasurably and dig his nails into Finnbar's trousers.

Those devilish claws are awfully close to the goods...

In the next moment the animal bounded to the floor and walked away imperiously, tail held high with all the haughty pride of a feline.

Genevieve rose and looked out the window. "Well, it is a beautiful evening and I am going for a quick jaunt- if you're of a mind..."

Finnbar promptly leapt to his feet and offered her his arm. "Delighted."

Together they exited the house through a side entrance and walked out onto the green sweep of lawn, which had taken on the golden hue of the sinking sun that blazed in the sky to the west of them.

Jones led the little group into a roomy, cherry-paneled drawing room that contained many shelves of books along its walls. Alvord, thoughts still lingering on Katherine, began listening more attentively and caught him mid-sentence.

"...commissioned by myself and executed by an young, itinerant negro artist whom I met in Cincinnati. Robert Duncanson is his name. He started, like most painters, with portraiture and still-life but has aspirations towards landscape painting. These are among his earliest attempts. He definitely needs to tour Europe in order to study the Old Masters, but just look at this work. The manner in which he blends romantic and naturalistic principles is impressive for a novice landscape painter. Can you see the style of Thomas Cole influencing his own?"

"I can," Alvord verified, peering more closely at the indicated painting, one that hung alongside several genre scenes by William Sidney Mount and George Caleb Bingham. "One can also detect a glimmer of Asher B. Durand's style. Although his sense of balance does need work; as you pointed out, a firsthand study of the Old Masters should remedy many such deficiencies."

Jones, partially lifting a dark eyebrow, regarded Alvord interestedly. "Are you an admirer of art, Mr. Rawn?"

"I would say that I am an admirer of landscapes more than anything else; art on the whole is a topic that I do not know enough about to accept the label of admirer. Whilst I dwelt in Manhattan I was a member of the American Art Union, receiving popular prints and art literature, as well as free admission to their exhibitions."

"Though as Police Captain, you no doubt could have gained free entry into such things anyway," Miranda purred, digging her nails into his arm just a bit.

Alvord fought the impulse to roll his eyes. He was fast tiring of this nonsense- that the girl was trying too hard was becoming painfully obvious.

It was at this moment, to Alvord's particular amusement, that Cerberus chose to bound into the room and, rearing up to his impressive full height, broke Miranda's stranglehold on his arm.

As if on cue, Alvord thought to himself appreciatively.

"*Damn it*, beast!" Jones roared, causing the dog to cow and seek out a dim corner of the room. "You see what I mean? He is defiant, this one. I am most sorry, Miranda."

Miranda, sullen and pouty-lipped, rubbed her arm where the large dog's head had broken her grip. Seizing opportunity, Alvord took a few casual sidesteps away from her, keeping all expression from his face.

A girl who could have been her sister piped up, apparently unconcerned with her sister's plight. "So can a black really paint in such a modish fashion? I would have thought that their capacity for creation was quite limited."

"I quote Samuel George Morton in his *Crania Americana*," Duddersfield swiftly chimed in, "'The Negroes have little invention, but strong powers of imitation.' So it stands to reason that some exceptional specimens among the sons of Ham could rise to such artistic heights. It *is* some rather fine work, is it not?"

"Aye," Jones agreed with a firm nod, "and painted by a man of sound character. And do you really buy into all that craniometric rubbish, Master Duddersfield?"

"Of course. It *is* science, after all."

Another man spoke, leaning close to one painting. "I

recognize a few of these locations. So he toured the Pictured Rocks shoreline, did he? And points west?"

The speaker was an older, imperial looking man who viewed the paintings with both hands clasped behind his ramrod-straight back.

"That he did. I covered the travel fees necessary to get him here from Ohio, as one can imagine that the income of a Negro painter is hardly conducive to such things," (here a smattering of appreciative laughter broke out) "and together we journeyed to a few sites that hold an especial meaning to me. Mostly the Pictured Rocks and a few spots along the Keweenaw."

"While we are on the topic of that region, Jones, I thought you might take a gander at a most anomalous artifact that one of my miners recently uncovered near Eagle Harbor. I left it with my hat out in the foyer..."

It was the older gentlemen, who left the room and returned shortly thereafter with something held in both hands. When the light of the chandeliers played off of its rusting length, Alvord saw that it was a sword.

Quickly his eyes assessed it. Leaf-shaped blade. Thoroughly rusted, anthropomorphic hilt. Total length of perhaps thirty-five inches.

"The blade looked to be cast in oxidizing iron, but look at that blueish-green patina on the part of the handle that is meant to resemble a man. It is of copper."

As Alvord had noticed, curving pieces of copper created the appearance of arms and legs on the sword's haft, which was crowned with a round, graven ball of copper that represented the head.

"Never have I laid eyes on an Indian weapon like this, and as some of you know I happen to collect them. This is something else entirely. Bears a passing resemblance to some Celtic swords I have seen. Jones, I figured you, with your matchless knowledge of the Upper Peninsula, might want to weigh in...?"

Jones, face unreadable, replied, "An unusual weapon, I will allow, but do remember that everything from Phoenician and Roman coins to medieval European swords to, even, Egyptian-style pyramids have been unearthed across our mystery-rich country. Indeed, a good many learned minds believe that it was Egyptians, Phoenicians, or people of ancient Greece that actually mined the copper here so long ago. If you recall, Major Rains, stone tablets bearing cryptic inscriptions are known to pop up ever and anon, some with writing curiously similar to that of such civilizations. Who knows what ancient races made forgotten landfalls on our shores before Columbus, voyages lost to the mists of history? It seems likely that Basques were fishing off the Grand Banks before 1492, and I'm told that the Scandinavians have ancient sagas of westward bound ships sailing beyond Greenland to unknown lands beyond."

Major Rains held it closer to him insistently. "But just look at its state of preservation! And see how highly wrought it is, with the details still clearly visible. Far from ancient, it looks as if it had been cast in times far more recent than the Iron Age!"

"Many things can factor into the preservation of artifacts..."

Alvord's brow furrowed ever so slightly. While most American imaginations leapt at the discovery of out-of-place artifacts, here Jones was distractedly brushing off this undeniably thought-provoking find...

"In what sort of location was it uncovered?" squeaked Duddersfield, round face agog as he wended his way around the other guests.

"It was picked up near one of the ancient mine shafts that dot the Keweenaw; the man claimed to have found it under a mantle of leaf litter, partially secreted beneath a boulder."

The young scientist pushed his glasses up higher on his nose. "Partially secreted, so it was partially exposed to the full force of the elements, which can account for the greater amount of rust on the first half of the blade. And look at the handle, it still retains some of the leather that was wrapped around it. Hmmm, it is very difficult to say with exactitude, but I would place its abandonment within a hundred years. Again, this is hardly my area of expertise, but a weapon in this condition..."

Richards, polishing his monocle, added, "Some of those ancient mineshafts the good Major mentioned are not nearly as 'ancient' as many are inclined to believe, you know."

Duddersfield's head spun 'round as if it were on a swivel. "Come again?"

The grave demeanor of Jones, Alvord noticed, seemed to deepen at Richards's words.

But just barely.

Richards quite suddenly found himself the cynosure of all eyes. Clearing his throat and straightening his cravat, he continued. "The bulk of the ancient, open-pit copper mines on the Keweenaw *are* in fact quite ancient. Exactly how old- who can say with any exactitude? It is atop such primary mines that many mining companies have set up shop on, for the ancient works were often quite accurate in their exposing of copper. Yet a small number of 'old' mines found by the current miners of the region appear significantly more recent and are of a different character altogether. Far from shallow, open-pit mines, they are deeper, more complex, and bear the unmistakable marks of modern tools. To that end, deep in the interior of the Peninsula a group of miners found a stash of chisels and single and double jacks that appeared to have been abandoned for a number of years. And if you recall, modern mining has only begun in earnest there since '45. Yet it still stands that mines complete with adits, crosscuts, winzes, and even some examples of cribbing pop up now and again, along with abandoned tools. Who were these miners?"

"The Injuns claim the copper is protected by wrathful *manitous*, or gods- they have ever attached superstition to the substance," supplemented the Major. "As we exploit the sacred metal for our own gain, so too do we invoke the ire of these entities. Rumors also abound about a mysterious, ill-known tribe that is killing and kidnapping mining men who stray too far from camp. And it so happens that several small groups of miners have been reported as missing. Stranger yet, I was told by miners who camped at what has become known as Miner's Beach in the Pictured Rocks that on perfectly still nights strange clanging noises, not unlike that of a hammer upon a blacksmith's anvil, can be heard faintly emanating from the interior. I might add that that beach is now avoided, with stories of disappearances, queerly abandoned camps, and weird fogs that sweep in out of nowhere being in fast circulation. Who knows what truths lie shrouded in mystery within that region-"

"Mystery, you say? Ah, if only they knew, eh Mr. Jones?"

The dinner party turned as one to assess the speaker, a rough, stubbly-faced personage who stood with folded arms and a prideful tilt to his head. Arrogantly, almost challengingly, he returned their stares. Alvord saw before him a dark-haired woodsman who had seen his share of action and privation, whose eyes held danger for any man who might decipher it. A man unafraid to fight and likewise unafraid to die, and one who had lived long enough alongside that mentality to think little of any man he happened upon.

So too, it would seem, he was a man with well-lined pockets- his attire and appurtenances suggested that he'd come into a recent windfall. New, unscuffed boots of black leather were complimented by a glossy belt of the same color, into which was thrust a brace of finely embossed Colt Paterson revolvers. Given their frame, Alvord figured that they were the .36 caliber model, like his own, rather than the underpowered .28. A thick-handled tomahawk with a gleaming blade hung from the same belt, looking to be of the very highest quality.

"Pollock," Jones greeted him frostily. "Wasn't expecting you for an hour at least."

His tone made it clear that Pollock's early arrival was undesired.

"Sorry boss, must've heard you wrong. Damn, that fodder smells good- this lot leave anything untouched?"

He looked around as if he expected a servant to bring him a plateful.

"I am trying to host a party, Pollock, one that you were not entreated to attend. You may go into the kitchen if you are hungry, but until my guests have departed, stay out of our way."

He stared unblinkingly at the man, face immobile.

"Yeah, sure thing boss." Leering at the dinner party, he turned to leave them but suddenly stopped dead.

"Marcel Durand! I'll be double dog-damned! Well just look at you, last of the goddamn breed, eh? What, the mountains getting a bit too rugged for you in your old age?"

Silently Marcel stepped forward, body language demonstrating that he had very little respect for the loudmouth before him.

"And- damn my taller and hide, you brought MacTavish along too! Nice little reunion we got ourselves here! This is just like a good ol' fashioned Company potlatch back in the day, ain't it boys?"

"Pollock," Marcel gave him a stiff nod. "Figgered you might be around."

Alvord took an immediate disliking to this man, whom he surmised knew Marcel and David from trapping days of yore. If the setting had been a mite less formal, he would be provoking a quarrel with this loudmouth right now, though Marcel would probably have beaten him to the punch, quite literally.

"You figured right. Glad to have you back in Superior country. But what brings you back? Last I heard the Rockies was your haunt these days."

"Come back to do a sight o' trappin'."

"Hmm, wonder where that might be?" Sarcasm dripped like poison from his mouth. "Only place that still harbors furbearers enough to be worth your while is the Pictured Rocks area. And let me guess, you'll pitch camp where you once did on Chapel Beach?"

"Yer off by more'n a few degrees."

Alvord, who knew that statement to be a lie, was impressed with the delivery of those false words. Even he half believed them.

"Where else, then? Believe you me, my fine French friend;

you'll want to be giving that site a pass. Unfit for occupation. Eh, Cadwallader?"

It was at this point that Alvord observed a distinct change in the bearing of Cadwallader Jones, the first overt display of emotion he had demonstrated. His face became one great sneer of purest contempt. Rarely had Alvord seen such darkness manifest itself on a human countenance.

"Behaving like an ill-mannered simian might be the way of things out in the woods, but under my roof you will either conduct yourself like a gentlemen or be forcibly removed."

His rumbling voice would brook no argument, and Pollock bowed his head in deference and took a quick step back.

"Alright, alright... to the kitchens I go. Won't happen again, boss."

"For your sake, Pollock, I'm glad."

Alvord wondered what business this coarse, bigheaded fellow had with Jones. Then again, Jones was involved in many different business ventures on the lakes, so who knew?

Pollack gave David a nod before locking eyes with Marcel and touching off a parting shot.

"Best of luck to you, Marcel. You'll be needing it if you go where I think you are."

"I don't much like yer tone."

"Care to change it?"

"As usual, yer tongue's outrunnin' yer ability, son."

"I'd like to see the day you try and test the latter."

"Keep pressin' and the last thing you'll see, *pissant*, will be my muzzle flash."

Marcel took a measured step towards him, hand casually dangling by the handle of his flintlock pistol.

Quite suddenly a murderous-looking Jones was between them, grabbing Pollock by his shirtfront and heaving him away from the dinner party in an impressive display of speed and power.

Pollock, having gone to the ground after being tossed, raised himself up with as much dignity as he could muster. "Sheesh, I got it, I got it..."

Red in the face, he tucked his guns deeper into his belt and took his leave, scowling deeply.

With a heaving inward breath that inflated his broad chest, Jones spoke to his guests in a voice that verged on eerie, it was so serene.

"So, where were we then?"

Chapter 24

"Were you in Ireland at the onset of the Famine?"

They were quite alone, sitting together at the top of the sloping lawn that overlooked the St. Mary's River, the current of which quickened in expectation of the churning rapids downstream. Genevieve sat upon a low stone bench, head inclined as the evening breeze pleasantly tickled her face, while Finnbar had parked himself nearby on the grass, gazing fixedly at the dancing water below. A long-stemmed piece of wild rye dangled from one corner of his mouth.

"Yes," he responded, voice containing the hollow aftertaste of disagreeable reminiscence. "I returned home in '43 after serving as a mercenary in the Uruguayan Civil War, or *Guerra Grande* as they call it down there. It's still raging, actually, but once my contract was up I readily took my leave rather than renew it, having had my fill of fighting a war that had no real bearing on meself me country. So I returned home to Cork and then completed my studies at Trinity College in Dublin."

He paused to cast an artful glance her way. "Strictly speakin,' the Church forbids Catholics from attending that institution, what with its proud Protestant legacy and Tudor roots. But in candor, I must admit that I can be terrifically clandestine when necessity dictates that I must."

"Ah, and I'd been wondering where that modesty was hiding. So you were in school then, when the Famine struck?"

He continued, pleased that his Catholic faith did not have a deterring effect on her. "I had recently returned home- studies complete, brain numbed, and all vestiges of creativity smothered by the musty world of academia. And by the by, exactly when the Famine began is actually a matter of conjecture. Some would posit that a series of crop failures starting in the 1770's marked its inception, with potato crop failure being universal in Ireland by 1839. But '45 was when the people of Erin really began to sag under the burden of food crisis. Unable to foresee the stubborn persistence of such hard times, many farmers reckoned that a wee bit of short-term starvation was preferable to using up all their rent money on food. If only they had known- for here, in 1847, it is as if the third Horseman of the Apocalypse has been loosed upon our country ahead of schedule."

"I have heard truly dreadful tales..."

"Aye, dreadful'd be the word for it." His pupils dilated as dark, ghastly memories winged their way into his mind. "People reduced to eating nettles and cabbage leaves whilst squatting in the rudest of shacks. Homeless men and women forced into hellish workhouses for meager pay. Folks dying by the thousands in roadside ditches, while orphaned children staggering about like animate skeletons clad in tawdry rags. In a short-viewed panic, unscrupulous landlords whose purses were feeling the strain conducted mass evictions, even when some people still had rent money enough. D'ya know that last month the Gregory Clause, named after that gobshite William Gregory," here he paused to spit bitterly upon the grass, "made it so that anyone who owns more than a quarter of an acre is now ineligible for any type of relief? A paltry quarter acre! Vociferous complaints have been made, but in Ireland the voice of the commoner is too often lost amidst the self-seeking cupidity of the well-born. Though not all affluent people acted as such; my family, with its ancestral wealth, did what it could to provide relief for people in our area. Other moneyed families and individuals have likewise done what they are able, but... what can a few really do to assuage the plight of millions?"

He made as if to continue speaking but instead fell silent, jaw tightly clenched and eyes blazing. A small, dizzying cloud of insects passed over him, but he hardly seemed to notice. Genevieve had never before seen such a searing look of intensity in a man's face; this hardly seemed the same jovial, cavalier Irishman with whom she had been whiling away the evening.

"And the upshot of it all is that Ireland is still a land of plenty." Finnbar blew out a deep, calming breath, trying to be grateful for the rarified company he was in, trying to appreciate the warmth of the lowering sun upon his back. "We produce wool and flax, we count among our exports wheat, oats, beef, and pork. Yet Sir Robert Peel's stubborn policy of continuing food exportation during this time of dire famine was embraced by those who followed in his wake. If only we could make wholesale use of our own resources and goods instead of shipping them off to other lands, we might well be able to heal *ab intra*. If only the money-grubbing bastards would put aside notions of political prudence and laissez-faire economic thinking and deign to spare us but a little genuine consideration... they'll have a rebellion on their hands if they aren't careful."

Finnbar became acutely aware of Genevieve's uncomfortable silence. Perhaps in his effort to give explanation to the situation he had unwittingly stumbled into the fiery realm of ranting. A tad embarrassed, he caught her eye and gave her a smile, however forced.

"Ah, no use perseverating over the matter, is there? Do pardon my intensity, m'dear."

"Of course, Mr. Fagan. And frankly, from what you have described this situation seems quite worthy of serious thought. Perhaps even intensity."

"For what it's worth, myself and my associates intend to usher in a new era of prosperity and independence for our country."

Considering his mysterious words, she watched as a lazily circling osprey suddenly tucked into a sheer dive, flattening out at the last moment to almost gingerly pluck a squirming trout from the water with its outstretched talons.

"Sounds ever so ambitious. But in the meantime you have taken to Bedouin ways?"

"Yes," he replied between appreciative chuckles. "I suppose that I have become something of a rover. My role in the ah, *movement* that my associates and I aim to put into action will be one of crafting nationalistic novels. So I decided that I would travel for a spell before returning home, gaining worldly experience and seeing how our people are taking to life in new lands."

A quiet, strangled noise caught in Genevieve's throat, one that implied an initial wish to speak followed hard by feelings of uncertainty.

"Out with it, lass. Nothin' worse than important thoughts left to simmer unspoken."

"Well, what if something were to entice you to stay?"

The Irishman's desire to appear composed wrangled futilely with his heartfelt satisfaction at her words. He angled his head away from her so as to hide the widening smile as it crept across his face. He felt a growing magnetism, one far beyond the superficial realm of physical attraction, towards this girl.

"As it has been said, nothing is certain but the unforeseen."

"I know you depart in a few day's time, but until then why don't you visit when you can?"

"That'd be grand, Miss Connolly."

Quietly they took in the encroaching evening with the warmth and intimacy of an unspoken understanding. The sundry noises of the nearby town and the miner's encampment seemed distant as the mellow light of the slinking sun sluggishly gave ground to lengthening shadows.

Glad to be free from Miranda's unabashedly pronounced

flirtation, Alvord welcomed the end of the soirée. Ever since the abrupt intrusion of that insolent Pollock figure, Jones had been increasingly distant, playing the role of host only grudgingly and speaking tersely when he spoke at all. And since Jones was the only one present aside from his own group whom Alvord actually liked, there was little enjoyment to be derived from the remainder of the affair. He found himself relieved when Finnbar rejoined the party with Genevieve at his side. Seemingly lost in thought, the Irishman approached Alvord and the two trappers, who sat apart from the main knot of dinner guests in a spacious parlor.

"Finnbar," Alvord greeted him enthusiastically, "ready to make good our departure? Conversation is far past its best."

Giving Cerberus, who maintained a vigil right next to Alvord, a few absentminded pats on the head, Finnbar nodded. "Alright then."

David nudged him with an elbow. "Not eager t'stay and chat with the ever-charming Miss Connolly?"

"We've chatted aplenty this evening; if you lads are of a mind to leave, we can go."

"I personally expected more of a struggle." Alvord could not resist. "Is the girl not hopelessly beguiled by your charm?"

"Let's just say that we got along famously and that this blessed son of Erin has an open invitation to this house; a privilege that I intend to take full advantage of in the days before our embarkation."

Marcel gave him a friendly thump on the back that nearly put him on his knees. "There's my Irishman! Sounds like a successful evenin' was had- yer off to a fine start, boy. Good fer you."

"You men about to be off?" It was Major Raines, flanked by Miranda and the woman whom Alvord took to be his wife.

"That we are. Nice meeting you Major, and I hope your colonization efforts on St. Joseph Island bear much fruit."

"Ah, many thanks, many thanks. But before you leave, I thought I would extend an invitation to you, Mr. Rawn, to join us a bit later in the evening. My wife would very much like to spend more time in your company."

At this Alvord frowned deeply. He had endured plenty of Mirand's simpering but had exchanged scarcely a word with the man's wife...

"Do you not mean your daughter?" he asked, indicating Miranda with a curt jerk of his head.

Raines shook his head in a lordly fashion. "I do not think you understand. Both Miranda and her sister here are married to me."

There followed a long-drawn silence as Alvord, completely thunderstruck, could find no words.

"That is profoundly disturbing," he declared in a voice shaking with anger and revulsion when finally he recovered his tongue.

"This is the frontier, man," the paunchy Raines quite unnecessarily reminded him in his Welsh accent. "Prudence takes on a different meaning in these parts. Things are done differently out-"

In a flash Alvord moved in and grabbed the man's pudgy hand as if he were shaking it. But anyone who could see Raines's fleshy face could easily decipher the agony thereon. Alvord applied more power yet, both feeling and hearing the damage being wrought. The Major gasped in a sharp intake of breath, unable to speak, and held onto his attacker's shoulder in an effort to stay on his feet. Alvord released his grip and in the next instant the man sank into a nearby chair, staring in stunned fashion at his throbbing hand.

Alvord leaned in and whispered sardonically into his ear. "Breathe not a word of this to our host, or next time I crush it for good and all. After all, this *is* the frontier, man."

He then led the way towards their host, spitting bitterly at Miranda's feet as he swept past she and her shocked sister.

I cannot vanish into the woods quickly enough... whether to my spirit's gain or loss I know not, but how I need to vanish...

Boots thudding loudly he approached Jones, who was surrounded by a knot of conversing guests but seemed distant indeed, gaze having drifted to a nearby window.

"Mr. Jones," Alvord spoke for the group, "we thank you for your singular generosity this eventide. I have heard men say much about Southern hospitality; obviously they have never ventured into the Old Northwest."

Jones rose and distractedly shook each of their hands, trying to appear pleasant but obviously preoccupied.

"It was nice to count you gentlemen among my guests tonight. Should you be in the area in the future, don't hesitate to stop by so we can arrange another dinner."

Finnbar heard his words but paid them little mind, for Genevieve, who was being conversationally assaulted by Duddersfield, had caught his gaze and he was blind as well as nearly deaf to all else around him.

Peering around the prattling young scientist's shoulder, she silently mouthed, *Help me!*

Chuckling quietly, he gave her a cool jerk of the head and

mouthed, *See you soon.*

Looking out the window again, Jones's blocky face took on a waxen immobility. "Gentlemen, my conscience compels me to speak... please reconsider your trapping grounds, if the Pictured Rocks area they truly be."

Marcel and David traded a swift glance.

Alvord's forehead creased slightly. "Whatever do you mean?"

"The Pictured Rocks are considered cursed ground by the Indians of this region. Sacred, it is true, but also haunted by the unpredictable gods that render it so."

"Never set much store in heathen superstition," Marcel grunted disinterestedly.

Jones eerie amber eyes regarded him almost tragically. "And as for the other strange rumors shrouding that and adjacent regions... I urge you to press not. Indian's fight shy of such places with good reason. I can't say with any certainty, but I get the distinct feeling that if a man were to delve too deeply into such mysteries, the attendant storm would sweep him off his feet and it'd be an awful long way to fall."

Marcel coolly returned his loaded stare, cigar idly smoking in the pinched corner of his mouth. "Do believe we'll be takin' our chances, but thanks."

"Well then, *bonne chance*," their host offered, with all the sincerity of a snake.

Chapter 25

From the world over they came to partake in America's first mining boom. Flocking by the thousands to Sault Ste. Marie, the gateway to Copper Country, they gathered in restive anticipation of transport to the famed Keweenaw Peninsula. To Copper Harbor, Eagle River, Eagle Harbor, and Ontonagon they would go, seeking the metal they were sure would make them rich men. Early on, the schooner *Algonquin* had enjoyed a monopoly on the large-scale transportation of miners to and from the Peninsula, but by now intense competition was to be had. Not too long into the game the *Ocean* and *Merchant* were put on rollers and hauled around the impassable rapids at the Soo, both being larger than the modestly sized *Algonquin.* But all three paled in comparison to more recent arrivals, like the 92-foot schooner *Napoleon,* converted into a steam propeller earlier this year, or the 280-ton steamer *Independence,* which held the distinguished title of first steamer to befoul the skies above the greatest of North America's inland seas.

But with their impressive cargo space, such crafts were also understandably hired out to transport mined copper back to the Soo. So those who sought cheaper and more immediate means of transportation could hire out parties of voyageurs to paddle them west via canoe or Mackinaw boat. Though confessedly slower than schooners or steamers, they could make upwards to sixty miles a day by canoe and, wind providing, a bit more by the small, two-sailed Mackinaw boats. Plenty of zealous men preferred this rapid course of action to idly waiting for room to open up aboard a larger boat.

Comically enough, the majority of this human surge could boast of no previous mining experience at all. Eastern storekeepers, soft-palmed clerks, hardy pioneers, lawyers and even ex-preachers could be counted among the ranks of the mining neophytes. Others, lured by the promise of riches, had rashly abandoned the lead mines in southwestern Wisconsin Territory in the hopes of striking it rich. And of the precious few among this ill-assorted horde who did harbor extensive mining wisdom and experience, most hailed from locations as far-flung as the diamond mines of Kimberly and the famed but dwindling copper and tin *bals* of Cornwall.

What had begun in 1771 with the abortive Carver-Henry Expedition, the first organized venture in the Copper Country, had finally developed into a mining bonanza the likes of which the United States had before never seen. The voluminous writings of geologist Douglas Houghton, who in the early 1840's documented his journeys along Superior's southern coast, sparked the copper fever that now drove men to pockmark the copper-bearing strata of the Keweenaw. Gold and silver would have been preferable to copper in the wishful minds of most miners, yet neither had been discovered in this country in any significant quantity. So if this new El Dorado happened to take the form of massive copper deposits they would take it, a bird in the hand being worth two in the bush.

It was Americans and Canadians who comprised the majority of the men both here and over on the Peninsula, but the number of European immigrants did not trail far behind. A smattering of non-whites was also present in the form of Indians, half-breeds, and even the odd Sandwich Islander. But it was the veteran miners hailing from Great Britain who drew the most praise and attention.

For the Cornish and Welshmen brought with them a vaunted tradition of mining knowledge and experience that dated back to the early Bronze Age. Their seemingly inborn understanding of the art was at a premium among prospectors and company owners, especially when paired, as often it was, with indefatigable work ethic and loyalty.

It also did not hurt that they would often accept woefully meager pay in comparison to the skill they brought to the table.

White or otherwise, skilled or greenhorn, only some among these miners realized that ancient diggings had unearthed copper long before their arrival in this roaring wilderness. And certainly none of them had any way of knowing that in total over 500 million pounds of the coveted metal had been extracted in olden times. So too were they ignorant of the fact that Lake Superior copper, the purest ever discovered and uniquely containing flecks of silver, could be found anywhere from the anomalous mounds and earthworks of Ohio to as far off as Guanaja Island in the Caribbean, on which Columbus had made landfall back in 1502.

The knowledge that they were entering upon a history as old, rich, and complex as that of the Copper Country would have meant little to these men even if they had grasped the true depth of it. For on the whole they were an impatient, ambitious lot whose myopic present-mindedness cared not a whit for much beyond the work to be done and money to be made in the here and now. Those that knew of the old mines sought only to use them as markers; these ancient pits were uncannily accurate in their pinpointing of copper deposits. The men who followed in the footsteps of those long-ago diggers took careful note of this. Many began seeing old mines in every moose-wallow and vernal pool.

Nearly as impressionable as they were determined, the more tender-footed among them fell victim to outwardly encouraging but often quite meaningless talk of ores, veins, and oxides, which they lent ear to in the rapt awe of the ignorant.

Yet even the Cornish, hardened copper miners though they might be, were admittedly bowled over by the size of the solid masses of pure, untainted copper they encountered. Until the discovery of Michigan copper, the Western world had always associated copper with other elements, necessitating the process of smelting, refining, and purifying in order to extract pure copper from its adulterants. But Lake copper was in fact so pure that a chunk of it could be drawn into wire without any smelting or refining. Even seasoned geologists who journeyed to the region were inclined to scratch their heads in bafflement.

Had foresight been a more common attribute among the workers, some might have perceived the telltale signs that this boom was already petering out. In the two years since the copper craze first seized the minds of men, over one hundred mining companies had taken form, a goodly number of which had already flopped with plenty of others poised to walk the same financial plank. The steepening cost of shipping ore to smelters down in Lower Michigan and Ohio, in combination with the cost of transporting ore to portage the Soo, was simply too much for many companies. Likewise were most prospectors beginning to give up, instead opting to work for the best-established and most lucrative mining companies like the Quincy, the Pittsburgh & Boston, or the Lake Superior Mining Company. In fact, the spring and summer of 1847 drew comparatively fewer men than years past, and more than half of those present came to work in the fissure mines of the companies that had weathered the buffeting storm of wild economic speculation, marginal initial returns, and panicky company stockholders.

For all intents and purposes, the copper rush was already past its zenith, having given way to localized commercialized interests; a single man stood little chance to strike it rich through prospecting. But who, after daring to entertain so lofty a dream, was willing to swallow so unpalatable a truth as that?

And so they would assail the marrow of the earth by dint of

chisel and sledge and blasting powder, stubbornly hoping to hit pay dirt. They would brave the cedar and tamarack swamps that one Florida prospector compared to the primordial fastness of the Everglades. And most would find at least a small amount of copper. But above all else they would find the ubiquitous presence of insects: the ticks and black flies and moose flies and, worst devils of all, the dizzying hordes of "Keweenaw Eagles," as the resident mosquitoes had been dubbed. Optimism firmly moored to the fact that as of 1847, Michigan was the only place on earth where pure, native copper existed in commercial quantities, these dauntless souls worked like men possessed.

And, given the time and money, they caroused in a manner that would have shamed the Devil's legions.

"Looks like a rollicking good time in these parts!" remarked Finnbar, head swiveling about like that of a child in a sweet shop.

He and the others were skirting the sprawling miner's encampment, where drink-inspired merriment and recreation made for a rather lively scene. Having come back east to the Soo from the Copper Country for supplies or simply amusement, these mining men made merry with an ardor that few could match.

Large bonfires were being set, as soon enough the sun would take its leave of this part of the world, and around them men drank, gambled, bragged, swapped yarns, whored, and fought or pantomimed fights past. Wrestling and boxing matches were underway, with massive rings of hoarsely shouting men indicating where the bouts took place.

The encampment lay roughly three quarters of a mile east (and downstream) of town, and Alvord was willing to bet that whatever form of law might exist in the Soo, it was inclined to give this place a wide berth. Although he had faced some dire situations as a patrolman in America's most corrupt and crime-ridden city, and beyond that in the city's bloodiest Ward (aptly nicknamed "The Bloody Sixth"), he would also freely admit that some situations were better left untended if no real harm was being done. This seemed to be one of them. And a good thing, too, for it would have been an awful lot of roistering to quell.

As if giving voice to his thoughts, Marcel observed with appreciation, "Yep, this has gotta be the most hellraisingest spot I did ever behold! Exceptin', of course, the Rocky Mountain Rendezvous. Wish you fellas coulda seen *that*. Dave, I tell you they made the Company potlatches of old look tame."

"I doubt ye nary a bit, auld friend. So Finnbar, that Genevieve seems to be a fetching gal."

"Aye brither," responded Finnbar in his best Scottish brogue, "she's a bonny lass and no mistake."

David threw back his grizzled head to unleash a merry chortle.

"She's not white, you know." Interest wormed its way into Alvord's comment, though quite uninvited. But he was in fact a bit curious as to how Finnbar felt about her mixed pedigree.

"Bah."

"You know I'm right."

"Come now, big fella," David admonished him mildly, "'tis a wee baltic of ye to say."

"David here is right, Alvord. That *is* a bit cold."

"What it is, my lovelorn Irish friend, is a bit honest. I seek not to her besmirch her character or make her out to be anything less than she is- she seems a good sort."

"Well you are right, I suppose. She is half Irish, one-quarter Chippewa, and a quarter Normandy French, which is essentially Celtic when you think about it. I am not overly bothered by her mixed blood, if that's what you're getting at."

"Chippewa are the handsomest Injuns if ye ask me," David averred. "Though I meself harbor no attraction to their womenfolk."

"Mmm," contended Marcel, "I'd say the Nez Perce are up there too. And fer the record, I *do* harbor attraction towards their womenfolk."

Chuckling, they kept walking east, following the course of the river. Upon encountering a putrefying quagmire over which a corduroy road of logs had been thrown, they quickened their pace. For the droning swarm of bloodsucking insects that engulfed them was unlike anything that Alvord had experienced. Mosquitoes blanketed their bodies and attacked whatever exposed flesh might be available.

Marcel, calmly puffing on a cigar, seemed to be the only one who was unmolested. David promptly lit one up as well, though Alvord had not seen him smoke up until this point. After breathing smoke over his limbs and torso, the Scot handed the noxious cheroot to him. Puffing inexpertly on it, Alvord blew smoke over his body and allowed a haze to envelop him. The bugs thinned out, with only persistent few launching occasional sorties. Finnbar hurriedly did the same with Marcel's cigar, and before long they were harried no more.

"So is that where we are heading to now? The Indian fishing village we paddled by earlier?" Alvord was suddenly conscious of the fact that he had been blithely following Marcel and David, not having bothered to ask what their destination was. Having been a leader of men for years, he realized that he naturally took command of most situations. But among Finnbar and Marcel, and now David, men he trusted without question, he did not feel the need. How nice it was to take a secondary role once in a while, not always leading but rather following at times, free to let your mind wander a bit because you don't have to be transcendentally concerned with the plan at hand or the actions of others. This he could get used to. In fact, his mind was uncharacteristically at ease, and so liberated it took note of just how pleasant this evening was; the languid warmth and the freshly blowing breeze that at times cut through it, the steadily brightening and multiplying stars rallied in the heavens above, the croaks of frogs, the chirps of innumerable crickets...

An instant later Cerberus gave a mighty tug on the leather leash that Jones had given him, providing Alvord with a jolt back into reality.

"*Heel*, beast." He gave the leash a sharp tug and brought the hulking pup back to his side. The dog whined a bit, but stayed at his side. Alvord noticed that the dog looked up at him at regular intervals, as if seeking approval.

Kneeling for a moment next to his new pet, Alvord scratched the animal's head affectionately. "Good dog. Good Cerberus."

He even fancied the hound's name: Cerberus, the multi-headed hellhound that served as a watchdog in Hades, employed to keep the souls of the dead from crossing back over the River Styx. He would grow to be a mighty dog, for even as a pup his sizeable frame was impressively fleshed out with muscle. He was tall too; already his head hovered around Alvord's hip and he was not a small man. Mercifully, the dog seemed to harbor no attachment towards Jones or the man's house, instead appearing to be happy as a lark as they walked into the darkening evening. His nose led him astray a bit, but after a while a few jerks of the leash were enough to keep him in check.

"Aha!" exclaimed a voice, shrill with excitement, from not far behind them. "How good to bump into you yet again! Off to the Chippewa camp, are you?"

They turned as one to verify what their ears warned their disbelieving brains about. Their suspicions were confirmed- it was the inimitable Duddersfield.

"I say, I left Jones's house after you lot did, yet here I am. You don't walk with a very brisk stride, now do you? Sort of maundering along, eh?"

Hand gripping his knife handle, Marcel turned to his group. "I could give 'im the dag right now, toss his carcass in the river, and I doubt the world would give half a damn."

These words he delivered half-jokingly... possibly?

Duddersfield heedlessly fell in with them. Clear-lens glasses had replaced his purple ones, revealing beady pig-like eyes that never ceased darting about.

"Ah!" he exclaimed exasperatedly, swatting at the harrying bugs around him. "These dratted flying pests! Still, I'm glad I quit that house when I did- that Pollock character began lurking about and I get the distinct impression that he's cast in a rather loutish mold."

Marcel gave a mirthless snort. "Well, you got him pegged right, son. Feller's no-account."

"How do you know the man, Marcel?"

The trapper scratched his dense beard thoughtfully as he replied to Alvord's question. "Me'n Dave worked with him back in our Hudson Bay days, and later when we trapped for Astor's American Fur Company."

"Aye," David reminisced with a scowl, "always a sly weasel of a man, much given t'lofty boasts and slights against others. An' always protected by powerful allies. What we used to call a flash in the pan- one who'll make a grand auld brag but is rarely around to back it up. Mind, he's fair deadly with a knife or tomahawk when it comes down to it, though."

"Yep, and s'got a bit more swagger in 'is step these days. Wonder what use Jones has of 'im?"

A contemplative silence followed his words, but was broken by Duddersfield after a bit.

"I could not help but overhear Pollock mention that Chapel Beach was your destination. Or at least he thought it to be so. Were you simply trying to mislead him, or do you in fact have another location in mind?"

"Naw, he was dead on. Just didn't want the bastard knowin' our business, is all."

"Spiffing! Since I intend to conduct a geological survey in that very vicinity, might I travel alongside you? Rest assured, I will pull my weight in camp, and will pilot my own canoe so that when I have concluded my survey I can transport myself back to the Soo. Plus, as I have other destinations in mind, I would only be with you for a short spell. I think you will find that my camping skills are quite protean and-"

"No."

The young scientist's face fell at Marcel's bluntly delivered rejection.

Finnbar, seeing his undisguised dejection, took Marcel aside.

"You won't even entertain the notion, trapper me friend?"

"I ain't playin' nursemaid to that human disaster."

"C'mon, lad. He'd certainly add some flavor to the crew. 'Twould be fun to have the oaf along."

The mountain man stared at him as if he were a madman.

"Just give it some thought. He's harmless."

Marcel merely grunted, taking a pull off his cigar.

"So what business do you have now among the Saulteurs, boy?" Alvord wondered how he would fare in the midst of red men.

"Ethnographic interests," replied Duddersfield vaguely.

The subdued, rhythmic throbbing of drums, the stamp of many feet, and sound of ululating cries met their ears presently- they were nearing the Indian encampment.

"Twill be nice to see your boyo again, eh?" David said to Marcel.

Looking at Alvord, Finnbar frowned confusedly. "You've a son, Marcel?

"Oh yeah," he grunted lightly, "musta forgot to mention..."

Ten minutes later Alvord felt as if he was strolling through a scene out of a James Fennimore Cooper story. Having, like many Americans, read about Indians and judged them according to that literature, Alvord's guard was understandably up as he entered upon a world unlike any he had encountered before. The underbelly of Manhattan certainly offered a body sundry glimpses into alien environments, but this? He realized with a start that red men outnumbered white in this location by a considerable margin... for the first time in his life his own race did not predominate in a situation.

It was more than a little shocking upon initial comprehension.

An acculturated remnant of Manhattan's Delaware Indian population still dwelled in parts of Brooklyn, the Bronx, and Staten Island, but were a far cry from these tomahawk-toting red men. They lived and dressed as whites for the most part, having been swept up by the inescapable tide of European-American culture.

Thieves, his mind cautioned him, recalling his readings on this matter. *Savages and heathens to boot. Besotted brutes whose logic could never be understood by white minds. Proceed with caution, Rawn.*

Eyes darting around suspiciously, he followed Marcel and David as they led the way through the camp. His eyes passed over their weapons, be they knives, tomahawks, or flintlocks. Quite a few Indians and some half-breeds passed by them, some looking them over curiously and others not bothering to spare them even a cursory glance. He did not detect much in the way of hostility lurking hereabouts. Perhaps a touch of pride or arrogance here or there, but he supposed some might be inclined to say the same of him.

Although he had read that Plains Indians could attain impressive heights, he had not been expecting these woodland Chippewa to be quite so tall. One of the men they encountered stood almost his equal in height, and on average they seemed to be a bit taller than whites.

The Indian village roiled with activity, matching in intensity the noisiness of the miner's camp. But the setting here was one not of unruliness but rather controlled chaos. It seemed that a feast of sorts was underway, with the trussed up carcasses of bear, deer, turkey, and smaller game being toted around. Though still quite full from dinner, a rush of saliva flooded Alvord's mouth upon detecting the savory aroma of roasting meat. They had passed into a considerable open area around which a circle of large, rectangular lodges was arrayed.

Dancing around a number of brightly blazing fires, Indian men and women stomped and whirled to the beat of many drums. The Indian band sat off to the side, pounding drums and shaking rattles crafted out of turtle shells. Others blew into wooden flutes and a few clasped tambourine-type instruments.

A cluster of young bucks stood proudly in the center of the gathering, wearing the pelts of various animals. The rest of the dancers cavorted around them, their movements a perfect visual accompaniment to the song being played.

Marcel stopped and, thick arms folded and face expressionless, watched and listened intently.

"Damn," he said, not directing the wistful words at anyone specifically, "wish I could play me an instrument."

Alvord took a moment to peer around him. Some white men, trappers and miners by the looks of them, were going in and out of a few smallish wigwam. The flushed, panting faces and disheveled clothing of those departing indicated to Alvord the unchaste nature of the amusements that were to be had inside.

A bare-chested Indian maiden threw aside the deer hide covering the entrance of one such wigwam and approached him, staring with bland inquiry. He noticed that she wore a burnished copper ring through her right nostril. She smiled, making sure that his eyes were upon her tattooed face before grabbing the sleeve of his coat. She gave it a gentle tug, as if suggesting that he follow her. When that occasioned his pulling the arm away, she chose another approach, head cocked to the side. To his revulsion she pointed to her nether regions before smiling at him again. He had been propositioned plenty by whores in his day but never quite so bluntly.

"She'll take coin r'booze," Marcel explained. "Not that it matters- I know you better'n that, friend. Yeah, some'll still debauch themselves like so, but it ain't near as bad as it was back in the days when they were in wholesale cahoots with the fur companies. Few bucks wanna see their wives used to that end anymore, but some still demand it of 'em fer extra money an' fire water. 'Course, sometimes they get so drunk they bite off the squaws' nose outta disgust or spite for what they've done."

"To love, to honor, and to cherish, eh?"

Alvord noticed Duddersfield silently gawking at the girl, who was admittedly enticing in face and form. She adroitly shifted her gaze from Alvord to the young, spellbound geologist.

"We're headin' over yonder- you comin' boy, or stayin' put?"

Duddersfield was a bit slow in replying to Marcel. "Oh, I ah... I will certainly come along! What reason might I have to stay, after all?"

"That lass's embrace comes rather readily to mind," Finnbar chimed in helpfully.

"Curious, isn't it, how some things are cultural universals?" Duddersfield tore his gaze away from the maiden, who was now cupping her small, shapely breasts together quite unabashedly. The red-faced lad turned to follow them, and Alvord fancied that he could almost see the smitten boy drool.

"Let us procure some libations, shall we gents? I'm parched," the odd fellow suggested.

"Aye, I too could go fer a wee swallae o' summat."

"Ha ha!" Finnbar roared at Duddersfield and David's words. "A sound proposition. We'll make Irishmen out of you boys yet!"

They moved on, slowly working their way through the crowds. Alvord noticed Finnbar scribbling away in his small leather notebook even as he walked through the village, dim lighting apparently offering no obstacle to him. Alvord followed his interested gaze; he seemed to be sketching and taking notes on the Chippewa wigwams. He too took a more careful look. Small saplings providing the interior and exterior framework in between which massive strips of bark were secured. Deer hides covered the doorways, which when swept aside revealed bulrush mats covering the floor as well as bear, deer, and wolf skin rugs.

They passed into a quieter section of the feast, where a large number of Indians sat watching the proceedings with a visible solemnity. These Indians stood in stark contrast to the others, with white man's clothing being the norm among them and wooden crosses hanging from the necks of many. Behind them rows of wooden cabins reared up out of the darkness.

Speaking rapid French, Marcel conversed with a distinguished-looking Indian in a white beaver top hat. "Looks like my boy is down by the river spearin' sturgeon by torchlight. Should be back in a bit. Al, we've been invited to go have a smoke in a nearby cabin? Yer invited, o' course, but I knows how ye hate smoky rooms and it might be a bit cramped in there..."

He knew from the trapper's tone that Marcel was in fact testing him, interested in seeing if he could retain his composure when surrounded by Indians without the assurance of their group at his side. Additionally, David had evinced no signs of being a hardened smoker, yet was going with them. Alvord did not mind- at least the Indians in his immediate vicinity seemed quiet and Christianized.

"I can wait here for the fishing party to return." He noticed that a well-worn path led down towards the river from their location. "Does your son speak English?"

Marcel had still offered no real information pertaining to his son, and Alvord and even Finnbar knew better than to press the reserved mountain man for details.

"Sure does. Arguably better'n me."

"Then there shan't be a problem. Do enjoy yourselves."

Marcel gave him an approving nod. "Much obliged, *mon ami.* See ya in a bit."

And with that Alvord was alone, excepting the company of Cerberus and nearly one hundred Indians bedecked in white man's clothing. He stood a bit uncertainly among them, attracting a few stares.

"I can appreciate your unease," said foghorn male voice with a French accent.

An older fellow dressed in a long, black robe sat on a log nearby. Sagging, fleshy bags under his eyes gave him a tired appearance, but a careful observer would have discerned the fierce glint of determination in those deep-set eyes.

"Forgive me, but if I am not mistaken this is your first time around red men? At least in so great a number?"

"No forgiveness required, Father. You are quite right."

He recognized the man's attire; the baggy black robe, silver crucifix, and white collar indicated to him that the man was a Jesuit Priest. Several times in New York Alvord had seen this brand of Papist priest, though they had been Irish rather than French.

"Your skills of observation serve you well. I am Father Bazin of the Society of Jesus- a Jesuit."

With a slightly flourishing sweep of the wrinkled hand Bazin bid him to take a seat. His at-ease manner seemed almost an insult to the frenzied activity around him, sitting as he was with his hands folded and toad-like face without expression.

After a moment's hesitation Alvord accepted the invitation, plopping down on the massive log next to the Jesuit. Cerberus lay rigidly next to him, casting a beady eye over the whirl of activity before them.

Alvord's natural Protestant distrust of Catholics had been tempered over the years by his working alongside them. Some of the finest men he commanded, in terms of both police work and moral integrity, had been Irishmen and Germans of the Catholic faith. In his youth he would never have considered sharing a conversation with a Catholic priest, but thirty-six years' life experience occasioned the softening of many such stances. The realization dawned on him that, despite having dealt with some Catholic priests in Manhattan, he had never really spoken with one at any length.

The Jesuit remained silent for a few moments, staring at the dance that now intensified in its speed and volume.

"A band of young braves undertook their first unguided hunt today. Having killed many animals, their success is the cause of this celebration. They call it the *Oshki-nitaagewin*, and it is an important rite of passage." His explanation, though not prompted, was nevertheless appreciated.

"Well I suppose that does warrant a *fête champêtre*."

Bazin laughed appreciatively at the use of the French term, the deeply creased flesh of his face jiggling a tad grotesquely.

"How many souls are gathered here? Well over a thousand, no?"

"Indeed. And many more shall soon arrive to receive their yearly payment from the government."

Alvord watched the nimble dancers and felt the priest's eyes on him.

"What brings you to the Soo?" The man's English, though accented, was still quite understandable. Which was a step up from many Frenchmen Alvord had met.

"A trapping expedition."

In one quick, sweeping glance, the priest's clever eyes sized him up. "You are new to that life, my son. Do you seek a fresh start?"

The man's incisiveness took him by surprise, though he did not let it show. "Merely a change, and the tranquility that only the wilderness can afford me."

"I bid you good luck, but must offer this- the wilderness has more perilous things to offer than change."

They lapsed into quiet again, Alvord stroking Cerberus's chest, upon which was emblazoned a white patch of hair in the shape of a diamond.

He looked over the assemblage, from the dancing red men and women to the sober Indians sitting nearby. "They are all Chippewa? Or do they call themselves Ojibwa or something similar?"

"*They* call themselves the Anishinabe, actually, meaning 'the first' or 'original people.' I am told that most Indian tribes grace themselves with a similar title. And you are right, for it is mostly Chippewa here with some Ottawa as well."

"What of these around us, dressed in modern garb?"

Bazin smiled as he looked upon them with the fondness of a father gazing upon his child. "They are the flock to which I tend, the more firmly Christianized members of the Saulteur Chippewa tribe."

Alvord considered them more carefully as they watched the goings on. None joined in the singing or seemed to be stirred in the least by the impassioned celebration.

"A tribe divided, I see."

"I seek to do what my bygone brothers and the Recollets before them sought to accomplish. I am bringing them out of the darkness of polluted ideology and into the light of truth. By slow degrees my congregation grows, both here and in the villages on the Canadian side of the falls."

"The Christianizing of the heathen, then? A mammoth undertaking."

"Indeed, but not one without its due rewards. Some of these men and women before you demonstrate piety the likes of which would shame many whites." Again he looked with fondness and pride over the Christian Indians. Then a brave, reeling under the weight of his intoxication, stumbled on by and a certain darkness passed over the priest's features.

"My order was despised in heyday of the fur trade. Wholesale dependency on the fur trade wrought catastrophic changes in both their culture and lifestyle. Indeed, the Saulteur Chippewa had a particularly nasty reputation for savagery when put to drink."

"Worldly sorrow, as St. Paul would label it?"

"*Precisely*. They rejected the Almighty in favor of a whole pantheon of more worldly gods. Drink, guns, furs... such are the idols to which they so blithely bow."

"*You adulterous people.*" Alvord quoted from the Epistle of James. "*Do you not know that friendship with the world is enmity with God? Therefore whoever wishes to be a friend of the world makes himself an enemy of God.*"

"What is your name?"

"Alvord Rawn."

"One to remember, I think." He reached behind him and produced a bottle of rum, which he offered to Alvord. Noting his hesitation, the Jesuit smiled.

"A small dram never hurt a white man. And it is good Caribbean rum, none of that New England swill."

They drank in sociable silence for a bit.

"You ever venture into the Pictured Rocks, father?"

The priest regarded him somberly. "No, never there. There exist neither roads nor trails along that section of the southern shore of the lake, and no Indians live there anyway."

"Do they really avoid it, as I have been told?"

"They often pass by the area and occasionally camp on the beaches there, but not before making careful offerings and prayers. They say supernatural guardians haunt those woods. Never do they stray far into those ancient forests."

"Ah. Indian myths."

Bazin cocked a bushy eyebrow. "Careful now, for among their myths is one claiming that Matchi Manito, the Spirit of Evil, tempted the first man and women with fruit from a forbidden tree found in the middle of a flawless, luxuriant garden. For this they were expelled from it."

Alvord frowned in curiosity. "Duly noted. So they do avoid the regions you mentioned?"

"That region and the interior areas of the Keweenaw. Before this copper madness, few men white or red would venture into those parts. In fact, in 1661 Father Rene Mesnard disappeared in the Keweenaw while searching for the Ontonagon Boulder. Indians will tell you that they are not surprised- horrible fates are said to have befallen Indians who stayed to far into that territory. Wild, disturbing tales of disappearances, dismembered bodies, even a tribe of painted cannibals. Copper for them is a revered metal and they regard it with superstitious awe. They are reluctant even to talk much about it."

"And when they do?"

The priest issued a scoffing laugh. "They say the gods from under the water bestowed it upon them as a pledge of good fortune. And one of their *manitous*, or gods, is said to live on a phantom island of solid copper out on the lake. It is curious; no matter how Christian they might seem, they will call upon this Missibizzi for aid. He is the one who would speak to them in a booming voice if they approached the ancient mines or sacred boulders, warning them to leave. I have rarely seen them so nervous as when speaking of the vengeful copper gods of the Keweenaw and Pictured Rocks area. And it is curious because no copper has been found in the latter..."

Bazin paused to look at him piercingly. "Why do you ask of this?"

"I have heard much about the area, and was just wondering." He had heard enough. None of this was very encouraging.

Changing the topic, Alvord asked, "So your inroads have borne fruit, then?"

Bazin continued speaking with relish; Alvord got the distinct impression that the old man did not get to talk to well-informed men very often. "Yes. But much work remains. The majority of them engage in but a little agriculture, content instead to chase the deer, to trap the marten and beaver, to spear fish and do battle with their enemies."

He looked up at gibbous moon with a rippling sigh. "A man reaches a certain age and begins to wonder how many more dawns he shall rise to greet, how many more full moons he will have the opportunity to bask under. And likewise how much good he has done in a world gone to Hell."

"Sometimes it seems overwhelming, does it not?"

"Better to light one candle than curse the darkness, my son."

These words Alvord regarded with meditative silence as the forms of the dancers cast jerky, flickering shadows upon his face.

Chapter 26

"Might any of you be Gaston, son of Marcel Durand?"

Alvord posed the question to a trio of men who had just come up from the direction of the river. Dressed in trappers clothing, they carried with them multi-pronged spears and a mess of freshly caught fish, with whitefish and sturgeon comprising the bulk of their harvest. A young man, spear resting jauntily over his shoulder, stepped further into the soft aura cast by the fires, his immobile face a landscape of shadow and unsteadily flickering firelight.

"Might I ask who wants to know?" requested an equanimous voice slightly laced with the accent that Alvord had come to associate with Indians.

The half-breed lad whom he assumed to be Marcel's son bore a passing resemblance to him. The piercing, close-set eyes of brown reminded Alvord of the mountain man's own canny pair, and they shared something of the same protruding brow. And his hair, to Alvord's surprise, seemed to be of a lighter shade than Marcel's. He stood a bit taller and straighter of leg, too; Marcel was a bit bandy legged.

"Alvord Rawn, a friend of his and a member of the trapping expedition he is organizing."

He saw the two other men glance at each other; he could not be sure but the look that passed between them appeared to be one of derision. Perhaps they simply did not see a trapping man before them, as had been the case with David.

"Is my father here?"

"Aye. He and the others are yonder having a smoke. So it is safe to assume that you are his son, then?"

The lad's eyes warmed and his face broke into an even-toothed smile highly reminiscent of his father. "I do bear that distinction. My name is Gaston."

"In truth, he has not spoken much on the matter, so I did not know what to expect."

"Yes, that would be my father." He stepped forward to clasp Alvord's hand in a firm shake. "Never one to waste breath on something as frivolous as conversation."

"Aptly put," Alvord chuckled easily.

The other two men came forward, both looking to be in their

late twenties or early thirties. Though of average height and lean, angular construction, the similarities between them ended there. One was a hatchet-faced white with shortly cropped blonde hair, while the other had a look of a Moor about him. He supposed the man might be an extremely dark Indian, but all of the red men he had encountered in this area were lighter of skin than this fellow. It seemed more likely that his blood was an admixture of Negro and Indian.

While Alvord stood assessing, he likewise felt cold eyes measuring him up.

"Lightfoot," the dark man offered in a scratchy voice, also shaking hands.

"Gordon," the other greeted stiffly, "pleasure to meet you."

That Alvord highly doubted. For it was with either suspicion or disapproval that these men regarded him, and whichever it might be they did little to disguise it. He was hardly dismayed by this; towards the opinions of most men he gave not a two-penny damn. In fact, suspicion he could understand and even endorse. These men did not know him, after all, and to be guarded in this specious, fallen world was a mode of deportment far preferable to blithe acceptance, the latter being the fool's approach.

"Regal looking beast," Gaston complimented Cerberus, who energetically licked his face as he knelt to pet him.

"Thank you. A recent acquisition of mine."

The boy, perhaps in his early twenties, seemed a jollier sort than his father. Not that Marcel was an unpleasant individual, but the easygoing manner of the son did contrast with the customary brusqueness of the father.

"My mother was half Chippewa, half Ottawa," Gaston freely offered, as if he could sense Alvord's curiosity as to his history. "When Marcel was younger he trapped the lands around Superior, where he met my mother. She died of smallpox not long after I was born."

Ah. Smallpox- an even greater scourge of the Indians than alcohol, though these days probably surpassed by syphilis. Alvord had been inoculated against smallpox as a youth, and he knew that Marcel had survived the disease while Finnbar claimed to be naturally immune.

"My father knew not of my birth- he left this region to trap in the Rockies shortly after I was conceived, but always I was raised hearing stories of his trapping and hunting prowess, and of his fearlessness as a warrior. When next he returned to these lands after many years' absence, I tracked him down and presented myself. He accepted me as his son then and there.

Back in those days a white man could sell or simply desert any Indian woman he married, and he did not even have that weak connection to my mother. Half Indian children were not even viewed as human by many of their white fathers, so it was refreshing to know after years of wondering that my own was a man of character."

It came as welcome knowledge that although Marcel had sired a bastard child, he had not regarded it with the cold indifference that other voyageurs seemed prone to.

"How old is your father?" Now that he thought about it, Marcel had never mentioned. One could discern that the dew of youth had long been shaken from his form, but with his hair showing no gray and a face like weathered leather, the man's age had been indeterminate until now.

"I don't know his exact age, but early to mid-forties is probably accurate."

They came to the cluster of wigwams where the others had gone to smoke. The hide door of one was swept aside and out came Marcel and the rest. Finnbar was putting his leather notebook back in his coat pocket while David bit off a monstrous chaw of plug tobacco.

Marcel's face, though hardly alight with vibrancy, still showed signs of happiness as he warmly embraced his son.

"Good t'see ye again, my son."

"And you, father."

A figure burst out of a nearby wigwam, inelegantly intruding upon this scene of reunion. Breathing raggedly, with his glasses askew and shirt disheveled, was Humphrey Demetrius Duddersfield. Lurching unsteadily, he headed towards a placidly flowing stream and plunged his head into it.

A bare-chested maiden came out of the wigwam to stare at him, with that curious absence of any discernible emotion that Alvord had seen in the faces of other Indians. Then, apparently bored with the situation, she went back inside and put the deerskin flap back over the entrance.

The hapless Duddersfield staggered to his feet, sweeping the sopping hair back on his head. Adjusting his glasses, he suddenly caught sight of their group, all of whom were openly staring at him. Still panting, he gasped in a half-stifled expression of shock and discomfiture.

Alvord shook his head stonily.

What a blundering oaf.

Quite unexpectedly, Marcel slapped his knees and doubled over laughing. He put one hand on a guffawing Finnbar to steady himself.

The Irishman too was also besides himself with laughter, but managed to choke out, "*Eth*, ha ha! *Ethnographic interests*! Ye've gotta be shittin' me!"

"Haw haw! Damn my tallow and hide! We'll make a man of you yet, eh Dudd?" Marcel thumped him soundly on the back. "Mayhap you'll be traveling with us after all!"

"First time away from home, son?" Alvord inquired drily.

The mining camp seemed, if anything, to have grown in rowdiness. Drunken pursuits were the order of the evening, be it boastful storytelling, fighting, or gambling. As regards the gambling component, a gang of miners was busily beating the piss out of two cardsharps who had swindled them out of their hard-won cash and then attempted to pull pistols when called out.

Gaston, Lightfoot, Gordon, and Marcel had talked at length about necessary equipment for their expedition, various trapping locations, and their impending departure. Talk concluded, Marcel, Alvord and the others made their way back towards town, pausing to watch a spirited wrestling match.

The men, and Irishman and a Cornishman, savagely wrangled with one another, demonstrating ample skill in a series of throws, locks, and trips. But at one point the Irishman grabbed a hold of the other man's jacket collar and arm and, spinning in a blur, sought to spike him. The Cornishman cleverly reversed it, and as he went down his Irish opponent flung out an arm to break the fall. A shriek of pain followed hard on the heels of the sharp cracking of bone. The Cornish spectators roared in triumph, the Irish in consternation. The Celtic passions of both sides were aroused, fired by gladiatorial ardor and forty-rod, a rotgut whiskey touted to be potent enough to knock over a greenhorn at forty rods. Fights ensued, most sloppy and quickly broken up.

Alvord watched the Cornish congratulate their champion on his victory. He had a bit of Cornish blood himself.

"A fine showing," he remarked to Finnbar. "A pity for your countryman, though."

"Aye 'tis, aye 'tis. And to a thievin' Cousin Jack, no less. Begging your pardon of course, mate."

"Of course." The Cornish had acquired the nickname of "Cousin Jacks" here in the states. Some speculated that it originated with Cornish immigrants frequently inquiring about work for their cousin Jack back home. Others pointed to the fact that the Cornish often greeted each other with the term "cousin," and Jack was the most common male name in

Cornwall.

The ring of men suddenly opened up to admit a mountainous figure. He stood but a little taller than average, yet was wider and more thickly set than any man Alvord had ever laid eyes on. The fellow must have been around three hundred pounds, possibly more, but not one you'd call fat. He seemed more beast than man, with a massive, ape-like face that called to mind crude caricatures rather than an actual human visage. There was something oddly atavistic about that miner, as if he belonged to a remoter age when men were altogether more primitive beings.

Spreading wide his lengthy, bulging arms, he threw back his square head and roared in a voice like a rockslide, "I am the best!"

"That there is Jemmy Tresize," a nearby miner informed them. "He's a Cornishman."

"Look at the size of him- his shadow weighs two hundred pounds! He looks a nasty brute, too," Finnbar observed.

"Aye, that he is," the miner assured them. "He does the work of ten men, drinks enough to lay low an elephant, and fights men by the group. He comes here to drink now when he has the time, for back at Eagle Harbor they won't sell him booze. Even though he only drinks on Sundays."

"Today is Tuesday," commented Alvord.

The man continued. "The cell at Eagle Harbor is too small for him, so they once chained him to a two hundred pound iron ball. When they went to check on him, he was gone, having picked the ball up and walked back to the bar with it!"

"I am the best! The *best*! Who among you dogs shall try me? I'll thrash any three of you!"

Alvord snorted and shook his head in disgust as the man made his brag. "Let us take leave of this place, shall we? I don't know about you fellows, but I am averse to the braying of braggarts."

"*Any four*!" roared Jemmy, pounding a ham-like fist against his barrel chest.

They made to leave.

"Hey! *Hey*, you there! Big fella! Fancy a match?" Jemmy mockingly enjoined Alvord.

He felt expectant eyes turn his way. "As it so happens, I do not."

As a rule he never fought for sport and certainly never for adulation- both came into play in this instance. It was not fear that drove him now but rather self-mastery. This was not a sort of man he much liked, the arrogant, the boastful. A sort he despised and would not lend much thought to.

"A pity, that is. Not fer your health, so much, but still..." The Cornishmen around him let loose with perfectly timed barks of loyalty laughter.

Alvord jerked his head to indicate that Finnbar, Marcel, and David should leave with him.

"Some never do grow up, do they?" he lamented loudly.

Jemmy chortled chestily. "Aye, just as some always recognize a bad deal when they see one. Have a good night, my cowardly friend."

At that Alvord turned on his heel without hesitation, slipping off his jacket and handing Cerberus's leash to Finnbar to the bellowed approval of the crowd.

In a low crouch, the colossus bared his stained teeth in a satisfied leer and reached out as if to shake hands.

"Fine stance you've got there," he remarked to his oncoming opponent.

"We're not wrestling," Alvord bluntly informed him, and without ceremony gave him a swift boot to the teeth.

Spoiling for a fight, was Jemmy? Well now he had one. He was going to hand this truculent brute a thrashing he wouldn't soon forget.

He then laid into the Goliath before him with a flurry of punches for which he had no answer. His last, a bone-rattling right uppercut that sent the man reeling backwards, should have put him down. But Jemmy's skull, which might well have been twice the size of his own, seemed impervious to the cracking blows being rained upon it.

The man stepped back with surprising swiftness, shaking his head clear and wiping the blood from the nasty cut under his left eye.

"Ye use yer maulies to great effect," Jemmy noted with a nod. Then he came in like a juggernaut, swinging punches of his own.

"Bash 'is brains in, Jemmy!"

"Watch 'is left, Jemmy!"

Ah yes, of course. The advice-dispensers, lively spectators of others men's deeds who would not dare to dream of standing against either combatant. Cowardly types who would run their mouths and do little else. He noted with approval that his own group stood tensed and watchful, but silent.

The rank staleness of Jemmy's beer-fouled breath washed over him as he sought to block or avoid the oncoming barrage of punches. He slipped a few of them, viciously counterpunching when he could, but the ones he blocked rocked him even though they did not land full-force.

When the man's boulder-like fist connected with his skull, he felt the world moving around him but his feet were oddly stuck to the ground. He was lucky- the bulky man's imperfectly thrown punches had a lot of weight behind them but lacked the essential, cracking knockout power needed to put down a tough foe with one blow. Perhaps realizing this, Jemmy moved in and, latching onto Alvord's coat, viciously dug a thumb in the meat just under his jawbone. He hit the pressure point he sought, but by then Alvord had recovered his senses sufficiently enough to bat the arm away and smash a stiff elbow into his enemy's blocky jaw. This he followed up with a thudding head butt into Jemmy's sternum, then ripped his head upwards so that the back of it connected with the man's chin.

The Cornishmen reeled away once again, spewing out the blood from his cut tongue.

"Know all the tricks, huh?" he noted with grim appreciation.

"Invented a few of my own."

He could tell that the Cornishman was used to overwhelming his opponents with his great size and strength, but Alvord was hardly his regular customer. Jemmy came in flat-footed and ploddingly, trying to get a hold of him, but with deliberate and well-placed jabs Alvord kept him at bay and controlled the distance. Fighting on the balls of his feet he danced laterally at times, at others backing straight away from blows and then stopping abruptly to catch the giant with sledge-hammer punches as he bulled in relentlessly. The man was trying to grab his shirt, for that was how throws and locks were accomplished in the Cornish style of wrestling. If those scarred, mammoth hands got a proper hold of him...

Alvord preferred fists as the appointed means of dispatching foes, having boxed with famed bare-knuckle fighters like Will Poole and Tom Hyer. But he had also been schooled in the brutal art of collar-and-elbow wrestling by some Irishmen he'd worked with in Manhattan. He could wrestle if it came to that, but at the moment he conceded that he'd rather not have it come to that. For once he faced an opponent stronger than himself, and perhaps every bit as experienced.

Jemmy rushed him with implausible speed for so large a man, hands darting in and out as he sought purchase on Alvord's shirt. Alvord used his forearms in short chops and sweeps to keep those awful hands away, alternately lashing out with punches that were ripping up the man's face but failing to fell him. Those very same punches had sent many a tough man to sleep but, sponge-like, Jemmy seemed able to absorb whatever he dished out. Though not a skilled striker, his durability was unlike anything Alvord had ever encountered. It reminded him of his older brother Anscom, who was a bit slighter in build than Jemmy but still a bull of a man who could take an extraordinary degree of punishment and wrestle with the best of them. Even though Alvord currently held the upper hand, his opponent's size and power was fatiguing. He must be careful. Faced with a relentless and dangerous fighter, Alvord could ill-afford to be anything less than absolutely wary.

The Cornishmen suddenly swatted his arms aside and bear-hugged him, lifting him off the ground and trying to squeeze the life out of him. And he was off to a good start. Already Alvord felt the breath vacating his lungs.

Fearing for his creaking ribs and spine, he acted swiftly. Jemmy had made the mistake of keeping his own face close to Alvord's, and for it he received a head butt that broke his wide nose. Alvord's forehead was stabbed with pain, but it paled in comparison to Jemmy's agony. The huge man dropped him presently, face a rictus of anguish, and Alvord stomped on his instep, hit him with a right uppercut, and hip-tossed him.

Or tried to. Jemmy, though in excruciating pain, somehow got a hold of him and reversed the move, so he ended up slamming Alvord into the ground instead. Both rolled to their feet, wary. Sucking in breaths of air, they looked for weaknesses to exploit, the light from raging bonfires playing ominously over their wrathful faces. Both men were only dimly aware of the swell of the crowd.

"Not bad," Alvord taunted, knowing full well that it was foolish to waste breath in such a fight as this but unable to resist, "for an inbred Cousin Jack."

He might have put up a confident front, but whispers of doubt began cropping up in the darker recesses of his mind.

There is always someone better, jeered a voice in his head, *always someone out there who has your number...*

The miner let out a furious howl and rushed him like an enraged bull. When he went for a takedown Alvord sprawled, but the man's size and momentum still drove him back and he fell with Jemmy's full weight on top of him.

Then the miner was bludgeoning his face with his fists, roaring like a madman. When he thought he had Alvord hurt, he drew back his right hand for a killing blow. Recruiting strength and ignoring the mass of pain that was his face, Alvord moved his head to the side and heard the meaty fist smash the rocky, hard-packed ground next to his skull. Jemmy's agonized cry was cut short when he received a quick punch to the throat, enabling Alvord to roll out from under him and scramble to his feet. Then, as Alvord charged in to drive his shoulder into the rising miner, he ran into a mighty backhanded blow swung with everything the man had. The force of that numbing wallop bent him sideways almost to the ground, but he just barely managed to keep his feet.

At the moment he was coming off second best, but in a fight the passing of each second brings change and opportunity should a man possess the ability to capitalize. So in the unguarded moment wherein the man stood admiring his own handiwork, Alvord pounced.

He followed up a crushing double-handed strike with lightning hooks and thunderous right hands, creating a storm that Jemmy simply could not weather. The Cousin Jack fell back, offering dogged resistance in the form of his own sweeping punches but rarely connecting well.

Alvord's next punch, thrown in what might have verged on desperation, caught the Cornishman's temple with a crack like a small caliber gun. Jemmy leaned forward, feet planted but face heading for the ground, and Alvord's subsequent right cross helped him on his way.

A few Cornish onlookers began moving in, apparently entertaining notions of interceding. Their leader, with a deep scowl on his face, strode boldly towards the fight.

But then David's knifepoint dug into the flesh over the man's ribs. "How 'boot we let the gents decide the outcome themselves? *D'ye ken, bucko*?"

The man *did* ken, and nodded slowly, his Adam's apple visibly bobbing as he gulped involuntarily.

Marcel, his own knife placed against another man's kidneys, gave a toothy grin. "Marvelous. Now why don't you jist sit tight whilst Al catawamptiously chews up yer friend there? Eh?"

Finnbar would have gladly lent further menace to the situation and probably a healthy dash of wit to boot, but at the moment he had his hands full restraining Cerberus. The dog strained at the black leather leash, snarling in dire fashion as he sought to get at Jemmy. An instant later, an unholy chorus of ululating cries shook the miner's camp to its core as chaos descended upon it.

Alvord, still feeling addle-brained but driven by cold fury, drove home his relentless attack as he brutally kicked the fallen giant in the ribs, sending him sprawling. Jemmy lay wheezing in the dust like a fallen buffalo while his enemy wheezed somewhere above him.

But at that moment Alvord chanced to see Marcel out of the corner of his eye. The trapper's head darted to the nearby wood line, and the expression that seized his face and body was one of utmost alertness.

A hail of arrows streaked out of the wood line and into the massed miners, meaty thumps indicating when they found their mark. The miner's howls of outrage and shock overtook the sibilant hiss of arrows, drowning out even the energetic war cries of their assailants.

In a move that shocked Alvord, who was sure his opponent was down for the count, Jemmy launched himself up, looking around wildly as men fled in blind fright.

"*Get down!*" The words leapt out of Alvord's mouth. His face was a mask of urgency as he forced his erstwhile enemy back to the ground.

Thoughts identical, they both rolled over to a cluster of barrels that would afford them some protection.

"This ain't over," Jemmy breathlessly but balefully assured him in that Cornish accent that so closely verged on being an Irish brogue.

"Stow your threats and we may yet live to greet the morn."

"And I'd urge you to stay down," he panted as Jemmy started to rise, "lest you seek death by arrow."

As if to punctuate his words, with a whisper an arrow lodged itself in the ground nearby.

"We can't just sit tight here!"

"Yes, we can. We have no means to retaliate as of now and must carefully consider the situation." He was worried about his friends, hoping they were not among the initial causalities.

"I sought only a wrestling match," the giant offered grudgingly as he took cover again, an unusual statement given the frightful circumstances.

"Then I suppose you should have employed less rebarbative words."

Jemmy considered him carefully as an arrow whizzed by. "Yer an odd 'un, huh?"

"Such aspersions have been cast my way."

Alvord hazarded a darting glance around the barrel he hid behind. Dark figures lined the wood's edge to the west. As did Jemmy he felt helpless at the moment, and as he watched he felt it afresh, along with a delicate tincture of what he reluctantly admitted was fear. For along that wood line a row of minute fires suddenly sprang into existence, looking for all the world like a swarm of lightning bugs glowing in unison.

Fire arrows, he realized in the instant before they were loosed.

As they showered down upon the bedlam that was the miner's encampment, Alvord regretted not having brought his Colt Walker revolver along.

A few of the fire arrows embedded themselves in some nearby casks, which with a hollow boom exploded in a spray of wood and briefly flashing flame. A four-inch splinter embedded itself in Alvord's leg, but it failed to dig deep and he yanked it out presently. Jemmy himself ripped out multiple bits of shrapnel, but had yet to offer even a grunt of discomfort. In unison, both stared at the barrels they lay behind for a moment before exchanging a look of intensifying panic. Moving quickly, they made a headlong dash for the west side of a ramshackle cabin, Jemmy taking a moment to powerfully hurl a sledgehammer towards the archers.

Alvord strove to get a better look at their assailants, but too many miners ran around blindly, too many arrows slashed through the night sky. And the bone-chilling sound of war cries added to the confusion all 'round.

Isolated gunshots then tore through the riotous night: it seemed that some of the miners were returning fire. Two more deafening explosions occurred, causing Alvord to wonder just how carefully the camp had been watched by the Indians now attacking it.

And then, *perdendo*, the violence visited upon them petered out, leaving in its place only the sounds of crackling flame and the drawn-out moans of the wounded. The Indian attackers had melted back into the darksome night woods, leaving panicked and befuddled men to make sense of the incident that had befallen them.

Alvord noticed Marcel, Finnbar, and David crouched behind a neighboring shanty and felt a flood of relief.

"You all alright?"

"Aye, shipshape," Finnbar shouted back.

Marcel and David, meanwhile, rushed out from concealment and towards a stack of rifles. Upon reaching them they snatched two up and raced towards the woods.

Looking at each other gamely, Alvord and Finnbar quickly followed the two trappers.

"What of Cerberus?" Alvord asked when he noticed the beast's absence.

Finnbar held up the snapped leather restraint by means of response. "Broke the damned thing, the mad-beast did. Was frothing at the mouth trying to get at our assailants. What in the bloody hell was that, anyways? I thought Marcel said the redskins 'round these parts were peaceable, and never killed whites."

"We shall see. I haven't an answer for it, but those could only have been Injuns."

The two trappers had stopped dead, apparently unworried by their proximity to the dark woods that might well still conceal the enemy. Squatting on his heels, Marcel was engrossed in his examination of an arrow. Not a man overly given to many displays of emotion, his rutted frown attracted Finnbar's attention.

"What gives, Marcel?"

"Somethin's up. Night attack makes no sense- a lot of Injuns, Chippewa included, won't attack at night."

"So are those Chippewa arrows, then?"

"Well, the dyed hawk and eagle fletching on the arrers is right, but..."

"What?" Alvord had never seen such confusion contort the man's face.

"Each warrior customizes 'is arrers, markin' 'em with lines by dint of a hot iron, and that part's oddly lackin'. They all look the same, not in the least personalized. And why'd they use arrers in the first place, when the Chippewa and other surroundin' tribes have flintlocks aplenty? They had guns as far back as when they ran the Sioux clear out onto the plains."

Cerberus reappeared, a shaggy gray phantom materializing out of the tenebrous night, dragging something out of the woods. The dog growled lowly as he did so, snout coated in blood.

"We got us a body!" David yelled excitedly, hastening over to it.

Still clutching the arrow, Marcel followed.

"Dog tore the blaggard's throat clean out!" David exclaimed gleefully, slapping Alvord on the shoulder as if the kill was his own.

"And we got another here!" A miner called out, beginning to drag it towards them. "A bullet took him through the neck!"

"War paint on the bodies is right," David explained after a moment's examination, "but look a' the faces, eh? That seem off to ye, Marcel?"

Their attention was momentarily diverted by the frenzied shouting from within the camp. The casualties were strangely few compared to the abundance of arrows pinned into the ground and various structures. Three dead, and perhaps twice that number wounded.

The miners were busy assessing their losses at this point, some doing so none too delicately.

"Just look at that arrow! Right through his blasted forebrain!"

Meanwhile, another group of miners had gathered weapons and, riling themselves up, were preparing what they considered to be a retaliatory assault on the nearby Saulteur camp.

"Heathen redskins! Blackguards one and all!"

"Damn straight!"

"I says we head to the camp and show them how white men fight!"

These words were met with wild roars of reinforcement.

"That will not be happening tonight," said a French-accented voice, loud but still quite in control of itself.

It was the Jesuit Bazin, his sagging visage calm and resolute. Upon hearing the tumult of the attack he had hastened over to investigate.

"Move aside, *priest*, or join in your "congregations" fate!"

"Aye, Papist. Don't impede justice lest you find yourself swept up in its dispensing."

"Kill this *Papist* and feel the wrath of the Church, *miner*."

At Bazin's words the crowd tensed, unsure of how to proceed. The priest continued with considerable sangfroid.

"Are you really so foolish as to think that the Saultuer Chippewa, or any of the Indians assembled here tonight, would seek to break a peace with this nation, one that has endured for so many years? If this attack was committed by Chippewa braves, it was by a band not here tonight. Most of these Indians are here to receive their payment from the United States government- why would they stoop to attacking a miners camp?"

A good bit of grumbling followed.

A bloodied Jemmy stepped forward. "Well, get to the bottom of it, priest, and report back to us. If any members of the group here are at fault, we demand retribution. Don't it say some such stuff in the Bible? Eye for an eye?"

Ignoring the latter statement, Bazin nodded sagely. "I shall question those present. I may even be able to have them do some tracking, to see what manner of war party attacked here tonight. In the light of day more answers shall be revealed, and retribution, if it is to be had, can more realistically be had."

Seeing that Bazin had masterfully diffused a potentially even bloodier incident, Alvord and the others continued their examination of the bodies.

"I mean t'say," David went on, "that'n there is a half-breed if ever I've seen, but one all done up in the manner of a Chippewa warrior."

"And look," Finnbar noted with amazement. "Alvord, Marcel, that tattoo bear comparison with any others we've seen lately?"

The second body bore several small but all-too familiar tattoos. They were identical in design to those they had seen on the two mysterious timber pirates' bodies after they had taken the *Hywell.*

"It does indeed," Alvord agreed. "You said they seemed almost Celtic in style?"

"Aye. And just look at the bows! Their short length and stout composition likewise reminds me of the Old World."

"Somethin's off," Marcel said firmly, running a hand over the bow. "Ain't like any Injun bow I've seen. What d'ya think, Dave?"

"Crivvens! Just look at how wide the weapon is! Never seen the like on any red man! What in the name o' Auld Clootie is goin' on here?" David demanded.

Alvord, Finnbar, and Marcel all traded troubled looks.

For the sands of this deepening mystery had most definitely been set to stirring.

Chapter 27

Cadwallader Jones awaited Pollock's arrival without the slightest indication of impatience, standing with his arms clasped behind his back as he stared hypnotically out the second-story window of the bowling alley he had patronized earlier. From this vantage he could just barely make out the orange nimbus of light that marked the roaring fires in the miner's camp. Every so often he caught sight of the uppermost reaches of the tongues of flame that created that aura.

Nearly an hour ago, whilst he stood in the very same spot, he had heard the hollow boom of gunpowder explosions. He had watched, a man aloof and detached, as the townsfolk down below began scurrying around like so many ants at the onset of the explosions. And he had waited, inexpressive, for the arrival of Pollock just as he did now.

Jones inwardly lamented what a pity it was that the downtown buildings obscured his view of the fire in its entirety, but tonight was hardly one to indulge selfish fancies. The importance of this night transcended any personal considerations.

Like any orchestrator of great events, the significance of what he had planned out so meticulously, of what he was now so close to bringing to fruition, had begun to consume him. He was, he conceded, being swept up in a tempest of his own creation, but oh, how serene the world would be after it passed howling over them...

It was a room dark and spare, the one in which he waited, a room highly conducive to the weighty matters he now mulled over. To gaze upon his face would have revealed an unsearchable expression, but it was only a lifetime of stifling emotions that allowed him to remain utterly composed.

For if what Major Raines told him tonight contained the seed of truth, then the *Hywell* had almost certainly been sunk on Lake Michigan. Partially submerged, the charred skeleton of a scuttled, one hundred and fifty foot timber schooner had been discovered by the Great Lake Patrol, though as of yet no details regarding the circumstances surrounding the ship's destruction were in circulation. What was known was that its ruined cargo of lumber had still been aboard along with many burned bodies, presumably of her crew, some of which also bobbed unceremoniously in the water nearby.

As a man unused to the intrusion of failure into his highly successful career, he was plagued with thoughts of how he could have prevented this blemish upon his record. His was generally a smoothly played hand... had he played an unwise card with this whole timber piracy venture?

Regardless, this minor failure had no bearing on the greater plan, and as only a few men knew of that shady enterprise aside from him, the world would be none the wiser.

Still, he wondered as to the fate of *Hywell's* crew. Did the entire crew share in the selfsame end of those found scorched or nibbled on by fish? For the majority of those rapscallions he could give a hang, but the two he had personally assigned to accompany the ship... those losses were noteworthy. And they were on him.

The door opened roughly behind him, slamming into the wall before being slammed shut just as loudly. Jones did not bother to take his eyes off the orange glow to the east.

"You are late."

Pollock rolled his bloodshot eyes. "Not by much, Jones. Just stopped to grab a quick bite and brew at-"

"*Pollock*," he spat the name in his cold, peremptory manner, "as you well know you were to report to me immediately following your rendezvous with our associates outside the camp."

The woodsman belched resoundingly and scratched his cheek's rough crop of stubble. Though he feared Jones as he feared few men, whiskey steeled his nerves and unsealed his tongue quite readily.

"No matter. I'm here now and all went well tonight. Sorry you had to wait, but I've had me a long day. Won't happen again, Boss."

"What have you to report?"

Pollock took off the belt containing the Colt revolvers laid it on a nearby table, taking a moment to clumsily light an oil lamp that threw a warm glow over the room.

"Met our contacts on the outskirts of the camp, as instructed. I led 'em to the best spot from which to launch an attack, then left to watch from a distance. They did what you said they would- attacked quick-like, left a few dead, couple wounded, a good bit of destruction and the entire camp rattled to the core."

"And the losses incurred by our associates?"

"Two, from what I could see. I was up in a pine where I had a fine view, and it seemed to me that two bodies was being examined. You won't believe who by."

Jones turned towards Pollock for the first time, though his eyes were downcast and he spoke as if to himself. "Two lost, eh? Well, we all knew some might fall. Those men will be remembered, their sacrifice shan't be forgotten, nor the role it will play in the grander scheme."

His employee impatiently cleared his throat. "*Hem, hem.* I said you won't believe who was looking at those bodies."

Those yellowish eyes, so like those of a lion, sought out his own. He firmly held the gaze, which he likened to staring down a catamount. There were times when Pollock tried to decipher the thoughts lurking behind those queer colored eyes. To no avail, though. The man's thoughts and emotions were carefully concealed behind a protective barrier that no man could scale or penetrate. It was beyond even the almost inhuman vacancy and absence of emotion that Indians were so damnably good at cultivating.

"Who might that be?"

"Marcel Durand, the mountain man dressed in white buckskins at your soiree. And the rest of that group, too."

Jones offered no answer but looked deep into the steadily burning wick of the oil lamp.

"Could be vexing, eh? He and MacTavish, the other-"

"Having *just* had them over for dinner, I believe I can recall whom the two trappers were. Continue."

Having just seen the still pool of his boss's impassivity ripple ominously, Pollock spoke with as much respect as he could muster.

"Of course, Mr. Jones. I was only saying that those two might notice that something is amiss about those bodies. Like myself, they can identify different Injun tribes by tattoos, piercings, facial features, hairstyles, clothing."

"I would not worry about it. As you know, the only paper in the region is run by a man who actually listens when I break words with him."

The look that followed was charged with meaning, one lost to the clouded sensibility of Pollock.

Crossing his thick arms in front of his chest, Jones sighed without opening his mouth. "Do you know why I chose you, out all the able men in this region, to aid me in this monumental endeavor?"

"Charm n'good looks might have something to do with it."

The frivolous attempt at humor passed by disregarded.

"I needed a man on whom I could rely unequivocally."

Is Cadwallader Jones complimenting me? Pollock wondered within the hazy confines of his mind, a tad confused but cautiously pleased with himself.

"One in whom I could place all my trust, with whom I could share the secret that has defined my time on this earth. One who would, like myself, take that secret to the very grave."

If the softly measured emphasis of that last word wasn't enough, something about the phrasing definitely should have given birth to a chill.

"So you are sure they will go to Chapel Beach?" he pressed Pollock, who knew he was referring to Marcel and that lot.

"Sure as shit. That French bastard scouted the area out in his youth, though he trapped there only a mite. There and behind the Sable Dunes, as well as Twelve Mile Beach are where they'll be found. Before they was wiped out, the Grand Island Chippewa always spoke of great game populations in the area, but no whites, half-breeds, or other Indians would dare hunt or trap the region."

"And you are certain they will divide their crew between those three spots?"

"S'what I'd have done. There are still plenty of furbearers in all those locations- a fact we both know."

"And you delivered the diagram I drew detailing their anticipated campsites to our associates?"

"'Course. Why, you worried Durand's crew might stumble upon something they shouldn't? They'll be well armed, and could inflict serious causalities if-"

"They will not. The region is too carefully patrolled, and lookouts will spot them long before they make landfall. And, if they press, then the full weight of the most puissant and guarded secrets within those woods shall be brought to bear on them."

"Huh?"

"Don't worry about it."

"Why not? I'm a part of this."

"Because," Jones answered, sounding patently bored, "it lies beyond the shores of your besotted comprehension. Just know that they don't stand a dog's chance. Nor, I fear, do you."

"Why's that?" asked Pollock thickly, still not able to fully grasp that his boss's self control was now only the sardonic semblance of such.

"Simply put, you have outlived your usefulness. Hardworking? Why yes, I daresay. Each week you use my flotilla to ferry more miners to the Copper Country, earning yourself money by the sweat of your brow and the stroke of your paddle.

Enterprising? You most certainly are, having come up with a number of sound ideas regarding both business and our special project. I chose you to come under my employ because among trappers you are canny, intelligent, loyal, and, up until recently, sober. But your periodic drunkenness is to the possible endangerment of those we seek to aid. I shudder to think what your ossified tongue might let slip in the crucial coming days, as if your comments at my dinner party tonight were not suspicious and detrimental enough. As is such, I have no further need of your services."

Jones paused and took a step towards the confused man, his overcoat swishing softly around his boots. "It did not have to come to this, a fact I do hope you understand. You could have chosen even relative sobriety and enjoyed a fruitful employment under me. Instead, you opted for dissolution and imbecility. A *costly* decision, Pollock."

"*No,*" Pollock whispered, a man very suddenly enlightened.

"Do stop talking."

An intricately carved club appeared in Jones's right hand as if by magic. It now occurred to Pollock just how physically menacing a man Jones was. He took two unsteady steps back and with fumbling hand drew and raised his tomahawk. He was shocked by the sudden turn of events, but even so he was not a coward. In a moment of clearness his mind raced, beginning to take into account the factors that were at play here. His pistols lay quite uselessly on the table nearby, if he could somehow get to them... ...

Jones, with dire deliberation, positioned himself between the warily circling Pollock and the pistols on the table.

"Boss, just what in the *hell* is going on here?"

He struck like a snake, batting aside Pollock's tomahawk with astonishing speed and landing an awful blow to his collarbone. The trapper went down to a knee under the force of it, gasping terribly, but being a veteran fighter he swung his weapon at Jones's leading leg. Jones merely lifted his leg up and out of the way as if he was bored, at the same time cracking the drunkard's skull with a backhanded swing that was accompanied by a hollow clunk.

Blood poured down into Pollock's eyes, but he could still see sufficiently enough to watch as his erstwhile boss lifted his weapon once more. A sharp spike protruded from of the base of the cudgel's handle, which in the next instant pierced the top of his skull.

"Speaking of Hell," Jones said conversationally, "be sure to give the Devil my regards."

"Evening." Jones greeted the thickset bartender downstairs.

"Same to you, old friend."

The shorn-headed man slid him a spruce beer before leaning his beefy arms on the bar. After a moment he cocked his head to the side, doglike.

"All go well upstairs?"

Jones replied without meeting his eyes. "Aye. The body is ready to be disposed of."

The bartender gave him a nod and a grin that were barely there.

"I'll see that it's taken care of."

"Many thanks, old friend."

Walking down the main road to where his horse was tethered, Jones noticed to his profound surprise that there was a decided spring in his step. Though it was dark he promptly checked himself. Once atop his horse, an exceptional dappled gray gelding, he urged him into a mud-slinging canter.

Jones barely saw the buildings pass by, or the people who milled around in the streets before him.

Manipulative power, he mused, could not sustain itself unless duly surrounded by and pandered to by the weaknesses of lesser beings. It was not enough to keep oneself abreast of developing events- no, it paid to be the authority who knew which direction events would tack *before* they unfolded. In the cozy delusion of their "enlightenment," some men of ideas would blithely liberate the bovine masses of this world from the shackles of their ignorance. Such men were laughably blind as well as deaf and dumb to the fact that the intellects and shrewd minds of this world were the wolves; predators who would rapidly starve once denied the attendance of that dumbly lowing herd.

In the rare, quiet moments wherein he indulged his streak of megalomania, he enjoyed likening his grand scheme to a game of chess. For in the parlous game he played, pretext was the coin of the realm. The ability to make a move and have your opponent think that it signified something else entirely came at a premium. The mining ventures, the shipping and ferrying services... such things were lucrative, but were also absolute necessities as he skillfully wove this tangled web together. Under the guise of those business ventures, he would set historic events into motion.

Most people he kept at arms length except, of course, when their businesses or connections might prove useful to him. Indeed, a number of them would prove valuable soon enough.

For important men would seek to publicize the turbulent events of tonight. And although he had the power to prevent it, he would let them, but not without making damned sure that it was crafted precisely as he wanted it in the "Lake Superior News and Mining Journal," the only newspaper in the region. Likewise would the Michigan Department of Indian Affairs wish to investigate the events of this night, and William A. Richmond would document the "Chippewa" attack on the miners. Knowing Richmond, Jones figured that in an effort to save himself some work the men would merely label the assault as one undertaken by a rogue band of Chippewa braves. Which would come as no surprise, since the Chippewa plainly detested the mining operations that they considered so much sacrilege. Their superstitious fear and awe of copper, so firmly ingrained in their culture, would make an attack on the assembled copper miners seem so very plausible.

In the end, Jones knew, all of these pieces along with some yet to be formed would come together to create a picture that would vindicate the totality of his existence.

Uninvited, a vivid image of Pollock's corpse floating facedown in the lake appeared in his mind. At this he allowed the shadow of a grin to flit across his granitic features. For, as he knew it would, as he knew it *must*, everything was proceeding as planned.

That which had remained hidden for centuries would be brought forth into the light. And oh, how it would dazzle.

Part Two
Terra Incognita

Et in Arcadia ego.

Latin: "Even in Paradise I exist."
Said of Death.

Chapter 28

In contrast to the madness of two nights past, dawn made slow inroads over a somnolent Sault Ste. Marie on the morning of their embarkation.

Alvord could not speak for the others, but as they pushed off the banks of the St. Mary's River he felt as giddy as a schoolboy. Well, nearly. Although a staid man by nature, on rare occasions even he had a hard time keeping his enthusiasm under proper rein. Although perhaps it was warranted in this instance, for here he was embarking on a trapping expedition that would take him to a remote and myth-haunted land. He, Alvord Rawn, city born and raised, poised to lose himself in the unfamiliar remoteness of the frontier.

After the passing of his family, he was no longer tethered to the city by ties of patriarchal responsibility. It was in that lonely span of time, during long hours spent in contemplative silence within the confines of his quiet home, that he first entertained serious notions of a frontier excursion. But while dreams were of the mind, realization rested in the hands. It was his own hands working in concert with those of Fate that had transmuted his gossamer dreams into the tightly woven fabric of reality. Had Fate not presented him with the opportunity to journey west to St. Louis this past spring, then Marcel and Finnbar would yet be strangers to him and he most certainly would not be sitting here in a thirty-foot canoe, his paddle keeping rhythm with those of trappers, half-breeds, and Indians.

He would never cease to miss his family, nor the years passed with them. In the joining of this expedition he sought not to vainly flee the taint of blighted past. It was with calm resolution that he chose this path. To have stayed in Manhattan would have been to set foot upon a steadily darkening road, one that indulged his more baleful proclivities. Indelible brands would have been seared onto his soul, joining those already borne. This journey had granted him a new lease on life and the prospect of this wilderness interlude was a welcome one.

The two days that had passed were relatively busy ones, what with their purchasing and readying of equipment and supplies. Marcel and David also busied themselves with recruiting more trappers; their ranks had swelled to thirty-seven men.

There had been much to do in the past two days in preparation for their departure. But when down time was to be had, Alvord and Finnbar wandered about the Soo with the ever-charming Miss Connolly acting as their guide. Her knowledge of local history proved impressive and was a welcome quality to two lovers of history like Alvord and Finnbar. During their walks they had seen the cabin in which the famed geologist, geographer, and ethnologist Henry Rowe Schoolcraft had lived in and worked from during his time as Superintendent of Indian Affairs for the region. His wife, the Scots-Irish/Ojibwa Jane Johnston of the pioneering Johnston family of Sault Ste. Marie, had shared in her husband's ethnographic interests, translating many traditional Ojibwa songs and poems into English.

Miss Connolly also brought them to the spot where Michigan Senator Lewis Cass, a former soldier and territorial governor as well as an explorer, had confronted and intimidated a Chippewa chief during the 1820 expedition to find the source of the Mississippi River, one that Schoolcraft had been a part of. The Indian chief had raised a British flag in his camp, one that Cass volubly demanded be tore down. Schoolcraft's recording of that trip, published as *Narrative Journal of travels Through the Northwestern Regions of the United States Extending from Detroit through the Great Chain of the American Lakes to the Sources of the Mississippi River in the year 1820*, was one that Alvord had recently reread in anticipation of their trip.

They were also shown the ancestral Chippewa fishing spots along the St. Mary's, where massive quantities of brook trout, lake trout, whitefish, and sturgeon were taken through a variety of methods. Alvord favored the night-fishing technique; in this approach torches were used to spot fish feeding near the surface and spears served as the tools of the harvest.

Alvord stole a glance at his Irish friend, who sat towards the front of a canoe to his left. Though his face was unreadable, he felt sure that Finnbar's mind was awash with thoughts of the Connolly girl. Well did he remember when he had first met Katherine, and the long hours spent reminiscing over the facets of her character that so appealed to him. Finnbar and Miss Connolly also seemed well matched. The two got along famously, much given to lightheartedness and playful bouts of intellectual sparring. They had spent much time together... Alvord wondered if the Irishman would be tempted to travel back to the Soo before the completion of their expedition.

His own mind returned to thoughts of their journey.

Marcel and David led their fleet, which consisted of a Montreal canoe, a bulky vessel over thirty feet long and six hundred pounds that required ten men to paddle it, as well as five Indian birchbarks that were crewed by four men each. Trailing behind was a twenty-foot bateau, a flat-bottomed craft with a shallow draft. Menacing looking swivel guns had been mounted on the bow and stern. The bateau was outfitted with a single sail, but relied more heavily on the two oarsmen and the rudder man. The majority of the traps, weapons, tools, food, and assorted sundries they needed for the expedition were stowed aboard this vessel.

Alvord's ears met with light splashing sounds from behind, and he turned to ascertain its source. He scarcely believed his eyes.

True to his word, Duddersfield had secured a boat for himself. But, in keeping with his odd nature, it was a boat unlike any Alvord had seen.

"Och, what in the divvil's name is that thing?" David asked in bewilderment.

"They call it a *kayak*," came Duddersfield's enthusiastic response. "The Esquimaux use it and I happened upon one in that old American Fur Company factory."

"Scarcely looks to be an eligible mode of conveyance," Finnbar remarked, doubtfully eyeing its extremely low draft.

Alvord himself sat towards the stern of the Montreal canoe and was glad of it. Plank seats in this craft afforded him a small degree of comfort; the smaller vessels were either knelt or sat in, but when one sat they sat directly upon the bottom of the canoe. Regulating his breathing and trying to move as fluidly as the very water around him, he ignored the throb in his knuckles that served as a token of his fight with Jemmy, and dug his paddle deep.

Fifty-five strokes a minute, fifty-five or you won't be keeping pace...

Two extents of land, separated by five miles of water, reared up over the lake just ahead of them. These were Point Iroquois, a sandy spit of land on the American side, and the rocky promontory of Gros Cap on the other- Lake Superior's very own Pillars of Hercules. Beyond them lay the vastness of Gitchi Gummi.

A momentary, reverent lapse in paddling transpired upon the flotilla's reaching of the headwaters of the St. Mary's River. The awesome sweep of Lake Superior, brooding and unlit, stirred something ineffable in the men and created a ripple in the pool of their collective consciousness. Confronted by the quiet majesty of the Father of Lakes, their insignificance loomed large.

Behind them lay the last vestige of civilization that they would encounter for some time. Before them lay the world's greatest lake and beyond that... the promise of self-discovery, the certainty of adventure, the possibility of death.

A fulgent glow to the east foretold of rapidly encroaching dawn. Alvord closed his eyes and breathed deeply of the invigorating flavor of freedom, reveling in the purity of the air that was untainted by the noisome stench of the city. How queer it still seemed, the absence of repellent odors that his nose long ago stopped paying mind to. He filled his lungs again, opening his gray eyes just as dawn's first energetic rays of light fell blazingly upon the earth, metamorphosing the landscape.

Some of the men began singing a paddling shanty in French, led by Marcel. The mountain man's gruff speaking voice translated into a fine, round baritone. The Indians did not join in with the whites but most of the half-breeds did. The words meant nothing to Alvord but the tune he found pleasing to the ear, particularly the chorus that the men roared out lustily.

"The refrain, what is its meaning?" he asked of the half-breed sitting in front of him.

The man, not breaking the rhythm of his paddling, turned his head back towards him. The long, blue toque cap he wore sported a tall red feather in it, which glowed crimson in the nascent sunlight.

"'It's the rowing that leads us to the high country.'"

The ghost of a smile drifted across Alvord's face as he looked out upon a world whose untamed, cobalt waters called to him ever so enticingly.

Chapter 29

An ocean. It might as well have been a bloody ocean. Alvord stood overlooking the staggering vastness of Lake Superior from what appeared to him the outermost rim of the earth.

The sweeping expanse of sandscape around him seemed wholly out of place on a lake. Indeed, he was strongly reminded of the dunes out on the south shore of Long Island, where he and Katherine had made many a trip to picnic and swim. Yet these undulating dunes dwarfed anything New York offered. The Grand Sable Dunes, *Na'gow Wudj'oo* in the Chippewa tongue, reared up steeply from the lakeshore, soaring at times to heights of three hundred feet. Not visible from the dunes but only fifteen miles to the west lay their destination, Chapel Beach.

Unhurriedly he looked east, then west, reckoning that the dunes took up a solid five miles of coastline. While mostly composed of pure sand from the pebbly beach to the upper edge of the bluffs, once on top the rolling dunes offered far more in the way of vegetation. Long dune grasses, scrubby bushes, and groves of stunted Jack Pines created an environment unlike any Alvord had clapped eyes on. The trees grew thickest in the troughs of the dunes, although even in the sprawling, prairie-like area to the west tiny pines dotted the land. Scattered among the vegetation, huge, sandy pits pockmarked the region as if haphazardly scooped out by some giant hand.

The tropical cast of the lake equally stunned him. Near the shoreline the enfeebled light of rapidly departing day was still sufficient enough to set the shallows to glowing a delicate sea green. This gave way to an aquamarine hue in the medium depths before melding into fantastic gentian blue further out.

Inhaling deeply, he watched the effortless soaring of a harrier hawk as it drifted over the massive open area to the west, its head darting to and fro as it sought a final meal before sundown.

What struck him most about the place was the silence, the astounding silence interrupted at times by the barest of breezes that stirred the sands and grasses. Even the sparrows and waxwings preparing for sleep in the nearby trees did so with none of their usual twittering or trilling, as if Mother Nature herself demanded their reverence in so sacred a spot.

Such was the sense of the sacrosanct in this place that Alvord felt as if he was rudely intruding upon it. He knew that as a mere man he could not accord that due measure of respect to such a scene as this. Aside from his suddenly insignificant-seeming presence and that of the crew on the beach far below, the colossal lake and dunes bore no other trace of human disturbance. And even so, it overwhelmed its puny intruders. A thing untamed and untamable, its grandeur stood unmarred.

The sand felt good underfoot. He wore a pair of recently purchased moccasins, which hurt the arches of his feet at first but now struck him as being more comfortable than any other footwear he owned. The hobnail boots he wore most of the time would have torn the bottom out of the birchbark canoes they piloted. His boots with soft India rubber soles might have been serviceable, but Marcel assured him that moccasins would serve him better while in the canoe. His back ached something terrible from paddling and being confined to a canoe for so long, but it was loosening up now that he was moving around.

Finnbar, a green silk headband circling his crown in a most rakish manner, gamely clawed his way up over the edge of the dunes. Walking over towards Alvord, he put his hands on his hips and exhaled deeply.

"*Whew.* What a bloody climb! But with a view like this as a reward, one can hardly complain. Just look at this place!"

They both did so silently for a few minutes. Camp had already been made for the night on the beach, so they had some time to kill before sundown. Most of their party seemed understandably content with simply resting after a hard day's paddling and indulging in a pre-snooze smoke, but after sitting in a canoe all day Alvord felt the need to do a spot of exploring. Finnbar, never one to rest easy while there was new turf to fossick about in, shared in the sentiment.

Marcel too surmounted the dunes, pausing for a moment to catch his breath before joining the others on the sandy hillock.

"When last I stood here, saw a serpent out there," Marcel informed Alvord and Finnbar with a nod at the lake. They regarded him skeptically, eyebrows raised.

"Come again?" Alvord asked.

"*Mishi-ginebikoog,* is what the Chippewa call it. Or *them,* I should say. Up thataways," he gestured northeast, "there's a place called Agawa Rock, on which are paintings of such serpents as well as the great water lynx, *Mishipeshu.*"

A knot rapidly developed in Alvord's stomach. "And you say you saw one?"

"Yep. Damn thing had to be forty foot, though given he was out purty far in the lake I reckon it's difficult to know fer sure. But it was a clear day, and whatever it was, it was big enough to get my attention."

"Might it have been a giant sturgeon?" Finnbar inquired. "David told me that-"

"Shit, Irishman. You figger I can't rightly identify a sturgeon?"

"What in the Devil's name was it, then?"

Alvord could tell by the note of strain in the Irishman's voice that he wasn't alone in his sudden unease. They were travelling upon this lake in flimsy canoes, ones easily dashed to bits by a beast of that size. Yet the notion of a giant serpent in this lake was fanciful at best... was it not? Then again, he had once taken his son Elihu to see the purported skeleton of a 114-foot sea serpent, displayed in Manhattan's Apollo Saloon by the paleontologist Albert Koch. The thought of that gargantuan, winding assemblage of bones, dubbed *Hydrarchos* by its finder, still gave birth to chills in his spine...

"Ah," Marcel shrugged carelessly. "Who knows what a lake this size might hold in its icy depths? Chippewa even talk of Nibanaba mermaids. Hell, I'd like to see me a mermaiden 'fore I give up the ghost..."

Coming back from his thoughts, he noticed of a sudden his companions' disquietude. "Maybe 'twas only a giant sturgeon after all. Wouldn't worry bout it, fellers. Think instead of tomorrow, when our hulls scratch the shores of a place that's had a hold of my soul since I first saw it."

The mountain man filled his thick chest with air, closing his eyes and titling back his toque-covered head.

"Wilder skeins fly in these parts, boys. It's like Mother Nature's tryin' to tell us somethin', tryin' to connect with us in a way that's been lost to the dust of ages... like somethin' long forgotten is stirrin' in our collective memories..."

Solemnly he looked out over the azure expanse of mirror-like lake. A picture of unfettered majesty, a bald eagle swooped down to neatly pluck a fish out of the water far below.

Marcel's beard twitched. "Hell, I guess that sums it up better'n I ever could."

They watched the sun slink steadily lower in the radiant sky to the west. Fidgeting and scuffing the sand a bit, Finnbar appeared ill at ease, which Alvord noticed after a moment.

"What's on your mind, Irishman?"

"My conscience compels me to tell you this, friend- during dinner that night Greeley spoke of your past when you left to grab a drink with Chicago's lawmen."

Alvord's face grew stony as he leveled his eyes at the steadily darkening waters of Superior. "And?"

"Well, we were informed of both your personal losses and the circumstances surrounding your expulsion from the force in Manhattan."

Finnbar noticed Marcel looking down at his feet as he made this confession. He knew the taciturn mountain man would not have offered up this information himself, figuring it something for Alvord to initiate talk of. But he simply felt obligated. Chalk it up to Catholic guilt.

Alvord's jaw clenched and a very ugly look passed over his austere features. "The losses are nothing to complain of. Of course it is no easy thing, that. Burying ones wife and offspring. Yet legions of people see disease and war rend their family apart. Such is the raw state of things. But the dark deeds of that night this March past…"

He paused for a second before continuing, the grim galleries of memory momentarily getting the best of him. "One of my patrolman, a young, up-and-coming Irishman named Andrew O'Farrell, was brutally murdered that night. A fine and noble specimen, a true credit to his people. Not long before this he had arrested a major player in an Irish gang, and because of that collar he met his end. The remaining gang members, seeing his arrest as blood treachery, waylaid him as he walked his beat late that night. The evidence suggested he fought savagely, but with the numbers they brought his fate was sealed from the get-go.

"We were informed of this by a witness to the deed not long after; the gang's trail still burned hot and we quickly tracked them down. Vengeance was meted out. O'Farrell death roused in me whatever demon generally lies dormant. I knew what protocol called for, but so too did I know that it might result in the impeding of wholesale vengeance. Steered by that darkness I was unwavering in my course; I led an attack and we slaughtered them to a man."

"*Abyssus abyssum invocate*- one Hell summons another. In my opinion you did nothing grievously wrong, Alvord."

Finnbar's words, though meant to provide balm to the wound, engendered a further contortion of Alvord's visage. He lowered his eyes in reminiscence.

"But I did, for many of the gang survived our initial onslaught and, bloodlust unsated, I ordered my patrolmen to aid me in dispatching them. I ordered them to kill defenseless men. Guilty, verminous men, but defenseless men. In war, *maybe*, but when you represent a city's moral code... in truth, it weighs heavy on my conscience."

"I'm with Finn. Heat o' the moment, you can't blame yerself fer somethin' like that. They had it comin', and reaped what they sowed."

Alvord's features grew unreadable. "It is our light that we should share with others, while keeping inner demons firmly tethered in the darkest recesses of our souls, lest they seek to assert their dominance."

All three stared at the still waters below, reflecting on past descents into shadow.

"Normally," Alvord continued, "I can dispense alibis by the bushel, but caught red-handed I could only admit my guilt. I lost my job, and the more I think about it the more I think I understand it. Had I acted alone, it might not have come to that, but having spread my darkness to my men..."

"So you seek rebirth out here, then?

"Aye, in short. And you, Finnbar Fagan? What seek you in this raw wilderness?"

The Irishman's eyes lost focus and his countenance grew uncharacteristically solemn. "Not all who wander are lost, Alvord."

Humphrey Demetrius Duddersfield hurled himself over the top of the dunes nearby. Raising himself up, he immediately began talking in a voice quite breathless.

"What an impressive example of a perched dune system! Just look at it!"

He brushed his hand over a tussock of thickly growing grass.

"Dune grasses growing in riotous profusion! And- zounds! *Tanacetum huronense-* Lake Huron Tansy! And- can it be? Pitcher's thistle? How I wish this execrable lighting was better- it is deucedly hard to see clearly."

"Take care not to fall, laddie buck," cautioned David, who had just reached the top himself and, arms crossed, stood watching the young scientist ferreting around taking soil and plant samples.

As if on cue, in the next instant Duddersfield slipped and tumbled back down the dunes, his dismayed cries echoing off the beach. Unable to halt his slow, rolling descent, his progress was stopped only when his unshapely body made contact with the distant beach below. Some of their fellow trappers pointed and guffawed loudly, a sound that only intensified when Cerberus, gamboling with the small, fox-like Indian dogs, impishly snatched up the geologist's cast-off hat and tore down the beach with it. Cerberus was better behaved these days, having responded well to Alvord's daily lessons in obedience. But what pup could resist the temptation of stealing a hat from a bumbling oaf of no consequence?

As it sank grandly, the sun's fiery path led it to the edge of the endless horizon. A molten ball sinking steadily into the absolute blackness of the water, it seemed to vainly struggle against the inevitability of the event. Great, feathery sweeps of clouds took on the subtle hues of the sunset like the incandescent wings of angels.

Daylight's last gasp took the form of a smoldering red sun pillar that blazed with otherworldly brilliance before dusk wrested control of the sky. Although Finnbar scribbled furiously in the failing light, the scene before them was beyond prosaic description.

Unearthly and sublime, it was a scene forever graven in Alvord's soul.

"*That*," he stated firmly, "was something."

Chapter 30

"This place is choice!" Finnbar declared excitedly, his roving eyes taking in the magnificent beach that stretched before them.

"That'd be the word fer it," concurred Marcel gladsomely as he looked upon the spot that would serve as their initial base of operations. Fondly he recalled the day when, the dew of youth still clinging fast to him, he had first beheld Chapel Beach. The site where the Jesuit missionary Jacques Marquette supposedly preached way back in the seventeenth century; a place feared and revered by Indians, half-breeds, and white trappers alike; where even now few dared to camp at all and those who did made damned sure to assemble the proper offering to the *manitous* that haunted this land...

The length of the beach spanned a shade under half a mile of shoreline. On its western edge it was bounded by a solid wall of rock that reared up fifty feet and jutted out into the lake with a dense, coniferous growth of trees carpeting its crown. On its easternmost side stood a most unusual geological formation, a true marvel of the forces of time and erosion. Wider at the top than at its base, it stood like a pulpit through which a network of interconnected tunnels had been carved. The marvelously sculpted rock would have been freestanding but for a short, narrow archway that connected it to the cliff of the mainland.

Just beyond this peculiar formation a small waterfall spilled merrily over the timeworn sandstone and onto the beach, forming a pool before winding its way to the lake. While hardly spectacular, the sight of water rushing out of the wall of tangled verdure added to the quaint charm of the location.

The sundrenched sand of Chapel Beach gave way to towering maples and birches one hundred feet from shore. An osprey, taking a moment to cast a wary glance around while it tore into a brook trout, spotted the incoming boats and took grudgingly flight, the shredded fish carcass flopping loosely in one of its talons.

Enchanting. Although he hated to employ the word even in the secure confines of his own mind, Alvord grudgingly admitted to himself that this word best served his unvoiced attempts to describe the place.

Their flotilla, diminished by half after having deposited smaller trapping parties at the Grand Sable Dunes and Twelve Mile Beach, was down to the Montreal canoe, one Indian canoe, the bateau, and Duddersfield's outlandish little craft. Which, as it happened, sliced through the water like a knife and even under Duddersfield's clumsy captaincy could easily paddle circles around the other vessels. The geologist had actually done so several times while talking of his skill in quite braggadocio a manner, until wordlessly Marcel fired his flintlock pistol and blasted off a small chunk of one of his paddle blades.

The canoes cut through the still, tropical-looking water and with the pleasing scrape of sand on birch bark made landfall. They had been paddling a paltry four hours since breaking camp at the dunes in the gloom of pre-dawn. Alvord, his arms and upper back now accustomed to the steady motion of paddling, felt fresh as a daisy, as if he hadn't paddled at all. Despite this, he was eager to put foot to *terra firma* once again. Long stretches of time spent in boats, even smaller craft, simply wasn't to his liking.

Gordon and Lightfoot leapt out of the Montreal canoe and along with some Indians whose names Alvord couldn't quite recall began pulling the boat up onto the shore. Without much talk everyone got out and started unpacking their gear and provisions, making camp with accomplished ease. He had noticed to his relief the egalitarian nature of their trapping party; while Marcel and David were undeniably in charge (the *chefs de voyage* in trapper lingo), orders were rarely dispensed and all present appeared to know what was expected of them. Accustomed to being in position of command himself, Alvord was worried he would chafe under the orders of other men. But this structure was one he could embrace.

He and a short, stout Indian he thought to be called Big Wolf unloaded the kegs of beans, hard biscuits, salted pork, flour, and rum together. He knew not if the man spoke English, but it mattered little at the moment. The fellow worked hard; while not as powerful as Alvord he determinedly hefted the heavy barrels and humped them along in an effort to keep up. Secretly, he had been hoping that Marcel and David would offer guidance when it came to dealing with red men, but at this point it seemed that he was being left to fend for himself in that respect.

Indians, he had noticed, walked with an outwardly lazy stride that covered a surprising amount of ground. They also raised their feet a lot higher than whites when they took a step. Their tracks too differed from a white man's, and not just by stride. Their toes tended to point straight, while a white man's angled outward. Since their embarkation Alvord had tried to start observing things from the viewpoint of a hunter and woodsman. And he had a long way to go, he knew. At times Marcel and David offered morsels of advice, but it was clear that he and Finnbar would have to learn a great deal on their own.

He and Big Wolf cleared the boats of foodstuffs and began hauling iron cooking pots and rolled-up tents onto the beach.

Finnbar, a stack of setting poles (used to secure traps set in water) precariously balanced across his arms, asked, "We making camp here on the beach or in the woods?"

"Here for now," David answered him between grunts as he and Marcel conveyed Marcel's large, secret box to the campsite. "Skeeters in the woods beyond'll do a number on ye come nightfall. Truly nightmarish, believe me brother. Flies can harry a fellow out here on the sands ever and anon, but 'tis far preferable. Plus we're close to a limitless supply of clean water and quality fishin' is to be had here."

"Fair enough. And for the love of Christ, Marcel, do ye intend to reveal the contents of that bloody box or not?"

The trapper gently set his end of the box down. "This is gnawin' away at you Irishman, ain't it?"

"Inquisitive minds demand to know. Back me up here, Alvord."

"He's right," Alvord admitted, folding his brawny arms across his chest, "I too have been wondering."

Gaston, peering closely at the crate, looked at his father humorously. "C'mon, father. Let's have it."

"Alright then. It's a raft."

"How is that?" Alvord was confused; how could a wooden raft, even taken apart, fit in that box?

"It's of India rubber."

"Ah," he nodded understandingly, "like the one used by the Fremont expedition back in '42."

"Yep. 'Cept instead o' tryin' to shoot the rapids of the Platte with it like a flock of damned fools, we're gonna use it fer leisurely fishin' and maybe transportin' supplies."

Cocking his head in bird-like curiosity, Finnbar's brow crinkled in confusion. "You bought and hauled that thing all the way up from Chicago for the mere sake of fishing?"

"Uh huh."

"So what now, do we set up camp and begin laying trap lines today?"

Marcel chuckled easily. "Stow that confounded Yankee work ethic of yers and prepare to enjoy yerself, Rawn. We'll get our campsite ready to go but that's about it. This day ahead of us is devoted to one thing and one thing only- *carousin'*. Trust me, we've got plenty o' hard work ahead of us, *mon ami*. Today let's have us a bit o' revelry, shall we?"

Alvord gave a sideways nod of understanding. "Let the revels commence, then."

So revel they did. After camp was made, rum and whiskey was broken out and distributed among the trapping party, most of whom gladly indulged. A few of the Indians declined, judgment plain as they watched their kinsmen drink greedily of the red man's bane. Instead they set up what appeared to be low altars near the wood line, upon which they carefully arranged tobacco, vermillion, and round copper beads.

"Do you think it wise to allow the Indians among us to imbibe?" Alvord queried uneasily, watching one of them guzzle one hundred and thirty proof rum from a tin cup. He'd heard that when booze presented itself, most Indians got piss drunk as a matter of course.

"Don't worry 'bout it," Marcel assured him unconcernedly, "we'll be in no danger. These Chippewa here are good sorts, even when put to drink. Me'n Dave chose these Injuns because of their character as well as their trappin' ability. They'll get a bit soused, no doubt about it, but them an' the breeds will behave themselves, they're a reliable lot. You should worry more 'bout Gordon and Lightfoot. Rum sponges the both of them, and rowdy bastards they are when possessin' of a bellyful."

Before they had consumed too much in the way of rum, Marcel suggested that he, Alvord, and Finnbar take a laid-back paddle west to see the rest of the Pictured Rocks.

"And I shall join you!" Duddersfield called out resolutely, snatching up a notebook and a steel pen. "This will give me a fair idea of which areas I should focus my study on. From what I've seen just here on this beach and the small cliffs we have passed, this place is geologically prime! The degree of uniqueness I have already taken note of-"

"What r'ye prattlin' aboot, lad? Rocks is rocks."

The geologist blinked owlishly. "No, Mr. MacTavish, they are most certainly *not*. Rocks are far more than mere chunks of aggregate minerals."

David bent down and, casually plucking one off the beach, scrutinized it with feigned interest. "Huh, coulda fooled me. But 'tis a pretty wee clod, I'll allow."

His words met with deep-throated laughter from the crew.

Duddersfield scowled acutely, his pig-like face flushing. "Your words are reflective of untenured thought, Mr. MacTavish.

Rocks, from the fortification agate you hold in your palm to the majesty that is the Alps, whisper the secrets of the ages to those of us who take the time to listen."

"Gee Dudd, that there's a thought so deep it carries with it a risk of drowin'" Marcel laconically observed to the hilarity of his fellows.

Duddersfield, his affront betraying itself in the stomping stride he employed, made for the boats.

"Dave, I'll give the lads here a quick tour, we'll be back in a couple hours."

"Sure thing, and while yer gone I'll look after the braw beastie, Alvord." He fondly patted Cerberus, who whined stridently as Alvord stepped into the canoe. But soon David and Gaston were cavorting about with the long-legged hound and it soon forgot its consternation.

"Kinda grabs ya, don't it?"

Marcel was quite right. The rocks here were of a more imposing character. In all his life Alvord had never felt more dwarfed and humbled in the face of Nature, which seemed here to be a tangible presence. Nearing three hundred feet at times, the weathered, multicolored cliffs stood like the insurmountable battlements of some colossal fortification. Just past their camp on Chapel Beach, a chain of sharply protruding escarpments appeared for all the world like a row of battleships heading out into Superior's forbidding wastes. Beyond them, the cliffs were more wall-like, although they did tend to bow outward a bit towards the bottom. It was clear that many different types of rock comprised the cliffs, as different colored layers were quite distinct even to the untrained eye.

"That owes to their composition," Duddersfield, though unprompted, enthusiastically offered. "The Precambrian quartz sandstone is at the base, upon which unconformably rests the Cambrian sandstone, which is followed by the more recent dolomitic sandstone that forms the capstone. Perhaps that would be of the Silurian period? Hmmm, some fossil specimens would certainly aid me in the pursuit of answers. Anyway, each layer weathers differently and at different rates of speed, producing the aesthetically pleasing, sculptured appearance. What a fine example of stratification; Charles Lyell would have a field day here."

"Cambrian and Silurian?" Alvord was unfamiliar with the terms.

"Period of geologic time established by Adam Sedgwick and Roderick Murchison respectively during their work on Welsh rock strata. Sedgwick named the former after the Latin name for Wales, *Cambria.* Murchison bestowed the other title to his proposed layer after the Silures-"

"Ah, one of the Celtic tribes living in the Welsh Borderlands during the Roman invasion."

"Why yes, Mr. Fagan! Right in one."

"Precisely how old do you believe the Earth to be?" A voracious reader of many topics that sometimes included science, Alvord no longer believed that the earth was only around 6000 years old, as he did when he was younger. Long hours spent in the station house lent themselves to reading and the mulling over of various ideas. Loosely familiar with but far from conversant in the theories of James Hutton, Charles Lyell, and William Buckland, it seemed likely to him that the world man inhabited was older than a mere six thousand years, Archbishop Usher's calculation be damned.

Dudderfield emitted a bad-mannered snort, not unlike that of a hog. "Good Heavens man, who could be sure of such a thing? But many, many millions of years if you do in fact care for my opinion."

"Whatever the case, it still stands that these cliffs, whatever there age may be, are spectacular in the extreme. What a testament to the creative powers of the Almighty. Even the Palisades on the upper Hudson, while loftier in spots, cannot hold a candle in the dark to these cliffs in terms of sheer majesty and splendor."

"Know what ya mean, Al. I myself am kinda reminded of the White Cliffs along the Missouri, 'specially since Miner's Castle just to the west of us bears a strikin' resemblance to Citadel Rock. But this place is altogether of a wilder aspect, less tainted by man."

But not entirely. Aside from their own presence they sighted a schooner and one steamer far out on the lake, no doubt heading up towards Copper Country. Still, the ships were so far off they hardly seemed to be intruding upon the scene. Never had Alvord seen so little boat traffic on so massive a body of water; the Atlantic Ocean he was familiar with was busier by far.

They passed a protuberant escarpment, out of which many large chunks had fallen over Time's inexorable course. Marcel had them angle back the Indian canoe they sat in so as it get a better look.

"Indian Head," he informed them with manifest pleasure, "said to be the physical representation of *Gitchi-Manitou* himself. That'll be the Great Spirit of the Injuns. They always leave tobacco offerings here when they pass."

Now that he mentioned it, Alvord had to admit that the rock really did resemble the profile of an Indian's face, right down to the curved, prominent nose.

Grand Portal, a soaring natural arch through which they paddled their canoe, was cave-like on the inside and could have easily accommodated a schooner of modest size. The cavern resounded with the gentle sounds of their splashing paddles, while the water playfully cast light upon the damp rocks.

In his kayak, Duddersfield went right up to the base of the cliff and touch it, muttering to himself all the while.

"What are the rocks sayin' to you, Humphrey old boy?"

The boy looked at Finnbar with a suggestion of madness stamped across his features. "Mr. Fagan, if only you knew!"

"Care to explain how all of those colors are present?"

Alvord looked over Finnbar carefully. The Irishman had his failings, but to say he was an unkindly soul would be to spout a black lie. Whereas Alvord and Marcel excelled in ignoring people whom they had had no desire to converse with, Finnbar went out of his way to bring up others' interests in conversations, to elicit speech from the timid and allay the awkwardness of the outcast.

"That, Mr. Fagan, can be attributed to the presence of iron, manganese, calcium and copper that seeps through the crevices in groundwater. When that water evaporates it leaves behind the mineral trace. The iron accounts for the red and brown, manganese is black, calcium is the white, and copper bleeds through in green."

He pointed east out of the cave towards a section of freestanding, crumbling talus that resembled the collapsed pillars of some prostrate ruin. "*Nota bene* that those fallen sections of rock are devoid of color. No groundwater seeps into them; they no longer hold minerals."

Even those colorless,s fallen pieces were gargantuan, akin to a colossal temple in ruin. It was as if on this very spot in the days of old that god and Titan met to settle accounts, leaving this rubble strewn in their wake.

"Just a minute... lads, have a look at this!"

Marking the sharp note of bewilderment, they obligingly scrutinized the section of rock that Finnbar gently ran his fingertips over. Upon the ancient sandstone, about four feet above the waterline, a short series of symbols were inscribed. Perhaps at one point in the past they had been more deeply etched into the rock, but every pounding wave and winter freeze brought with it the mirthless laugh of a thoroughly unawed

Nature as it scorned the futility of man's congenital desire to be remembered.

"Hmm," Duddersfield ruminated, lifting his purple glasses to peer at them carefully, "a pictograph of some sort. Chippewa? Or another tribe? Perhaps Ottawa?"

"Nope," Marcel chimed in gruffly, peering at the rows of symbols with narrowed, suspicious eyes. "No woodland tribes I know of leave markin's like that."

"Can you liken it to the symbols any other tribes?" Duddersfield pressed. "Could it have been the Sioux or Fox or another tribe that inhabited this area in bygone days?"

"Mmm, mayhap. Can't rightly say, but somethin' in my gut tells me no. They ain't like any Injun scratchings I've seen."

Finnbar stroked his chin thoughtfully, on which a bristly growth of light red hair was sprouting. "It... *damn*, this smacks of madness even inside me own noggin... but it looks to be *Ogham.* Coincidental how we were just speaking of Wales and the Silures."

"Ogham?"

"Ogham is the runic alphabet that was used to write the Old Irish language, as well as the Brythonic languages. Call me bat-shite crazy Alvord, but if ye were to ask me I'd say these runes are of European origin. And, more specifically, Celtic origin."

Alvord nodded sagely. "Well, legends do exist telling of European landfall on American shores preceding by far the arrival of Columbus."

"Curious symbols..." Finnbar thought aloud.

"And it just so happens that you can decipher them."

"And on what do you base that astute assumption?" asked the Irishman drolly.

"A undemanding deduction," Alvord responded forthrightly. "I can see it in the way you intently scrutinize the runes whilst forming silent words with your lips."

"There's our detective. But yes, you happen to be right. Part of me formal studies focused on Runology, Ogham being among the runic alphabets I delved into. I suppose I am tolerably proficient at deciphering them."

Marcel used his paddle to stave off the rock wall their canoe drifted towards. "Well, might ye apply that 'tolerable proficiency' towards translatin' the things?"

Finnbar promptly obliged the arisen question. "*Beyond these walls shall our legacy endure...* again, don't quote me on it, and that's just me paraphrasing, but that's what I'm gleaning from it."

"But what is meant by those words?" Alvord pressed, a thrill of fascination passing through him. It was as if something of great, looming significance reached out to them from across the yawning gulf of ages.

"Search me, auld mucker of mine."

No one broke words for a moment, the idle slap of water against rock and the screeching of gulls replacing their spoken thoughts.

"Blimey, this certainly sets the mind to wondering," Finnbar finally said in breathless wonder.

In pensive silence they resumed paddling.

Here and there bushes and even smallish trees grimly clung to impoverished existence on the cliff face, but the rock faces were mostly without significant vegetation. In one spot a natural amphitheatre of stone with heaping talus piles beneath it served as a rookery for raucous legions of wheeling gulls and sunning cormorants that stretched out their wings to dry. Bald eagle nests were a common sight atop the patriarchal white pines whose crowns could be seen from below, and along the cliff tops were the abundant aeries of falcons.

Due to some recent, sustained downpours, the many waterfalls were flowing with uncommon intensity for this stage of the summer. Some ran down the length of the rocks in a white froth while others shot over the edge of the cliffs and straight into the lake. They canoed right past the iridescent spray of several, letting the fine mist cool them down in a welcome respite from the scorching midday sun.

Sea caves were numerous throughout their journey, and cautiously they entered a few. Beaches were few and far between, but every so often they would encounter one. Mosquito Beach, though sandy in spots, was half comprised of rippling bedrock that Duddersfield assured them was the fossilized wave activity of an ancient ocean. Nearby another sandy spot gave way to bedrock that stretched forth in the shallows like a natural pier before abruptly plunging into fathomless depths.

Miner's Castle, a soaring, palatial formation complete with two turrets and oddly Gothic in appearance, was where they turned back.

"That there is Grand Island," Marcel let them know, pointing to a sprawling landmass just to the west. "Grand Island Chippewa used to live there, now I hear that a former ship captain owns land there, in addition to a feller named Abraham Williams and 'is family. Heard tell he's even got a warehouse and water-powered sawmill somewhere in there."

"Hemming us in on all sides, aren't they?" Alvord quietly mused, tearing into a chunk of salted pork.

Paddling back past the sublimity of the cliffs as they stood silent vigil over the Prussian blue expanse of lake evoked a positively exhilarating feeling in Alvord's spirit. Not even the mist-shrouded, lonely wastes of the Lakes District in England, which he visited once in his boyhood, could bear comparison.

Never had he felt a greater affinity with nature and, indeed, God. For over the bare grandeur of this place God himself seemed to preside. Through the simmering, transparent shallows, tabular rocks lay strewn like sunken altars, strengthening this mood of veneration.

The India rubber raft floated in the crystalline water three hundred yards out from Chapel Beach, soothingly bobbing with the rhythm of the ripples that passed under it.

Looking over the side of the peculiar craft, Alvord reckoned that there had to be seventy feet of visibility in these waters. The raft was positioned directly over a steep drop-off, where the lake fell off into yawning depths.

Upon returning from their tour of the Rocks, Marcel suggested that the three of them take the raft out for a trial run. It had taken the three of them a labor-intensive half-hour to inflate the raft with a fireplace bellows, but Alvord admitted that the reward far exceeded the effort. The India rubber raft, though pungent, afforded them a vast degree of comfort. It easily accommodated the three of them with a good deal of room to spare (they had invited David but the Scot voiced doubt as to the seaworthiness of the rubber vessel).

A number of lines hung off the side of the raft, the ends of which were fastened to baited hooks that were suspended at various depths.

"No stint o' fish in these parts. Not quite as plentiful as they are in Michigan or Huron, granted, but damned if these fish ain't a sight bigger on average. They got what we call coasters- fat ol' brook trout that range the coastal waters of the lake. Plus there's sicowet, a kind of lake trout. Fatter n'tastier than yer standard laker by far. Its name means, 'that which cooks itself' in Chippewa, and its aptly named."

Men fished from the shorelines, with Duddersfield proving himself quite adept at fly-fishing. The fact that a large stream fed into the lake right by their camp boded well for such an endeavor, for fish congregated to feed in such areas. Although it had been decreed that no work needed doing today, some Indians and half-breeds led by Gaston were busily setting up fishing weirs and drift gillnets at that spot and on the far side of the beach, where another, smaller stream also joined Superior.

Gordon and Lightfoot were sparring each other in the French *savate* style, which involved a variety of kicks and punches, with kicking being the favored mode of attack. Earlier they had wrestled with David, but after being schooled several times each they moved on to drunkenly beating the piss out of one another.

From the raft they drew in a goodly catch of fish, brook and lake trout mostly with the odd whitefish and walleye being drawn in. Marcel even succeeded in snagging one of the prized siscowet, a trout so fat it looked ill, that was taken from a far greater depth than the other fish.

After using it himself, Finnbar passed his pouch of opium to Marcel, who promptly sprinkled the yellow-white substance into his cup of whiskey.

"That stuff is highly addictive," Alvord warned, having wrestled with a bout of addiction to it following a broken arm.

"Deliciously so," Finnbar agreed cheerfully, drinking deep of his laced drink. Marcel followed suite.

"That goes right to the head, don't it?" the trapper leaned back and contentedly stared up at the flawless sky above. "Damn, but a man can lose himself out here."

Looking around, Alvord silently concurred before re-baiting a hook with a piece of trout stomach, an incredibly life-like bait once placed in water. It was as he dropped that hook into the water that he noticed a distinct gleam in the cliffs by the beach, like that of sun upon metal. Shielding his eyes to get a better look, he could have sworn he saw through the waves of shimmering heat a figure up on those cliffs, holding what might have been a spear. But with the swiftness of a single blink it was gone, leaving him to wonder if he wasn't seeing things. He had quaffed more than his fair share of rum, after all, and the sun glinting off the water could have created the mirage.

"You see somethin' Al?" Marcel, noticing Alvord's intent stare, immediately swept the cliffs with his sharp brown eyes.

"Thought I saw a figure up on the cliffs, but in the next instant it was gone. Might have been a trick of the light."

Convinced that such was the case and drowsy with contentment, Alvord leaned his head back against the pungent rubber and let the sun's weakening rays warm his face. An odd tingling feeling, not one merely derived from the intake of rum, clung to his breast. Most uncharacteristically, he struggled to keep a childish grin from sliding onto his face.

He realized with a start that for the first time in years, he was well and truly happy.

They paddled the raft back towards camp with a mess of fish to their names.

As they slid onto the beach a tall Indian jogged out of the woods, triumphantly holding up a large snapping turtle by its tail.

"Mikinaak!" he triumphantly roared to those on the beach.

"Cram *that* into yer meat bags," ordered Marcel, handing a steaming bowl of turtle soup to Alvord and Finnbar after the turtle had been cooked.

"Savory meat. Its taste recalls that of lobster," Alvord noted as he gnawed on a hunk. Wild onions had been used in the making of the soup, lending it a flavorful broth.

"Never dined on the latter," replied Marcel, broth spilling onto his unruly beard, "but I agree that it's fine. They did this good and proper too; left the shell in the pot while it cooked. Adds to the flavor."

Before the sun was spent Finnbar helped Duddersfield collect rocks from beneath the small waterfall, amazed at their diversity. With childlike abandon they both scooped up the wildly diverse rocks that the young geologist readily identified.

"Jasper! Carnelian! And just look at that chalcedony! Prehnite and zeolite as well!"

There was a breeze now, one that kept the bugs off of them. Alvord threw his cork mat and Mackinac blanket right on the sand near the fire and gingerly lowered himself onto it. Having eaten and imbibed a mite more than he had anticipated, his stomach bulged to an embarrassing extent.

Marcel fell onto his own blankets next to him, putting his hands behind his shaggy head and sighing contentedly.

"Shit, what a day! Barrin' the unforeseen, I'd say we got a hell of a trappin' expedition ahead of us."

Fireside talk soon grew subdued, supplanted by booze-induced snores of stentorian volume. Laying on his back, Alvord gazed up at the stars, arrayed in greater numbers than he had ever seen. They shone with an intense luster, some burning coldly while others merrily blinked in the empyrean.

That night, in the secluded fastness of Lake Superior, the soothing lilt of waves lapping at sand ferried him towards the realm of dreams.

Chapter 31

Back on civilization's fringe, in the dining room of Van Anden's Hotel, Cadwallader Jones edgily sipped his spruce beer while he awaited the arrival of his venison tenderloin. Van Anden's, aside from offering the most fashionable accommodations in Sault Ste. Marie, also boasted the finest eatery in town. Both points would have been hotly contested by the proprietors of its rival establishment, the nearby St. Mary's Hotel, but the simple truth of the matter was that the former easily surpassed the latter on both scores. Run by Mr. Joshua Van Anden, this stately but unpretentious hotel had been established along with the St. Mary's to accommodate the steady influx of miners, speculators, and businessmen that copper fever had occasioned.

Although the exceptional skills of his own personal cooks more than satisfied his palate, Cadwallader Jones occasionally ventured into town with Genevieve so as to dine out. This he did for her sake; he realized that a young woman like Gen would grow understandably restless if confined to their home, spacious and comfortable though it might be. The Jane Austen novels she favored all depicted characters of refinement enjoying the finer things in life in the rarified air of patrician settings. Jones's manor wanted for little in the way of refinement, yet aside from that the setting of Sault Ste. Marie was a far cry from patrician.

But for now, until he had the time to bring her east, an occasional dinner in this backwoods town would have to suffice. Yet ever since the miners had become an overshadowing presence in the Soo, it was with increasing reluctance that he descended into its throbbing heart with her at his side. Not that all of them were bad sorts, but that a distasteful element lurked within their ranks was simply undeniable. A man of quiet but unshakable confidence, it was not personal safety concerns that sorely vexed him; Genevieve, being the magnetic beauty that she was, drew more than a little male attention. To her credit the lass handled such situations with the utmost aplomb, the poise that exemplified her character betraying none of the transparent artificiality that was the poise of many women. In smooth stride did she shrug off the overt ogling of men, a credit to her composure but not likely to deter the offending parties.

True, she had been in town quite a bit without his supervision in the last few days, but the Irishman and that Rawn character whom she showed around town seemed very solid sorts, fellows he trusted to manfully defend her honor if it came to that.

Although the population of the Soo had swelled in the last two years, white women, particularly those of Genevieve's station and magnificence, were still few and far between. Men feasted starved, bestial eyes on her in a manner that consequentially brought out the beast in him, that beast of a nobler streak that eyed with loathing the baseness of his peers. The brasher one's he occasionally cowed through bluntly intimated promises of bloodshed, yet how often could he realistically afford confrontation and still be taken seriously as a businessman? The behavior of those fiends, though deplorable, always fell short of crossing the line that would move him to violence. For Jones, the massing of power whilst simultaneously avoiding the glare of publicity was an indispensible element of life. A creature of shadow at his core, he remained as inconspicuous as a man of his importance could hope to be.

With unreadable eyes Jones look out upon a world hateful to him, a world of men for which he held little fondness, one that he knew would do anything for self-satisfaction. So with all the sleekness and assurance of a confidence man he played that world for all it was worth. Some of man's millennial foibles had to be endured, others crafted into tools so as to ensure the triumphant execution of his plan. For now, he needed to uphold his reputation as a peerless businessman and serious player in lake commerce whose sangfroid in such matters was reflected in his daily comportment. And soon it would pay off and the dividends of a lifetime's work would be magnificently realized...

"What business have you at Copper Harbor, Mr. Jones? Does one of the company presidents seek your counsel once again? Or perhaps merely the depth of your pockets to combat their own financial dearth?"

Spoken in a tone that revealed she had observed his mind a-roaming, Genevieve's question succeeded in snapping him back to reality.

"You know how I feel about the copper mania, Gen- a studied glance at the logistics reveals that for all its brag it is simply unsustainable. Yet a select few of the companies will realize handsome profits. So aside from the start-up funds I lent several of the more promising companies, I will not blithely pour my savings into their ventures. Unless, of course, they can firmly convince me of their capacity to stand the acid test of time. I go there to discuss the cautious expansion of our operations with the Pittsburgh and Boston Copper Harbor Mining Company as well as the Jackson Mining Company, so as to hopefully ensure the success of my initial investments. But they must in large part handle their own financial crises."

"Will you use this opportunity to broach the subject of your proposed canal plans?"

Answering her, he smiled thinly. "Should the situation allow for my doing so without appearing overly ambitious, then yes my dear. At present the portage and freight hauling business is booming, so much so that it makes sense to wring as much out of it as possible before my canal plans become cemented in reality. Recall you the hauling of the schooner *Uncle Tom* past the rapids back in June? I made a mint off of that; until a canal is truly viable, with both private and government money and resources properly aligned as they were in the funding and creating of the Illinois-Michigan Canal, it makes sense to focus more on the portage business."

"*For dynamism, while an indispensible part of business, need always be tempered by the blunt acknowledgement and assessment of variables both principal and minute*. Does that not sum it up?"

A twinkle of humor appeared in his eyes. "You've been reading my manuscript, have you?"

Behind her veil a mischievous smile took form. "You should not leave it sitting around if you don't wish for inquisitive eyes to peruse it, Mr. Jones."

"Fair enough," he admitted with a short chuckle that she and she alone could elicit from him.

"As though you aren't already hopelessly over-tasked? So how long have you labored over this business philosophy tome of yours in your 'free time'?"

"Two months of writing firmly backed by a lifetime of firsthand experience," he responded briskly. "But enough about that, Gen. Let us turn to you. Over-tasked though I may be, I can still plainly see that Mr. Fagan's departure has weighed heavily on you. You miss the company of the Irishman, then?"

She did indeed miss the Irishman, from his spiked red hair and gold-accented, cavalier grin to his unpretentious intellect. She found herself pleasantly reminiscing on their conversations, particularly those relating to literature. Finnbar conducted himself with all the charm and polish of a Continental gentleman straight out of a novel, but the honest realism of his temperament she found more mesmerizing than any imagined character.

"I would be remiss to say that he has not lingered on my

thoughts of late."

Although the gray veil shielded her face, Jones readily detected the unhappiness contained within her response. The knowledge of what fate was almost certainly going to befall that witty Irishman weighed heavily on him, but what more could he have done? He had tried to warn Mr. Fagan and the others... ah, it would not do well to dwell on it. Had they heeded his earnest warning they could have avoided the horrors that lay in store for them in the tractless gloom of the forests within the Pictured Rocks. But who knew? Perhaps Marcel had been telling the truth and their destination was not Chapel Beach, which he hoped for Gen's sake was the case.

"Well hopefully he will emerge unscathed from the wilds, and then you two could-"

In a voice that would have been loud even out of doors, an inebriated miner rudely interjected.

"C'mere girl, let's have us a dance or two, eh?"

Genevieve, prim and aloof, did not even deign to fix her eyes upon the man.

"I am not of a mind to dance, thank you sir. Good day."

The miner evinced so signs of comprehension, instead stumbling closer.

"C'mon, I seek only to twirl you around a bit."

"You'll do nothing of the sort." Jones informed him coldly. "Do us all a favor, miner, and take swift leave of this place. Your presence here is as distasteful to us as it should be embarrassing to you. And even in your dissipated state you should recognize that expecting her to dance with the likes of you is an insult to common sense."

"Why don't you listen to the man, Daniel?" a fellow miner hastily counseled him.

The sot, his weathered and bewhiskered face ruddy with the overindulgence that likewise made him deaf to Jones words, swayed in place and tried in vain to fix his insouciant leer on Genevieve.

"Pretty one, ain't she?" he said thickly, giving seemingly unconscious voice to the thought. The other miner half-heartedly attempted to grab his arm but the drunk shook him off.

The face of Cadwallader Jones did not flush with rage, nor did it even glower at the whiskey-saturated miner before him. He merely leveled his tawny eyes at the man in a manner that would have chilled the blood of a wolf and spoke in firm but controlled tone.

"Because you are so obviously a man of scanty perceptions, I am affording you one final chance to turn on heel and leave."

It was at this point that, oblivious to the dire warning those strange eyes and chilling voice so clearly communicated, the miner attempted to grab Genevieve's arm.

He didn't get very far, Jones saw to that.

Like a coiled spring release from its tension Jones sprang at the man. A long-bladed knife materialized in his right hand, the keen edge of which whipped downwards to neatly sever the man's outstretched fingers. The miner's lust instantly gave way to panic, panic that froze into stillness as his mind, clouded though it might be, wholly comprehended the full measure of his mistake. He stared in immobile silence at his hand, now a stump from which sprouted only half a thumb, and from which spouted fine geysers of blood.

With glacial coolness Jones stepped back and observed his foe. As if he was not quite willing to accept it as reality, the miner stared at his ruined hand and the severed fingers on the floorboards, one of which still twitched spasmodically. Then, as if fighting gravity the entire way down, he lethargically fell backwards onto the floor.

The miner's last sight before unconsciousness swallowed him up was the face of Cadwallader Jones, whose unblinking stare and half-concealed sneer filled the gradually diminishing field of his vision.

"Well miner, that was infernally foolish of you, now wasn't it?"

He then took a purposeful step towards the other miner who, slack-jawed with shock, put his hands out in placatory fashion and quickly retreated.

The smell of blood slammed into Genevieve's nostrils. This was not the first man Jones had maimed on her behalf. In fact, she'd been witness to more significant consequences. Once when she was thirteen a half-breed trapper cornered her in a stable where she had been petting the horses. Then too had Jones, her guardian in more ways than one, descended on the offending hand in a fury cold and calculated, and therefore all the more lethal. He had carried her wracked and weeping body from the scene of that interrupted crime, while two men were required to bear the stiff, mangled body of the half-breed out of the stable.

And then, just as now, the chilling look of delight that manifested itself on his normally impassive face caused a wholly irrepressible shudder to course through her.

Noticing her alarm Jones placed a comforting hand on her shoulder. "He left me no choice. My only regret, Gen, is soiling your riding jacket."

On the light green of her riding coat a fine mist of blood had been sprayed, which settled on the fabric like droplets of morning dew set ablaze by the rising sun. Her lips trembled uncontrollably and burning tears welled up in her eyes. At the moment she was exceedingly glad of the veil that shielded her unnerved face from view.

As he went over to explain the situation to an aghast Joshua Van Anden, Jones realized that under the ponderous weight of his various responsibilities his soul was beginning to sag. He had quite lost his cool a moment ago, and in recognizing this a very foreign emotion took hold of him- *fear.* He had come too far for a pathetic lapse in self-mastery to compromise his plans. He must bring to a swift conclusion his plot, for increasingly the beast within him threatened to snap its tether.

And that was a beast he could ill-afford to loose upon the world just yet.

Chapter 32

Owain Derog Crowder, stirred from the comforting fog of his slumber, awoke to find his place of detainment in an agitated state. As was often the case these days, when he first began regaining awareness the clinging power of the dream world deluded him into thinking that he was free from this waking nightmare. But alas, in a moment's time his outer senses reasserted themselves. Reality gave him a stiff slap across the face and inexorably forced him to reenter the harshness of its realm.

"Jesus wept," he groaned in unreserved misery, rolling over to look out his cell.

The two men who a moment ago sat guarding his cell dashed from the room like shadows fleeing the consuming power of pure darkness. The confusion of voices beyond the walls of this cheerless prison spoke wildly in that queer tongue, so recognizable yet just warped enough to make wholesale comprehension of it impossible...

He cocked his head as the tumult outside crested. By now he knew his infernal captors well enough to know that little rattled them to such an extent. What, then, was this hullabaloo all about? Was this something to do with him? Were these barbarians working themselves into a blood-fueled frenzy in anticipation of dispatching him? Was this it, then, after he had proven himself useful to them, had put his skills as a physician to good work among their sick and injured? He centered himself with a few deep breaths, eventually regaining control over his emotions.

Many would have been driven mad were they to find themselves in his predicament, but him- never. Insanity was a great leveler among men and something, therefore, to be avoided at all costs. Despite the maelstrom of horrors he had been swept into he refused to give in to panic, as he had seen some of the other prisoners do. Or former prisoners, more properly put. After watching them meet their savage, untimely ends Crowder clung even more desperately to his acumen and dealt with each day as it winged its way toward him. Dwelling on the past, fearing the future- what good could come of such things? Intellect and sangfroid would carry the day as always they did.

Rising to his feet, he placed his hands around the wooden bars of his cell and listened closely.

The Babel outside reached its apex only to be swiftly brought down several decibels by a voice that cut through it like a blast of Arctic wind. Not shouted but nevertheless potent, not alarmed but rather forceful in its composed delivery of words, that chilling voice was one Crowder had grown to fear of late.

Through the tiny windows of the domed structure in which he was held captive, he listened raptly as the cold voice continued assuaging the masses, transforming their distressed chatter into attentive silence. At length some other voices cut in, which sounded to Crowder like the questions being put forth, but he was too far away to be sure. The impassive voice grew slightly louder as it delivered a concise speech, one concluded with the steady, ceremonious clanging of weapons and the heavy stamping of feet.

And then with startling abruptness it was over, plunging Crowder's world into silence. He slumped against the cool stone of his cell, mind churning with conjecture.

That night no drums were played, no ululating songs or chants floated through the muggy summer air. In the pit of his cramping gut Crowder knew that something big, something sinister, was poised to go down.

But what?

Chapter 33

He rose early, so as to greet the dawn. Never having been one to languish abed, this particular morning found Alvord more eager than usual to busy himself. As the wanton indulgence in food and liquor that characterized their camp last night was a sin he most assuredly shared in, he determined that a healthy dose of exercise would serve as an acceptable penance while concomitantly doing his body some good.

Thus driven, he ignored the throbbing mass that was his brain and the sourness in his gut and, stumbling to the water's edge through stubborn volition, thrust his head into the lake. Bracing in its temperature, the water instantly snapped him out of his stupor. He took a moment to gulp some down and rinse the staleness from his mouth. Refreshed, he rose and rubbed the accumulated crust of a night's sleep out of his eyes, taking a look around their camp.

Partially risen, the sun just barely shed its muted glow over a somber, fogbound Chapel Beach. But even as he watched the fog began to lift, several rays of strengthening sunlight sliced through it like celestial blades. Before long the remaining gold-infused, fibrillose wisps of vapor rose heavenward, appearing to Alvord a legion of souls departing from this world. In its wake the robins and towhees, first harbingers of the morning, gave vent to their dawn songs.

While the sun burnt off the last of the stubborn blanket of fog a hawk floated in lazy circles over the cliff that marked the far end of the beach, while nearby several gulls sent their shrill cries across the water. Below them a magnificent gray fox prowled cautiously around the rivulet that ran into the lake under the cliff. The haunting call of a nearby loon caused the fox to look up sharply, and upon noticing Alvord it slipped ghost-like back into the gloom of the forest. He silently wished it luck, for soon these woods would be a veritable deathtrap for he and his furbearing brethren. The newly arrived trapping party would see to that.

Tossing and turning, coughing and farting, most of that trapping party still lay wrapped in the embrace of Morpheus. One Indian had already clawed his way back to consciousness and squatted before the dormant mound of ash that had been one of their fires, sullenly poking at it with a stick. The two half-breeds who had taken the last shift of watch saw that Alvord was up for good and gratefully fell onto their Mackinaw blankets.

He kicked off his shoes and readied himself for laps up and down the beach. This is how he used to run back in New York. After his family had departed this world, he would take a rowboat to Coney Island and occasionally even Brighton Beach, where he would run barefoot in the sand and exhaust himself swimming and exercising. It had proved cathartic, he supposed, in the days when those losses were freshly felt.

Before he commenced running, however, Duddersfield appeared at his side, briskly trotting in place. The unshapely geologist brought his knees up as high as he could, breathing in short, irregular puffs. His glasses he had left behind; those beady little eyes and flushed, quivering jowls again calling to Alvord's mind the image of a bipedal pig.

"You may want to try what I'm doing," he suggested between breaths, "it's not good to run without dynamically warming up the muscles involved beforehand."

And with that he was off, kicking up an inordinate amount of sand as he ran down the beach with every bit as ungainly a gait as Alvord had imagined. Sandpipers and plovers took startled flight before him, squeaking their displeasure.

Shaking his head in wonderment, Alvord broke into a slow, even stride.

Humphrey Demetrius Duddersfield- may the world never again see his like.

Twenty minutes later he leaned over, sweaty palms on his knees as he tried to steady his breathing. His chest heaved mightily, lungs strained after a particularly intense run. Peeling off his soaked shirt he strode leisurely across the beach. Towards the water's edge, the large-grained sand gave way to colorful pebbles of infinite variety.

"Water in the shallows here is alright," Marcel called from behind him, "but you dive down too deep and its colder'n a witch's tit."

The camp was more fully alive now, with those still sleeping beginning to stir and those already up getting fires started. The fox-like Indian dogs chased inquisitive gray jays away from the camp, voicing their excitement in that strange yip that seemed to be as close to barking as they could verge on. Still lounging on Alvord's blankets, Cerberus paid them no mind.

"I haven't much experience with witches' tits," Alvord ruminated wryly.

"Well I have, and can firmly attest to their frostiness," offered

Finnbar, who also began stripping down. When he started removing the lower half of his undergarments, Marcel offered words of caution.

"Whoa, hold hard there Finn. Wouldn't go doin' that."

"Ye wouldn't?"

"Hell no, son. There's trout and pike in there as could take off yer cod and knackers all in one go if they see 'em danglin' about. Yeah, even yer unappetizin' Irish package, so wouldn't risk it."

"Duly noted," Finnbar replied crisply.

They swam in the pure, crystalline water for some time, with many of the others joining them. The Indians were superlative swimmers, better even than Alvord who swam on a regular basis during the more clement months.

A spirit of lightheartedness prevailed; they had hard days ahead of them so it made sense to enjoy this singular scene of peace. Floating on his back, Alvord stared up at the endless droves of dragonflies that cruised the sky above them in frenzied search of flies and mosquitoes. He tried his best to push from his mind thoughts of the serpentine *Mishi-ginebikoog* and the great water-lynx *Mishipeshu* of Chippewa lore.

Unable to shake off that primal pulse of trepidation, he swam back into the sea-green shallows. Duddersfield was standing in the water nearby, staring as if transfixed to the north.

"What's on your mind, Humphrey?"

"Well Mr. Rawn, I don't know if you are aware but somewhere far, far to the north of us the Franklin Expedition is currently lost. Or at least that's the rumor. You know, the British expedition to find the Northwest Passage?"

Most everyone knew about that expedition, but that it was currently being given up as lost was news to Alvord.

"Unlucky bastards. An inhospitable place to be adrift, the Arctic. At least I would assume."

"Indeed it is. Let's hope your trapping venture fares better."

"Oh, I'm sure we'll make out alright." Yet even as the confident words left his mouth, a fleeting image of those anomalous petroglyphs flashed through his mind, followed promptly by the memory of the figure he thought he'd sighted among the cliffs above camp.

But he quickly pushed such things out of his mind, focusing instead on the adventures that awaited him.

"You didn't make a fire when you got up." Gordon's tone bluntly communicated his disgust to Alvord. The trappers glared sharply at him, bleary-eyed from the night's festivities.

The three half-breeds who acted as the self-appointed chefs were busily preparing breakfast over the now crackling campfires.

"Jawbeance was setting one as I rose."

"We have more than one fire. First few men up are to each get one going. Camp etiquette."

Alvord nodded thoughtfully. "Very well then. I shall bear that in mind, and will be sure to do so in the future."

Gordon gave a *humph* of decided skepticism and stomped away, apparently unsatisfied with his reply. Watching him go, Alvord sighed hopelessly. He was growing awfully tired of the man's juvenile posturing.

They feasted avidly on a breakfast of cooked trout, sturgeon, and thin-sliced potatoes mixed with onions.

"I could get use to this, the breakfast of a voyageur." Finnbar belched loudly, sipping on some steaming coffee. A number of their party stood in a circle drinking the fragrant substance that Alvord had never developed a taste for. He supped tea instead, which he knew to be better for him anyway.

"We ain't proper voyageurs, actually," Marcel told him.

"We're not?" Alvord asked confusedly. While always portrayed as inferior to the mountain man in American literature and art, the title of the voyageur was not one that he minded. What were they then if not voyageurs?

"Nope. Coeur de bois, actually. *Runners of the woods* in French. Voyageurs is licensed trappers, while Coeur de bois ain't, instead bein' unlicensed, independent trappers. We're circumventin' the system."

"Hmm." As one who was chary of adhering to rules and systems he found fatuous, Alvord could appreciate that.

Gordon misinterpreted his amusement as disdain.

"What," he snorted, "you gonna arrest us all, *Cap'n* Rawn?"

Moving in a blur Alvord backhanded him sharply across the face, promptly sending his body crashing to the sand. Gordon rolled to his feet after a moment's recovery with murder in his eyes. He tried to advance but Lightfoot put a restraining hand to his chest.

"Let it be, brother."

"Naw, let 'im have at, Lightfoot," ordered Marcel, who paused to release a dry bark of a laugh, "if the fool really fancies a go."

"Greenhorn or not, I don't brook shit from pissants like him," Alvord firmly informed the camp, his shirt doing little to disguise the tensed muscles of his chest and shoulders. "He has slighted and pressed me a few times- I have responded diplomatically but he may now have a go if he likes, at his own peril."

His smoldering gray eyes, fiercely reflecting the glow of sunlight off the lake, did not stray from those of the heavily breathing trapper. The Indians watched both men intently, their tattooed faces offering no indication of their thoughts.

"We have reached a collision of opinion here, Gordon. You are convinced that I do not belong in this outfit, and I firmly believe otherwise. So what'll it be, trapper? You going to brazen it out, or back off and keep a civil tongue in your head?"

For a moment it looked like Gordon might indeed brazen it out and charge him, but like the passing of a tempest the moment passed and he stormed off in high dudgeon.

After breakfast Alvord brushed his teeth with his boar bristle toothbrush and carefully ran dentifrice through his teeth. Running wet hands through his dark chestnut hair, he observed that most of the trapping party was having another round of coffee. He decided to read for a bit and saw that Finnbar and Duddersfield had already beaten him to the punch.

He knew Finnbar to be tearing through Herman Melville's breakout book *Typee* at the moment, which in a fictional manner recounted the author's time spent in the Marquesas Islands in the South Pacific. The Irish writer intensively studied every book he read and took detailed notes on them. Despite this he still read rather quickly, devouring more books than Alvord, who preferred to savor what he read.

Duddersfield, meanwhile, was absorbed in the pages of the most recent addition of Charles Lyell's *Principles of Geology*, and nearby on the sand sat *Geological Observations on South America* by Charles Darwin and Martin Lichtenstein's, *Reisen im südlichen Afrika*. Munching stolidly on some of those horrifically bland Graham crackers made popular by dietary reformer Sylvester Graham, the young scientist was wholly consumed by his reading.

Alvord grabbed the book he was currently working through, *Letters and Notes on the Manners, Customs, and Condition of the North American Indians*, a compendium of the observations of the famous frontier painter George Catlin as he traveled extensively through the West and encountered a wide variety of Indians. There was one passage in particular that Alvord currently scoured the book for, one that pertained to the enigmatic Mandan Indian of the Upper Missouri. Often cited as being an unusual tribe among the red man by early explorers, the Mandan had dwelled in permanent, walled villages filled with large, earth-covered lodges. This alone qualified them as strange, for Alvord had never read of other tribes employing this mode of protection except in the Southwest or in Mexico. In his mind fixed, wall-enclosed societies stood as largely a white, European concept while Indians favored mobility, which allowed them to freely follow game populations. For obvious reasons, the rumors abounding in this region about tribes of light skinned demons drew him to this section.

After a few moments spent fixedly searching, he located the sought-after passage.

A stranger in the Mandan village is first struck with the different shades of complexion, and various colours of hair which he sees in a crowd about him; and is at once almost disposed to exclaim that "these are not Indians".

There are a great many of these people whose complexions appear as light as half breeds; and amongst the women particularly, there are many whose skins are almost white, with the most pleasing symmetry and proportion of features; with hazel, with grey, and with blue eyes, -- with mildness and sweetness of expression, and excessive modesty of demeanour, which render them exceedingly pleasing and beautiful.

Why this diversity of complexion I cannot tell, nor can they themselves account for it. Their traditions, so far as I have yet learned them, afford us no information of their having had any knowledge of white men before the visit of Lewis and Clarke, made to their village thirty-three years ago. Since that time there have been but very few visits from white men to this place, and surely not enough to have changed the complexions and the customs of a nation. And I recollect perfectly well that Governor Clarke told me, before I started For this place, that I would find the Mandans a strange people and half white.

The distracted flipping of several pages brought Alvord to Catlin's hypothesis on the matter.

It would seem from their tradition of the willow branch, and the dove, that these people must have had some proximity to some part of the civilized world; or that missionaries or others have been formerly among them, inculcating the Christian religion and the Mosaic account of the Flood; which is, in this and some other respects, decidedly different from the theory which most natural people have distinctly established of that event.

With thoughts of bygone things still percolating in his mind, Alvord readied his equipment for today's foray into the unknown.

Chapter 34

"Well, time to take the plunge, then."

Alvord, standing next to Finnbar atop Chapel Rock, cast a dubious glance down at the water-laved, rocky span of beach thirty feet below before regarding the Irishman curiously.

"Plunge into the *woods*, that is. Come now, Alvord me mucker, by now ye must surely know that I delight in the ebb and flow of life far too much to go and off meself? Plus, think of the remarkable genius I would be depriving the world of, the wit, the dash, the vim, the *verve*-"

"Are you quite finished?"

The sun was more significantly risen, casting a heat-induced shimmer over the sands of Chapel Beach and a silver-white sheen upon the diminutive waves out on the lake.

Finnbar swung his torso back and forth gingerly, his vertebrae issuing tiny cracks as he did. "Well, I for one could do with a fair bit o' fossicking about. Got drunk as a lord last night, did I. Still trying to figure out how you brought yourself to take exercise this morn'."

"Compulsion of conscious, I suppose you could say. Though it has its appeal, I simply cannot allow myself to loll and laze the day away after a bout of overindulgence."

"Aye, 'twas quite the session we had ourselves, was it not?"

Alvord grinned in fond remembrance of a day well seized. "'*Twas*."

The Irishman shuffled his feet as he stared at the slowly assembling trapping party below them. "You understand this whole trapping business yet? I still feel like the pair of us are neophytes in the midst of hardened professionals."

"Well, in all fairness we are. But come now, Finnbar. You of all people should know that if a body acts confidently enough, people will automatically assume you know what you're doing."

"Specious comportment is the coin of the realm, eh?"

"Indeed it is."

With wary steps they crossed back over the short, narrow archway of rock that connected Chapel Rock to the cliffs of the shoreline.

"You know," Finnbar remarked interestedly, "should this archway collapse," (here Alvord took the few final steps off it with a brisker stride) "Chapel Rock will still be connected to the mainland by the roots of that young pine that grows atop it. See how the nexus of roots stretches across?"

Alvord did indeed see, and gave a half-chuckle at the thought. "That would make for an odd sight. So do you really think that the Jesuit Marquette preached atop it in the days or yore?"

"Who knows? But it makes a fine pulpit, does it not?"

"The question is- would his Holiness Pope Pius IX approve?"

Finnbar offered him a look of polite bafflement. "How in the bloody hell would I know the answer to that?"

"Fair enough. After all, he is the 'Holy Father' and you merely a-"

"Lethally suave Irishman with a small arsenal of wit at his disposal."

Unable to muster a suitable rejoinder, Alvord simply led the way back down to camp in silence.

Marcel spoke loudly in his gravelly voice so that all present could hear him. They stood near the edge of the beach, where the sand rose in a short acclivity to meet the forest. On the beach before him he had etched into the sand a rough schematic of their trapping expedition.

"So, on our way to this spot we dropped off small exploratory parties here and here."

With a stick he indicated the cluster of half-circles that represented the Grand Sable Dunes and the smooth span of Twelve Mile Beach.

"I've never trapped either location, nor has any soul that I know of, so Dave'n I figgered that smaller outfits could scout the land before reportin' back to us here. The reason we're using Chapel Beach as our base of operation is that I scouted these lands back in my youth and did a mite 'o trappin' here. Place was fair teemin' with furry bank notes of all varieties back then, and to the best of anybody's knowledge no one else has laid so much as a single trap in this locale. Even at the height of the fur trade and inter-company competition, the major fur companies gave it a pass."

"Aye," remarked David drolly, "funny how talk of vengeful gods and unexplained disappearances keeps the sane folks away."

The camp chuckled darkly at this, even the Indians. Upon inquiring into the matter of the legends shrouding this area, Alvord and Finnbar had been informed that Indians had long considered the place cursed, a land haunted by malevolent gods or *manitous*. Compounded by stories of disappearances dating back to the early days of the Jesuits, so ingrained was their fear of it that soon men red and white alike gave it a wide berth. Yet the Indians, half-breeds, and white men of their trapping party all claimed to harbor no dread of the region and its fearsome legends. Alvord was with them, never having been one to let superstitions stand in the way of enticing potentialities.

Yet his mind, especially adept at identifying inconsistencies in peoples' stories after years of police work, could not stop asking itself- if these men professed no fear of this land, why was it that none of them had ever attempted to trap here before now?

"There are two small rivers that flow through this beach," Marcel continued. "We got what I'm callin' Chapel Creek yonder," he indicated the nearby stream that gave way to the small waterfall, "plus that unnamed trickle on the far end o' the beach. I once followed that to a small lake. Plenty of swampland to the west of it, too. Cut sign aplenty during my perambulations."

"Virgin land prime for the taking." Gordon said with an unchaste leer.

Marcel offered him a toothy grin. "Ye might say that, Gordon. Plus, if you follow Chapel Creek up a ways, it leads to another, far larger lake. A body o' water that big with a decent sized outflow, it stands to reason that there are least a few tributaries feedin' into it. So today we focus our efforts on scoutin' out those two areas."

Idly tracing the two deep scars on his forehead, David pointed to the north end of the larger lake Marcel had drawn. "We reckon that the lake might be fed by streams flowing north into it. Marcel made it but a little ways up its eastern bank afore turning back without coming across any, so perhaps they're further yet."

"Nothing like going in half-blind," Gaston quipped.

Marcel grabbed his crotch in mocking response. "Bite the back of 'em, you young cuss. I was only one person so's I didn't cover a lot of ground, but in the little saunterin' around I did I got me an eyeful o' prime real estate."

"Your father saunters?" Finnbar quietly asked Gaston out of the side of his mouth.

"Oh, you should see him go."

They fought down boyish chuckles as they continued listening.

"That's why we're here durin' the height of the summer, to scout the land 'fore we lay serious trap lines. Each day we push further into the interior, eventually making camp by late August, when its cooled off and the skeeters ain't suckin' blood by the gallon, we'll set our hands to the task of establishin' major trap lines.

"So then, me boyos," David said, surveying the trapping party with his thumbs hooked into his broad leather belt and his head tilted back self-confidently, "once we know the lay of the land better, we'll draw us up a grand auld plan. But for today, we break off into small groups and branch out. So set a few well-placed traps, tip over some meat if ye happen upon it, but haul yer arses back here by dusk."

"Plus," he added with a crafty sidelong glance at Marcel, "we'll get to see if Marcel's fancy eastern traps'll get the job done."

"I take exception to that, you scoundrel of a Scot. I'm tellin' ye, this Miles Standish feller outta Manhattan makes better traps than Thomas Moore himself, better by far'n the old American Fur Company traps what you lot use up here. Cheaper, too- only two bucks a piece. Eastern traps is quality, I'll make a believer outta you yet. Ramsay Crooks came to prefer Standish's traps over the one's outta the Michilimackinac trap emporium."

Amidst idle chatter they assembled their gear and hefted their bulky packs, assembling in the cool shadows of the overarching maples, birches, and pines. Soon everyone was ready to depart save the two men who would serve as camp watchers and Duddersfield, who elected to stay behind and continue focusing his survey on the beach.

"And as you may know," here Marcel paused to cut his deep-set eyes at Gordon, "Al and Finn here ain't trapped before. Some occasional bits of advice wouldn't go amiss."

"I think you're underestimating my peerless skills of observation and intuition, Marcel. The delicacy of detail is not something lost on me."

"Really Finn, 'cause from where I'm standin' there's plenty those peepers of yers are blind to."

"Ah," the Irishman scoffed dismissively as he began stepping forward, "and pray offer an example of this alleged obliviousness. What's escaped me notice?"

"The fact that that's a grave yer about to set foot on."

Finnbar's moccasin paused in mid-air as his eyes swept downward in surprise. Below his foot was a gently sloped mound of sand and leaf litter. Large fragments of bark lay scattered around it, and what appeared to be rotting stakes poked out of the sand.

"See these pines around the grave?" Gaston pointed the modest sized trees out. "Look at how perfectly they surround this patch of earth. They were planted there as saplings, picketing the grave, and now they have become part of the forest. Those rotting stakes were used to support the bark that formed the low roof over the body. I'd say that it was at least fifty years ago that this women was buried."

"Woman?" Alvord saw no indication of gender before them. Then again, he ruefully conceded that had not even noticed the grave.

"Aye," David confirmed, "woman indeed. Do ye not see that pit o' paddle sticking outta the sand there?"

He did not- not at first glance, that is. But after a moment's careful inspection his eyes studied more patiently one of the partially jutting stakes. It terminated in an odd, unnatural shape...

Damned if that isn't the rotting handle of a paddle.

Gaston bent down and touched the handle. "Women were always buried with the tools of their daily routines- like paddles and carrying straps, to ensure that the drudgery of this life would carry over into the next. For men, tools of the hunt and war would be displayed instead."

Finnbar frowned deeply in a rare display of perplexity. "I thought no man would tarry on this stretch of beach, much less take the time to bury a body on this 'haunted' ground."

"The Grand Island Chippewa, who lived on that island I showed you yesterday, did not fear the Pictured Rocks as others. They gen'rally kept their distance, but were unafraid to make use of these beaches and fishing grounds. They're mostly dead now... war and disease made short work of them... real good folks, too..." Marcel's voice trailed off.

Alvord met Finnbar's gaze, which communicated the same thought that

We've got a lot to learn.

"Worry not, lads, this stuff'll come with time," David assured them, discerning the concern on their brows.

Alvord looked past his wiry form towards the woods. The interior that lay beyond that rustling row of trees summoned him on a primal level. Here he stood, Alvord Rawn, formerly of Manhattan and a lifelong city-dweller, poised to plunge into *terra incognita* and harvest a bounty of furs amidst tales of maleficent gods and unexplained disappearances...

This expedition had real potential.

Chapter 35

The first large game animal Alvord ever felled had been a deer, a feat accomplished while hunting with his older brother Anscom in the Pine Barrens of New Jersey during his youth. And it seemed awfully long ago indeed that he had, in a moment of raw inexperience, lifted his eyes from the rifle's sights the instant before he squeezed the trigger in nervous anticipation of the shot. The lead ball tore its path through the crisp air to strike the four-point buck in the spine, a near miss. With its backbone blown almost in half, the pitiable animal had been rendered crippled, unable to rise again, but its desperate, fruitless thrashing and the manifestation of sheer terror in its eyes turned his stomach. With clumsiness born of haste he had been forced to reload the Pennsylvania-Kentucky Rifle and bring mercy to the suffering creature, cursing himself all the while for bungling the shot.

That mistake was not one he repeated, not even now, when it was a black bear in his sights rather than a deer.

The country that he and his group explored seemed almost too perfect to be, with airy, virgin stands of maple, beech, white and yellow birch, and elm interrupted at times by the shadowy intrusion of primeval pine and hemlock groves. Along the unnamed creek cedars stood in solemn rows, their entangled canopy rifted only by the occasional questing ray of sunlight. In the hardwood sections of woods the forest floor was carpeted by a vibrant and extraordinarily diverse array of wildflowers and orchids. The variety of Nature's palette graced some flowers with muted tones, while others blazed with hues of such intensity that they threatened to scorch the land. Here and there old or storm-damaged trees had fallen, but against so picturesque a backdrop they seemed to be intentionally placed there, and in no way disturbed the sense of Edenic perfection this place radiated.

It was from behind one such log that Alvord had glimpsed the patch of fur, fur black as pitch and readily visible against the overwhelming green of the verdant forest.

He'd signaled to Lightfoot to stop while slipping behind the trunk of a mighty elm before he was spotted. Motioning for the rest of the group to halt and take cover, the swarthy trapper had urged him forward with a jerk of his head, indicating that it was Alvord who should proceed with the shot.

This was the first bear he had encountered in the wild. Twice in Manhattan and again in St. Louis he had seen "tame" bears and their handlers. But seeing such a beast in its natural habitat was another matter entirely.

Trundling idly along, the bear revealed more of its bulk, its head and shoulders coming around the end of the log. Alvord judged the distance to be around eighty yards, which was about the extent to which he felt comfortable shooting. He knew that mountain men were known to make shots at distances of over three hundred yards, but such feats of marksmanship were beyond him.

Bringing up the octagonal barrel, he shouldered his .53 caliber Hawken rifle and set the smooth black walnut of its stock against his sweat-coated face. His senses sharpened upon aligning the rifle's sights just behind the bear's shoulder. The cloying mugginess of the forest washed over him, the chirping of birds and droning of mosquitoes he heard more acutely. Taking a short breath and letting it slowly, evenly leak from his lungs, he squeezed the trigger and in the next moment the gun barked. A cloud of pungent smoke instantly blotted out his view of the beast.

Through the ringing in his ears Alvord could hear the bear barreling through the woods ahead, and with the rest of the group he raced to where the bear had stood. Sure enough, lung blood so vividly red that it seemed unreal coated the churned up area, and a widening trail of it led south.

In no time they had followed the crimson rivulet to the dying animal.

"A true monarch," Alvord noted in somber admiration as he watched it breathe its last. His bullet had flown true, shattering the bear's shoulder and massively damaging its lungs. The light went from the bruin's eyes as a whitish film crept over them, much in the way the radiance of a star might diminish with the encroachment of dawn.

Lightfoot's face betrayed his pleased curiosity at Alvord's admiration of the animal he'd slain.

"Yeah, that he was. Damn near four hundred pounds I'd say." Gordon might be an inflexibly obdurate man, but Lightfoot appeared to be softening his stance regarding Alvord's greenhorn status.

The Indians each stepped forward and shook the dead bear's paw, muttering something in their native tongue.

"They're paying him homage," Lightfoot informed Alvord in

his raspy voice.

He saw.

Following the winding course of Chapel Brook alongside David and Marcel, Finnbar took a moment to adjust the green headband that had slipped down his forehead. Tightening the sweat-soaked silk around his head, he continued following his two friends deeper into the welcoming embrace of the wild.

His head swiveled around almost of its own accord, his eyes unable to keep up with his brain's fervent desire to visually document all around him.

Hunting was not unknown to him before now. On his Uncle's estate in Killarney he had pursued the great red stag as well as boar. Likewise, during his time in the Uruguayan Civil War did he and his fellow mercenaries hunt for meat. But wilderness this intact and unsullied? No. Never in all his born days had he walked amidst such primordial majesty.

Brook trout swam in abundance in this slow-moving section of Chapel Creek, the telltale flash of sunlight on scale indicating their presence. Passenger pigeons, totally unbothered by the trappers, could be found in such riotous profusion that twice he killed individuals with his rifle butt just to see if he could. Up in the tangled lacework of canopy a variety of birds lent their voices to the natural melody that the forest resounded with.

The two groups had gone their separate ways, each following a watercourse toward their respective sources. It was hoped that from the lakes a ganglion of tributaries would lead them to other lakes, or at least ponds and swamps. With Marcel and David in the lead, Finnbar kept pace with Gordon, two braves and three half-breeds, one of whom was the likeable Gaston. For all of Marcel's gruffness, his son was an easygoing sort with whom Finnbar got along famously.

The abrupt, cracking report of a rifle reverberated through the open woods around them. The two groups were still quite close to each other at this point, separated by only six hundred feet of forest, but the roar of the gun made that margin seem closer by far.

"Sounds like that lot is off to a good start!" Finnbar declared excitedly.

"Hope it's an elk," Marcel confessed. "Haven't sank my teeth into a good piece of elk fer a couple o' months now."

Finnbar licked his lips. "Sounds good t'me. What other game have we in this area?"

"Deer, moose, bear, woodland caribou, hare, turkey, grouse, all manner o' waterfowl... hell, might even be a stray herd of woodland buffalo around."

"I've heard plenty of talk of them. They're said to darken the plains in massive herds out West."

Marcel snorted crassly. "Shit son, you ain't lived 'til you been caught in a buffalo stampede."

"In that case, I must see about getting stuck in one then..."

"*Saganosh*," an Indian hailed Finnbar by their moniker for him, which much to his chagrin meant "British."

Alvord they referred to as *Chemoquemon*, or American. Of the two titles he'd gladly opt for the latter, but why settle for either when the most glorious of earthly titles, that of Irishman, was his very birthright?

The brave, Walks With Thunder, handed him a cheroot and motioned for him to light it.

"Smoke keep bugs away," the tall Chippewa promised him, puffing on his pipe. Finnbar had to admit that once he lit up the bugs gave him an acceptable berth.

The mosquitoes along this riparian setting were unspeakably bad, descending in hellish clouds upon the trappers. Having smeared their bodies with foul-smelling bear tallow, the Indians appeared to be targeted less. Or perhaps they were simply more stoic in their dealing with the airborne vermin.

"Hey Finn. Take a good squint at that." Marcel squatted on his heels, pointed at a muddy stretch of ground next to the stream.

"Wolf?" Finnbar suggested upon seeing the large track.

David shook his head. "Nay, Irishman. 'Tis the pug-mark of a panther. See how round the track is, and the fact that no claw marks show?"

"Yep, and the track of a wolf has but one lobe on the leadin' edge of the main pad, while a panther" (Marcel pronounced it 'painter') "s'always got two."

Finnbar scanned the woods, trying to picture a lion prowling about. "Do believe I'll be keepin' me eyes peeled for him."

"Damn!" Marcel suddenly lifted his toque hat and ran a distracted hand through his hair. "That reminds me- forgot the largest traps back in camp. Thought my pack felt light."

"Och, no worries," David reassured him. "Ye and I'll go back for 'em. Twon't take long if we leave our packs here and hare it."

"True enough."

Dropping their packs up against a rock, they began loping through the woods back towards camp, looking every bit as natural as any beast of the wild.

The others continued walking, this time in stealthy silence. Finnbar tried hard to conceal a grin of boyish enjoyment. Who knew what their next step might bring them face-to-face with? Around the next bend in the willow-fringed river could be a moose, a panther, a bear- even a bloody buffalo!

Ah, but for the thrill of the hunt!

It was Alvord who gutted his kill, but a half-breed named Defago and the Indian Big Wolf skinned and quartered it with effortless speed and deftness. He took careful note of their technique, flitting eyes hoping to retain every detail.

They and the other Indians ate the liver on the spot, offering pieces to Lightfoot and Alvord, who declined. Alvord, not one to sample even cooked liver, was hard put to restrain his distaste as they greedily tore into the raw organ.

Defao and Big Wolf also offered to hump the meat and hide the short distance back to camp and then regroup with the others at the headwaters of the nameless stream. In this heat meat had to be cooked, salted, or smoked in a hurry, otherwise it would spoil. Alvord voiced his intention to bring the meat back to camp himself, but they had insisted. Maybe it was out of respect for his first kill? Or perhaps they doubted his speed and ability to find his way back to the group? Whatever the case, his objections fell on deaf ears. Their packs emptied of traps, Defago and Big Wolf transferred the *makowiiyaas*, or bear meat into them and departed. That left Alvord, Lightfoot, and two Chippewa bucks, Jawbeance and Osho-gaz.

Re-shouldering his sixty-pound pack with a grunt, Alvord followed Lightfoot as they cut back over to the creek and continued following it towards the lake from which it flowed.

Jawbeance sported a peculiar looking cap, one made from pelican throat skin. David had told him earlier that it made for light and airy summer wear. Yet atop a human head, its uncanny resemblance to the skin of a certain part of the male anatomy was a bit much for Alvord. Otherwise he actually envied the Indians' attire; breechcloths and buckskin leggings with only a loose-fitting vest over their torsos. But no white man would expose so much of himself even in the privacy of the wilderness, and even most half-breeds opted for clothing of a more concealing character.

Still, as he wiped the sweat from his face he could not restrain a pang of envy. His canvas trousers were thoroughly soaked, as was the light cotton shirt over which he wore a black oilskin vest.

"So," Lightfoot asked him in a manner that implied consultation, "what do you think of this stretch of water?"

"I defer to your expertise in such matters."

Lightfoot dark faced broke into a crooked smile. "I'm asking your opinion, Mr. Manhattan. What do you see here?"

Gray eyes sweeping over the frothing swiftness of the brook, Alvord spotted a pile of mussel shells on several rocks that jutted out of the water.

"Otter midden," he responded astutely, recalling some distant relative of his pointing that out to him during his trip to the Lakes District of England so long ago. He had been what, eleven or so? A tidy span of time had passed since then, but the lesson had stuck.

Lightfoot's smile broadened by a few degrees. "Right in one. What next?"

"Ah, set a trap? Is not otter pelt among the most profitable these days?"

"Uh huh. Unseasoned but a quick study, eh? Alright then-let's see how well you set traps, pilgrim."

From his pack Alvord unfolded two No. 4 traps that they laid at this site. One they placed at the bottom of an otter slide that had made smooth mud of the riverbank. The other soon rested on a rocky stretch of creek bed near several piles of tubular otter scat.

They moved on and soon glimpsed through the trees the sparkling water of Little Chapel Lake. Here they waited (in a protective cloud of tobacco smoke) for Defago and Big Wolf, who came trotting toward them a short while later.

From here they fragmented the group, with Alvord and Osho-gaz trekking along the eastern shoreline of the lake. Defago and Jawbeance would work their way up the western shore, while Lightfoot and Big Wolf stayed put at the headwaters of the little creek they'd followed in to lay more traps and scout out the immediate vicinity.

"*Chemoquemon*, puck-a-saw," said Osho-gaz, whose nose and cheekbones were among the sharpest of any man Alvord had seen. His ears and nose, pierced and adorned with copper, were illuminated by a golden sunbeam, as were the copper armbands he sported.

He half-smiled at Alvord's uncomprehending expression. "Stop and have smoke."

Alvord shook his head politely. "I do not smoke. But if you desire to we can stop."

The man regarded him curiously; few indeed were the men who did not smoke in this country, particularly trappers.

Upon continuing their march they happened upon a broad stream energetically feeding into Little Chapel Lake. They followed its course, soon happening upon a fork. Osho-gaz went left, Alvord right after exchanging nods of good luck.

It was a shadow-dappled pine and hemlock copse he stealthily walked through, with a spongy bed of their needles lending silence to his measured steps. He strayed from the bank of the stream a bit, reveling in the quiet majesty of the forest.

He was quite alone, and upon this glorious realization he basked in the irreplaceable feeling. The distant, dolorous cry of loons out on Superior, the throaty trilling of gray treefrogs, the throb of the cicadas: what welcome substitutes to the acoustic affronts of the city! Such a scene of untarnished wilderness he had seen only in the paintings of Thomas Cole, Asher B. Durand, and their breed of landscape painter. Tilting his head back, he closed his eyes and filled his chest with the leafy air of the forest, a pleasant warmth flooding his body as he did. Upon opening his lids he saw through a gap in the canopy the gibbous moon hanging palely in the aquamarine sky.

He paused a moment atop a steep, thickly treed knoll with his rifle cradled easily in the crook of his arm. Carefully surveying the woods before him, he casually leaned against a soaring white pine, batting away a venturesome mosquito. He ran a hand against the deeply grooved bark of the ancient tree whose canopy might well have been two hundred feet above him.

"An old lord of the forest," he whispered to the benefit of none but himself.

The way in which his voice carried alerted him to a strange fact. The forest was suddenly achingly, almost *intolerably* quiet. The birds ceased their chirping, the squirrels their rustling.

Yet suddenly the birds resumed their calls, but something was different about these... something that even his greenhorn ears were attuned to.

Although he was hardly in his element, something struck him as unusual. Disquieting even. Instantly he was on his guard.

The birdcalls sounded once more, songs that were similar to those he had heard earlier but somehow their slightly different pitch troubled him.

His outward senses could not confirm with any certainty what his primal senses raised their hackles at. Had it not been for years spent patrolling the dismal bowels of Manhattan's underworld, dealing with fiends in human form and relying on instinct as much as anything else, he might have been inclined to let his modern-day logic override this rousing of immemorial awareness. But so conditioned, he did not.

A good thing, too. For at that moment, by degrees swift and

sudden, the world passed from the realm of the sublime to that of nightmare.

Chapter 36

The blanketing humidity was untroubled by even the faintest stir of air. Portentous in its hushed expectancy, a deafening silence pervaded these woods. As a droplet of sweat glided off Alvord's nose, a noise to his left garnered his straining attention. At once recognizable and unexpected, his mind struggled to place it with any exactitude.

And yet...

Thump- there it was again. He knew, *he knew*, that sound...

An unsettling jolt of familiarity coursed through him.

Alarm bells clanging within his brain he stole forward, the soft carpet of club moss underfoot cushioning his footfalls. Rounding the trunk of a colossal hemlock, his eyes met with a shocking sight.

Although the dense canopy of the mature stretch of beech forest below him made for a shadow-dappled setting, a few penetrative rays of light that seemed to doubt their own effectiveness illuminated the shocking scene before him. Alvord's blood ran glacially cold as he stared at the supine form of Osho-gaz. The brave lay lifelessly on the leaf litter fifty yards away, the froth of the gurgling stream right next to him taking on a rosy hue as copious quantities of his blood spilled into it. A dark pool of the crimson fluid had collected under the brave's caved-in skull, and the long spear protruding from his torso let loose a spray of more blood yet as its wielder put his foot against the Indian's corpse and with a low grunt withdrew his weapon.

Alvord automatically began raising his rifle, but stopped when more dark figures silently joined Osho-gaz's killers. There were at least five of them clustered together now, a number that might at any moment enlarge. He needed to ignore the adamant, fiery impulse to avenge the Indian's death so as to take stock of this perilous situation.

For who knew what manner of evil lurked unseen in the leafy gloom?

The weapons they brandished sent questions racing to his mind- were not the swords, spears, and clubs they clutched decidedly non-Indian? But if they weren't Indians, then what in the Devil's unholy name were they? Exactly what unguessed madness had he stumbled upon? His imagination searched in vain for an answer. There were simply too many imponderables at play here.

Cursed land, he then recalled Marcel's glib words with a deepening feeling of dread.

As if to drive those words home, forked tendrils of ground-hugging fog snaked through the trees behind them, threatening to engulf the men. *Otherworldly* was the first word that came to Alvord's mind as he watched its progress. Its movements were far too kinetic to match those of any naturally occurring fog he'd ever seen, appearing instead like some hydra-headed beast that consumed all in its path.

Taking a slow step back to conceal himself behind the hemlock, his foot sank in an old squirrel midden, where the arboreal rodent had piled dozens of pinecones at the base of the tree. The hearty crunch that resulted quickly alerted the killers to his presence.

In prompt, awful unison their shaggy heads swept his way. As the fog began to dissolve their forms they started towards him at a run. Shouldering the Hawken he prepared to fire so as to lessen the odds against him, but the sound of muffled, approaching steps interrupted him. Reacting purely on instinct he ducked low, feeling the cool rush of air on his scalp as a weapon swept over it. He thrust blindly behind him with the butt of his rifle, an action rewarded by a thud and a sharp intake of breath.

But something felt wrong, it was as if he had struck metal instead of flesh and blood...

With speed borne of desperation he whirled around to confront his foe. What he beheld did nothing to diminish this realm of terror he had been swept into. Nor did it do anything to assuage mankind's age-old fear of the unknown that vexed him so.

A squat, bearded fiend stood before him, with a face painted black and a body protected by what appeared to his unbelieving eyes to be a now-dented copper cuirass. A broad-bladed ax was being brought back into position after a missed swing.

Faced with an enemy in close quarters, Alvord's spirit rose against the mystery and peril to confront the situation at hand. Stepping forward, he smashed his rifle against the bearded man's chin with force enough the break both his jaw and the wood of the gun's butt. Hurriedly he exploded into a fast run. An arrow whizzed by his face, just a hairsbreadth off its mark, and another imbedded itself in the ground half a stride in front of him.

He heard outraged imprecations nearby, which spurred him on to greater speeds. What he believed to be a spear failed to pierce him after smashing into his pack, a cumbersome burden he shrugged off without losing speed.

A hollow roar cut through the forest, not unlike the blare of a horn but far deeper and more resonant. It was, he knew, the signal for this ambuscade to graduate to its next bloody phase.

Alvord Rawn was not one to quail at the sight of brutalities, nor one to flee from danger, but he knew that an attempt to stand and fight the rest of these men would be suicidally foolish. Pride wrangled with reason, and lost.

So on he ran.

Coward! Hissed a reproving voice in his head.

Run, Rawn, a sterner, equanimous voice contended. *Run like the Devil's own legions spewed from the flaming bowels of Hell are after you.*

Fear stimulates the imagination. It causes men to seize upon their most fanciful fears and expand on them, to develop new ones that would provoke jealousy from even the most original of minds.

Alvord frantically tried to collect his jumbled thoughts. But the armor-clad fiends that silently pursued him through the woods, coupled with the unearthly fog and monstrous howling sent a cold chill of fear rippling through him. With a start he felt the rising panic, that emotion so foreign and odious, well up in his throat.

Vengeful copper gods, Father Bazin's disbelieving phrase came rushing back to him, doing little to alleviate his mounting trepidation.

Nonsense! The dominant voice in his head insisted. *They are but men- and already you have put one to ground.*

He moved fast in the manner of a desperate man, but in his own mind the trees were not flying by quickly enough; he felt as if he was trapped in that awful species of nightmare in which you run from something dire on the most leaden of legs, frantically urging yourself onward but knowing all the while that you are not moving nearly fast enough...

Through the wall of trees up ahead he caught a glimpse of Little Chapel Lake. Lightfoot and Big Wolf might still be alive; perhaps these painted devils had not reached them yet. Surely those two had heard the hollow roaring of that unknown instrument; perhaps they'd made hurried tracks back towards camp.

But no- there they were, locked in a frenzied, mortal struggle with two opponents as others closed in around them.

Trying to control his stertorous breathing, he raced towards them as dark, phantasmal forms flitted through the pines to his right. Further on, more of his pursuers fanned out and began circling towards the lake, the menacing wall of creeping fog not far behind them.

They were trying to corral him.

As the thought swept through the storm of his overwrought mind, a sword-wielding foe dropped out a tree not far from him and advanced. Alvord waited until he was a mere five feet away before discharging his rifle. Though hip firing in a something of a panic, he got lucky and the lead ball took the painted devil in the stomach, unleashing a warm spray of blood that fell like mist onto Alvord's hand as he flew past the wounded man.

Blood- mere men indeed, then.

Lightfoot, hard-pressed and with a snapped off arrow stuck in his side, was about to be put to the sword when he saw the splintering remnants of Alvord's Hawken dashed against the skull of his brutish assailant.

Alvord dropped the ruined rifle and, seizing the longhaired man whose spear sought the shifty Big Wolf, ferociously bum-rushed him into the base of a girthy beech without breaking stride.

"RUN!" he roared in animalistic desperation, charting a course that had not yet been blocked by the hounding enemy force.

They required no second bidding. Seeking desperately to lose their pursuers, they ran pell-mell through a thick section of forest that favored their undertaking. But although the thicket provided cover, the trees and bushes of the undergrowth were like a thing alive, seeming to hold them back with spindly fingers. The shrapnel injury to Alvord's right thigh received a few nights back stung smartly, and his pounding feet were taking a dreadful beating through the lightweight moccasins. But he was alive. Forcefully and desperately alive.

They had gotten patently lucky in surviving the initial, bewildering onslaught. But in Alvord's experience luck was not apt to hang around for long after gracing you with a particularly heavy dose of its draught.

According to Cicero, self-preservation is the first law of nature. The three men lent credence to the belief as they strained every nerve in their desire to get back to the beach. It was hardly a desirable state of affairs, but at the moment it was every man for himself, and Devil take the hindmost.

Chapter 37

Standing knee-deep in the cool, cloudy shallows of Chapel Lake, Finnbar could not help but wonder what thoughts might plague the mind of Mother Fagan, could she see her highborn son mucking around so. Poor dear, she had ever harbored delusions of Finnbar becoming a professor, a lawyer, or (saints preserve us!) a clergyman if he chose to pursue a career at all. But alas, his adventurous spirit and undeviating desire to write simply did not allow for the serious contemplation of any such options. Not yet at least. Sure, not too long ago he had found professordom to hold some allure, but at present he reckoned that if he did want to formally teach it would be later in life, once he'd exorcised the wanderlust that firmly possessed his soul.

Using his feet to depress the springs of the No. 4 trap beneath him, he then used the butt of his knife and hammered a thin bait stick into the mud of the shoreline just above the trap. This he scented with the yellow-brown castoreum that he and each other trapper kept in a small tin container. A technique first applied to the trapping of beaver by the Nepissing, Algonquin, and Iroquois among other eastern tribes, the musky fluid contained within the bladder of both sexes proved an irresistible allure to the creatures.

A long setting pole secured the extended chain of the trap in three feet of water behind him, which would keep the trap held fast once a beaver was caught and tried to escape. When an inquisitive beaver came to inspect the castoreum it would inevitably spring the device. With the steel jaws clamping down on it, the animal would make for deeper water as it normally did when under duress, where the weight of the trap would soon drown it.

"Not bad for a first attempt, Irishman," Gordon was forced to admit, running a hand through his sandy blonde hair. He stood atop the large beaver lodge nearby, which sat ten feet from the shoreline over a drop-off point in the lake.

"But," the veteran trapper added sharply, "the trap rests a touch too deep under water. Try and keep it around eight inches."

"Eight inches. Gotcha. A figure I'm use to working with

anyway."

Laughing appreciatively, if somewhat grudgingly, Gordon waded back to shore. He himself had just set a trap on a beaver run, a shallow channel in the reeds the beasts used as a path to bring them from water to land and vice versa.

Gordon's head turned northwest, in the direction of Little Chapel Lake.

"Wonder what them trigger happy boys felled earlier. Fancy a bet on what critter will supply our supper?"

Having emerged from the woods, Gaston and the rest of their group made their way across grass that fringed the northern end of the lakeshore.

"Well if they missed, at least we still have this," said Gaston with a cheeky grin. He tossed the sopping muskrat carcass he carried at Gordon, who spun to avoid it.

"Clubbed her over the head in that swampy stretch yonder," Gaston jerked his head towards the marshlands they had crossed at the headwaters of Chapel Creek. "Also found something strange over there, looked like the frame of some sort of vessel..."

His hawk-like eyes of reddish brown squinted in deep thought before he continued. "But it's ancient, nearly crumbling, and it was probably just left by Indians in days long past. I'll warrant that it was unusual though, the frame was awfully rounded for any Indian craft... never mind it- I'm telling you Gordon, this place is fair crawling with fur. Damned if I've ever seen the like. You wouldn't believe the amount of sign we cut in just that little jaunt we took. And this muskrat here- I nearly stepped on the damn thing. No fear of men at all. It's like the stories the white heads tell of the old days."

Gordon squinted through the sunlight at a pair of massive swans swimming placidly together out on the sparkling lake. Turning back towards the men on the shore, his hard-bitten face broke into a rare smile.

"Yeah, kinda reminds me of that one spot over in-"

Although there was simply nothing he could have done to prevent it, Finnbar saw the arrow before it struck. Almost lazily it arced out of the wall of trees, whining through the air before thudding in Gordon's left eye. The arrowhead tore through the socket and out the other side of his skull before its lethal progress was halted.

Gordon did not go down immediately. Keeping his feet for an instant, his wasted, slack-jawed face blankly stared at those around him. It was merely a blink, Finnbar *knew* that, but with the black fletching of the arrow jutting from his left eye it looked for all the world as if the dead trapper winked at him with his right before falling backwards.

A deep, resonant boom, not unlike the sounding of some great trumpet, rang out from somewhere to the west and rendered silent the splash that accompanied Gordon's fall. More arrows flicked out of the woods, finding their marks in one of the Indians. Like greased lightening Gaston threw himself behind a rock. Finnbar and the other two half-breeds likewise took swift cover, as did Walks With Thunder. Suddenly it seemed all too real to him, that seemingly far-fetched talk of disappearances and copper gods and malevolent entities haunting this Heaven-forsaken land...

In a moment of contemplation Shakespeare's Macbeth had mused, "Present fears are less than horrible imaginings."

But an interfusion of the two?

Had the mists of legend solidified into fact? He had little time to lend this much thought, because legend, fact, or something in betwixt, a world of carnage was heading his way.

"*What in the hell is this?*" Gaston yelled in a panicked voice. Each man was armed but seemed unsure of how to proceed. Caught on the receiving end of the element of surprise, a moment of uncertainty passed between them as arrows slashed through the air, keeping them pinned. Apparently no guns could be counted among the enemy's arsenal, and for that Finnbar was grateful.

Recalling his mercenary days, Finnbar tried to center himself. Much as he loathed the role of leader, someone needed to take the reins here, and quick...

He chanced a quick peek around the log he hid behind and took in a cold eyeful of reality. A dozen or more dark, armed figures streamed out of the wood line fifty yards away, while arrows zipped over their heads to keep them pinned. The arrow-riddled body of the fallen brave gave birth to a terrible idea in his scrambling mind. Those arrows could easily have found lodgment among their whole group in one fell swoop, but instead they had all been directed at the dead Indian whose name he could not quite recall...

They're toying with you, Finn, making you wait for Death and basking in your fear all the while...

Fear was indeed thrusting its icy fingers into his heart, but of a sudden the old, familiar childhood stories of Irish heroes like Brian Boru and Conn of the Hundred Battles returned to him. Like a driving wind passing over coals did they rouse his martial ardor. And in that moment he decided that fear would be cast aside, death embraced, and battle joined.

Rolling out from cover in a prone position he squeezed off a round and dropped one of the hostiles, but nearly took an arrow to the face doing so.

Men. They were men after all, for surely a phantasmal deity would not be laid low by a mere gunshot?

The cracking gunshot and well-placed bullet did nothing to deter the others, whose ominously silent progress brought them ever closer to the beleaguered trappers' cover.

Men. But what manner of men were these? Wielding the weapons of medieval Europeans and clad in copper breastplates, the men they faced were beings wholly out of place and hailing from across a vast gulf of time. They were baffling anachronisms that left a host of questions in the Irishman's probing mind.

There was no time for such musings, for those anachronisms were nearly upon them.

In a blurring motion Walks With Thunder rose and with a double-handed grip hurled his tomahawk, which lodged itself in the nearest man's copper breastplate but failed to bring him down. A spear carved a meaty strip of hair and flesh out of the brave's scalp. Evincing no signs of pain aside from a muffled grunt he swiftly knelt behind the log that shielded he and the half-breeds from the hail of arrows.

Acting in unison, the two half-breeds broke cover and made for the forest in the direction of camp, but in the twinkling of an eye they were cut off and cut down by a foe that sprang out of the woods they sought to enter. They attempted to fight with tomahawks and knives, but Finnbar watched in mute shock as their murderer skillfully wielded a long handled axe and made easy, almost contemptuous work of them.

"Let's GO!" Finnbar used the momentary distraction caused by the two fallen half-breeds to his advantage.

That cavernous noise assaulted his ears once again. Whatever the doleful blast was, he could not help but feel as if it was sounding their doom. But never having been one to sit around and blithely wait for events to unfold before him, he would have a hand in authoring this one too.

They shot out from behind their cover, discharging what guns they had at the trees that the archers loosed arrows from. This gained them a moments respite from that threat, but the nearest attackers continued pursuing them, as did the man who had just butchered the half-breeds.

Gaston deftly reloaded his rifle on the run, pausing a moment to snap a fast shot. He grazed one of their pursuers in the shoulder but barely even slowed him. Never had Finnbar seen men advance so fearlessly in the face of gunfire. Gaston then caught up with Finnbar and Walks With Thunder, running with reckless intensity across the open, marshy area they had crossed earlier at the north end of the lake.

Four times arrows shrieked past their heads, but served only to boost their already grueling pace. Constantly and unpredictably shifting the angle of their flight, the trio confused the archers behind them. Finnbar fully expected at any moment to feel an arrow slam into his back. Gritting his teeth against the clinging dread of that anticipation, he focused on keeping up with the others, whose long strides were creating a widening gap between them.

Fear and desperation driving them across the spongy ground of the marsh, they soon found themselves among the dark lanes of trees that Chapel Creek plunged into. They chanced no backward glances lest they lose a step or two, preferring instead to simply pray that their feet prove swifter than their antagonists'.

Within the forest the sharp cracking of a stick garnered Finnbar's attention. To his profound alarm, his eyes swept over another clutch of enemies up ahead, angling towards them at a fast clip. Some wore the copper cuirasses he'd seen on the brutes by the lake, but the frontrunners were clad in light, gray-green leather jerkins. All had devilishly painted faces, with black on the cheeks and forehead and a startling crimson around the eyes. Tattoos that looked awfully familiar to him curled and wound around the skin of their arms and torsos. The fact that he was close enough to discern these details did little to slow his racing heart.

He and the others veered away sharply, and through the smooth gray trunks of the beech grove before him Finnbar caught sight of the gleaming blue that marked the big lake. Digging deep into his energy reserves, he strove to keep up with Gaston and Walks With Thunder, whose prowess in running definitely exceeded his own. Both ran fleetly and sure-footedly on the uneven forest floor, while Finnbar found himself getting tripped up on roots and undergrowth. They followed the serpentine creek northward, with ever more lake-blue becoming visible through the green of the forest.

They were getting close to camp now. His lungs felt as if they might burst through his ribcage and his legs were leaden, but soon they would reach the beach where a defensive position could be taken up. Between the cover to be had there and the abundance of guns they might just be able to repel these wretched, paint-spattered devils. Or at least hold them off long enough to make a tactical withdrawal in the boats. Marcel and David had been making their way back to camp, and surely they would be on their guard after hearing their volley of shots and the dreadful blaring sound.

Yes! He could hear the gunshots issuing from camp now, Marcel and the David must have been making a stand alongside the camp keepers. Plus, some of the others might-

Mother of shite! Alvord and the others, he hadn't even thought of them until now. Had they too been caught unawares in this sanguinary ambuscade? Did his friend yet draw breath?

He collected himself and with much effort forced his mind elsewhere. Reminding himself that Alvord Rawn was a man who would take an awful lot of killing, he shrugged off his gnawing concern as best he could.

Preceded by a conspicuous whirring sound, something wound tightly around his ankles, bringing him down like a sack of potatoes. Spitting out leaf litter he looked down at his feet and saw that a rope with weighted ends had snared him, not unlike the *bolas* he had seen used by the *gauchos* in South America. Fingers fumbling in panic, he frantically tried to extricate himself. As he did so his eyes darted around him, seeing nothing that offered much in the way of reassurance. For in a scene that hailed from the realm of nightmare a wall of fog rolled towards him, and through its nebulous mists he saw figures flitting around, heading his way.

Emerging from the fog to take clear form was a large, infernal-looking canine that bore down on him so swiftly he had no time to react. It charged in to sink its stark-white teeth into his right arm, which blossomed with sharp pain. Howling in rage, he savagely dug his thumbnail into the hound's wild eye before it started shaking its head and causing severe injury. In reaction to this the shaggy gray beast released his arm and fell back, and in that moment he drew his straight-edged dagger. When it renewed its attack, fangs bared and hackles bristling, he thrust the weapon into its throat. Still it came forward, bulling him over. Then he heard a hearty crunch and felt the percussion of whatever had been sunk into the dog's skull. The animal was powerfully thrown off of him by Gaston, while Walks With Thunder retrieved his tomahawk from its blood-spurting skull.

"Just go!" Finnbar fiercely urged them both. "I'll catch up!"

"*C'mon!*" Gaston urged, pulling him to his feet. But with the bolas still firmly wrapped around his legs the Irishman was unable to locomote with any dexterity and nearly toppled over.

"I said GO!" Finnbar roared, roughly shoving Gaston onward

and turning to face their oncoming enemies. The men, grimly silent in their approach, came at them just ahead of the encroaching fog. Gaston and Walks With Thunder stared at the formless, white-gray wall of mist and the enemies it contained in abject horror and disbelief.

"Rally with the others at the beach!" commanded Finnbar over his shoulder in a voice that would have shamed many a drill sergeants'. To his relief he heard their rapid footfalls take them towards camp. No need for all of them to die here, just because he himself was unable to run. The weighted ends of the bolas had smashed into the meat of his calves with deadening force; the bones felt unharmed but his numbly throbbing muscles would not have served him well towards that end.

So here he would stand, straight-backed and proud, for Finnbar Francis Fagan of County Cork would be damned if he was going to pass mildly into the great unknown. Here, remote from the eyes of men, Death would single him out this day, but it would have to extract him from a heaping pile of enemy carcasses. The kindling wrath of the Irish resurged in his breast, and giving vent to a crazed roar he began fighting as only a man with nothing left to lose can.

He dipped to neatly avoid a club swing and in the same move used the keen edge of his blade to sever the entangling bolas. He rammed a hard shoulder into the man with the club, sending him crashing into a tree where his face met the trunk in a spray of blood. A spear thrust missed his stomach by a hairsbreadth, and as it swept by him he grabbed its haft and yanked hard, sending its wielder stumbling towards him. The wickedly sharp, doubled-edged blade of his knife slipped under the bastard's copper cuirass and deep into the flesh of his abdomen. Hot blood cascaded onto Finnbar's hand and as he attempted to retrieve the knife his lubricated hand slipped right off its handle.

"Fuck!"

Though mortally wounded, the burly savage punched him squarely in the face and with a shove sent him flying backwards into a tree. Skull throbbing, the Irishman countered with a desperate flurry of punches, beating him to the ground and stomping his face into oblivion whilst screaming like a madman. Picking up a cut section of the bolas he swung the metal weight to which it was still attached hard into the face of an oncoming combatant, instantly flooring him.

Not a bad start, he had to admit, but the power of numbers was beginning to make itself felt.

One of the pack laid a hard club stroke across the back of his legs, ducking to avoid the metal weight that Finnbar's reactionary swing sent his way.

Another pricked his back with a spear point, just deep enough to produce a considerable stab of pain and unleash a stream of blood but failing to strike anything vital. His retaliatory slash found naught but air as his assailant danced nimbly away.

They seemed almost to be toying with him, as a cat might a sorely wounded prey item. There were quite a few of them and they came at all angles, and worse yet the roiling fog had fully engulfed him. Finnbar spun around frantically, trying to orient himself in the chilly, enveloping cloud. A panic threatened to seize him, for this suffocating mist lent a claustrophobic feel to an already precarious situation. Dark, fog-swathed forms darted all around him, and unable to face them all he found himself exposed. A sword sliced him shallowly on one side while a club thudded into his back a second later. Then a man charged him head on, bowling him over. With a scissor motion Finnbar used his legs to bring the man down, and his upheld blade pierced the copper of his breastplate to find the heart. There was reward in the grinding sound of metal piercing metal.

The two men, one crossing the threshold of death and the other resigned to the same fate, locked eyes for the briefest but weightiest of moments. In his furious death rattle the slain foe spewed hot blood into Finnbar's face. The smell and taste of iron clung to him as the oppressive weight of the newly minted corpse held him down. Rolling the body off of him, Finnbar's skull was immediately assailed by a spear butt. Here followed a dizzying bombardment of queer colored lights, and when he recovered his sight he found himself on the ground.

Head lolling over to the side dazedly, he saw the fog swirling through the forest of legs around him. Then one of those legs drew back and came at him fast, and no more did he see.

Alvord's lungs begged him, *implored* him to stop running with every step. This entreaty he simply could not oblige, and indeed he urged his screaming legs on to greater speeds. Startled by his sudden appearance, a velvet antlered buck deer sprang out of its bed and bolted, and oh how he wished for its fleetness of foot!

He had pulled ahead of Lightfoot and Big Wolf by dint of long, ground-devouring strides and great leaps when the terrain was conducive to them. Not by a great margin did he lead but one large enough to make him wonder if perhaps he should check on them.

Swiveling his head back he saw them, still sprinting with single-minded intent. He saw that they seemed to have outpaced the prowling fog but behind them, between the crooked trunks of the Jack pines he could make out the wraithlike forms of their chasers.

Lightfoot and Big Wolf met his eyes, their own both containing the same message: *For the love of God- keep going.*

While he ran he tried hard not to worry about Finnbar and Marcel. Little good would it do to fret over their fate at the moment.

The woods here were open and airy, the sandy soil home to the root systems of the pure stands of Jack pines that formed the forest. They were nearing the camp- the lake was becoming increasingly visible. If they stayed this straight course they would emerge from the woods near their encampment, where he hoped some of the others had escaped to.

Furnishing hope towards that notion, Jawbeance and Defago came pelting towards them from the woods off to their left.

Good. How many other survivors would emerge from the haunted wilderness behind them was a matter on which he cared not to prognosticate. But Jawbeance and Defago had, so together they would make the beach and take up a defensive position.

But no! From a dark section of forest materialized a pack of gray, snarling dogs.

Was that Cerberus among them? Alvord asked himself in a moment of wild speculation.

No- the beasts looked quite similar in outline but ultimately more wolf like in appearance. *En masse* they brought down Jawbeance and Defago and began tearing into them. Then a sharp whistle pierced the air and the dogs drew back hastily. Looped ropes flew out of the woods and, snaring the two trappers, dragged them away screaming.

On Alvord ran, knowing full well that to try and aid those two was to invite capture or death. Up ahead another band of attackers coming from their right began cutting them off. Hemmed in on nearly all sides, they were forced to swerve to the left, toward the western edge of Chapel Beach. Again Alvord felt as if he was being herded, but ever-shrinking options left them little choice.

The ground beneath his feet inclined a bit as the woods became thicker, harder to navigate. With a tearing sound a dead spruce limb ripped a strip out of his sweat-soaked shirt and scored his side. He ignored the stinging pain and continued crashing through the dense undergrowth like a juggernaut.

A grouse burst out from under his feet in a pulsing explosion of wings and feathers but he paid it no mind. He could hear Lightfoot and Big Wolf just behind him now; they were smaller and more easily able to worm their way through this infernal thicket.

The stunted evergreens abruptly gave way to a narrow, sparsely vegetated cliff edge, one that hovered some forty feet over the tropically hued water. Alvord realized that this was the rearing wall of rock that marked the western boundary of Chapel Beach. To the right lay the beach, although the cliff jutted out into the lake one hundred feet or more. On the left was a wide cleft in the rock that some ancient geological process had carved out. The edge of the cliff overhung the water below, creating something of an alcove. They were trapped here, then, on this narrow peninsula with a horde of murderous tribesmen closing in on them.

Lightfoot and Big Wolf exploded out of the dense wall of green behind him.

"Can't run for much longer," Lightfoot panted raggedly, holding his side where the broken-off arrow had pierced him. He'd been lucky; the projectile had stuck him head-on and appeared to have missed the ribs. Flesh wound though it might be, it bled freely and obviously caused the man no small amount of pain. His dusky, grimacing face had lightened to a startling ashy color.

"Convenient," Alvord replied between gasps, gesturing towards the cliff with his drawn Elgin Cutlass pistol. Amazingly, the gun had remained tucked into his belt during their pell-mell flight through the woods. His new Bowie knife also remained in its sheath, and this too he drew and made ready. He lamented not having taken along his Colt Walker this morning, but he had wanted to travel light and figured the birdshot he had loaded the Cutlass pistol with would make for a better small game gun.

Thunderous volley fire from the direction of Chapel Lake gave him heart. Good- not everyone had been caught with their breeches 'round their ankles.

The three men had little time to regroup and formulate a plan. Alvord could hear their enemies approaching, cracking sticks and shoving past the sharp, interlocked conifer boughs. He wanted to get an idea of how many men they faced, for to jump into the water below was a move that would leave them exposed, but to stand and fight might very well offer worse odds.

He offered no words of command or encouragement to the

other men, opting instead to simply step out in front of them and receive the enemy.

The first of their adversaries appeared, extracting themselves from the entangling foliage. A lean spearman leapt over a fallen pine only to be wounded and dropped by the deafening blast of the Elgin Cutlass pistol's birdshot load. Another one of those massive hounds came springing out of the undergrowth and bounded at them, but Big Wolf's tomahawk swiftly ended its advance. Yet as the squat Indian bent over to yank the weapon free, a fresh wave of enemy combatants freed themselves from the thicket and charged them. These fighters fought without the benefit of the copper cuirasses some of the others wore, and quickly did they close the distance. Alvord smoothly tossed Big Wolf his Bowie knife and stepped forward to meet them.

One warrior, wielding twin, long bladed knives, rushed out in front of the rest and came at Alvord. The first slash he slipped and, driving his shoulder into the man's gut, rose up powerfully and sent him flipping over his back. His body smashed hard into a tree but upon sliding down to the ground he was immediately on the attack. Still on his knees he sent a knife blade slicing towards Alvord's calf, but this the battle-hardened former police captain skillfully stepped over. He then brought his fist crashing into the man's bearded chin, putting his lights out with bone-crushing force.

Turning quickly to face the onrush, he barely dodged a spear thrust. The spearman's green eyes leered death at him as he kept coming forward, trying to topple Alvord with his body.

At this he failed. Standing like an expertly built redoubt Alvord lowered a shoulder and his powerfully set frame took the man's feet out from under him as his forward progress was instantly halted. The well-honed knife blade of the Elgin Cutlass Pistol found the flesh under his sternum and was then driven up into his heart.

Ripping out the blood-coated steel Alvord saw Big Wolf viciously battling a large, bearded fighter. Both men bore blood-seeping wounds but the Indian was getting the worst of it. And more enemies still were closing in on them fast- a decision needed to be reached. They had no choice... choice was a luxury they could ill afford at the moment.

"*JUMP!*" he bellowed above the tumult. He judged the water to be plenty deep but prayed he wasn't mistaken.

Barreling forward, he gave Lightfoot a stiff shove that sent him staggering past a wind-blasted pine and over the cliff's edge, and took heart as he watched the unfearing Big Wolf take the leap right after. Alvord jumped last, but not before an enemy leapt forward and determinedly clung to his body as his feet left the rock.

His stomach rose to meet his throat as was wont to happen during a jump from this height. Wrangling with the foul-smelling savage in mid-air, his head began angling down until his feet were skyward and his face would be the first thing to make impact.

Shimmering brightly in the midday sun, quite rapidly did the turquoise water come up to meet him.

Chapter 38

Humphrey Demetrius Duddersfield distractedly pushed his glasses further up the bridge of his nose, an annoying necessity that the steadily rising temperature occasioned. His face gleamed with sweat and his pudgy, snout-like nose was no exception. Plus, the mounting humidity caused the lenses to fog up, lending further frustration to the activity of reading.

He sat cross-legged in the Indian manner in his tent, over which he had draped a finely woven mosquito veil of muslin. The sand flies that patrolled this beach possessed a rapacity matched only by their relentlessness. While the veil kept them at bay, if he were to step out of the tent he knew they would instantly descend upon him unless he took the proper precautions. Although he abhorred the stench of the camphorated oil that served as a useful repellent against them, he was desirous of leaving the tent to take some fresh air. With a long-suffering sigh he began applying the vile substance to himself. The Indians and some white woodsmen made what was known in trapping parlance as a smudge, which was smoke born of a fire fed with evergreen boughs and certain lichens. The ashes of this they then smeared over their bodies along with bear tallow in an effort to keep harrying insects away- perhaps he too should give it a go? Just because a culture was indigenous did not mean its remedies were ineffectual. Aboriginal solutions to adversity posed by their environment were often ingenious in the extreme, utilizing natural resources in ways that were simply beyond the ken of any white man.

With reverence he set down his copy of *Strata Identified by Organized Fossils* by William Smith, the Father of English Geology. Sighing hugely and rubbing his beady eyes, Duddersfield slipped out of his tent, casting a wary eye around for Cerberus, who kept stealing his round, short-brimmed hat. He was beginning to think that Alvord's reprimands of the hound during such incidents were halfhearted at best. There the gray beast was, sitting and watching some nearby cormorants with his head cocked in youthful preoccupation.

He walked past the two Chippewa camp keepers who busied themselves constructing a primitive fur press out of maple logs. Already the industrious pair had set up a number of drying racks for meat and stretch racks for pelts. On those drying racks were slices of bear meat cut from the carcass that some of the others had brought back to camp earlier. The braves had to keep chasing their fox like dogs away from the meat, although it seemed more play than serious behavior. Despite Duddersfield having found no evidence of selective breeding among the Chippewa, most of their dogs were of this small and fox-like variety. Half-wild and rarely given to barking, these animals were used in various ways and even eaten in times of dearth. It was rumored that some specimens of the Hare Indian dog, also called the Mackenzie River dog, were occasionally used by the Indians this far south of the northern wastelands of Canada in which they were commonly used in the coursing of small game. John James Audubon had encountered, painted, and described them, and Duddersfield was eager to lay eyes on one himself.

The Chippewa were a fascinating people. So far they had been neither decimated nor driven off their ancestral lands, making them one of the more successful tribes. Tall, handsome Indians, it was said that the Lake Superior Chippewa were less inclined towards alcoholism than most other red men. Of particular interest to Duddersfield was their engraved birch bark scrolls called *mide-wiigwass* that contained ceremonial and mystical instructions of the Grand Medicine Society or *Midewiwin.* Such scrolls constituted perhaps the closest thing to written documents among Indians north of Mexico. He wished to examine some of the sacred objects before his time in this land came to a close, but so far his attempts had been met only with suspicion.

"*Paw-gwa-be-can-e-ga*!" The nearest Indian hailed him affably. This was the title they had graced him with, one that meant "He who employs himself among the rocks." Henry Rowe Schoolcraft had enjoyed the same moniker during the 1820 government expedition to find the source of the Mississippi. Led by then-governor of the Michigan Territory, Lewis Cass, the expedition had passed by this very spot. Looking out across the lake he tried to imagine that flotilla.

At this he failed. He was possessing of a rather poor imagination, after all.

Duddersfield had pored over Schoolcraft's journal kept during that journey, but could find no evidence that he ever explored this section of the South Shore. Perhaps those nonsensical rumors of supernatural guardians had kept him away... ah, all it meant to him was some virgin land to document. Sure, the late Douglas Houghton had allegedly poked around this vicinity while scouring the South Shore for copper deposits, but having pored over Houghton's writings he uncovered only a cursory mention of the Pictured Rocks. He and the legendary Houghton actually shared the same alma mater, the Rensselaer School, and Duddersfield had eagerly scrutinized the man's journals and various writings. As they had the same formal education and field training it made sense to him to do so.

It was his hope that this shoreline and its ill-frequented interior would yield some unexpected mineral riches. A find like that would land him a reputation for sure. His aim was to become a geological consultant for state funded geological surveys. These studies increasingly blended scientific, patriotic, and economic objectives and were in high demand in this, the age of rising mineral importance. The copper boom here in Michigan might be the most fashionable of the mineral extracting ventures in this country, but the vast bituminous coal deposits in western Virginia and Pennsylvania were grander in scale and more lucrative in nature.

His porcine face warped into a scowl. That was the way of things, wasn't it? Men of learning and science were only valued by the bewildered masses when their hard-won knowledge and talents were suddenly at a premium. Science for science's sake was but a confusing concept to their untutored minds.

But it still stood that his own aptitude and expertise were needed in many parts of the country. And no new mining activity occurred without a detailed state geological survey being conducted. Or he could even work alongside prospectors if he preferred, seeking to uncover new mineral deposits. That was really how one accrued a proper degree of fame in the world of American geology. And as a devotee of William Smith, whose practical application of stratigraphy had garnered him widespread acclaim, Duddersfield simply knew with the most unpretentious of certainty that he could pull off such a feat.

He cast his dim-sighted gaze towards the lake, where far out a shimmering mirage made it look like some sort of citadel protruded from the depths. Such mirages were due to the contrast of air and water temp, for even in the summer months Superior remained cool and unwelcoming, although in the shallows it did warm up a bit.

Hearing the buzz of voices, he looked back towards camp and saw Marcel and David trotting out of the woods and back into the camp. They were at least three hundred feet away and his vision was none too good even with glasses, but he could tell they were collecting a few additional traps. The expedition must be off to a capital start, then. One of the camp keepers disappeared into the woods, holding what he believed to be a snare.

He continued walking, lengthening his stride. For the second time that morning a shot rang out, this one deeper in the interior and not quite so cracking. He paid it no mind and stayed his course. His destination was the district of sandy alluvium at the mouth of a small creek that had its origin in Little Chapel Lake. Its lively flow met the lake at the very edge of Chapel Beach, where the sheer wall of yellowish sandstone rose forty feet into the air. After a few minutes of walking he reached it, scattering a flock of grackles that pranced around its base. Eagerly he knelt down and began examining the wealth of unconsolidated pebbles washed down by the current.

Red jasper, pearly-pink thompsonite, mottled brown and white gypsum, feldspar, ferruginous quartz- how singular an assortment! And the agates- oh the agates! This constituted the most diverse presentation he had ever beheld. Carnelian agates, peeler agates, sagenite agates, eye agates- uncharacteristically, he knew he would need to consult his notes, for some of the more unique specimens defied even his ability to categorize.

He did not linger long but inspected and collected a few specimens and stashed them in his geology kit. There existed even in just this little stretch of beach a whole host of sardonyx. Collecting a good deal of them would be in his best interests, for this mineral was favored in the crafting of cameos, wherein a raised relief image was carved into the stone and set in jewelry. As cameo jewelry was both fashionable and expensive, cameo-worthy sardonyx could be sold for a handsome profit. Before rising again he broke out his notepad and with his steel pen scribbled across its pages.

Clumsily he splashed across the mouth of the creek and examined the heavily striated rock face before him. He would do well to keep an eye peeled for red hematite and iron pyrite, which the iron ore up in the Keweenaw and around Marquette often contained. With a motion that bordered on a caress he ran his hand over the ancient formation. After scrutinizing a section in meditative silence, he gave the rock a curt nod. Removing the rock pick from his kit, he began chipping a projecting piece of it off in movements sharp and precise but far from powerful. It was while gradually hewing a chunk from the cliff that the fluttering dispersion of a flock of pigeons distracted him. Peering into the dim forest from which the creek flowed and the bird had been startled, his bespectacled eyes fixed on an unexpected sight.

Half in shadow hovered a face, the visage of which was

further obscured by the dark paint smeared over it.

Odd. Aside from the two camp keepers, all the others Indians in their party were out trapping and exploring. But perhaps one of them had returned? And it did not look like the one camp keeper who had left to set that snare, as his face had been unpainted.

Raising a hand in uncertain salute, he received only a disquieting smile in return. Something about that smile did not sit well with him. Faintly, laboriously, the cogs of his scanty intuition shook off their dust and began whirring.

Another rifle blast from the interior, quickly succeeded by a clattering volley of gunfire, struck a resonant chord of fear within him. His perception of the situation grew increasingly clear until perfect clarity was achieved.

That wasn't one of their Indians staring at him.

He then found, to his eternal mortification, that suddenly it was not just one but rather a cluster of leering, paint bedaubed faces gazing at him from the shaded forest. Silently they began their approach.

Recalling every tale of Indian savagery and torture that his memory could muster, Duddersfield turned from them and began dashing back towards camp, which lay over four hundred yards away. At present that distance seemed awfully far indeed. When he saw the savages give chase he let loose with a scream, hitting a note that would have garnered the envy of many a prominent soprano. For a few seconds all was mad scrambling as he sought to reach the camp that seemed impossibly far away. Trying madly to make his feet move even faster in the shifting sand, he shrieked again as a man came at him from the side and went to run him through with a sword.

At the last possible moment he tripped over a piece of driftwood and went down hard, with the savage staggering into his body and tumbling to the sand himself. Another gunshot rang out from somewhere in the forest to the south, and then a few more, these far closer.

The warrior who had fallen over him was then struck by a bullet and never rose from the sand. Another man, closing in on Duddersfield with an upraised club, took a round to the arm and spun to the ground, his wound brightly coloring the beach.

Marcel, David, and the camp keeper had taken notice of his predicament and opened fire, saving his life in the action. Shambling back onto his feet he resumed running, still beleaguered yet bolstered by the fact that the others were safeguarding his approach to camp. Had Duddersfield not suffered from a thoroughgoing lack of martial prowess, he might have ditched his geology kit and snatched up the fallen sword or club, but no plan short of wholesale flight crossed his frantic mind.

A few more shots rang out from the camp and chancing a glance behind him he saw that they had deterred the brutes, who veered off towards the sandy hill that led up to the woods.

Through fogging, purple tinted lenses he also saw a disorderly group of men spill over the northern edge of the pine-clad cliff he had just been working toiling under. Bodies flailing, they plunged towards the mirror-calm surface of Gitchi-Gummi.

Gulping air and churning his plump legs, Humphrey Demetrius Duddersfield, mostly a skeptic when not an open critic of God, silently petitioned the Almighty for mercy and aid as he strove towards what safety their camp might offer.

What a world of goddamn contrast he lived in. One minute Marcel Durand was peacefully listening to the tinkling, ethereal call of the hermit thrush, the most beautiful birdsong in nature by his reckoning, and the next he was opening fire to save a beleaguered Duddersfield. In the moment after that he was quickly taking cover, for out of the corner of his keen brown eye he caught sight of an archer in the nearby woods. Lucky thing, too, for in the next instant a hail of arrows came streaking out of the maples and beeches, and the very air was palpitant with their humming arrival.

He hurled himself down behind a barkless pine log that the lake had spat out in some bygone storm. Several such logs had been set around the campfires to serve as rough benches, and now they acted as a redoubt that saved the lives of the three men crouched behind them.

David and the camp keeper, the Indian called Kattawa, had instantly noticed Marcel's reaction and shadowed his movement; in doing so they very narrowly dodged becoming human pincushions.

As they recovered their wits Marcel had already fired his rifle at the new threat and was hurriedly reloading. Kattawa had been the first one to notice Duddersfield's plight, and he and the others had opened fire to cover his getaway.

David rose to a knee and discharged his own gun into the woods, narrowly missing his target. Kattawa crawled over to a box and, dragging it back over to their line of defense, wrenched it open. Out came additional rifles, charged and ready to go, along with some six-shot, Model 1839 revolving shotguns and flintlock pistols.

Rifle primed and ready, Marcel popped up and squeezed off

another round, this time showering an archer with slivers of the yellow birch he stood alongside.

They had cover for now. Yet it was a paltry space of sixty feet separating them from their assailants. Should they be charged, no- *when* they were charged, they would be swiftly overrun. But it would be costly to the enemy and the enemy seemed privy to that fact, and it was the only thing that was buying them time.

A shrill, keening noise rapidly gained in volume. Turning to confront it David found a screaming, red-faced Duddersfield, around whom arrows flew but found no mark. The bumbling geologist tripped and stumbled forward, an arrow shrieking through the air where his head had been a moment before. He rose spitting sand and made it to the log bulwark, but as he went to leap over them an arrow lodged itself in the ample meat of his buttock. With a gasp he froze and hung over the dead tree, his face taut and pallid.

"C'mon, laddie!" Exposing his torso, David grabbed and bodily dragged him inside the half-circle of logs. Like angry wasps did arrows fly around him, one actually tearing a hole through his shirt. In a flash he and Duddersfield were safely behind the wooden line of defense. With a deft movement he snapped off the arrow in the geologist's rump, leaving only a few inches of shaft protruding. Without a word he thrust a brace of pistols into Duddersfield's sweaty palms before rolling back over to his previous position and removing Alvord's Colt Walker from the former police captain's pack. This he placed next to him and began reloading his rifle.

Marcel, David, and Kattawa did not need to consult with one another to know that each man would keep a number of loaded guns next to him in preparation for the inevitable charge. When their adversaries broke ranks it would serve them well to have a stash of loaded and primed weapons at hand.

Two of the bowmen had climbed into the trees and began loosing arrows at a steep downwards angle, overcoming the barrier of the logs. One struck the prone Kattawa in the side of the calf, slashing off a decent bit of muscle. Grabbing the revolving shotguns, Marcel and David sent a withering fusillade of buckshot rocketing into the trees, sending the mangled bodies of the venturesome archers back to earth.

The arrows ceased flying. While momentarily a welcome thing, what the lapse ultimately betokened was far from comforting. Duddersfield, aloof from many of life's actualities, failed to grasp the gravity of its meaning. But that gravity was one intensely felt by the other three men. Gripped by a terrible sense of expectation, in unison they rose to a knee and restlessly awaited the next bloody phase of this assault.

The charge, when it came, was not the chaos of screaming men they anticipated, but an oddly organized onrush of a dozen that held form and deadly purpose. To his profound surprise, Marcel noted wooden shields among the men. Shields were used as defensive weapons among the Plains Tribes, but then only on horseback. Many tribes of this region had once used moose-hide shields in battle. But wooden ones?

Never.

Beards too he noted among them. Beards, which Indians did not grow save for a humble growth of chin and mustache hair at best. And the armor, the copper armor- no Indian of this land employed them in battle.

What exactly, then, were these bearded men before him?

You know damn well what they are, you fool of a trapper. You led these men here and due to your own arrogance your hands are forever stained with their blood. There was a reason men never trapped here, the very reason behind all the tales of evil and disappearances. You've gone and invoked the wrath of the copper gods, Marcel Durand.

And may Heaven show you mercy.

This realization staggered his initial disbelief. Indian legends were not something he often heeded... yet here was legend made flesh before his wondering eyes.

Fear made its presence felt by the shallow, rapid intake of his breath. A lifetime of experience warned that Fear was threatening to defer to its accomplice of old, Panic. Stifling that emotion, he let the enormity of the situation rouse in him anger, letting it fan the kindling fires of his rage.

Boldly did they come forward, as if they reckoned that easy pickings were to be had. Or perhaps, even, that their targets would turn and flee before them.

Born of adversity and a life lived according to reputation, Marcel's pride bristled at the thought. He was supposed to flee from these men? *He*, who had walked through the Garden of the Gods? *He*, who had thrice beheld the hallowed Medicine Wheel? *He*, who had watched in voiceless wonder as the wild horses raced across the fiery sands of the Red Desert?

As sailing types were wont to say- *fuck that.*

Faster than credulity would allow he fired his rifle and two pistols, dropping a pair of warriors. Having thinned their ranks, the Marcel plunged headlong into his next move. Face a contorted mask of fury, he flew out from behind the log, hurling himself into a blurring forward roll and rising among his advancing foes, knife and tomahawk things alive in his deft hands. Blood singing in his head, Marcel let loose all the brutal wrath of a mountain man.

In the space of a breath an armor-clad attacker was down, spurting blood and breathing his last.

He drove his heel into the chest of the next inbound man, denting his copper cuirass and dropping him. A shield split his forehead open but on he fought, spinning away from the blow to engage another man, who was instantly disarmed and then felled by seamless twin action of the tomahawk and knife.

Gods be damned- they bled and died like men. Sneering his satisfaction at the fact, Marcel Durand hurled himself like a man possessed at the growing stream of enemies.

Chapter 39

By shifting the weight of the struggling man he clasped, at the last possible instant Alvord managed to nearly invert himself. While his face was no longer directed at the water, his body still hit at a slight pitch. With a muffled rush of bubbles the breath left his lungs.

Mind fleetingly set adrift by the impact and bracing temperature, he sank swiftly and unresponsively. A second later the urgency of the situation overrode his dazedness and he was fighting once again, driving his heel into the nose of the man beneath him and unleashing a vaporous cloud of blood that hung in the water like a many-armed beast. Tenaciously he clung to Alvord's pant leg, but another kick broke his grip and sank him a few feet deeper into the water. Through water-blurred vision Alvord saw him begin clawing his way towards the light overhead.

Alvord broke the surface with a loud gasp after a few powerful upward strokes, emerging to find Big Wolf aiding Lightfoot in reaching the beach. He soon caught up with them, and grabbing Lightfoot with one arm he used his other to propel them towards shore. Over the sounds of splashing water and sputtering men could be heard the crack of gunshots in the direction of their camp.

They stuck close to base of the cliff, which afforded them some degree of cover. Twice arrows came at them from above, but the angle was off and they sliced harmlessly into the water beyond them. So thick was the growth of trees and underbrush atop the peninsular rock that the archers couldn't find openings to fire from. Frustrated yells communicated that their enemies were on the move, fighting back through the brush-choked forest to reach the beach.

Their feet found the firmness of submerged bedrock, and together they waded through the water alongside the base of the formation from which they had leapt. Warming this section of lake with its shallow flow was the nameless brook that was the outflow from Little Chapel Lake. Surging through it, they soon hit the beach.

A peek behind him assured Alvord that the man whose nose he'd crushed was in single-minded pursuit, a knife gripped between his bared teeth as he paddled towards them. He would be dealt with shortly, but for now they needed to devise a hasty escape plan.

Running across the beach and making the camp was a doomed enterprise. That much was plain. His vision had always been sharp, and through the shimmering heat Alvord made out a frantically fleeing form, not one of the attackers but who he guessed to be Duddersfield by the stride. Two bodies lay on the ground behind him- friend or foe Alvord could not say. The geologist was poised to join a small group of others among the logs and boats that marked their camp. The din and smoke of gunfire marked their bivouac. At least three men were firing from behind the large logs they had used as crude benches. For now, it seemed, their rapidly fired weapons were keeping the raiders at bay.

Too close for comfort, six copper-clad warriors began trickling out of the forest in pursuit of Duddersfield. This reinforced the reality that their traversing the beach would be a foolhardy undertaking. Alvord and the others stuck to the shadows of the cliff, waiting for them to make progress down the beach. If they were caught out in the open by a group that size…

The inescapability of this situation sparked a very primal brand of fear within him. The oppressive feeling of being trapped was one that rattled even his rigid composure. Grimacing bitterly, he resolved to make himself master to it and take action. The tranquility of Chapel Beach had given way to a grim scene of desperation, and Alvord needed to find his place amidst the chaos.

"Run or swim?" he quickly asked of Lightfoot.

"Swim," Lightfoot rasped in a tight expulsion of breath. If appearance outwardly expressed his pain with any accuracy, the man was in a great deal of it.

"Big Wolf. Help him swim. Get far enough out into the lake so that you'll be hard to spot. Swim down the shoreline to where we have our boats. We will make a tactical withdrawal from the beach using them. I will meet you there."

The issuing of orders and effortlessly assumed air of authority reminded him of his days on the force in Manhattan. Leadership was an integral part of his being, at times a dormant quality yet one easily seized upon in times of necessity. It might be havoc on all sides, but his mind was now locked tight within its own impulse to wrest order out of disarray. Fear and hesitation were no longer considerations and had in fact been completely divorced from his awareness. Action swift and resolute was the only thought pulsing through his brain, which had centered and sharpened in response to the roiling chaos around him.

Alvord Rawn was in his element, and gloriously so.

"What of you?" The Indian queried, his night-black eyes curious despite the danger all around them. His cheekbone had been laid bare to the bone and his right arm bore a shallow cut but otherwise he appeared in decent shape.

Alvord sodden beard could not conceal his satisfied grin. Without replying he turned and faced the water, where their chaser was poised to make landfall.

The warrior splashed noisily onto the shore, face spattered with bright blood that dripped from his face in watery droplets. Fury danced in his eyes, around which crimson paint still clung in patches. Knife in hand, he let out a wrathful hiss and advanced in a half-crouch.

"Go." Alvord urged the others over his shoulder.

They moved past him and back into the water, although once in the lake they did turn their gazes back to watch the outcome of the impending fight.

They were not kept waiting.

The Elgin Cutlass pistol had somehow remained clutched in Alvord's hand during and after the jump from the cliff. The pistol's twelve-inch blade had served him well in the past, and he readied it for action.

Knife held low, his opponent came in fast. Alvord steeled himself, having seen enough of the hand-to-hand fighting skill of these men to know that they were better than any he'd seen.

The long-bladed knife swept towards his face in a blurring, shallow arc. This he met and deflected with the Bowie blade of his pistol, turning it in the next instant to slash at his enemy's skull. The man slipped the blow, but failed to avoid the return swing. The keen knife-edge bit through flesh and into bone, scraping against the latter with a grating noise that Alvord felt more than he heard.

Cheek a mass of flensed skin, the man still sought to kill him. Alvord took a looping punch to the face but instantly countered, and the arterial spurting that instantly followed served as a sanguine indication that his blade had found his enemy's femoral artery. Another swing severed the tendons of his opponent's knife-hand.

Mortally wounded but still defiant, the warrior leaned forward and brutally sank his teeth into Alvord's chest, biting clear through the black oilskin vest. He was rewarded with the metallic taste of blood and a deep grunt of pain from his adversary. Yet a second later something pierced his unarmored gut. Staggering backwards, he blindly flailed his left arm again.

The desperate blow struck a jaw of granite but then a meaty fist found his sternum, producing the awful cracking of bone. Spewing blood, the crimson-stained warrior teetered backwards onto the pebbly beach.

As the man convulsed in a death-induced paroxysm, Alvord noticed something that struck him like a blow to the stomach. The lake water had taken from his victim's face most of the garish war paint. The skin beneath, while bloodstained, was undeniably pale.

He had slain a white man.

He had slain a very tough, very skilled white man at that. As ludicrous as it sounded, it added up- the beards, the armor, the light eyes he'd caught fleeting glimpses of. Not Indians but rather white men did they face, a savage host of white men in obsolete garb here in the uncharted desolation of Upper Michigan. Here, where Alvord had stumbled upon some dark and forbidden secret, the undivulged essence of which he longed to divine. There were strange tattoos upon the arms of the dead man, and these too jogged some recent memory that he had no time to consider.

Sheathing the Cutlass Pistol, he pounded across the beach to the forest. If he survived this fracas, he would have plenty of time to ruminate over what the bloody hell this all meant. Survival, however, was not going to be cheaply purchased.

Among the trees he would approach their camp, and give any pursuing foes the slip. The beach was too exposed, too obvious. He would be easily picked off by any nearby archers. Sure, there were enemies amid this shadow-shrouded forest of pine, but at least here there was cover to be had, as well as a chance of outmaneuvering any pursuers. There was also that baffling wall of fog he'd encountered earlier, which would offer additional concealment should it appear in these woods. Although he reminded himself that Death lurked among that fog as well...

His strides were long. Foot placement he was highly conscious of, not wanting to draw attention to himself with mindless noise. Twice he caught sight of groups of running men through the disorderly aisles of tree trunks, but they were a ways off and did not take notice of him.

It was a distance of four hundred yards back to the camp. Sticking to the thicker patches of forest, he used the undergrowth to mask his movements. In little time he was a mere seventy yards from the spot where Marcel, visible in the red calico shirt he wore, had established a rallying point with some others. Together they poured lead into the woods before them, using the logs as cover against the arrows that were fired in return. The group of savages that had been pursuing Duddersfield lost a man to a bullet and sped back into the woods before any more losses were incurred. They passed only twenty feet from a crouched, observant Alvord, who was concealed in the middle of some young cedar trees. He had both the Cutlass Pistol and his silver-handled knife in its leg sheath, but he drew neither.

Patiently he waited for them to pass deeper into the forest. That blaring hornlike sound he heard once again, this time much closer than before. The pack of men was heading in that direction, perhaps joining up with a larger force in preparation for an organized, large-scale charge. That would have been his course of action if his situation were reversed.

Flickering movement by the beach garnered his attention. His fears had been made reality- in tight formation the white brutes were sallying forth to charge the camp. Marcel, after touching off three rounds in such rapid succession that Alvord could scarcely believe it, forsook the cover of the logs and met them head on, knife and tomahawk in hand.

He tore his eyes from the scene. He needed to get down there without delay.

Confident that no enemies were nearby, he burst through the scale-like leaves of the cedars and resumed running. The camp was within reach.

Alvord broke cover and stepped out into the heat of the sun-drenched sand. He tore down the beach, satisfied that he would soon be in thick of the action.

Without warning a knot of men crashed through the woods to his right. An Indian he recognized as one of the two who had stayed back at camp fled from four warriors. One of them hurled a spear that stuck into the brave's hamstring, bringing him down by the base of a boulder. Rounding on his pursuers like a wounded animal, the Indian began grappling with one of the men, hacking wildly with a knife.

The rest took notice of Alvord and stepped out onto the beach. They came at him as one, their paint-enhanced expressions of malice evincing signs of self-assurance as well.

Alvord changed his course so as to meet them. He might be out of his element in this wilderness setting, he might indeed be a greenhorn whose presence did little to benefit this trapping expedition. But meeting spite with rage, and violence with bloodlust of his own?

Well now, that was a language in which he was long

conversant.

On his countenance an expression more sneer than smile formed, though this he was not conscious of. He did not slow his pace as he neared them. Onward he went at an easy lope, confident as a saint before judgment. Breath came easily, awareness slowly expanded. Acutely did he notice the clothes that clung wetly to his form, the shifting sand beneath his moccasins. So too did he spot an eagle soaring over the lake out of the corner of his eye, but like most else he perceived he lent it no thought. Instead he focused on the gray-haired, lean-visaged warrior who led the staggered formation of men by several paces and the position of those closest to him.

The bearded axe he clutched swept towards Alvord's neck but Alvord was already inside his guard. He grabbed the axe man's weapon and with a quick twisting motion wrested it out of his hands and pulped his face with its butt.

Disdaining death, he walked in to meet the rest. Walked, not rushed, and as he did this he observed the merest flicker of indecision in their demeanors.

He who hesitates is lost...

The axe he automatically tested the balance of and found it to his liking. His other weapons were sheathed and stayed that way, for the axe trumped them in terms of sheer brutality.

His next movements were not planned but rather reactionary. Deftly batting aside the flashing swords of his opponents he gained an opening, driving home the axe. It pierced a copper cuirass and rammed through the organs beyond, lodging itself in the man's spine. He did not bother to wrench the weapon out and simply let the handle slide out of his hands as the man slumped to the ground. Ducking to avoid a sword swing, he kicked the other man in the groin with such force as to lift him off the sand. With the butt of his drawn pistol he clipped that man's skull, felling him.

He moved on at a brisk pace to help the Indian. After a hard fight the Chippewa brave had dispatched his enemy and rose from the ground, breathing heavily and bleeding badly from several wounds. He began to say something to Alvord but just then a large, dark figure dropped down from atop the boulder he leaned against.

No sooner did the newly arrived enemy hit the ground then was he in motion.

With remarkable speed the Indian reacted to this sudden appearance, but in a flash his knife-arm was broken and sticking out an unnatural angle, and his head was being rammed backward into the rock. As his limp body fell towards the earth the savage caught him by the hair and with a swift, decisive motion broke his neck.

This happened very quickly, allowing Alvord no time to intercede. He stopped advancing so as to properly size up this formidable new adversary, and drew his knife.

The man turned to face him, visage displaying only a small fraction of the war paint that coated the faces of the others. A short sword hung from his belt, but he made no move to unsheathe it. He was lightly dressed, with no copper armor. In its absence was bulging, almost freakish musculature that the black leather vest he wore did little to contain. Alvord had never seen so well developed a human form; the man's tanned arms and shoulders rippled with dense, corded muscle.

Rarely had he seen a man of so cool a demeanor, so utterly in command of himself. As a former leader of men Alvord recognized that bearing and realized that in all likelihood it was the warlord of these wildmen.

He stood but a little taller than average, with a square head that matched his physique. A blondish beard coated his chin, quite at odds with the raven black hair of his head. But the most conspicuous quality of his appearance was the dark brown eye patch of what appeared to be snakeskin that covered his right eye.

The remaining eye, Alvord noticed, roved over him in return, cold and calculating in its appraisal.

It was a fleeting moment of mutual inspection. When it passed they rushed one another without ceremony.

Swinging both blades across his right side, Alvord sought to wound the man in the thigh and arm. Instead, he found his wrists firmly grasped and wrenched. In a flash the weapons slid from his hands. Enraged, Alvord yanked his right hand free and dealt him a sharp blow across the face. Using his fist as a hammer he smashed the man's other arm away from his and then grabbed him by the vest. Spinning fast, Alvord used his momentum to throw the man up into the smooth face of the boulder he'd leapt down from. His enemy's back made hard contact with it, but in an unforeseen and lithe maneuver the man arched his spine like a cat as he fell towards the ground and propelled himself off the rock with his feet.

Hands outstretched, he came flying at Alvord, who was unprepared for the move and suddenly found himself flat on his back with a fist zooming towards his face. Recovering his wits, he grabbed a hold of the man's sinewy arms and exerted his strength to its fullest extent. Though he fought Alvord's grip with all the might he had, the one-eyed warrior found himself locked in a stalemate and for an instant they simply glared at each other, the glacial blue of his eye locked on Alvord's stormy gray ones. Without much subtlety he jerked his head back to deliver a head butt, but when it came Alvord shifted his own head so that it was the top of his skull that was struck rather than his face. A sharp twinge stabbed his neck but he knew the other man was hurt by the sudden limpness in his body. He jerked an elbow into the bastard's jaw and then threw him off his body, delivering short, choppy punches to his face. Before he could land a finishing blow the wind was knocked out of him from a vicious heel-kick to the stomach. Then the warrior was rolling away and sinuously rising to his feet.

Alvord too got up, wheezing slightly as he sought to catch his breath. They were out on the beach now, the man's roll having taken them from the cover of the forest. His stomach dropped when he noticed two of the three men he had faced beginning to stir, wounded but not down for the count. If he didn't hurry here would find himself outnumbered in what was fast becoming the most frenzied fight of his life. He had not been defeated in a brawl since his early youth, and the consequences of losing this one were more dire by far than a mere blow to his reputation.

Again they clashed. With a blurring motion the savage drew his short sword, Alvord having regained the pistol. Sparks flew as they dueled with rabid speed, Alvord being at a distinct disadvantage. The Elgin Cutlass pistol was cumbersome in comparison to a properly balanced blade. To slow the pace of the savage he used his left hand to jab in between the play of their blades, drawing blood from his enemy's nose and, he saw, eliciting a frustrated rage from the man.

Landing punches abruptly became tricky. Now privy to the pattern of slash-punch, the cyclops before him constantly weaved back and forth like a serpent preparing to strike.

His blade flicked out and swept the pistol from Alvord's grip. Behind the sword swing he shot out a crippling kick that caught Alvord in the liver and bent him over. With a triumphant hiss the strapping warlord moved in smoothly, sword poised for an upward thrust.

Doubling up his fists Alvord swung with all the strength he could muster, moving with swiftness that surpassed his opponent's. Caught coming in, his foe took the crashing blow to the chin and was rocked to his very foundations. The sword flew out of his grasp and he spun in a full circle before falling to a knee. Quite unexpectedly he hurled himself forward to throw a shoulder into Alvord's groin, putting him down once again.

Shaking his head clear, the man charged in and leapt at Alvord like a big cat going in for the kill. Just in time Alvord caught him on his feet and tossed him back.

Gunshots had been ringing out during the duration of their fight, but Alvord became aware of the most recent two only because of the sand they kicked up right into front of his adversary. The man was in the process of getting to his feet when two bullets whined into the pebbly beach just short of him. The fellow's bulk belied his incredible agility, Alvord had to give him that. Lithely he performed a backwards roll that took him close to the wood line and out of the line of fire. He landed on his feet, the brilliant blue of his stare frigidly regarding Alvord.

Their clash had reached an abrupt and indecisive end. Just starting to recover his wind, Alvord dimly heard his name being yelled over the crack of gunfire, but took a second to lock eyes with an exceptionally worthy adversary.

"There will be another day," he assured the one-eyed warrior between breaths.

Phantomlike, the powerfully framed man melted into the shadow-dappled woods, painted face betraying nothing.

Snatching his knife and bloodstained pistol out of the sand, Alvord sprinted towards the chaos that was their camp.

Hopelessly outnumbered and facing dreadfully skilled enemies, three times Marcel had been driven back. Hot blood, both his own and otherwise, lent a deeper hue of red to his torn calico shirt.

In response to his maniacal charge, David and Kattawa had grabbed whatever guns were near and began discharging them as quickly and accurately as human limitations allowed. Wielding Alvord's Colt Walker, David employed a marching fire, advancing at a controlled pace while laying down suppressive fire. His bullets killed two, wounded another, and had others seeking cover. When the last round was fired he solemnly drew his dirk and tomahawk and readied himself for death.

Kattawa hung back, wounded in the leg and unable to move well. Firing a revolving shotgun, he too gave the advancing fiends cause for concern.

Bawling like a scorned squaw, Duddersfield unexpectedly reared up from behind the logs and fired his two pistols in one go, actually hitting one of the attackers point-blank and striking the wooden shield of another.

With confusion adding to the psychological toll of their sudden casualties, the enemy forces paused and fell back.

Driven by purest panic, Gaston and Walks with Thunder came pelting out of the woods along Chapel Creek, clearing the little waterfall with a mighty leap to land in the pool below. Hard on their heels were a pack of enemies, who likewise leapt into the pool that their quarry hurriedly crawled out of. Together Gaston and the Indian raced towards camp, where they saw the others fighting. One of the men behind them nearly closed the distance but was intercepted by Cerberus, who bounded into him and began mangling the man's face before being thrown off. Much like people, some dogs are born fighters. It was such with Cerberus. He nimbly danced around a sword swipe and renewed his attack with the dauntless vigor that had given his ancestors a fearsome reputation as war dogs.

The charge had been momentarily halted and the painted men fell back to regroup. Three souls had been sped to the afterlife by Marcel, who now dodged around a spear and expertly hooked his tomahawk under the man's shield. He drew him in with a powerful inward jerk, swinging the Bowie knife in low upward arc into his groin.

A sword streaking towards Marcel's unprotected back was blocked by the rifle of Gaston, who took a vicious kick to the sternum in return. Walks With Thunder threw a shoulder into the swordsman and sent him staggering, buying them enough time to drag Marcel back towards camp, where David waited. Dirk red with the blood of a wounded foe, the Scot bled from a stomach wound as he helped them drag a struggling Marcel back behind the logs. Lusting for blood and crazed by the heat of battle, the trapper hurled oaths at the retreating force as he strove to go after them.

Gaston held him down and talked sense to him while David and Kattawa began fiddling with a fifty-pound keg of gunpowder. They opened the plug in its top and shoved an oil-soaked cloth into it. Kattawa hastily struck a match and, after David began herding the others towards the boats behind them, touched it to the rag before joining the rest of them.

Marcel, wits recovered, urged them to flip the India rubber raft up and use it as a massive shield, which was a good thing because right then a hail of arrows hissed after them. Following the fusillade was a long line of warriors, shield-to-shield and coming in fast.

Alvord saw the surging warriors spread into a skirmish line and rush the breastworks, threatening to breach them. He raced them to the lake. His friends were clustered around the boats at the shoreline, using Marcel's raft as a giant shield against the arrows.

In mid-stride an earsplitting explosion occurred, an upsurge of towering flames and smoke that blotted out the camp. Such was the force of it that it blew Alvord off his feet. He quickly shot up, ears ringing and vision hazy. Marcel and the others must have blown a keg of gunpowder, and although it had not appeared to inflict any enemy casualties it had knocked down the frontrunners and thrown confusion their way. He took advantage of the lull and sprinted the last leg into camp.

They put their shoulders into the bateau and pushed with all they had, desperation augmenting their strength. Their other vessels were hopelessly riddled with arrows and spears but the bateau was of stouter construction. Their feet deeply scoring the sand beneath them, bit-by-bit the boat moved. With a thud and a bestial roar Alvord was suddenly among them, his broad back against the boat and legs pumping furiously.

Spirits renewed by the arrival of a friend, they felt the boat gain buoyancy a few agonizing seconds later. Coat blending with the gray of the smoke, Cerberus charged in out of nowhere and with a graceful leap entered the boat.

The sulfuric smoke from the powder was beginning to diminish, stirred by the wind that had come out of nowhere. Likewise was the water beginning to churn as if stirred by some unseen agency so as to mirror the wild scene on the beach.

Through the swirling veil of smoke Marcel saw the armored men beginning to collect themselves.

"We gotta shove off now! We don't stand a dead Dago's chance if we stay here!"

"Finnbar?" Alvord inquired between breaths.

Marcel merely shook his head, unwilling to reply. At this Alvord's mind reeled. A friend's life reduced to a mere nod...

Armed figures were heading their way, having recovered from the force and upheaval of the explosion.

Clambering into the bateau along with the rest, Alvord and Walks With Thunder grabbed the oars and began rowing at a grueling pace. The turbulent water surged over the sides of the craft in an icy sheet while the wind began blowing them southeastward, towards the easternmost edge of Chapel Beach but also back towards shore on a sharp angle. Gaston leapt up and slashed the ropes holding the boat's sail up, and with a rushing sound it unfurled and filled with air.

Gasping like spent beasts, Lightfoot and Big Wolf suddenly hauled themselves over the side of the boat to the surprise of the others; in all the tumult Alvord had forgotten about them, but against the odds the rugged pair had made it to the boat. The gasping Big Wolf immediately snatched up a rifle and spat lead at their assailants.

Kattawa desperately manned the tiller but without warning slumped over, an arrow in his sternum. David laid his body down and took over, one hand staunching the flow of blood from his own hemorrhaging stomach wound. They were right near Chapel Rock now, with a swarm of enemies in hot pursuit. By slow degrees the boat began turning in the direction they needed it to, but they were awfully close to shore.

Alvord noticed an archer run around the bulk of Chapel Rock, arrow notched. He dove over the prone and shivering form of Duddersfield to grasp the swivel gun mounted on the ship's stern. It was a massive, oversized musket that he manned, already primed and ready to fire. Drawing back the massive hammer with both hands, he centered the sights on the archer, whose bow was rising.

He was a mere twenty yards away, and his body disappeared amidst a shuddering, reddish spray after the gun's buckshot found its mark.

Meanwhile, Marcel had moved to the bow of the ship and was turning the cast iron tube of the other swivel gun, a one-pound cannon, towards the shore. More enemies swept out of the forest and from the base of Chapel Rock began firing arrows. Touching the matchstick to the fuse, Marcel brought the one-pounder to bear on the nearest pair of archers, and with a hollow roar that shook the boat the ball was spat. It struck Chapel Rock next to them, showering both with a punishing hail of flaked rock.

Then they were past, the wind and waves subsiding as if by miracle and the rain reduced to a drizzle. Behind them the section of lake by Chapel Beach still raged with waves, as if a confined storm hung over it.

Rain fell in torrents as Alvord looked back at the beach where the attackers stood watching. The insidious fog coursed through the trees and poured onto the sand, rendering spectral the arching birch and maples limbs. As it enveloped the beach entirely, Alvord watched as the stout figure of the one-eyed warrior gradually deliquesced into formlessness, sword pointed directly at him.

This he looked upon in misery, in anger... in defeat.

In resigned silence they made their way eastward, spirits trudging through the dreary wasteland of broken dreams.

One arm propped up against the smoking cannon, Marcel

stared hypnotically in the direction of Chapel Beach, taking full stock, Alvord knew, of a trapping expedition gone hellishly awry.

Chapter 40

Something stirred on the edge of the shadow-strewn timber. Genevieve Connolly just barely caught it on her left periphery, and turned her head to more fully examine the sudden movement. Her lively olive eyes flicked over the shaggy hemlocks and the smooth bark of the stately beech in the hopes of ascertaining what it was.

Nothing.

Her mind must have been playing tricks on her. Just as well. She did not want any distractions, for she was having a capital time strolling down this lonely stretch of beach with Finnbar. There the Irishman was, his left arm intertwined with her right as he moved with the leisurely swagger of a self-possessed man. The sun glinted off his dark red hair, lending an almost angelic air to his roguishly handsome appearance. That same sun failed to shimmer on the brooding waters of Lake Superior off to their right. Something about the foreboding cast of the lake elicited a current of unease in her. In its primordial absoluteness Gitchi Gummi stubbornly refused to reveal even the smallest of her secrets. But there was nothing to fear so long as she had Finnbar Fagan of County Cork at her side.

The pair spoke not a word, content to let the screeching gulls and lapping waves provide a dialogue. No stranger to bungled attempts at courtship, Genevieve was ever so refreshed by the unshakable confidence of this soigné Irishman. There was no uneasiness, no bluster, no stammering attempts at conversation. Coolness and acumen marked his speech, which when delivered with that enchanting lilt produced a languorous warmth in her chest.

But just now, his companionable silence suited her every bit as much as his engaging talk did.

They passed a killdeer and to her surprise the generally querulous, skittish little shorebird did not flee and harass them with its wild cries, instead staring at the forest with unusual intensity.

Finnbar followed its gaze across the beach where sand met tree root, face unreadable.

"I must go, lass." His tone was plaintive, so much so that it made her sad in turn. "There is something required of me."

She frowned slightly, a shallow rippling of her usually smooth forehead. “An important something, Mr. Fagan?”

“Aye,” he replied slowly, voice sounding distorted and far away, almost as if he spoke through a sheet of water. “We were brought here for a purpose. You don’t bring in the big guns for a wee dust up, now do you?”

We. He must be referring to Alvord and Marcel. Perhaps they were already in the forest?

“Good luck,” she offered, her voice also monotone and distant.

He reached out and gave her hand a reassuring little squeeze before striding off towards the woods. An irresistible urge to follow him came over her, to follow him right into the heart of that untamed wilderness. She watched him go, and with a start her eyes detected that irregular motion again among the solemn tree trunks. Then, with a demonic howl that shook the woods, a blurry, massive *something* swept out of the trees in a dark wave, instantly engulfing Finnbar.

Reality quite suddenly seemed flimsy and unreal, a thing dreadfully distorted by forces unseen and unknown.

Genevieve opened her mouth to scream but no sound issued from it. So too did she attempt to flee from the menacing, vaporous thing before her but to her abject horror she found herself rooted in place and unable to oblige the urgings of her brain.

The shapeless, indefinable cloud was upon her in a flash; she was wholly enveloped by it. She felt herself being borne aloft, and after a moment the darkness cleared.

For an instant she hung perfectly still in the air, impossibly high above the lake. But only for an instant. As she began plummeting face-first towards the boundless depths below, her stomach fluttered so violently she though she might be ill.

She should be screaming, she knew that, but oddly no ragged exhalation accompanied her seemingly endless descent. She merely stared at the ominous water that rushed up to meet her and awaited the inevitable impact.

The voice of Cadwallader Jones, resounding like some great bell tolling doom, filled her ears in the seconds before she made impact.

The storm will sweep you off your feet and it’s an awfully long way to fall.

Face gleaming with the cold sweat of nightmare, Genevieve awoke in the act of inhaling a great lungful of air. Staggering off the Persian blue couch on which she had been slumbering, she caught herself on the ornately carved mahogany side table that stood just below a mirror. In this mirror she peered into the twin abysses of her dilated pupils. They offered no assurance or hope in their inky absoluteness. But in a moment's time the black of her eyes hurriedly constricted in response to the aura of golden light around her. She finally caught her breath and steadied herself, watching as the pulsating vein in her forehead slowly disappeared along with the flushness of her face. Genevieve knew she was not falling and had never been, yet a vestige of that unsettling feeling still remained.

The nap she had just violently started from was not planned, but rather one induced by the duel effect of a sluggishly paced section of *Sense and Sensibility* and the slanting beams of sunlight filtering in through a nearby window. In combination, the monotonous text and drenching warmth of the sun's rays had been her ushers to the hazy landscape of sleep.

Her Chippewa kinsmen set great store in dreams and visions. Indeed, they would even induce them at times so as to try and discern what symbols they held, what glimpse of the future they might offer.

Yet her own nightmare was nothing of the sort, it was just a frightening concoction of her tired mind. There was no way it could have been a-

Premonition, the voices of her ancestors seemed to call through the void of ages.

But so dreadful was the nature of her nightmare, so steeped in inescapability, that she resolved to regard it as simply a dream and nothing more. She did not care to think about what meaning it could hold. For nothing good could be derived thereof.

Her thoughts turned to Finnbar- could he in fact be facing some sort of dire predicament? After all, he was out pitting himself against the wilderness. Should she be worried? Would she ever clap eyes on him again? Could-

"It was a dream, Gen," she told her clammy face in the mirror, the firmness of her tone implying that to even consider it as anything but would be the very height of absurdity.

The ward of Cadwallader Jones sat back down on the lavish couch and heaved a shuddering sigh, expelling along with the air the last traces of fear that clung to her breast.

Yes. Naught but a dream.

Chapter 41

The events of the day had left Alvord and the others sapped of energy. Its sail furled for the moment, the arrow-riddled bateau bobbed in gentle measure with the lake one hundred feet out from the cobalt pebbles of the shoreline. As the lowering sun stared down at them like some great, unblinking eye, their own eyes intently scanned the dunes and the glowering darkness of the forest. Intent as only those praying for a miracle can be.

But for now the towering sand offered as little hope as the grim row of trees that the sun did not seem to penetrate.

So on they floated, minds steeped in thoughts morbid and speculative.

Earlier today they had learned of the fate of the men they dropped off at Twelve-mile Beach two days past. That band of trappers had planned to initially make camp at the broad, shallow mouth of a creek that emptied into Superior. Upon their approach to the spot, they had seen no evidence of that group having camped there. And the canoes were nowhere in sight.

Perhaps, they had wondered among themselves, those men had already pushed further into the unknown by following the creek?

But then Gaston had tripped over something buried in the sand, and his foot pulled up a half-burned log. Which might have confirmed their suspicions, had it not been heavily stained in sand-specked blood.

They then fanned out and kicked up more sand around the area, revealing patches of blood-soaked beach over which fresh sand had been spread. Cementing matters was Marcel's discovery of an arrow that had missed its mark, identical to the ones sunk into their boat.

In a crouch, the somber mountain man rolled it between his fingers before angrily snapping it in two. "Likely caught 'em unawares here in camp. Ambush style. Like what would've happened to us under different circumstances. Equipment and boats were hauled away to cover up the attack."

They were down to only a few guns with next to no ammunition, a couple of knives and a tomahawk. The cannon had been reloaded but that would do them little good on foot. They dared not court further disaster by venturing into the interior. Of the many things these unhallowed woods might hold for them, slaughter was prominent among them. They opted instead to press on to the Grand Sable Dunes, where they had dropped off the first party of trappers.

The first party's canoes were on the beach, which was possibly a good sign, and their small camp was orderly, betraying no signs of an attack. Marcel had tried to hail them with a few booming "Halloo" call, but they went unrequited.

The wait continued under the watchful sun, a gnawing feeling of hopelessness pervading those who waited.

No grievances were issued about their having sat there for two hours. Nor was anything mentioned about the somewhat cramped conditions engendered by eight men, a large dog, and a human carcass all sharing a twenty-foot boat. A variety of wounds marred them all, but not a complaint was to be heard as they bore their pain silently.

Thankfully there was no shortage of cool water on this, the Father of Lakes, and the men drank it and cooled their sore bodies. This blessing came at a small cost, because their overcrowded vessel was taking on water. Not badly, but at times they did have to use bailing sponges to keep the leak at bay.

It owed to the wherewithal of the dead Kattawa that they were able to both eat and tend wounds. The fast-thinking Indian had snatched up two packs during the frenzied retreat to the boat, one of which contained some venison jerky and flavorful pemmican. The other pack was full of medical supplies, which were put to good use once they had put sufficient distance between themselves and the maledict place that was Chapel Beach.

Alvord inwardly lamented, selfishly he knew, that neither of the packs were his. His truncheon had been in his pack. After fourteen years of dependable and rather frequent use, his trusted weapon was lost.

Ah, no matter. There were far more important things to apply concern to at the moment.

A fire platform on the raised forward deck was put to use and water was boiled in an iron kettle to sterilize the wounds, the needles, and the silk thread. The cut David had taken to his stomach had initially bled a copious amount. Yet once slowed it proved to be a long but relatively shallow wound. It did require stitching, however. This Marcel tended to with deftness and precision that astonished Alvord. He'd seen seasoned physicians do poorer jobs. Grimacing tightly throughout the procedure, the tough Scot had merely taken a quick look at the stitches in the aftermath and given a nod of thanks. In a similar manner were

Big Wolf's slashed face and Walks With Thunder's scalp wound mended.

Duddersfield and Lightfoot had both taken arrows. The projectiles had been snapped off so they would not bang against anything and worsen the wounds. Lodged deeply in the generous flesh of Duddersfield's posterior, the arrow would have to stay inside the young geologist until they could receive professional medical assistance at the Soo. This news he accepted with a nod and a moan, his pale face a canvas of poorly concealed agony. Lightfoot, however, insisted that Marcel attempt to dig his arrowhead out.

"Caught me as I was spinning around, and didn't sink too deeply. See? Hit my possibles bag first."

"Alright, but I'm gonna have to slice open a bit of flesh along your side to remove it."

"Have at," Lightfoot had grunted, grimly staring out into the lake. And damned if he let out more than a single grunt throughout the entire procedure, which proved successful.

So at this point everyone was fed, if only meagerly, and the worst of the wounds were dealt with.

A westerly wind had initially favored their undertaking, but it had died down to an intermittent breeze that the hot, tired men relished as they watched the land for any sign that their fellow trappers might yet live.

A fact that dogged every man's thoughts was spoken, punctuating the drear of their silence.

"Those men were white," Big Wolf said in his awkward English.

His words were met with a low murmur of assent by his peers.

"The weapons, the armor... never have I seen the like." Gaston frowned deeply. "Were they the *manitous* spoken of by the tribe? The *osuwahbik manitous*- the gods of copper?"

He looked inquiringly at Big Wolf and Walks With Thunder.

"It would seem." Walks With Thunder said in a dull voice, his sharply featured face devoid of all expression. "We trespassed upon their holy ground and we were punished. And that great sound- it was the voice of *Missibizzi* that has long kept Indians away from such places. He is the chief servant of Matchi Manito, the Spirit of Evil."

Big Wolf silently nodded his agreement.

"But they dropped like men," David pointed out. "I meself dirked one, and the bastard was flesh and blood same as you and I."

"Maybe they didn't really die," Gaston hollowly mused,

staring off into the distant horizon. "Could be that they can resurrect themselves, like in some of the stories. And the storm-where the hell did *that* come from? Not to mention that fog that came out of nowhere."

"It was an atmospheric phenomenon unlike any I have witnessed," supplemented Duddersfield in the first words he had spoken since their frenzied exodus from the beach. He lay on his stomach atop some blankets, countenance wan and strained. "And the way it just abruptly ended once we were past the beach... I can offer no rationalization."

"*Manitous*," Gaston said in a voice scarcely above a whisper.

Marcel, sitting with his back propped up against the mast, simply lowered his shaggy head.

"I have another explanation." Alvord was scratching the long, regal neck of a restless Cerberus. "I intend no insult to the legends of the Chippewa, but I think I might know what lies at the heart of this."

"What's yer mind pieced together, laddie?"

"Well David, it begins with the legend of the Welsh Prince Madog, or Madoc as he is more commonly called, who according to legend-"

A gunshot tore through the air, its origin to the south, beyond the Sable Dunes. Another followed shortly thereafter. Then nothing.

There followed fifteen minutes of unbroken silence as each man strained his eyes trying to perceive any sign of their comrades.

Nothing encouraging presented itself. Their focus began to wane.

"*There!*"

The word leapt out of David's mouth as he rose from his seat to point up at the crest of the dunes.

Two figures leapt over the sandy rim of the two hundred foot dunes and began half-running, half-falling down the malleable slope. In shadows of the fading light it was difficult to see with any clarity, but instinct told them those men were part of their expedition.

Without speaking, Alvord and Big Wolf manned the oars and began propelling the boat towards the beach their fellow trappers would soon reach.

But those two were soon followed by four more figures, whose descent down the sloping height of the Grand Sable Dunes was far more controlled as they moved with graceful bounds and slides.

Blind to the desperate scene as he rowed, Alvord

commanded himself to ignore the throbbing bite wound on his chest and the sharp pain his midsection was laced with after his clash with the one-eyed warrior.

"Close enough, they got archers!" Marcel roared.

The others began yelling for the men to come to the boat in both English and Chippewa. Alvord turned to see what was going on. They were close to the beach now, and he had a clear view of unfolding events. He watched in helpless dismay as a black-painted enemy expertly loosed his spear in mid-bound, lodging it into the back of one the their trappers. The man's twitching body made hard contact with the beach below and he moved no more. The other man, an Indian by the looks of him, dove into the lake and began a frantic swim towards their boat. When an arrow sliced into the water by his face, he redoubled his efforts and in no time he was being hauled into the bateau. Alvord and Big Wolf, aware of the arrows that were being launched at them, began furiously paddling back out into the lake.

Guns were fired around him but Alvord could not see if they were effective.

Up in the bow Marcel touched off the cannon. With a roar and fiery discharge it spat its one-pound ball up into the dunes, where it tore into the sand right next to an archer poised to shoot at them. The cannonball carved out a chunk of dune next to the man and sent sand spraying all around him. The slope shifted beneath his feet and he tumbled down the dune for a ways before recovering himself.

Alvord looked back and saw two of the painted warriors staring at them from the beach while the other two released arrows from the dunes that fell just short of their mark. Then fog, that animated, insidious fog, spilled over the rim of the dunes. Soon the vapor wrapped them in its obscurity and the arrows ceased flying.

The speared trapper behind the warriors on the beach still stirred. They turned and began walking towards the dunes and the approaching wall of mist when one of them, in a move that seemed almost an afterthought, brought his axe crashing into the man's skull, finishing what the spear had started.

Then that section of the Grand Sable Dunes was no more, replaced by the sinuous sheet of fog that ran like a white-gray waterfall over its sands.

"Jesus, Mary, and Joseph," David whispered in awe as he beheld the awesome sight.

"What happened to ye?" He then asked the Indian in a loud voice, holding the man by his shoulders.

"Maji-manidoog! *Maji-manidoog!*" The brave stared at the Scot as if looking right through him.

"Devils." Walks With Thunder solemnly translated, offering the quivering man a swig of the small amount of whiskey they had.

"Any other survivors?" Alvord pressed.

"No," Gaston told him after posing the question in his native tongue. "None but him. They fell upon them like demons and he barely made it out of the initial attack."

Of the thirty-seven man they had come with, a mere nine made it out with their lives. Or so it seemed. Alvord harbored a dim hope that prisoners had been taken; he had seen Defago and Jawbeance being dragged away by ropes, still quite alive. Finnbar still had a chance if such was the case, he had to cling to that faint hope...

Alvord and Marcel took the next rowing shift. Alvord had been rowing since Chapel Beach, but felt that the activity might ease his turbulent thoughts. The others, exhausted by the tumultuous day, curled up where they could and grabbed some shuteye.

Rowing in easy unison, the two friends shared not a word until Marcel broke the silence in a voice of shame that Alvord had never heard him employ before.

"Al, I ah-"

"Don't." Alvord swiftly cut him off. "We all knew of the stories. And in the back of our minds we all knew there existed the remotest possibility of them being true."

The normally stoic mountain man hung his disheveled head in regret. "But Finn and the others..."

"They took captives, I saw it. Someone knew we were coming," Alvord firmly insisted. "There is no way that bunch could have located all three of our groups and then coordinated an attack in so rapid a manner. They were informed of our plans."

"*Jones*," growled the mountain man into the gloaming. It was a thought that warranted further deliberation, but neither gave vent to any.

As the moon took the reins from the sun, they paddled in silence. In the inky blackness of eternity the stars marshaled in their millions, but their merry twinkling lent no gladness of spirit to the two men who tenaciously rowed away from the scene of horror they had been lucky to escape.

Chapter 42

Copper Harbor, Keweenaw Peninsula. Dusk

Hemmed in by the illimitable span of Lake Superior to the north and a low-lying chain of mountains to the south, Copper Harbor held the title of America's mining capital. And in terms of yield and product purity, this rough-hewn boomtown perched on the northernmost tip of the Keweenaw could justly claim world supremacy.

A collection of rude log cabins sat in the town's nucleus, the sturdiest dwellings at hand save for the building on Porter Island in the harbor where the permit-dispensing Government Agent dwelled. Of course, the large company boardinghouses held most of the men, but those not attached to any company were lucky to call a log cabin home. The rest of the abodes of the miners were a jumbled assortment of hastily erected shanties and white canvas tents, many of which lay close to the water's edge. The propitious discovery of the Cliff Mine, the mother lode of all the region, transformed what had been an isolated prospectors' camp into a vigorous mining district.

Copper Harbor was the destination of most of the mining men who came to rip the red metal from the marrow of the earth. Of the boomtowns spawned by the copper craze, Copper Harbor offered the largest bay and bore the greatest resemblance to an actual town, and for that it was considered headquarters of the Copper Country. From this rallying point men would either commence working or go west to the neighboring boomtowns of Eagle Harbor and Ontonagon, or north to the rich fishing grounds off Isle Royale if mining was not their aim. All travel back and forth to the Soo was done by boat, mostly schooner and steamboat. Not a single roads or even trail system linked the two.

The bulk of Fort Wilkins, built in 1843 to protect early prospectors from Indians, lay swathed in the gloom of the dusky twilight. The fort had been deserted earlier this year when its garrison had been called to the front in response to the exigencies of the Mexican War. The Chippewa, it turned out, had no real interest in molesting the white miners despite the fact that they were defiling a land and substance the natives regarded with superstitious reverence. But still the fort stood, unimportant as it was unoccupied.

A dingy little post office stood nestled among bawdy houses, dram shops, taverns, and warehouses along the muddy primary lane, and nearby an apothecary was closing up shop. Work had ended for the day, and a steady trickle of haggard-looking men emerged from darkening rows of birches and evergreens, their weary strides and slumped shoulders souvenirs of battles raged against the copper ore.

These were overwhelmingly single men, most ranging in age from late teens to late thirties. No room existed here for tethered fellows, nor bodies anything less than robust. Before long they would shake off the accumulated dust of a day's toil. And in turn the town would shake with the din of their carousing as they drank, gambled, whored, and fought their way towards a night's sleep in their company boardinghouse.

Twelve accursed bucks a month for accommodations offering little in the way of comfort or privacy.

Mosquitoes whose dimensions earned them the moniker, "Keweenaw eagles" descended upon the miners in Biblical numbers, as if they hadn't been dreadful enough during the daylight hours. The region no longer resounded with the repetitious click of hammer and hand-held drill, and the boom of blasting powder would not be heard again until dawn. Those sounds were replaced by the howls, hoots, chirps, and shrieks of a cacophonous orchestra whose conductor held harmony in no high regard. Wolves, bears, and panthers prowled the primeval forest, which expelled all but the stoutest of souls from its depths once sunlight was extinguished.

While no longer quite at her rawest, Nature around the Keweenaw reclaimed its ascendancy by night. And for the miners who labored among the invasive diggings, existence was as frugal and often as tenuous as it was for the beasts they shared the Copper Country with.

Few and scant as they were, the ungraded streets of Copper Harbor bore the congestion of thousands. Miners were understandably the majority, but those of other stamps were present too. Saloonkeepers, half-breeds, trappers, and the whores who stood as the only representatives of the gentler sex shuffled by one another, faces rendered dark and inscrutable by the erratic shadows of the torches that lit their way. Lace-frilled gamblers idly made their way to preferred camps and watering holes, having left the familiarity of Mississippi side-wheelers to leech what they could from the copper mania. They knew well that where men rose each day hoping to strike it rich, so too existed the mindset of the gambler. Turning your back on the familiar to seek metal riches was a gamble in and of itself. How straightforward it was for such a venture to translate nicely into gambling of a more common variety. The well-situated cardsharps hardly had to exert themselves. Demoralized men, dreams ground down by every stroke of the hammer and hearts heavy with disappointment at having been denied a windfall, would ever prove easy prey.

Indeed, a careful observer might have noticed that more people were currently leaving the Copper Country than entering it. As rabidly pursued as it had been in the previous two years, prospecting was unsustainable for the average man. And it was the notion of prospecting that had drawn thousands to this land in the first place. But by the end of 1846 many men had taken their leave of the region, disheartened at not having found the El Dorado it had been touted as. The days of intrepid fellows pushing into the interior in the generally forlorn hopes of finding a rich vein were drawing to a grudging close. The realization that prospecting had become the province of professionals dawned on an ever-increasing number of individuals. Yet even among the hardened professionals success owed as much to luck as to skill. Of the hundred or more mining companies that had sprung up since the bonanza, only a handful remained active.

And so it was that the majority of men who came to the Keweenaw now came to work for those few companies that had found their footing amidst wild speculation, uncertain financing, and fierce competition. Most of the mining companies that had not tanked in the opening season were now in possession of productive mines. Faith undimmed even by the severity and privations of a Lake Superior winter, they clung to existence as grimly as the wind-tortured pines atop the rocky precipices they sunk shafts into.

The owners of two such companies sat in a dimly lit room with Cadwallader Jones, whose brooding gaze was leveled not at them but out towards the twilight, where the nascent moonbeams played off the idly rippling water of the harbor.

"Jones? *Jones*? Might we be so bold as to request your exclusive attention during this meeting? The matter at hand is rather a serious one."

Jones unhurriedly turned his luminous eyes on the men seated in a half-circle before him. The sizable room of the two-story hotel they sat in was mostly dark but for the glow of the candelabras that had been centrally placed.

"I assure you I heard all, Mr. Hayes. You needn't fret."

Though spoken in a tone that might have passed for affable, John Hayes received that last word exactly as it had been presented- a transparent insult.

Hayes was seated with his trusted business partner, James Raymond, as well as Captain Edward Jennings, their veteran Cornish mining engineer. Jennings ran operations at their now-famous copper source, the Cliff Mine, which had catapulted their formerly humble Pittsburgh & Boston Mining Company into major player status.

The chairs of this trio were set conspicuously apart from the chairs of the two other men who had come to see Jones. Those two were Philo Everett, owner of the Jackson Mining Company, as well as his chief engineer and forgemaster, Ariel N. Barney.

All were worn-looking men, faces tanned and weathered. Unchecked stubble coated the cheeks of those who normally shaved, while the facial hair of the others was approaching unkempt. Yet they had dressed well, in quality frock coats and vests of various shades and materials.

Hayes leaned forward in his chair, elbows on his knees and eyes aflame with the blazing intensity of a man whose overwrought mind demanded answers.

"We seek only to impress upon you the enormity of this gathering. It was your idea to meet at this late hour, Jones; so too was it your stipulation to meet with both companies simultaneously."

He jerked his balding head sharply at the men of the other company, unwilling to divert his stare from Jones. He eyed the lake baron with a pinched face, in the manner of a starving predator.

Clearing his throat gutturally and spitting onto the floor, Philo Everett also leaned forward into the yellow-suffused atmosphere of the candlelight. His face, sharp-featured and square, was bordered by a trim, graying chinstrap beard unattended by a mustache. The organizer of the Jackson Mining Company, Everett was unique in that he mined for iron rather than copper. This did not make Hayes and Raymond direct competitors of his, but he resented their success and secretly feared that they would come to covet his mineral before long. Hayes and Raymond suffered from similar misgivings.

"Mr. Jones. As a businessman you value brevity, a feature that I for one can appreciate. It is no secret to either party here that the other is in need of additional funds. I mean not to sound unctuous, but you built for yourself a commercial empire from scratch- surely you can sympathize with our current financial-"

"I don't suggest you hold your breath if it is pathos you are waiting for. My store of it has long been depleted."

Jones paused a moment for his words to take full effect before setting his thick arms on the cluttered desk he sat behind. Hands folded musingly, he awaited a response with his trademark impassivity.

Raymond scratched his dark stubble as he spoke, sounding very unimpressed by Jones's words. "*Pathos*? Hardly, Jones. Our company seeks only the means to take action. It is our fervent wish to rapidly expand in the coming year."

"Then you shall be ruined by its end."

The mining men swapped worried looks. Haughty and imperious as he could be, Cadwallader Jones knew his craft. This was not a man to speak blithely, nor one to be frivolous in his investments. The money he had sunk into each company had sustained them through difficult times; they would do well to hear him out.

Hayes snorted much like a disgruntled horse might. "We shall be ruined by its end anyway if circumstances do not change. Our investors in Pittsburgh and Boston won't listen, preferring instead to look down their noses at us from their distant perches. Even after we've amply demonstrated that we are poised to reap the riches of this boom, they refuse to acknowledge anything aside from their initial investments that have gone largely unreturned."

Jones nodded in what actually appeared to be an understanding way. "It is the law of diminishing returns, I fear. Many stockholders grow tightfisted in response to the profit slump that initial expansion engenders. It is the way of the world, such as it is."

Leaning back in his chair with a creak, he ran a hand through his thick, backward swept hair. Surprising all present, he issued a sympathetic sigh.

"Not all men possess the gift of foresight as we do. Frustrating at times, is it not?"

Again, the mining men exchanged sideways glances, this time mingling mild perplexity with self-satisfaction. Was Cadwallader Jones, shadowy Great Lakes mogul, really suggesting that he shared a bond with them, that they were birds of a feather?

Behind his inexpressive mask Jones smiled inwardly at their puerile naïveté. They were the struggling entrepreneurial spirit personified, admirable but all cast in a similar mold. Look at the lot of them, exultant after one little compliment. He knew their lofty delusions as well as he knew their pragmatic fears, and these he played to with all the dexterity of a master manipulator.

"It is frustrating," Everett swiftly replied, "so we must work together to overcome it."

"Indeed," supplemented Raymond, his tired face eager and full of hope. "And possessing of foresight as you are, you can surely see how we need funds for equipment, mine facilities, the recruiting of workers, and living quarters for them. Additionally, there are-"

"Don't bludgeon me with the particulars." Jones spoke in a perfectly level tone that caught them off guard. He so enjoyed this, lifting their spirits only to drag them down a moment later. The resultant churn of converse emotions did such funny things to a man's face.

"I am aware of what needs to be done. But you would seek do it on too grand a scale. Don't overreach. I think Pope said it best-

Like kings we lose the conquests gain'd before,
By vain ambition still to make them more;
Each might his sev'ral province well command,
Would all but stoop to what they understand."

"Pope was commenting on the role of the critic, not the fate of the mining man," retorted Hayes, temper flaring. "And I'll remind you that you don't own controlling shares of our companies. Don't try and tell us how to run our operations."

Jones looked at him in barely visible entertainment. "Who tipped you off about the Cliff vein after your initial Copper Harbor leases proved unsustainable? Who sold you the land rights for the parcel that now holds the vaunted Cliff Mine?"

Hayes did not reply. He did not have to. For it had been Jones.

"You were naught but a wealthy druggist from Cleveland who had journeyed to the Copper Country after reading the voluminous geological writings of Douglass Houghton. Despite your zeal, had it not been for me you would still have failed as so many others did."

Philo Everett smiled his appreciation at that, but Jones had only a sneer for him.

"Amused, Everett? He laughs best who laughs last. For who dropped you the hint that the Chippewa Chief Marji-Gesick had knowledge of iron ore near Teal Lake? Me. You and your partners knew nothing, *nothing*, of mining. You were a clueless storekeeper-cum-miner who had dismally failed in the copper game. But again, your drive was what I recognized. 'Twas neither an instance of skill nor a gift of fortune that aided your respective endeavors. It was *me*. You would do well to remember that."

Jones breathed deeply, watching Everett take a conciliatory pull from a hip flask and Hayes look at the floor in bitter embarrassment.

"Through my aid you've both secured productive mines. A fine start- most companies wore themselves into nothingness attempting to develop unprofitable parcels of land. Now present me with a logical plan of attack. Development schematics. Financial projections. Cost analysis. In a word, *sway me*."

"We shan't be divulging company secrets this night." Raymond gave Everett and Ariel Barney a look askance.

"I possess the permits for most of the viable land surrounding your current operations. I will not sell either of your companies' land that is adjacent to the others. I am not looking to pit you against one another, obviously. Such would be to the detriment of my initial investments. Nor do I foresee any natural conflict between your companies in the near future. One mines copper in this region, while the other seeks iron down at the Jackson Location in Marquette. Wariness is understandable here gentlemen, but trust me when I tell you that you have nothing to fear from each other in terms of sabotage. While struggling to keep ones head above the water, it is awfully difficult to plan for much else."

That was a good one. That would appear in his book for sure.

"In short, you are too busy with your own affairs to meddle in the affairs of others."

"The Cliff Mine continues to produce," offered Edward Jennings suddenly in his curious Cornish accent. He had remained aloof from all the accusatory talk; his curt and precise voice was reflective of his blunt, all-business mentality.

"We begin to drill deeper, still finding copper aplenty. Our mines grow larger and more complex, and show no signs of being exhausted anytime soon. By the autumn we will be able to repay our investors. Yourself included."

"Welcome news, Mr. Jennings."

"We continue to recruit from the coalfields of Pennsylvania. We've contracted Welsh and Cornish labor too."

"No Irishmen?"

The Cousin Jack laughed hollowly. "Bad blood between us and the micks. Of the two I choose my kinsmen, as we are simply better copper miners."

Jones nodded his approval. "The Cornish prove exceptional workers, arguably better than even the Welsh."

"If it were iron, lead, coal, or gold, the Welsh would prove our equals. But copper is mined only in a few localities in Wales, whereas in Cornwall the widespread copper and tin bals have produced for centuries. And better yet, the copper mining industry in Cornwall is poised to collapse due to outside competition, so we can expect a steady influx of Cornishmen seeking work. Many will be experts in modern drilling techniques and blasting, given our history of deep mine operations. Which is precisely what is beginning to develop here."

Jennings stopped speaking to take a drag off his cheroot. He regarded Jones silently, stroking his red beard.

"Splendid. And you say production is steady?"

"Aye. This month we're close to matching the 500,000 thousand pounds of copper removed from the Cliff Mine last July. And who knows when another 100,000-pound solid mass of copper will show up as it did last year? But my employers are right- once they can afford additional equipment the income will soon exceed expenses. Drastic expansion, as you stated, may prove detrimental. Yet additional equipment is still needed to expand even in a more modest capacity. We very much need the money we ask for. Here are my proposed expansion plans. If they seem too ambitious I would be amenable to suggestions."

He rose and handed Jones a few sheets of paper.

Good. At least this Cornishman had a square head on his shoulders. If it came down to it he might be able to restrain the impetuosity of his employers.

"Everett? What of your company? I see that you've rid yourself of that bungling fool McNair- a decision I heartily approve of."

Everett turned and gave Ariel Barney a pointed nod, indicating that he should be the one to speak. Barney straightened his slouchy frame and spoke up in a scratchy voice.

"I've been tasked with the construction of the Carp River Forge, having taken over its supervision from McNair. And by take over I might as well reveal that I am essentially starting from scratch. That 'bungling fool' as you described him was just that- he knew nothing of forge construction and as a result the forge won't be finished and producing 'til early in '48 I'd reckon. As of now the dam is complete, eighteen feet high and spanning the length of the Carp River. The waterwheel is still under early construction. With the eight proposed fires and forging hammer, we will need additional funds to commence working. But once in place, the supply of iron we will have mined shall be well worth the effort."

He produced a folder that Jones flipped through under the glow of the nearest candelabrum. He nodded faintly to himself, eyes flicking over the schematic and projected costs of the forge construction.

Both companies would benefit immensely from the knowledge and competence of their top engineers, he noted.

After taking a moment to drink in the uncomfortable silence, further deepened by the palpable atmosphere of anticipation, he spoke. "Based on the reports of your engineers, I will come to your aid this time. But be warned- this will be my final contribution to you both until serious dividends are realized. Additionally, in the coming months I will be drawing up plans for a canal at the Soo. Upon its proposal, I expect all of your support.""

"Of course," said Hayes and Everett jointly, taking a moment to shoot each black, distrustful looks.

"Aided in no small measure by your ambition and rapacity, this money should sustain you. I shall send it upon my return to the Soo, the respective amounts being based on the projections given to me tonight as well as my own judgment. Hayes and Raymond, I would leave you with this: I am sincere when I suggest you don't overreach. Once you have weathered this storm and are able to expand beyond what you are limited to now, don't let passion sway thy judgment. And at all costs you need to avoid producing a surplus of copper that drives its value down, gentlemen. The market remains uncertain and if a too great a surplus comes about the results might well be catastrophic."

Everett expelled a lungful of tobacco. "And what of us? As you will see upon closer examination of that report, we wish to prospect into the unexplored region east of Marquette, towards the place the Indians call Munising."

Jones collected his fine leather valise, putting the reports inside as he digested Everett's words.

"No." He spoke bluntly and rose a commanding figure, with a well-muscled frame, long coat, and imperious bearing.

As he went to leave, Barney blurted out the question that both sets of men were asking themselves. "Mind tellin' me why not?"

Sparing him a moment, Jones stopped and answered, his face obliterated by shadow. "I have personal interests in that area. Leave it be and work the areas you already own."

"We've found signs of mining activity whilst scouting the area around our lease, Jones." Everett found it impossible to restrain his malicious curiosity. “And not just ancient diggings. We’re talking iron-mining activity within the last hundred years. Some are obviously more recent yet. Do you wish to comment on that?”

“Not particularly.” His impatience mounted and he headed for the door.

Hayes, Raymond, and Everett all grinned at one another knowingly.

Everett was the one who pressed, incited by the scent of vulnerability. “Might this have anything to do with the fact that your ship has been seen anchored off the Pictured Rocks, near Mosquito and Chapel Beach in the wee hours of the morning?”

Barney and Jennings slowly looked at one another. That last morsel of info was one that neither engineer had been privy to.

Jones stopped in his tracks and turned to stare at them wooden-faced, self-furious but wholly unwilling to betray it. He would not raise hackle and play the part of the cornered wolf, but would rather assert himself calmly and without the least indication of ill-temper.

“Reasons unascribable, then?” Raymond joined in mockingly, confident that they had Jones back on his heels.

Jones dropped his valise and walked towards them purposefully, and their bodies visibly tensed. He positioned himself right in front of them.

“You are all teetering on the brink of insolvency. Without my financial backing you have no company.”

“You truly believe that keeping others in the dark is a proper way to do business?” Hayes was livid.

“That has long been my creed.” The grim shadow of a smile flitted across his face.

Everett could not curb his desire for answers. “What secrets are you hiding out there? What viper lays coiled under that stone?”

“One coiled indeed, and ready to strike at the slightest sign of threat. Bear in mind the stories of prospectors penetrating deep into the interior, never to return. Bear in mind the parties of miners who vanished en route to the Keweenaw after setting camp on the wrong beaches. Recall the legends this region is steeped in. And for your own sake, act on every fear you have ever harbored while out in the gloom of these hallowed woods. Ignore not the shiver that creeps down the spine when you feel the watchful eyes of the forest upon you.”

They all knew precisely what he referenced. He turned with finality to leave.

"Vanished, like that vanished Welshman Crowder?" Barney asked bravely.

"Meddlesome and underhanded, wasn't he Barney?" Jones spoke briskly over his shoulder. "And dealt with accordingly. Don't end up on the wrong side of things, gentlemen. The consequences could be... *disadvantageous*."

He left them to their ruminating, boots rapping authoritatively on the uneven floorboards of the hallway. In the darkness of that corridor he indulged a grin that had been threatening to manifest itself in the last moments of the meeting.

For the words of those men contained no consequence. When you held the proper cards, there was never a need to fear those around you, posturing be damned.

And what an intoxicating feeling it was.

Chapter 43

With time, the pressure of the tiny pebble sticking into his face graduated to a dull ache, which summoned Finnbar to consciousness. As the shutters of his perception creaked open bit-by-bit, the various other pains in his body seared and throbbed that pebble-born ache into nonexistence. His whole being was alive with pain that drew a drawn out grunt from him as he rolled over.

"Have a nice nap?" a droll voice inquired from somewhere nearby.

"Aye, slept like the dead." He might have just regained his awareness, but Finnbar Fagan would be damned before he'd let that stand in the way of promptly dispensed wit.

"Irish?" the man wished to know.

With a stifled groan Finnbar dragged himself to his feet, staggering into a wall of wooden bars.

"Guilty as charged," he replied through clenched teeth.

His hands closed around those bars for support. A quick look around told him that his situation had not improved. It was a jarring sort of revelation, for he was alive but in a jail of sorts, one with a low, domed ceiling cleverly constructed of rock. Tiny apertures that he supposed passed for windows dotted the walls, but as it seemed to be night the only luminosity that he and the other man were afforded came from a small, crackling fire in the middle of the room.

"Who might you be?" Finnbar asked of the man, who languished in the shadows of an adjacent cell.

"No one of consequence." The fellow spoke in a Welsh–accented voice that, while retaining some of its rock-ribbed cynicism, was so without hope that even a deeply ingrained pessimism offered little in the way of reassurance.

"I'm in rarified air, then. Lovely."

"And who might you be, Irishman?"

"Finnbar Fagan, originally of Cork, lately of wherever the road might take me."

"Ah. A wayfarer bold."

Their words of courteous, albeit dry badinage were making this dismal scene more bearable. Misfortune shared in is misfortune lessened.

"Was on a trapping expedition but-" here Finnbar gingerly touched the spot where a sword had nicked his side, "looks like that has come to a rather abrupt halt."

The other man stepped forth from the shadows, allowing the fire to shed its light on his features. He was lean-visaged, more so than Finnbar, with a sly hook to his nose that went well with his crafty, almond shaped eyes. Dark haired and fair skinned, he was around average height and build. A careful student of body language, Finnbar also observed the brooding slump in his shoulders that reflected physically the desolation in his voice.

"They bore down on you like a north wind, did they not?" His light blue eyes were locked on Finnbar in forceful curiosity.

"Indeed they did, Welshman," Finnbar replied absently, testing the strength of the wooden cell and finding it extremely sturdy. "Took a few of the bastards with us, though."

"You did, did you? Personally?"

"Aye."

"Good man," the fellow approved with a stiff nod, reminding Finnbar of Alvord.

He casually stepped forward to the wall of wooden poles that separated their cells.

"Well, Finnbar Fagan," he extended his hand through the bars, "the name's Owain Derog Crowder."

"A name as Welsh as dairy farming."

Crowder chuckled deeply as they shook, shaking his head in appreciation. "Always glad to make the acquaintance of a fellow wit."

"Always glad to propitiate the illusion. So, how did you come to find yourself sequestered in this charming little gaol?"

The Welshman snorted mirthlessly. "They attacked my mining crew west of here, near the place they call Marquette."

"A copper seeker?"

An amused contortion of facial features followed his question. "Woe to mine wallet, if so. Copper is a passing fad, the dimmed hope of this age. A few will get rich off it whilst the rest are scattered to the wind. 'Twas iron I sought."

"Any of your crew make it?" There was a wooden bucket in the corner of Finnbar's cell that he gladly emptied his bladder into.

"Nary a soul. Decent bunch too, as far as men go."

Crowder looked down slowly, and Finnbar could tell that he replayed the instance of his capture in his mind.

With great effort he tried to recall anything after his being knocked out. It came back to him in brief, nonlinear flashes.

The occasional, dim, and scarcely remembered flickering of

consciousness while being dragged along in some sort of sled. Towering trees on all sides. The dank odor of the painted men around him. And something unpleasant being forced down his mouth, some vile concoction that tastes like rotting grass...

"Cup of cheer?" his fellow prisoner offered. "A low quality port by my assessment."

"Hey, any port in a storm, lad."

"Spoken like a true son of Bacchus, Irishman!"

He passed the goatskin *bota* bag through the bars, whereupon Finnbar gratefully poured a salubrious measure down his parched throat. He then dumped some on his bitten arm, and the shallow cuts his torso bore. The bite, he was glad to see, had just barely broken skin.

"They are a thieving bunch, and pilfer the camps and corpses of those they kill. This must have been among some unfortunate bastard's belongings. But his past misfortune is our present gain."

"You are a captive, yet they gift you with wine?"

"I have proven my worth among them. In another life I was a physician, or a sawbones as these colonial brutes call it. Additionally, I speak their tongue."

Finnbar's wandering stare shot over to the man and remained fixed.

"In a manner of speaking," Crowder quickly amended. "After all, we are kinsmen of sorts."

Finnbar had been working up to asking who in the bloody hell they had been taken captive by. He had not wanted to simply blurt the question out and thereby seem anxious, but he decided that now would be a fitting time to go ahead.

"The beards, the armor, the weapons. And the architecture," he added, eyes sweeping around the room again. "All wildly out of place here in the wilds of Michigan. Anachronistic, ye might say. And I saw light eyes on one of the men I laid low. You say you speak their tongue, that you are kinsmen to them- by this do you mean-"

Owain Derog Crowder sat down against the wall of his cell and stared into the dancing flames of the fire as if peering back into some remoter age. Beyond the windows of their jail, drums began pounding out a wild beat as an eerie, lilting chorus rose heavenward.

"Aye. Move over Christopher Columbus."

The Irishman's eyes widened involuntarily. "So what we're dealing with is-"

"The legacy of Prince Madog ab Owain Gwynedd. Or Madoc, as most know him by."

"*Shite*," uttered Finnbar with vehemence, and he too sank down against he wall in wonderment.

Chapter 44

"They are, as you can imagine, a rather clannish lot," Crowder explained as the confusion of noises beyond their cells reached fever pitch.

"I suppose seven centuries of warfare, exodus, and relentless persecution will do that to a culture," he continued in his bored drawl, apparently unconcerned with the tumult outside.

"What's with all the ballyhoo out there, Owain?"

"You're better off seeing it with your own two eyes, lest you deem me a madman for my explanation."

Rapid footsteps approached as the awful wail of some unknown instrument joined the infernal ensemble outside. A cold shiver of fear, involuntary and hastily suppressed, passed through Finnbar as he awaited the appearance of his captors and whatever fresh hell they brought his way.

Five men swept into the room and stopped abruptly before the small, glittering fire in its center. Its orange glow washed over them, throwing their faces into sharp relief. One of them, armed with a spear, had skin that quite contrasted with the flickering shadows around him.

"Mark you his shade?" Crowder asked. "White as the driven snow, Finnbar. And the others? Lighter by far than any Indian, lighter even than most half-breeds, but not quite white. This lost tribe of Madoc's appears to have occasionally interbred with Indians."

Crowder was right- that there was Indian blood among them was noticeable. The nose of one swarthy man had an Indian cast to it. Finnbar had heard of the legends of Madoc- shite, who hadn't? But to be bearing witness to that very legend... God above, he was scarcely willing to believe his eyes.

"Interbreeding with friendly tribes or perhaps captive Indians taken in warfare, this far flung Welsh colony avoided the taint of inbreeding whilst taking on the taint of red blood. Notice the amber eyes that some of them bear? The rarest of human eye colors, but apparently one passed down through generations within this micro-population."

Finnbar bristled at that one, as Genevieve Connolly's bloodline was similarly "tainted," but just then the guards moved in and opened his cell door. He watched interestedly as of them inserted a long, square piece of what looked to be copper into the thick, wooden dead bolt that held shut the cell door. With a deft turn of the grip on the end of the copper piece, the lock was sprung.

"Clever," he muttered under his breath.

Two long-bladed spears were leveled at him menacingly. One of the men, his light eyes intense as they bore into Finnbar's, beckoned him forward. Finnbar cast a questing glance over at Crowder, hoping for some advice.

"Don't attempt anything foolhardy; they won't hesitate to make mincemeat out of you."

Truth telling, Finnbar harbored no such inclination. Outnumbered, wounded, and quite possibly still shrugging off the effects of a sedative, he knew that discretion would be the better part of valor here.

"So, we dead men?" mused Finnbar offhandedly.

"Likely as not."

The Irishman chuckled bitterly, more to quell the mounting sense of panic than for the sake of humor. "Gallows humor, eh?"

The apparent leader of the group of Welsh Indians held up his hands and placed them outward and close together, then indicating that Finnbar should ape his movement. He did, and his hands were promptly tied together with rope. Crowder was likewise removed from his cell and bound, and then with spears at their backs the two captives were marched down a narrow, torch-lit passageway before emerging into the riotous night.

The scene that confronted them was more horrible in aspect than any macabre imaging of Edgar Allen Poe's and more barbarous by far than any of James Fennimore Cooper's. The mounting tempo of the pounding drums struck a chord of foreboding within Finnbar's breast. He had found himself in some pretty sticky situations by far, but *strewth*, this one certainly took the biscuit.

A roaring bonfire blazed in the center of a spacious, open area of hard-packed dirt. The fire flung its light all 'round, but beyond its radiant aura stalked the tenebrous shadows of the night. Arrayed crowdedly outside the flames, forming a massive ring of humanity that wildly throbbed with the thudding drums was the lost tribe of Madoc. Dressed in dyed buckskins and furs, in a manner that recalled ancient peoples of Europe, the throng howled their delight at the appearance of the captives. Finnbar's overwrought eyes caught the glint of flames on copper jewelry as he was pushed forward as a break in the crowd formed to admit him.

The instrumental was odious enough to the ears, but the chorus! Not merely some barbarous chanting but actually a song of sorts. The voices of the chorus sang in many different parts rather than in unison. It might have been discordant but somehow each of these self-contained elements managed to coalesce into a blood-chilling dirge.

"Sort of strains credulity, don't it?" asked Crowder, smiling thinly.

Finnbar, stupefied into a bout of uncharacteristic speechlessness, could only stare at the roiling madness around them.

Five men bedecked in long robes of what looked like white wolf pelts stood before the fire, their hooded heads all the more portentous in their obscurity. Hands raised towards the heavens, they chanted words that were drowned out by the cacophonous jumble of singing and instruments. A gnarled and ancient oak, low-growing but massively thick of limb, loomed over them like some beast from the realm of myth.

Finnbar had heard tell of some surviving pockets of pagan ritual back in the Old Country, where berobed figures would enact the ancient Druidic ceremonies. And when he had attended Trinity College, there had been whispers of secret societies searching for the key to the old magic.

But here, in the New World, the tradition had been preserved by this single tribe of transplanted Welshmen? It strained credulity indeed.

More captives were brought into the circle and made to stand next to Finnbar and Crowder. This new group of captives contained eight or so men. To his surprise he saw Jawbeance and Defago among them, and gave his fellow trappers a nod of recognition once they noticed him. He saw the panic in their eyes and wondered if it showed in his own.

For at the moment he felt like the captured Samson in John Milton's *Samson Agonistes- eyeless in Gaza at the mill with slaves...*

Crowder, for his part, seemed perfectly undaunted.

"You've been here before, haven't ye Welshman?"

"I have."

"So you've survived this sort of ceremony. What are we to expect?"

"I am not so arrogant as to presume to know. They are more pent up than I have ever seen them before. Might have something to do with the casualties they incurred today. Expect anything."

The Irishman felt panic clawing its way up his throat. He

choked it back, but it went down his gullet as a shot of rotgut whiskey might.

The music and singing abruptly ceased. The priests solemnly approached the line of bound captives.

Here we go... don't give them the satisfaction of screams or begging, steel yourself for whatever comes next, Fagan...

From their ranks the priests took four white men with the look of miners about them.

Finnbar watched breathlessly as the ritual began. So too did the fire-bathed, paint splattered faces, more than he could count, watch eagerly from their hushed circle as the priests again raised their hands and gave vent to intonations of a magic he had long thought bygone.

The little that he had heard of the Welsh language came back to him in the lilting imprecations of these incongruous New World druids. At a pause in the flow of chanted lines, five warriors came forward, all armed and moving with the confidence of seasoned fighters. One of them, the most broad-shouldered of the bunch, paused a moment to look over Finnbar and his fellow captives.

He looked around him with the air and conceit of a king.
Under a black leather jerkin this raven-haired warrior's frame was imposingly fleshed out with muscle, more so even than Alvord. His large skull sat atop a bull neck that showed thick, corded sinews when his chiseled face swiveled towards the prisoners. An eye patch covered his right eye, giving this brute an even more diabolical appearance. He turned to face them, his scathing sneer deepening as he looked each of them in the eye. Murder shone in the glacial blue band encircling the man's iris.

It was far from comforting, and for a moment Finnbar thought the man might draw his sword and began hacking them to bits.

"Eyes down, Irishman!" hissed Crowder, his voice for the first time sounding shaky and ill at ease.

Finnbar complied, and soon the man turned on his heel and strutted towards the druids, whose chants gained in intensity.

"Do *not* cross that man," he was warned. "He is their warlord, a fearsome creature who will not hesitate to physically break you in half."

A rope was cast over the most accessible limb of the old oak, a noose dangling off one end. Some of the warriors positioned a man directly under it while they made sure the other captives did not budge. The noose was forced over the chosen man's neck, whereupon he began screaming pitiably. But with a sword at his throat he chose not the struggle. One of the druids daubed something on the man's forehead, and a moment later the rope was hauled up. This did not break the man's neck nor, Finnbar realized, was it meant to. The rope simply held him a few inches off the ground the priests stood back, waited for his violent thrashing to subside. When the man could only feeble resist, his throat was cut with a long bladed, ceremonial dagger produced by one of the druids to the obvious delight of the crowd. Eyes agleam with bloodlust, the Welsh Indians watched as their holy men gathered round the spot where the man's lifeblood gushed to the earth. Pointing at and tracing certain bloodstains, they talked among themselves in subdued voices.

"*Scrying,*" whispered Finnbar in disbelief.

"Good God!" Defago declared, as nonplussed as Finnbar. Jawbeance said nothing, simply staring wide-eyed and open-mouthed as the gruesome spectacle played out.

These men were attempting to discern future events by scrying, the reading of blood, in which they analyzed the pattern in which it had fallen. Some of the legends surrounding Druidic practices touched upon blood magic as a prevalent way to see past the obfuscating fog of the present and into the future. He watched, oddly spellbound, and they peered into the blood and, perhaps, into the very fabric of time.

In the same manner were the three other captives ritualistically murdered, although once they had seen the brutal fate of the first man the others struggled ferociously, having to be beat into semi-consciousness beforehand. The brutish one-eyed warrior dispensed bone-crunching blows; Finnbar did not fancy being on the receiving end of them.

As the warriors removed the carcasses, the priests threw something into the fire and it began emitting black, acrid smoke. They then stepped back and began bellowing incantations, hoods thrown back and heads inclined. Their hands began making strange patterns in the air around them, and a few minutes later Finnbar heard the distinct patter of rain. Heard, not felt, and looking closely he could see the exultant druids dancing in the contained rainstorm they had just conjured. For it was only over them that the rain appeared to come down and come down hard. As their chanting continued it changed, becoming deeper and less ululating. The rain ceased as swiftly as it had begun. In its place a tendril of fog, just like that queer fog that he had been caught in earlier, appeared and hovered above the sorcerers. This spindly tendril they appeared to manipulate through hand gestures until it blossomed into a hydra-headed cloud that settled over them. It wove around and in between the priests before rising once more and deliquescing into nonbeing above the fire.

Slack-jawed, Finnbar tried to slow the frenzied pulsing of his heart.

"Saints preserve us!" he breathed in abject wonder, for his world no longer bordered on reality. "This is sheer, bloody madness!"

"Well its no cotillion party, now is it?" Crowder said, unexpectedly shaky in his delivery of the words. "The laws of nature are being altered-"

"Nay- they are being uprooted. Those murderous fiends wield elemental power! This is some ungodly shite!"

"I suppose you are closer to the mark. This isn't some parlor trick, nor a charlatan's hocus-pocus. Nor are they vainly making offering to gods who don't exist. This is something else entirely. Something responds to their fervent prayers and sanguinary offerings. I'd wager it has helped them cling to existence all these years."

As with the adventure down in St. Louis this past spring, Finnbar Fagan had once again been drawn into the howling vortex of a staggering mystery.

He shook his head in helpless bewilderment at the fact. "So that was the grand finale, was it?"

"Yes," Crowder answered, his stare fixed on a small group of women that had assembled nearby, "but it appears that we are to be a part of the aftershow."

"And what, pray tell, might that be?"

"You much disposed to wenching, Fagan?"

An odd question at a time like this, but he replied, "Ever and anon."

"Well get ready to wench to your heart's content, the only charge being our captivity. Hope your feeling frisky, Irishmen."

Finnbar's head shot over to the cluster of topless females who were now arrayed in two rows and moving his way. Their appearance was similar to that of the men, with varying degrees of skin, eye, and hair tone. But the majority of these women were on the lighter side of the spectrum. The lurid music picked up again and they broke into a sinuous dance, erotic if ever he'd seen.

"Ye've gotta be shittin' me?"

"Irishman, I shit thee not. They appear to be breeding back towards pure white, and you, with your fair complexion, no doubt qualify." As if to drive his point home, Jawbeance and Defago were roughly herded away from them, back towards the cells from which they had emerged.

The bare-chested tribeswomen continued their unhurried approach, weaving ever closer through exaggerated copulatory movements.

"So this is some sort of fertility rite?"

"I have some other choice words for it, but yes."

Finnbar's agitated mind instantly strayed to Gen with her smile as bright as the midday sun, but in an effort to maintain his sangfroid he bitterly quipped, "Well, I suppose even captivity can have its perks..."

Part Three
A Gathering of the Worthies

Fear the reckoning of those you have wronged
Norse Proverb

Chapter 45

They had rowed the night through. This strenuous labor was divvied up into shifts among those who bore lesser injuries. At the moment, Walks With Thunder and Gaston leadenly propelled the boat towards the docks of Sault Ste. Marie. They were in the dancing rapids of the St. Mary's River now, and mercifully close to their destination. Aided by their knowledge of the currents in this section of river, the Chippewa brave and the half-breed were stoic in the face of unspeakably cramped backs and shooting hunger pangs. It was midday or damn close, and their meager rations had witnessed depletion once the men breakfasted.

As could be readily deduced by each of their appearances, the past night had been hellacious. Sleep came to them in fits, with frequent nightmares jolting men from sleep. At least the wind had proven sympathetic to their cause, helping them along during most of their miserable nocturnal voyage. Likewise did the moon, unharried by clouds, steadily shed it light on Superior's gloomy waters.

Alvord and Marcel had doggedly rowed into the wee hours of the chilly morning. Knowing that if they stopped paddling they too would succumb to fitful slumber, Alvord and the rugged trapper beside him had spoken barely a word and stopped only to swig some water. Each sensed the other's searing rage, but what good would words do them when they needed to get back to the Soo posthaste?

So they'd saved their breath for the task at hand.

It was one of those times that passed like some interminable nightmare, more miserable in the moment than the mind could ever hope to replicate in memory.

But then Big Wolf and Walks With Thunder had awoken and insisted on taking over. The others rose soon after, whereupon the tiller was then unlashed and manned, allowing them to take full advantage of the wind.

Soon after that Sault Ste. Marie was in full view, as well as the promise of getting off that cramped and uncomfortable bateau.

On the British side of the Soo Alvord saw with hollow, disinterested eyes the Hudson's Bay Company depot. Its moldering storehouses, blockhouse, sawmill, and canal and lock showed signs of neglect visible even from a distance. Then Whitefish Island, the pine-clad bulk of which took up a decent span of river between the American and Canada shores, blotted out their view of the latter.

With David controlling the rudder, Gaston and Walks With Thunder skillfully directed them through a gap between the seven-foot high docks of the American Fur Company and those of the adjacent McNight Brothers & Tinker warehouse. A fishing sloop as long as their bateau had been poised to make entry into that landing area before being unabashedly cut off, and its crew began angrily upbraiding the exhausted and unconcerned remnants of the offending trapping party.

Their threats and chastisements fell upon decidedly deaf ears. The bateau slid past the wharf of McNight Brothers & Tinker, where ships of all kinds would transfer their freight onto the rails of the portage road. From there they would be hauled north to the head of the rapids, to waiting Lake Superior craft.

The sound of wood scraping against sandy shore was music to their ears. Alvord and Gaston leapt out of the boat first to drag it ashore, followed closely by an ecstatic Cerberus whose young sighthound mind and frame had been cooped up for far too long. The Indian who had survived the Grand Sable Dunes assault was hard on his heels, and he began running towards the Chippewa village without bothering to look back.

The badly wounded were gingerly helped off. David could manage alright, but Lightfoot and Duddersfield were hurting. Alvord could no longer feel much of his upper body, but with numb arms he lowered the bravely grimacing scientist onto an empty, sizeable cart on the portage tracks. He would have expected a complainer in Duddersfield, yet the young man had not dishonored himself since being wounded.

"*Oh God*," he breathed shakily when the broken-off arrow brushed up against the side of the cart.

"Sorry, boy," said Alvord apologetically. "Be brave."

"I know, but Lord in Heaven does it hurt..."

A tear slid out from behind his glasses and Alvord knew the pain was poised to get the best of Duddersfield.

"Hang on there, Dud, we'll get ye fixed up good'n proper." Marcel turned to Alvord as Lightfoot was also loaded into the cart. "Gotta get these fellers to a sawbones quick-like, Al."

"Nearest one?"

"Just up that way," answered Gaston, pointing at a modest cabin dwarfed by the considerable Hopkins Hotel.

"Good, let us-"

"*Hey!*" a voice full of vinegar yelled.

They turned to see two fishermen and a handful of rough-looking warehouse workers stomped their way over.

"Of the goddamn lot of you, is there even one decent set of eyes? Because we'd been given clearance to enter when you cut us off!"

The approaching group of men was rounded on so fiercely that they stopped dead in their tracks.

In no mood at all for nonsense, Alvord picked up one of the rifles and with one hand pointed it at the lead man's snarling face. "Shut your sniveling mouth or I blow it out the back of your skull."

He cocked the hammer for emphasis. Beside him, Walks With Thunder already had his knife out.

"What seems to be the trouble, gents?" A well-dressed man stepped under the door of the neighboring American Fur Company warehouse.

"I'll be damned," acknowledged Marcel gruffly. "John Livingston."

Livingston's eyes swept over the scene cautiously. "S'been a while, Durand. That little trapping expedition of yours went south, did it? Oh, word travels fast in a one-track town. Speaking of which, that cart is ours; use it to transport your wounded to the nearest doc. Free of charge, naturally."

Marcel bristled at the sarcastic mention of his failure, the depth of which that coiffed bastard knew not, but chose to merely accept the help.

Livingston then addressed the other group. "As for you lot, clear out and get back to work. I'd hate for anyone's superior to hear of this little misunderstanding."

Alvord lowered the rifle as the other men dispersed, obviously cowed by Livingston's sudden appearance.

"Much obliged, Livingston. See ya around."

"No doubt, Marcel," he agreed dryly. "So now you know the reason why that place has been given a pass by all in the trade for centuries, don't you?"

Marcel let the comment pass unanswered.

Normally animal labor conveyed such carts up and down the portage road, but as none were attached to this cart they put their aching shoulders into it and soon it was squeaking its way down the track.

They passed by retail stores, dramshops, blacksmiths and barbers, with patrons flooding in and out of them like bees from a hive. The crowded street around them produced many a question as to what they were doing, but no answers were issued.

They loudly burst into the small but tidy physicians shop, but the young doc, who sat with his back to them as he read over some papers was not to be startled.

"Just a minute," he rapped out over his shoulder, "I'll be with you gentlemen in just a minute."

"Pardon my lack o' civility, doc, but get yer ass up outta that chair *now*," ordered Marcel in a deep growl containing no patience at all.

The man rose instantly, appearing totally unsurprised at the scene before him.

"Who is worst hurt?"

"That'd be Dudd, right here. Took an arrow in a place he's not used to displayin' publicly."

The doc immediately went to work, demonstrating competence and clear-headedness. He had an apprentice too, an even younger redheaded kid whose quiet efficiency was of great help.

The piercing screams were eventually replaced with whimpers; the poor geologist's face was so white as to be ghostlike. The entry wound had to be widened before the arrowhead, which was designed so that it could not be easily pulled out, could be removed. The resulting pain could only have been nauseating, and Alvord was frankly surprised that the young scientist had not lost consciousness. Even the laudanum he'd been dosed with could partially only dull the pain caused by the lancing of his flesh.

Gaston had offered his hand to the horrified Duddersfield during the dreadful procedure, which was now released sore and throbbing due to pain-wracked scientist's desperate grip.

"You did well, Dudd," he said to the panting man.

"You fellows are in rough shape," the physician remarked indifferently as he dropped the offending arrowhead into a pan with a clatter.

"We're the lucky 'uns, lad," David assured him.

The wounds Marcel had sutured were all inspected by the man, whose name was Mansfield. The mountain man's handiwork received a compliment from the doctor, although he did insist on additional stitching for Big Wolf's lengthy facial laceration. The brave consented, but bluntly refused anything for the pain. Lighfoot, possessing of no such disinclination, was heavily dosed with laudanum and made to lie down on a bed to rest. Cerberus, free from any perceivable injury, curled up next to him and in seconds was dozing.

Alvord was concerned about the throbbing bite wound he

had taken to the chest, for human bites could be as bad as those of wild animals. He had the doc cauterize it, having seen what bites could do during his time on the job. He feared the infection and potentially lethal fever it could cause.

"Someone was intent on removing your pectoralis," Mansfield briskly observed, though he did not ask how it had been received. Young but seasoned, he asked patients only the questions he needed to.

"Gaston, you keep Dudd an' Lightfoot some company," Marcel instructed as Mansfield began taking a look at the more minor injuries among them. "You other fellers want to meet up at the Injun camp in an hour?"

They nodded their agreement.

"You not come?" Walks With Thunder wished to know.

"There's somethin' that needs doin'. Al and me'll go tend to it."

He offered no further explanation, and promptly led the way out into the fast flow of the sunlit street beyond.

Chapter 46

"I'm going back," said Alvord and Marcel simultaneously, each addressing the other.

They ceased walking and regarded one another seriously, each recognizing that of the legions of men that walked this earth, few would willingly return to the site of such recent loss and vividly recalled terror.

Alvord smiled tightly, recalling Finnbar's words. "*Abyssus abyssum invocate-* one Hell summons another. And I propose that in response to that attack we raise an unholy hell of our own."

A game grimace overcame Marcel face. "Blood fer blood has long been my creed."

That code was one held by Alvord as well, and within it a mentality that would cease only in death.

Marcel put forth his hand.

"Time to dig up the tomahawk, *mon ami.*"

"Agreed."

Alvord's palm met the rough hand of the mountain man and they shook forcefully.

They continued their course north on Water Street, striding past groups of rough-talking miners. Their talk of trifles seemed patently immaterial to Alvord, whose mind was consumed with questions, anger, and worry.

"Jones." He stated simply. "You suspect him as well, Marcel?"

"Yep. First explanation that leapt into my mind, and if life's learned me anything at all it's that you trust yer gut."

"Good man. I am of the same mind, and have been piecing this together all night. The strangely tattooed warriors on the timber pirate vessel were the first clue, along with that surviving pirate's tale of strange fog and weather that he tenuously connected with those savages. Colson questioned the survivor, asking about a man named Jones."

Marcel nodded strongly. "Uh hu. Then we saw similar lookin' bodies in the aftermath of the miner's camp attack, painted in Chippewa fashion and usin' Chippewa style bows and arrers- but there was somethin' off about those arrers, they was-"

"Generic. You and David stated that they bore none of the

individualized markings that Chippewa arrows should have. And that odd sword present at Jones's dinner party, I recall him brushing it aside in order to change the subject. How I cannot say, but he has something to do with all this."

"Granted, but he's a problem fer another day. Now Al, I'd hazard that you got more'n a couple questions bouncing around yer skull about exactly what it is we're dealin' with. I would see 'em answered, so we're gonna seek out the one man who might be able to furnish those answers. Lucky fer us he resides nearby."

"And who is the fellow in question?"

"Goes by Thurgood, ain't sure of his first name. I know the feller a bit, but always dismissed him as *non compos mentis*. He was cap'n of the *Otter*, a Hudson's Bay Company fur schooner used on Superior durin' the Company's heyday."

"And this man had dealings with those white savages?"

Marcel's dark eyes grew distant as his mind drifted towards the past. "They say he showed up at the Soo half-mad and mostly dead in the spring of '24, blatherin' about how his ship was caught in a storm around the Pictured Rocks. Claimed white devils summoned the storm, and in the aftermath the tribe wiped out the survivors of the wreck but took him captive."

Alvord's interested was immediately aroused. "Yet he escaped?"

"Yep. And then somehow found his way back here without the use of any trails. His claims were shrugged off as the ravings a madman, though the Indians heard 'im out, readily speakin' of copper gods and trespassin' upon cursed ground. He's a hermit fishmonger now, lives to the north of town."

"You thinking he could lead us to their village?"

Marcel's jaw clenched firmly and the glint of fierce resolve smoldered in his eyes.

"Aye. And to vengeance."

They quickened their pace, resolute and hungering for information and the means by which to rescue their Irish friend if yet he lived, or wreak terrible retribution if he did not.

From a bird's eye view the frontier town straddling the river was little more than a colossal anthill through which swarmed the attendant colony. In all the hustle and bustle, the unwavering course of two fast-walking men went unnoticed. The pair lent it no thought, but it still stood that those they passed knew nothing of the enormity that accompanied their steps, nor the realm of arcane horror they were poised to plunge back into.

Elijah Thurgood strung the lifeless trout and whitefish on the iron hooks above the smoking fire that he then stoked with kindling of red maple and black cherry.

His task accomplished, he plopped down on the grassy knoll that his modest cabin rested atop and let his eyes take in the quiet majesty of the country around him. He lived at the end of a small peninsula that jutted out into the headwaters of the St. Mary's, and a lovelier spot he defied anyone to find.

The pellucid water of the shallows gave way to an increasingly intense aquamarine that only lessened upon its approach to the distant Canadian shoreline. Those were some of his prime fishing grounds, from which he derived a livelihood. Beyond the shore, sharply outlined against the horizon were the Hiawatha Highlands that dominated the lands beyond. It was rugged country, appealing to the eye, but on the whole his passion was the water. Thurgood was no woodsman, and left the interior to those suited for it.

The life of a fishmonger; now that was one for him. He kept to himself, lived by himself, and by the sweat of his own brow earned enough to get by. He wanted nothing more from life except, truth telling, a slightly larger vessel. In quiet moments his mind would occasionally drift towards thoughts of the goodship *Otter* and his bygone days of captaincy, but nightmares came hard on the heels of such thoughts so he generally curbed them.

Legless with liquor, a half-breed approached him and in slurring fashion requested a brace of whitefish. This he gave the man for a fair price; too numerous were the whites who would cheerfully rip off Indians and half-breeds when the vapors of alcohol clouded their judgment.

The half-breed went his way, passing two men who approached the cabin. The pair, one tall and the other a shade shorter and broader than average, walked with conviction, noticed Thurgood. They also bore the blue and yellow mottling of recent bruises as well as fresh cuts on their faces...

In the next instant he recognized the shorter man, and from the mists of the pasts came a jolt of fear that he had a tough time suppressing.

The two men stopped a few feet away from him, expressions grave. Grave and expectant, actually. And he knew precisely why.

"Marcel Durand," he acknowledged stiffly. "S'been a while."

"We can ditch the pleasantries, Thurgood."

Thurgood then knew what would come next and wished to God it wouldn't.

The worn-looking trapper's eyes burned into his. "Congratulations, you ain't a madman after all."

Thurgood's heart pounded like the drums his memory involuntarily recalled.

"Where did it happen?" he asked, not genuinely curious but needing to know all the same.

"Chapel Beach." Recent loss and dark memories hung heavy on the words.

"You boys had best come into my cabin then. We've much to speak of."

He turned and led the way, bowing to the fact that the past he longed to forget was rising, serpent-like, from its lair.

Chapter 47

Alvord and Marcel stood in Thurgood's small but well constructed cabin. The smell of fish guts and smoke that greeted them weren't odors that Alvord particularly cherished. Fishing nets were piled neatly in one corner of the room, and nearby rows of bookshelves were stuffed with volumes. Their gray-haired host poured himself a measure of whiskey and took a nerve-steadying drink. Gulping down the remainder with a wince, he afterward seemed to notice his churlishness and offered his guests the bottle.

After the nightmare they had endured, both gratefully accepted the liquid comfort.

"You fellows look a sight and could no doubt use a bevvy," said Thurgood reflectively. "I take it you didn't come here just to say hello.

He regarded them more closely. "You were lucky to escape. Not many who trespass upon that land do so. How many of your party made it back?"

Marcel heaved a ragged sigh and, deferring to his aching back and conscience, wearily slumped into a chair. "Our trappin' party got real tore up."

Alvord took another face-blanching swig of whiskey before handing it back to Thurgood, who drank deeply of it.

Looking him over carefully, Alvord spoke. "You've dealt with the white savages, then?"

"Aye," he replied in the *scouse* accent of Liverpool.

"And the conclusion you arrived at...?"

Thurgood gazed into his eyes perceptively. "The selfsame one you're dying to have verified."

Alvord felt his heart accelerate. If what he was about to hear was true, then they were peering into the depths of a mystery so profound that it would impose a radical rewriting of the history books. No longer aware of his soreness and fatigue, he waited for the delivery of the next words with the insuppressible expectancy that accompanies the uncovering of forbidden knowledge.

Thurgood's coffee-colored eyes grew distant, as he peered into the musty chapters of the dimly remembered past. "What you encountered on Chapel Beach was legend made flesh- the legacy of Prince Madoc."

He'd known it. Alvord had known it ever since his battle-churned brain had seized a moment's reflection. The light skin and eyes, the Celtic tattoos, the Old World weaponry and armor... it all added up to this- a white tribe of Welshmen hidden in the desolate wilderness of Upper Michigan...

He quickly drew in the reins of imagination and returned to the present.

"I agree. How did you arrive at this conclusion?"

The man gave a chuckle that was half snort. "I was their captive for a couple months during the fall of '23 through the winter of '24. Got me a view from the inside looking out."

The man had an insider's view of the enemy. A better edge they would not be afforded. Alvord maintained a keen silence, thirsting for more information.

"I captained a Hudson's Bay Company fur schooner here on *Gitchi Gummi* in those days. Impelled to employ more aggressive business strategies due to increased competition from the hated Northwest Company, the HBC higher-ups financed the construction of six schooners. The *Speedwell, Invincible, Otter, Mink, Recovery,* and *Discovery,* were to drop off and pick up fur cargoes at various stations. Because St. Mary's Falls at Sault Ste. Marie rendered it impossible to bring large vessels from the lower lakes into Superior short of a grueling portage, these six ships would bring speed and efficiency to Superior's fur trade. Initially the venture had seemed promising, yet I now opine that it was all a tragic mistake, a senseless waste of lives and money. One by one, ships all came to rest on the lakebed excepting the *Speedwell.* My own craft, the *Otter,* was sunk off the coast of the Pictured Rocks in November of '23, near the spot they call Mosquito Beach. We were heading east to the Soo from Fon du Lac on a late season run- the last run of that season, as it happened- when a storm was conjured that ended up scuttling my boat."

"*Conjured?*" Marcel raised a bushy eyebrow.

Thurgood, who had been staring at the floor while he spoke, leveled a cynical gaze at him. "Nothing strange happen during the attack on your party? No creeping fog, no bizarre weather coming out of nowhere?"

"*Shit,*" the mountain man spat, "you mean to tell me-"

"Yes. They have Druids among them that wield elemental power. I know it sounds like madness in a story already rife with it, but Madoc must have had Druids in his ranks when he landed at the mouth of the Mississippi a world ago in 1170."

Alvord frowned. "I thought the Druids were killed off by the

Roman legions during the invasion of Anglesey, on the isle of Mona. Tacitus wrote of it."

"That he did, but to this very day the stain of Druidism clings to the Old Country. Pagan rituals are still in use, in places well hidden from prying eyes. The white robes you saw the Welsh Druids wearing points to the ancient Right of Taghairm, in which the aim is the evocation of spirits for various purposes. They burn meadowsweet, long used in pagan rituals. Vervain and mint are used here just like they were in Europe. They use what I believe to be Jimson weed to induce visions, an important element of Druidic ritual. Madoc must have had Druids in his ranks- indeed, I have sometimes wondered if he was a sort of pagan, religious dissenter and as a consequence cast out of Wales."

"Who *is* this Madoc feller anyway? I've heard the name thrown around a bit over the years but it don't mean much to me."

Alvord was surprised to hear this. The legend of Madoc was known to many Americans, if only vaguely.

Instead of answering immediately the former schooner captain tossed each of them a smoked lake trout, which both men tore into as if suddenly recognizing their intense hunger. Alvord peeled off a pinkish-orange colored strip of flesh from along the trout's backbone. This he greedily shoveled into his mouth, marveling at the richness of its flavor.

"It would appear that this is old news for your friend here, but I'll relate the tale to you as best I can. Feel free to supplement..." His voice trailed of as he waited for a name.

"Alvord Rawn."

"Quite a name. Would that we met under less trying circumstances, friend."

Thurgood took down some more whiskey to wet his throat. Alvord could tell this was the most the aging hermit had spoken in some time.

"There exists a legend that in 1170 AD a Welsh prince named Madog ab Owain Gwynedd took three hundred followers and sailed to Mobile Bay in Alabama, where a Welsh colony was established. Disheartened by the civil wars caused by his brothers' incessant infighting, which ensued after their father's death, he chose to leave his strife-torn homeland. Having commanded his father's fleet, Madoc (as his anglicized name is pronounced) was a seasoned sailor and today is the patron saint of Welsh fishermen. Legend tells of specially designed vessels that he had custom made for the daunting journey."

"How'd he know there was anything here? Folks knew nothin'

of the Americas that long ago."

"We cannot say with certainty how long peoples have known of land to the west of the Old World. As early as 800 BC Hanno of Carthage sailed west from the Pillars of Hercules for thirty days. It was said by Aristotle that Carthaginians actually colonized a land west of the Pillars; in a similar manner did Didorus speak of Phoenicians doing the same."

Alvord spoke up, recalling past reading. "Artifacts of both cultures as well as that of Greece and Rome have been found in the Americas. Of their authenticity I cannot speak with any authority, but I know finds have been made."

Chewing a piece of fish contemplatively, Marcel spoke. "Thought it was reckoned that you'd fall off the edge of the world back in them days."

"A pre-Socratic Greek named Anaximander knew the earth was round in the time of the ancients."

Alvord cut his eyes at the bookshelves. Thurgood knew his stuff; those books were not wanting for use, he surmised.

"It is a myth that sailing into deep water was universally avoided. Generally avoided- perhaps, yet there have always been those dauntless souls among us who are driven to plunge into the unknown, to see what lies beyond the horizon."

"Strikes me as a sight more dangerous than keepin' operations close to shore."

Thurgood chuckled mildly. "Your landlubber is showing, trapper. Sailing close to shore holds just as much peril, take it from a sailor born of sailors. Anyway, further along the road of history we have the intrepid Vikings. They pushed ever westward, into Iceland, Greenland, and eventually a place they named Vinland. It is thought by some historians that Vinland was North America, exactly where is not known. And if these Norsemen knew that land existed to the west of the British Isles, then Madoc would have likewise known owing to his partial Danish ancestry."

Alvord posed a question he thought fitting for a former ship's captain. "In your opinion they had ships capable of making the crossing?"

"Indeed they did. According to the Welsh bardic tradition, Madoc financed the building of a few ships, the exact number of which is debated. One of them was christened *Gwennan Gorn*. Stags horns were used to fasten the boards instead of nails so as to not interfere with the compasses."

"*Compasses?*" Alvord could not restrain his skepticism. "A bit early in history for those, from what I've read."

His words met with a look of amused approbation from the

fisherman. "According to popular belief, yes. It is thought that Flavio Gioja invented the compass in the 14th century, but in truth he was simply improving upon earlier models. The Vikings actually employed crude compasses, floating a sliver of lodestone on a wooden chip in a bowl of water. Not too long after, the same technique was used during the transportation of Crusaders to the Holy Land. But compasses do not make the sailor, let me tell you. To navigate by the heavens was a method seized upon by most cultures, and the Druids themselves were no mean astronomers. Madoc may have utilized the Canary Current from the direction of Madeira to the coasts of Florida and Alabama. Some bards claim he made a return trip to Wales after an initial exploratory expedition so as to collect more followers. If so, he could have ridden the Gulf Stream back up to the British Isles. Despite contrary claims, the direction of the trade winds and prevailing winds were well known even then, as was the North Equatorial Current. If you look at it carefully, the ocean steamers have adopted the courses of sailing vessels, and for a reason."

"If what yer sayin' is true, then ol' Columbus was late by a few hunnerd years, eh?"

"Marcel, the Basques were fishing the Grand Banks over a hundred years earlier than Columbus. Much ink has been spilt considering exactly who "discovered" the Americas. And on the topic of Columbus, a popular Spanish belief in his time was that of the *gente blanca*, or white people who inhabited the southeastern part of what was to become the United States. Some said Columbus was outfitted with a chart and knew what he was heading towards in 1492- a land already discovered. It has also been asserted that he happened upon the ancient, crumbling wreckage of some bare-ribbed ships at Guadeloupe. Some of Madoc's fleet, perhaps? But the truth stands mute in the face of a tangled historical thicket."

"So," Alvord asked, endeavoring to be staid despite his undeniable excitement, "They came and colonized at the mouth of the Mississippi, then?"

Thurgood shrugged hopelessly. "Who's to say with any certainty? The archeological evidence points to that, but they could just as easily have ended up somewhere along the Atlantic coast. Personally, I am inclined to believe that they used the Mississippi as a route of travel to escape persecution from hostile Indians, and from there utilized both the Missouri and Ohio River systems. A line of ancient fortifications can be traced along both routes. In fact, an antiquarian by the name of Thomas S. Hinde claimed that a number of skeletons clad in breastplates bearing the mermaid and harp coat of arms of Wales were found not far from the Falls of the Ohio, on an island near Jeffersonville, Indiana. He heard from local Indian tribes that a long-ago, large-scale battle took place there between red men and white men that forced the Welsh colonists northward. He also asserts that a Welsh fort once existed on what is now called the Devil's Backbone, which is located near that very site."

"Stands to reason," Alvord concurred, stroking his beard in reminiscence. "During my journey to St. Louis last year I stopped in Cincinnati. A museum there houses pottery from the earthworks and tumuli around the Ohio River Basin. The vases, cups, pitchers and pots were all apparently kiln-made, yet no Indian tribe is known to employ kilns. The frontier painter George Catlin saw this too, and linked it to the Welsh. He also cited the ancient fortifications found throughout that region and locations along the Missouri River as evidence of bygone European colonies."

"Yes, Catlin has proven a rich source of information and speculation regarding the progeny of Madoc's pioneers. You know his thoughts on the Mandan of the Upper Missouri River, then?"

"But of course." Somehow talking this over was rendering the situation more bearable, making their enemies seem all the more human and therefore subject to mankind's myriad vulnerabilities. "He pointed out that a goodly number of the Mandans bore European features, and built walled villages unlike other Indians. They employed a scallop-shaped boat nearly identical to the Welsh coracle, and were reputedly capable of manufacturing exquisite blue glass beads, much valued by trappers and worn around the neck."

Marcel scratched his facial hair as he mulled over their words. "I've beheld such beads. You know, the Mandan *were* lighter'n other tribes, though it was tough to tell sometimes between the bear grease they put in their hair and their paint-besmeared faces. And in those walled settlements of theirs they lived in round lodges of earth and stone. Never seen aught like it among the red man. Their women were some of the handsomest I've ever clapped eyes on, and a goodly number of 'em definitely looked to be infused with white blood. The pox wiped 'em out in '37, almost to a man..."

Thurgood walked over to his bookcase and ran a finger over the books' spines lovingly. Rowdy laughter and occasional gunshots could be heard outside, but at this moment in time the world of these three men was confined to that lonely, fish-reeking cabin on the outskirts of town.

"Piecemeal, the saga of the Welsh Indians can be assembled through various accounts, and it is something I have attempted to do since becoming their captive and slave so many years ago. Hell, I think it's the only thing keeping me sane..."

His face grew stormy for a moment before he continued speaking as if automatically. "David Ingram sailed with Hawkins, preying upon Spanish and Portuguese ships in the Atlantic. In 1567 his vessel was shipwrecked on the Mexican coast near Tampico. Along with some fellow castaways he apparently walked from there to New Brunswick in eleven months, where a French fishing vessel picked them up. Ingram reported certain tribes using a variety of Welsh words, enough so to make it significant. The tale of the Rev. Morgan Jones is more interesting yet. Captured by the Doeg Tuscarora in 1660, he faced almost certain death at their hands. But when he began praying in his native tongue of Welsh, he was spared-and then spoken to in broken Welsh by his very captors."

"This is all good'n well," Marcel cut in distractedly, "but what's with this talk of Druids and magic?"

"Druids were the holy men of the ancient Celts. Some lore indicates that Madoc was born with a clubfoot or some other physical blemish and was to be killed as an infant as a result. That was the way of things back then. His mother instead took him to Pendaran, an old Druid who raised the boy until he was sixteen and presented to his father, the king. And the Druids, most conveniently, had long spoken of lands to the west of Britain. Pre-Christian Celtic paganism is still deeply rooted in Wales, more so than any part of the British Isles. Their Christianity took on a mystic taint that drew from the cult of Druidic paganism that flourished alongside it. Fantastical though it incontestably is, there are modern-day Druids among the ranks of the Welsh Indians right here in Michigan. They wield elemental power, summoning fog or rain that is used to mask attacks on those intruding upon their homeland. Just as my ship was sunk by a violent storm that came out of nowhere."

"What happened after your capture?" Alvord pressed.

The old ship captain's body was racked by a great sigh. "That, m'boy, is where the story takes a turn for the truly bizarre."

Chapter 48

"They *bred* you?" Alvord's incredulity spilled out of his mouth in a sputter.

"Uh hu," Thurgood replied straightforwardly. "With the fairest women of the tribe. Who knows how long they have been endeavoring to breed back to white? Indian blood is most certainly among them, doubtless from past alliances with friendly tribes or captives taken in raids. The Indians of this region regard both the tribe and the region they inhabit with superstitious awe, so it's probable that that admixture of blood dates back to earlier times, when the tribe, forced from one locale to another due to incessant warfare, was desperate for alliances with any tribe that would have them."

"So let me get this straight, Thurgood," said Marcel in as tactful a voice as he could muster. "You tellin' us you was *raped* by *women*? Seems to me that ain't somethin' a man can force."

The former captive snorted in good humor. "Don't I know it! I was drugged by the Druids—and the concoction produced the desired effect, let me tell you. I've never heard of anything that could replicate the results of whatever they gave me, but suffice it to say that it got the job done. Who knows have many bastards I sired in those months? Some of the menfolk were not wholehearted advocates of the plan, but the Druids overruled them."

Alvord, who could scarcely believe his ears and would have brusquely disbelieved such a tale if he weren't face-to-face with its weaver, steered the conversation in another direction. His Victorian sensibilities were sagging under the weight of this uncouth revelation.

"What was the village like- its location, its design? And how did you manage to escape such a hell?"

"Sounds like an agreeable hell to me," mumbled Marcel.

"If it is still where it was when I escaped, the village lies at the confluence of two small rivers. Almost directly south of Chapel Beach. Yes, you gentlemen descended into the heart of their stronghold. It is a walled village set atop a gently sloping hill- this is not a traditional hill fort as was built by the Celts of long ago, much less severe a hill is it set atop. The ramparts are camouflaged, painted natural colors and patterns and festooned with moss to make them blend in. The village is a sizeable one, home to hundreds, which is larger than what I expected from so secretive a tribe. But you must realize that no one ventures into the interior as you attempted to. There is mile after mile of game-filled land that does not see the boot prints of whites nor the moccasin of the Indian. Some degree of European culture persists- they have blacksmiths for instance, and the buildings are of stone. They mine too, copper and iron. The Welsh have ever been great mining people. In fact, I think that is how they ended up here at the edge of the world- they heard stories of ancient copper mines in this region and migrated here, whereas others of their kind went west on the Missouri River to become the Mandan tribe, which took on more of an Indian identity."

He paused to drink more whiskey. "And how did I escape such a place? Luck, I suppose. They were planning on killing me; I have no doubt of that. Once my shoulder injury healed they used me as a slave to work the maize, bean, and squash fields, but I could tell my time was nearly up by the way they began treating me. I escaped when their vigilance wavered. I was left working in the fields, toiling alongside the women. The men guarding the fields went to investigate what I think was a woodland buffalo in the nearby forest, and I simply slipped away in the direction I knew to be east. Running like Old Scratch nipped at my heels, through woods and streams and swamps, I somehow evaded capture and found my way back to the Soo through that wilderness, though I was delirious upon my arrival here. I believe they always kill their captives after a while, so as to avoid situations like mine. They wish to retain their identity as the malevolent copper gods- they want to remain wreathed in mystery and seen as something more than human. Gods that seemed to move with unholy speed and attacked under the cover of fog. It is a brilliant defense mechanism, one strengthened by their use of occult magic. Once they arrived here in Upper Michigan, they became perceived as more than mere men. So fearsome and clandestine that they became known as evil *manitous*, the descendants of Madoc and his pioneers carved out not only land for themselves but also a reputation that would ensure none would encroach upon them. Until now. With the mining craze hemming them in on all sides, it is only a matter of time before they are forced to reveal themselves to the world. Funny how when Michigan was awarded three quarters of Upper Michigan as a compromise after the Toledo War, it acquired far more than merely a desolate, Indian-inhabited wilderness."

"So," he said summarily, "there you have it. The truth, as far as I can see it, but still one smothered in surmise as Shakespeare once said. In initially relating my story to others I made the mistake of expecting sympathy from my fellow man, and in return was labeled addle-brained."

"Yeah, sorry 'bout that Thurgood." Marcel stood and rolled his stiff shoulders, which issued sharp cracking sounds. "You sure know yer stuff as regards them Welshmen."

"Most interesting," Alvord mused, his hand on his chin. "This will constitute a rewriting of history. Forget some Catholic Italian claiming this land for Spain. Americans will seize upon the verified story of Madoc, exemplar of the northern European pioneering spirit."

There were more important things at hand, which he now addressed.

"I saw men being captured during the attack. Indian and white alike. The white man was a friend of ours, a red-haired Irishman who was last seen alive by members of our party. You think he might be spared so as to be bred?"

"If your friend was indeed captured then he may well draw breath. For now."

Marcel grabbed the bottle of whiskey and took a final dram of it. "Well then boys, we might as well hop to it."

"Quite right," concurred Alvord.

Thurgood was confused. "What do you mean?"

"We need you to lead us back there, Thurgood."

For a moment the fishmonger stared at the trapper in mute disbelief.

"*What?*"

"We have a score to settle with them," Alvord explained calmly, instantly on the same page as Marcel. "From here on out its blood for blood. We need you to lead us back there."

"You would have me return to the site of such past horror? To where my crew was slaughtered and I taken prisoner? That's an awful lot to ask of a man."

In that moment Marcel and Alvord both recognized a streak of resolution in the man, one that greatly surprised them both. This was, after all, an insane idea at best.

And suicidal at worst.

Thurgood gulped loudly, then clenched his jaw in defiance of trepidation. "A regular pair of hell divers, aren't you?"

"There's worse things to be in this life," Marcel pointed out solemnly. "Lend us aid and see your past losses avenged. I can see it in yer eyes you ain't no coward."

"No, I am not." The old mariner sat down and ran a hand through his long crop of graying hair. "Damn, but this is madness…"

"And as is such, you're in the very best of company," Alvord told him.

He smiled inwardly. He had not reckoned on having a guide to take them back to that cursed land… suddenly the notion of rescuing Finnbar did not seem quite so hopeless.

Thurgood pursed his lips, scratching the old scar on his cheek. "I know that you, deaf to rumors of demons in the woods, once trapped the area, Marcel. How extensively did you explore it?"

"Just a mite. Saw it was teeming with fur but each time I went in there it felt like eyes were on me. Knew of the Injun legends and other stories, includin' yers, but forgive me if I thought you was addled. Lookin' back, seems I was lucky to make it out alive…"

"Well at least you have some knowledge of the area. We shall need it. I recall my escape, and I think I can lead us back to their village, if it is still at the same spot. And then…?"

"We'll be outmanned, but I'll be damned if we'll be outgunned," Marcel stated fiercely.

Thurgood gave him a quizzical look. "How are we going to acquire such munitions?"

The mountain man allowed himself a dark chuckle as he turned his gaze toward the deserted Fort Brady.

"Got a good idea o' where to start."

Chapter 49

He'd gotten to see more of the village today. Once the fertility ceremony reached its conclusion, Finnbar and Crowder had been roughly ushered back into their cells. Yet in the night the guards had summoned Crowder, anger made evident by the threats that easily pierced the language barrier.

Afterward Finnbar had lapsed back into a heavy sleep, still shrugging off the side effects of whatever vile substance he'd been made to drink before engaging in the lurid saturnalia earlier. But shortly thereafter the guards burst back into the room and dragged him to his feet. He was not without grave doubts as to whether he would return to that cell or not. Feeling violated and resigned, what fate awaited him he had not much cared. Over death he had achieved a sort of supremacy- an enlightened numbness towards the concept had taken hold of him. His suspicions were misplaced, however. Crowder, it turned out, had been bidden to put his medical skills to use. In the aftermath of the assault on Chapel Beach, a number of Welsh Indian warriors bore significant injuries that only one skilled in modern medicine could properly remedy. Finnbar was put upon to act as Crowder's assistant, aiding him in his ministrations.

The Druids had apparently been doing what they could before being displaced by Crowder. They gave vent to their displeasure of this, but were overruled by a fierce, imperial looking woman with dirty blonde hair. All present deferred to this young Valkyrie, whom Finnbar took to be the queen or chieftess of the tribe. Irate but silenced, the murderous high priests could only watch in dismay as Crowder succeeded where they had failed.

Medical supplies had apparently been taken as spoils during the course of the tribe's raids. Crowder made full use of them; indeed, Finnbar could recall the night only in a fragmented barrage of gory bandages, bloodied forceps, stitched flesh, and sweating, grimacing men. The awareness that some of these warriors might have been wounded by his very hand was but a vague one.

After hours spent assisting Crowder's curative efforts, the exhausted Irishman had snatched a few winks before being dragged outside once more. At sword point, he and Crowder were guided past chattering women with baskets slung across their backs and eel spears clasped in their hands. Flocks of giggling children strayed close, multicolored headbands encircling their foreheads. Peering up at the captives with the irrepressible curiosity of youth, some even ventured to try and touch the foreigners before being chased of by the ill-tempered guards. Men with fishing nets and large, barbed hooks and bows and arrows headed passed them by, not sparing them a glance. The villagers wore the light buckskins as would an Indian tribe, but also wore some thin furs and varying amounts of copper and gemstone jewelry. Most men were bare-chested in the sticky summer heat, revealing more than a few Celtic style tattoos, and while the women were more modestly attired, the children were often naked or close to it.

After the frothing insanity of last night, Finnbar's mind boggled to hear the cacophony of screams and devilish chants supplanted by the dulcet sounds of happily chatting voices and the laughter of young ones. With bleary, half-lidded eyes he took in his surroundings, scarcely willing to believe them. The walled village he was a prisoner in was a vast, dirt-floored throwback to Europe's Early Middle Ages. A fifteen-foot high stockade encircled the sprawling town, complete with bastions from which bow-toting sentries kept vigilant watch. Tree trunks of six inches diameter or more formed the stockade, and reinforcing those upright, sharpened stakes was a layer of dried mud or clay, which lent it further sturdiness.

The ground sloped gently up, though it culminated in a sudden, artificially raised mound of earth atop which sat an august castle of wood and stone.

"Reserved for high-ranking tribesmen and the Druids," Crowder, following his gaze, quietly informed him.

They passed by more modest buildings constructed of narrow logs, clustered in some cases, others set apart. Women sat out in front of many, tending to a variety of quotidian tasks. Fragrant smoke curled lazily from openings in the center of the moss-covered roofs, up into the ethereal blue that appeared to Finnbar freer and more unfettered that ever it had.

With their metal weaponry and armor it should not have come to him as a surprise, yet when he saw a considerable blacksmith's shop Finnbar could scarcely believe his eyes. The repetitious clanging emanating thereof bespoke a busy day. A number of well-muscled men filtered in and out, bringing in what he believed to be copper and iron ore from a towering pile of the substances that sat nearby.

Long legged, wire-haired dogs of varying colors loped easily alongside them. They actually resembled larger versions of Cerberus but were decidedly more wolf-like. Especially in the eyes, those dagger eyes that took note of Finnbar's every move. But even they scattered when a wild-eyed woman, blade in hand, rushed him shrieking dire imprecations. The guards fended her off as gingerly as possible, one of them hugging her and talking soothingly into her ear. Like a witch of fairytale, the woman drew back her fist and then punched it his way and released it as if casting a hex on him.

"Husband no doubt died in the attack on your trapping party," Crowder theorized.

A tad unsettled by the widow's ferocity, Finnbar continued his observations. The whole place bore an unmistakable resemblance to a *motte-and-bailey* castle, which had been brought to the British Isles by the conquering Normans in the 11th century. So effective were they militarily that the Anglo-Saxons and Celts they employed them against were quick to adopt the style. On the far side of the town, which Finnbar could just barely see from where he stood, he watched a primitive gate creak open to let out a group of women. Through the dim lanes of trees revealed by the open gate, he glimpsed the suggestion of an expansive crop field beyond.

Look at this place, there must be hundreds living here... of all the times to be bereft of me journal...

As if reading his mind, Crowder said, "They don't seem as susceptible to white diseases as Indian tribes; no doubt their European heritage plays a role. So their population is healthy and stable."

"How is it that they speak Welsh that you can understand? Would not their language have become bastardized by time and isolation?"

"Don't underestimate the persistence of the Welsh language. It has endured in the face of time, diasporas, and persecution. It predates and has survived both Greek and Latin. The Welsh spoken today is thought to be very similar to the Welsh of our earliest ancestors."

At last, they were made to sit in the low, wooden stands overlooking a small arena. Well over a hundred people, mostly older men, awaited the next bout. The three remaining miners who had escaped yesterday's ritualistic butchery had faced butchery of another order, serving as sword fodder for the tribe's young warriors.

"How're you faring?" a dog-tired Crowder wished to know, tearing his eyes from the scene. "I reacted badly to that potion of theirs the first time I supped it."

"You mean the rape elixir? It's exacting a toll on me as well."

"Rape elixir? Think of it more as a vehicle to carnal delights that evade all but the most decadent of men in this life."

"A thin distinction."

Defago and Jawbeance were now herded into the arena like cattle. The chatter of the crowd abruptly ceased- two fledgling warriors were loosed upon the trappers to the roar of the crowd. Watching the miners die had not dulled their appetite for blood. In the fighters swooped, a ravening pair armed with swords.

Crowder observed the proceedings owlishly. "At least they arm the men who die in this arena."

"Aye," Finnbar snorted mirthlessly, making his derision plain, "in the spirit of fair play..."

"True, staff does not stand equal to steel, but at least they can die honorably, free to fight until their last gasp if they so wish."

He was right, Finnbar reasoned silently. At least they died in a warlike fashion, a nobler end than suffered by their luckless peers. Finnbar's stomach twisted into a dread-induced knot as he watched the youthful warriors descend upon his trapping mates. Licking his dry lips, he forced himself to watch.

Jawbeance, a full-blooded Chippewa, skillfully ducked under an overly enthusiastic sword swing to jam one end of his staff into his opponent's kneecap. Meanwhile Defago, facing a spearman, spun to avoid a thrust and swung his staff in a blur, cracking it in half against the back of the young warrior's skull.

The spectators were mute for an instant. In a flash both Welsh Indians had been skillfully brought to the ground, much to the chagrin of the crowd that was suddenly all froth and teeth.

"Why are we being made to watch this?" Finnbar demanded of his fellow captive, fearing what would happen next.

"If I were to speculate, I'd say that its so we know what awaits us. So as to deepen that acquired sense of hopelessness. Or perhaps to reassure us that we will have a chance to go out on an aggressive note."

Warily the two trappers backed off, standing shoulder to shoulder as they looked around uncertainly. Finnbar knew what they were thinking. To kill the fallen youths would bring them a fleeting moment of satisfaction, but what horrors might await them at the hands of tribe if they did so? So they hesitated, poised and ready for whatever came next.

For a moment it was silent but for the sound of nervous, labored breathing. Many eyes in the crowd swept up towards the highest row of benches, where the young blonde woman sat alongside the one-eyed warlord and a retinue of women and rugged-looking guards. A man bent over and whispered into the warlord's ear, but his superior simply shook his blocky head, face impassive.

The two young warriors slowly rose from the ground to the delight of the onlookers.

"You know those men," Crowder stated more than he asked, observing Finnbar's clenched jaw.

"Part of me trapping party, they were. Poor bastards..."

"They are giving a fine account of themselves. For that they will be honored with a quick death. Lucky thing... I once saw them set their hellhounds on some men who refused to fight."

The fallen warriors regained their desire to kill and lunged in again, teeth bared. Faces unmarred by paint or tattoos, it was easy to discern their rage, and underneath that layer of emotion the apprehension at having been so easily dealt with. Intent on compensating for their lame gambit, they launched a vigorous secondary assault.

But Jawbeance and Defago were waiting for them.

The spearman found naught but air once again as his thrust missed Jawbeance's face by inches. The Indian, having jerked his head away from the questing blade, grabbed the spear by its haft and pulled the warrior towards him. Dipping low, he sent his shoulder thudding into the man's waist before rearing up and tossing him over his back.

Defago deftly parried his enemy's hacks and stabs with the staff, slowly giving ground. A slicing attack found the meat of his thigh but his enemy's footwork left him leaning forward, chin outstretched. The half-breed brought one end of the staff whipping around and crashing into his sparsely bearded jaw, soundly flooring him. Without admiring his own handiwork, Defago limped over towards Jawbeance and his combatant, who were going at it hammer and tongs. After tossing the young fighter, the Chippewa brave had rounded on him. But his foe recovered his wits with impressive speed, and from the ground sent the blade of his weapon up into Jawbeance's stomach. The brave ripped out the spearhead with a grimace and moved in for a kick to the face. The Welsh Indian rolled to avoid it and, drawing a knife, deeply slashed the Chippewa's calf. Letting out a fearsome cry of mingled pain and rage, Jawbeance stomped on the man's hand, breaking bone. He then brought the staff down with both hands into his sternum, and was positioning himself for a killing blow to the throat when Hell descended upon that arena.

With inconceivable speed and agility the warlord exploded into action, hurling himself off the ten-foot high bench on which he sat. Once his feet found earth he flung himself into a forward roll, which brought him next to Defago. The wounded half-breed he swatted like a fly with a mighty backhanded blow, sending him flying into the wooden wall of the arena. He then forcefully ripped the staff out of Jawbeance's grip. The Indian rounded on him ferociously but was hit in the chest with a punishing, open-handed blow.

Defago recovered from the shot he'd taken and snatched up his unconscious enemy's sword. Four times he swung it as this new and powerful assailant, who dodged around the sun-glinting blade with the ease of one whose confidence did not waver. The warlord then disarmed Defago with a blurring move and in the next moment sank the weapon through his ribcage and up into his heart.

Jawbeance, spewing blood and clutching his damaged chest, rose with a shout of anger and hurled himself at the indomitable one-eyed fighter. He snatched up the spear and after a sidestep that his opponent did not bite on plunged the weapon towards the unruffled figure of the warlord. The heavily muscled Welsh Indian caught the spear with his right hand and with a dexterous inward spin broke off its tip. The charging Indian could not stop his momentum and as he passed the cyclops the man rammed the spearhead into his kidney, wrenching it out to then insert the blade into the back of his neck. The brave Chippewa trapper slunk to the ground, his body raising a fine cloud of dust from the earth.

It was over. Predictably enough the crowd bellowed its approval, although the one-eyed warrior did not acknowledge it. Instead he sneeringly looked up at Finnbar, as if to say, *You're next.*

"I am sorry for your friends," consoled Crowder. "That is Cadoc. He is their warlord and, from what I have gathered, also heads their mining operations. That brute led the pack that wiped out my mining party. Have you ever seen the like? None stands his equal in hand-to-hand combat."

Finnbar stared after the departing form of the muscle-bound soldier. "I know one who might give him a run for his money."

Later that night, lying on his back and staring up at the ceiling of his cell, Finnbar broke the preoccupied silence that had reigned for some time.

"I'm getting out of here."

"The sex that bad?"

"I jest not, Crowder."

"Don't be fatuous, Finnbar. To contemplate escape from this place is among the rosiest of delusions."

"Do you prefer to stay here contemplating the drear prospect of imminent death?" Finnbar rolled his head towards the man and glared at him defiantly.

Crowder shook his head dejectedly. "No, not really. But a failed attempt would land us a fate *worse* then death."

"Even if we don't escape, if my friends yet draw breath they will come looking for me." He indulged a fleeting thought, one of seemingly indomitable Alvord and indestructible Marcel coming back to unleash all the fury of Hell on his captors. "Few forces on this earth will stop them, mark ye my words."

"And if you do escape? What then? Do you have any idea how far we are from *anything*?"

"We cannot be all that far from the coast. It took them but half a day to drag me here from where they fell upon me and my fellow trappers. If we can pull off an escape from here, we follow the first stream we encounter to the coast and head east along it. Even if it's a hundred miles, we can hoof that in a few days if we march day and night. Might even be able to flag down a ship or something."

"If the bugs don't kill us first."

"So be it then, the wilderness can take me. But my death shan't go unsung at the hands of these barbarous shites."

They fell silent once more, their thoughts their own. Set adrift by the events of the past two days, Finnbar's nimble mind pondered a myriad of things. Certain things about this tribe did not add up. Sure, they could have been raiding mining camps and offing those who strayed too close for years. But how did that account for the abundance of modern items among them. The pots and pans he'd seen were all very contemporary looking, as were at least some of the sword and knives, and their fishing hooks. He could have sworn that he'd seen a woman light a fire with a set of Lucifer matches, while a bunch of canned provisions sat next to her... but in honesty everything came back to him in such a blur. And yet... by the blacksmith's shop he *knew* he'd beheld a wealth of modern mining equipment- why would they keep items like that close at hand?

Long and hard did he wrangle with such thoughts. Then Cadwallader Jones materialized out of the gloom and, *a presto*, the skeleton fleshed itself out.

Chapter 50

As the lazily flickering flames more clearly illuminated the visage of the unaccompanied Jones, a bombardment of thoughts and speculations wove themselves into a single, unifying deduction: Cadwallader Jones was the tribe's link to the outside world. It explained Jones's ominous warning regarding the Pictured Rocks region as readily as it revealed why so many items belonging to modernity had found their way into the Welsh Indian village. In a flash Finnbar also recalled the strange, tattooed bodies they had found among the timber pirates, when he had first heard the name Jones spoken in connection with Great Lakes commerce. Cadwallader Jones, he was sure, acted as the middleman between the two worlds, and exactly why and how Finnbar felt would soon be divulged.

"And thus entered the principal actor in this farce," Finnbar spat, hatred blossoming on his face.

Quite unbothered by his vitriol, Cadwallader Jones countered serenely.

"Less the actor and more the director, truth telling."

"You goddamn Judas," the Irishman pronounced with deadly intensity. His temper flared like a wind-stirred prairie fire, aided in part by what he suspected to be the stirrings of opium withdrawal. "You welcome me into your home only to let me and my fellows walk into this bloody fate? You're beneath my contempt, you shit-encrusted arseling."

"That'll be rather enough churlishness out of you, Mr. Fagan. I did warn you about your trapping destination, if you recall. And who have we here? As I live and breath- it can't be Owain Crowder! It has been awhile, my would-be competitor. I do trust you find your accommodations suitable?"

"Bugger off."

Jones tilted his shadow-dappled head to the side and tut-tutted as if dealing with fractious children.

"Come now, gentlemen. Let not civility desert us over current predicaments. I am not entirely at fault for your precarious situation. After all, you both found your way to this village by way of very unfortunate incidents."

"A very unfortunate incident indeed," Crowder made answer cynically, "and one I can only explain on the basis of a highly improbable coincidence-"

"Namely?"

"The fact that I am a Welshman taken captive by the lost tribe of the legendary Prince Madoc."

Jones's lips curled upward in the phantom of a smirk. "Well done, Mr. Crowder. Most discerning. But then again, you are a shrewd one, aren't you? Much like Mr. Fagan here. *Him* I like, however. And in all honesty, I am sorry that you have been swept into this realm of arcanum, Finnbar. Little comfort it offers you, I know, but I am sorry."

His manner was unaffected, genuine. Despite his mounting rage, Finnbar felt oddly compelled to believe him as his words had the ring of truth about them. He tried calming himself, for as of now there was no proper outlet through which to channel his anger. He found that the thought of the vengeance he was going to visit upon Jones had a tranquilizing effect on him.

He regained some of his customary swagger, leaning against the bars of his cell nonchalantly. "You're in cahoots with these white savages, are you? Birds of a feather, eh?"

Jones stared daggers at him and took a meaningful step forward. "You should accord me some respect, Finnbar. Should I suggest you be thrown to the dogs or roasted alive, the tribe would happily oblige me."

The Irishman ignored his words but held the penetrating stare. "So you manufactured faux Chippewa arrows of your own, then, for the attack on the mining camp at the Soo? And had warriors from this tribe daub Chippewa war paint on themselves so as to further nourish the illusion?"

He had struck a chord. Jones could not suppress his surprise at the incisiveness of the statement.

Finnbar drank deep of the small, verbal victory he had won.

"Clever I'll allow, but imperfectly done, *Mister* Jones. Not quite transparent, but to the discerning eye a cleverly devised sham took form. My trapper mates immediately saw through the ruse, noticing the imperfections of the arrows. I meself saw the European cast to the bows. Not the famed longbow of yew, but rather the elm short bow. Interesting to think that after all these years, the Welsh short bow is still in use an ocean away..."

Well-defined jaw muscles clenched in anger as Jones reflected on how his seemingly watertight deceitfulness had not been without flaw.

Finnbar capitalized on the shift of conversational power and continued to press.

"And as it happens, on me way up to the Soo my companions

and I encountered a ship bearing the name of *Hywell.* Welsh name, no? A ship used, as it were, in the black industry of timber pirating. Attacked that band of arse spawn, we did, butcherin' them to a man."

"Deservedly so," chimed in Crowder with perfect timing.

"And amidst the mangled corpses we found two of your pathetic Welshies."

He glanced at Crowder. "No offense, mate."

"Oh, none taken."

"And before he gasped his last, one of the other pirates mentioned certain... *atmospherical anomalies* that occurred whenever it seemed that all was lost. He attributed such puzzling incidents to those two mutilated savages of yours. Any thoughts, Jones?"

"Yes," his interlocutor replied fiercely, tearing his sinister gaze away from the fire. "My thoughts are aligned with the key concepts of self-preservation. The end justifying the means. The bitter and ruthless struggle for existence weighed against the horror of oblivion."

He inclined his strong, weathered face, stuffing his hands deep into the pockets of his long oilskin coat.

"Do you know that I have never divulged my whole story to another soul? Nary a single one. And many are those who lust after it, without even being attuned to the darker realities therein. The depths of my solitude have stayed unplumbed. Duplicity, manipulation, and above all else secrecy have been the coin of the realm in my line of business. But tonight- ah, what the hell? You see, gents, I am not merely an outsider acting as a go-between for this tribe. I am *of* it."

Finnbar felt a thrill of the fantastic pass through him like a bolt of lightning.

"Here in the seclusion of this village I was born, what year exactly I can't rightly say. Whatever the case, it is fair to say that by this time the seed of Madoc had observed the increasing expansion of white America. You might think us bound to this region out of fear of discovery, but that was not always so. True, since our arrival in Upper Michigan we have used the unpopulated Pictured Rocks area as our center of operations."

"But of course," Finnbar cut him off brusquely. "*Beyond these walls shall our legacy endure.*"

Jones looked at him, impressed. "You saw the inscription on the rocks, did you? And translated it, too? Well done, Irishman. And regarding that legacy- indeed it has endured. Yet we were once on the Keweenaw and near Marquette as well, where our mining operations flourished for several hundred years. But with the coming of more and more whites we grew wary. True, we shared the same blood, but years of persecution and warfare made us leery of any strangers. If history is any indicator, we were not dealt with very mildly. A large group of newcomers with strange customs and different colored skin in a land of warlike peoples? I'd imagine it was only our doggedness, skill in battle, and the carefully preserved Druidic magic that kept us alive all these years, and damned if we did not trust even those who looked like us and hailed from the distant land it was rumored we came from.

"Anyway, at a certain point the white man was making his presence felt even on Superior, and on the Lower Lakes, which the more temerarious men of the tribe sometimes travelled to, they saw the waters suddenly teeming with fur sloops and schooners, and eventually the monstrosity that is the steamship. The fur trade sent Indians and white trappers probing into regions the red man never frequented, making it difficult to maintain our obscurity.

"You see, it was only the Grand Island Chippewa with whom we traded and allied with. They were a peaceable tribe that dwelled mainly on Grand Island, to the west of here. They had few dealings with other Chippewa and had no problem acting as middlemen between us and the rest of the region. We gave them copper and iron in exchange for goods we could only acquire through raiding or trade with other tribes. Unwilling to pursue the latter, we let the amiable Grand Island tribe do it for us. They met with disaster, though; sometimes around the turn of the century they were goaded into fighting the Sioux along with other Chippewa bands. After years of maintaining their peace, and our secret, the men of the tribe all died heroically save one, Powers of the Air. He survived and still lives, actually. He continues to hold his silence regarding the truth behind the copper gods, the *osuwahbik manitous* lurking in the Pictured Rocks wilderness."

"The truth," Finnbar interrupted once again, "is that you are naught but a flock of half-breed, pagan savages evincing no signs of civilized living, including Christianity or even something so basic as animal husbandry."

Jones sneered his distaste at those words. "There were no printed Bibles when we crossed the Atlantic, you fool. How were we to preserve such a complex religion through mere word of mouth without hopeless distortion ensuing? And as for animal husbandry- what native North American animals have Europeans domesticated, hmm? The rabbits and hare- no, too unruly. The deer? Far too panicky and unwilling to breed in captivity. Grouse or turkey? Too flighty by far. And to attempt all this while endlessly shifting locations to avoid persecution at the hands of countless savage nations? While dwelling in wastelands and swamps and places most humans would cringe to even pass through? You rave, Irishman. Our existence has hung by a thread since first we made landfall those hundreds of years ago. At the hands of necessity some things fell by the wayside.

"As I was saying," he continued, composing himself after a passing shudder of rage, "after the Grand Islanders tribe dissolved, a plan was devised wherein a young, fair-skinned member of our tribe would be sent to live among the whites, posing as a white child brought up by savages. It happened frequently enough back then. I spoke the Chippewa tongue without flaw, and was seen as the ablest candidate. So at the age of nine I was made to wander into the Soo, looking lost and hungry."

Finnbar stood in rapt silence, listening. For the story being related to him was one that had his literary mind firmly in its thrall. It was like entering upon the world of the fantastic, like poring over some forbidden volume.

"I was taken by some Hudson's Bay Company trappers down to Detroit, Michigan. They knew of a wealthy man whose ethnographic interests might well lead him to adopt me. It worked, and I tell you now the plan could not have followed a smoother course. For although I was young, I was chosen for my mental acumen and carefully educated on my mission for months before my departure from the tribe. I was to find out what made white men more powerful than Indians, and to ascertain whether or not the Americans would accept us as their own. And, most importantly, if possible I was to rise to some degree of power and influence so as to aid the tribe, to end its era of secrecy and isolation. Well, my adopted father, after grilling me with questions regarding my fabricated Chippewa upbringing, saw fit to write an article on me and then send me off to boarding school in the East. Seeing from the start that education was the key to my advancement, I pursued further studies in New York and Boston, studying history but dabbling in business all the while. When my adopted father went to dust, I was left a tidy sum of money, with which I was able to implement many business ideas I had in mind for the Upper Great Lakes. Timber piracy was one of them, and yes, those two slain men were my kin, one of whom was trained in the ways of the Druids. They voluntarily aided my endeavor. By using my position to garner wealth and power, I have played my role and protected my people through a number of decisive maneuvers."

Smirking at Crowder, he asked, "Why do you think I went to all that trouble, eh? Approaching you, gaining your trust, selling you the parcel of land, and furnishing you with a fake map? I knew your ambition would lead you to seeking iron one way or another, thus compromising my tribe. For if you found iron somewhere close by, who knows what sort of floodgate that might have opened? I own much land in the area, but not enough to ensure that you and your ilk would not spread dangerously close to this place."

"Yeah, and what of the Jackson Mining Company, doing precisely what I sought to?"

"Those men are deep in my pocket, Crowder. You would not have been so easy to keep under rein. They mine in one spot and have been instructed to stay away from certain areas."

"So you are the one who outfitted your tribe with modern mining tools?"

"Why yes, Finnbar, although they have, ah, *appropriated* other such tools from miners who camped a bit too close to our borders for comfort. Under the leadership of their one-eyed warlord, Cadoc, they mine with all the competency of the more recent Welsh immigrants to this land."

"Why?" Crowder demanded. "Why would they keep mining and risk exposure?"

Jones frowned confusedly. "Well, when we reveal ourselves to the American government, we want to be worth something. We can't simply be another primitive Indian tribe whose concept of wealth does not jive with the white, European definition. We want to demonstrate our productivity, our capitalist streak. A large quantity of copper and iron will serve that end. We wish to keep our lands, and if history is any indicator that will be difficult. Indians tribes have historically struggled to do so in the face of white greed. Our horn, the voice of the dreaded god Missibizzi, would not be enough to deter their avarice as it has deterred Indians for centuries. Why do you think we are breeding back towards white? We wish to appeal to prevailing American views on race. If we present as a hearty but beleaguered white tribe with origins reaching all the way back to the legendary figure of Madoc, we stand a better chance at keeping the land that had become our home. It won't take America long to realize that the lands we claim as our own are home to metal riches. We can mine that ourselves, we will demonstrate, and over time acculturation will transform the tribe into true Americans. Such is our only hope for survival. Civilization is knocking on our doorstep, and we must act judiciously lest we be deemed some inferior race of polluted white blood that lays claim to rich mineral land. And that brings us to the recent attack on the miner's camp- we want to present the Chippewa as enemies of America. *They* are the ones attacking helpless miners in Copper Country, not us. We simply point to a mutual enemy and in doing so form a bond between us and the U.S. government."

Jones began pacing back and forth in front of the fire, head down in thought. He indulged in a moment of silence, listening to the sounds of the villages beyond the walls of this dismal cell.

"We don't dare court publicity, not just yet anyway. In the fullness of time, after more careful planning had been done. Meanwhile, my tribe likewise seeks to preserve our lands and perilous secret from the encroachment of whites until we decide to reveal ourselves. With the disappearance of many a trapper, white or otherwise, it seemed to whites that the Indian legends of Missibizzi, spiritual defender of this land, were indeed true. And some escaped our lands to return with tales of sword-wielding, copper-clad devils who attacked with the fog. Even the mighty Hudson's Bay Company eventually found it fruitless to send trappers into our territory. Crowder, you might recall how Doctor Douglass Houghton, the first state geologist of Michigan, drowned in '45 off the Keewenaw? That was Druidic power in action, summoning the storm to kill the man in the hopes of ending his geological surveys. In that they succeeded, staving off the arrival of even more miners and buying us more time."

"Just another entry in your catalogue of evils."

"*Practical* evils, Finnbar. And that brings me to you. It was not my intent to kill you, yet recent events have forced my hand.

"Then for shit's sake stop pontificatin' and get on with it, lad."

Jones looked at the Irish captive almost tragically. "You would have been such a good fit for my Gen, too. More's the pity. I do hope you understand the underlying principles behind all this. They simply will not let you go, for fear of spreading the word of their existence. In two nights there will be a ceremony commemorating those lost fighting against your trapping party. You will both be offered up to the spirits by way of blood sacrifice. For my part, I will inform the holy men to make it quick."

Cadwallader Jones, equal parts savior and devil, turned with a swish of his overcoat and was gone.

Chapter 51

It did not show, but the impatience with which Alvord waited to board the steamer *Napoleon* gnawed away at him as a wolf on a kill.

Not helping matters was the roaring maelstrom of thoughts that was his mind. Try though he may, he was not immune to anxiety. The mission they were poised to embark on, one in which they would be going into nigh on blind, harried him relentlessly. He was a man who did not much care for surprises; they could expect many in the perilous homeland of the Welsh Indians. He surmised there would be many. There were not variables in this situation so much as there was a lengthy catalogue of unknowns. Fear of the unknown would not subdue his spirit, but neither would it entirely fade away.

Success in this scenario would be questionable. As would their survival. He readily conceded both points, and in their straightforwardness he found tonic to his disquiet. Hopes kept afloat mostly by the promise of retribution, he was as steeled towards the prospect of death as he had ever been. But that was not to say he did not expect to emerge victorious, even in the face of daunting odds. They did, after all, have many elements on their side, that of surprise not the least of which. Outnumbered they would most assuredly be, but that prospect did not deter men of their resolve.

Marcel, features equally indecipherable, stood nearby along with Thurgood and Gaston. Of the men who had survived the harrowing attack on Chapel Beach, only Gaston was physically able to join them.

Their supplies lay at their feet, contained within some rucksacks and a long wooden box. They had a few surprises of their own for the murderous Welsh tribe...

Alvord cast his gray eyes up at the flawless morning sky, which reflected in no way the darkness that currently shrouded their lives. They waited alongside gangs of rough-talking miners with their meaningless talk of trifles; what topic could possibly seem important to him now, when his friend was probably a captive of the savages deep within the Pictured Rocks?

"Don't tell me you're heading *back*, Durand?"

John Livingston, directing a crew of American Fur Company

employees who were busily unloading a freight cart, looked at the weathered mountain man as if he could barely believe his eyes.

"Then I won't," Marcel replied flatly.

Livingston walked over to them, astonishment stamped across his stubbly face. "Marcel, you were lucky to emerge with your life last time- most who stray too close to that region aren't as lucky."

"Wouldn't worry 'bout it."

"You could have asked us for help in this matter, Marcel." Livingston's calculating gaze lingered on Alvord. "You seem understaffed."

"We'll manage just fine."

The man's face contorted into a sneer. "You enlist his aid in this, some greenhorn? A bloody *mangeur de lard*?"

Marcel turned to face Livingston squarely. "The game's changed. From here on out I'm huntin' scalps, and to that end I prefer his company to yours. Make yersef scarce, Livingston."

His hand hovered about his Bowie knife meaningfully. Shaking his head in disbelief, Livingston moved on.

Herd-like, the anxious crowd began shuffling its way onto the ramp that led up to the steamship. As Alvord drew nearer the boat, a voice hailed him that, while mellifluous as a human voice could get, struck a note of dread in his heart.

"Mr. Rawn! What are you gentlemen doing back here so soon?"

It was Genevieve Connolly. Of course they would encounter her, of all people. A sinking feeling took hold of his gut as him mind instantly strayed to Finnbar. Composing himself, he turned around to face her. She sat in a light barouche carriage piloted by a man in servant's livery and borne along by two horses. She lifted her thin black veil to get a better look at him.

He lied straight-facedly, glad for the years spent as a patrolman and private detective, where truth often had to be distorted for the sake of exigency.

"Marcel and I had to make a quick trip back for supplies." He indicated the rucksacks and wooden box.

Setting aside her parasol, she peered at him and Marcel more closely.

"Whatever happened to your faces?"

The faces of both he and Marcel bore a conspicuous array of cuts and bruises. And although he'd washed as much blood from his clothing as possible, some noticeable stains remained.

"Just a little commotion within our own ranks, but we sorted it out just fine."

"And Finnbar? He did not join you?"

He prayed that his face did not betray his unease. "He elected to stay behind and do some exploring. He sends his regards, naturally."

"Al," Marcel reached up and tapped him on the shoulder. "We gotta board."

To his dismay he saw that the girl was no fool. Her mind did not know precisely what to make out of the scene before her, but that something was amiss she definitely grasped.

"Just for my own edification, Mr. Rawn- what exactly is in those bags and box?" She did not bother to conceal her suspicion, or if she did then she did a poor job of it.

"Ah, precious cargo." He flashed her a reassuring smile, using teeth, which he rarely did. "Don't worry, Ms. Connolly. All is well. We merely forgot a few important items and were forced to make a trip back. Shall I inform Finnbar that you send your best?"

Still wrangling with the entire situation, she smiled back and answered, "But of course. And tell him that I hope to see him soon."

"Fair thee well, Ms. Connolly." With an encouraging nod he turned and strode up the crowded ramp and onto the ship's deck. He did not need to look back to be sure that her gaze was upon him.

With thoughtful eyes Genevieve watched the converted schooner *Napoleon* depart, its recently added smokestack befouling the sky above it. The shriek of the steam whistle cut through her troubled thoughts for an instant. She told her driver to urge the horses onward, and to the repetitive rattling of wheels she considered what she had just seen.

Her chance encounter with Alvord and Marcel was rife with unsatisfactory explanations. Instinct was not a word much applied to the nature of a young lady, but what else could be warning her that something was terribly amiss?

With a shudder she recalled her recent nightmare, how the formless darkness from the woods had consumed Finnbar. Shaking the image from her head, she wondered what sinister truths lay behind Alvord's evasive words.

Chapter 52

Having grown accustomed to piloting a large and stately vessel, Captain Elijah Colson felt no pride in arriving at the Soo in the twenty-foot Mackinaw boat that he and Mick had taken north. In all candor the sleek, two-masted craft had served them well, but their entrance into the frontier village was somewhat less than impressive. Still, as his boots squelched into the ankle-deep mud of the bank, he indulged a conspiratorial grin.

After reaching Cleveland following the battle with the timber pirates, Colson found himself down more than half his men. Some had been killed in the frenzied fight, but plenty more refused to work under his employ any longer, outraged by his decision to launch that bloody but triumphant assault.

Colson was not hurting for money, and decided to take time off to pursue a recent theory of his. His quest had brought him here, to the periphery of civilization- and more importantly, to the hometown of Cadwallader Jones.

This was no arbitrary whim. Rumors of the cutthroat lake baron's involvement in various dark enterprises on the Great Lakes dogged the man, timber piracy being but one of them. However, most of those doing the speculating were singularly busy men, higher ups in the world of Great Lakes commerce. Mostly older fellows, they might possess both shrewdness and enough ears upon the water to be aware of Jones's shadowy ventures, but what they lacked were the knackers to personally look into it. A truth buttressed by the fact that none so far had made even a stuttering attempt at bringing Jones to justice.

So he was going to do it for them.

Unlike most men, Colson knew evil. He did not speculate on it, nor did he harbor any delusions regarding it. He simply knew it. As a sailor in the Royal Navy in the Pacific, he had encountered evil firsthand, had witnessed man's iniquity and maliciousness vividly manifest itself before his very eyes.

And always had he loathed it.

Some would count him among the crazy folk of this world. Others would dismiss him as a man athirst for conflict and blood. Both parties would be decidedly mistaken- it was his keen sense of right and wrong that drove him to this.

Mick insisted on accompanying him, and for the stolid

Irishman's presence he was thankful. To face a mighty obstacle alone was to invite fear and doubt. With a reliable someone to watch your back, even daunting tasks seemed altogether doable.

His mind strayed to the past. He had met Jones once, in Detroit. A meeting brief and curt, one facilitated by a kindly merchant who was a mutual acquaintance. This was shortly before Colson had been privy to Jones's shady reputation. Yet even then he had perceived the underlying darkness. And with it a nettling, assumed superiority so ingrained that he had a hard time coping with it even for a few minutes.

Something nebulous and ominous surrounded the outwardly legitimate mercantile efforts of Cadwallader Jones.

And come Hell or high water, Captain Elijah Colson was going to find out what.

Chapter 53

Not long after the *Napoleon* crossed paths with the eastbound schooner *Algonquin*, a young lad of sixteen noticed a faint change come over the group of men he had been surreptitiously watching. If he had to guess he'd say they were a rough-and-ready lot, with cuts and bruises marring their tough, weather-beaten faces. Guns, knives, and tomahawks filled their belts, and were carried with a natural sort of ease. The tallest among them was an imperious man, broad of shoulder and fierce of countenance. When the light of diminishing day caught his beard it glowed a deep-hued red.

The young man, hired to work the Copper Falls Company holdings, had been observing the cluster of four men, envious of their tough demeanor and interested in how they interacted. Yet they uttered not a word, eyes glued on the rocky shoreline some two miles to the south, eyes bearing the suggestion of some great and imminent undertaking. Moving as one, they suddenly and mutely shot each other looks that transmitted a mutually arrived upon decision.

Of the four, a half-breed and an older man charted a course towards the staircase that led up to the pilothouse, while the other two headed towards boiler deck and engineers' room. The tall man brushed by him, not overly rough but still enough to send the younger man stumbling a step of two. The grim-faced fellow offered no words of apology and kept walking alongside his burly trapper companion, to what end the boy knew not.

"Cease feeding the fire," Alvord demanded of the nearest engineer in his best police captain's voice, letting the order rumble from deep within his chest.

"Yeah, says who?" the ash-coated man shot back at him sneeringly.

"Says my friend here." Alvord pointed a sawed-off shotgun at the engineer's disbelieving face. "And he is not one to brook much in the way of haggling."

The gleaming face of the engineer broke into a sweat of another kind. At this range there would be no missing, and his aggressor's face harbored no mercy.

The room was hotter than Hell's furnace, heated by the large fires into which two cords of wood were fed each hour. Stacks of wood and backup coal filled most of the room, contributing a feeling of claustrophobia to the searing heat of the place. Four pipes ran from the fires into the boiler room, where the fire-tube boilers were heated up by the hot gasses from the wood or coal.

The other two engineers promptly dropped their shovels and stepped back from the fires. The man with the gun in his face looked down the barrel a bit crossed-eyed.

"What is this?"

"Wouldn't worry 'bout that, son," Marcel urged him. "Just follow our orders and all will be fine. If you don't, I toss this in with the boilers." He dug a grenade from out his torn, dirty shirt, and casually tossed the fist-sized iron sphere up before catching it in his palm. With his other hand he caressed the wick fitted into the top.

"You suicidal or something, trapper?"

"Care to find out?" Marcel grinned deeply, revealing the gap where a lower incisor once sat.

"Those tanks are under pressure! The ship can't withstand an explosion like that! She'll go down!"

Alvord broke into a chuckle, but it was not a happy sound. "Then I suppose you'd best just heed our advice."

They quit stoking the fires, and Alvord heard the grinding of gears that meant Thurgood and Gaston had succeeded in getting the Captain to stop the vessel.

From five miles and hour the ship slowed to nothing, generating an outcry on the part of the other seventy or so passengers. This reached fever pitch in the next moment, when Alvord and Marcel led the engineers out onto the main deck at gunpoint, meeting up with Thurgood and Gaston, who had with them the nonplussed ship's Captain and First Mate.

They grouped up by the massive side-wheel paddle that propelled the *Napoleon.* Nearby, a large rowboat was suspended by ropes, which they carefully loaded their gear into. Keeping some of their guns trained on the befuddled horde of men before them, Alvord and company proceeded with their plan.

"Tell them to give us some space," Thurgood instructed the pallid-faced Captain.

"Keep back!" the man shrieked wildly.

"Lower that rowboat," Gaston told the engineers and First Mate in growl reminiscent of his father's. "And hop to it."

He nudged the nearest man with his gun's muzzle, keeping a wary eye on the crowd. Most were simply shocked but some looked livid, and could be armed.

"Where are you going?" the First Mate demanded. "This is a

wasteland! There's nothing out here!"

Marcel snorted without humor. "Friend, you'd be surprised."

The boat splashed almost merrily into Superior, and Alvord and Thurgood used ropes to quickly lower themselves into the bobbing craft. Training guns on the Captain and other men, they waited until Marcel and his son were safely aboard before shoving off. Alvord and Thurgood vigorously manned the oars while Marcel and Gaston kept their rifle sights on the Captain and First Mate, who had been instructed to stay on the edge of the steamboat, easy targets if shooting had to be done.

Alvord caught some wide-eyed kid watching them dazedly; he realized numbly that he was engaging in a blatantly criminal act. Oh well. Dark deeds awaited them in yonder woods, and now was hardly the time to fret over examples set.

Alvord and Thurgood rowed in frenzied unison, the icy water spilling over the sides in hissing sprays as they cut through two-foot waves. With each splash of oar upon water, the scent of victory mingled with the stench of death. For at the moment, that was their lot in life.

Victory or death.

For a few moments a stunned silence presided over the steamboat and its occupants following the whirlwind hold-up of the vessel. So audacious and sure of themselves had the four rogues been that the entire ordeal had lasted but a paltry ten minutes. Numbly, the Captain ordered that the engines be restarted and soon they continued their northwestern course towards the Keweenaw Peninsula, still not entirely sure of what the hell had just happened aboard his ship.

Alvord and the others reached the shoreline as the sun began to set. It was not a proper beach they made landfall at but rather a tiny, rocky cove sparsely fringed with sand. They hauled the boat up and out of the water, dragging it into the woods with them.

That night, only the smallest of fires warmed their bodies and kept the bugs at bay in the rocky hollow that served as their bivouac. The food they unhurriedly chewed might as well have been ash for how much they tasted it.

Sleep, when it came, was fitful and full of the potential dangers that tomorrow would hurl their way.

Chapter 54

On the fog-strewn morning of the next day, Cadwallader Jones did not walk through the doors of his manor so much as he glided. There was vigor in his self-satisfied stride, a certain buoyancy that he generally lacked. While most assuredly a man of unshakable confidence, Jones rarely let that confidence transmute into an outward display, even after a victory had been won.

But today- ah, what a capital day it was! He could breathe easy knowing that the threat of both Crowder and the Chapel Beach trapping expedition had been neutralized. A pity about Finnbar, but at the unfortunate Irishman's expense the safekeeping of the tribe was secured for a little longer, buying him some much needed time. His plan was not ready for fruition just yet... there would be much to considered and put into effect in the coming days and weeks.

At present he could bask in the comfort of two more brilliant victories scored. As in a game of chess, he maneuvered as best he could to keep his beleaguered king from being engulfed by enemy forces. And today, two more enemy pieces exited the board, victims to his masterful manipulation of the game. He felt like whistling.

As he absently handed his overcoat to a servant, his surging pack of hounds swarmed him *en masse*, overjoyed to see him after his absence. He bent down and engaged them in some rough play, his large form barely visible beneath the wiry gray coats of the massive beasts. They had need of exercise, he could plainly see. Perhaps he and Gen would take them out onto the backfield and let them gambol under the oaks for a while. In a swift moment of reflection he realized that he had been denying himself even small, quotidian joys lately. True, he was a man burdened by the ponderous weight of his people's future, but even he could set aside a little time here and there to indulge in life's simple pleasures. And also to fulfill his duties as a Guardian, an obligation that often yielded to his many other commitments.

Ars longa, vita brevis, after all. Art is long and Time is short. Time imposed limitations on men, and by the time a craft was mastered sometimes there was not enough time to leave behind a desirable memory of oneself. Of his professional and clandestine responsibilities he knew he was adept, but he was not sure if he'd perfected the craft of being a proper Guardian.

"Gen!" He hailed jovially as his ward strolled into the room.

His thunderous voice elicited a smile from Genevieve, whose head was cocked curiously at his unexpectedly gladsome aspect.

"Mr. Jones! This day finds you in fine spirits! How did the business of-"

"Bah! Belay that talk of business, Miss! Come- let us bring these exuberant hounds outside presently, before they bring these walls crashing down around us!"

A slightly flummoxed Genevieve followed as he briskly led the way outside. She could not remember the last time she had seen him so animated.

"Just look at them go!" The amber eyes of Cadwallader Jones followed the powerful movements of his coursing hounds.

"It appears that the servants did not keep them sufficiently entertained while you were gone," Genevieve speculated as she too watched their gleefully cavorting pets.

"Noble beasts, and useful too- I might take them to the Grand Sable Dunes sometime and let them course deer. There is enough open country there, it would be a sight to behold..."

"I should like to accompany, Mr. Jones."

Given the clear nature of the day, the sounds of town, though muffled by the hills and trees, could still be heard. Hearing the strident blast of a steam whistle, Genevieve recalled her puzzling meeting with Alvord and Marcel yesterday.

She informed him of it airily, curious to see what he thought. "By the by, Mr. Jones, yesterday morning I ran into Alvord Rawn and Marcel Durand, two of our guests at your recent dinner. They were back in the Soo and I happened upon them during a carriage ride."

Her Guardian's broad smile wilted like a flower exposed to flame.

"*What?*" He spat out the word as if it were an obscenity.

"Is something the matter, Mr. Jones?" His anger, only partially submerged beneath the pool of his self-mastery, confused her. He had no reason to be alarmed or perturbed by the reappearance of Alvord and Marcel. Yet here he was, his usually passionless face mingling both emotions. Unused to seeing Jones evince much in the way of emotion, she was almost frightened by his immediate and vehement reaction.

"No, no," he comfort her in a voice returned to composure,

but still his queerly colored eyes flared with chilling intensity. "But what reason did they give as to being back so very soon?"

She summoned up their conversation in her mind. "Well, Mr. Rawn said that he and the others had come back for some supplies they had overlooked. Strange though, is it not? Most of those men were hardened trappers- would not a lifetime of experience have left them wholly prepared for such an expedition? I can't imagine them forgetting any essential. And I doubt it is a leisurely paddle back to the Soo from where they are. He was oddly evasive about the contents of their baggage, too..."

"How many of them made the trip back?" Jones kept his question casual while his mind raced with potentialities.

She thought for a moment. "Four, I believe. There was Mr. Rawn and Mr. Durand, and a half-breed as well as an older fellow, a local fisherman if I am not mistaken."

Jones stomach dropped as if he'd stepped off a cliff. *Thurgood.* He knew he should have snuffed the hermit out years ago, but he had always seemed so harmless, just an escaped captive of the tribe thought to be stark, raving mad by most folks.

"And when you came upon them, what were they doing?"

"Waiting to board the steamer *Napoleon.* I thought that odd as well... canoes are what trappers generally use."

Another detail popped into her head, one that she had nearly forgotten. "And they seemed rather worse for the wear, I must say. Mr. Rawn and Mr. Durand both sported bruised and cut faces, and their clothes were ripped and quite stained."

"I suppose," Jones spoke from within the protective carapace of his regained self-control, "it is possible that some supplies were lost en route to their destination. I would not worry, Gen. They came across as very competent men."

He felt a faint stirring of conscience as he thought of the doomed Finnbar, but in the next instant reminded himself that Thurgood was, almost beyond conjecture, leading Alvord and Marcel back to the village. Against the odds those two had survived, and now planned to visit vengeance upon the tribe. Some inner demon told him there could be no other scenario.

And it was one that he and he alone needed to handle.

"Well Gen, I believe the beasts have had taken enough exercise. One of my fishing vessels has need of repair- hit a reef up on the Canadian side and was barely able to limp its way home. I need to go take a look. And unfortunately, after that I have to venture down to St. Joseph Island; since our dinner Major Raines has asked me to come down for the sake of consultation on a number of matters regarding the island's development. I hope to be back in two nights, though it may be a bit longer."

Both stories were bald-faced lies hastily applied to the situation, and although he hated lying to her it was an unfortunate necessity.

"But you only just returned."

"I am truly sorry, my dear. After this business is concluded I am taking some time off. Perhaps we can do some sailing, do a bit of traveling? We could go to Detroit, or even Cleveland if you're of a mind."

She restrained her childlike disappointment and gave him an understanding smile. "That would be most enjoyable, Mr. Jones."

They returned the dogs to the house. Nearly as quickly as he had arrived, Cadwallader Jones was gone, leaving his lonely ward to her isolation once more.

The heavyset bartender at the bowling alley Alvord and his friends had patronized just a few night ago met Jones in a backroom of the establishment.

"What ho, old friend?" he asked of Jones, settling into a leather chair with a creak.

Jones did not mince his words. "I am poised to embark on a mission... not entirely sure I will be returning. I do not expect failure but those I face are going to take a lot of killing, I can tell."

He cast his amber eyes down in thought. "Should I fail, you know how to proceed, old fried. And please give this to Gen for me. She deserves to know."

He let a deep gulp of air inflate his chest and handed the other man a sealed envelope. "Now, to business."

The bartender scratched his ear along the scar where the upper rim had been bitten off.

"You'll need shoulder-hitters," he observed sagaciously, passing Jones a much-needed spruce beer.

"Precisely. Killers. Cutthroats. Fighting men whose guns can be bought. How long before you can assemble such a group?"

"Of those sorts?" The husky fellow chuckled. "Depends on how full the bar is."

Fifteen minutes later a ragtag assortment of evil-looking men awaited the arrival of Jones in that same room. Some knew him by name and reputation; others didn't and didn't give a damn, eager for whatever opportunity this stranger could offer them. To men as thoroughly unscrupulous as themselves, murder and mayhem meant naught but coin jingling in their purse.

The door flew open and in stepped Jones. Blocky jaw set grimly in the dusky gleam of the oil lamps, he looked every bit as formidable as the unsavory batch of Hellspawn before him.

"What offer have you got for us?" asked one of the men roughly.

"One you've heard before- cash for blood."

Exchanging looks of maleficent satisfaction, the men hunkered down to hear Jones out.

Chapter 55

"*Humphrey?*" Genevieve could scarcely believe her eyes as the doctor led her into a back room. He closed the door on his way out, leaving her alone with the recovering Duddersfield.

For his part, Duddersfield could scarcely believe his own, and very much wished they were betraying him.

"Miss Connolly!" he squeaked, embarrassment fighting its way through the pain. "What brings you here? How did you find me?"

She noticed the conspicuous bandages on his posterior and politely averted her gaze. "I recently overheard two of our servants talking about a trapping party that just this morning returned to the Soo after being attacked by Indians. Fearing that it was the expedition yourself and Finnbar were part of, I hastened into town to seek them out."

Her eyes fierce, inquisitive slants, she ceased speaking and awaited an answer. A dark-skinned man snored softly on a bed nearby, but she paid him no heed. Between her mysterious encounter with Alvord and Marcel yesterday, and now Mr. Jones's peculiar behavior this morning, her mind was athirst for answers.

Tears slipped freely from the beady eyes of the young geologist. "If it is Finnbar you seek, then I..."

Duddersfield had never been in a situation like this in all his life, and knew not what to say. Instead he looked at her helplessly, as if begging her to not press any further.

"*Mr. Duddersfield,*" her voice cracked like a bullwhip, "I know you have sustained injury and my heart goes out to you, but I need to know what happened, please..."

He collected himself and through more tears spoke truthfully. "It was dreadful, Miss Connolly, a scene hewn from nightmare and one that any of us were lucky to escape..."

David, meanwhile, was at a nearby groggery looking to buy a bottle or two from the bartender. As he paid for the whiskey and rum, he overheard a voice that attempted to be casual while barely restraining its keenness.

"And Jones, you say, went into a nearby bar and soon emerged with a crew of cutthroats?"

The canny Scot turned and saw two men, one blonde and the other dark-haired, conversing intently with a miner.

"That's what I'm telling ya," the miner insisted thickly, "and then they all boarded one of his schooners and went up into Superior, although that I heard secondhand. But from close friends and good sources."

"And what of t'other stories ye were tellin' us?" the dark haired men asked in a thick Irish brogue. "Ye wager there's fact in 'em?"

"Uh huh," the miner was adamant as he took a sip of gin. "It's known that while he's a rich businessman with a good image among those who matter, here in the Soo he's got a tarnished rep among some. Tales of competing fishing vessels sunk in the night and tales of timber piracy."

Here the blonde and dark haired man shared knowing looks.

"There's talk of his shady business up in the Copper Country as regards land sales, as well as the disappearance of those who stand in his way. Hell, a feller named Crowder, seeking iron rather than copper, was recently lost along with his whole crew after buying land from Jones in the Marquette Range."

The man paused to snap his fingers dramatically. "Just like that, gone. A crewman who was away at the time found their campsite, and he found blood and other signs of a struggle. It's well known that Jones wishes to control the expansion of the iron mining business in Marquette- bastard pretty much owns the Jackson Mining Company, the only iron seekers of note."

"Hey lads," David approached them affably. "The name's David McTavish. I meant not to eavesdrop, but if its Jones ye fancy information on, then ye'd do well to folla me."

The two men promptly paid for the miner's drink, as well as another round, and then walked with David out of the bar.

"Elijah Colson," the tough-looking blonde fellow offered in his Liverpool accent.

"Mick," grunted the other man.

"A pleasure, gents. Ye be seekin' information on Cadwallader Jones, eh?"

"Aye," Mick told him, choosing to trust the Scot though he had just met him.

"Towards what end?"

After days of nonstop travel Colson was in no mood to beat around the bush. "To bring him to account for the evils he's perpetrated. He is a fiend in human form, and many innocents have suffered and perished because of his illegal enterprises. So what news have you of the man?"

David, having survived the harrowing beach assault and

eager to piece this puzzle together, was equally all business.

"Me'n my trappin' crew got thrashed by a strange tribe of savages, and a few of the survivors linked Jones to the attack."

"By thrashed, you mean-"

"I mean most fell brutally to sword, spear, and arrer."

"Hold hard," Mick said, deeply frowning in revelation. "Cap'n-weren't Marcel, Alvord, and Finn headin' up this way to trap?"

"Ye knows them boyos?" a bewildered David asked.

"As coincidence would have it," said Colson, "it was my ship that they rode north from Chicago. We encountered timber pirates along the way, and they aided us in bringing that crew of fiends to justice. That timber ship was thought to be financed by Cadwallader Jones."

David nodded sagely. "After the attack Marcel and Alvord spoke of two warriors aboard the pirate ship that were cast in the same mold as the savages we faced in the Pictured Rocks. They looked white and were tattooed in the same manner, according to them."

"And they figured that Jones was involved in the attack on your expedition?"

"Aye Mick, as he tried to dissuade us from trappin' that area when he heard aboot it. They also think, and I along with 'em, that Jones somehow tipped off the tribe, tellin' 'em of our camp locations. For we had three camps separated by a number of miles, and all were struck on the same day. Didn't seem logical that we could have been found out that quickly without them knowin' we were comin', d'ye ken?"

Colson certainly did. "Where are those fellows now?"

"Went back to rescue any possible survivors. Finnbar was last seen alive by two of our party, and it seems that they were taking some captives. I took a wound to the breadbasket, else I'd be there with 'em."

"So the Irishman may be dead?" Mick asked remorsefully.

"Aye, that he may. But somehow, I think he lives. Somethin' tells me that the luck of the Irish will pull that 'un through."

They entered the physician's practice and went into the back room, where they found a teary-eyed Duddersfield conversing with Genevieve Connolly.

"That's Jones's young ward," David informed the two men under his breath.

Genevieve turned towards them, her own eyes welling up with tears.

"Mr. McTavish! Humphrey has informed me of the tragedy. I am so very sorry..."

"Och, lass, 'tis not me ye need to show pity to."

"So Finnbar," she said, on the verge of breaking down, "he may have, he may be-"

The trapper gently placed a calloused hand on her shoulder. "Come now, lass, worry not. Marcel and Alvord, they wouldn't have gone back if they didn't think him still among the livin'."

"Humphrey mentioned that you all think Mr. Jones has something to do with this?"

The Scot clenched his jaw, wishing very much that the wee slip of a thing before him had not gotten involved here. "I am sorry, but he may well be. Where is he now?"

She hesitated.

"Please tell them what ye told me, Miss Connolly," Duddersfield requested kindly but firmly.

"Gone, he's gone. He came home this morning from the Copper Country and was in so jolly a mood, such as I have rarely seen. It almost frightened me. But now I am highly concerned and a bit confused. Because Mr. Jones claimed that one of his fishing vessels needed repair and that after checking it he would be going down to St. Joseph Island for a few days. Yet upon checking his schedule I found nothing of the sort written down."

Colson's forehead knit in thought. "Why did you check his schedule, Miss?"

"Because he records every responsibility he has therein and he simply never diverts from it. I felt the need to check it because, as I told you, his behavior was so very out of character this morning, and upon mentioning that I had seen Alvord and Marcel his attitude changed with startling swiftness. His eyes turned to wrathful slits, though he tried to mask it. Then he asked me questions about them and what they were doing, and suddenly he left, offering those excuses I just informed you of."

"M'dear," Colson spoke softly, "I mean not to speak ill of your Guardian, but it seems that his ship was spotted heading towards Superior earlier today. Sordid are the reputations of the men who went with him."

She felt the breath catch in her throat as a knot of dread coiled in her stomach. Sinking into a chair, she tried to contain herself. Cerberus laid his wiry head on her lap soothingly, and his presence was of aid. She was very close to breaking down, but she did not want to get hysterical in front of these men, two of whom were strangers...

"What does this mean?" She asked in a trembling voice.

"It means, lass, that it is very likely that Cadwallader Jones is somehow deeply involved in this. I ask ye to not worry unduly aboot this, for if we're wrong we'll soon find out."

"What is going to happen? Are you going to kill-"

"Only if it comes to tha'."

The world seemed to be spinning around her, much the way her brain felt inside her skull.

"Where shall I go, then? How can I go back there?"

"I can't imagine the man meaning ye any harm- I think ye should stay there, Miss Connolly. We'll seek ye out when it's over."

David turned to Duddersfield. "Ye rest up there, Dudd me boyo. As fer the three of us, we got us some business in the Indian village."

Colson seemed taken aback. "Indian village- what do we need there?"

"Ye boys want blood or at the very least justice, right?"

"Aye," replied both of them promptly.

"After tha' timber pirate business, I know neither of ye shirk bloodshed. So here is my proposal. Yer a cap'n of yer own ship, right? I can get us an American Fur Company sloop. Ye folla me?"

Colson and Mick looked at each other and nodded in unison. Both intended on bringing down Jones in one fashion or another, but neither had expected things to fall into place quite so quickly and neatly.

"Aye lad, that we do." Mick affirmed with a dark chuckle.

"And in the Indian village is t'other ingredient needed fer this plan."

Big Wolf and Walks With Thunder were resting, letting their scalp and facial wounds knit up. Both men lounged and idly smoked outside a longhouse in the Chippewa village, and watched impassively as David approached with two strangers.

"Ye boyos healin' up alright?"

"Yes," Big Wolf answered, rising along with the other brave to meet the two new faces. "And you, McTavish?"

"Och, 'tis but a wee scratch compared to some wounds I've had. I've got somethin' to ask of ye fellas."

The Indians stared at him with inscrutable faces as they waited for his request.

"You two up for a little dust-up on Superior? Marcel and those who went with him are in danger. These gents here are Colson and Mick. They're game lads, and they and meself need a crew in a hurry. We'd be honored if ye two joined us."

"Warriors." Walks With Thunder stated instead of asking.

The Scot nodded fiercely. "We got room for at least eight, if ye can make it happen."

"I shall spread the word of scalps and glory to be had," Walks With Thunder said simply, and he and Big Wolf moved off to raise a war party.

Chapter 56

Night fell swiftly, aided by the wispy clouds that subdued the waxing moon's burgeoning luminescence. Soon the only light in Finnbar's cell emanated from the ever-present fire in the center of the jail.

This he took no note of, because he was rather busy writhing in his death throes.

His body convulsed in sharp paroxysms of pain, and white froth spilled out from between his lips along with inhuman notes of agony. Fingers locked in claw like positions, his hands scratched at something unseen.

Crowder began frantically shouting for their guard in Welsh, hands banging against the bars of his cell as he helplessly watched his fellow prisoner thrash about. The guard rushed in alone, as nearly all other tribe members were at the ceremony for their dead warriors. Looking wildly around, the young man followed Crowder's frantically pointing finger to Finnbar's supine form. He made as if to turn and get help, but Crowder yelled something desperate sounding in Welsh and he paused, uncertainty creasing his devilishly tattooed face. Crowder yelled more insistently still, and the man took a decisive step forward and, removing the copper key from his belt, unlocked Crowder's cell.

The door swung wide to admit the prisoner, who dashed over to Finnbar's cell and hurriedly signaled for the guard to unlock it. He visibly faltered, looking back towards the shadows of the corridor that led to the exit. Crowder's undulating Welsh lilt grew more insistent yet. At last the guard grudgingly sprung the lock on Finnbar's cell. He made Crowder go in before taking a few tentative steps forward to see what was going on, spear at the ready.

Allowing confusion and curiosity to override his wariness–this was a mistake the man was destined to never make again.

Finnbar exploded into action with speed that exceeded an unsuspecting mind's ability to react to. In a flash the Irishman had seized the spear by its haft and pulled the Welsh Indian into his cell, smashing him into the far wall. He then snatched up the fist-sized rock he had dug out of the earthen floor and charged like a man with precious little to lose. His approach was momentarily halted when the guard, both hands on the spear, punched outwards and cracked Finnbar in chin with the wooden length of the weapon. When the guard sought to follow this up with a strike from the spear's butt, Finnbar wildly ducked it and bulled in, swinging his arm in a tight arc to bring the rock into hard contact with his enemy's face. Teeth and a chunk of tongue exited his mouth along with an outpouring of blood. Crowder moved in, deftly drawing the long knife from the fallen man's belt and inserting it through his ribs and up into the heart with surgical precision. A sharp intake of breath gave way to a few wet, rasping gasps before the man's life was spent.

"Sterling performance there, not nearly as histrionic as I expected it to be," Crowder remarked dryly. "Now what?"

"*Now what?!* Now's our bloody chance, man!"

Ignoring the sharp throbbing on his stubbly chin, he wiped the spittle from his lips. The "seizure" had been a deliberately affected condition on the part of Finnbar. And he took a second to silently thank the Almighty for the nearly flawless efficacy of that ruse. Wrenching the knife blade from the dead guard's chest to an arterial spurt of blood, he handed it to Crowder, picked up the spear and at a stealthy crouch led the way down the corridor that danced with the flickering shadows of distant flames. The tribe was gathered in its hundreds near the center of the village, in the large, open area where the sacrifices occurred. The pulsing of lurid music, so dirge-like that at times it sent chills pulsing through his body, had indicated to him that the time to act was nigh. He knew he must strike before the celebration reached full swing. Delicate timing was of paramount importance, for to have attempted escape too soon might have resulted in their being spotted and captured. He needed the whole tribe distracted by the initial stages of the ceremony, so much so that they would not notice that he and Crowder had given them the slip until they found the empty cells. Empty but for the fresh carcass of the guard.

They slunk unperceived along the edge of the darkness, bodies crouched low and legs pumping at high speed. They knew not if there would be dogs around; the prospect of blindly running into a pack of those ravening curs was hardly a pleasant one.

As they sped through the darkness, Finnbar came to a halt so abrupt that Crowder ran smack dab into him.

"Just a second- 'tis something I need to retrieve from these pilfering primitives. This structure here is where they cache stolen objects, I saw it yesterday."

"*What*? Have you lost it, Finnbar?" Crowder demanded in

hoarse incredulity. "You some kind of madman?"

"Aye, if popular opinion is to be lent any credence. Just give me half a mo'," he insisted firmly, and disappeared into the low, domed building.

Inside were several heaps of stolen possessions, some soaring upward towards the ceiling in the manner of stalagmites. Aiding his endeavor, however, was the fact that his own possessions, along with those of his group, were very recent acquisitions. He grabbed a nearby torch and peered into a modest pile of items that included kettles, axes, and traps. He saw no guns, else he'd have armed himself accordingly. Rooting through the stuff, he soon felt his hand brush against leather.

"Paydirt!" he muttered to himself. He made sure it was indeed his black leather journal and not some other book before he stuffed it into his shirt pocket. Nearby he also found the push-dagger that Alvord had gifted him with, still in its ankle sheath. He strapped it on, and as he prepared to leave something else caught his eye. Protruding from the corner of a pack was a gleaming something that caught the light as only metal can. Grabbing it, he removed the item from the bag and placed it more closely under the light.

It was Alvord's copper-tipped truncheon.

Taking the briefest of moments to admire the brutal weapon, he ran his hand over its length, feeling the narrative chips and dents along its length. He knew in that moment, as he gazed upon that symbolic messenger of Fate, that this would not be an hour of folly. For although they were well beyond the pale of civilized laws, justice was on their side.

He reemerged just as Crowder was about to leave him and make a go of it on his own.

"What in the blazes made you do that?"

"A tickling fancy. Now let's shake a leg out of here, eh?"

"Is the plan the same? We still heading towards the rotting part of the wall they're repairing?"

"Aye."

"And once there, we kill any nearby sentinels and exit via that spot?"

"That's the general idea, yes. But who knows how it will play out? Like me Uncle Pat used to say, 'Ye can dig a canal bed, but ye can't always make a river follow its course.'"

"Zounds, but that's pretty fucking daft, man."

Ignoring him, Finnbar pushed onward. Like specters they floated from building to building, hoping beyond hope that this all-or-nothing gamble would not prove to be their undoing. The darkness was their principal ally, but in its enveloping embrace also lurked every doubt and fear they harbored.

Atop a projecting bastion, the sentinel guarding the section of wall that was undergoing repair peered out into the inky gloom that encircled the village. He could have sworn that he just heard something out there. His eyes were not yet fully adjusted to the darkness; that would take a little longer yet. His ears, however, were finely attuned to the sounds of the night woods, and that had not sounded quite natural to him. Yet the wailing of voices and simultaneous blaring of instruments from deep within the village made it difficult to focus as clearly as he generally did...

He doubted he had anything to worry about, though. This village had remained a secret for so long, none had dared attack them in centuries...

Two arrows took him hard under the chin, angling upward into his brainstem and instantly rendering him lifeless. His body slumped forward onto the sharpened top of the palisade, the short bow in his grasp sliding down onto the wooden floor of the defensive wall.

Marcel and Gaston dropped their bows, pleased with the accuracy of their shots in the poor lighting. They had been out in the dark for long enough to allow their natural night vision to set in, but it was still a risky business. Picking up grappling hooks, they twirled them as they eyed their target and then dexterously cast them upward. The metal flukes had been wrapped in cloth to muffle the sound of their impact. It was not a tough toss, and both succeeded in finding purchase on the top of the fifteen-foot wall. Alvord and Thurgood moved in, shotguns secured to their backs and pistols stuffed in their belts. They used the ropes to scale the wall, with Alvord athletically surmounting it far sooner than the older fisherman.

Once atop the wall they scanned their surroundings, seeing other sentinels off in the distance. They propped the body of the dead man up against the wall, making him look as lifelike as possible. Then they lowered more ropes down, and the wooden box was tied fast and slowly pulled up to the bastion. Throwing it open, they began hastily assembling their weaponry as Marcel and Gaston noiselessly ascended the ropes.

From the deserted Fort Brady they had amassed a formidable arsenal consisting of rifles, shotguns, hand grenades, and a goodly number of Congreve Rockets. When they went to the Fort to appropriate weapons, they found to their convenience that the two guards stationed there were busy getting drunk in town.

It had been pathetically easy to break in and raid the armory. And what firepower it had afforded them.

The Congreve Rockets, invented in 1804 by a British Colonel named William Congreve, would lend them a nice edge. The rockets themselves were foot-long iron cases that utilized black powder as a propellant. These rockets were secured to seven-foot wooden guide poles, and launched from a small metal bipod.

Rockets at the ready, they mentally regrouped and prepared for the next phase of this audacious campaign.

Tracking down the village had been far easier than anticipated. Thurgood had rightly believed its location to be not far from Chapel Beach, at the confluence of two large brooks that Marcel felt eventually fed into Chapel Lake. The former captive had acted as their Virgil, leading them through a Dantesque portal towards an infernal kingdom. Sticking to the shadows and thickest sections of forest, they were prepared to be intercepted at any moment by a horde of enemies. Yet it had not come. As stealthily as was possible they had continued making their way south, state of mind part predator and part potential prey item. They had been able to locate the village with their ears long before they set eyes on it, and had waited for the cover of darkness to move in. In a fantastic feat of confidence and skill, Marcel had scaled a prehistoric pine and spied on the village using a spyglass of Thurgood's. He had roughly determined the location of the lightly guarded prisoner-holding structures and also a spot in the wall where rotting stockade posts were being replaced. That spot was close by, and would provide a secondary avenue of escape should "Plan A" go up in flames. Much to their satisfaction, what appeared to be most of the tribe was in full congregation towards the center of the sprawling village.

So in they swooped.

The ceremony continued unabated now, and under the cover of that unearthly music Alvord and Marcel stole forward, lions prowling in the dark. Low slung, they sought out the deepest shadows to aid them. Gaston and Thurgood were to stay behind with their weapons and eliminate any sentinels who discovered their position. A set of stairs led down from the stockade, which Alvord and Marcel crept down, each keeping his head on a swivel. They each had two pistols in their belt and a shotgun slung over their back, but in their hands they carried the age-old tool of the assassin- cold steel. Marcel opted for his trusted tomahawk and Bowie knife, while Alvord carried a Model 1832 Foot Artillery Sword appropriated from the Fort. This hefty shortsword resembled the ancient Roman *gladius*, with a straight, double-edged blade of twenty inches. And just like that ancient design, it was a fearsome weapon to both cut and thrust with. The blades of both men were liberally smeared with ashes from last night's fire to avoid reflecting light.

Movement up ahead caught Marcel's keen eye, and he motioned for Alvord to stop. Wraithlike, both men drifted behind a large kiln, poised and ready.

Through eyes still adjusting to the night, Finnbar thought he saw a group of figures some thirty feet in front of them. He knew not how many. It seemed to him they were moving, possibly in the opposite direction. After a whispered conference with Crowder, it was decided they would risk it, as the rotting section of gate was not far off. Leveling the spear in front of him, he advanced at a determined trot. This could very well be it, for if even a small group of enemies lay ahead it could prove too much for them.

At the sound of rapidly approaching footsteps Alvord and Marcel sprang out from behind the kiln, weapons at the ready and minds set on blood and blood alone.

A spear nearly took out Alvord's right eye. As he swiftly ducked he felt the draught of the blade tickle his hair, and in the next minute he lunged forward in a punishing tackle. His shoulder made hard contact with a stomach, which he was glad was not sheathed in a copper cuirass. The man he attacked exhaled with a loud *whoosh* and went down with Alvord on top of him. Alvord was promptly fetched a hard clout to the face. Ignoring the blow he brought his sword up and prepared for a killing thrust but-

"*Alvord?*" came the breathless gasp of disbelief.

In utter disbelief Alvord heard the now-familiar *Alvaird* of none other than Finnbar Fagan, whose brogue-imbued voice he had never been so glad to hear.

"None other."

"Wasn't sure ye'd be making it, friend."

"Oh ye of little faith."

Relief flooding him like a tidal wave, Alvord helped his friend up.

"Damn, remind me never to run afoul of ye, mucker," Finnbar said ruefully to Alvord, hand on his bruised stomach.

Alvord glanced to his right and saw that Marcel had pinned a grimacing white man by placing his foot on the prone fellow's throat.

"Howdy, Finn."

"Marcel Durand! Now it's a party!"

The mountain man spared no more time to rejoice in their reunion.

"Let's light a shuck outta here, boys!"

He powerfully yanked Crowder to his feet and began running towards the wall in his bowlegged gait. They all followed his lead.

Finnbar was scared, he admitted as much to himself, but there was newfound strength to be had with the auspicious arrival of his friends. Sure, they were in the black heart of enemy territory and hopelessly outnumbered. But with Alvord Rawn and Marcel Durand at his side... Fate itself might struggle against them in vain.

For the space of about twenty seconds they ran in silence. They had nearly made it when two things happened very quickly. An inhuman howl of outrage cut through the air from the direction of the cells. A few seconds later, the roar of gunfire broke out from atop the wall. Onward they ran, towards what scene they knew not.

Gaston and Thurgood were beset on both sides. Arrows hummed through the night, launched by sentinels who had detected their presence. With Marcel in the lead, the others took the stairs in a series of bounds and joined the beleaguered men, using the walls of the bastion for cover.

Without pause or talk they joined the battle, grabbing the surplus of loaded guns from the wooden box. With the increased firepower the attacking sentinels were quickly driven back. But their small victory was short-lived. Howling for blood, a horde of enemies poured out of the village and towards the wall. The white-robed Druids led the way, furious at having found that their human sacrifices escaped. In short time they would be to the wall.

"Ye may be wanting this if they close, Alvord." Finnbar held out the truncheon.

Alvord took it, surprise barely registering. "Let's avoid that possibility entirely, shall we?"

And with that he set a Congreve Rocket on its bipod and aimed it down at the approaching swarm of Welsh Indian warriors. Finnbar was dumbfounded by the presence of rockets, but recovered swiftly and helped Crowder and Marcel set more up as Gaston and Thurgood poured lead down at their enemies. Due to the darkness and chaos their shots were none too accurate, but it was making men more wary and slowing down the surging enemy tide.

It had been an unspeakable bitch, transporting these rockets through miles of woods. But now they paid big dividends.

"Let 'er rip!" an exhilarated Finnbar yelled to Alvord, who touched a matchstick to the nearest rocket's fuse. It sparked with a loud sizzle that was soon joined by others. The first rockets took flight with a shriek and a surprising amount of flames. In succession the rockets streaked towards the Welsh Indians, a few inflicting gruesome causalities while others went rogue, exploding as they made contact with buildings or the ground. There were two different varieties, one with a conical top and one with a rounded, and Alvord was not sure which was which but one kind exploded on impact while the other was incendiary and started small fires.

They did not delude themselves into thinking that with these weapons they would take out the attacking force. But the rockets did impart something vital- confusion and distraction.

More rockets were set up and sent off, intensifying the chaos below. Most of the warriors scrambled for cover, but undeterred a small contingent raced towards the stairs. Gaston distributed their supply of grenades, and the fuses of these were lit. Through the flitting forms, fires, and spiraling rockets, Finnbar caught sight of the white-robed Druids huddled behind a building, desperately trying to rally men. Drawing back his arm, he hurled his grenade as he had never hurled anything before.

He lost sight of it in the gloom, but as he watched the Druids suddenly looked fixedly at something next to them on the ground. The subsequent explosion and flaring of orange light constituted the most rewarding feeling he'd ever basked in. The other men likewise heaved their grenades, which did not deal as much death as hoped for but effectively kept their enemies pinned and apprehensive.

"Time to go!" Alvord roared about the tumult. More sentinels closed in on them from other sections of the wall, and arrows and spears were beginning to strike disturbingly close by. Thurgood, Crowder, and Gaston were on the ropes heading towards freedom, with Alvord, Finnbar, and Marcel touching off one last salvo of rockets before retreating.

A few bold warriors, heedless of consequence, charged towards the stairs with death in their eyes. The mighty one-eyed warlord led them. Brandishing his tomahawk, Marcel took a step forward and loosed it with practiced ease and bad intentions. The warlord weaved under it with blurring speed, but it deeply imbedded itself into the forehead of the man behind him.

"Ha ha!" Finnbar cackled madly. "Bleedin' deadly!"

Alvord adjusted their last rocket, an incendiary, aiming it at the knot of warriors on the stairs. It came up short but starting a fire that prevented them from continuing their approach. The trajectory of that rocket bought Alvord and the others enough time to half fall, half slide down the ropes that brought them safely to the other side of the wall and all the frenzy that was inside it.

Propitiously, the moon broke through and bathed the forest in its soft glow. Taking advantage of this, the six men ran full tilt through those ancient and myth-strewn woods, leaving behind the fiery carnage that was the Welsh Indian village.

To a place of doom they had brought a darkness of their own, and within that darkness burned the flames of vengeance.

Chapter 57

After a seemingly endless night of all-or-nothing running through the night woods, Alvord and the others had made it to their boat. Somehow they had managed to avoid the warriors who desperately sought to track them down along with the dogs whose howls were chillingly close by at times. Their plan was one of unabashed simplicity: run like hell. Never once had they stopped for rest. No- every man jack of them had run for hours on end, enduring the bugs, branches whipping them in the face, and the unshakable feeling of being intercepted by enemy units at any moment. At some point they had lost their pursuers, having made full use of the advantage of darkness and the orientation of Marcel.

As the sun began its ascent into the eastern sky, they forcefully shoved off that nameless, desolate little beach and rowed towards the safety of Superior's vast expanse. As it was early yet, a dense fog languished above the water. Once they had put sufficient distance between themselves and the shore they ceased paddling, exhausted and very much in need of rest. Their legs and feet ached something terrible, the numbing effects of fear and exhilaration having long worn off. In the calmness of the lake and its fog they basked, reflecting on just how lucky they had been to not only escape that churning Hell but escape unscathed at that.

"Well," said Finnbar, unsurprisingly the first to speak his mind, "damned if we didn't pull that off with a touch that would've made Midas green with envy."

"Agreed," Alvord wearily assented. "Whose your friend here?"

"Owain Crowder," the man introduced himself, equally weary.

The others grunted by way of introduction.

"I am formerly of Wales and, if irony is alive and well, no doubt a distant relation to some of those primitive shits we left behind. Many thanks for the aid there, impeccable timing..."

"You were held as prisoners, correct?"

Finnbar snorted. "Second incarceration of me life, Alvord. I'll take the St. Louis jail over that place anytime."

"You escaped on your own, then?" Thurgood was interested in their story, having once done it himself.

"This maniac of an Irishman here tricked some guard into thinking he was apoplectic. The fool actually let me out of my cell to aid him, and once Finnbar's cell was opened we took the guard by surprise."

"Sounds about right," chuckled Marcel, recalling their own prison break a few months back.

"So," Crowder continued, "your rescue coincided with our own escape efforts, the result being that dazzling fireworks display."

"Eat your heart out, Francis Scott Key," Gaston quipped, and they all had a tired chuckle.

Towards the notion of paddling no one lifted a finger, content with resting a bit longer. For an hour they let the ruddy, strengthening sun kiss their drained faces, feeling the subtle waves rock the boat ever so gently while shorebirds wheeled in the air above them. The fog began lifting and quite rapidly at that, dematerializing in the face of the burning sky above. This revealed the distant shoreline, so outwardly beautiful yet home to such horrors...

No one even made a move for the bread, pemmican, and salt pork that sat in a bag on the boat's bottom. Alvord found himself in a stupor unlike any he'd experienced. Having been denied proper food and sleep for days during which he'd been straining his body to its limit, he had achieved that leaden state of being wherein mind and body have been exhausted for so long that they think it the normal condition of things. In the same way Marcel suffered from that torpidity of the senses, resisting the urge to surrender to sleep as it urged him to accept the tenderness of its embrace...

Their rowboat bumped into something that nearly capsized it. For a panicked second Alvord's taxed brain leapt to the Indian legends of the *Mishi-ginebikoog* serpents and *Mishipeshu,* the great water lynx, but when he looked up he saw that they had struck a ship, a sleek, three-masted schooner that towered over them. Heads hung and eyes half-lidded, they had all failed to sight the vessel as during its phantom approach it cleverly made used of an intact section of nearby fog.

Nobody moved. It seemed injudicious to do so, given that at least a dozen guns were trained on them. At the center of the menacing figures that loomed above the rowboat stood Cadwallader Jones, whose usual severity of mien communicated nothing good to them.

A rope ladder was dropped, splashing into the water right next to their boat.

Jones's foghorn voice rang out across the calm waters.

"Please climb aboard, gentlemen. I would have words. Were I you, I would not attempt anything brave."

Not sure what else to do, they all followed his request. None knew exactly what to expect. If he wanted them dead, they'd be riddled with bullet holes, right? Somberly they climbed up the rope ladder. When all had made it they were directed to stand by the mainmast. Guns were lowered but kept at the ready. The men gripping those guns had the looks of thugs and killers about them. Alvord counted twelve, and another three other men who looked like ordinary sailors who hung back from the uninviting scene.

To the sailors Jones turned, face maintaining its usual degree of impenetrability. "Any sight of that fur company fishing vessel off the starboard side?"

"Nay, Cap'n," one of the sailors responded. "Lost her amidst the fog."

"Ah, no worries then."

"What do you want with us?" Finnbar demanded brashly. "We've got no patience for melodrama, if you're going to off us just get it done."

"Soon enough, Mr. Fagan."

Alvord tried to slough off the blanketing feeling of lassitude that still clung to him. He hated to admit it, but for perhaps the first time in his life he felt wearily resigned to his fate.

"Gentlemen, with the exception of Mr. Crowder here, whom I find to be a reprehensible human being, I never meant you harm. Mr. Rawn, Mr. Durand- surely you recollect that I warned you to give the Pictured Rocks a pass? My earnest advice met with gruff disregard. So what choice did I have but to alert my people as to your impending arrival? It was a pity, you seem like decent men, but my loyalty is, and has ever been, to my tribe."

Alvord watched the hired killers glance at one another, confused.

"He's one of them, lads," Finnbar informed the others. "He came to our cells two nights back and revealed all. As a youth he was sent to live among whites, to learn of their ways and find the source of their power and success in this land, so as to help secure the future of the tribe."

Jones heaved a world-weary sigh, his broad shoulders heaving pronouncedly under his overcoat.

"I just want you to know that you left me no choice. Had my words been heeded, then this tragic drama would never have been set in motion. So-"

"Quit trying to justify this to yourself and get on with it, you bombastic prick." Alvord, his rage rearing its head at seeing this bastard trying blame them for all this, felt the blood pump hot through his veins. If he was going to die, it would be with enemy blood fresh on his hands. From the corner of his eyes he noticed Marcel, Finnbar, and Gaston all shift their weight slightly, readying themselves for a charge. Their synchronized thought caught the attention of some of the hired thugs, who began raising their guns.

In that brief moment, which passed with dreamlike sluggishness, Alvord saw bodies hurl themselves over the other side of the ship, behind Jones and the other men, and he knew the time to act was upon them.

For he knew not how or why, but that was Elijah Colson leading the way.

Alvord charged with a bestial roar, thoughts of fatigue forgotten. The others followed his lead, each seeking out a gun-wielding foe. Shots rang out but not from the men they faced. In fact, two of them dropped, crimson stains sprouting on their shirts. The rest were understandably distracted by this, and some of them turned to assess this new threat.

Alvord made a beeline not for Jones but for a man right in front of him, who hip fired his rifle and missed him by a hair.

It was a costly miss.

Still at a run, Alvord swept aside the smoking rifle and head butted him so hard that his nasal bone was driven clear into his brain. The tremendous force of it rocked Alvord, but shaking his head clear of stars he sought out a new opponent.

Colson, Mick, and David, he saw fleetingly, were among a contingent of Chippewa warriors who, afraid to continue firing their rifles and bows because of the confusion before them, drew melee weapons as they swept in with rowdy war whoops.

Alvord smashed a rifle butt across a man's face before an Indian axed him from behind. Likewise working in unison with their rescuers, Marcel, Finnbar, and the rest fought like cornered animals. Though lesser in number, the Indians proved more than a match for those they faced.

However, in the next moment Cadwallader Jones entered the fray with a club trailing in his hand, and the men nearest him fell back under his withering onslaught. As good as the Indians were, he was their equal. He batted aside a tomahawk while weaving under a knife thrust, coming up in a lunge to hammer a skull. At the base of his club a wicked spike had been imbedded, and in a blurring spin he now sunk it into another brave's forehead. Wrenching it out he shouldered an oncoming Big Wolf to the ground. The doughty Chippewa lashed out with his tomahawk and sank its keen edge into the meat of Jones's thigh. The large man's howl of pain converted into one of fury and he brought his ornately carved club down at the Indian's face. Big Wolf rolled out of the way. David came at him swinging a rifle stock, but Jones merely grabbed it over David's grip and with a powerful jerk sent him skidding across the blood-spattered deck.

Jones saw that his crew would soon be decimated, and resolved to at kill as many foes as was in his power before Death winged its way towards him. Club raised, he swept towards a Chippewa warrior who was grappling with one of his men. As he readied himself for a killing blow he felt something strike him from behind. It burned coldly within him at first, but as the accompanying pressure grew it turned white-hot. Then he felt the wave of warm fluid run down his back and knew he'd been dealt a grave blow. Rounding on his assailant he beheld Finnbar, whose knife was still lodged in his back. He struck the Irishman a sledgehammer punch across the face, which opened a cut on his cheekbone and sent him down hard. From across the deck Walks-With Thunder tossed his tomahawk to Gaston, who sunk its blade into Jones's falling club and yanked it from his grasp. Jones backhanded Gaston and sent the half-breed reeling away with a broken nose, then took a moment to drag the knife out of his back. So great was the pain that when he drew its full length out it slipped from his trembling hand. He had no time to retrieve it, for Finnbar was upon him again like an undersized predator trying to fell his larger quarry.

He and Jones pummeled each other with fists, with Jones's strength fading but still demanding respect. He rocked Finnbar to his very marrow with a thunderous right hand, but with one eye closing and his nose pouring blood the Irishman laid into him with desperate punches. Through blurred vision he saw Jones falling back dazedly. In a blind fury he rushed in and tackled the larger man to the ground, shocked at how solid Jones was. Jones sharply elbowed him across the chin and, rolling away, Finnbar drew his push dagger. As Jones tried to rise the Irishman threw himself forward and with the full force of his weight behind him punched the dagger into his enemy's heart. Seizing Finnbar's arms, Jones pulled him close in something of an embrace, his amber eyes locked onto his vanquisher's.

"Take care of her," he wheezed horribly, "promise me that much."

"Aye," Finnbar gave surety to him in a breathless voice. Jones looked at him thankfully, relief flooding his rough face before a certain vacancy took hold of it.

"There is really no time for this... so much to be done... I simply haven't the time for this..." Jones spluttered, choking on his own blood.

As Finnbar watched the light go from his eyes, and in that moment comprehended the full measure of his foe, an enemy unlike any he'd encountered.

For the dying enigma before him was not one driven by avarice nor inborn malevolence. His lot in life was one that demanded he tread the barrier between two worlds, neither of which he wholly belonged to. A life steeped in secrecy and isolation was his, even when surrounded by others. In trying to become the savior of one world he became something cold, manipulative, and unknowable to the other. He had pledged his entire existence on this unforgiving earth to the furtherance of his people. And in death he had achieved the highest honor of his vocation- that of martyrdom.

Chapter 58

"So that, m'dear, is the whole of it. I am sorry beyond the measure of words."

Finnbar sat holding Genevieve's quivering hand in Jones's parlor room. An uncomfortable hour had been passed there as they had attempted to explain the extraordinary events leading to Jones's death. The girl had tried to put on a brave face, but sorrow won the day. Fat tears rolled down her tremulous cheeks despite her best efforts, and her body was racked by the occasional sob as she hid her face in Finnbar's handkerchief. They all understood her misery and confusion. Her world had, after all, been very swiftly turned on its head.

The Irishman looked at Alvord, Marcel, and David miserably. None of them knew quite what to say, and stared at the ground uncomfortably.

"There, there," he comforted, putting an arm around her. "I know this isn't easy, but 'twill be all right, I promise. We shall have a lawyer look over Jones's will once it is located, I am sure he made provisions for you, Genevieve. And again, we will have those sailors testify that Jones hit his head, fell overboard, and in the fog and confusion his body was lost to the lake."

It was an inefficient sop to her emotional state, but he felt obligated to say it anyway.

"But everything I thought I knew, *everything* I put trust in... it was all a lie. His actions- all those people killed... and to think that you nearly joined their ranks... oh, your poor face, Finnbar..."

She stopped speaking as more sobs set in. Finnbar, whose bruised face was indeed an artist's palette of post-fight shades of purple, yellow, and blue.

Giving the others a pointed nod, Alvord rose and they followed him, leaving Finnbar alone with her.

"Here lass, take this." He produced a gold ring in which two hands clasped a heart, which was surmounted by a crown.

"What is it?" she asked confusedly.

"'Tis a Claddagh ring. The bestowal of these rings is an old Irish tradition, and it symbolizes friendship and loyalty. I would like ye to have it, and I meself will wear its partner."

She smiled and reverently put it on her finger, but the ease it brought her could not outweigh the grief and confusion she still felt.

"I thank you, Finnbar, and shall wear it with pride, but Mr. Jones, I just cannot stop thinking about how he-"

"There is no denying the life he led. But he did love you, Gen. His dying words left that very clear."

Through shimmering tears she looked at him confusedly. "What did he say?"

Finnbar gazed upon her affectionately and, putting a hand to her face, wiped some tears away. "He told me to look after ye, lass."

Kissing her hand tenderly, he left.

Colson, Mick, Thurgood, Crowder, and Gaston waited for them outside the manor, throwing sticks for Cerberus and the other dogs to chase.

"How'd the girl take it?" Colson inquired earnestly. "Can't have been easy..."

"It wasn't," Finnbar admitted. "It'll take time, that's for sure."

They began walking back towards town, Alvord whistling for Cerberus as the rest of the dogs were brought in by Jones's servants, who it turned out had no idea of his secret life and now faced uncertain futures after his death.

"You reckon this is the end of it?" Marcel posed to Alvord, his voice implying that he himself doubted it.

"Knowing what I do now about Cadwallader Jones... something tells me this is far from over."

Purposefully, the burly bartender from the bowling alley strode out from the wood line, taking a moment to watch the receding forms of Alvord and the others. Striding through the knee-high grass of the field near Jones's manor, he reached the road and followed it to the doorstep, stonily watching the grackles scold him from the pines. He rapped upon the door firmly, taking a step back as he waited to be received. A tired-looking servant opened the door and asked his business.

"I have come to offer my commiserations to Miss Connolly."

The servant visibly hesitated, wishing that Finnbar and the others were still here in case this man's intentions were unpleasant. Honestly, he had no idea how the man even knew about Jones's death, for he himself had just been informed.

The man held up a sealed letter.

"Cadwallader Jones gave me this to give to the girl should he not return. I knew not his exact business, but I feel bound to let her have it. I don't know if it's a mere letter or perhaps his will..." his voice trailed off artfully, letting the servant's mind race as his eyes flitted over Jones's familiar seal.

"Do come in, then, sir. Your name?"

"Grigor will do just fine."

He waited patiently in the entrance hall for the servant to return with Genevieve. His interest strayed to a painting by a fellow named John Martin. Though he had never heard of the painter, the scene was one he knew well. Entitled *The Bard,* it depicted a romanticized scene from the English King Edward I ruthless conquest of Wales in the 13th century. Convinced that the bards, or professional poets of Wales, would keep old memories alive and one day incite rebellion, Edward ordered them all slaughtered. The sublime painting depicted the last of the bards, who had retreated to a craggy precipice overlooking a turbulent river far below. The King and his mounted forces were on the other side of the river from the berobed bard, who flung curses at them from the ledge. Tripe harp in hand, he was as defiant as the rock of the Snowdonian Mountains around him.

He was not a learned man, but this part of history was one that fascinated him. Grigor recalled and recited the last verse of the Thomas Gray poem also entitled *The Bard*:

Enough for me: with joy I see
The diff'rent doom our fates assign.
Be thine Despair and sceptred Care;
To triumph and to die are mine."
He spoke, and headlong from the mountain's height
Deep in the roaring tide he plunged to endless night.

"Excuse me?" Genevieve came into the entrance hall just as the last line fell from Grigor's lips. "How may I help you, sir?

She recognized him from town, but did not know the man.

"My name is Grigor, Miss Connolly." He bowed deeply, if not quite urbanely. "I own a bar in town. Firstly, I would like to offer my deepest sympathies for your loss."

He held forth the letter. "I was instructed by your Guardian to present you with this should he not return from his business out on the lake."

She took it from his hands, feeling fresh tears threaten to spill from her eyes yet again.

"Forgive me, Miss. I know it is a fresh wound. I would have given it some time, but there are things I need to do, and soon."

She shook her magnificent head. "This is no fault of yours, sir. Please, let us repair to the sitting room."

She led the way as Grigor shuffled behind her at his customary speed. She gestured that he take a seat and then perched atop one herself. That two male servants lurked in adjacent rooms did not escape her notice, nor that of her guest.

"I understand their concern, but I don't aim to hurt any of you, nor steal anything from this house."

Looking him over, she was apt to believe this thickset man. His was a rough but honest-looking face, and even the partially bitten-off ear failed to lend him a fiendish appearance.

"Why did Mr. Jones entrust you with this letter? Did you know him well?"

"As well as any, I suppose. We counted one another as a man to trust- I reckon even a friend."

"Do you know the circumstances surrounding his death?" Her voice, scratchy from crying, failed to belie her burning curiosity.

"I can guess, as I knew what business he was looking to tend to."

"As I was just informed of this myself by the only men who know it, how do you come to possess the information?"

He bow his shaven head humbly. "As a bartender I keeps an ear to the ground, Miss."

He thumbed his disfigured ear.

"I see." Genevieve felt strong and fearless at the moment, and was almost rapping out her responses to him. "Is that all, then?"

"You've come to hate him, huh?"

"He was a fiend in human form!" she hissed like a serpent. "His whole life was a black lie!"

Grigor leaned back folded his hands patiently. "His life, as it were, was marked by some, ah, deplorable necessities. Look here, I ain't putting his name in for sainthood, but now that you know his whole story, to say that he was not a great man would be an unpardonable insult. Men with far less on their plates than him have done far worse things in this life."

Her eyes widened in sudden shock. "Wait... 'now that I know his whole story'- do you mean that...?"

His eyes met hers almost apologetically. "Did you really think they would send only one? That the future of the entire tribe would rest on the shoulders of one individual who had no backup? Not so- I was sent out just as he. I stayed here at the Soo to act as his and the tribe's eyes and ears in this region, which I could do real easily from the bar I eventually opened. I was second fiddle to Jones, as you lot called him."

Her heart raced- the man made no move to hurt her, nothing in his entire demeanor suggested ill will, but..."

"What it is you want?" she asked nervously, her voice nearing a whisper.

He merely handed her another envelope.

"I need you to give this to the trapper Marcel Durand. Or David MacTavish, either one will do. They are then to deliver it to the chief of the Saulteur Chippewa, and tell them to stick around and listen to its contents. Important instructions have been provided therein."

"If you live in town, why not do it yourself?" she shot back at him defiantly.

Grigor chuckled dryly at her sass. "I told you. I *was* second fiddle to Jones. That makes me main fiddler at the moment. Time for me to resin up the bow, Miss."

He rose and left without saying goodbye, leaving her thunderstruck on top of grief-stricken.

She then opened and read Jones's letter to her, which explained his extraordinary personal history as well as the life of shadow he'd been forced to live. He made no excuses for his actions, instead merely relating the truth of the situation. Towards the end he addressed her on a more personal level, and at this her grief only deepened as she came to fully grasp the tragic complexity of the man she had viewed as a father figure.

Tears blurring her vision, she read on.

Words seem but cheap as I earnestly apologize for being an inexpert and often distant Guardian. Dearest Gen, I initially decided to become your Guardian for purely selfish reasons. Firstly, it made me appear more human to others, for only a man possessing of compassion would take in a child. No longer was I Cadwallader Jones, cold and enigmatic Great Lakes baron. No- I was now Cadwallader Jones, paragon of empathy. Your mere presence enhanced my character as it appeared to outsiders.

But another reason existed. It was my fervent hope that raising you, that learning to love and nurture, would tether me to whatever decency and morals I yet retained after a life of secretive plotting and cutthroat business. In this I was not disappointed. Watching you grow into a remarkable young woman not only kept me from wholesale malice towards mankind- it was also a rare honor the likes of which I did not deserve to be accorded in this life. You buoyed me above the beckoning shadows of my own distorted psyche. For that I thank you, my treasured Gen.

You should also know that I eventually came to regard you as a daughter rather than a ward. So too were you my only true friend on this earth, and for that I am forever grateful.

So easy it is to become a demon when you will brook no impediment to the salvation of those you protect. We wage war against our personal darkness, lest we be wholly consumed by it. You were my light, Gen, that twinkling light upon the distant shore that guided me through the straits of life as directly as was possible. I did not lead a life to be proud of, but I shudder to think what I might have become had I been bereft of your gladsome influence. Remember my story, and if ever you are called upon to be a beacon of hope to others, don't let the fear of failure lead to the shriveling of the soul.

In this fallen world, they often come in quick interchange.

Eternally yours,

C. Jones

Casting aside the letter, Genevieve put her face in her hands and wept like a child.

Chapter 59

Chippewa encampment. Dawn of the next day.

"How could this possibly take so long?" Alvord asked irritably of Father Bazin as they watched the proceedings in the Chippewa village. "This is rather cut and dry, is it not?"

"Oh, but it is not. You see, there is no single, unifying chieftain among the Chippewa. Those who live around here are mostly Saulteur Chippewa, but there are bands far to the north and west too. In fact, the far-ranging Bungee band has taken on many Plains tribe characteristics, including mounted buffalo hunts. A far cry from the woodland hunters and fishermen in these parts, I daresay. Among so diverse a people no single chief holds sway. Indeed, individual villages and even families retain much of their autonomy. At the moment, Marcel and some others are trying to gather warriors for the upcoming battle, as they were instructed to by that letter Marcel presented them."

"So not all are willing to fight?"

The Jesuit chortled deeply. "Not all are willing to believe the enemy human."

"And you, Father? You think that it's gods we are to face?" Alvord looked at him with a half-smile.

"No, my son. From what you have told me, I think they are simply men who were forced to become brutal, cunning savages or face extinction. It has, perhaps, made them something more than average men. Something altogether more bitter and ferocious. But as for gods- there is but one, and He brooks no rival."

Alvord grinned his appreciation at the priest's words. He liked the man; he had a sense of calm assurance and wisdom about him that did not lend itself towards the puffed-up pomposity that he'd observed in some men of the cloth.

Shaking his grizzled head, David left the considerable assemblage of hot-blooded young war chiefs and wizened-faced elders to go sit by Alvord and Bazin. He sat gingerly, for fear of pulling stitches.

"What news, David?"

The Scot shook his head darkly. "Nothin' good. At this point I'm rightly scunnered with all that gob. I'm without much delicacy in such matters. But Marcel- that gent's got a way with the red man."

Alvord watched Marcel addressing the semi-circle of prominent Indians, speaking in their tongue but talking with his hands just as much. Most of the younger men stood by stonily, but a few, with eagle and hawk feathers hanging from their long hair in honor of enemy kills, listened to him raptly.

"Can't the chief of the Saulteurs convince *his* warriors to fight?"

David bit himself off a chaw of plug tobacco. "Should stand to reason, Alvord, but it don't. Shamans and war chiefs decide things regardin' general warfare. A band chief has no coercive force at his disposal; his control over each situation hinges on personal prestige and the demands of the moment. But the good news is, a war party can be raised and led by any fighting man with a sufficient reputation."

"Which is what Marcel seeks to do?"

"Aye. And his reputation is a fearsome one. We shall see what comes of it, for while he is respected, not even a bona fide war chief can compel band members to join an expedition."

Alvord glanced around the village, where a knot of black-painted women were wailing and immolating themselves as they lamented the loss of their men in the customary Chippewa fashion. Kattawa's body, the only one recovered from the beach assault, was being prepared for burial alongside the two braves lost during the attack on Jones. Hair braided and dressed in glittering finery, their send off to the celestial hunting grounds would occur shortly before sundown.

"One would think that with these freshly felt losses, they would be clamoring for blood."

"Some certainly are," David assured him. "But others are still wary, there is talk of angering *Matchi Manito*, the Evil One. They think they need to appease him rather than fight. They feel that the *osuwahbik manitous*, the copper gods, are agents of his wrath."

Alvord ground his teeth in anger at the memory of the Chapel Beach attack. Soon enough those "copper gods" would feel the agent of *his* wrath.

Bazin spoke up in his frog-like croak. "Their Mide priests of the *Midewiwin*, the Mystic Doings Society, tell them the same. But there are young, angry warriors who want blood and care not for fairy tales. They know it is men they face and just need numbers enough to do it."

Alvord's eyes swept over the Indians who sat intently watching the council. "It is fortunate then that so many of the tribe are here at the Soo now. What drew so many?"

"Yearly payment from the government," answered David.

"And it is fortunate for sure. T'would take a long time indeed to organize a council this size, and some chiefs might simply not show. As it stands, many of those from Canada and the Wisconsin Territory are unconcerned with this matter. Feel as if it's not their problem."

A murmur of assent could be heard from the council. After taking a puff off an ornate ceremonial pipe along with the rest of the assembly, Marcel came over to them, frustration contorting his countenance.

"What's doing?" Alvord eagerly sought the information.

Marcel *humphed* scornfully. "What's doin'? It been decided that this here has to wait 'til tomorrow because Kattawa needs burin'. But I got Big Wolf, Walks With Thunder, and another young Saulteur buck of vaunted reputation what will rally to me, and they promised to spread the word among warriors seekin' vengeance."

The mountain man handed Grigor's letter to Alvord. "What time we supposed to meet that bastard?"

"Noon."

"Best go grab Finn and get a move on, then."

Big Wolf, Walks With Thunder, and the other Chippewa brave joined them, as did Father Bazin.

"Father," Marcel pointed out gruffly, "this sorta thing ain't really fit fer priests.

The unsightly old Jesuit regarded him equably. "Are you so forsaken that a man of God finds no place among you?"

Nothing more was said of the matter.

Chapter 60

As was dictated in Grigor's letter, they met the man at the headwaters of the St. Mary's River as the summer sun reached its zenith. It was a large fur barge on which they convened for the purpose of hashing out the details of the looming battle. For battle there was to be- Grigor's letter contained within it a brash challenge to the Chippewa.

The Montreal canoe Alvord rode in swung round to come abreast of the barge. He jumped out along with some others and made fast the canoe, watching his back as he did. Waiting imperiously for them on the barge's far side was Grigor and a small contingent of Welsh Indians. Conspicuous among them was the strapping one-eyed warlord, whose remaining eye flared upon recognizing Alvord.

The rest of their party exited the canoe and together they approached the enemy group. They took a moment to add their weapons to the pile that their enemies had started. Peace would prevail for today, if only to ensure the bloodshed of tomorrow. Finnbar, who had earlier been spending time with the grieving Miss Connolly, saw the one-eyed warrior staring daggers at Alvord.

"Large chap there doesn't seem overly fond of you," he quietly mentioned to his friend.

"Nor should he be."

Their group came to a halt, and for a moment all was hard, distrustful looks. No overt signs of aggression could be seen, but a keen eye would have perceived the hostility that simmered just under the surface.

"Who invited the blackrobe?" Grigor jerked his head at Bazin.

"I invited myself," Bazin informed him calmly. "Have you or your people retained any Christian traditions, my son?"

Grigor chuckled pityingly. "No, old man, we have not. We're devout pagans, if you must know. And our gods actually lend an ear when we entreat them."

Now it was Bazin who had himself a mocking chuckle, but Grigor appeared only amused. He stared with a slight grin and cocked eyebrows at the priest, beefy arms casually folded across his chest.

"What it is?"

"One would think that your people, having endured so much persecution and suffering, would have turned to the Lord. Instead you ran into the Devil's open arms."

Something sinister swept across Grigor's face. "Maybe the Devil was willing to lend an ear to us."

Bazin laughed again, shaking his head so that his sagging face swayed side to side like bull's dewlap.

"Somethin' funny, old man?"

"Honestly, it should not be, not from a priest's perspective. But with the knowledge I now have of you, I will now make no move to restrain my Christian Indians from fighting you. You unashamedly bear the Devil's brand; I now see no reason to try and talk peace to my flock."

Bazin turned to Marcel. "Your ranks swell, trapper."

"Much obliged, Padre."

Task accomplished, Bazin stepped back and folded his hands in his robe demurely.

"Alright, let's not get lost in righteousness here. To business, eh?" Grigor took a step forward. "Who am I addressing?"

At this Marcel took a leisurely step ahead, looking very unimpressed with Grigor. "That'd be me."

"*You* speak on behalf of the Chippewa?"

"Last I checked I'm headin' the war party."

"Our main feud is with the redskins."

"Why's that, now?"

The hefty fellow chuckled, as if the question were idiotic. "Many moons ago, we were persecuted and eventually driven out of Lower Michigan by these savages. So after all these years we will face them in open battle, and in cuttin' 'em down we'll avenge the memory of our ancestors."

This did not add up to Alvord, whose police mind sensed a lurking motive. Their beef should be with he and the others who had attacked the Welsh village...

"You there, big fella," Grigor pointed to Walks With Thunder. "Come forth and receive our challenge in your tongue. I don't want anything lost in translation."

The tall Indian stepped forth with poise.

"Take this message back to your chief."

Grigor nodded to one of the Welsh Indians, who began speaking to Walks With Thunder in what Marcel recognized as flawless Chippewa. He saw Big Wolf exchange confused looks with the other Indian, looks that soon changed to those of rage as they listened to the speech.

It did not last long. Walks With Thunder stared death at the man he'd been listening to before taking his place next to

Alvord.

"What did he have to say?" he asked the Indian.

"Much. He say my ancestors were dogs and that he and his people will drink from our skulls." The Indian turned his piercing black eyes on Alvord. "His scalp will grace my lodge pole."

Said Grigor to Marcel. "If it is you who leads them, then listen up. The Grand Sable Dunes- noon, a week from today. Smack dab in the center of those sands is the largest dune, you can't miss it, trapper. We're bringing three hundred warriors, and we intend to fight in the old way: hand-to-hand."

They could field three hundred warriors? Alvord wondered just how many of these people there were.

"We'll honor that," Marcel promised nonchalantly, and Alvord felt a thrill pass through him. Hand-to-hand was his preferred mode of carnage, after all.

"You and your crew here are welcome to join, we'd love to steep our hands in your guts after what you did to our village."

"Sounds good," replied the mountain man, so casually he almost sounded bored.

Grigor, possessing none of Jones's grace, spat on the deck of the barge. "We're gonna paint the sands red with your blood. You hear me?"

"Loud and clear, Your Corpulence," Finnbar assured him with a smirk and rigid half-bow.

For a moment each side stood glaring at the other. Alvord held the blistering gaze of the warlord until the two parties broke. He collected his weapons and returned to the canoe with the others. After they pushed off, the Welsh began punting the barge out towards Superior, where one of Jones's schooners waited for them.

"Well, this should be interesting," Finnbar considered out loud.

"A fight for the annals, not to be missed," agreed Alvord.

"Think of it, no? An extant, ragtag group of displaced Welshmen forging their destiny amidst the wilds of an uncharted North America? Much like Lucifer in Milton's Paradise Lost, they are tragic rebels in a world of ruin."

"And we the agents of that ruin. They are bloodthirsty savages and shall be dealt with as such."

"Aye, lad! This is downright poem worthy!" the Irishman exclaimed excitedly.

"You ready for round two with that eye-patched feller?" Marcel bluntly asked Alvord.

"He acquitted himself well in our first meeting. I look forward to escorting him to the afterlife."

The boat traffic on this section of river was significant for Superior, and many had seen the meeting on the barge. But none could comprehend the enormity of the events that tension-filled summit had set in motion.

Chapter 61

"Let's hope they don't renege on the deal and break out those bows of theirs," Finnbar voiced his concern as they lounged on the grassy bank of the St. Mary's. He, Alvord, Marcel, David, and Gaston had just concluded their training session for the day. Sparring with blunted weapons comprised the bulk of that training, although they did wrestle and box as well.

Gaston scoffed at him. "I'd rather face a few pointy arrows than guns, which they don't seem to have."

"Bows can be formidable weapons," Alvord interjected mildly. "Benjamin Franklin, who was no dunderhead, theorized that if the patriots had been proficient in the use of English longbows then the Revolutionary War would have been more easily won."

Nearby, Crowder and Thurgood shared a bottle of rum, with the Welshman talking to the fisherman about expanding his operations now that Jones's fishing fleets no longer had a stranglehold on the Whitefish Bay area.

"That un's mind never stops workin'," Marcel said of Crowder.

"Aye," agreed David amusedly as he ran the edge of his ancestral claymore over a grindstone, "nor scheming."

Five miners approached them unhurriedly, one of them being the hulking Jemmy Tresize. Upon seeing him Alvord sighed and wearily rose to his feet, tired from a day's training and none too eager to brawl with the beastly man. However, he angled his body towards Jemmy and began raising his fists.

"Easy there big fella," the Cornishmen spoke diplomatically, "I seek no quarrel with ye. Here, I brought a peace offering. Have a pasty."

With his oversized fist he bizarrely extended a basket of Cornish pasties, small meat-and-vegetable baked pies.

"What then might you want?" Alvord inquired coolly after accepting the basket.

"There's been whispers of eldritch things in the mining camp," Jemmy casually answered him. "Talk regarding the attack we suffered recently, in which one of me mates was killed. Some says twasn't Injuns what attacked us after all. If fact, some says the Injuns are plannin' a good old-fashioned dust up against those rumored to be behind that attack."

He ceased speaking and silently awaited a response.

Propping himself up on an elbow, David theatrically cocked a quizzical eyebrow. "Eldritch talk for sure, by the sounds of it. What concern of it is yours?"

"We wants in," the behemoth stated simply.

A smirk of satisfaction slid onto Alvord's face as he heartily shook the man's enormous, calloused hand. Maintaining that smirk, his gaze drifted west, where Madoc's progeny gathered their furies.

Later that night: Over a hundred miles to the west, the one-eyed warlord Cadoc stood atop the smooth, expansive cliff top of Grand Portal Point in the Pictured Rocks. With his remaining eye he took in the moon-flooded world before him. Upon those vast, somber wastes of Superior he stared, like a poet searching for his muse.

The night was clear and, although eclipsed by the glory of the moon, the stars also lent their light to the scene. From out of the wood line fifty feet behind him drifted an imperial female form. The figure padded silently across the sandy cliff top, knowing that Cadoc would be aware of her presence despite her stealthy movements. She came up next to him and looked out upon the shimmering lake.

"Brangwen," he greeted the young, blonde-haired ruler of the tribe, a direct descendant of Madoc himself.

"A call to thought?" She asked in the Welsh Indian tongue, her question verging on the rhetorical.

"There is much to think of." For so large and powerful a man, his voice was soft and dulcet, like the rustling of wind through dry grass.

"I'll grant you that, Cadoc. What plagues your mind and ruins your sleep?"

Her own voice was fluid, with an indescribable quality to it that was found very attractive to the opposite sex.

"It is the plan. Everything hinges on its flawless execution, and it has been both altered and accelerated because of recent events."

"The death of Jones," she said sadly. "A true pity. We owe him everything- he always did well by us, and without him none of this could be achieved."

"The subsequent attack on our village is more troubling yet. Our location and therefore our security has been compromised. Each day we risk another attack. The Indians will seek to wipe us out now that they know us for what we are, and since their death we have not the magic of Holy Ones to protect us any longer. I know that Grigor needed this week to make preparations, but our position remains a perilous one. Tomorrow I lead our force towards the Great Dunes to make camp near the battle-site, but I will breath easy once we have met our enemies upon the sands."

She touched his powerful arm gently, but still he did not look at her. "You can come with us, you know. There are men making the journey but none such as you, no true leader. There will be tasks for us where we go, mining included-"

"I cannot. That life is the furthest thing from my desire."

"What it is you want then, Cadoc?"

Finally he turned his blazing blue eye towards her. "I want to die, Brangwen. And die well."

She said nothing in reply, letting him continue.

"The path set before you and the others is not one I can walk. I am a warrior, and will depart this world as such. The refuge you seek, the life you will be forced to lead... it is not for me. That is why my soldiers and I embrace death in two days time. It is not about restoring honor to our people, it is not about the past of our ancestors- it is about serving the tribe in the present, and in doing so choosing how we die."

Brangwen let out a cynical half-chuckle. "And if, which would not surprise me, none can bring that death to you?"

"There is one who will be there, a force to be reckoned with. He will be a more deadly enemy than I have faced yet. And should any of us survive the battle, we shall seek death somewhere else, for in it lies our only freedom. This world hems us in on all sides, having no place for us any longer. So we will oblige it by fading like ghosts from its stage, knowing that our legacy lives on."

The beautiful tribal leader gave him a tragic little smile. "You are a noble man, Cadoc. Rest assured that your son will know of your deeds, and grow to be a man you would be proud of."

Cadoc turned and gently placed his mighty palm against her stomach. He returned her smile, his remaining eye locked on hers.

"They will continue to look up to you, particularly once their whole world has so drastically changed. Lead them well, Brangwen."

Although she still smiled, a tear ran down the pale skin of her face. She stood on her tiptoes and tenderly kissed him on the lips. As soundless as a cat on the prowl, Brangwen moved off, leaving Cadoc to his reflection.

The rocks, untroubled by thoughts of such magnitute, maintained their lonely vigil over the gleaming water of the lake.

Back at the Soo, Alvord stared up at the formless black of his tent's ceiling. He could not sleep, and it had nothing to do with the frogs, the crickets, or any of the other night sounds that the woods around the Indian encampment resounded with.

His mind slowly but unalterably strayed across a gulf of time to a scene from years earlier, in Manhattan. His wife Katherine was still alive then, and he lay next to her in the cozy fastness of their bedroom. Like now, he was wide-awake and broodingly pensive.

In her firm but mellifluous voice, she spoke to him. Through the mists of recollection he almost fancied that he smelled her.

"Alvord, what troubles you my love?"

"I would rather not speak of it."

She was the wisest person he had ever met, and was never one to indulge his occasional bouts of melancholia. "You are many things, Alvord Rawn, but a brooding fool is not one of them. It will lessen the burden on your heart if you simply talked to me."

A moment of unbroken silence passed between them before Katherine spoke again.

"Is it Isabel?"

They had lost their youngest child to a cholera outbreak four months earlier. The suffering that that disease had visited upon their daughter was forever seared into their souls. The only consolation, and a deficient one at that, was that Isabel had passed swiftly and her agony was short-lived.

"Aye, in part. But it began when we lost Bridget."

Their second-born child had died before her first year passed. They found her one morning in her truckle bed, rigid in the way of the dead. The physicians had not been able to offer any satisfactory explanations as to why.

"Alvord, even you cannot deal with such losses like some cold, inanimate hunk of granite. They invariably take a toll, and to ignore that is unwise."

He sat up, looking down at his rugged, scarred hands. Turning them over, he stared at his palms before clenching them into massive fists.

"I fear that I am losing control, Katherine."

She had gently placed her smaller, silken hands over his own; that detail would never slip through the cracks of his memory.

"What do you mean by that?"

"Violence. Killing."

"Such things, while unfortunate, are sometimes unavoidable aspects of your occupation. You are a patrolman and a detective, Alvord. And the very best among them, what's more. Being vigilant and dauntless, its stands to reason that violence and killing find you more than others."

He turned and looked at her with the eyes of a haunted man.

"I enjoy it, Katherine. It has nothing to do with law or justice or vengeance or circumstance- I have actually begun to derive enjoyment from it. Grim and awful enjoyment."

Her eyes suddenly distant, she let him speak.

"After Bridget, it was as if something took root inside of me and now it's growing, fed by more recently felt loss..."

"So fight it. Keep it at bay." She paused and considered her next words carefully. "But don't altogether lose it."

Her wisdom had confused him. "What do you mean? Is this bloodlust not the lure of the Devil?"

"Mayhap it is, but sometimes the Devil's devices come to be turned against him. They become the very instruments of his undoing."

"So you do not think me evil for this?"

"No, Alvord," she had said to him across the darkness. "It just makes you a singularly dangerous man."

Chapter 62

It was a truly beautiful day.

The midday sun shone merrily upon the Grand Sable Dunes, which rose silent and sublime from Lake Superior's mirror-calm waters. High above the sands a turkey vulture hung motionless, a ragged patch of black outlined against the cerulean sky beyond. Insects droned and birds twittered idly among the dune grass and stunted trees. A deer, feeding as casually as any wild beast can afford to, noticed with a start the line of upright figures that suddenly crested a dune's rim just to the east. Another group appeared to the west- feeling threatened, the animal raised its feathery white tail and silently bounded across the sands to the refuge of a nearby copse of trees. The solemnly convening men ceased walking, and there was something sinister in the act.

It was a beautiful day and there was killing to be done.

Alvord felt as if he and his compatriots had entered upon a scene of stark unreality, but it was one that he could embrace without hesitation. For there they were, Madoc's Legacy, ranged along the far rim of the dune just one hundred yards away. With the glint of sun upon weapons and burnished copper armor, they waited.

Taking a rough count, he reckoned the enemy's number to be around three hundred, as promised. Their own numbers were approximately the same: the boldest and most decorated warriors among the Saulteur Chippewa, along with some hell-roaring half-breeds and whites. Alvord unhurriedly shifted his gaze from the assembling ranks of enemies to the boundless lake that might have been monotonous but for the richness of its hue and immensity of its scope. A steamship left its frothy wake two miles off shore as it chugged its way west towards the Keweenaw, but it might as well have been a world away.

He returned to the moment, letting his eyes settle on the Welsh Indian warlord, whose strapping build and regal bearing were evident even from this distance. As he watched, Alvord saw the man look left, then right. Appearing satisfied with the bold assemblage of warriors around him, he stared across the sands directly at Alvord as he slowly lifted his long-handled war club skyward.

With the wail of some unearthly instrument, the ranks of the enemy began their pre-battle pageantry. Weapons clashed against wooden shields and copper breastplates at regular, ominous intervals. That awful horn that had sounded during the attack on Chapel Beach was given voice once more, pulsating the sand beneath their feet. Drums were rhythmically pounded and shrill flutes played, while the men shouted forcefully, baying for blood.

Alvord but sneered at their antics. They wanted blood, did they? He'd give it to them. He'd drown them in a frothing torrent of their own. He'd steep his goddamn hands in it.

He had an edge, he supposed. Because towards the notion of living or dying he simply didn't spare a damn. For if he died today then he would write his own epitaph upon these sands in a turgid stream of enemy blood. Somehow the Romantic in him almost pitied those howling, bloodthirsty men across the dunes as they braced for their final act of derring-do. The approaching hand-to-hand battle with these ancient white colonists was one wholly out of place and time, the whole scene came off as so very anachronistic...

But the devil on his shoulder did not pretend to care.

The Chippewa now gave vent to their own shrieking, ululating war cries, and soon the air hung heavy with death threats and proclamations of fearlessness. As the warlord had, so too did Alvord look to those on both sides of him. Finnbar stood to his left, breathing heavily and looking murderous, while Marcel, composed and prepared, was on his right. On Finnbar's other side stood Big Wolf, who at that moment turned his freshly scarred face to Alvord. He had thin red lines painted vertically on his face like streaks of blood, and the fringed crest of his dyed-red porcupine roach rose above the eagle feathers that completed his headdress. A bear-claw necklace hung around his neck.

"Walk well," he said simply.

Next to him was Walks With Thunder and Thurgood, who desperately wished to be a part of this battle. The fisherman had old scores to settle. Lightfoot too had insisted on joining them, despite his still-mending arrow wound. On Marcel's right were Gaston and David, who both watched the proceedings with cold, bleak eyes. Aside from a handful of white miners and half-breeds the rest were Chippewa Indians, mostly Saulteurs, with mohawks shaved and faces fearsomely tattooed and painted.

Alvord allowed himself a terse smile. For these were men to draw blood beside.

The noise of defiance rose in volume. It wouldn't be long now.

It suddenly struck Alvord as it hadn't before. And it was not dread that it inspired but reflection. If he breathed his last today it would be here of all places, here on these resounding sands on the outer rim of nowhere...

In response to the sentiment, deep within him something primal reared its head and made known its awful power. And in that power was dominion over death.

"How's that poem coming, Finnbar?" he wondered aloud. "You said this day was poem worthy."

Still staring straight ahead, Finnbar instantly began reciting.

Stirrings of madness call us to the fore
To raise War's banner high above this place
A land well-steeped in mystery: what's more
Upon these hallowed sands 'tis gods we face.

Recalling deeds of heroes long to dust
We know they may exist on either side
But who will Fortune with her crown entrust?
Who swept up in Oblivion's dark tide?

The prospect of Eternity looms large,
Too ponderous to balance, or to weigh.
We steel ourselves for this impending charge,
And shall press ever onwards- come what may.

At Finnbar's words a tingling warmth that originated in Alvord's heart soon spread to his head and the rest of his body. The hairs on his arms and legs stood rigid and his muscles convulsed ever so slightly as a shiver born not of fear, but of exhilaration passed through him. His head buzzed and the blood sang in his ears. He inclined his head, closed his eyes, and drank it in- for it was absolutely intoxicating.

"Come what may," he repeated in a whisper to the expansive sky above. "Well done, Irishman."

Marcel slowly nodded his approval of the poem.

"Boisterous lot," he commented, idly testing the edge of his new, fearsome tomahawk. "Let's see if we can't find the yeller in 'em."

David chuckled menacingly, his lengthy Scottish claymore resting easily on his shoulder. "Aye, brother. And the red."

Someone bumped into Alvord from behind, whom he saw to be a young Chippewa brave, face screwed up bravely but still subject to involuntary quivers of fear. He sidled in next to Alvord, breathing irregularly. The smell of fresh vomit hung around him. Jemmy and his miners passed a bottle of rum down the line of fighters, from which men took sips to bolster their courage. Alvord merely passed it along without sparing it a glance, but the young brave next to him gulped more than his share.

Alvord looked down at him, and noticing this the lad met his eyes.

"When this gets underway, you stick close, boy."

Father Bazin stepped out from the ranks of Indians and in a stentorian voice began reciting a prayer in Latin. Alvord bowed his head and prayed for God's blessing along with the other Christians present. Prayer concluded, the Jesuit took his leave, and howling silence presided for a moment brief and weighty as the rest of the men entreated whatever gods they held dearest. Alvord smiled sardonically when he saw the Welsh warlord lower his weapon to level it directly at him.

The inevitable battle was preceded by a final roar from each side, but the charge itself was mostly breathless. Men streaked down the sides of the dune towards its level bottom, where two armies would collide.

With the poetic clash of weaponry, they met. Bodies thudded into one another and Chippewa moose hide shields met those of wood. The Welshmen were dire hand-to-hand fighters, and the Chippewa, whose fighting had grown more long-ranged as they acquired firearms, were at a slight disadvantage overall. Weapons found their marks, and horrific death screams rang out over the tumult. In the opening seconds the luckless fell alongside the less skilled, the first wave of casualties. The seemingly impenetrable tranquility of the Grand Sable Dunes was convulsed by the savagery of battle, and Death prowled the sands.

His boots rasping against sand and dune grass as he made his descent into the dune, Alvord focused on his breathing and the enemies who pounded towards him. Wielding a large gunstock war club in his right hand and his artillery short sword in his left, he did not sprint to meet the enemy as many did. It had nothing to do with cowardice or lack of zeal. He simply knew how quickly the lungs strained under the stress of battle, and had no desire to be gasping for air before this thing was well and truly underway.

Men were already fighting just in front of him, Finnbar included, and over them a Welsh warrior made a fantastic leap. Upon landing he promptly ran an Indian through and then charged Alvord, bloodied spear at the ready.

Without losing speed, Alvord blurredly spun around the spear thrust and jammed his sword point-first into the side of its wielder's neck. Its edge scraping vertebrae, he slid the sword out and boldly waded into the thick of it.

Alvord found himself fighting alongside Marcel and David, the course of the initial clash having driven Finnbar off to their left. The two trappers fought like madmen, weaving in and out of questing enemy weapons like wisps of smoke. The fearsome claymore was as lethal in David's hands as the tomahawk and Bowie knife were in Marcel's.

A snarling man leapt at Alvord, sword aloft, but the battle-hardened former patrolman simply booted him in the chest, denting his copper breastplate with a hollow thud. The man went down hard, hacking up blood. With a harrowing underhanded swing the gunstock war club split his face open and sent his carcass hurtling backwards into two of his fellow warriors. Before they could recover Alvord was upon then, spinning his club so that the iron spearhead positioned on the elbow of the curved weapon faced forward. This he swung with deadly purpose into the skull of one man as he sent his sword streaking into the other's chest.

Freeing both weapons with a decisive tug, he flexed his brawny shoulders and bellowed his fury at a knot of approaching foes.

"*Come to me!*"

Something whizzed past his face and in the next moment he saw a huge Bowie knife buried into the frontrunner's shoulder, just above his shield. Alvord did not need to check to know who had flung the weapon so lethally. In his agony the wounded man stumbled and fell. One of the other warriors tripped over him and his face met Alvord's mightily swung club. His lifeless body flipped head over heels into the others, who fought to get out of Alvord's way.

"*Haw*!" Marcel exclaimed as the tide of the battle moved away from them. "You've got the hair of the bear today, Al!"

That was fitting. Before the battle Alvord had actually smeared bear grease on his joints in the Indian manner, as it was thought to limber one up. The Romans had done likewise, with bear and lion tallow, always beasts of power. And damn, but he felt fluid and strong.

As they took some wind-restoring breaths, David shot past them and cleaved a shield with a swipe of the claymore, mangling the arm holding it. Struggling to free the blade, the Scot took a retaliatory club swing. As weapons rose to deliver killing blows, Big Wolf, Walks With Thunder, and Thurgood swept to his rescue. Fiercely driving the Welsh warriors back, they bought David a moment to recover and retrieve his weapon. Marcel helped him up swiftly, having to block a sword stroke a moment later. He sent the man reeling away with a gaping knife wound to the leg, but he himself took a knife in his thigh. David skewered the bawling man with a desperate thrust as he and Marcel limped over to join Thurgood and the two Indians. Back-to-back, they formed a formidable fighting ring. Alvord moved on; those men fought well as a unit, but as for himself, he needed room to swing.

Men died in droves, and during the initial onslaught the lines of battle were quickly blurred. In some spots there were no longer any ranks at all, and men fought each other singly and in groups. In such jumbled confusion, the man next to you was not necessarily on your side.

Brandishing both his weapons, Alvord swung across his body, and while his opponent did expertly block the blows, he was flattened by their raw power. The young Indian Alvord had stood alongside went to lance the man but he agilely rolled into the brave, taking out his legs. From his knees the Welshman raised his sword, which Alvord sent sailing out of his grip with a hard-swung blow. As the young brave grappled with the man, a group of fighting men drifted between they and Alvord, so he sought out a fresh foe. There were so many struggling figures around him that often he only engaged an enemy for a moment's time before the unpredictable flow of the fight bore them along.

Blood-drunk, Alvord felt an eerie elation settle over him in this scene of roiling carnage. Delivering a debilitating head butt to another comer after parrying an axe swing, he flipped a charging enemy over his back into the lethal spear of a waiting Chippewa brave. A Welsh Indian dual-wielding a sword and an axe engaged him, and their ensuing clash was a feverish one. Alvord took a cut to his shoulder and a thrust wound to his stomach that only his heavy, oilskin vest prevented from being grievous. Crossing his weapons, he violently drove them forward and deflected the oncoming axe back into the man's painted face. He then took the skilled warrior's leg out from under him with a kick, and an Indian swiftly caved in his skull with a ball-head club, giving Alvord a nod before moving on.

As he stood taller than most, Alvord rapidly scanned the area and saw a knot of Welsh Indian warriors ferociously repulsing oncoming enemies. Cutting down Chippewa fighters like a scythe through wheat, they left a growing stream of dead and dying men in their wake. A dozen or so of the most skilled men on each side accounted for a disproportionate number of deaths, and he knew that taking out that group could very well change the tide of the battle.

Letting rage more fully possess him, Alvord scattered men like ninepins as he hurled himself headlong at that group, hoping to find the one-eyed warlord among them.

Stepping over the convulsing body of a dying Indian, Finnbar regrouped with Gaston and Lightfoot. His breathing was ragged, as was theirs. Having gained a moment's respite by cutting a bloody swath through enemy lines, they took a knee behind the sparse foliage of a stunted Jack Pine, one of the only blemishes on this otherwise fitting battlefield. Finnbar felt as if his lungs might collapse- he had expended far too much energy on the charge and the initial, brutal fighting. He recalled that in battle the Romans had rotated their troops to keep them fresh, and now he knew why. For at present, fatigue rendered him terribly vulnerable and helpless, and whilst in the heat of battle there is no feeling more awful nor keenly felt.

He was not alone in his exhaustion. Gaston and Lightfoot both sucked wind as well, chests heaving as they struggled to slow their breathing. Above the din of battle they all heard an animalistic roar and, seeking its origin off to their right, beheld a blood-drunk Alvord dealing death to all comers.

"Crazy bastard's on the warpath," Lightfoot said in amazement.

"Still, I wouldn't say we're winning," stated Finnbar, eyes flitting over the battle. Watching for just a few seconds demonstrated that the Welsh Indian's skill, armor, and weaponry proved a match for the speed and skill of the Chippewa and their allies. Some of their enemies had weapons lodged in their copper breastplates but still fought on.

Having regained some of their wind, they rose just as an attacker leapt over the tree and sent his sword into the meat above Lightfoot's collarbone. The trapper savagely dented the man's temple with his ball-headed war club as Gaston knifed his kidney.

"Goddamn... piece... of... *shit*!" Lightfoot said through gritted teeth in between club swings.

"You alright?" Gaston asked, watching the blood seep from his new wound.

His words were ignored. "Let's move."

They went to rejoin the main fray when a strident whirring sound assaulted their ears. Finnbar saw a Welsh Indian perched atop the crest of the dune, where earlier their entire force had assembled. Above his head the man whirled something in a blur that emitted the piercing sound. In a flash

Finnbar took stock of the situation, and his stomach soured as it suddenly dawned on him...

"NO!" The word had barely left his mouth when a considerable pack of the massive Welsh Indian dogs tore across the dune, towards the far end of the sandy basin where some of the Indians were actually driving the Welsh back. After them came at least twenty men, who also angled across the sands to join the fracas.

"Jesus Christ!" Gaston spat in disbelief.

Finnbar's mind raced while his heart spasmed with fear. "C'mon, we've got to flank them!"

Kicking up sand, they tore across the dune. From their location they managed to skirt the throbbing heart of the fight and pursue the dogs and men that now fell upon the suddenly outnumbered Indians. This was on the far right side of the battle, where the Chippewa had just gained the upper hand. They now faced a new and terrible threat in the dogs, to say nothing of the fresh warriors that loomed in their wake.

Finnbar, Gaston, and Lightfoot doggedly pursued the newly arrived warriors. In mid-stride Gaston snatched up a fallen spear and put into it every ounce of strength he had. The spear zipped through the battle-stirred air and took a Welsh Indian through the jaw. The other warriors engaged the Chippewa braves, who fought with the affronted wrath of those who knew they'd been deceived. Not only were they now outnumbered, but frenziedly fending off the massive hounds to boot. Things looked inexorably bleak, but a second later Finnbar and the others fell upon the Welsh Indian flank. Hacking and stabbing furiously, they felled five enemies before they knew what hit them. Capitalizing on this state of flux, the Indian's counterattacked with renewed vigor, spears and tomahawks finding flesh.

"That's our cue!" shouted Elijah Colson as he saw the Welsh Indian reinforcements break their cover of a small pine forest above the sprawling dune. Drawing his cutlass and Alvord's Colt Walker, he led the way after removing the leash and muzzle from Cerberus. The snarling dog shot out in front of them, moving with awe-inspiring power and agility.

He, Mick, Crowder, and fifteen gun-toting Chippewa warriors and half-breeds came pelting out of the aspen grove they were watching the battle from. It was on Alvord's advice that they followed the Chippewa war party to the dunes. The former police captain had not trusted their enemies to honor the terms of battle, and thank God he had acted on that stabbing of instinct. On his orders, Colson was to be ready to lead the other men but was not to join the fracas until the enemy's deception unfurled.

No holds were barred after this. With a rousing yell they thundered into the battle's roiling core, ready to make up for the enemy's perfidy or die in the attempt.

Alvord saw the Welsh Indian reinforcements, but with satisfaction knew that Colson and his force awaited just such a happening. He focused on his own life-and-death struggle. With one disarmed enemy clinging to him like a leech, he frantically fended off another man's sword. He lost a weapon but gained an opening when he sunk his war club into the sword-wielder's copper cuirass in a death-dealing blow. Biting the ear off the man who tried to wrestle him, Alvord finally shook the bastard off. Arms a blur, he alternately punched and sliced the man's face into a mass of raw, mutilated flesh and bone.

This was no battle- it was a goddamn bloodbath. And Alvord Rawn was in his element.

As a sword hissed towards his face Alvord shoved it aside after catching it on his own blade. Someone smashed into him from behind and he stumbled forward half a step. The swordsman punched him in the cheekbone with his weapon's pommel before drawing the blade down slantwise across Alvord's chest and ribs. Again, the oilskin vest offered him some measure of protection and the steel did not bite too deeply, a fact that cost the swordsman his life. Alvord severed the tendons of his sword hand with a strong downward hack and then, throwing a shoulder into him, picked the screaming man up. He ran for several steps with the man in the air, using his helpless body as a battering ram against two Welsh Indians who had teamed up against a hard-pressed miner. The bone-rattling impact sent them all to the ground hard, and as Alvord got to his feet he saw David dirk a rising foe. The blood-drenched Scot tossed Alvord his claymore, his telling gaze revealing that an enemy approached from behind. Although ragged of breath and fatigued, Alvord promptly turned and swung the two-handed sword for all he was worth. The force of it divested the oncoming attacker's head from his body with incredible ease.

"Swung like a true MacTavish!" the Scot approved, catching his weapon as Alvord threw the awesome sword back his way.

Alvord heard a deep-throated bellow and saw the colossal Jemmy Tresize nearby, with a Welsh Indian clinging to his back and another two seeking an opening before him. But they were not willing to get too close to his two-handed sledgehammer, which he wielded with one hand as if it were weightless. With his other monstrous hand he hurled the man on his back to the ground, stomping in his chest cavity. Alvord moved in and slashed into the spine of one of Jemmy's attackers. This freed up the miner to charge like a raging bull, and in the blink of an eye he had laid the other assailant low with crushing blows of the hammer. The sword cut he took to the chest hardly seemed to faze him as it seeped blood down his shirt.

"Not dead yet?" he shouted to Alvord with an exhilarated grin.

Breathing heavily, Alvord smirked in reply and charged alongside Jemmy, towards where their forces were battling the fresh wave of enemy troops that included the deadly gray hellhounds.

Finnbar, Gaston, and Lightfoot had made an initial difference. But the dogs- oh, those fucking dogs! They were the devil to take down. Twice Finnbar sunk his knife into the animals, up to the hilt. Yet it was only when he buried the spike on the ball of his ironwood club into a canine skull that he garnered the fruits of his labor. The beast crumpled but another took its place, and he was once again giving ground frantically, dodging the massive, frothing jaws. Gaston and an Indian came to his aid, but even after a lance had been sent through its ribcage the beast reared up and tore out the Indian's throat.

These beasts had Irish wolfhound blood or something close, and Finnbar knew that wolfhounds were once feared as war hounds, their prowess on the battlefield surpassing even that of mastiffs. This he acknowledged as he found himself pinned under the wounded wolfhound with its blood and saliva dripping teeth inching closer to his face with every snarl. His failing grip dug into the dog's muscular throat but did not deter it. He realized in horror that the beast was poised maul him.

But then bursting upon the scene was Cerberus, sinking his teeth into the larger dog's face and shredding it with a gruesome rending of flesh.

The Chippewa nearby had formed a rough shield-wall and were slowly falling back. The more numerous Welsh had a shield-wall of their own and hurled themselves at their foes, who continued yielding ground grudgingly. Hard-pressed by a sea of enemies in front of them, none of the Chippewa chanced a look behind them. They had been backing up the gradual slope of the far side of the dune. The rim of it was also part of another, smaller basin right beside, this one shallow but sheer-sided, and comprised purely of sand. The rim began collapsing under their weight, and seeing this the Welsh Indians pressed their offensive, relentlessly pushing them back. With yells of shock and dismay over thirty Indians fell down the shifting slope, along with Finnbar, Gaston, and Lightfoot.

The Welsh Indian shield-wall roared its triumph and began launching spears at the easy targets below them. But at that moment Alvord and Jemmy thundered into them, with Marcel, David, and a tight formation of Indians at their back. The two forces met; most men who still retained the ability to fight were here, joined in close-quarter battle.

The moments that followed were sheer butchery.

Part of the Welsh shield-wall turned to face Alvord and Jemmy, who barreled into them with such impetus that shields splintered and men toppled backward into the sand pit from the shockwaves. The sandy rim of the pit gave way again once the two forces met atop it, and some of the Welsh Indians began spilling into the basin, where Finnbar and the others were waiting for them.

The exhausted Irishman doled out thudding blows with his club, his world so narrow that he was no longer a thinking, reasoning being. The fact that never before had he been a part of so insane a battle did not cross his mind. Survival and the killing it would take to achieve that end were his sole thoughts and they were more like an animal's impulses than a man's rationalizing. One fallen warrior held up his hands imploringly but Finnbar did not even register the act. He heard the crunch of bone behind him and looking back saw the sightless eyes of Lightfoot, whose brain leaked out of his skull like an egg yolk. An enraged Finnbar fought on. He was knocked to the ground at one point, whereupon he lost his spiked club but snatched up a sword and immediately resumed swinging when he regained his feet.

All around Finnbar in the shifting sand pit, men sliced, battered, and wrestled each other in a barbaric dance of death. Above him the remaining men of both sides frenziedly sought to bring this blood-soaked battle to a close.

With twin strokes of his short sword Alvord struck a man's head from his shoulders. He paused to rip out the thin knife the man had jammed into his side and then drew his truncheon form his belt. Shouldering the decapitated body into more enemies, he saw Jemmy make a mad dash for the one-eyed warlord, whose mighty club had created a tangled pile of corpses at his feet. Rushing out to meet him in the open space he had created, the warlord made a lissome leap over the charging miner, who tackled naught but air. The one-eyed warrior's club butt was rammed into Jemmy's spine before the weapon pulverized the head of another miner. To Cadoc's surprise, the now-weaponless Jemmy bulled into him, driving home a stiff left hook followed by a looping but punishing right hand. He fell to the earth hard but nimbly rose to bring his mace thudding into Jemmy's chest, and the wounded miner stumbled back before tripping over a carcass his feet got tangled up in.

Alvord was upon Cadoc after that.

His sword swing was meant to take the cyclops in the neck, but at the last moment he saw it coming and jerked his head back. Alvord missed and as a consequence felt the butt of his enemy's huge mace collide with his ribs. He went down but shot his leg out, striking the man on his kneecap. This he followed up with a truncheon thrust that dented his foe's copper cuirass and sent him staggering backwards. Alvord rose swiftly but too many men came between them. The Welsh Indian's poisonous, one-eyed stare lingered on him for a second's time. Then, with a collection of tough-looking followers at his back, the warlord led the way around the pit to a grassy area below, where they would regroup.

Gunshots ran out. The Indian and half-breed reinforcements took careful aim and quickly evened out the odds against them. Colson emptied the Colt Walker into the archers who were targeting enemy outliers on the battlefield. He and Mick then led the other reinforcements in a sweeping charge that turned the tide of the battle on the dune's rim. Mick slit a man's throat and raised his flintlock at the approaching Welsh warlord, but the man closed the distance between them with a lightning roll. He rose with a knife in his grasp, which he plunged into the spot where Mick's chin met his throat. The blade pierced his brain, killing him instantly. With an incensed roar Colson swung his cutlass at the man, who bobbed under it before shouldering him off the rim of the dune and into the cauldron of chaos that was the sand pit. He and his elite warriors continued fighting their way to the grassy meadow below, where Destiny would seize them.

Gaston and Finnbar were faced with a tall, brawny foe who had them both on their heels. Gaston flung a knife that lodged itself in their opponent's breastplate, but it did not stop the man from doling out minor injuries to them both. It was only when David leapt down the side of the pit and dropkicked the Welsh Indian in the side of the head that he was put down.

Out of nowhere a sword sliced through the air, messily lobbing off Gaston's left hand at the wrist. Wound hemorrhaging blood, Marcel's son simply stared at it a moment before collapsing in a heap. Marcel saw this from above, and like

Heaven's wrath he descended upon the guilty party. He disarmed the man with a deft move using his knife and tomahawk, severed his fingers in the act. He then looped his tomahawk blade up into the shrieking man's groin and relished it for a grim moment before unleashing his lifeblood with an expeditious slash across the throat.

Crowder joined him, breathless and eager to quit the savage fighting, and together he and Marcel addressed Gaston's appalling wound.

Alongside the Chippewa, Finnbar and Gaston had won the corpse-strewn, blood-bespattered pit.

The pit had been taken at the cost of much blood, but there still remained the warlord and his elite retinue. They were now outnumbered, and their enemies lusted after their death. Alvord was part of the surging charge towards them, but as they neared the doomed warriors, three archers appeared at the top of the dune and interrupted their progress with an outpouring of arrows. This diverted attention from the knot of warriors, who took advantage of the disruption and mounted an attack of their own.

Alvord was on a collision course with the warlord when two Welsh war dogs tackled him to the ground. One had his vest in its teeth and was shaking its head frenetically while the other clamped down on his leg. He struggled to beat the gargantuan beasts off, and would have probably failed had not Cerberus entered the fray with the force of a thunderclap. His body slammed into the dog biting Alvord's vest, sending it rolling away with scraps of material in its mouth. He then rounded on the other dog, slashing into him with ferocity Alvord had never seen equaled in any animal. In a flash the Welsh dog's ear had been torn off, and this bought Alvord enough time to drive home a stiff kick to its face. He then rose, turning just in time to catch the other beast as it mounted another attack. Weaponless, Alvord swung a stiff left hook into the animal's bloody jaws. Up it came again, but this time he charged the animal and pinned it. Hands on its throat, he wrapped his fingers around its esophagus and squeezed as he had never squeezed before.

Having opened up several gaping wounds on his larger opponent, Cerberus was fighting like a berserker. But when he went for the throat the dog succeeded in shaking him off and, rearing up, brought the younger dog crashing to the ground. Although near death, the beast sought Cerberus's jugular. Big Wolf appeared out of nowhere, the many injuries lacing his body not slowing him down. He clubbed the dog twice on its skull, and it's dead weight collapsed in a heap on top of Cerberus. Turning and seeing a Welsh Indian warrior poised to spear the struggling Alvord, Big Wolf lunged and sold his life at the dearest rate.

The spear thrust blew threw his ribs and into his right lung, a death stroke for sure but not enough to stop the indomitable brave from exacting revenge. His ball headed club crushed the offending hand in one blow, and smiling broadly he imbedded his knife in the man's painted temple.

Finished throttling the hound, Alvord rushed over to him as he slumped, still smiling, to the ground.

"Walk well," were his dying words to Alvord.

The fight had reached its last sanguinary stage. The archers had been dealt with, and only two Welsh Indian warriors stood alongside their warlord, Cadoc. Dauntlessly they sallied forth a final time into overwhelming odds, and only consummate skill and uncanny luck allowed the warlord to survive it. Standing alone, his remaining eye looked around him coldly. There was undiminished pride and superiority in his stature as he gazed upon the dunes and the lake, the sky and the woods, and the enemies gathering before him.

In an uncharacteristic move, he actually smiled.

Four Chippewa fighters and a half-breed gathered around him, like wolves on an elk. Working together, they counted cheap coup on him with their hands and coup sticks until he lopped off one of their arms at the elbow and in his next move shattered a man's knee with his mace.

This elk had fangs.

In a lethal surge of action Cadoc renewed his attack, his sword and mace working in lethal unison. Having one eye did not seem to effect his fighting multiple opponents; indeed, his fighting style seemed tailored for it. He briskly ducked under a hatchet and, throwing an arm into the back of another man's legs, rose and sent him flipping into the air with an explosive burst of upward power. His next moves, all lithely decisive, brought down his assailants with astonishing rapidity. Cadoc used his sword to impale and lift a dying enemy, holding the weapon vertically. Exerting his strength to its fullest, he mockingly held the skewered, dying man up with his sword arm and took a few steps towards his few remaining enemies, who backed up in awe.

"*He is mine!*" Alvord declared in a voice that rolled through the Grand Sable Dunes like a peal of thunder. Breathing heavily, he stared challengingly at the Indians and other men. They all heeded his words, even Jemmy. Solemnly they backed up a few steps, clearing out a space for the two peerless warriors.

Both men readied themselves for the Homeric fight before them, from which only one would walk away.

Fate had them by the throat.

Chapter 63

The grassy area they stood upon was closer to the lake than the original field of battle. Indeed, they were not far from where the dunes fell steeply away towards the distant beach below.

His shirt and vests reduced to tatters, Alvord took a moment to simply rip what remained of them off. He then stood there bare-chested and straight-backed, his imposing figure laced with old scars and the rawness of new wounds.

In a surprising *beau geste*, Cadoc dropped his weapons and undid the fastenings of his dented copper cuirass and the protective leather shirt underneath it. He shrugged the armor off to reveal a massive and rippling physique underneath. Unlike most of his fellows, his body bore but one tattoo. Three downward pointing, double-lined triangles interlocked over his heart. Slowly he bent down to retrieve his weapons, eye locked on Alvord. He then rose and rolled his massive shoulders. Leaning over like a predator poised to attack, he flexed his brawny torso and let out a sibilant hiss.

Alvord's weapons were at the ready. In his left hand the blood and gristle coated short sword dangled easily. Around his right wrist was entwined the bolted leather strap of his truncheon, and there was a reassurance in its familiar weight. His fingers instinctively found the worn, carved grooves in the weapon's hickory handle.

They were well matched, both still languishing in their prime, and made all the more deadly by a lifetime of fighting experience. They stared at one another in a moment of weighty anticipation, twenty paces separating them. Simultaneously they charged.

As Cadoc drew near he athletically juked right, left, right again and then somehow spun to the outside off his right leg. This landed him beside Alvord, who felt a nettling sting on the back of his left shoulder. Whirling about, he swung his sword and just barely missed his opponent's satisfied face.

They broke. Alvord could feel the blood running down his back in hot trickle. He'd been nicked.

First blood to the Welshman.

There is no man more dangerous than he who realizes that, despite all his exertions, his time on this earth is short. Infused with that sense of the inexorable, Cadoc pressed his attack with almost inhuman strength and speed. With mace and sword working in lethal concert he bore down on Alvord relentlessly, who in the opening seconds of the contest had no choice but to reluctantly give ground, exerting his martial prowess to its fullest. His opponent came at him with a cold, deliberate fury that, combined with his strength and extraordinary skill, was damn near unmanageable.

Powerfully deflecting the deadly mace with his sword, Alvord punched out with the truncheon and the copper-tipped weapon smashed into Cadoc's sternum. This gained him the briefest of respites from the furious onslaught, but a blow that had incapacitated many a lesser man did little to even slow the warlord down. His weapons a blur, he suddenly had Alvord on his heels again, his sword point opening up a scratch across his taller adversary's chest. He whirled his club and sent it streaking at Alvord's legs, but Alvord leapt back and lifted his leading leg into the air to avoid the potent swing.

Alvord rushed forward, batting aside the sword blade. Still advancing rapidly, he shouldered Cadoc to the ground and moved in for a kick. Dropping his sword, the warlord took a double-handed grip on his club and punched it outward, its shaft meeting Alvord's incoming shin.

Alvord stumbled back as lancing pain shot through his leg. He knew his shinbone had been compromised, but it would still bear weight. Yet for the moment it felt leaden, as if his brain no longer had full control over its movement.

Again they broke, seeking breath.

Without warning Cadoc darted in with a ferocious roar, his recovered sword angling towards Alvord's face. Alvord whipped his head back and felt the draught of the blow on his blood-encrusted beard. Cadoc maintained his advance and sought to impale his adversary's body. With flawless footwork Alvord stepped aside and trapped the questing blade between his sword and truncheon. With a push-pull maneuver he sent his enemy's weapon skidding across the ground. He jammed a cracking elbow into Cadoc's granitic chin, setting him back on his heels. A follow-up sword stroke opened a diagonal slash across the warlord's abdomen. But when Alvord attempted a move on his blind side, Cadoc hooked the head of his club behind Alvord's neck and with an explosive spin drove him to the ground with it. Wielding the mace with both hands now, he pressed his attack. Alvord was still on his knees when the first underhand sweep came his way, and as he crossed his weapons and blocked it the force of the blow not only sent shuddering shockwaves through his hands and arms, it also drove him up and onto his feet. Sliding backwards in the grass besprinkled sand, he parried and ducked under the next barrage of club strokes with consummate skill. He landed two solid truncheon blows in the process, battering Cadoc's shoulder and fresh stomach wound. But in the face of this ferocious offensive, he felt himself flagging. He drew breath with increasing difficulty, and his limbs felt tight and sore. The injury to his leg was affecting his mobility; he must see this *affaire d'honneur* to an end soon.

Sensing his fading strength, Cadoc laid into him with punishing club strokes, finally succeeding in landing a significant strike. As he swiped at Alvord's head, he let the momentum of the swing spin him around. He figured that Alvord would advance to take advantage of his exposed back, and he was right. Swiftly falling to he knees, Cadoc heard a weapon hum through the air above him. He thrust the mace directly backwards, making hard contact with his enemy's stomach.

The impact knocked the wind out of Alvord, and further aggravated a knife wound he'd sustained earlier in the fight. He lurched rearward, wheezing horribly, and could not react quickly enough when the warlord lashed out with the butt of his club. It took him solidly in the temple, and in an explosion of otherworldly light he was felled.

Finnbar stepped forward meaningfully, but putting a firm hand on his chest Marcel restrained him.

"Ain't our place, son."

Colson did his best to restrain Cerberus, who snarled wrathfully as he tried to intercede.

Involuntarily, the onlookers collectively experienced a sharp intake of breath. Their champion was in an awfully perilous position...

Alvord was keenly aware of Cadoc readying himself for a *coup de grace* somewhere above him, in the same way that he was conscious of the fact that he had sand in his mouth. These were things he registered, but working far faster than unfolding events was his memory. For although unbidden, a decisive memory furnished itself within his mind at this crucial moment.

He was back in Manhattan, training with his old swordmaster, an aged German named Maximilian Schuller. They had just sparred after studying the ancient German *fechtbuchs*, or sword fighting manuscripts. Alvord had perfected his *sturzhieb*, or plunging cut technique that day, but it was the talk with Schuller afterwards that stood out to him now.

"Study und practice ist all good und vell," the swordmaster had assured him. "But vhat no book can teach, vhat no training can combat, is vhat you are naturally blessed vith. Inequality ist the first natural law among men. Vhen faced vith one as skilled or better zen you, vhen no opportunity presents itself, you must make use of those natural advantages. Zhat may be the only thing vhat lets you walk away from such contest."

Shaking off the clinging mists of injury, Alvord hurled himself into action. He instinctively rolled away and scrambled to his feet, narrowly avoiding Cadoc's deathblow. Rising unsteadily, Alvord realized that he did in fact have a few natural advantages in this fight. Strength alone would not avail him, for in that regard they were evenly matched. But he was the taller man. So too was his reach superior. What he needed, therefore, was a weapon that played to these advantages.

Although still reeling from the effects of the blow to his head, Alvord moved as if automatically and was on his feet and inside Cadoc's guard with speed that shocked all present. With a firm hand he caught the club low on its shaft and stopped its downward progress with an extraordinary application of strength. Shocked beyond measure, Cadoc hesitated for an instant. Alvord quickly twisted the club out of his grip and sent him reeling backwards with a vicious shot from the heel of his hand. It severed the leather band of his snakeskin eye patch, and in his rage he laid into Alvord with a right hand that had him stumbling away. Alvord kept backing up, turning to those nearest him.

"Sword!" he yelled to David, who without hesitation tossed the mighty claymore aloft.

Alvord caught it and turned back towards Cadoc, who was retrieving his weapon. His head was angled away, and after he brought a hand up to feel his fresh wound he turned with baleful deliberation towards his foe. This revealed a right eye socket that was a scarred, hollow mess, a token no doubt of some bygone fight with beast or man. But his left eye was aflame with anger, its brilliant blue searing into Alvord like hellfire.

Having survived the initial onslaught, Alvord ignored his ringing head and aching wounds and took full stock of the situation. In that moment, one of stark gladiatorial clarity, he saw laid bare in his enemy's eye and body every fear, weakness, and opening. These he exploited in the moments that followed with the same savage adroitness that had made his a feared name in the Manhattan underworld.

Summoning the last reserves of his strength, he strode forward briskly and engaged his worthy adversary with all he had, making full use of his superior reach. The sword flashed in his hands, and riposting expertly, he opened a sizable cut on the warlord's shoulder. Cadoc was the one on the defensive now, and frantically so. When he was again able to attack, Alvord fiercely turned aside his weapon. He had detected a few patterns in Cadoc's style: a tendency to lean in slightly with his strikes and therefore be off balance, along with some occasional missteps in his footwork when advancing quickly. Utilizing his own footwork, Alvord feinted, stepped back diagonally, and caught Cadoc coming in with a stiff strike from the claymore's pommel.

Gaining some space and time by booting his unrelenting combatant in the gut and smashing him with his club butt, Cadoc tried to recover his ascendancy in this fight. But, feinting an overhand hack and turning it into a mid-level sweep, Alvord laid Cadoc's right bicep bare to the bone. Howling in pain, the warlord smote him in the face with a one-handed swing, and although it rocked him Alvord did not let it ruin his momentum.

Knowing that with the passing of each second he was at a bigger disadvantage, Cadoc launched a final, desperate attack.

Alvord was waiting for him.

In German it is called the *Zornhau*, or Wrath Hew. The angle of a man's shoulders is always telling, and if one can anticipate precisely how an enemy weapon will be brought to bear on him, he can implement a series of strong, decisive maneuvers against it. In an overhand chop Cadoc brought his club humming towards Alvord's skull just as he'd predicted. Alvord thrust his sword out to both stop the club's course and aim his sword point at the warlord's face. Cadoc forced his sword aside before it struck him, and then had to hastily block a counter riposte on the other side of his body to which Alvord had smoothly sidestepped. A third sword stroke was instantly being aimed down at his right knee, yet this too he succeeded in preventing. But he had unwittingly played into Alvord's hands. In responding to those moves he had opened up his guard, and with his feet staggered there was little he could do as Alvord spun to his left side and flenced the meat off the outside of his thigh. Although grievously injured, he still tried to parry the faultless underhanded cut that came next, but in its power it hewed the shaft of his mace in two and opened him up slantwise from hip to chest.

Cadoc lashed out with what remained of his weapon, actually

landing a hard strike to Alvord's arm. But then his body grew intolerably heavy, and he sank to his knees as if gravity had suddenly intensified tenfold. Blankly he stared at the blood pooling in his upheld palms, before placing them on his mortal wound to prevent innards from spilling out. He then turned his disbelieving gaze to Alvord, whose panting visage regarded him gravely.

The Welsh Indian warlord, letting out a blood-spewing half chuckle, jerkily nodding his head in acceptance of his manner of death. Baring his neck, his good eye soared heavenward and as he awaited the *coup de grace* he looked calm and free from any earthly pain.

With a deft motion Alvord drove the claymore's tip through the base of his throat and into his spine. Cadoc gasped and gurgled wetly, and as Alvord watched as the light winked out from his eye.

Deed accomplished, the exhausted and bloodied victor turned towards the spectators, who stared at him in wonder. None among them had ever borne witness to a showdown of that caliber or intensity. He saw the young brave he'd stood beside before the onset of the battle; his face was now a mask of utter hollowness as he fixed his vacant gaze on Alvord.

No longer an innocent, his mind dimly registered as he sank to his knees, utterly spent. *Irrevocably stained by the sin of Cain.*

The post-battle sounds came to Alvord in a flood. Dazed from extreme exertion and his throbbing wounds, he heard crying, screaming, and praying men as if from a great distance. Crows and ravens cawed in gruff contentment, already pecking the eyes out of corpses. The few remaining Indians dispatched wounded foes, taking no prisoners but a number of scalps. The rank smells were more forceful to him: the metallic odor of blood mingled with the cloying stench of open stomach cavities, the voided excrement of dead bodies, and the musky odor of those still living.

As he and the others eventually wandered the body-strewn field, he watched Father Bazin tending to the wounded along with Crowder, and administering Last Rites when necessary. At one point a corpse sat bolt-upright and trashed about right next to Alvord, a delayed but final firing of nerve impulses.

Thurgood was found dead, impaled by a spear. His sword was thick with blood. Mick too had been laid low, and a weeping Colson sat near his body, head cradled in his hands. Big Wolf had selflessly given his life for Alvord, and Lightfoot had fallen during the insanity in the sand pit. Gaston would live, thanks to the swift intervention of Crowder, but when Marcel tried to talk to him he said nothing. Instead, he silently regarded the bandaged stump where once a hand had sat.

Jemmy was the only surviving miner. The colossus was marred by a number of wounds, enough to kill the average man twice over, but was somehow still on his feet.

"Well fought," he commended Alvord. "You're a perilous 'un with a blade."

"As you're a perilous one without." They shook, two former rivals brought together by the inescapable pull of greater circumstances.

Alvord suddenly saw several Indians huddled around the lifeless body of Cadoc. One fiddled with something by the slain warlord's chest, while the others hung around reverently. The echo of words spoken by Horace Greeley a world ago in Chicago came back to him as he hastened over there. As he suspected, they were cutting out Cadoc's heart so as to eat it, thus paying him the greatest tribute they knew. Upon seeing Alvord, they solemnly offered him the first piece.

He did not cannibalize his fallen foe, but as he watched the Indians reverentially devour Cadoc's heart, he realized with a start that he actually comprehended their doing so.

After an hour, a large war party of Indians and half-breeds arrived at the dunes from the west. It turned out that Thurgood had furnished them with a map, and they had planned on raiding the Welsh Indian village and destroying every vestige of it while the battle raged. Yet upon finding it they found only the charred remnants of the walls and structures within. Not a soul was present- the village had been abandoned and put to torch.

After their wounds had been dressed, Alvord, Finnbar, and Marcel came to stand on the edge of the dunes, where they mercifully collapsed and looked out upon the water contemplatively. All of their bodies were sore as never before. Gaston had been heavily dosed with laudanum, and slumbered peacefully nearby with a totally sapped Cerberus curled up next to him. A blood-covered David slumbered too, having succumbed to battle fatigue.

"You were right, Alvord," Finnbar said through swollen lips and the taste of dried blood. "They did try to pull a fast one on us. Just as the Chippewa attempted some skullduggery of their own. How'd ye know?"

His friend sighed tiredly, the sun setting his red beard to blazing. "Because at its core, the butchery visited upon these dunes today was not about honor or avenging the memory of ancestors. It had everything to do with buying the rest of the tribe as much time as possible."

The others cast their puzzled gazes at Alvord, who continued explaining in a voice scratchy from roaring.

"When you informed me of Jones's plan to eventually approach the U.S. government on behalf of the tribe, I knew that after our attack on the village a bolder course of action had to be adopted by them. For as was proven today, the Chippewa would seek to exterminate them once they knew of their location and true identity as mere men, not untouchable creatures of myth. They were quite suddenly vulnerable, and Grigor knew it. It stands to reason that they would strike the village around the time of the battle, when the warriors were away. It would be easy pickings."

"Where'd they go, then?" Marcel frowned in thought. "Deeper into the interior?"

Alvord simply jerked his head out towards the lake, where five schooners sailed steadily east in tight formation.

"No bloody way..." breathed Finnbar.

"Were I a betting man, I'd say that was Jones's fleet with Grigor at the helm, heavy laden with hundreds of passengers."

"We can try to catch them, head them off at the Soo," Finnbar insisted fiercely after Alvord's statement. "After all this, they deserve punishment."

"Do they really?"

Contemplative silence met Alvord's softly spoken words, and they let him speak.

"Women and children, perhaps along with some men who weren't fighters to begin with? Not guilty of much except trying to exist, as far as I can see it. And the Druids? Killed to a man by that well-cast grenade of yours, Finnbar. As for Grigor, the man seeks only to save his beleaguered people."

Alvord let his gray eyes stray to the lake once more.

"Justice has been meted out to the guilty parties, trust a copper on that."

"Where do they go, then?" Finnbar wondered aloud.

Alvord's face grew distant. "I know where I'd go."

Marcel's throat exorcised a few desiccated chuckles.

"What is it, Marcel?"

The battered, tousled mountain man turned his head towards Alvord, scrutinizing he and Finnbar in an odd, indefinable sort of way. Then he redirected his dark eyes back towards the lake.

"A rogue mesmerizer in St. Louis, now this business with a lost tribe o' Welsh Indians... it gets a body to wondering... what else is waitin' out there?"

Wordlessly they leveled their weary gazes northward, where the seemingly infinite expanse of Superior's blue depths merged with the distant horizon.

The northern lights made a rare appearance in the summer sky that night. It was, according to Chippewa legend, the souls of the worthy dead dancing in perpetual delight across the cosmos.

Epilogue

The Irish Sea. One month later

They had put many, many leagues behind them in the past month of ceaseless travel, but Grigor was far more concerned with the remaining half a league their fleet of clipper ships would cover. The apogee of modern sailing technology, these clippers served them well during their Atlantic crossing, and now they delivered them within sight of their coveted destination.

He stared hypnotically at the weathered coast they approached. His lips curled into a pleased grin, for they had a serviceable wind at their back- it wouldn't be long now.

Watching a pod of bottlenose dolphins effortlessly pacing their ship, Grigor lapsed into deep thought to the tuneful lapping of wave against copper-sheathed hull.

In death, Cadwallader Jones had still managed to play his final hand. And at every turn Grigor could not help but marvel at the breathtaking scope of the genius, organization, and far-sightedness of his kinsman. He himself had shrewdly helped with planning their mass departure well in advance of it, but Jones had been a veritable mastermind. As was in keeping with their plan, Jones made available to Grigor the majority of his fortune in the form of gold. Then, following the folder of detailed instructions Jones had supplied him with, he affected the tribe's evanescent disappearance from the New World. The week leading up to the showdown at the Grand Sable Dunes had been one of frenzied activity. Grigor traveled down to Sarnia, Ontario to negotiate with some of Jones's former business associates, succeeding in securing passage for he and the others from the St. Mary's River down through Lake Huron. Jones had done well to curry favor with the right men: with a quick glance at Jones's authorization papers and a bit of coin greasing their palms, they had granted Grigor a well-crewed flotilla with which to traverse the Lower Lakes.

As a result, their exodus from Michigan went as smoothly as so momentous an undertaking could possibly go. Grigor had led a group of Jones's Lake Superior crewmen to Mosquito Harbor in the Pictured Rocks, where a shelf of barely submerged bedrock projected into the lake, forming a natural pier. Disguised in white man's garb, the tribe had boarded Jones's personal fleet of schooners, riding them east as the battle raged up in the dunes. Upon their arrival in the Soo, they had waited for the cover of darkness to disembark the schooners and walk the length of the rapids, at the base of which they boarded their waiting ships.

And in doing so they had most assuredly crossed the Rubicon.

Those ships had carried down them length of Lake Huron and then straight through the St. Clair and then Detroit Rivers, into Lake Erie. From there it was on to the vaunted Erie Canal, where again Jones directed his actions from beyond the grave. A canal boat owner who owed Jones a favor outfitted them with four large canal boats that took them towards New York *en masse*. Still languishing under the sheltering aegis of Jones, they had arrived in New York a travel-weary lot. Sedulous cultivation of allies once again carried the day, with a shipyard foreman directing them to their waiting ships, five sleek crafts known as extreme clipper ships- the fastest vessels of their day. Jones had purchased them just last year, in case their original plan fell by the wayside. And to Jones's gift of foresight they were all indebted.

Before long they were harnessing the power of the Gulf Stream, heading north. Fate had cheerfully smiled upon their astounding enterprise. That was a belief he clung to with tenacity.

Moving with her customary feline stealth, Brangwen joined Grigor at the helm of this, their lead vessel. She appeared tired and strained but had not lost her air of authority, nor her marked delicacy of feature. Under her light dress, a gentle swell was beginning to show. Beaming as the wind set her dirty blonde hair to dancing, her cobalt eyes swept over the alien landscape before them.

"It almost seems like a scene from the dreamworld, does it not?"

Grigor rested his thick forearms on the ship's railing and breathed deeply of the salty air before replying in their native tongue. "Aye, that about sums it up. A real feast for the eyes. Ironic thing though, no? When our predecessor left this very port, his dream lay to the west, from which we've come."

Rhos-at-Sea, Conwy County, Wales, lay waiting for them. The location was a neat but almost negligible little fishing village situated upon a broad expanse of gray, sandy beach. Bryn Euryn and other hills rising behind it bore the mark of farms, with hillside meadows so green they might have been painted. Sheep grouped in flocks so grand that even from this distance the white of their fleece could be seen. To the far right, a craggy uprearing of rock from the benign sea was the mountain of Little Orme. Beyond its swell was the distant height of Great Orme, a productive site of copper mining. It was a markedly clear day, and if they chanced to glance northward they could have made out the Isle of Man seven miles away.

"Llandudno lies in between those mountains, a great mining district. People known as the Romans mined it in the long ago, and recently it has been revived. Our men will find work there, our contact assured Jones."

Brangwen frowned confusedly. "Why did we not make landfall there, then?"

"This place is more desolate, don't want too many prying eyes around when we disembark. Anyway, considering that Madog left this very bay over six hundred years ago, I thought it fitting."

She nodded, pausing briefly before delivering a pointed query.

"What do you think has become of Cadoc and the others?"

"Exactly what they wanted, Brangwen. Victory in death. I suspect Cadoc met his end well, awash in the blood of his enemies."

Broodingly, she looked down at the churning, white-gray froth produced by the ship's slicing bow. "I still struggle with his decision."

Grigor nodded understandingly. "I know. But the original plan was compromised as soon as your village's location was. Things never would have been the same. For some men, living in fear is no way to live at all. Cadoc and the others sought out a useful alternative, one that served both our purposes. Knowing there was an upcoming battle that would empty our village of fighting men, they rightly anticipated that the Indians would postpone their attack until then. That granted me time to make preparations and get everything we needed in order to execute our fallback plan. Without their sacrifice we may very well not have escaped."

He rubbed a hand over his stubbly head and bewhiskered face.

"There will be many changes. You will no longer be regarded as royalty, although you will very much find yourself in the role of leader. In due time all will adjust to this new land, but they will need your guidance. We still have much money for now, but everything hinges on our ability to do something productive with it."

"You are our only connection to the outside world. Surely you have some ideas we can implement quickly?" The stirrings of unease betrayed itself in her tone.

Grigor cast a sidelong glance at her. "I am fair at furnishing both independent and constructive thoughts. But Jones- *there* was a man with a complex mind. His suggestion was that we look to establish in this region what they call *seaside resorts*. They are a growing trend, apparently, places where the wealthy come to get fresh air and escape the affronts of the city."

"But for now...?"

"Many people from this region have relocated to the Americas in recent times, as has happened all over Wales. Wealthy landowners are starved for tenants able to make rent each month, as well as able bodies to work the land. One such local landowner was Jones's contact, a distant relative of yours, as Fate would have it. We will find lodging with him, and our men's mining prowess will be prized in the mines at Great Orme. Women can find work around our contact's various farms and fisheries. New skills must be learned, and learned quickly."

Placing a hand on her stomach, she turned and peered into his eyes steadfastly. "I will do all that I can to aid our people in this time of transition."

Braking sharply after a steep dive, a Northern Fulmar glided above the ship's bowsprit, as if guiding their fleet towards the steadily approaching shoreline.

Grigor was not a learned man, but poetry was his one intellectual passion. He devoured it, the lilting magic of rhythmic words calling to his soul as it did to the Welsh bards long before him. He began reciting his favorite poem aloud, one written by the English poet Felecia Hemans. Entitled "Prince Madoc's Farewell," it went like this:

Why lingers my gaze where the last hues of day,
On the hills of my country, in loveliness sleep?
Too fair is the sight for a wand'rer, whose way
Lies far o'er the measureless worlds of the deep!
Fall, Shadows of twilight! And veil the green shore,
That the heart of the mighty may waver no more!

Why rise on my thoughts, ye free songs of the land
Where the harp's lofty soul on each wild wind is borne?
Be hush'd, be forgotten! For ne'er shall the hand
Of minstrel with melody greet my return.
-No! No- let your echoes still float on the breeze,
And my heart shall be strong for the conquest of seas!

'Tis not for the land of my sires, to give birth
Unto bosoms that shrink when their trial is nigh;
Away! We will bear over ocean and earth
A name and a spirit that never shall die.
My course to the winds, to the stars, I resign;
But my soul's quenchless fire, O my country, is thine.

Grigor and Brangwen put foot to beach a half hour later, and with the scrape of boot upon sand, the legacy of Madog ab Owain Gwynedd had come full circle.

Historical Note

The notion of a far-flung, Pre-Columbian Welsh colony establishing itself in North America nine centuries ago is one that has attracted both supporters and detractors among mainstream historians and archeologists. Proponents of this theory recognize that legends of light-skinned Indian tribes speaking a language akin to Welsh can be found in profusion in the historical record, alongside archeological evidence suggesting the presence of a people quite unlike the Amerindians.

Atop Lookout Mountain in Alabama stand the crumbling remnants of an ancient fort, asserted by some experts to be nearly identical in design to Dolwyddelan Castle in Gwynedd, North Wales. Gwynedd, it should be noted, is the presumed birthplace of Prince Madoc.

In Georgia's Fort Mountain State Park stands a plaque that recounts the old theory of how the ancient stone wall from which the park derives its name came into being. It quotes early 19th century Tennessee Governor John Sevier in stating that Cherokee Chief Oconostota believed "a people called the Welsh" had constructed the wall as part of a larger defensive fortification built atop the mountain to deter hostile native forces.

For if Madoc and his followers did in fact make landfall on our shores, their history in this land was no doubt fraught with hardship and peril. Numerous Native American legends and oral histories in the South and Midwest make mention of a mysterious race of pale-skinned, bearded people with whom their ancestors warred against and, in some instances, decimated. If the documentation of 18th and 19th-century historians is to be lent credence to, the Cherokee in particular had extensive oral history regarding their ancestors' wars against pale-skinned tribes with a name that sounded like "Welsh." So too did the Shawnee and Iroquois. In fact, according to their oral traditions they once formed an inter-tribal coalition that launched a costly but ruinous attack on a well-established Welsh settlement at the Falls of the Ohio River, near present-day Louisville. As Elijah Thurgood informs Alvord and Marcel, a highly respected 19th century antiquarian by the name of Thomas S. Hinde stated that across the river at Jeffersonville,

Indiana, six skeletons with breastplates were unearthed in 1799. The armor, he claimed, unmistakably bore the Welsh coat of arms- the mermaid and harp. So persistent was the legend of Madoc that President Thomas Jefferson instructed Lewis and Clark to keep an eye out for a peculiar tribe of light-skinned Indians during their celebrated exploration of the Louisiana Territory.

Yet as skeptics are quick to point out, this potent archeological evidence, along with many other reported artifacts, have been rather conveniently lost to history. But in those days, personal reliquaries and cabinets of curiosity were very much in vogue among the wealthy and intellectually inclined. Zealous collectors of archeological oddities would not have thought twice about adding an ancient sword or rusting breastplate to their collection. These collections had a way of swiftly dispersing or disappearing entirely upon the death of their owners. Additionally, the looting of Native American burial mounds was a rampant practice in our nation's early history, and it stands to reason that looters could have easily pilfered many a Welsh artifact from the aforementioned sites.

The geographic locations of these sites are in keeping with the theory that Madoc's colonists engaged in steady northward migration along the Alabama, Tennessee, Ohio, and then Missouri River systems. I chose to secrete my own Welsh tribe in the vastness of Upper Michigan's wilderness, which even by 1847 was less tamed than many sections of the American West. In fact, given its seemingly boundless tracts of uninhabited woodland, it seemed to me to be one of the few places in the country that could realistically conceal a secretive tribe.

I would like to note the historical figures presented in this book. Some characters presented, like Horace Greeley and Abraham Lincoln, are easily recognized. Others not so much, and I therefore feel obligated to mention the names of the men who appeared in the book and who with much sweat, blood, and grit sought to reap their fortune through the Copper Boom. Business partners John Hayes and James Raymond of the Pittsburgh & Boston Mining Company did in fact exist, as did their adept Cornish mining Engineer, Edward Jennings. So too did owner Philo Everett and forge master Ariel N. Barney of the Jackson Mining Company, two enterprising men who with admirable foresight sought iron rather than copper. The meeting of these men with the fictional Cadwallader Jones was as fictional as Jones himself, yet the obstacles that both companies are mentioned as facing were quite realistic at that stage in the Copper Boom. For me the most intriguing character that did in fact exist is the colorful Jemmy Tresize. The colossal Cornishman was a renowned, if feared figure in the Copper Country the 1840's. All of the qualities of his character that are mentioned in the book, from his work ethic to his drinking and fighting habits, are historical tidbits that my research unearthed.

In presenting the Welsh Indians as a copper mining people, I am in no way proposing that Madoc and his pioneers can be pointed to as the original copper miners of this land. The dates simply do not jibe: the earliest of the ancient copper mines around Lake Superior have been radiocarbon dated anywhere from 5000 BC to 1200 BC, predating by far Madoc's purported journey to the New World. So too were the techniques employed by the earliest miners a far cry from those of High Middle Age Welshmen. The shallow pits and various stone implements unearthed at Upper Michigan sites would not have been used by a people like the Welsh, who had been accustomed to working with iron for some time. But even taking into account the primitive tools, the first wave of copper miners excavated a staggering quantity of the precious metal from the Keweenaw Peninsula and Isle Royale, with some estimates ranging as high as 1.5 billion pounds. If such figures verge on truth, then the copper miners of old had a very large, very reliable market fueling their ventures. And as was stated in *Madoc's Legacy*, Lake Superior copper, easily identified due to its matchless purity, has been found in abundance all over this land, with samples recovered as far off as Mexico and the Caribbean. Those miners of bygone days utilized the intricate, continent-spanning Amerindian trade network to widely circulate their valued product.

Around 5000 open pit mines once existed across Upper Michigan. Although it is variously claimed that ancient Egyptians or Minoans somehow mined the region, the evidence points to a vanished race of early American Indians who unfortunately left little in the way of burial mounds, tools, or other indicators of culture. I do, however, think it interesting that a few railroad workers whom I interviewed stated that during their maintenance of rail lines across the Upper Peninsula in the 80's and 90's, sinkholes were a recurring problem. Some of these sinkholes were pronounced to be old mines by geologists, which showed signs of being far more complex than the shallow pits dug by the original copper miners. These mines, once explored in a preliminary fashion, were summarily filled in for the sake of progress, their stories being forever blotted out.

Luckily, ours is a nation rife with mysteries. Some have been solved, others endure to this very day, and who can presume to know how many lie yet uncovered beneath the dust of ages, awaiting discovery?